Books by Natalie Babbitt

Dick Foote and the Shark

Phoebe's Revolt

The Search for Delicious

Kneeknock Rise

The Something

Goody Hall

The Devil's Storybook

Tuck Everlasting

The Eyes of the Amaryllis

Herbert Rowbarge

The Devil's Other Storybook

Nellie: A Cat on Her Own

The Devil's Storybooks

NATALIE BABBITT

SQUARE
FISH

FARRAR STRAUS GIROUX

SQUARE

FISH

An Imprint of Macmillan

For information, address
Square Fish, 175 Fifth Avenue, New York, NY 10010.

Square Fish and the Square Fish logo are trademarks of Macmillan and
are used by Farrar Straus Giroux under license from Macmillan.

ISBN 978-0-312-64158-0

Originally published in the United States by Farrar Straus Giroux
First Square Fish Edition: April 2012
Square Fish logo designed by Filomena Tuosto
mackids.com

P1

AR: 5.6 / LEXILE: 970L

Contents

The Devil's Storybook

Wishes 3

The Very Pretty Lady 13

The Harps of Heaven 21

The Imp in the Basket 37

Nuts 47

A Palindrome 53

Ashes 63

Perfection 73

The Rose and the Minor Demon 79

The Power of Speech 91

The Devil's Other Storybook

The Fortunes of Madame Organza 105

Justice 113

The Soldier 121

Boating 127

How Akbar Went to Bethlehem 135

The Signpost 143

Lessons 149

The Fall and Rise of Bathbone 155

Simple Sentences 165

The Ear 175

From his brimstone bed, at break of day,
    A-walking the Devil is gone,
To look at his little snug farm of the World,
    And see how his stock went on.

Over the hill and over the dale,
    And he went over the plain;
And backward and forward he swished his tail,
    As a gentleman swishes a cane.

ROBERT SOUTHEY (1774–1843)

The Devil's Storybook

WISHES

O N E   D A Y when things were dull in Hell, the Devil fished around in his bag of disguises, dressed himself as a fairy godmother, and came up into the World to find someone to bother. He wandered down the first country road he came to and before long he met a crabby farm wife stumping along with a load of switches on her back.

"Good morning, my dear," said the Devil in his best fairy-godmother voice. "It's a fine day, isn't it?"

"It's not," said the farm wife. "There hasn't been a fine day in the World in twenty years."

"That long?" said the Devil.

"That long," she snapped.

Now, it was the Devil's plan that morning to make a nuisance of himself by granting wishes, and he decided there was no time like now to begin. "See here then," he said to the farm wife. "I will grant you one wish—anything at all—and that ought to cheer you up."

"One wish?" said the farm wife.

"One," he replied.

"Very well," said the farm wife. "Here's my wish. Since I don't believe in fairy godmothers, I wish you'd go back where you came from and leave me alone."

This wish caught the Devil off guard and before he knew it he had landed with a bump in his throne room in Hell. Up he rose, his hair on end with anger. "That's one I'll get someday, anyway," he said to himself, and back he went to the World to find another victim.

The next soul he met was a very old man who sat under a tree staring away at nothing.

"Good morning, old man," said the Devil in his

best fairy-godmother voice. "It's a fine day, isn't it?"

"One of many," said the old man. "One of many."

The Devil didn't like this answer at all. It sounded too contented. "See here then," he said to the old man. "I will grant you one wish—anything at all—but I can guess what you'll choose to wish for."

"What's that?" said the old man.

"Why," said the Devil, "seeing as your life is nearly done, my guess is you'll wish to be a boy again."

The old man pulled at his whiskers for a while and then he said, "No, not that. It was good to be a boy, but not *all* good."

"Then," pursued the Devil, "you'll wish to return to young manhood."

"No," said the old man. "It was good to be a young man, but still—it was difficult, too. No, that wouldn't be my wish."

The Devil began to feel annoyed. "Well then," he said, "surely you'll wish to be once more in your prime, a hearty soul of forty or fifty."

"No," said the old man, "I wouldn't wish that. It was good to be forty and good to be fifty, but those times were often hard as well."

"What age will you wish to be, then?" barked the Devil, losing his patience at last.

"Why should I want to be any age but this one?" said the old man. "That was *your* idea. One time is as good as another, and just as bad, too, for that matter. I'd wish for something different—I don't know what —if I really had a wish."

"Well," said the Devil, "I've changed my mind anyway. You *don't* have a wish."

"I didn't think I did," said the old man, and he went back to staring away at nothing.

The Devil ground his teeth and smoke came out of his ears, but he went on down the road until at last he came to a vain young man in fancy clothes riding on a big brown horse. "Good morning, young man," said the Devil in his best fairy-godmother voice. "It's a fine day, isn't it?"

"Indeed it is, dear madam," said the vain young man, taking off his hat and bowing as well as he could from the saddle.

"Well now," said the Devil, "you're such a fine young man, I think I'll grant you a wish. One wish, anything you like. What do you say to that?"

"A wish?" cried the vain young man, dropping his hat. "Anything I want? Can it really be true?"

"It can," said the Devil, smiling. "What will you wish for?"

"Dear me!" said the vain young man. "Anything at all? I could wish to be rich, couldn't I!"

"You could," said the Devil.

"But on the other hand I could wish that all the girls would fall in love with me," said the vain young man, beginning to grow excited. "Or I could wish to be the Crown Prince. Or the King! I could even wish to rule the whole World, as far as that goes."

"You could," said the Devil, smiling more than ever.

"Or I could wish to stay young and handsome forever," said the vain young man.

"You could," said the Devil.

"But wait!" cried the vain young man. "Perhaps it would be better to wish for perfect health. What good are all those other things if you're too sick to enjoy them?"

"True," said the Devil.

"Oh, dear," moaned the vain young man, wringing his hands. "What to wish for! What to choose! I shall go quite mad, trying to decide! Health, power, money, love, endless youth, each a perfect wish all by itself. Sweet fairy godmother, I wish you'd *tell* me what to wish for!"

"If that's what you want, all right," said the Devil with a smile as big as the moon. "Most people think the best wish of all is to wish that every wish they ever wish will always come true."

The young man's eyes grew round and his cheeks paled. "Yes. Yes!" he said. "They're right, of course.

That *is* the best. All right, so here I go. I wish that every wish I ever wish will always come true."

"Too late," said the Devil gleefully.

The young man stared. "Too late?" he cried. "But why? You said I could wish for anything, didn't you?"

"I did," grinned the Devil. "That's true. But you used up your wish when you wished I'd tell you what to wish for!"

And with the young man's wail of chagrin ringing in his ears, the Devil went back down to Hell, well satisfied at last.

THE VERY PRETTY
LADY

THERE WAS a very pretty lady once who lived all alone. She didn't have to live all alone; she was so pretty that there were many young men anxious to marry her. They hung about in her dooryard and played guitars and sang sweet songs and tried to look in through the windows. They were there from dawn to dusk, always sad, always hopeful. But the very pretty lady didn't want to marry any of them. "It's no use being loved for the way one looks," she said to herself. "If I can't find someone who will love me in spite of my face, then I will never marry anyone at all."

This was wise, no doubt, but no one is wise all the

time. For the truth is that the very pretty lady rather liked the fact that she was pretty, and sometimes she would stand in front of the mirror and look and look at herself. At times like that she would be pleased with herself and would go out to the dooryard and talk to all the young men and let them go with her to market and carry home her bags and packages for her. And for a long time afterward they would all look a good deal more hopeful than sad.

But most of the time the very pretty lady stayed inside her cottage, feeling lonely regardless of all the young men in the dooryard, longing for someone who would love her as she wanted to be loved.

Now, after a while, one way or another, the Devil heard about the very pretty lady and he decided that she was the very thing he needed to brighten up his days in Hell. So he packed a satchel of disguises and went up to have a look at her.

He had heard how very pretty she was, but no one had told him that she never let anyone inside the cottage. He went disguised as a beggar, but she wouldn't open the door. He tried appearing as a preacher and then as a king, but that didn't work either. So at last he simply disguised himself as one of her suitors and hung about with the others waiting for market day.

When the pretty lady came out at last, the Devil walked beside her all the way to town, looking at her every moment, and he carried back the heaviest package. By the time she had gone inside her cottage again, his mind was made up: she was indeed exactly what he needed in Hell, and he had waited long enough to have her.

When night came and the sad and hopeful young men had all gone home the Devil threw off his disguise and wished himself into the pretty lady's bedroom with a puff of red smoke and a noise like thunder. The pretty lady woke up at once, and when she saw him she shrieked.

"Don't be alarmed," said the Devil calmly. "It's only me. I've come to take you away to Hell."

"Never!" cried the pretty lady. "I shan't go and there's no way you can make me."

"That's true," said the Devil, "there isn't. You have to come of your own free will when you come before your time. But you'll like it so much down there—you'll be the prettiest thing in the place."

"I'm that already, right here," said the pretty lady, "for all the good it does me. Why should I go away to have the same thing somewhere else?"

"Ah, but in Hell," said the Devil, "your beauty will last forever and ever, whereas here it can only fade."

For the first time the pretty lady was tempted, and the Devil knew it. He fetched a mirror from her bureau and held it up in front of her so she could look at herself. "Wouldn't it be a shame," he coaxed, "to let such a pretty face go to waste? If you stay here, it can only last fifteen or twenty more years, but in Hell there is no time. You will look just as you do now till the stars fall and a new plan is made, and we all know that will never happen."

The pretty lady looked at herself in the mirror and felt, as she sometimes did, that it *was* rather nice to be pretty, but in the nick of time she remembered what it was she really wanted. "Tell me," she said. "Is there any love in Hell?"

"Love?" said the Devil with a shudder. "What would we want with a thing like that?"

"Well then," said the pretty lady, pushing away the mirror, "I'll never agree to go. You can beg all you want from now till Sunday, but it won't be any use."

At this the Devil grew very angry and his eyes glowed like embers. "Is that your final word?" he demanded.

"That is my final word," she answered.

"Very well!" he said. "I can't take you against your will, that's true. But I can take your beauty. I can, and I will." There was another clap of thunder and the Devil disappeared in a cloud of smoke. He went straight back to Hell and took all the pretty lady's beauty with him, and he tacked it up in little fragments all over his throne room, where it sparkled and twinkled and brightened up the place very nicely.

After a couple of years, however, the Devil grew curious about the lady and went up to see how she was getting along. He arrived at her cottage at twilight and went to peer in through the window. And there she was, ugly as a boot, sitting down to supper. But candles lit the table and she was no longer alone. Sitting with her was a young man just as ugly as she, and in a cradle near her chair lay a very ugly baby. And the strange thing was that there was such love around the table that the Devil reeled back as if someone had struck him.

"Humph!" said the Devil to himself. "I'll never understand this if I live to be a trillion!"

So he went back to Hell in a temper and tore down all the lady's beauty from the walls of his throne room and threw it away, and it floated up out of Hell into a dark corner of the sky and made itself, more usefully, into a new star.

THE HARPS OF
HEAVEN

THERE WERE two brothers in the World once
named Basil and Jack—Basil was the fat one—a pair
of mean, low, quarrelsome fellows who hated each
other right from the start and would never have stayed
together if it weren't for the fact that no one else
could stand them for a minute. They had begun to
fight when they were babies and fought all their lives,
so that one or the other was always black and blue;
but still they had gone into business together and had
managed to become quite famous, at least with the law,
for they were positively the best thieves in the World.

There wasn't anything that Basil and Jack couldn't

steal if they wanted to, and most of the time they wanted to. Then they would sell what they stole and spend all the money on whiskey and iodine, the first to get them ready for a fight and the second to patch them up afterward. But one night they went too far, for each in secret had bought a pistol, and in the middle of the fight they shot each other dead. However, this drastic event made very little difference between them, for when they arrived at the gates of Hell, which happened almost at once—there being no question in anyone's mind as to where they belonged—they began another fight on the spot over who should go in first.

When the Devil heard all the commotion, he was pleased as punch. "It's Basil and Jack!" he said to himself. "And not a moment too soon!"

Now, what the Devil meant by that was this: there was a peevish piano teacher in Hell—sent down for nagging—whose principal quarrel with the place was the music. There was bound to be better music in Heaven, she said, since they had so many lovely harps there, while in Hell, she said, there wasn't even one harp, lovely or otherwise.

The Devil had been stung by these remarks, for he was proud of Hell. But it was all too true that he had no harps, and he had decided that the only way to get a good one was to steal it from Heaven. And the only way to do *that* was to send up Basil and Jack. "If anyone can steal a harp from Heaven, it's Basil and Jack," he said to himself, "and now at last they're here!"

So, as soon as the brothers were settled in, the Devil had them brought to his throne room. "Basil and Jack!" he said joyfully. "Basil and Jack at last."

"That's us," said Jack.

And Basil said, "None other!"

"Splendid!" said the Devil. "I've got a job for you." And he went on to tell them the problem.

Well, the brothers were just as glad to get busy again, so they heard the Devil out, and the whole thing appealed to them hugely.

"That's the stuff," said Basil.

And Jack said, "Right!"

"You'll need a good plan, though," said the Devil. "A really good plan."

"Nothing to that," said the brothers. "There's no job anywhere too tricky for *us*."

"So I've heard," said the Devil, "and I hope it's true. I've set my heart, such as it is, on having a harp in Hell. I can't go up myself—they'd know me in a minute. But you two can do it if anyone can."

So Basil and Jack thought up a plan, and the plan was to disguise themselves as angels. "We'll just go up all sweet-like," they said, "and pretend to have lost our way. Then we'll slip in, grab the merchandise, slip out, and be back in time for supper."

"Splendid!" said the Devil, and he gave them the costumes they needed and sent them on their way.

It took a good while to get there, for they had to pass round the World on the way, and the wings the Devil gave them took time to get used to. But at least they didn't fight, for neither wanted to spoil his costume, and after a while they arrived at the gates of Heaven, out of breath but full of confidence.

Now, confidence is all right, but it isn't everything, for at this point things began to go wrong in ways that the brothers had never in the World expected. Here they were at the gates, but a Person was sitting there with a harp at his side, and this Person looked at them, looked at their costumes, smiled, and said at last in a gentle tone, "Why, it's Jack and Basil, isn't it? Let's see now. *You* must be Basil, because Basil is the fat one, and *you* must be Jack. What brings you up this way?"

"Oh," said Basil.

And Jack said, "Well . . ."

"Never mind," said the Person at the gates. "I already know why you've come. And I must say you look very nice in your costumes."

No one in all their lives had ever called the brothers nice, and Jack had it in mind to say, "Nuts!" But he didn't quite dare, somehow, and Basil just stood there with his mouth open.

"You're here for a harp," said the Person at the gates. "Well, that's all right. There are plenty of harps in Heaven, and this one here beside me is for you. There isn't any need to steal one."

"Oh!" said Jack.

And Basil said, "Well."

And they were both severely disappointed.

But the Person at the gates only smiled and picked up the harp—a small triangular harp made of gold, with cupids carved on its frame and strings like sunbeams—and handed it to them. "Goodbye then," said the Person at the gates.

So Jack took the harp and off the brothers went, back round the World to Hell.

It took a good deal longer to go down than it had to come up—a fact about which one may draw one's own conclusions—and the brothers, who were already cross about missing the chance to steal, soon grew bored with flying and began to argue.

"Here," said Basil. "Let *me* take the harp for a

while. There's no reason *you* should get to have it all the time."

"I'll be hanged if I will," said Jack. "You'd only drop it."

"Selfish!" said Basil.

And Jack said, "Clumsy!"

"Donkey!" said Basil.

"Pig!" said Jack.

"You're another."

"Am not."

"Are too."

And right there in the air between Heaven and Hell, Basil and Jack began to fight.

It was a glorious fight, with a great tearing of costumes, and a great snatching out of feathers from wings, and a great noise full of yells, thumps, swats, and wallops; and right in the middle was the poor little harp, yanked this way and that like tug of war.

They fought all the way back to Hell and arrived at last in terrible condition.

"Where's the harp?" said the Devil, who had heard them coming. "Hand it over." He took it away from them, cradled it in one arm, and ran his thumb across the strings.

But instead of sounding sweeter than zephyrs, the harp gave off a discord that made all three of them wince.

"*Now* see what you've done with your silly fighting," said the Devil. "My harp's all out of tune!"

"Oh," said Basil.

And Jack said, "Well."

"And I don't know how to tune it!" said the Devil.

"Neither do I," said Jack.

And Basil said, "Me either."

And that, of course, was that, for the pity of it was that there wasn't a soul—no one in all of Hell—who knew how to tune a harp from Heaven, not even the piano teacher.

"Well," said the Devil to Basil and Jack, "you'll just have to go back and get another."

"If you say so," said Basil and Jack.

"I do," said the Devil.

So back they went just as they were, in their ragged costumes, and the flying was harder than ever with so many feathers missing from their wings. But still they got there at last without too much complaining, and found the Person still sitting at the gates.

"Why, Jack and Basil! Here you are again!" said the Person.

"That's it," said Jack.

And Basil said, "Right."

But they were more than a little embarrassed.

"You've come for another harp, I expect," said the Person at the gates, observing the tears in their costumes.

"Right," said Basil.

And Jack said, "That's it."

"Nothing easier," said the Person. And he took another harp exactly like the first one from under his robe, and held it out to them.

This time Basil took the harp and off they started once again for Hell. But after they had been flying for a while, Jack couldn't stand it any longer. He gave Basil a poke and said, "I never saw anything so silly as you holding on to that harp."

"Says who?" said Basil.

"Says me," said Jack.

"Says pigs," said Basil.

And they were off again, fighting like a frenzy.

This time, however, in the middle of the fight, just when things were getting really satisfying, Basil dropped the harp. Down it fell, straight toward the World, and landed—clunk!—on a mountaintop.

"I told you so," said Jack.

Well, they flew down and found it and took it round the World to Hell just the same, and when they gave it to the Devil, he was very upset.

"Look at this harp!" he said. "It's all bashed out of shape! No one could play a harp in this condition."

"Someone can patch it up," said Basil.

"Ding it out with a hammer or something," said Jack.

But there wasn't a goldsmith in all of Hell who knew how to work on a harp from Heaven, and the piano teacher stood to one side and looked scornful.

"Back you go," said the Devil to the brothers. "One more time. And this time you'd better do it right."

"If you say so," said Basil and Jack.

"I do," said the Devil.

So back they had to go once more, and this time the Person at the gates sighed and shook his head when he saw them. "Jack and Basil!" he said. "Can it really be you again?"

"That's it," said Jack.

And Basil said, "Right."

But they were more embarrassed than ever.

"Well," said the Person at the gates, "there's one harp left. I hope you make it through with this one." And he handed them the third harp, went on into Heaven, and shut the gates behind him.

So Basil and Jack took the harp between them, with both holding on to it, and started back down again toward Hell. And this time they got all the way round the World before anything happened. In fact, they were almost to Hell when Basil's wings, which were in far worse shape than Jack's, came loose from his costume and there he was with no way to keep from falling except to cling to his half of the harp.

"Leave off!" cried Jack, flapping his own wings hard. "You'll drag us both down!"

"I can't leave off!" said Basil. "If I do, I'll fall."

"So fall!" said Jack. "Better you than both of us." And he tried to pry Basil's fingers loose from the harp.

They made quite a picture, there in the air above Hell, grappling and struggling, and in the midst of trying to get a safer grip, Basil snatched at the harp strings and pulled them right out like straws from a broom.

And that was the way they arrived back in Hell, Jack with the harp and Basil with the strings, and the

Devil was so angry that his horns smoked. "I'll go myself!" he bellowed. "And take my chances!"

"No use," said Basil.

"There's no harps left," said Jack.

"This was the last one," said both of them together.

And the pity of it was that there was no one in all of Hell who knew how to put the strings back into a harp from Heaven.

So the Devil had to give it up, angry or not. And to punish Jack and Basil, he made them take piano lessons from the peevish teacher—thereby punishing her as well, since the lessons went on for hundreds of years and the brothers never could learn anything but scales, no matter how much they practiced. And of course she made them practice all the time.

But the Devil kept the harps in his throne room just the same. "At least," he said to himself, "no one can say I don't *have* any." And he pretended to everyone that he could fix the harps any time he wanted to, but just didn't want to for now.

THE IMP
IN THE BASKET

THERE WAS a clergyman once who was a very good and gentle man. He scrubbed the steps of the church every day and made his own candles for the altar, and he believed that everyone was just as good as he was himself. No matter how terrible the things were that people did, no matter how often they pounded each other and murdered each other and robbed and cheated and kicked their dogs, he would only sigh and say, "Ah, well, it was all a mistake, I'm sure. They didn't mean to do it." And he would say a prayer for them and was always sure they would mend their ways sooner or later.

One morning when the clergyman went out to scrub the steps of the church, he found a basket waiting and in the basket was a baby. "Aha!" said the clergyman. "Someone has left this baby here for me so I can raise it in the church in the ways of goodness!" And this pleased him very much. But when he picked up the basket and looked more closely, he saw that the baby was no ordinary baby. "Dear me!" he whispered. "Why, this baby is an imp! No doubt about it. A devil's baby with skin like a pepper, and the basket reeks of brimstone!" He set it down again at once, in horror, but the imp peered up at him so sweetly, smiling and smiling, that the clergyman was at a loss to know what to do. He left the basket where it was and went inside the church to sit down and have a talk with himself.

"A baby is a baby—helpless and in need of protection."

"Yes, but *this* baby can only grow up to be a demon!"

"And yet, suppose I could prevent that. Just suppose. Shouldn't I try?"

"Nonsense. It's been sent by the Devil to tempt me."

"Perhaps. But, on the other hand, it could have been sent by God to test me."

"That would be a test, to be sure, turning red into white."

"There now—it's starting to cry out there. It's hungry, no doubt, and tired after its journey."

"Its journey! What am I saying? Why, it must have come up straight from Hell."

"Nevertheless, a baby is a baby. I must do what I can."

And so, still unsure as to whether he was right or wrong, the clergyman carried the imp home to his cottage behind the churchyard.

Now, the clergyman saw at once that he would have to have food for the imp. "For," he thought, "a baby is a baby and mustn't be let to starve." So he hurried to a nearby farmhouse to buy a pail of milk.

"What!" said the farmer's wife. "A pail of milk? You've taken on a child at your age?"

"I have," said the clergyman nervously. "A baby. Left on the church steps."

He didn't say the baby was an imp. He was not at all sure what the farmer's wife might do when she learned about that. But his silence did him no good, for the farmer's wife turned business-like at once. "I'll come along and see to the little mite for you," she said. "What do *you* know about babies after all, an old bachelor like you?"

"No, no!" said the clergyman hastily. "I'll figure things out, no doubt. Don't trouble yourself."

"Twaddle," said the farmer's wife. "It's no trouble." And he couldn't put her off.

When they came to the clergyman's cottage, the farmer's wife stopped suddenly and sniffed. "Brimstone!" she said. "Smoke and brimstone! Quick, save the baby—your cottage must be on fire!"

But it wasn't. When they went inside, the smell of brimstone was very strong, but everything was peaceful. The imp had gone to sleep in its basket. The farmer's wife went right away to look at it, and when she saw what it was, her mouth fell open. "Why, it's a devil's baby!" she gasped. "An imp!" And she turned and ran out of the cottage. "A devil!" she yelled as she ran. "A devil at the very doors of the church! Help! Help! We'll all of us be cursed!"

"No, wait!" cried the clergyman, wringing his hands in the doorway. "Stop! It's only a baby, and a baby is a baby, isn't it?" And he was quite overcome with doubt.

But the farmer's wife went running all around the village, raising a great crowd of people, and in no time at all they were gathered round the clergyman's cottage. "Come out!" they demanded. "Come out at once and leave the imp behind. We'll burn the cottage down and the imp with it. It's the only way to get rid of it."

When he heard this, the clergyman was horrified and his doubt dissolved. "You can't do that!" he answered firmly. "A baby is a baby, imp or not. Helpless, and in need of protection. And anyway, perhaps the imp can be raised in the ways of goodness. The Devil was an angel once, wasn't he? So there must be hope, even for an imp!"

But the people said to each other, "He's mad! He's out of his senses!" And they called to him again: "Come out and let us burn the cottage down!"

"Never," said the clergyman. "I can't abandon a baby, imp or not. If you burn down the cottage, you must burn it down with both of us inside."

The people conferred among themselves and decided it was too late to save the clergyman anyway; the Devil had most certainly possessed him. There was only one thing to do. They brought a torch and set fire to the cottage with the clergyman and the imp, both of them, inside.

The clergyman stood holding the basket as the flames shot up around him, and prayed a long prayer, for he was very much afraid. But the imp woke up and when it saw the smoke and fire it clapped its little hands and crowed with delight.

Outside, the people stood back from the heat and watched the cottage burn, and now it was their turn to doubt. "Of course it *was* only a baby after all, and suppose it *could* have been raised in the ways of goodness," they said to each other. "Just suppose."

However, it was far too late to put out the fire, for the cottage was small and dry. The roof began to buckle and then it fell in, and the walls fell in around it. But when the smoke cleared, there stood the clergyman in the middle of the mess with his eyes tight shut, entirely unharmed, and the imp and the basket were gone.

The people were amazed, and then they were thankful, and then they were jubilant. "A miracle!" they cried. "Our clergyman has been saved by God from death!" And as a gesture of their relief and gratitude, they went to work at once to build a new cottage so the clergyman could have his own place once again.

The clergyman took up his life and duties without a murmur, but for a time he was greatly troubled. Had he really been saved by God, as the people supposed, or had he perhaps—just perhaps—been saved by the Devil? However, he never spoke of this question to anyone. He continued to make candles for the altar, and every morning he came out to scrub the steps of the church. He had noticed at once, of course, the sooty spot on the top step where the imp's basket had rested, and he tried very hard to scrub it away. But no matter how hard he scrubbed, the spot remained as clear as ever. So at last he brought from inside the church a pot of sickly ivy and set it there. The ivy flourished, standing on the spot, which was strange; but the clergyman scrubbed around it every morning and was glad of it anyway, and to the end of his days he never saw another imp.

NUTS

ONE DAY the Devil was sitting in his throne room eating walnuts from a large bag and complaining, as usual, about the terrible nuisance of having to crack the shells, when all at once he had an idea. "The best way to eat walnuts," he said to himself, "is to trick someone else into cracking them for you."

So he fetched a pearl from his treasure room, opened the next nut very carefully with a sharp knife so as not to spoil the shell, and put the pearl inside along with the meat. Then he glued the shell back together. "Now all I have to do," he said, "is give this walnut to some greedy soul who'll find the pearl in it and insist on opening the lot to look for more!"

So he dressed himself as an old man with a long beard and went up into the World, taking along his nutcracker and the bag of walnuts with the special nut right on top. And he sat himself down by a country road to wait.

Pretty soon a farm wife came marching along.

"Hey, there!" said the Devil. "Want a walnut?"

The farm wife looked at him shrewdly and was at once suspicious, but she didn't let on for a minute. "All right," she said. "Why not?"

"That's the way," said the Devil, chuckling to himself. And he reached into the bag and took out the special walnut and gave it to her.

However, much to his surprise, she merely cracked the nut open, picked out the meat and ate it, and threw away the shell without a single word or comment. And then she went on her way and disappeared.

"That's strange," said the Devil with a frown. "Either she swallowed my pearl or I gave her the wrong walnut to begin with."

He took out three more nuts that were lying on top of the pile, cracked them open, and ate the meat, but there was no pearl to be seen. He opened and ate four more. Still no pearl. And so it went, on and on all afternoon, till the Devil had opened every walnut in the bag, all by himself after all, and had made a terrible mess on the road with the shells. But he never did find the pearl, and in the end he said to himself, "Well, that's that. She swallowed it." And there was nothing for it but to go back down to Hell. But he took along a stomach ache from eating all those nuts, and a temper that lasted for a week.

In the meantime the farm wife went on to market, where she took the pearl out from under her tongue, where she'd been saving it, and she traded it for two turnips and a butter churn and went on home again well pleased.

We are not all of us greedy.

A

PALINDROME

THERE WAS an artist once who was so kind and good and loving that everyone who knew him liked to say he was "the best fellow in the World." But the pictures he painted struck a lot of people as being most remarkably evil, for they all showed blank-faced men and women hopping about with their clothes off, or chopping each other into little pieces, and in general behaving in ways unacceptable to decent society.

In spite of this, the people who knew him, loving him as they did, were more than willing to accept and admire the artist's pictures. He was very skillful after all, quite a master, and some of his friends, believing there is good and evil in everyone, liked to think that all the evil in the artist came out in his work and left behind nothing but good in the man himself.

Now, the Devil knew about the artist's pictures and thought they were magnificent. Sometimes, in fact, he would come up out of Hell in the middle of the night for the sole purpose of hanging about in the studio, admiring them. "Wouldn't it be splendid," he would think to himself, "if we had such a fellow for Number One Artist at home!" And then he would go away shaking his head, for he knew, as well as he knew anything, that the artist was too good a man to end up at an easel in Hell.

The Devil pondered this problem off and on for a long time and after a few years he had an idea. The artist had completed thirty-seven pictures. "When he makes it to forty," said the Devil to himself, "I'll just go up there and steal them all and hang them down here in my gallery. Forty is enough, anyway. And then I'll steal all his canvas, paints, and brushes, and even his easel—after which we'll just sit back and see what happens."

The artist didn't know of the Devil's plan, of course. He went on calmly with his work, creating pictures of unmatchable evil, and whenever he went out, little children would follow him and birds would perch on his shoulders, and people would say: "Here comes the artist! What a good fellow he is, in spite of his terrible pictures—surely the best fellow in the World!"

It wasn't long, however, before the fortieth picture was completed, and when that time came, the Devil, true to his plan, sneaked up out of Hell and stole the whole kit and caboodle. He dropped the easel, brushes, and things in a dusty corner of his throne room, but he hung the pictures in his gallery and they were a huge success, with streams of the damned and all manner of major and minor demons filing through every day to study them approvingly over a cup of punch.

Up in the World the artist, meanwhile, was baffled

by what had happened. He asked around his village, but no one knew anything at all about the disappearance of the pictures, and even less about the theft of the easel and the rest. The artist grew very worried because he was a poor man who earned the money for his tools by digging holes, since no one ever bought his pictures, and he knew that he would have to dig holes for a very long time before he had enough money to begin again.

"Lovely!" said the Devil when word came to him in Hell of the artist's distress. "Now we shall see what we shall see." And he sat back and smiled and waited.

As day after day went by, with no more pictures to work on and nothing to do but dig, the artist began to alter. He stopped smiling, and chased little children away when they tried to follow him, and shooed the birds from his shoulders. He grew silent and ill-tempered and even cast off from the friends who loved him. And when he walked scowling in the village, the people would move out of his way and say to each

other: "Here comes the artist. What a terrible fellow he is after all, just like the pictures he used to paint!"

The Devil was enormously pleased by these developments. His plan was working perfectly. "I'll have the fellow himself in the end, as well as his pictures," he said, and he sat back and smiled and waited some more.

One day, however, as the artist was digging holes in the earth, he came to a rich layer of clay. He scooped out a large lump and put it aside, and when the day was over he took it home to his studio. All night he worked with it and when morning came he had finished a little statue. Strange to say, however, the statue showed a mother bending over to touch a small child clinging to her skirts, and the mood of it was one of great goodness and love.

This was the beginning of a new life for the artist. He modeled more and more small statues, similar to the first, and people liked them so much that he sold every one and didn't need to dig any more except when he needed more clay. Soon he could afford to work in stone, and as his fame spread, he was asked to carve fine marble statues and these in time could be found in every great church and courtyard in the land.

But the artist's ill temper grew worse and worse as his statues grew more and more loving. He became at last quite the opposite of what he had been before. And the people who had once been his friends, still believing there is good and evil in everyone, said it seemed as if all the good in the artist came out in his work and left behind nothing but evil in the man himself.

The Devil was hard put to understand what had gone wrong. On the one hand he was well pleased with the kind of man the artist had become, but at the same time he was disgusted with the statues. "That fellow is as useless to me now as he was before, and I don't know what to do," he said with a gnash of teeth. "So I will do the best thing: just forget all about him."

And that's what the Devil did. He forgot about the artist altogether and turned his attention to other things. As for the artist, nobody knows what became of him.

His paintings are admired in Hell to this day, and his statues are admired in Heaven, but the man himself seems to have been lost somewhere in between. No matter. He's sure to have plenty of company.

ASHES

THERE WAS a very bad man once, a certain Mr. Bezzle, who made a great deal of money by cheating shamefully, and on his death, which happened all of a sudden and was the plain result of too much roasted pig, his wife had his body cremated and kept the ashes in a silver urn on the mantelpiece, where it was nice and warm. This was entirely appropriate, though she may not have known it, for her husband had gone directly to Hell when he died, and was every bit as nice and warm there as his ashes were up in the World.

Now, it happened that Mrs. Bezzle, grown lonesome with her husband gone, took on a large, ill-mannered dog to keep her company. "He's got whiskers and he snores," she told her friends, "so it's just like having Bezzle back again." She was devoted to the dog and spoiled him dreadfully, even to the point of allowing him to gnaw bones in the house, though this practice was a great annoyance to the housemaid, whose task it was to keep things tidy.

One day, on coming across a greasy pork bone on the hearthrug, the housemaid, in a fit of temper, seized it and flung it into the fire, where it burned away to ashes with no one any the wiser. And then, on the next day, when the housemaid was at her daily chores, the handle of her broom bumped Mr. Bezzle's urn and down it fell onto the hearth, spilling that bad man's earthly remains into the fireplace.

"Horrors!" said the housemaid, and then she looked around. Mrs. Bezzle was nowhere in sight. "Oh, well," said the housemaid, and she knelt down and carefully scooped the ashes back into the urn with the fire shovel.

This was all very well, perhaps, and one way out of a bad situation, but the trouble was that some of Mr.

Bezzle's ashes had got mixed with the ashes in the fireplace; and some of the ashes in the fireplace were the ashes of the pork bone which the housemaid had thrown into the fire the day before. So what happened was that the pork-bone ashes got into the urn too, where they clearly didn't belong, and no one knew a thing about it.

Next morning, down in Hell, the Devil was sitting in his throne room writing poems when Mr. Bezzle came in and demanded an interview.

"What's the problem?" asked the Devil, going on with his writing.

"Problem?" cried Bezzle. *"Problem?* Why, look for yourself!"

So the Devil looked and saw that a large pig had come in with Mr. Bezzle and was standing pressed against his legs, looking up at him fondly.

"What are you doing with that pig?" asked the Devil.

"What am *I* doing?" cried Bezzle. "What is *it* doing? That's the question. See here now. Everything's gone along well since I came down. Good company, plenty to eat and drink, a nice room all to myself. Then yesterday this pig appears out of nowhere, follows me about like a puppy, and even insists on getting into bed with me. I don't know where it came from, and I don't know why or how. Do you?"

"I haven't the least idea," said the Devil.

"Well, something has to be done," said Bezzle, trying to push the pig away, though this seemed to be entirely useless, seeing as the pig merely pressed the closer and continued to gaze up at Bezzle with a look of great warmth and affection in its little red eyes.

"It's a nice enough pig," observed the Devil, peering at it, "and quite attached to you, evidently."

"Never mind that," said Bezzle. "Just do something. I really don't want to spend Eternity stomach to stomach with a pig."

"I'll ask around," said the Devil. "No doubt we can figure things out."

So Bezzle went away, the pig at his heels, and the Devil called in a couple of scholars, who looked through a couple of books; and the next day, when Bezzle came back, the Devil said, "It appears that you must have been buried with the pig, somehow or other."

"Impossible," said Bezzle. "I was cremated. And my wife keeps my ashes in an urn on the mantelpiece."

"Oh?" said the Devil. "Well, still, you're mixed up with the pig somewhere along the line. It's the only explanation."

"Then I'll just have to get unmixed," said Bezzle, moving his feet so the pig—who of course was still with him—wouldn't step on his toes. "One more night like the last two and I'll be crackers."

So the Devil went up to the World to Bezzle's house and when no one was looking he stole the urn, brought it down to Hell, and dumped out its contents in a quiet corner. "Well, there they are," he said to Bezzle. "You'll have to pick out the pig's part yourself, assuming you can tell the difference."

"There's got to be a difference between my ashes and a pig's," said Bezzle. And he set to work at once with high hopes, tweezers, and a large magnifying glass.

Day after day Bezzle sat in the corner, working away, while the pig rested its chin on his knee and gazed at him, and after a year he had separated a thimbleful of ashes that he thought must be the pig's because they were a slightly different shade of gray. After two years, and two thimblesful, it appeared that he was right, for the pig seemed less attentive. Its gaze was sometimes distracted from Bezzle's face, and it took to spending an hour or two, now and then, wandering off by itself. Bezzle was delighted, and attacked his work with fresh vigor.

And then, after three years, when the task was nearly done and the pig was only coming by for lunch, Mrs. Bezzle's housemaid died of ill temper and arrived in Hell, still clutching her broom. And the first thing she noticed was the two piles of ashes, left alone for

a moment in the quiet corner where Bezzle had been laboring so long.

"This place is a mess," said the housemaid.

And she swept the two piles into one pile, swept the one pile into her dustpan, carried it all out, and buried it by the gates.

All Bezzle ever knew was that one minute the ashes were gone and the next minute the pig was back full time. Still, after a while, when the first rude shock had worn away, he grew resigned to having the pig around. They were together day and night, after all, and there was nothing for it but to make do. But Bezzle, in time, did more than that. He found that the pig was really rather good company and altogether his best friend in the place. Before a hundred years were out, he had even managed to teach it to play gin rummy, though it cheated shamefully. As for the housemaid, she settled down in another part of Hell and kept her fireplace—and her hearthrug—shining clean.

PERFECTION

THERE WAS a little girl once called Angela who always did everything right. In fact, she was perfect. She had better manners than anyone, and not only that, but she hung up her clothes and never forgot to feed the chickens. And not only *that,* but her hair was always combed and she never bit her fingernails. A lot of people, all of them fair-to-middling, disliked her very much because of this, but Angela didn't care. She just went right on being perfect and let things go as they would.

Now, when the Devil heard about Angela, he was revolted. "Not," he explained to himself, "that I give a hang about children as a rule, but *this* one! Imagine what she'll be like when she grows up—a woman whose only fault is that she has no faults!" And the very thought of it made him cross as crabs. So he wrote up a list of things to do that he hoped would make Angela edgy and, if all went well, even make her lose her temper. "Once she loses her temper a few times," said the Devil, "she'll never be perfect again."

However, this proved harder to do than the Devil had expected. He sent her chicken pox, then poison ivy, and then a lot of mosquito bites, but she never scratched and didn't even seem to itch. He arranged for a cow to step on her favorite doll, but she never shed a tear. Instead, she forgave the cow at once, in public, and said it didn't matter. Next the Devil fixed it so that for weeks on end her cocoa was always too hot and her oatmeal too cold, but this, too, failed to make her angry. In fact, it seemed that the worse things were, the better Angela liked it, since it gave her a chance to show just how perfect she was.

Years went by. The Devil used up every idea on his list but one, and Angela still had her temper, and her manners were still better than anyone's. "Well, anyway," said the Devil to himself, "my last idea can't miss. That much is certain." And he waited patiently for the proper moment.

When that moment came, the Devil's last idea worked like anything. In fact, it was perfect. As soon as he made it happen, Angela lost her temper once a day at least, and sometimes oftener, and after a while she had lost it so often that she was never quite so perfect again.

And how did he do it? Simple. He merely saw that she got a perfect husband and a perfect house, and then—he sent her a fair-to-middling child.

THE ROSE AND
THE MINOR DEMON

T H E R E   W A S   a minor demon once, a wistful, sentimental creature who really didn't belong in Hell at all,
though Heaven knows there was nowhere else for him
to go. And the Devil was embarrassed to have him
around because he was so different from everyone else.
So a job was found for him which kept him out of sight,
and this job was to guard the Devil's treasure room.

The minor demon worked at his task every day, which
is to say that he sat in the treasure room with nothing
to do, since no one ever came near the place; and while
he sat there, he would fall to mooning over all the
thousand objects that filled the shelves, everything from

silver pitchers to golden calves. But the object he mooned over most was a large porcelain vase which had a lot of roses painted on it. The roses, he thought, were lovely, all colors of the rainbow, and he wished like anything that there were roses just like them in Hell.

But there were no roses of any kind in Hell, or rainbows either, for that matter. And yet, the more he mooned about it, the more the minor demon wanted some, and at last he went to the Devil to ask if he could have a garden.

"Well now," said the Devil. "That's a funny thing to ask for. What in the World do you want a garden for?"

"I just want to plant things," said the minor demon. "Flowers."

"Flowers?" exclaimed the Devil. "What kind of flowers?"

"Oh," said the minor demon nervously, "just some roses or something."

"Ugh!" said the Devil. "Roses? In Hell? Where did you get an idea like that?"

"From the porcelain vase in the treasure room," said the minor demon, and then he blushed a darker shade of red than he was already. "I guess," he confessed, "I've got a soft spot in my heart for roses."

"What kind of a minor demon are you anyway?" said the Devil in exasperation. "A soft spot? In your heart? You haven't got a heart. And as for soft spots, you know what they say about that. A soft spot in an apple means it's going bad, and one bad apple can spoil a barrelful. So let's have no more talk about soft spots and hearts. Or roses, either. Roses are entirely out of the question. If you really want a garden, you can have one, I suppose, but you'll have to plant sensible things. Like henbane or hemlock or aconite."

"All right," said the minor demon sadly, and he went away to a quiet place and hoed up the ground and planted henbane and hemlock and aconite and even a little deadly nightshade. But he wasn't satisfied, not even when all the things he had planted grew like weeds, which is after all exactly what they were. For he still wanted roses.

At last he could stand it no longer. He crept out of Hell one night, which was quite against the rules for minor demons, and made his way up to the World, where everything was sweet with May; and he stole a little rosebush and brought it back down and planted it at the back of his garden, with the hemlock growing up tall around it to hide it from view.

The minor demon was amazed at his own daring and trembled very much to think what might happen when the deed was discovered. But for a long while no one suspected that the rosebush was there. Even the Devil, passing by, admired the hemlock and the deadly nightshade, and told the minor demon that the garden was a good idea. But then one morning one of the buds on the rosebush opened into a blossom, white and silky as a baby's fist.

The minor demon was enchanted when he saw the

blossom, but right away he was frightened too. For although it was just like the roses on the porcelain vase, and most enormously pleasing, it had one thing the painted roses didn't have, and that one thing was fragrance. The minor demon hadn't known about the fragrance. And now the air all over that part of Hell was rich with it.

Up rose the Devil in his throne room, sniffing like Jack in the Beanstalk's giant, except that he didn't say "Fee fie foe fum." Instead, he said, "What's that smell?" and wrinkled up his nose. And he trailed around, up and down, looking for it everywhere.

But the minor demon, afraid that exactly this would happen, had hurriedly picked the single blossom and buried it, so that the fragrance drifted off at last and disappeared.

"Humph!" said the Devil. "Must have been a bad dream." And he put it out of his mind and went back to his usual business.

The minor demon grieved for the buried flower.

"But what else could I have done?" he reflected with a sigh. And next morning, of course, the same thing happened again. Another blossom opened, spilled its fragrance, and had to be picked and buried.

This time, however, the Devil knew that the smell he smelled was not a dream after all. "It's that pesty minor demon, that's what it is," he said to himself. "He's got a rosebush in that garden of his or I miss my guess. And tomorrow I'll catch him red-handed."

So the morning after, the Devil got up early and went directly to the minor demon's garden, where he found that the smell of roses was powerful indeed. And of course it took no time at all to uncover the rosebush, back behind the hemlock, with another heavy blossom nodding on its stem. Not only that, but there crouched the minor demon in the very act of picking it.

"Aha!" cried the Devil triumphantly. "What have we here?"

The minor demon was a wistful, sentimental creature, to be sure, but still he could be quick when he had to

be. So, although he trembled, he thought for an instant and said, "It's harvest time. I'm harvesting my thorns."

"Thorns, my grandmother," said the Devil. "That's a rosebush."

"Oh no, sir," said the minor demon. "Excuse me, but this is a *thorn* bush. Why, just see for yourself. It's got many more thorns than blossoms. I planted it especially, and I'm giving all the thorns to you when the crop is in."

"Indeed!" said the Devil. "Well, the fact is, that white thing you're holding there happens to be a rose."

"Dear me!" said the minor demon. "Is it really? Isn't that a shame! And the thorns were so ideal."

The Devil knew perfectly well that the minor demon knew the bush was a rosebush. And what's more, the minor demon knew the Devil knew he knew it. But still, the idea of a crop of thorns was appealing to the Devil, for thorns were useful in a number of ways. So at last he merely shrugged and said, "Very well. You can be my first and only thorn farmer if you want to.

But pull up that terrible rosebush at once and plant a nice big cactus instead. Oh, and while you're at it, take a can of black enamel and give that porcelain vase a good thick coat. There'll be no roses of any kind in Hell as long as I'm around."

So the minor demon had to pull up the rosebush and throw it away and plant a cactus behind the hemlock, and this made him very sad. And it made him even sadder to paint the porcelain vase. Still, he knew he was lucky to get off with so small a punishment, so he tended his garden without another murmur and harvested many a bumper crop of thorns.

He kept on guarding the treasure room as well, though it gave him no pleasure to look at the porcelain vase now that it was painted black. And then one day long after, the Devil came in for some reason or other, and when he saw the vase, he said, "What's that ugly thing doing in here? Take it out and throw it away." For he had forgotten all about the roses.

Well, the minor demon did as the Devil asked. He

took the porcelain vase out and dropped it on the trash pile. But when it landed, it broke into a great many pieces and some of the black enamel chipped off. And there, on one of the fragments where the paint had come away, a rose was clearly visible, looking white and silky as a baby's fist.

Then the minor demon took the fragment and filed down its sharp and jagged edges, and carried it home to keep under his pillow forever and ever. And in this way he had a treasure of his own, which made Hell a little nicer place for him to be even if he didn't belong there, since Heaven knows there was nowhere else for him to go. The painted rose wasn't as good as the real thing, of course, but still it was better than nothing. And knowing it was there under his pillow made the minor demon happy in a small and secret way that no one ever knew about but him.

THE POWER OF
SPEECH

A LOT of people believe that once a day every goat in the World has to go down to Hell to have his beard combed by the Devil, but this is obvious nonsense. The Devil doesn't have time to comb the beards of all the goats in the World even if he wanted to, which of course he doesn't. Who would? There are far too many goats in the first place, and in the second place their beards are nearly all in terrible condition, full of snarls, burrs, and dandelion juice.

Nevertheless, whether he wants to comb their beards or not, the Devil is as fond of goats as he is of anything, and always has one or another somewhere about, kept on as a sort of pet. He treats them pretty well too, considering, and the goats give back as good or as bad as they get, which is one reason why the Devil likes them so much, for goats are one hundred percent unsentimental.

Now, there was a goat in the World once that the Devil had had his eye on for some time, a great big goat with curving horns and a prize from every fair for miles around. "I want that goat," said the Devil to himself, "and I mean to have him even if he has to be dragged down here by his beard." But that was a needless thing to say, and the Devil knew it, for animals, and especially goats, are nothing at all like people when it comes to right and wrong. Animals don't see much to choose between the two. So, Heaven or Hell, it's all one to them, especially goats. All the Devil had to do was go up there, to the cottage that the goat called home, and lead him away.

The only trouble was that the old woman who owned the goat was no dummy. She knew how much the Devil liked goats and she also knew how much he hated bells. So she kept the goat—whose name was Walpurgis—tied up to a tree in her yard and she fastened a little bell around his neck with a length of ribbon. Walpurgis hated bells almost as much as the Devil did; but there was no way he could say so and nothing he could do about his own bell except to stand very still in order to keep it from jangling. This led some passers-by to conclude that he was only a stuffed goat put there for show and not a real goat at all. So many people came up to the old woman's door to ask about it that at last she put up a sign which said: THIS IS A REAL GOAT. And after that she got a little peace and quiet. Not that any of it mattered to Walpurgis, who didn't give a hoot for what anybody thought one way or another.

The Devil didn't care what anybody thought either. But he still wanted the goat. He turned the whole problem of the bell over in his mind, considering this solution and that, and at last, hoping something would occur to him, he went up out of Hell to the old woman's door to have a little talk with her. "See here," he said as soon as she answered his knock. "I mean to have your goat."

The old woman looked him up and down, and wasn't in the least dismayed. "Go ahead and take him," she said. "If you can do that, he's yours."

The Devil glanced across the yard to where Walpurgis stood tied up to the tree. "If I try to untie him, that bell will ring, and I can't stand bells," he said with a shudder.

"I know," said the old woman, looking satisfied.

The Devil swallowed his annoyance and tried a more familiar tack. "I'll give you anything you want," he said, "if you'll go over there and take away that wretched bell. I'll even make you Queen of the World."

The old woman cackled. "I've got my cottage, my goat, and everything I need," she said. "Why should I want to buy trouble? There's nothing you can do for me."

The Devil ground his teeth. "It takes a mean mind

to put a bell on a goat," he snapped. "If he were *my* goat, I'd never do that. I'll bet a bucket of brimstone he hates that bell."

"Save your brimstone," said the old woman. "He's only a goat. It doesn't matter to *him*."

"He'd tell you, though, if he could talk," said the Devil.

"May be," said the old woman. "I've often wished he *could* talk, if it comes to that. But until he can, I'll keep him any way I want to. So goodbye." And she slammed the door between them.

This gave the Devil the very idea he was looking for. He hurried down to Hell and was back in a minute with a little cake into which he had mixed the power of speech, and he tossed it to Walpurgis. The goat chewed it up at once and swallowed it and then the Devil changed himself into a field mouse and hid in the grass to see what would happen.

After a while Walpurgis shook himself, which made the bell jangle, and at that he opened his mouth and said a very bad word. An expression of great surprise came over his face when he heard himself speak, and his eyes opened wide. Then they narrowed again and he tried a few more bad words, all of which came out clear and unmistakable. Then, as much as goats can ever smile, Walpurgis smiled. He moved as far from the tree as the rope would allow, and called out in a rude voice: "Hey there, you in the cottage!"

The old woman came to the door and put her head out. "Who's there?" she asked suspiciously, peering about.

"It's me! Walpurgis!" said the goat. "Come out here and take away this bell."

"You *can* talk, then!" observed the old woman.

"I can," said Walpurgis. "And I want this bell off. Now. And be quick about it."

The old woman stared at the goat and then she folded her arms. "I had no idea you'd be this kind of goat," she said.

"To the Devil with that," said Walpurgis carelessly.

"What's the difference? It's this bell I'm talking about. Come over here and take it off."

"I can't," said the old woman. "If I do, the Devil will steal you away for sure."

"If you don't," said the goat, "I'll yell and raise a ruckus."

"Yell away," said the old woman. "I've got no choice in the matter that I can see." And she went back inside the cottage and shut the door.

So Walpurgis began to yell. He yelled all the bad words he knew and he yelled them loud and clear, and he yelled them over and over till the countryside rang with them, and before long the old woman came out of her cottage with her fingers in her ears. "Stop that!" she shouted at the goat.

Walpurgis stopped yelling. "Do something, then," he said.

"All right, I will!" said the old woman. "And serve you both right. If I'd known what kind of a goat you were, I'd have done it in the first place. The Devil deserves a goat like you." She took away the bell and set Walpurgis free and right away the Devil leaped up from the grass and took the goat straight back to Hell.

Now the funny thing about the power of speech is that the Devil could give it away but he couldn't take it back. For a while it was amusing to have a talking goat in Hell, but not for very long, because Walpurgis complained a lot. He'd always been dissatisfied but being able to say so made all the difference. The air was too hot, he said, or the food was too dry, or there was just plain nothing to do but stand around. "I might as well be wearing a bell again, for all the moving about I do in this place," said Walpurgis.

"Don't mention bells!" said the Devil.

This gave Walpurgis the very idea he was looking for. He began to yell all the bell-ringing words he knew. He yelled them loud and clear—clang, ding, jingle, bong—and he yelled them over and over till Hell rang with them.

At last the Devil rose up with his fingers in his ears. "Stop that!" he shouted at the goat.

Walpurgis stopped yelling. "Do something, then," he said.

"All right, I will!" said the Devil. And with that he changed Walpurgis into a stuffed goat and took him back up to the old woman's cottage and left him there in the yard, tied up to the tree.

When the old woman saw that the goat was back, she hurried out to see how he was. And when she *saw* how he was, she said to herself, "Well, that's what comes of talking too much." But she put the bell around his neck and kept him standing there anyway, and since the sign was still there too, and still said THIS IS A REAL GOAT, nobody ever knew the difference. And everyone, except Walpurgis, was satisfied.

The Devil's Other Storybook

THE FORTUNES OF
MADAME ORGANZA

THERE WAS a fortuneteller once who wasn't much good at her work. No matter who came to her door to get a fortune told, she could never think of any but the same old three: "You will meet a tall, dark stranger"; "You will take a long journey"; and "You will find a pot of gold." She went through the usual rigmarole, with a crystal ball and chanting, all in a gloomy little parlor lit with one candle, and she even wore a turban with a big glass jewel glued to it, right on the front where it showed. But of course, though this was very nice, the fortunes themselves were what mattered, and since none of them ever came true, it wasn't long before no one came to her door at all and she was forced to take in washing to keep herself going. But she kept the sign on her door saying FORTUNES BY MADAME ORGANZA—though her name in fact was Bessie—just in case.

Now, it happened that one dark night a couple of burglars eased through the village with a satchel of money stolen somewhere else, and they hid themselves in a barn, where in the morning they were discovered snoring away by the farmer; and he ran them off with a pitchfork so all-of-a-sudden that they had to leave the loot behind, buried in the haymow, and didn't dare go back.

Later the same morning, the farmer hired a milkmaid, who, being new to the place and no one thinking to warn her, went off with her first day's wages to get her fortune told. Madame Organza put on the turban, lit the candle, muttered and hummed for a while, and then said, "You will find a pot of gold."

"Goody!" said the milkmaid. And, tripping home, she climbed the ladder to the haymow to have a little peace and quiet for planning what she'd do when she was rich. And of course she sat down on the burglars'

satchel and pulled it out and opened it, and there was her gold, great handfuls of glittering coins, just as her fortune had predicted.

"Well! Goody again!" said the milkmaid. She closed up the satchel, climbed back down the ladder, and went to find the farmer. "Please," she said, "does this belong to you?"

"No," said the farmer, "it doesn't."

"Goody three!" said the milkmaid. "It's mine, then, and just what Madame Organza said I'd find." And she let the farmer peek inside at the gold. Then she went away to the city to begin a new life, and was never heard from again, though the farmer thought he saw her there, some time later, rolling by in a carriage, with plumes on her hat and a little white dog in her lap.

But in the meantime her story spread all over the village, and such a noise was made that down in Hell the Devil pricked up his ears and said, "What's that hullabaloo?" And when he found out what had happened, he smiled a big smile and straightaway went up to the World to see what he could do to cause a little extra trouble and confusion, for he'd guessed that

Madame Organza's business would be taking a turn for the better.

This was indeed the case. The line of people waiting to get their fortunes told stretched clear to the river and halfway back, with everyone so excited that everything else was forgotten. Cows were left unmilked, pigs unslopped, and bread sat so long in ovens that it burnt away to cinders. And Madame Organza, believing, herself, that she'd somehow got the knack of it at last, was telling fortunes at a great rate, though the fortunes were only the same old three from before.

During the days that followed, thanks to the Devil's interference, the village changed completely. Twenty-two people found pots of gold and went to live in the city, which they soon found dismal to the utmost but were too proud to say so. Another thirty-seven went off on long journeys, ending up in such spots as Borneo and Peru with no way at all to get back, and so they were forced, for a living, to chop bamboo or to keep herds of llamas in the Andes.

All the rest had met with tall, dark strangers who hung about, getting in the way, and looking altogether so alarming in their black hats and cloaks and their long black beards that the villagers remaining were afraid to stay and hurried to move in with relatives in other villages, which caused no end of bad feeling.

At last there was no one left but Madame Organza and the strangers, and since the strangers had the orphaned cows and pigs to care for and didn't want their fortunes told, Madame Organza put away her sign forever and went back full-time to being Bessie. She took in the strangers' washing, all of which was black, and made the best of it she could without complaining. And she put her crystal ball in the garden, where it showed to great advantage, out among the pansies, whenever the sun was shining.

JUSTICE

THERE ARE few surprises in Hell. At least, the Devil has seldom been surprised—except for the time when someone spotted a rhinoceros.

"Absurd," said the Devil.

"I know it," said the major demon who'd brought in the news. "Nevertheless, I went and looked myself, and it's out there all right, large as life, with a hole right through its horn. It's out there shuffling and snuffling and breathing hard, and I'd say it looks impatient."

"I wonder what it wants," said the Devil. "Well, never mind. Perhaps it will go away."

Now, on this very day a man named Bangs arrived unexpectedly in Hell. Bangs was a mighty hunter who in life had crept about the wild parts of the World, shooting off his gun and making possible a steady stream of elephant's-foot umbrella stands and rabbit-fur muffs and reindeer-antler coatracks and other lovely, useful things, till on the day in question he backed by accident into a boa constrictor. And the boa constrictor, seizing both the opportunity and Bangs himself, constricted the hunter so hard that, before he knew it, he found himself at the gates of Hell, out of breath and very much surprised.

"This is a piece of luck!" said the Devil when Bangs was sent in to see him. "As it happens, you're the very type we need. We've got a rhinoceros loose, and we can't have it snorting about, upsetting people. Go out and catch it. Then we'll pen it up and charge admission."

"Well now," said Bangs, who'd recovered his breath and his swagger, "I don't put much store in bringing 'em back alive."

"Bangs, Bangs," said the Devil. "You've got a lot to learn. Guns are no earthly use down here. You'll have to do the job with a net. But be careful. This rhinoceros has a hole right through its horn and I'm told it looks impatient."

"A hole right through its horn?" said Bangs, turning pale.

"That's the situation," said the Devil.

"Dear me," said Bangs. "I may be the one who made that hole."

"I wouldn't be a bit surprised," said the Devil. "Now, run along and do what you're told."

So Bangs had to take a big rope net and creep out into the wild parts of Hell to look for the rhinoceros, and it goes without saying that, without his gun, he was very much afraid he would find it. He looked all the rest of the day and never saw a thing, but he could hear the shuffling and the snuffling and the breathing hard, always just out of sight. At sundown, however, he was setting up his tent when out through the bushes burst the rhinoceros, like a bus downhill with no brakes, and it chased Bangs all night long, up and down the wild parts till daybreak. And then it disappeared.

This happened three times in a row, and at last Bangs dragged in to see the Devil. "Look here," he said. "I'm supposed to be chasing that rhinoceros, I know, but instead, somehow, it's chasing me. It chases me all night long, and then it disappears. I can't go on like this—I'll be worn to a frazzle."

"Go on?" said the Devil. "Of course you'll go on. You'll catch it sooner or later. I'm depending on you, and I don't want to see you again till the job is done."

So Bangs dragged back to the wild parts. He tried to sleep in the daytime, but this was hard to do, what with the shuffling and the snuffling and the breathing hard always just out of sight. And as soon as the sun went down in the evening, the rhinoceros would burst through the bushes and chase him up and down till morning.

After three weeks of this, Bangs was worn to a frazzle, and so were his boots. He gave up the chase altogether and took to living as wild animals do, always watchful, always listening, sleeping with one eye open. And he dug himself a hole to hide in. But as sure as he came out at night to cook his supper, there was the rhinoceros, and off they would go, pounding through the wild parts till the sun came up at dawn.

"Well," said the Devil after a while, "I guess Bangs is doing the next best thing. He may not be catching that rhinoceros, but at least he's keeping it busy."

"True enough," said the major demon.

"Might as well leave him to it, then," said the Devil. "Pass the word that the danger's taken care of."

So the major demon passed the word and everyone felt relieved. And every month or so the Devil sent someone out with fresh hay for the rhinoceros and a new pair of boots for Bangs—just to keep things even.

THE SOLDIER

THERE WAS a soldier once who had nothing at all to do because, though he'd often been to war, at this particular time there wasn't one to fight in, anywhere around. So he did what he could—he kept his sword shiny, and polished his boots, and he practiced marching on an open road, up and down, up and down, with his plumes and tassels bouncing and the buttons on his jacket flashing in the sun, and the sight of him was altogether splendid.

One day the Devil came along, disguised as an old, old man with a weak knee and a strong crutch, and he stopped when he saw the soldier. "I say!" exclaimed the Devil. "What an elegant picture you make!"

The soldier gave him a smart salute. "Thank you, old man," he said. "I'm practicing my marching."

"So I see," said the Devil. "But why aren't you off somewhere, fighting?"

"There's no war anywhere to fight in, dash it," said the soldier, with a sigh.

"Don't despair," said the Devil. "Something will turn up soon."

"I hope so," said the soldier, "for there's nothing I like even half so much. I've seen some lovely wars, old man, some lovely wars."

"Ah!" said the Devil. "I don't for a moment doubt it."

"I fought against the Turks at Heliopolis," said the soldier proudly.

"Yes?" said the Devil. "I was there."

"Well—but I also fought in the Santo Domingo Rebellion," said the soldier.

"I was there," said the Devil.

"Indeed!" said the soldier, with a frown. "However, *I* was with Napoleon at Austerlitz."

"I was there," said the Devil.

"Hmm," said the soldier. "You've seen a few campaigns yourself."

"Oh, yes," said the Devil. "In fact, I never miss one."

"Then," said the soldier, "I suppose you'll say you were there at Waterloo."

"I was there," said the Devil.

The soldier raised one eyebrow. "Come, come, old man," he said. "Next you'll be telling me you fought in the Siege of Troy and went with Caesar into Gaul!"

"That's right," said the Devil. "I was there."

The soldier tried to hide a smile, for he didn't at all believe what he was hearing. But, deciding to be polite, he said, "It seems I've got a ways to go to match you."

"Yes," said the Devil, "you do."

"Well," said the soldier, smiling once again behind his sleeve, "I must be getting on with my marching. Perhaps we'll meet again at the next great battle."

"Perhaps we will," said the Devil, "for I'll certainly be there." And he moved off down the road, leaning on his crutch, and didn't try at all to hide his own smile.

BOATING

SOME PEOPLE think Hell is dry as crackers, but this is not the case. There are four nice rivers inside the walls, and a fifth, called the Styx, that flows clear round the place outside.

Hell has the Styx the way castles have moats, but there isn't any drawbridge. Instead, you have to come across the water on a ferryboat run by a very old man named Charon. Most of the time Charon does his job all by himself, but it happened one day that he came to the throne room with a problem.

"What's wrong?" said the Devil, putting aside the novel he was reading.

"Why," said Charon, "they're having some kind of

fuss in the World, in case you didn't know it."

"They're always having fusses in the World," said the Devil with a yawn. "What of it?"

"Well, whatever sort of fuss it is," said Charon, "they're coming down in droves and I can't keep up. You'll have to lay on another ferryboat."

"You don't say!" said the Devil. "That's splendid! I'll come and take a look."

And sure enough, there were hordes of people on the far side of the Styx, waiting to get across. Some of them were quite put out to be kept there cooling their heels, and wouldn't stay nicely in line for a minute. And what with their birdcages, boxes, and bags all piled and getting mixed, the confusion was indescribable.

"I'm doing the best I can," said Charon to the Devil, "but you see the way things are."

"Hmmm," said the Devil. "Well now. I'll give you a hand myself. It looks like fun."

He called for a second ferry—which was, like Charon's, more of a raft than a boat—and, climbing aboard, seized the pole and pushed out cross-current into the river Styx. He wasn't as good at it as Charon, not having had the practice, but still arrived not too long after at the opposite bank, where all the people were waiting.

"Ahoy," said the Devil. "Women and children first." And since there weren't any children—indeed, there never are—three old women stepped onto the raft, which was all there was room for, and off they started back across the river.

"And who, my dears, may you be?" asked the Devil, eyeing their silks and feathers.

"We're sisters," said the first old woman. "The last of an important old family. The sort of people who matter."

"We can't imagine what we're doing here with all these common types," said the second.

"It's all a terrible mistake," said the third.

"Indeed!" said the Devil, with a smile. "I'll have someone look into it."

"I should hope so," said the first old woman. "Why, we can't put up with this! Look at these dreadful people you've got coming in—riffraff of the lowest sort! It would appear that anyone at all can get in."

"We can't be expected," said the second, "to mingle with peasants and boors."

"Never in the World," said the third.

"It's true," said the Devil, "that we do have every class down here. But so, I've heard, does Heaven."

"I don't believe it," said the first old woman. "Not Heaven."

"You must be misinformed," said the second. "Only the best people go to Heaven."

"Otherwise," said the third, "whyever call it Heaven?"

"An interesting point," said the Devil. "Why, indeed!"

And all the way across the river Styx the three went on protesting and explaining.

When the raft at last scraped up before the gates, the sisters refused to get off. "We simply can't go in," said the first old woman. "I'm sure you understand."

"Oh, I do," said the Devil. "I do."

"Not our grade of people in the least," said the second.

"Look into it for us, won't you?" said the third.

"We'll just wait here and catch the next boat back."

Now, the river Styx flows round the walls of Hell in a wandering clockwise direction, and a long way round it is, too, which will come as no surprise. And though the current isn't swift, it's steady. So the Devil, disembarking, put his pole against the ferry and simply shoved it out again so that the current bore it off, turning it gently in circles, with the sisters still on board. And then he went back to his throne room and sent a minor demon out to give a hand to Charon. For the Devil had had enough and wanted to finish his novel.

Years went by, and dozens of years, with the sisters still floating round the walls of Hell. Every once in a while, in the beginning, the Devil would remember them and go out when it was time for them to pass. And as they came along, he could hear their protestations, steady as the current of the Styx.

"Ragtag and bobtail," they'd be saying. "Waifs and strays. Quite beneath contempt! Commoners, upstarts, people of the street. Not our sort at all." And they would say, "There's been some mix-up, certainly. Why don't they get it straightened out?"

Sometimes they saw the Devil standing on the banks, and the first old woman would call to him, "Yoo-hoo! I say, my good man—have you made inquiries concerning our situation?" And the Devil would wave and nod, and watch as they slowly circled by and disappeared. And then he would smile and go back through the gates for a nice cold glass of cider. But after a time he forgot the three completely. This was not because he was too busy to remember. No, indeed. He forgot them because they weren't the sort of people who matter.

HOW AKBAR WENT TO
BETHLEHEM

THERE ARE no camels in Hell. You might suppose
there would be, for camels have shocking bad tempers;
they were crabby to begin with, when everything was
new, and they're just as crabby now. The only thing a
camel does from morning to night is sulk and moan
about in the desert, kicking its children—who always
kick back—and complaining in a voice that is not at
all agreeable. But still, there are no camels in Hell.
Not anymore.

Once, long ago, when Hell was getting settled, there
was a camel there, a great, ragged beast named Akbar,
and the place was just to his liking. He was the Devil's
special pet, and could go where he pleased, growl-

ing and grumbling and curling his long, split lip at everyone. "Oh, Akbar," the Devil would say, "what a satisfaction you are!" And Akbar would sneer and show his yellow teeth, the picture of disrespect, and the Devil would laugh and let him get away with it. So it seemed like a nice arrangement.

Then one night when it was winter in the World, a strange light appeared in the sky that had never been there before. Everyone in Hell observed it, and they all crowded into the throne room—major and minor demons, and imps of various ages—to find out what it meant.

The Devil had seen it, too, and was very much upset, though of course he didn't let on. "It's only a star," he said. "You've all seen stars before."

"But not like this one," said the demons. "Never one like this. We don't know what to make of it!" And one of the youngest imps began to cry.

"It's nothing, I tell you," said the Devil snappishly. "Go along to bed and leave me be."

But when they had gone, he climbed to the roof of his throne room and stared at the strange new light in the sky above the World, for he knew very well what had happened. A baby had been born up there who was going to be nothing but trouble for a long, long time to come. "Confound it," said the Devil to himself. "And just when I was getting on so well!"

Now, although this event was a terrible thing for the Devil, he still felt a certain curiosity. So, one dark night soon after, he dressed himself as an Arab, climbed onto Akbar's hump, and away they went up to the World to see how things were going. They wandered up and down among the little towns and found them all so quiet and serene that the Devil felt encouraged. "No fuss here," he thought. "It all seems just the same." But he didn't dare go to the one small town where the strange light glowed the brightest.

It happened, however, that soon they arrived at a wild and dry sort of place with cold black sand, and wind that made the Devil shiver, huddled on Akbar's hump. And, wandering there to think things over, the Devil saw at last three beasts, not far away, striding by on the crest of a rounded dune. Camels they were, like Akbar, but hung with bells and tassels and richly patterned rugs. They held their heads high as they came, and on their backs, on saddles made of skins and polished wood, were riders in robes of pale, soft wool woven into stripes and fine designs, with wide, embroidered borders traced in gold. Gold was on their fingers, too, and round their necks, and one wore a thin gold crown. Their faces were lit by the glow that hung low now in the sky, and they were leaning toward it, eager and intent.

"Look at that," said the Devil to Akbar. "They're going *there*, to see that baby, or I miss my guess." And he tried to look scornful, but the sight made him very uneasy.

However, instead of sneering with him, Akbar made a sound in his curving throat, a gentle sort of bleat. And then, quite suddenly, he dropped to the big, knobbed knees of his two front legs, pitching the Devil off onto the sand.

"What's this?" cried the Devil. "How dare you!"

But Akbar continued to kneel, with his ragged head tipped down, till the royal camels disappeared from sight. And then he reared upright again, and this time

made a great, glad, bubbling sound like a trumpet full of milk, and strode away alone in the wake of the wonderful three, off toward the strange new glow.

"Confound it!" yelled the Devil. "*You* can't go!"

But Akbar could. And did. And the Devil was afraid to go after him.

Next morning, down in Hell, everyone said, "Where's Akbar?"

And the Devil said, "Who cares? We don't want *his* sort here."

And never again did he try to keep a camel.

THE SIGNPOST

THERE WAS a pair of sweethearts once named Gil and Flora who believed they were in love. But, in fact, they were not a bit good for each other. They were always quarreling over nothing, and would go for days quite red in the face, refusing to speak to each other. Then they would make it up, and things would be fine until the next argument. At last they had the worst argument of all, and Gil said to Flora, "I've had enough. I'm going away to the inn at Argo and I'll wait there seven days. If you can promise you'll never argue again, send me a message and I'll come back and marry you."

And Flora said, "You can go to the inn at Argo and

stay there forever, for all I care. Because it's you that argues, not me."

So Gil went off quite red in the face and started on foot down the road.

Now, the road went along for many miles and then it divided in two, going east to Argo and west to a town called Woolfield. There was a signpost at the split, with arrows pointing the way to each. And when Gil arrived at the signpost, he headed east and came in time to Argo, where he went to the inn to wait.

Four days went by, and at home Flora stewed and fretted and missed Gil more and more. Finally she could stand it no longer. She wrote a note to him saying, "Come back right away and marry me, and I'll try never ever to argue." And she hired a messenger with a fast horse who went galloping toward Argo with the note tucked into his vest.

But on that very day the Devil was walking about in the World, looking for ways to make mischief, and came by chance to the place where the road divided. "Well!" said the Devil. "Here's a nice idea." He switched the signpost around so that the arrow for Argo pointed now to Woolfield, and the arrow for Woolfield pointed instead to Argo. And then he went on his way, whistling a little tune, and so far as anyone knows never passed that way again, at least not for years and years.

Meanwhile, Flora's messenger came galloping along and, arriving at the signpost, turned west, thinking he was heading for Argo. And of course, after a while, he arrived in Woolfield instead and went to Woolfield's inn to look for Gil. But though he searched it from top to bottom, he could find no trace; so he sat himself down to have a mug of ale and catch his breath before he turned back to Flora with the news that Gil was gone.

While this was going on, Gil stewed and fretted at the Argo inn and said to himself, "Four days! And I miss her more and more. I'll just go and marry her, arguments or no." So he left the inn and hurried back along the road, coming at last to the signpost. "Egad!" he said. (In those days people often said *Egad*.) "Egad, what's this? I haven't been in Argo at all but in Woolfield. And it could be that Flora has sent a message already and I wasn't there to get it!" Off he went at a run toward Woolfield, thinking he was headed right, this time, for Argo. And on the way he might have passed the messenger coming from the other direction, but the messenger had ridden his horse into a meadow to drink at a little stream, so they missed each other entirely.

Gil arrived at the Woolfield inn, and he waited out the last three days. But no message came. "Well, that's it, then," he said. "She doesn't want me back. I'll go away to the city and seek my fortune." So that is what he did.

And the messenger, arriving home, told Flora that Gil had been nowhere to be found. "Well," said Flora, "that's it, then. He doesn't want me back. I'll have to marry someone else." So that is what *she* did.

And a peddler who knew both Argo and Woolfield came along soon after and set the signpost straight.

Gil found his fortune in the city and married a lovely girl named Belle with whom it never occurred to him to argue. And Flora married a lovely man named Carl with whom she lived in peace without a single quarrel. And down in Hell, the Devil, who'd long since forgotten the signpost, heard of these two happy couples and said to himself, "Disgusting. How do such things happen?"

LESSONS

THERE WAS a sharp-eyed parrot once who lived
with a doting old woman and was her pride and joy.
His name was Columbine, and instead of growing up
with pirates, and learning all kinds of nasty language,
he had spent his youth with a clergyman and acquired,
in his earliest lessons, another kind of language altogether. Then, having outlived the clergyman—for
parrots survive to amazing great ages—he moved to
the old woman's cottage, where he learned to say things
like "Sweetheart, kiss me quick," and was just as well
content. Still, Columbine was no sissy. He was big and
shrewd and liked things on the up-and-up. And to keep
them that way, he sat all day on his perch in the old

woman's window, with his eye peeled, and he watched for trouble.

The old woman's cottage was on the main road, and all day long the carts went by, and the wagons, and people on horseback or muleback or clumping along on foot, going from here to there and Heaven knows where else. And Columbine looked hard at everyone. When someone went by who looked suspicious, he'd say "*Oh*-oh," or "Look out," or sometimes even "Lock the doors!" But there wasn't any need for locks with Columbine around. He was better than any lock or bolt, or even any watchdog, just by the way he sat in the window with his eye peeled.

Now, one day it happened that the Devil came down the road disguised as a strolling musician with a fiddle under his arm. Columbine saw through the costume in a minute—that's how sharp his eye was—and he squawked, "It's the Devil! The Devil! Fire! Flood! Pestilence! Run for your lives!" And while he was squawking, he flapped his wings something awful, and hopped up and down, and made such a racket that the old woman hid under the bed.

The Devil stopped in the middle of the road, right in front of the cottage. "Shh!" he hissed to Columbine. "Hush up, you wretched bird—you'll give the game away!" But Columbine wouldn't hush up; he went on flapping, with his feathers every which way, squawking out his warnings at the top of his lungs. And of course the people in the road went running off in great alarm and confusion. Horses reared, carts were overturned, and even the mules were in a hurry. And soon there was no one left except the Devil, alone and feeling foolish, with the fiddle under his arm.

"Drat," said the Devil. "That ties it. There's not a soul in sight."

Columbine calmed down. He closed one eye and said, "Pretty bird."

"You there," said the Devil. "Suppose I were to trample your beak in the dust?"

"Bibles," said Columbine, very cool and clear.

The Devil backed off a step. "What?" he said, surprised.

"Church," said Columbine. "Church and chapel. And cathedral."

The Devil backed off even farther.

"Parson," said Columbine. "And priest. Parson, pastor, priest, and preacher. And *Pope*."

"Whoo!" said the Devil with a shiver. And he took himself off in a cloud of smoke and went back down to Hell.

The road soon filled up again with traffic, and the old woman came out from under the bed and went on baking bread. And Columbine sat on his perch and preened his feathers, but he kept his eye peeled just the same, for he was not so pleased with himself that he thought of neglecting his duty.

Down in Hell, the Devil trampled the fiddle in the dust and said to himself, "Someone ought to teach that bird a lesson." But, of course, someone already had, thank goodness.

THE FALL AND RISE
OF BATHBONE

THERE WAS a little, sweet no one of a man once, named Bathbone, who was not quite right in the head, for he thought he was someone else—a famous opera singer of the time called Doremi Faso. No one was sure how Bathbone had got this notion. He had never sung a note in his life, though he hummed sometimes, and on top of that, there was the fact that he was little and sweet, whereas the real Doremi Faso was quite the opposite, with the shape and weight of a walrus and the ego of several roosters. Still, here was Bathbone, sure they were one and the same.

Faso, though famous, was not a very good singer. His

voice was big and deep, but big and deep like a moose at the bottom of a well. He was only famous because someone important had once *said* he was a good singer, right out in the newspapers, printed in type and everything, and after that nobody had the nerve to say he wasn't. But Bathbone didn't know this. He was only sure that he was Faso and that Faso was he, and no amount of talk could change his mind.

Things went along this way for quite a while, and then one night Faso met his end at the opera when he gave himself a stroke on a high note he had no business trying for, and he turned up in Hell at once, ego and all, to begin a long series of concerts. Meanwhile, his death was reported in the newspapers. Bathbone, reading of it, was very much astonished. "What can this mean?" he said. "Here I am, the great Doremi Faso, as hale and hearty as ever. How can they say I am dead?" He took to puzzling back and forth on a bridge across a river, waving his arms and mumbling, while he tried to figure it out. And it wasn't long before he waved and mumbled himself right off the edge and into the water, where he drowned. But the newspapers ignored this second loss and ran, instead, a story about someone who'd grown a four-foot-long mustache.

Now, when Bathbone fell off the bridge, there was a hasty conference in Heaven. And it was decided that Bathbone had better go to Hell and get himself straight as to who he really was. For in Heaven they like you to know that kind of thing and be content with it. So Bathbone arrived at the gates of Hell, still mumbling and wet from head to foot, and was sent to see the Devil.

"What's this?" said the Devil.

"It is I," said Bathbone, "the great Doremi Faso."

"Oh, no, it isn't," said the Devil. "We've got one of those already. I know about you. You're Bathbone, that's who, and you're dripping all over my carpet."

"Sir," said Bathbone, drawing himself up as tall as he could, "I am not Bathbone. My name is Doremi Faso and my death was reported in the newspapers."

The Devil looked annoyed. "Bathbone," he said, "you're not quite right in the head. Now, listen. You don't belong down here, and we don't want you. You're much too little and sweet. But I've been informed you have to stay till you get at the truth on this business of who you are. So I'll tell you one more time: you're not Doremi Faso. The real Doremi Faso has been down here for a week. He's giving a concert right this very minute."

"I don't believe it," said Bathbone.

"Then come and see for yourself," said the Devil.

So off they went to the concert hall. And there on the stage was the real Doremi Faso, bellowing out some song or other, and striking remarkable poses. But the rows and rows of seats were empty—not a single soul to listen—and no one to play in the orchestra, either. All the instruments lay silent, though on some of Faso's high notes a cello, leaning in a corner, shuddered its strings faintly.

"See?" said the Devil.

But Bathbone said, "That can't be Faso. That man up there is a terrible singer. And, for another thing, there's nobody here to listen. Why, people come in droves to hear the great Faso sing."

"Not down here they don't," said the Devil with satisfaction. "Down here, no one ever comes."

"Just my point, if you'll excuse me," said Bathbone. "The singer on that stage is an impostor."

"You're a stubborn man, Bathbone," said the Devil. "Well, all right. We'll schedule a concert for you. Tomorrow, after you've got dried out. And then we'll see who's who."

The next afternoon, the concert hall was full, and roared with the sound of laughter and talk, while up and down the aisles, hawkers were selling peanuts and beer. In the orchestra pit, the musicians were tuning their instruments with a dreadful discord of tweets, blats, and scrapings. The racket was immense, and in the midst of it all, the orchestra conductor came up to Bathbone, who was waiting in the wings, and said, "So—what are you planning to sing?"

And Bathbone said, " 'Out of My Soul's Deep Longing.' "

The conductor made a face. "The Devil won't like that one very much," he said, "but if it's what you want, we'll do it." He went away and, appearing below in the orchestra pit, lifted his baton. The chandeliers went dim, the shadowy great hall fell silent. And Bathbone, full of confidence, stepped out onto the stage. Down came the baton, up rose the music, with the flutes and violins fighting for the melody. And Bathbone began to sing:

> *Out of my soul's deep longing,*
> *These little songs come winging*
> *Like wee feather'd birds...*

He had never sung a note before. His voice came out little and sweet, not big and deep like Faso's, and took him so much by surprise that by the time he'd got to "wee feather'd birds" he simply stopped, unable to manage one more note, and the truth swelled up in his heart like a great balloon and exploded, leaving him shocked and limp. "Why, they're right," he exclaimed to himself. "I'm not the great Doremi Faso!"

The people in the audience stood up, jeering and throwing peanuts, and when they got tired of that, they all filed out and went about their business. Even the musicians and the orchestra conductor wandered off, leaving Bathbone quite alone in the middle of the stage, feeling very sad. "I guess," he said aloud, "I'm only Bathbone after all."

As soon as the words were out of his mouth, a blaze

of light leapt up, and Bathbone vanished, simply disappeared, and was never ever seen in Hell again. And when the Devil was told, he said, "Good. That's done, then."

Bathbone is singing now in a glee club in Heaven with his own name—B A T H B O N E—on the posters, and the people come in droves to hear him. He is famous there for the songs that require in their solos a little, sweet voice, and the flutes and violins are something wonderful.

Oh, and by the way, the real Doremi Faso still sings every day in Hell, and has got an audience at last—a walrus and several roosters. They go through an awful lot of peanuts, but they seem to enjoy the music.

SIMPLE
SENTENCES

ONE AFTERNOON in Hell, the Devil was napping in his throne room when a frightful hubbub in the hall outside brought him upright on the instant. "Now what?" he barked. "Can't I get a minute's peace?"

The door to the throne room opened and a minor demon stuck his head in. "Sorry," said the minor demon, "but we've got two new arrivals here and they're giving me fits with their entry forms."

"Show them in," said the Devil darkly. "I'll straighten them out."

So the minor demon brought in the two and stood them before the Devil, where the first one, a shabby, mean-looking rascal, dropped his jaw and said, "Well, I'll be sugared! If it ain't Old Scratch hisself!"

And the second, a long-nosed gentleman, opened his eyes wide and said, "Dear me—it's Lucifer!"

Now, the Devil isn't fond of fancy names like Lucifer, preferring simply to be called "the Devil" or, once in a while, "your Highness." And he certainly dislikes all disrespectful terms, of which Old Scratch is only one. So he scowled at the two who stood there, and said, "See here—I like things peaceful in Hell. We can't have all this rattle and disruption."

At which the two said, both at once, "But—"

"Hold on for half a second, can't you?" said the Devil testily. He turned to the minor demon. "What've you got on the pair of them so far?" he demanded.

The minor demon consulted the sheaf of papers he'd brought in with him. "This one," he said, pointing with his pencil to the rascal, "is in for picking pockets. And that one"—pointing to the long-nosed gentleman—"is down for the sin of pride and for writing books no one could understand."

"Well?" said the Devil. "That sounds all right. What's the matter with that?"

"But it's not a question of their sins," said the minor demon. "We've known about those for years. What it is is what happened up there that finished them off, don't you know. And I can't get their stories straight on that."

"Oh," said the Devil. "All right." And he turned to the two, who'd been waiting there, glaring at each other. "You," he said to the rascal. "What's *your* story?"

"All I know is," said the rascal in a whiny voice, "I was mindin' my own business, out on the public streets, when this lardy-dardy lamps me and commences screechin' fit to blast yer ears. Thinks I, 'This cove is off his chump,' so I do a bunk. But he shags me, and we both come a cropper in the gutter and sap our noodles, and—well—that pins the basket. Next thing I know, I'm standin' here ramfeezled and over at the knees, and he's comin' the ugly like I'm the party responsible."

"What?" said the Devil.

"If I may be permitted," sniffed the long-nosed gentleman. "What actually transpired is that this squalid and depraved illiterate was on the verge of appropriating my purse when I observed the action at the penultimate moment. And whilst I was attempting to apprehend him, we both seem to have stumbled on a curbstone, with resultant fractures and contusions, and I find I've been deprived of my life—and my hat—in a most abrupt and inconvenient fashion. Surely I can't be censured for reacting with extreme exasperation."

"What?" said the Devil.

"I think what they mean is—" began the minor demon.

"I know what they mean," said the Devil. "That one tried to pick this one's pocket. Just write it down like that."

"Chalk your pull, there," cried the rascal. "You've got it in the wrong box. Maybe I was on the filch, sure, that's my job. But I wasn't after this poor, mucked-out barebones, not for toffee. I know his type. More squeak than wool, you can stand on me for that. A barber's cat like him ain't never got a chinker to his name. Why, I'd go home by beggar's bush if I couldn't pick better than that!"

"What?" said the Devil.

"He means—" the minor demon tried again.

"I know what he means," said the Devil. "He means he *didn't* try to pick the other one's pocket. A misunderstanding. So just write it down like that."

"Oh, now, really," exclaimed the long-nosed gentleman. "I must protest. I tell you, I saw this felon's grubby hand reaching for my purse. I am not in the habit of misinterpreting evidence supplied by my own observations. Why, the meanest intelligence could easily discern that the fellow's a thoroughgoing prevaricator!"

"See what I mean?" said the minor demon to the Devil.

"I see," said the Devil.

The rascal stepped a little nearer to the Devil. "Look here, yer honor," he said. "I don't want to tread the shoe awry and chance yer gettin' magged. But it's above my bend how a chap with yer quick parts could hang in the hedge when it comes to separate between brass tacks and flimflam. I mean, this underdone swellhead could argue the leg off an iron pot, but it's still all flytrap. Take it from me."

The long-nosed gentleman stepped forward then, himself. "I'm cognizant of the fact," he said haughtily, "that I'm not by any stretch of the imagination in Paradise. And it may be that I'm naive to expect impartiality. All I can do is to iterate the unembellished fact that I observed what I observed, and what I observed was that this clumsy brigand tried to rob me."

The rascal narrowed his eyes. "Handsomely over the bricks there, puggy," he said in a threatening tone. "Clumsy, am I? Just because you've got yer head full of bees, that's no reason to draw the longbow. You never twigged me doin' *my* kind of work. Even if I was on the dip with a piker like you, you wouldn't twig me. When it comes to light fingers, I'm the top mahatma. No one ever twigs me. So play Tom Tell-Truth or else keep sloom."

The long-nosed gentleman's face turned very red. "Sir," he said in a strangled voice, "your impertinence is beyond all sufferance. I wouldn't dignify your statements with rebuttals if it weren't that I have such respect for veracity. And the plain, unvarnished truth is, you attempted to commit a felony."

The Devil clapped his hands with a sound like a pistol going off. "That's enough," he said. "I've heard enough. The plain, unvarnished truth is there's only one crime here: neither of you can speak a simple sentence."

And at this they both stopped short to gape at him, and both said, *"What?"*

The Devil turned to the minor demon. "Write down," he said, "that what happened was they both tripped over their tongues."

The minor demon nodded. "Very well. And what shall I put for their punishment?"

For the first time, the Devil smiled. "We'll put them in together, in a room designed for one," he said. "And there they'll stay till it all freezes over down here."

So the two were led away, both sputtering with shock, and the minor demon folded up his papers. "I do admire that punishment," he said to the Devil.

"Thank you," said the Devil, settling back to get on with his nap. "It was the simplest sentence I could think of."

THE EAR

THERE WAS a clan of very silly people called the Pishpash once, ages and ages ago, who took it into their heads to carve a huge stone idol at the top of a hill, and when it was finished, they sat and sang it songs with words like *zum zum zum*, and they gave it offerings of turnips, which grew wild in the area around. The idol had the head of a hairless man with ears as big as washtubs, and its body was shaped like a horse sitting down, and needless to say, it didn't care a bit about turnips—or anything else, for that matter. So the turnips went bad, lying there in heaps, and they smelled something awful. Nevertheless, the Pishpash kept right on piling new turnips on top of the old, and believed something good would come of it. Nothing did, however, and at last a minor earthquake tipped the idol over. Its body was broken to bits, and the head cracked off and rolled like a boulder down the hill, coming to rest with one ear up, one ear down, out on a level plain below. The Pishpash were put off by this, and took it for an evil omen, so they packed up their bowls and spears and babies and wandered off, no one is sure exactly where, but it doesn't matter because, although the Devil found them entertaining, they were all of them very silly, and good riddance to the lot. The head, however, remained behind and lay there so long that the earth began to cover it up, until finally, after hundreds of years and a lot more minor earthquakes, it was buried under three or four feet of soil.

By that time, things were civilized. A village had appeared, and a great many little farms, and everyone mostly raised turnips, since they grew so well there. And one day some new people came to the place and picked out a spot for farming that was near where the idol's head lay resting underground. These people were a father and a mother and their big, slow son,

Beevis. They put up a shack to live in, and next they tried to figure out where to dig a well.

"It ought to be over there," said Beevis.

"No, here," said Mother, "next to the shack."

"Not here," said Father. "Too risky. Beevis would only fall into it."

"Would not," said Beevis.

"Probably would, at that," said Mother.

"Would *not*," said Beevis, who had got his feelings hurt. "You never listen to me." And this was true. They didn't.

In any case, the end of it was that Beevis was sent to dig the well exactly at the spot where the idol's head was buried. The digging took a while because Beevis was big but he wasn't very strong, and with his feelings hurt he wasn't inclined to hurry. "They never listen to me," he said, this time to himself, as he chunked away at the soil with his shovel. Still, slow as he was, after a little while he had dug down to the place where his shovel went *chink* instead of *chunk*. "Rock," said Beevis. He brushed away the soil at the bottom of the hole to see how large the rock might be, and there, exposed to the sunlight after all those years and earthquakes, was the Pishpash idol's ear, big as a washtub but plainly an ear for all that, and altogether unexpected.

Beevis climbed out of the hole and stood gazing at the ear for a long, long time, so long that at last his father came over and stood beside him.

"Why aren't you digging, Beevis?" said Father.

"There's an ear down there," said Beevis.

"What?" said Father.

"An ear," said Beevis, pointing. "Down there."

So Father looked and saw the ear as plain as day at the bottom of the hole. And then they both stood gazing at it.

After a while, Mother peered through a window of the shack and called, "What in the World are you doing?"

Father beckoned to her, so out she came and looked down into the hole. "What's that?" she said.

"It's an ear," said Father. "Beevis found it."

"It's ugly," said Mother.

"Button your lip," said Beevis. "It'll hear you."

And indeed, at that very moment, a minor earth-

quake shook the ground just hard enough to make their feet tingle.

"It heard you," said Beevis.

After this, they went inside the shack to talk it over.

"It's a dangerous ear, that's clear enough," said Mother. "If it can make the ground shake."

"Likely so," said Father. "What do you think we should do?"

"I think," said Mother, "we should cover it up. Fill in the hole again."

"No!" said Beevis. "That ear is mine. I found it, and I like it."

"Cover it up, Beevis," said Father. "It's the only thing to do. Go out right now and fill in the hole."

"You never hear a word I say," said Beevis. He went back out to the hole and stood there, looking down at the ear. *"Zum zum zum,"* he crooned softly so that no one but the ear could hear him.

"Fill in the hole, Beevis," called Father from the shack, so Beevis picked up his shovel and pretended to begin. But when they weren't watching, he took some boards left over from the shack and laid them across the top of the hole and covered them over with dirt so that it looked as if he'd done what they told him. And then he went and dug the well in quite another spot, on the opposite side of the shack.

The weeks went by with no more earthquakes. Beevis and Mother and Father plowed their field and planted turnips and nothing more was said about the ear. But every night, when the old folks were asleep, Beevis would creep out and uncover the ear and talk to it. He told it all his troubles, and he tried out all his thoughts about life and the World, and the ear, lit up by moonlight shining into the hole, would listen to every word. And every night he would croon to it ever so softly— *zum zum zum*—before he covered it up again. But he never gave it turnips, for Beevis wasn't silly like the Pishpash.

These midnight meetings with the ear did a lot for Beevis. He began to feel more confident. He stood up straighter, and wasn't nearly so slow.

"Beevis has changed since we came here," said Father to Mother. "He's turning into quite a man!"

"Fresh air, hard work, and healthy food," said

Mother, who was cooking up turnips at the stove. "That, and no mollycoddling. That's what's done it."

So of course it was clear they didn't understand at all.

And then one night, while Beevis was out in the moonlight, talking to the ear and explaining his dreams for the future, Mother woke up and went to the window and saw him. "Beevis!" she called. "What in the World are you doing?"

"Phooey," said Beevis to the ear. "Looks like the jig is up."

But not at all. No sooner were the words out of his mouth than a more-than-minor earthquake shook the land so hard you'd have thought the whole place was a dust mop. The shack fell down, and so did Mother, and out on the other side, the walls of the well collapsed. And Father got a bump on the knee when the stove fell over. But Beevis, standing by the ear, wasn't so much as toppled off his feet, and the walls of the ear's hole stayed firm.

Next day, when they'd calmed themselves down, Mother said, "It's an evil omen. We'd better leave this place. It's no good after all."

And Father said, "Beevis, pack up what's still in one piece and we'll move along."

"I'll pack," said Beevis, "but I won't leave. I like it here."

For once, they heard him. "But, Beevis," said Mother, "how will you manage without us?"

"I'll manage," said Beevis. "I'll manage very well. It's time."

And it was. Beevis managed. He waved goodbye to Mother and Father and sent them on their way. He rebuilt the shack and dug a new well. Then he pulled up all the turnips and planted beets instead, and became a successful farmer. And he made a round sort of cover for the ear's hole and told people it was a dry well and to keep away, which they did, having no reason not to. And every night, unless it rained, Beevis went out in the moonlight and told his hopes and joys to the ear. And every night the ear heard every word.

Go Fish!

GOFISH

Natalie Babbitt

What did you want to be when you grew up?

When I was a preschooler, I wanted to be a pirate, and then when I started school, I wanted to be a librarian. But in the fourth grade, I got my copy of *Alice in Wonderland / Alice Through the Looking-Glass* and decided once and for all that I wanted to be an illustrator of stories for children.

When did you realize you wanted to be a writer?

I didn't even think about writing. My husband wrote the story for the first book. But then he didn't want to do it anymore, so I had to start writing my own stories. After all, you can't make pictures for stories unless you have stories to make pictures for.

What's your first childhood memory?

I have a lot of preschool memories, all from when we lived in a little town just south of Columbus, Ohio. I kind of remember sitting in a high chair. And when I was a little older, I remember seeing Jack Frost looking in through the kitchen window. *That* was pretty surprising.

What's your most embarrassing childhood memory?
I don't remember any. I'm probably just suppressing them all.

What's your favorite childhood memory?
I think I liked best the times when my sister and I would curl up next to our mother while she read aloud to us.

As a young person, who did you look up to most?
No question: my mother.

What was your worst subject in school?
Arithmetic. I think you call it math now.

What was your best subject in school?
Art. And after that, English.

What was your first job?
It was when I was a teenager. I worked in what we called the College Shop in a big downtown Cleveland (Ohio) department store called Higbee's. But after that, I mostly worked in the pricing department of a washing machine factory.

How did you celebrate publishing your first book?
I don't think I did anything special. By that time, I was beginning to get over my absolute astonishment at having found my editor in the *first* place. That was the most wonderful moment of all.

Where do you write your books?
I think about them for a long time before I actually start putting words on paper, and I think about them all over the place. Then, when I'm ready, I work at my computer in my workroom. But before, I always wrote them out longhand, sitting on my sofa in the living room. I wrote

on a big tablet, and then I typed everything, paragraph by paragraph, on my typewriter, making changes as I went along.

Where do you find inspiration for your writing?
I mostly write about all the unanswered questions I still have from when I was in elementary school.

Which of your characters is most like you?
The main characters in all of my long stories are like me, but I think Winnie Foster, in *Tuck Everlasting*, is most like me.

When you finish a book, who reads it first?
Always my editor, Michael di Capua. His opinion is the most important one.

Are you a morning person or a night owl?
Neither one, really. I'm mostly a middle-of-the-day person.

What's your idea of the best meal ever?
One that someone else cooked. And it has to have something chocolate for dessert.

Which do you like better: cats or dogs?
Cats to look at and to watch, but dogs to own.

What do you value most in your friends?
Good talk and plenty of laughing.

Where do you go for peace and quiet?
Now that my children are grown and gone into lives of their own, I have plenty of peace and quiet just sitting around the house.

What makes you laugh out loud?
Words. My father was very funny with words, and I grew up laughing at the things he said.

What's your favorite song?
Too many to mention, but most of them are from the '30s and '40s, when songs were to *sing*, not to shout and wiggle to.

Who is your favorite fictional character?
No question: Alice from *Alice in Wonderland* and *Alice Through the Looking-Glass*.

What are you most afraid of?
I have a fear that is very common when we are little, and I seem to have hung on to it: the fear of being abandoned.

What time of year do you like best?
May is my favorite month.

What is your favorite TV show?
I don't watch many shows anymore—just CNN News and old movies.

If you were stranded on a desert island, who would you want for company?
My husband, Sam.

If you could travel in time, where would you go?
Back to Middletown, Ohio, to Lincoln School on Central Avenue, to live through fifth grade again. And again and again.

What's the best advice you have ever received about writing?
No one single thing. Too many good things to list.

SQUARE FISH

What do you want readers to remember about your books?
The questions without answers.

What would you do if you ever stopped writing?
Spend all my time doing word puzzles and games, and practicing the good old songs on my piano.

What do you like best about yourself?
That I can draw, and play the good old songs on my piano.

What is your worst habit?
Always expecting things to be perfect.

What is your best habit?
Trying to make things as perfect as I can.

What do you consider to be your greatest accomplishment?
Right now, it's a picture of a man in a washtub, floating on the ocean in a rainstorm. I'm really proud of that picture.

Where in the world do you feel most at home?
That's a hard question. My family moved away from Middletown, Ohio (see the question/answer about time travel), when I was in the middle of sixth grade, and we never went back. Even after all these years, though, Middletown is the place I think of when I think about "home." I've lived in a lot of different places, though, and liked them all, so I don't feel sorry for myself. It's just that the word "home" has its own kind of special meaning.

What do you wish you could do better?
Everything. Cook, write, play the piano, everything.

What would your readers be most surprised to learn about you?
Maybe that I believe writing books is a long way from being important. The most important thing anyone can do is be a teacher. As for those of us who write books, I often think we should all stop for fifty years. There are so many wonderful books to read, and not enough time to get around to all of them. But we writers just keep cranking them out. All we can hope for is that readers will find at least a little time for them, anyway.

Willet Goody's father has disappeared.
With the help of his tutor, Willet is determined
to discover the truth about what happened.

Hidden treasure, a gypsy séance, and a frightening
exploration of a tomb all help unravel the mystery in
Natalie Babbitt's *Goody Hall*.

CHAPTER 1

The blacksmith stood in the door of his shop and
sniffed the May breeze hopefully. "There's something in the air, no doubt about it," he said to himself
with satisfaction. "Something's going to happen." He
fixed a pipeful of tobacco and lit it contentedly, sort-
ing over in his mind a number of possibilities. There
was the baker's daughter, Millie, who had been in
love with the new parson all winter and was said to

be pining away because he refused to notice her. Perhaps she would throw herself off the church roof —that would be interesting! There was Alf Hulser's son Fred, who had been jailed for stealing a cow— maybe he would try to escape. And then, wasn't it time for Pooley's barn to catch fire again? It burned to the ground about once every five years. The blacksmith scanned the skies for signs of a storm. Lightning was always good for starting fires. But the sky was clear, so he leaned against the door frame and thought about the last fire. "Five years ago exactly," he nodded to himself, counting back. "One of the best fires we ever had." And it had happened the very day before that rich fellow Midas Goody fell off his horse and killed himself.

"Yoo-hoo there!" called a voice. The blacksmith peered down the street through a cloud of pipe smoke and saw a big, heavy woman dressed in black hurrying toward him. "Good morning, Henry!" she said breathlessly as she came up. "What are you standing out here for? Let's go inside. I've been marketing all morning and I want to rest up before I start back to the Hall."

"Come in then," said the blacksmith, "and tell me the news."

The big woman in the black dress was the blacksmith's sister and her name was Dora Tidings. *Mrs.* Dora Tidings. "A widow—a very respectable widow," the villagers declared, "who supports herself by keeping house for that woman out to Goody Hall. *You* know the place, like a regular palace—if you like palaces. Well, Mrs. Goody's rich, all right, but it takes more than money to make a fine lady, and that poor little boy of hers, cooped up away from natural play and exercise, although they do say he's a regular holy terror. Mrs. Goody hasn't changed her ways one bit since her husband was killed so suddenly that night, and no one ever saw her shed a tear over him. Not that anyone ever knew much about them, coming out of nowhere the way they did—but he was a fine gentleman, you know, or at least that's what Dora Tidings says."

What Dora Tidings said counted for a good deal in the village. She was the only one who could be depended upon to pass along the news about the rich Mrs. Goody and her son, and she enjoyed her importance so much that she stayed on and on at Goody Hall, with no one to help her except the gardener's daughter, Alfreida, who came in afternoons. Not that gypsies were ever much help, the gossip ran, and there was certainly gypsy blood in those two somewhere. All right, so maybe they *did* have a cottage all their own at the edge of the village instead of the usual gaudy caravan, but still—once a gypsy, always a gypsy. And, of course, nobody in her right mind would hire one to do anything, let alone be a housemaid or a gardener. So there had to be something very strange about that woman out there and someday, the villagers said to each other, Dora Tidings would find out what it was.

"She's got a new bee in her bonnet," said Mrs. Tidings to her brother the blacksmith as she sank gratefully onto a nail keg inside the shop. Mrs. Tidings always referred to her employer, Mrs. Goody, as "she."

"Yes?" said the blacksmith encouragingly.

"Well!" said Mrs. Tidings. "She's decided she needs a tutor for that boy, Willet. She's taught him his reading and numbers already, but now she wants him to learn a lot of other things, so she's going to look for a tutor. I asked her—I said, 'Why don't you send that boy to school in the village?' And *she* said she didn't want to do that because Willet wasn't used to having a lot of other children around and they might make things hard for him. But it isn't that, of course. What she's thinking is the village children aren't fancy enough for a Goody."

"Where is she going to find a tutor in these parts?" asked the blacksmith.

"I'm sure *I* don't know," said Mrs. Tidings, looking upward and shaking her head.

"By the way, Dora," said the blacksmith, leaning forward. "Isn't it just five years ago that Midas Goody died? Remember? It was right after Pooley's barn burned down last time."

"I should say I do remember," said Mrs. Tidings. "Yes, five years almost to the day."

"She'll be putting flowers at the tomb, I suppose," said the blacksmith with a sour smile.

Mrs. Tidings folded her lips. "Not her, as you very

well know. Not so much as a petal. Nothing in all the years I've been with her. It certainly is a strange way to behave."

The blacksmith was silent, thinking ahead to his own tomb. He always pictured it heaped with roses and washed on a regular basis by the gentle tears of his own devoted wife. He thought anxiously of that wife for a moment and a small doubt occurred to him that made him even crosser with the mysterious Mrs. Goody. "You're right, Dora," he said. "It certainly is a strange way to behave."

CHAPTER 2

Spring in those long-gone times was exactly like spring today, of course. Some things never change. The birds were just as merry, the grass as tender, and the air had that same exciting lightness which threatened, if you breathed too deeply, to lift you right up off the ground. One morning not long after, a baggy young man came down the road from the village, and in spite of his heavy satchel he half bounced, half glided like a large balloon, gulping great lungfuls of May as a thirsty man gulps water, and letting them out again in blasts of shapeless song. He had been singing all the way from the village, swinging the scuffed old satchel from one hand and gesturing with the other from time to time when he felt the song required it, and his long face was blissful and absorbed.

Just as he reached for the fortieth time a particular place in the music which sounded like "Merrily, merrily shall I live now," but wasn't quite that, somehow, he came to a sudden bend in the road and the song ceased abruptly. "Aha!" said the baggy young man. "This is the place. It must be." And he put down the satchel and went forward.

It was a house that had stopped him, a beautiful house that rose up from its dewy square of barbered lawn like a wedding cake on a green tray—a house so white and frilly with chiseled wooden filigree and balconies, so rich in scalloped eaves and dormers, so decked with slender columns and peaking, bright-tiled roofs that it would have stopped anyone. It was a lacy handkerchief, a valentine, a regular seafoam of a house, and the baggy young man stood quite still in the middle of the road and looked at it for a long time. Then he went up to the gatepost and peered into the square of brass that was fastened there. *Goody Hall*, the square announced in a soft gleam of letters. Yes, that was the name they had given him in the village.

"If it's talking work you want," the blacksmith had said, "they're looking for a tutor out to Goody Hall. It's quite a place. My sister's the housekeeper. Why don't you go along and see about it?" But after the baggy young man had gone, the blacksmith remarked to a friend, "I don't think they'll want the likes of *him*, though. What a queer duck! Not a whisker on him anywhere!" And he stroked his own sooty beard complacently.

To which the friend replied, "Well, they're strange themselves at Goody Hall, aren't they? Fellow like that ought to suit them just right. I don't see why your sister stays on out there year after year."

The blacksmith picked up his hammer. "Oh well,"

he said, smiling modestly into his beard, "she's full of curiosity, you know. Also, the pay is good. But mostly it's curiosity."

"Yes," said the friend, "I can understand that."

But the baggy young man had heard none of this and now he was leaning on the gate and looking at the beautiful house with a sort of hypnotized pleasure. As he stared, his mind's eye squinted and he seemed to see himself coming out of the tall door, a new and polished self in an elegant black suit. He watched this self pause on the verandah, pluck a blossom from a flowering shrub that leaned there, and hold it delicately under his nose. Then the scene enlarged. A crowd of ragged people appeared at the gate, clutching their thin coats under their chins. "There he is!" cried the ragged people. "There he is! Bless you, sir! Bless you!" He saw himself striding down the long gravel path to the gate and now he was pressing a gold coin into each outstretched, careworn hand. "Bless you!" cried the people.

A bird chirped loudly nearby—the bubble burst— the pretty scene dissolved. The baggy young man rubbed his forehead and frowned. "Oh no, you don't!"

he said severely to the house. "I don't even *want* to be that sort of a fellow. I'm here to be a tutor, re-member, not a lord." And he picked up the old satchel firmly, opened the gate, and started up the path.

The beautiful house was set in equally beautiful, well-kept grounds. Off to the left, against a high hedge, a formal garden glowed moist and vibrant in the morning sun. Daffodils bloomed there now, and sturdy hyacinths, and a wide band of red tulips like a bright sash against the green of the hedge. Far to the right, at the edge of the lawn where a well-mannered wood began, stood a magnificent iron stag, its branching head tilted to listen and one slender foreleg lifted. The baggy young man paused and smiled. "Better run away!" he called to the stag. "Whoop! *Hey*—watch out! Hercules is here!" But the stag continued motionless, looking off over his head with its cool, indifferent iron eyes, and the baggy young man laughed and nodded to himself and went on up the path.

The next thing that happened happened so sud-denly that it took a few moments to piece it together afterward. There he was walking calmly up the path when all at once there was a terrible crash of dishes from inside the house, the door burst open, and a small figure shot out, bounded down the steps, and ran right into him with a great bump that sent them both over backward. The satchel went spinning off into the grass and burst open like a ripe melon, a portion of its contents erupting onto the grass.

The baggy young man sat up and blinked, and the boy who had knocked him over sat up and blinked, too. They got to their feet, brushing gravel from the seats of their pants, and looked at each other warily.

"Who are *you?*" said the boy at last.

"I've come about the tutoring," said the baggy young man. "My name is Hercules Feltwright."

"Hercules?" said the boy. "Really? What kind of a name is that?"

"An unkind kind of name," said Hercules, "but I've learned to accept it. What's *your* name?"

"I'm Willet Goody," said the boy. "I live here. This is my house."

"Then it's you I've come to tutor," said Hercules Feltwright.

Willet Goody looked with interest at the long face

of the baggy young man. "How come you don't have any whiskers?" he asked. "Everyone has whiskers. My father's got yellow ones, a beard and everything."

"I like myself better this way," said Hercules. "Is your mother at home?"

"You'll see her in a minute, I expect," said Willet. "I just tripped old Dora and made her drop the breakfast tray, and she's gone to tell, the way she always does."

"Who's 'old Dora'?" asked Hercules.

"The housekeeper, Mrs. Tidings."

"Ah! The blacksmith's sister?"

"That's the one," said Willet. And then he pointed toward the gaping satchel. "What *is* all that?"

It was indeed a strange assortment lying about on the grass, but Hercules Feltwright was not apologetic as he went to repack. He called off the names of things as he put them back into the satchel. "Two embroidered vests. One cloak. Five pairs of tights. Hat. Box of paint. Another hat. False beard. Cat skin. Three under . . ."

"Wait!" Willet interrupted. "Wait! Can I see that cat skin? Where did you get that cat skin?"

"I'll tell you about it sometime," said Hercules. "Not now. Three undershirts. And—a book."

"What's the book?" asked Willet.

"Plays," said Hercules. "Shakespeare." And he closed up the satchel.

"Plays?"

"Yes."

"What for?"

"Pleasure."

"Oh," said Willet, seeming surprised. And then he said, "I don't like to read."

"That's too bad," said Hercules. "What *do* you like to do?"

"Well," said Willet, "if there was a dog around, I'd be pretty busy, but I'm not allowed to have one."

"That's a shame!" said Hercules. "Why not?"

"They scratch up the flower beds and shed hair all over the furniture," Willet explained. "So—I mostly just tease Mrs. Tidings."

"Hmm," said Hercules. "I thought perhaps it was an accident that you tripped the dear old soul."

"Bugfat," said Willet. "I meant to. And she's not

a dear old soul. She's big and her face is red and she's always watching."

Just then a soft voice called from the verandah. "Willet? Willet. Up here, please."

"That's my mother," said Willet. "Come on."

When Hercules Feltwright saw Mrs. Goody standing in the doorway of the beautiful house, he felt that there was something out of place. Here was the house, shining like a jewel box way out here in the country—the fact that it was there at all was surprising enough—and when the box was opened, it revealed, not a diamond necklace but a slice of bread. He would have had a hard time defending this impression, however, for Mrs. Goody was rather small and handsome and she wore a dressing gown drenched with lace. If you went by her appearance, she was not like a slice of bread at all, but rather a frosted muffin in a fluted paper cup. "But it was never the way she was dressed or anything like that," he always said afterward. "It was something about the anxious way she stood there, as if she were afraid someone was going to come and tell her she'd have to move along."

When he had climbed the steps and stood before her, he bowed and said, "Good morning. My name is Hercules Feltwright—I've come about the tutoring."

"He has a cat skin in his satchel, Mama," said Willet, coming up beside him. "I like him. Can he stay?"

Mrs. Goody frowned thoughtfully at Hercules. Her eyes were very blue and a little sad, he thought. "How do you do, I'm sure, Mr. Feltwright," she said. "How did you know I wanted a tutor? Well, never mind that. But you don't look like a tutor, do you? You don't look like . . . any profession in particular."

"I hope I only look like myself," said Hercules Feltwright.

Mrs. Goody's blue eyes narrowed. "Whatever do you mean," she asked, "by that remark?"

Hercules Feltwright stared. "Why, nothing!" he said hastily. "Nothing at all! That is, I *am* a teacher, truly I am, and I hope to be a good one."

"Very well," said Mrs. Goody, relaxing a little. "But—can you teach the proper things?"

"What things did you have in mind, ma'am?" asked Hercules with care.

Mrs. Goody looked taken aback. "Why, *you* know," she faltered. "The *proper* things. Whatever it is that tutors teach. I want Willet to be a gentleman. All children his age have tutors. That is," she added rather grandly, "all *wealthy* children."

"Oh," said Hercules. "Yes, I think I can teach him things like that."

Mrs. Goody turned to Willet. "Go in and eat your breakfast, Willet," she said. "And apologize to Mrs. Tidings. Do it nicely, mind you—she's very angry. You're a thoughtless, selfish boy to cause her so much trouble." But instead of frowning, Mrs. Goody's eyes went soft as she gazed at her son, and she smiled in spite of herself.

"I'm sorry, Mama," said Willet, and he smiled, too.

"Oh—and, Willet," said Mrs. Goody, "I have to go up to the city again this morning. I'll be gone the usual three or four days, I expect. I wish I didn't have to go, my love."

"Never mind, Mama," said Willet. "It's all right if Hercules is here." And he ran into the house.

Mrs. Goody turned back to the baggy young man. "He seems to have taken quite a shine to you," she said, giving him another long and thoughtful look. And then she seemed to make up her mind all at once. "I guess you'll do. Bring in your satchel and I'll ask Mrs. Tidings to show you to your room."

"Why, that's splendid," said Hercules Feltwright happily. "I'm very glad. This is my first tutoring position, but we'll get along, I'm sure, Willet and I. And it's such a beautiful house!"

At that, Mrs. Goody did something he was to remember for a long time afterward. She put out a hand and touched the shining brass knocker on the tall door, and she said with surprising fierceness, "Yes, it is. It *is* a beautiful house. It's everything in the world to me."

There was a moment of silence. "Hmm," said Hercules Feltwright to himself. Then he cleared his throat. "Excuse me," he said aloud, "but is Willet's father at home? Shouldn't I meet him too?"

Mrs. Goody's face changed. "Midas Goody is out there," she said abruptly, pointing across the lawn. "In the tomb beyond the hedge. He's dead."

"Dear me! I'm very sorry!" said Hercules.

"Don't mention it," said Mrs. Goody in a cold voice.

"Don't mention it ever again. He's dead and that's all there is to it." Then she gathered the skirts of her dressing gown around her, and her first, softer voice returned. "Go and get your satchel, Mr. Feltwright," she said. "I'm glad you've come." And she turned and disappeared inside the beautiful house.

READ ALL OF THE
NEWBERY AWARD—WINNING TITLES
AVAILABLE FROM SQUARE FISH

Thimble Summer
Elizabeth Enright
978-0-312-38002-1
$6.99 U.S. /$7.99 Can.

The Cricket in Times Square
George Selden and Garth Williams
978-0-312-38003-8
$6.99 U.S./$8.99 Can.

Everything on a Waffle
Polly Horvath
978-0-312-38004-5
$6.99 U.S.

I, Juan de Pareja
Elizabeth Borton de Treviño
978-0-312-38005-2
$7.99 U.S. /$8.99 Can.

The Cow-Tail Switch
Harold Courlander and George Herzog
978-0-312-38006-9
$6.99 U.S. /$7.99 Can.

Young Fu of the Upper Yangtze
Elizabeth Foreman Lewis
978-0-312-38007-6
$7.99 U.S. /$10.25 Can.

Kneeknock Rise
Natalie Babbitt
978-0-312-37009-1
$6.99 U.S. /$8.50 Can.

Abel's Island
William Steig
978-0-312-37143-2
$6.99 U.S./$8.50 Can.

A Wrinkle in Time
Madeleine L'Engle
978-0-312-36754-1
$6.99 U.S./$8.99 Can.

SQUARE FISH

WWW.SQUAREFISHBOOKS.COM
AVAILABLE WHEREVER BOOKS ARE SOLD

READ THE KAREN HESSE NOVELS

AVAILABLE FROM SQUARE FISH

LETTERS FROM RIFKA

Rifka knows nothing about America when she flees from Russia with her family in 1919. But she dreams she will be safe there from the Russian soldiers' harsh treatment of the Jews. On her long journey Rifka must endure a great deal: humiliating examinations, deadly typhus, murderous storms at sea, and separation from all she has ever known and loved. And even if she does make it to America, she's not sure America will have her.

ISBN: 978-0-312-53561-2
$6.99 US / $8.99 Can

WISH ON A UNICORN

Mags wishes she could live in a nice house with a mama who isn't tired out from work. She'd like a sister who's normal and a brother who doesn't mooch for food. And once in a while she'd like some new clothes for school. Then her sister finds a stuffed unicorn, and Mags's wishes start to come true. She knows the unicorn can't really be magic, but she's not going to let anything ruin her luck— even if it means believing something that can't possibly be true.

ISBN: 978-0-312-37611-6
$6.99 US / $7.99 Can

PHOENIX RISING

Nyle's quiet life with her grand mother on their farm is shattered the night of the accident at the nuclear power plant. Nyle's world fills with disruptions, protective masks contaminated food, and mistrust. Things become ever more complicated when "refugees" from the accident take shelter in Nyle's house. But Nyle doesn't want to open her heart to them. Too many times she's let people in, only to have them desert her. If she lets herself care, she knows they'll end up leaving her, too

ISBN: 978-0-312-53562-9
$6.99 US / $7.99 Can

SQUARE FISH

WWW.SQUAREFISHBOOKS.COM
AVAILABLE WHEREVER BOOKS ARE SOLD

Read all the magical novels by
Natalie Babbitt

Available from Square Fish

"An ingenious story with unforgettable fictional characters, crossing paths with well-known historical ones. I learned a lot from this book, the main thing being that I could never write one."

—Larry David

"*Second Street Station* is a great read. Following Mary Handley through this Victorian adventure makes you feel like you've found some lost Sherlock Holmes story. It's impressive that the characters, many based on actual historical figures, are always funny, but the greatest delight is the mystery itself."

—Matthew Weiner, creator of *Mad Men*

Second Street
STATION

Second Street
STATION

A Mary Handley Mystery

Lawrence H. Levy

B\D\W\Y
Broadway Books
New York

Published in the United States by Broadway Books, an imprint of the Crown Publishing Group, a division of Penguin Random House LLC, New York.
www.crownpublishing.com

BROADWAY BOOKS and its logo, B \ D \ W \ Y, are trademarks of Penguin Random House LLC.

Library of Congress Cataloging-in-Publication Data
Levy, Lawrence H.
Second Street Station : a Mary Handley mystery /
Lawrence H. Levy. — First edition.
pages cm
1. Women detectives—New York (State)—New York—Fiction.
2. Murder investigation—Fiction. 3. Brooklyn (New York, N.Y.)—
Fiction. I. Title.
PS3612.E9372S43 2014
813'.6—dc23   2014021004

ISBN 978-0-553-41892-7
eBook ISBN 978-0-553-41893-4

Printed in the United States of America

Book design by Anna Thompson
Cover design by Tal Goretsky
Cover illustration by Scott McKowen

10 9 8 7 6 5 4 3 2 1

First Edition

To my daughter, Erin,
whose belief in me and this story kept me going;
to my son, Josh, who inspired me;
to my wife, Fran, who is my love;
and to my nephew Zachary who I know would be proud.

Second Street
STATION

PROLOGUE

The Boston boat was late, and the Frenchman was livid. He should have followed his natural inclination to travel by land from Boston to New York. True, it was 1876, but even in this modern age he knew sea travel was at best unreliable. Yet, those who were *au courant* in Boston (everyone in that infernal city thought they were *au courant*) echoed the same sentiment: "Take the boat from Boston to Greenport, Long Island, then the train to Manhattan. That's the fastest route by far."

Well, his journey on this godforsaken boat had not only turned out to be much longer than expected, but the weather was treacherous and the waters of the Long Island Sound were far choppier than when he had crossed the Atlantic.

As the Frenchman flexed his right hand, cramped from clutching the large suitcase by his side, he looked around, the nostrils of his aquiline nose flaring with disdain for his surroundings. Since it was suicidal to venture up to the deck, most of the passengers were crammed into the saloon, though precious few were in the mood to imbibe. The crew,

whose forced smiles and fake good humor were so grotesque they made unctuousness seem genuine, had distributed buckets to those who felt the urge to vomit. Many did, creating a chorus of sounds that bounced off the ship's walls, amplifying the noise to unbearable levels. If hell had a choir, this was most definitely it.

So these are the new breed of "Hardy Americans" who would rule the world, the Frenchman thought, allowing himself a small, derisive snicker.

"Yes, I suspected you might find that little tidbit amusing," said the fat woman, adding a shrill of a laugh so high-pitched that the Frenchman found a need to shield his eardrums. She was crushed up against him on a bench and had been talking incessantly, completely oblivious to his attempts to ignore her.

The fat woman had boasted of being from the upper crust of Boston society and of being able to trace her family origins back to the *Mayflower* and beyond. The Frenchman wasn't impressed. To him, Boston's upper crust was at best middle in London and no more than third-rate in Paris. Still, he felt obliged to reply.

"*Oui,* Mrs. Campbell. *Très drôle.*" He hoped this would end it, but he knew it was unlikely.

"Please, call me Hermione."

"If you wish." *And if that will shut you up.*

It didn't. "I'm so glad you agree." She nodded toward his suitcase, which had the words "Property of" emblazoned on its side along with the Frenchman's name. "Ah, your first name is Louis. May I take the liberty of calling you Louie?"

The Frenchman cringed. He didn't know what annoyed him more—her unabashed impudence or her ignorance.

Since "Louis" is pronounced "Louie" in French, there was no need to ask such a question unless you were an imbecile. It reeked of arrogance that the people of this upstart nation would deem it unimportant to learn the most rudimentary elements of the world's languages. Of course, it was precisely this single-minded arrogance that could lead America to being a world power, but it would most assuredly also lead to its downfall. He gave them no more than a century, a century that would be filled with catastrophic changes. Catastrophic. He turned toward the fat woman and nodded. Once again, she shrilled with glee. He prayed they'd reach port soon, or he too would need to request a bucket, and not because of the rough sea.

The downpour bordered on torrential as the Boston boat pulled into the Greenport harbor on the northeastern end of Long Island and docked. The passengers scurried off the boat, but the Frenchman was weighed down by the two large suitcases he was carrying. As he plodded along, his thin, spindly arms unable to move, it was impossible to also hold an umbrella. A hat would have to do to shield him from the rain, and it didn't.

The fat woman was already ashore and was instructing the carriage driver on the finer points of loading her luggage while a servant held an umbrella over her, keeping her perfectly dry.

God, how the Frenchman despised her! As he stepped onto shore, she waved.

"*Au revoir,* Louie. Perhaps one day I will see you in Paree."

With this, the Frenchman lost his footing. It took considerable maneuvering and the luck of finding a railing nearby to prevent his fall. Muttering angrily to himself, he

lifted the two large suitcases he had dropped and moved as fast as he could to the nearest available carriage.

"The Greenport train station, *s'il vous plaît,* and be quick about it," he ordered the driver, spraying some water with his words while attempting to load his luggage. The driver slowly hopped down off his perch to help him.

"Let me get that for ya, guvnor," the driver said. "Don't you fret. They always wait for the Boston boat." The driver secured one suitcase on the outside rear of the carriage and was about to take the other with his name on it when the Frenchman pulled it back possessively. The driver raised both his hands.

"Have it your way, guvnor. It should fit nicely on your lap," he said, knowing that it wouldn't.

As the Frenchman squeezed inside, the top of his suitcase pressed tightly against his chin, his mind wasn't on his discomfort. *A cockney carriage driver on Long Island?* he thought. *It makes an interesting combination, rather interesting indeed.* He conceded that maybe there was something to be learned from this melting pot. It was this singular thought that occupied his mind as the carriage pulled away from the dock on its way to the train station.

About five yards away, there was another carriage waiting, lurking in the shadows, hidden by the darkness of the evening and the pouring rain. All that could be perceived of the passenger inside its cabin was the silhouetted outline of a large bowler hat. The Bowler Hat had been given an assignment, and as always, he was fastidious in his devotion to detail. It wasn't really necessary though. He could tell from first glance that his assignment was soft, beneath his level of expertise and not really worth being out in this

weather. He tweaked the brim of his new bowler hat, glad he had spotted it earlier that day in the town store. At least he would net something positive from this job. The Bowler Hat sighed, then knocked twice on the roof with his cane. The carriage lurched forward and, after sliding on a patch of mud, was on its way.

~

Boarding the train with his luggage in the downpour was no small feat, but with the driver's help the Frenchman managed to get everything on. The passenger compartment was neat, clean, and, most important, devoid of any other passengers.

At least this part of my journey hasn't been muddled by the Americans, the Frenchman thought.

He speedily relieved himself of his sopping wet overcoat and hat, carefully hanging them on a rack at the far end of the compartment, hoping they'd dry by the time they arrived in New York. His suit and shirt were manageable, but his shoes and socks were soaked. He removed them, wrung out the socks, and hung them up as well. Barefoot and comfortable, the Frenchman had one final chore to perform before he could relax.

He picked up the suitcase he had kept at his side the entire trip, the one with his name on it. The Frenchman placed it on the passenger bench across from him and unlocked it. Inside was a large boxlike object. With the delicacy of a munitions expert handling nitroglycerin, he removed it from the suitcase and sat down, ever so gently placing it on his lap. He examined it carefully to see if any damage had

been done when he had dropped the suitcase on the dock. None was perceptible, but he would soon see. Reaching inside the suitcase, he pulled out a metal bar with a handle at one end. He inserted the metal bar into a hole in the box and began turning the handle over and over. Finally, a foil cylinder on top of the box started to spin, and a scratchy voice could be heard reciting what sounded like some sort of nursery rhyme in French. Relieved, he sighed. Nothing had been harmed! The Frenchman's demeanor instantly transformed as he listened attentively to every single sound, nodding his head and tapping his bare feet to the musical cadence of the rhyme. When lightning illuminated the car, he turned to the door without breaking rhythm. He was surprised to see it was ajar.

Staring at him from the hallway was a twelve-year-old blond girl with the bluest eyes he had ever seen. The girl was clearly spellbound by the Frenchman's amazing toy. Her excitement was so contagious it would easily have melted the most jaded of hearts. Carefully placing the box on the seat next to him, the Frenchman stood up and slammed the door in her face.

~

The Bowler Hat sat patiently in his compartment. There was no rush, no worry. Everything was planned out. Jobs like these were nothing if not predictable, emphasizing the paradoxical nature of his work. His employers insisted his implementation be boring and uneventful, whereas he craved a challenge. He doubted whether any would present itself this night. For the moment, his hat rested on the bench

next to him. He was of indeterminate age, a plausible thirty, yet forty-five was certainly within the realm of possibility. Besides being thick in the chest, there was really nothing remarkable about his looks. Depending on his dress, he could easily pass for a businessman, a waiter, or a factory worker, and that was fine with him. Anonymity was his ally.

He checked the pocket watch in his vest. Nineteen minutes had passed since the train left the station. It usually took about twenty minutes for people to find their seats, register any complaints with the conductor, then settle in for the long haul. Restlessness would come later as passengers wondered what kind of time the train was making, young men began to troll through the cars inventing excuses to speak with pretty girls, and husbands were finally able to extract themselves from their families and venture to the bar. *Actually, a shot of scotch would be nice,* he thought. *Afterward.* The anticipation of a reward would stave off the boredom and keep him focused. The Bowler Hat figured he now had twenty-two minutes before the train cars began buzzing with people. That was more than sufficient to accomplish his job. He always allowed extra time but rarely needed it. He was that good. No need to look at his watch again. It was time. He stood, straightened his vest, put on his hat, and grabbed his satchel.

～

The Frenchman answered the knock at his door thinking the little blond girl had returned to bother him. This time he would shoo her away for good.

"I don't appreciate little snoops—"

Before he could finish, the Bowler Hat was upon him,
using his left foot to shut the door. With one hand covering
the Frenchman's mouth and the other at the back of his
head, the Bowler Hat broke his victim's neck with one violent twist. The Frenchman sagged to the floor. The Bowler
Hat shook his head in disgust. He was right. Soft. He had
hoped for some sort of surprise, a modicum of resistance,
something. But it was not to be. He sighed, then promptly
switched gears. Any distraction during a job could prove to
be costly. The Bowler Hat was his own toughest taskmaster.

He opened his satchel, removed a rope, and as he tied a
noose, he focused on the scotch he'd be savoring sooner than
he had anticipated. He could almost taste it.

As the Bowler Hat left the compartment, the suitcase
with the Frenchman's name on it in one hand and his
satchel in the other, he suddenly felt a presence. The corridor had been empty—he had checked—but now someone
was behind him. Careful not to move too hastily, because
that would look suspicious and force him to take action,
he slowly glanced back, and what he saw almost made him
laugh.

A little blond girl no more than twelve, was coming
down the corridor. This couldn't have been better if he had
planned it himself. He had purposely left the compartment
door open because he wanted the Frenchman to be found.
How perfect it would be for the announcement of his death
to come from a hysterical child. It was dark, and even if the
girl had seen him, she would be too distraught to remember any details and too young for anyone to pay attention
if she did.

Just as he was about to leave, lightning flashed through

the car again, revealing something that concerned him—the little girl's piercing blue eyes staring right at him. He could read people instantly. It was what he did; it was his job. And her eyes betrayed not only intelligence, but an awareness beyond her years. This was no ordinary little girl. She was different. He stepped toward her, but someone else was already entering the corridor. His moment of opportunity had passed. As he swiftly moved into the next car, his mind already back on his scotch, he looked back and caught a glimpse of the little girl entering the Frenchman's compartment. He paused, but there was no screaming, no hysterics. He was right. She was different.

1

What could Senator Conkling have possibly been thinking? The Blizzard of 1888 struck in March and had brought the entire Eastern Seaboard to a virtual standstill. Telegraph and telephone lines were snapped, public transportation was shut down, and all businesses were closed. Thirty-foot snow drifts piled up against buildings and blocked streets in Brooklyn and New York City, making normal, everyday life almost impossible. Absolutely nothing was untouched by what was dubbed the Great White Hurricane. So, what could have possessed the former New York senator to go for a stroll that had resulted in his falling ill and presently being on his deathbed?

Mary Handley couldn't get this thought out of her mind. It was odd. She knew there had to be some skewed logic behind his illogical behavior, but absolutely no one was questioning it. She didn't think anything untoward had happened to him. Wondering about it was just a mental exercise, the kind to which she kept gravitating: questioning the inexplicable until it was explained. She had no illusions

that anyone would take her musings seriously, no matter what she had concluded. She was a woman and poor, and therefore nothing she said could possibly be of import. As she had been told many times, she should confine her interests to family and children or trivial pursuits such as theater and art.

On occasion, when a man would feign interest in her opinion, it usually meant he was flirting. Though her appearance was offbeat, at twenty-four, Mary was quite attractive. Her nose was somewhat long and her chin a bit short, but her thick blond hair and penetrating blue eyes more than compensated for it. But no physical description could do Mary justice. She had a magnetic aura about her, fueled by her strong spirit and her unquenchable thirst for knowledge, that only those purely interested in the superficial could possibly miss. Much to Mary's chagrin, her mother, Elizabeth, was one of them, and she could often be heard saying, "My Mary falls just short of being pretty."

Looks aside, no one could question Mary's intelligence, and though being patronized or dismissed by a society that valued individuals based on gender or money infuriated Mary, she had learned to live with it. She knew that the world was governed by many prejudices, and she also knew that if she dwelled on that fact, her anger would prevent her from accomplishing anything.

Mary didn't mind living in a tiny one-room apartment with a minuscule corner kitchen. She didn't mind that her tenement building was on Elizabeth Street, in one of the worst sections of Brooklyn. Nor did she mind working for slave wages at the Lowry Hat Factory, a death trap where health hazards abounded. What she did mind was her boss,

the Widow Lowry, who thought her ability to thrive on the misery of others made her superior. Though often tempted, Mary never challenged the Widow Lowry yet refused to kowtow to her, and thus received fewer working hours than those who did. Still, her continued employment there was a testament to her restraint. She viewed the Lowry Hat Factory as a mere stop on the way to achieving her life's plan. One day, against all odds and the prevailing wisdom, she would get her opportunity, and she needed to be ready. Her patience and determination were exemplary, for she had harbored this ambition for quite some time, ever since she took the train from Greenport to New York City when she was twelve.

That night, Mary and her family had been returning from a summer weekend at a farm on Long Island owned by the parents of their neighbors and very close friends in Brooklyn, the McNishes. The families had a lot in common: both sets of parents were Irish immigrants, and all the children were first-generation Americans. The weekend was supposed to be a respite from the intense heat of another Brooklyn summer and a chance for the children to experience the country, but thunderstorms and pouring rain had kept them indoors, where Mary was forever under the watchful eye of her extremely critical mother. Elizabeth had known for a while that Mary was "different." After all, the girl admired such figures as Darwin and that Elizabeth Blackwell woman with her fancy medical degree, and Kierkegaard, whoever that was.

"The girl's gone all loony. She wants to be a scientist or a philosopher or both. Imagine that," she whispered to her good friend Abigail McNish. Elizabeth sat next to Abigail on the train, their husbands, Jeffrey and Archie, in the seat behind them, and their children in front of them. At thirty-five, Elizabeth's sensible hairstyle and matronly clothes didn't entirely obscure her natural good looks. As a young woman, she had allowed herself to be more stylish, and many men had taken notice. But it was Jeffrey who had charmed her and stolen her heart. In hindsight, it had crossed her mind more than once that she should have ignored her emotions and aimed higher, a mistake she hoped to help Mary avoid.

"If anyone can do it, it's your Mary," replied Abigail. Her daughter, Sarah, and Mary had grown up together and were the best of friends. Sarah would never be as bright as Mary, but she admired Mary's intelligence. It wasn't that life hadn't also blessed Sarah. With her jet-black hair, porcelain skin, and large, soulful eyes, Sarah was more classically pretty, which Elizabeth never hesitated to point out.

"The one who's special is your Sarah," she responded, again in a low voice. "Mark my words. With her beauty and easy disposition, she's going to land herself a fine husband one day. A very fine husband."

And that summed up Elizabeth's attitude. She felt that marriage was the only realistic way a girl could advance herself, and that it was her job as a mother to bring Mary's two feet down to earth "for her own good." If it meant belittling her ambitions, so be it. There were precious few opportunities for women and almost none in the lofty fields to which Mary aspired. But her mother's negativity just made Mary's resolve stronger. As a result, they were always at

odds. Nonetheless, Elizabeth was unprepared for what happened next. Loud and clear, a voice rang out and reverberated throughout the car.

"Pick it up, Sean. Pick it up, or I'll box your ears, you jealous shit!"

Elizabeth closed her eyes, hoping she was wrong about the voice's origin. This would have been an unacceptable exclamation for any man outside of a rowdy saloon, and here it was coming from a twelve-year-old girl.

Mary's expletive was directed at her brother, Sean, and he had done his best to earn it. After losing to Mary in a game of chess, he had thrown a tantrum and had knocked the chess set to the floor. He was a full two years older and a boy, and the prevailing wisdom had taught him that boys were smarter than girls. Yet, with Mary as his sister, he had learned firsthand that the prevailing wisdom was not always correct. Whether it was at chess or anything that required a reasonable level of mental acuity, Mary outwitted him time after time. He kept trying as if his absent male superiority would one day magically appear and help him defeat her, but it never did. He had to settle for being annoying (something at which he excelled) or getting her in trouble. Either one put a smile on his face.

None of that mattered to Elizabeth. Avoiding public embarrassment was paramount, and her daughter had just made her bathe in it.

Mary had a vast vocabulary for a girl her age and was definitely aware that proper society frowned upon certain words. Because of her mother's constant scrutiny, she normally kept her true emotions in check, but these pent-up feelings inevitably led to occasional outbursts. What added

to the ease with which swear words rolled off her tongue was that society's obsession with such words didn't seem logical to her. If they added the appropriate emphasis to what was being said, she saw nothing foul about them. What was foul was using words to lie, to deceive, or to render harm. And what was most certainly foul was the taste of soap. In no time Elizabeth was at Mary's side with a full bar. She always kept one in her pocketbook for disciplinary reasons.

"You know what to do with it, girl, and don't be stingy," commanded Elizabeth, her Irish accent more pronounced when she was upset.

As Mary took the bar from her, Elizabeth glanced at Sean, who was slouching. He immediately sat up as straight as he could. Then, having done her duty, Elizabeth returned to her seat, holding her head up high as if daring someone to say something about her, her family, or her mothering skills.

Mary looked at Sarah, whose large, round eyes were full of empathy for her friend and the daunting task she had ahead. They had always confided in each other, revealing their most personal thoughts and feelings, but now all they could do was exchange looks and shake their heads at the annoying smirk Sean was wearing. Mary soothed herself, though, with the knowledge that any satisfaction he felt over getting her in trouble was the result of flawed logic. Mary had no intention of eating any of the soap.

As soon as her parents and Sean weren't looking, Mary slipped away. Her idea was to carve up the soap to make it look like she had been eating it. The task at hand was to find someone with a pocketknife. With rain pounding against the train, thunder exploding, and lightning occa- sionally illuminating the darkness, it became an adventure

where Mary imagined ghosts and demons popping out of every crevice. She had stopped at a large window to gaze at the foreboding weather when a passenger appeared out of the blackness and startled her. She spun about, and it was then that she noticed the Frenchman's door ajar for the first time. If Mary hadn't been so scientifically oriented, she would have thought his contraption magical. There had to be an explanation for it. So on her way back, after an extremely friendly conductor had helped her carve a jagged masterpiece she was sure would fool her mother, she hoped to find his door ajar again. Though he was mostly hidden in shadows, she spied an austere-looking large man wearing a bowler hat exiting the Frenchman's compartment. They locked eyes for a brief moment, but her attention was more drawn to the door that he had left open. She decided that it was worth risking another sampling of the Frenchman's bad humor for a second look at the contraption.

When she entered the compartment and saw the French-man with the noose around his neck, her mind kicked into an analytical mode. She had never seen a dead body before. Her parents had shielded her from going to the wake of her aunt who had died in childbirth, yet Mary behaved as if this experience were a common occurrence. She was sure the Frenchman was dead, but she checked his pulse anyway. Nothing. The poor man was gone all right. There was nothing she could do for him, so she looked around the compartment, taking a visual inventory. She saw the clothes that were hanging to dry and a suitcase, but where was that strange object that made the sound? She had no fear, no emotion, just a desire to find out what had transpired. It was not until the adults arrived that hysteria broke out.

"Little girl, you need to get out of here," a man with a pipe said as he looked wildly down the corridor, but Mary didn't budge. "Conductor!" he screamed. "Somebody get the conductor!"

"Jesus, Mary, and Joseph!" the conductor cried upon seeing the Frenchman hanging there. "Someone help me get this poor soul down."

By now a crowd had gathered. Too many rushed forward to help, although more stayed back, frozen by the sight of the dead Frenchman. The noise level and the size of the crowd were multiplying. Taking charge, the conductor pointed to three men.

"You, you, and you, help get this man down." As they promptly jumped to, the conductor turned to the crowd. "Ladies and gentlemen, please go back to your seats. There's nothing to see here, just a poor fella who killed himself. Let's give him some of the peace that he obviously did not find in life."

As the passengers dispersed, the conductor felt a tug at his side, and he turned to see the little girl he had helped carve a piece of soap.

"This is no place for you, child. Go back to your mother."

"But, Mr. Conductor, sir, this man did not commit suicide."

"You mean, you saw . . ." And the conductor paused for a moment to choose his words carefully. He was talking to a child. But Mary was too quick for him.

"Not exactly." And Mary explained about the man with the bowler hat, whom she hadn't seen that well, and about the object that made sound, which was no longer there.

The conductor realized he was dealing with a little girl

who had a big imagination and ordered her once again to return to her mother.

"But it makes no sense, Mr. Conductor. Why would a man take off his shoes to hang himself? Why would he hang clothes to dry he wasn't ever going to wear again?"

The conductor had no answer, but he also had no time to deal with a child's logic. "He was probably crazy." And he gave Mary a gentle push into the corridor, then closed the door.

Word of the Frenchman's suicide had traveled fast and was already the topic of excited conversation when Mary returned to her car and calmly announced she had actually seen the dead man. Her family and friends were anything but calm. Immediately forgetting the swearing incident and the soap, Elizabeth hugged Mary, doing her best to soothe her young daughter, who really needed no soothing. In this rare burst of warmth from her mother, Mary informed her that she'd had a change of heart.

"I no longer wish to be a scientist or philosopher, Mother."

"Really?" said a relieved Elizabeth, thinking this awful incident may have somehow netted a positive result.

"I've decided I want to be a detective."

Elizabeth flinched. This daughter of hers would never give her peace.

Mary spent the rest of the trip trying to think of reasons why the dead man would have taken off his shoes and hung up his clothes before killing himself. There were none. She was sure he had been murdered.

~

It was a few days past the Blizzard of '88, and everything in New York and Brooklyn had reopened as the city regained its legs. In a way, Mary had welcomed the blizzard. The Lowry Hat Factory was shut down, and though the loss of wages hurt, her Franklin stove kept her room warm, and she had time to catch up on her reading.

Having been denied a college education ("It's for the wealthy," her mother told her, "and even if we had the money, why waste it on a girl?"), Mary was a sponge for all knowledge. When their children were young, Elizabeth and Jeffrey had splurged on an *Encyclopedia Americana,* hoping Sean would aspire to higher education of the type that would pay off, such as medical or law school. To their dismay, Sean's passion for academics was tepid at best. Mary reacted differently, devouring the material, reading each volume from cover to cover. She loved science, and Thomas Edison became one of her idols. She began following him when he revolutionized the incandescent lightbulb in 1879 and admired him for his creative genius and hard work.

Mary's appetite was larger than the encyclopedia, and books were expensive. The occasional birthday or Christmas present did little to satisfy it. So Jeffrey befriended the owner of a bookstore that was a few doors down from the butcher shop where he worked. The owner had devoted a small section of his store to secondhand books, most of which were from his own collection. He was pleased to hear Jeffrey's daughter was such a voracious reader, and he gave him access to any of the books in the secondhand section. The owner reasoned they had already been read, so it would be no calamity if they were read again before someone bought them. So began a tradition in which Jeffrey

would come home with a twinkle in his eye, and Mary would know he had a special present for her. As a result, Mary was exposed to a wide variety of writers, from Dickens to Dostoyevsky to the Brontë sisters, Shakespeare, Milton, and beyond.

Elizabeth disapproved. "It's sure to give her false hope," she lamented to Jeffrey. "Disappointment and heartache are the only things she'll get out of all this reading."

It didn't matter. Even if Elizabeth was right, and Jeffrey suspected she probably was, he couldn't deny Mary the pure pleasure she derived from learning, nor could he deprive himself of the pride he felt over having a daughter with such wondrous abilities. He hoped that when disappointment came later in life, the knowledge she was gaining now might somehow help her be strong enough to handle it.

Luckily for Mary, advancements in all facets of book publishing and production had lowered the price of books. They now came bound in leather or cloth, or wrapped in paper, the last being the cheapest. The bookstore owner was still kind enough to lend Mary books, but the selection was limited. She found that if she skipped a meal here or there, she could save up to buy a paper-wrapped book.

Mary's reading list betrayed her passion for forensics and detective novels. There were so many scientific journals and books randomly strewn around her little one-room apartment that it looked like the Great White Hurricane had struck inside.

"It's all part of my decorating scheme," Mary would quip. "This may look like the work of a slob, but if you look closer, you'll realize it's my way of giving color to an awfully drab floor."

Though the city was back to work, Mary wasn't. The Widow Lowry's response to Mary's lack of total subservience was to lessen the number of days she worked, but the quirk of fate that allowed the Lowry Hat Factory to reopen on one of her off days didn't upset Mary. Though it would strap her further financially, any day without the Widow Lowry was brighter, and it gave her more time to read.

She was lying on her couch (actually her bed marginally disguised to look like a couch), engrossed in *Beeton's Christmas Annual,* which contained a serialized version of *A Study in Scarlet,* a first novel by a relatively new author, Sir Arthur Conan Doyle. When the distinct odor of burned French toast interrupted her reading, she bolted for the stove and grabbed the frying pan with her bare left hand.

"Shit!" she screamed as she dropped the pan, then ran to the sink. She flipped on the water, threw her hand under it, and sighed as the cold water soothed the pain. Mary's four-letter exclamations had been tempered over the years. Her mother and society had seen to that. But at times like these, a healthy "Shit!" did her a world of good.

Someone started banging at the door. She decided not to pay any attention to it. The water felt too good. The knocking persisted.

"Mary, it's Kate. Are you okay?"

Mary smiled. Kate Stoddard worked with Mary at the Lowry Hat Factory. She had a similar room upstairs and had become a good friend. They weren't as close as Mary and Sarah McNish had been, but she and Sarah no longer saw one another as much as they would have liked to. Their feelings hadn't changed, and in time of need they would most

certainly rush to each other's aid, but Sarah was married to a lawyer and had two children. She was busy raising them, and their lives had taken different paths.

Kate Stoddard was a brown-haired girl in her early twenties who had a penchant for the dramatic and was easily excitable, often in a very folksy, noncosmopolitan way. A country girl from Haddonfield, New Jersey, she tried to dress and look as sophisticated as possible in order to assimilate into the big city. But her origins always shined through, and Mary wasn't alone in thinking that the dichotomy was charming.

Kate was careful to shield her family from her "scandalous" life in the big city. She made regular trips to the Twelfth Street Post Office in Manhattan to pick up mail from them. Mary had accompanied her once. It seemed like a senseless journey.

"You should have your mail delivered instead of coming all the way here."

"My parents run the general store in Haddonfield. They're very small-town."

"And they don't want their baby living in scary old Brooklyn."

Kate nodded, smiling. "I presently rent from an elderly couple in New York who refuse all mail delivery."

"And they believe that?"

"Haddonfield. I left that hopelessly rural town, and they think I'm crazy."

Kate always entertained Mary with comments about her origins or about her adventures in the big city. She found Kate refreshing compared to the average hardened

city dweller. So in spite of how good the water felt, Mary wrapped a wet washrag around her left hand and answered the door.

"Did you burn your breakfast again?" Kate whispered.

As Mary nodded, embarrassed that it had happened yet again, neighbors started emerging from their apartments. Kate took over.

"It's okay, folks. Nothing serious." She lifted up Mary's left arm. "Just a burnin', cussin' fool."

Mary pulled Kate inside and shut the door, both of them laughing.

"My poor mother would be scandalized."

Kate walked straight to the scene of the crime and picked up the charred French toast. "Pitiful, simply pitiful."

"What's even more pitiful, that's supposed to hold me till dinner."

Kate threw the French toast in the garbage, used a towel to pick up the frying pan, and put it in the sink. "Kiss up to the Widow Lowry, and she'll give you more hours."

"There's a limit to what I can stomach. That woman's a sadistic, dishonest . . ."

"I know. A real . . ." And, uncomfortable with such language, Kate lowered her voice to a whisper and spelled out, "B-i-t-c-h."

"Why, Kate, I believe I've been a bad influence on you."

With a glint in her eye, Kate replied, "Well, not all bad."

Mary blanched, feeling guilty at having forgotten. "Of course, I'm sorry. How did your big night go?"

Nonchalance didn't fit Kate, yet she tried it anyway. "Oh, nothing significant, except he's having his mother's ring sized to my finger."

This announcement was accompanied by a look of complete and total joy. Almost simultaneously, the two friends screamed. Mary hugged Kate.

"Oh, Kate, I'm so happy for you!!"

Kate broke away from Mary and danced around the room. "All of Haddonfield's gonna be abuzz. I came to New York, got me the perfect man, and we're gonna have a perfect marriage and perfect kids."

"You ought to be ashamed, Kate Stoddard. You left out the perfect grandkids."

Kate pointed to a large locket around her neck. "Their photos are goin' right here, in Grandma Stoddard's locket."

"Nothing like planning ahead, but right now you're late for work."

The reality of her everyday life dawned on Kate and snapped her out of her reverie. She rushed to the door but turned before leaving.

"Just think. Pretty soon I won't have to work anymore for that . . . b-i-t-c-h."

Mary was happy for her friend. She had no idea that it was the last happy moment they would share.

2

Mary wasn't joking about her burned breakfast. After the debacle of the French toast, she had nothing to eat until dinner. She had enough money to pay the rent that was due the next day and buy two cans of soup, one for dinner that night and one for the next. If she wanted something to eat before then, she could either go to her parents' house and be degraded by her mother or visit Sean, who was a policeman at Second Street Station. Neither choice was pleasant, but Sean was decidedly the lesser of two evils.

The irony of Sean's becoming a policeman didn't escape Mary, though she didn't believe he had chosen that profession as a protruding middle finger to their life-long sparring. Sean lacked the makings of a professional man, and the police force was no stranger to young men of Irish descent. The current joke was that you had to kiss the Blarney Stone in order to get in. Besides, the hostilities between Mary and Sean had been reduced as they got older. Not living in the same house had helped, but more significantly, Sean felt less threatened by his

sister. After all, he was on a career path, and she was going nowhere.

Mary lived in a part of Brooklyn where violence was common, but that never gave her pause when she ventured out. Learning to defend herself was not an option for her but rather a rite of passage.

Growing up in late nineteenth-century Brooklyn was hardly conducive to a happy life for an intelligent girl with a sharp wit. School had been a nightmare for Mary. She had often been ridiculed and physically bullied simply for being cleverer than her tormentors. Mary likened school to Dante's *Inferno,* thus adding to her schoolmates' anger because she could reference something they had never heard of or couldn't understand.

Much to her credit, Sarah, who in marked contrast to Mary was very popular, always defended her friend, but her parents insisted that she switch to a parochial school and Mary was left to stand on her own. She wasn't the only outcast at school, but she had little in common with the perennial-oddball group who took the brunt of the abuse. Luckily, there was one girl in her class with whom Mary had formed a genuine bond.

Tina Chung had immigrated to the United States from China with her parents when she was three. In spite of her perfect English—and she spoke better than most of the other children—they still mocked her speech and constantly made fun of her name.

"You know how the Chinese get their names? They throw a stone into a pot and if it goes ping, ching, or chung, that's the name they pick." Inevitably, this pronouncement was followed by a cacophony of giggles.

Mary didn't become friends with Tina because she felt sorry for her. She was drawn to Tina because she was smart, and they could discuss topics in which few children their age had any interest. After school, they often went to Tina's home, where they would speed through their homework, then pursue other interests, which ranged from playing spirited games of chess or whist to conducting scientific experiments, and to inevitably discussing the works of great writers. Tina and her parents lived in a basement apartment of a brownstone. In exchange for rent, Tina's father, Wei, did handyman work, and her mother, Xin, performed cleaning services for the owners, who lived upstairs.

Wei was aware of the prejudice and hostility his daughter was encountering and wanted her to feel proud of her heritage. He personally schooled Tina in the rich history and traditions of the Chinese people. Wei possessed an old Chinese charm that had been passed down from generation to generation in his family. It dated back to the Ming Dynasty. It was attached to a gold chain, and he wore it around his neck. He told Tina that one day it would be hers, and she could pass it on to her children so they'd always know where they came from. Tina loved the charm and was thrilled at the prospect of carrying on the family tradition. Mary was also fascinated by it and asked Wei what the Chinese letters on the charm meant.

"Ji qing ru yi," he told her. "It means 'May your happiness be according to your wishes.'"

This saying struck Mary as especially relevant to her life since her mother and everyone else seemed to want Mary's happiness to be according to their wishes, not hers. The

words stayed with her for years to come and often helped her focus on her goals when others cast doubt upon them.

Tina was nine years old when, after a particularly tough day at school, Wei took her into the backyard of the brownstone.

"It is time for you to learn the art of jujitsu."

Wei was a jujitsu master and a very fine teacher. One day Mary watched him give Tina her lesson and was enthralled. She approached Wei and bowed.

"Mr. Chung, I would be greatly honored if you would take me on as a student."

Wei was charmed by Mary's humility and her respect for Chinese culture. He had never experienced that with an American child. Mary genuinely admired the Chungs and their traditions. She worked hard and learned quickly.

Sean had the dubious distinction of being the first one to experience Mary's new abilities. When he was unable to best her mentally, he would occasionally try to exert his physical dominance. In the backyard one day, Mary warned him: "I wouldn't do that if I were you, Sean. I won't tolerate it."

"Oh, you won't tolerate it," he said, mimicking her, then went for Mary. In no time, she had flipped him to the ground.

Sean was in a state of disbelief, but he dismissed it as luck and charged harder at her. As a result, he went down harder. After two more good thumps, his disbelief was replaced with sad resignation at having lost his last bastion of dominance over his sister.

A few years later, Wei got an opportunity to open a laundry business with his brother, Huan, in San Francisco and decided to move his family there. By then, Mary had become

proficient in jujitsu, enough so that the bullying at school had changed to whispers behind her back. Ideally, physical supremacy wasn't the way Mary had wanted to earn respect, but it certainly made her situation better, both at home and at school.

As Mary turned the corner onto Second Street, she stopped and took a deep breath. About thirty-five women were picketing in front of Second Street Station, carrying signs that read HIRE FEMALE POLICE OFFICERS, YOU NEED POLICEWOMEN, etc. Mary's views on the women's rights movement presented her with a dilemma she hadn't reconciled. She was all for women's rights, but she despised organized groups in general, feeling that by their very nature, they lowered their intelligence level to that of the least intelligent member.

Mary approached the precinct and began to climb the stairs. One of the organizers, Amanda Everhart, spotted her ignoring their picket line. She was a well-dressed woman in her thirties who came from an upper-class family. Her father was a lawyer and her husband was a newspaperman. Both men approved of her activism and encouraged her liberal views. She was adamant about her cause and certain that she was right. Mary would not go unchallenged on her watch.

"Join us, sister," Amanda called out. "We'll change the world."

"Get them to outlaw corsets," Mary replied, "and I'll be a lifetime member."

"It's your future, too, sister."

What bothered Mary most about these women was their self-righteous tone. It didn't seem to enter their minds that

some people had to spend their days trying to scrape together enough just to exist.

"Protest is a luxury, and the womb that bore you was obviously more privileged than the one that bore me . . . *sister.*"

As Mary entered the police station, Amanda wasn't insulted, nor was she deterred. Instead, she was intrigued and impressed by Mary's fire.

Bedlam had taken up permanent residence in Second Street Station. The place was in a continual state of panic, and the policemen reflected it.

"Most of them scurry around with great purpose as if desperately seeking an unoccupied toilet," Mary had once joked to Kate.

Mary's observation was certainly true this day. Some of the policemen had criminals in tow, mostly poor men and women. Either the wealthy never broke the law or they had the means to avoid the consequences of breaking it. A handful of people were there to report crimes, trying their best to find a free policeman. All these activities created a noise level that was insufferable, but insufferable was the norm.

"Doctor!" screamed a badly bruised man with a large cut on his head. He was alone, handcuffed to the arm of a bench. "Doctor!" But no one came.

Mary spotted a policeman struggling with a prostitute who was arrested not for selling her wares but rather for stealing her customer's gold watch. The policeman's name was John Russell, a wiry but deceptively strong man with a

quick temper who looked most comfortable with a sneer on his face.

"Get your hands off me. I'm a lady!" she protested.

"And how much does a lady cost nowadays?"

"I wouldn't know. Ask your mother."

Officer Russell slapped her before she could start laughing, and he slapped her hard. It wasn't the slap that prompted Mary to step forward. It was something else.

"Excuse me, Officer," Mary started to say, "but it seems—"

"Get lost!" Officer Russell screamed. "Only one whore at a time!"

He then smacked the prostitute with such force it knocked her onto the bench behind her. His smirk indicated he enjoyed doing it. Most women when faced with this situation would have been either scared or insulted or both. Not Mary. She calmly looked into Officer Russell's eyes, decided this man did not deserve her time, and moved on.

"Doctor!" the man on the bench screamed again.

"This isn't a place for ya, Mary."

Mary turned to see Police Sergeant Billy O'Brien. He was fifty, balding, and pudgy, but no one ever judged Billy by his appearance. The man was full of life and defined Irish charm.

"Why, Billy, you look so spiffy I thought it was the commissioner himself."

"Do I? Now, why am I gettin' the feelin' you're wantin' somethin'?"

"I'm here to see Sean."

Billy smiled impishly, then shouted toward the stairs that led to the basement. "Sean Handley, there's a mighty fine-lookin' lass inquirin' about ya!"

In seconds, Sean came charging up the stairs, still buttoning his messy uniform. He had grown into a handsome young man and was brushing back his hair with his hand when he spotted Mary and disappointment registered on his face. Billy laughed, then winked at Mary and left them alone.

"Doctor!"

Sean took Mary aside, talking hurriedly. "I'm in it over my head, Mary. The pipes in the basement burst. It almost flooded the evidence room and I—"

"I was hoping you'd take me to lunch," Mary said, cutting him off mid-excuse.

He stared at her and shook his head. "All those brains and not a plug nickel."

Just then, all eyes in the station clicked toward the doors as Chief Patrick Campbell entered. In his forties, heavy but solid, Chief Campbell was not only their boss but probably the best policeman in all of Brooklyn. He was tough on crime and tough on his men, yet there wasn't one policeman in that precinct who didn't aspire to be him or at least earn his respect. Greetings of "Hi, Chief" and "Morning, Chief" rang out as he walked along.

Billy approached with a copy of the local newspaper, the *Brooklyn Daily Eagle*. The headline read, CAMPBELL VOWS TO CLEAN UP BROOKLYN, and right below it was a newspaper artist's rendering of Chief Campbell scowling.

"Made it again, Chief. Charmin' picture."

Chief Campbell grimaced, unwittingly looking exactly like the drawing. The grimace was Chief Campbell's trademark. It kept his men on their toes, and he was keenly aware that no one wanted to see a happy chief of police.

They would think him ineffective or daffy. Though labeling him as merely grumpy would have been a disservice. He was smart, perceptive, and somewhat witty when in the mood.

Sean shoved some money into Mary's hand as he saw Chief Campbell approach.

"Now, get going," Sean said, then abruptly turned away from her. "Morning, Chief."

"Doctor!" the man on the bench moaned again. He was not giving up.

"Officer Handley, do my ears deceive me," Chief Campbell said, "or did you just tell this charming young lady to shoo?"

Sean was flustered, while also flattered Chief Campbell actually knew his name. He wasn't aware that the chief made it his business to know everyone in his precinct.

"Yes, sir, I did. I mean . . . Sir, this is my sister, Mary."

"Ah, now it's clear. A pleasure, Mary." Chief Campbell extended his hand and they shook.

"Doctor!"

Chief Campbell turned and barked, "Get that man a doctor or shut him up!"

Policemen from all over the station converged on the man to do the chief's bidding, making Officer Russell's struggles with the prostitute more apparent than they had been.

"Russell seems to have his hands full," Chief Campbell noted. "Too bad he hasn't figured out what handcuffs are for."

"He's probably waiting for Mrs. Mead to come over," Sean explained. Men weren't allowed to search female

suspects, and since there were no policewomen, they often used Mrs. Mead, who worked at the laundry across the street.

"Good," Mary said. "She'll find the weapon the woman has stashed."

"A weapon?" Chief Campbell asked.

"Right leg, under her garter," Mary explained matter-of-factly. "Her hand hasn't left there since I came in." Mary noticed Chief Campbell's surprise. "I tried to warn him, but he's averse to women. His mother denied him her breast, I suspect."

At that point, Mrs. Mead, a harried older lady, entered the station. "Does anyone know where Officer Russell is?"

"Ah, Mrs. Mead, finally!" Officer Russell sighed and turned toward her.

With Officer Russell's back to her, the prostitute saw her opportunity. She lifted her dress and unsheathed a knife that was exactly where Mary said it would be.

"Russell!" Sean yelled.

Officer Russell turned just in time to stop the prostitute from planting the knife in his back. Two policemen ran over and helped subdue her, then cart her away.

Mrs. Mead shrugged. "Can I go back to the laundry now?" There was no answer, and she left.

Chief Campbell nodded his approval to Mary, who smiled, then turned and left.

"Your sister's very observant, Handley," the chief commented. "Rather remarkable for a young lady."

Sean was too lost in the history of his relationship with his sister to be pleased with the praise. Once again she had

bested him, and at his work, too. By now he had accepted this occurrence as a fact of life, but he didn't have to like it.

"The mind of Sir Isaac Newton, the sass of a rebel, and the purse of a street urchin," Sean said, then returned to the basement and its leaky pipes.

Chief Campbell absorbed his words and watched as Mary walked out the door. No one saw. It was practically indiscernible, but a hint of a smile crossed Chief Campbell's face.

3

Thomas Edison was nervous, and he despised J. P. Morgan for it. Edison had known Morgan for years. Morgan had first hired this "telegraph boy turned inventor" to put electric lights in his Fifth Avenue mansion. Since then, their relationship had grown. Edison inventions backed by Morgan money had made them millions. Yet Edison always felt uncomfortable around Morgan. That was by design, not accident. Morgan thrived on others' discomfort. It was what gave him his edge. Edison knew Morgan's infamous cold stare was nothing more than a cheap device, but it always worked on him. Still, Morgan was the man with the money, and money was the reason Edison had asked Morgan to meet him at the Pearl Street Station one sunny day in the middle of March 1888, just a few days after the blizzard.

Four men walked along inside the gray, cavernous building as six huge DC electricity dynamo generators chugged noisily. In addition to Edison and Morgan, there were Charles Batchelor, Edison's right-hand man, and Charles Goodrich, Edison's bookkeeper. Almost fifty-one, Morgan was the eldest

and about a decade older than the others. Edison led the way. Having to talk loudly to be heard above the generators, he was feeling more self-conscious than ever about trying to sell Morgan. Internally, he was miserable. Externally, he was expansive and positive, bordering on boasting.

"Each one of these jumbo dynamos produces enough electricity to power twelve hundred lights. Imagine, twelve hundred, and that's just the beginning. The power production begins—"

Morgan cut him off. "Across from city hall, Joe Pulitzer's planning to put up the largest building in the world. That's all I need to know."

"Both commercial and residential. The demand is endless, J. P.," Edison added.

"How much more do you need?"

Morgan had known all along what Edison wanted. Once again, Morgan had made him feel like a bumbling amateur, but he was prepared. He motioned to Goodrich.

Charles Goodrich was an unassuming man with a slight build. As he fished for the cost breakdown he had prepared, he was more concerned with something else.

Morgan had a purple-tinted nose that was also deformed, the results of rosacea, a chronic skin disease he'd had his whole life. He was self-conscious about it and had gone as far as having the discoloration hand-brushed out of photographs. Edison and Batchelor had dealt with Morgan many times, so they were used to it. Goodrich wasn't.

Goodrich gave Morgan the paper, desperately trying to avoid looking at his nose, which made what he was doing all the more obvious. Morgan studied Goodrich but decided to let it pass. He gave the paper a cursory glance.

"I'll send a man over with a check."

"Thanks, J. P.," said Edison, and they shook hands.

"Next time, Tom, skip the science show. I don't understand it, and I don't care."

Having sufficiently chastised Edison for wasting his time, Morgan left. Edison's minor irritation was overshadowed by their success.

"That was rather quick," Edison commented, catching Batchelor's eye.

"I'll say," Batchelor replied, and the two of them started laughing. Goodrich joined in, making sure his enthusiasm level was a notch below the other two's. He viewed himself as a mere employee, much further down in the company's hierarchy. To avoid offending anyone, he almost always opted for bland.

Their celebration was short-lived. Unexpectedly, out of a shadowy section of the Pearl Street Station, Nikola Tesla emerged and stood next to a generator. In his early thirties, he was tall—six foot two—weighed a slight one hundred forty-two pounds, and had intense blue-gray eyes. He was a brilliant scientist and also very combustible. He had a strong sense of right and wrong but little aptitude for business and was even less adept at human relations. He began clapping his hands loudly and deliberately, the clapping taking on a mocking tone.

"Well, well, the Wizard of Menlo Park," said Tesla, his accent revealing his Serbian origins.

Batchelor was concerned. Edison noticed this, but he was unruffled.

"My lab's in West Orange now," Edison calmly corrected him.

"No more Wizard then. How about Hack?"

"Ah, still as charming as ever, Nikola."

Edison wasn't taking Tesla's bait. Unlike his interactions with Morgan, he could handle Tesla with ease. Tesla was first and foremost a man of science and believed that in the end all that really mattered was the quality of the work. He didn't understand what Edison knew so well: business could make or break any invention. That was why Tesla's superior AC electricity was lagging so far behind Edison's inferior DC. Mistakenly thinking it would get a rise out of Edison, Tesla pointed derisively to the DC dynamos.

"Much ado about nothing," he said.

"Reading Shakespeare now? I'm impressed, Nikola. Come, let's have some wine, and we can talk about old times."

Edison took Tesla by the arm, but Tesla pulled away, frustrated his attempts to unnerve Edison had failed and more upset that he could never make any headway with him.

"I want my money, Thomas! You promised me, in front of these men!"

Irate and indignant, Tesla pointed to Batchelor and Goodrich. Edison now had Tesla exactly where he wanted him. He casually turned to the two men.

"Did I? Go ahead, speak up, gentlemen." Neither responded.

Having given Edison the ammunition to outmaneuver him, Tesla felt like a fool.

"You're scum, Thomas! You're all scum!"

Tesla stormed off. Edison and Batchelor shared a smile. Edison was especially pleased, having reassured himself that

his clumsiness with Morgan was an anomaly. It was time to leave. They turned to Goodrich, who seemed bothered.

"Is something troubling you, Goodrich?" Edison asked.

"Me, sir? No," said Goodrich, whose behavior suggested the opposite.

"Take a stand for once, man. Now's the time. You're quitting anyway."

Not wanting a confrontation at this time, Goodrich was afraid to state what was on his mind. Trying to redirect the conversation, he assumed a deferential tone. "I've built boardinghouses that need my attention. We're not all trailblazers, sir. We can't all be Thomas Edison."

"No, I suppose not," Edison mused, his head seeming to grow a few hat sizes.

Goodrich naturally thought he had avoided a touchy situation. It lasted a mere fraction of a second, but if Goodrich had seen the pointed glance Edison gave Batchelor, it would have shaken him to his very core.

4

The Bowler Hat pulled his horse and buggy onto the main street of Pithole, Pennsylvania, stopped, took off his hat, and dusted it. It was the same bowler he had purchased in a Greenport, Long Island, shop twelve years earlier. A haberdasher had done some minor repairs on it since then, but otherwise, it was still in good shape. He had grown fond of this bowler like some become attached to an old robe, and he hoped to wear it for many more years.

The Bowler Hat looked around. The one saving grace was that he didn't have to deal with snow. Being in western Pennsylvania, Pithole had avoided the Blizzard of 1888. But if ever a town fit its name, it was Pithole. Only rubble remained where many of its buildings had once stood. Of the structures that were still recognizable, roofs had caved in, windows were shattered, and doors had fallen off their hinges. Weeds grew freely in the middle of the street, and a strong wind blew dust everywhere. Pithole was completely deserted, the quintessential ghost town.

When oil had been discovered in Titusville a few decades earlier, the influx of wildcatters to Pennsylvania mirrored the California Gold Rush. Oil strikes were plentiful, and Pithole became a boomtown. That was then. Unlike Titusville, Pithole had run dry, and everyone had left in search of dreams elsewhere. Then an immigrant farmer made an unexpected strike, a very rich one. Albert Zuckerman was his name.

A Jew farmer in the middle of nowhere, the Bowler Hat thought. *Lucky bastards. Money follows them wherever they go.*

Not so lucky this time. The Bowler Hat had been sent by the Oil Trust to "negotiate a settlement," and that wasn't good news for Zuckerman.

"Hi there, mister, you lost?"

The voice came from the right of the horse and buggy, and the Bowler Hat realized that whoever it belonged to was hardly concerned about his predicament.

"No, just resting before moving on."

The Bowler Hat slowly turned to size up the competition. He was five foot eight or nine and average weight with sunken eyes and several days' beard growth. Standing in front of what used to be the assessor's office, Sunken Eyes jumped to the street to avoid the broken steps. The Bowler Hat could tell he was shaky. He figured it was probably from nerves or drink, or a combination of both, but one thing was abundantly clear. There was no way Sunken Eyes would have enough guts to approach him alone.

"No place to rest here, unless you're partial to having splinters in your ass."

This voice was from the left, and it came from a balding

man with a thick mustache who stood in front of an old stable on the opposite side of the street from Sunken Eyes. He had a huge barrel chest and was wide all over. The Bowler Hat immediately pegged Mustache as a man who would be valuable in a bar fight but would lose any advantage in open space, where it wasn't easy to simply grab a man and muscle him.

As the two men slowly approached, the Bowler Hat waited to see who else would present himself. These two certainly weren't the brains of this unit. As expected, a third voice was heard, this one from behind.

"In his own crude way, what my friend was trying to say is, this godforsaken place offers nothing. But I'm sure you didn't mistake it for Philadelphia."

"Hardly," the Bowler Hat replied, playing along. Trying to keep track of the first two, he turned to get a look at Number Three. As he did, the wind swirled up, and he caught a mouthful of dirt. The Bowler Hat coughed and spit it out.

Number Three laughed, gesturing grandly. "Ah, the March winds. Welcome to Pithole."

The man was capable of sarcasm, something that was certainly beyond the reach of the other two. He was tall and slim and carried himself with total confidence. The gun belt he wore with a holstered Colt .45 tilted just to the right indicated he was a pretty fair shot. Now it all fell into place. Number Three was the leader and probably the most dangerous. The strategy was simple. Send Sunken Eyes and Mustache as a distraction. Then Number Three could come from behind and use his skills to finish the job. If he saw

that the opponent was too formidable, he could just leave and make a clean getaway. Either way, Number Three was at minimum risk. He had found partners who were either desperate or stupid. Probably both. But then, who else would be residing in Pithole?

The Bowler Hat knew he only had seconds to decide on a course of action. He viewed this trio as a chicken, with Number Three being the head. Once the head was gone, the other two might run around for a while, but it was just a matter of time until they realized they were dead and dropped to the ground. Still, it meant at some point he would have to get out of the buggy, so gunfire was out. It would spook his horse, and he had no desire to spend the rest of the day chasing after him.

He started coughing. "Yes, grand place, Pithole, garden spot of the world." His coughing became more pronounced as he ducked back into the buggy and out of sight.

Number Three quipped, "I see our little town has already gotten to you." But all he heard in return was a few garbled words accompanied by loud coughing. "You all right, friend?"

Number Three stepped next to the rear of the buggy on the right side, pulling a knife out of his coat pocket and signaling the others to attack. Laziness is a strong motivator. They also preferred not to use guns because they, too, did not want to chase after the horse and buggy.

"I'm coming in with some water," Number Three said. "I have a canteen in—"

Unexpectedly, with shocking accuracy and speed, a large dagger ripped through the canvas of the buggy, cutting its

way deep into Number Three's ear and piercing his brain. He stood there, frozen, blood pouring out of every orifice in his head. Then, his mouth still open, he fell to the ground, the handle of the knife protruding from his ear.

Moving faster and more efficiently than any human being these two men had ever seen, the Bowler Hat landed a blow to the windpipe of the charging Mustache that caused the man to fall back, desperately gasping for air. He then caught a glimpse of Sunken Eyes, consumed with fear, frantically fumbling for a gun in his coat, and he leapt from the buggy. With one powerful blow, he broke Sunken Eyes's right arm in two places, dislodging the gun. As Sunken Eyes fell to the ground, writhing in pain, the Bowler Hat heaved the gun as far as he could. He was about to put Sunken Eyes out of his misery when he got hit from behind with a force that felt like a fully powered locomotive.

Mustache had recovered faster than the Bowler Hat had anticipated and now had him where he definitely didn't want to be—in close, against the stable wall, where Mustache could use his strength to his best advantage. As Mustache pressed against the Bowler Hat, holding him there while punching away at his body, the Bowler Hat had one thing on his mind: limiting the damage until he could find a way to separate. He tucked his elbows into his body, making many of the blows glance off his arms. After a while, he began to slowly sink to his knees as if Mustache's punishment were taking its toll. And it was, but not as much as he let on. Then he summoned up all the strength he had in his thighs to push upward as hard and as fast as he could. His head crashed into Mustache's fleshy chin, causing him to stumble back a step or two. That was just enough room

for the Bowler Hat to free himself. Now out in the open, this fight would radically change.

Mustache rushed the Bowler Hat with all he had, but he quickly stepped to the side and punished him with blows to the face. Mustache kept charging like a bull, and like a very skilled matador, the Bowler Hat made him pay dearly. Finally, his face bruised and bloodied, Mustache stumbled to the ground, exhausted. Very businesslike, the Bowler Hat kneeled down, wrapped his arm around Mustache's neck, and squeezed the life out of him.

As the Bowler Hat stood over the body of Mustache catching a slight breather, he heard a gunshot, promptly followed by his horse's whinny and the noise of it galloping off with the buggy. The warm, burning sensation in his right arm meant he had been shot, but that wasn't what angered him. He knew that the bullet had exited his arm, doing very little damage. What angered him was that after all this effort he would still have to chase down his horse and buggy. He turned and glared down the street.

Sunken Eyes had dragged himself over to Number Three and had taken the Colt .45 out of its holster. Defying all probability, he had somehow been able to shoot with his off hand and hit his target. The Bowler Hat headed straight for Sunken Eyes. He was the one with the gun, but Sunken Eyes still panicked. As he reeled off shot after shot, the Bowler Hat rolled to the ground to avoid the bullets or pressed himself against the stable wall to become a smaller target. It worked, yet each shot only succeeded in making the Bowler Hat angrier. It meant his horse would keep running, and it would take that much longer to catch him.

Finally, Sunken Eyes ran out of bullets. The Bowler Hat

moved toward him with the alacrity and purpose of a man who has finally found the pesky gopher that has been burrowing holes in his garden.

"Please don't!" Sunken Eyes pleaded, but the Bowler Hat did and soon Sunken Eyes had joined his comrades. The Bowler Hat pulled his knife out of Number Three's ear and wiped it clean on Sunken Eyes's shirt. He then cut a piece out of Number Three's coat and tied it around his wound.

An unsettling thought entered his mind. Could it be he was slipping? It did happen to men in his profession. Five years ago, might he have dispatched these three losers more quickly and with less trouble? Hell, three years ago, or two. But the Bowler Hat was never one to dwell on his own mortality. He dismissed this notion as ridiculous and looked down the street. He couldn't see the slightest trace of his horse and buggy, not even a cloud of dust. That meant he had a very long hike ahead of him.

That Jew Zuckerman better not give me any trouble, he thought as he looked at his knife, *or I'll circumcise him a second time.* He sheathed the knife and trudged down the empty streets of Pithole, leaving the three lifeless bodies for the vultures.

5

It was Mary's first day back at work after the blizzard, and it was not easy adjusting. The Lowry Hat Factory seemed bleaker and more depressing than usual, which made it more difficult for her to focus on her long-term goals.

Like many of its brethren in the garment industry, the Lowry Hat Factory was a sweatshop, but its working conditions were even more deplorable than the norm. It was located in a basement of an old grain storehouse, and there were forty girls and women from age eight to fifty lined up in rows and packed into a space that should only have accommodated fifteen. They worked twelve-hour shifts and were paid a few pennies per piece. Cockroaches and rats were commonplace, there was no heat in winter, and the ventilation was abysmal. Come July and August, workers often fainted on the job.

The Widow Lowry ran this abomination like a sadistic jailer. She was a large, powerful-looking woman in her late forties who, though considerably overweight, carried it well. She used her size to physically intimidate her workers.

"She looks like she ate all the food her employees couldn't afford to buy," Mary had remarked to Kate one day after work.

"Did you hear about her husband?" Kate had shot back, reciting workplace lore. "He was so afraid of her he killed himself rather than ask for a divorce."

Rumors abounded. If you polled the employees, they would swear when the Widow Lowry shot out of her mother's womb the doctor was so scared he fainted.

The Widow Lowry made it her business to regularly patrol the floor, checking to see if anyone was wasting her money, her mere presence enough to make her workers quiver. She would stroll through the aisles, inspecting the work and invariably stopping at some poor soul to humiliate her. On this particular day, she stopped at a thirteen-year-old girl who sat in front of Mary.

She stood over her and glowered, making the girl so nervous she kept sticking herself with the needle. She then grabbed the hat on which the girl was working.

"You call this even stitching?!"

The girl was too terrified to answer. The Widow Lowry tore the hat apart and held it up for everyone to see.

"I'm deducting this from her pay! I won't tolerate shoddy work!"

The girl was reduced to tears, which only fed the Widow Lowry's disdain.

"What are you waiting for? Get another piece, you idiot!"

The girl ran to get one as the Widow Lowry glared at the workers, establishing her dominance. All the ladies cowered, with one notable exception—Mary.

The Widow Lowry had been watching Mary for some time and was sure she needed an attitude correction. So far, Mary had been smart enough not to show any defiance. She did her work and kept quiet. But the Widow Lowry abhorred indifference. If it spread, it could become insolence, and then where would she be?

"Do you have something to say, Miss Handley?"

Mary kept working and didn't say a word. This woman wasn't going to get her to say or do anything she didn't want to say or do. She had dealt with bullies all her life, and the fact that the Widow Lowry was a woman didn't make her any different.

"Come on, Miss Handley, we're all friends here." She gestured, indicating the whole room. "Everyone would love to hear what you have to say." But Mary remained silent.

"Don't for one moment think I don't know what's going on here," the Widow Lowry opined, putting on her wisest look. "You think you're better than me, don't you?"

Mary glanced at Kate, who sat next to her. Kate saw what her friend was thinking and frowned, shaking her head as if to say, "Don't do it." But Mary knew a simple negative response would not satisfy the Widow Lowry. She had made her hostility public and in order to save face, she was not going to stop until Mary cowered before her.

"No," Mary said, then looked directly at the Widow Lowry. "I don't think I'm better than you. I know I am. We are all better than you."

Gasps ran through the room faster than a rabbit trying to avoid becoming dinner. The Widow Lowry did a slow burn before totally imploding. A string of invectives burst

from her mouth. Not all of them were intelligible, but the word "fired" popped up often enough. That was a problem, but Mary was fairly certain she could find a job in another sweatshop in a reasonable amount of time. *Well, fairly reasonable,* she thought, and possibly in one less oppressive than the Lowry Hat Factory. *One would be hard-pressed to find one worse.*

Mary looked at Kate, who shook her head in disbelief. Mary shrugged and walked toward the exit, smiling. She felt very good about what she had just done. After all, if you didn't call a pig a pig, it might never know it was one.

When Mary reached the door, her smile faded. She remembered she was having dinner that night with her parents.

6

Although both Mary and Sean had moved out, Friday night dinner at the Handleys' was still mandatory. If not with an iron fist, Elizabeth ruled her family with an iron tongue, her verbal lashings being more painful and leaving longer-lasting scars than any physical beating. To be fair, Elizabeth truly believed she knew what was best and was trying to steer her children in the right direction when they veered off course. Unfortunately, instead of a stiff wind to right the ship, she often used a hurricane.

The Handley home was a small wood-framed house in the Fort Greene section of Brooklyn, which was filled with Irish immigrants in similar houses. Not far from the waterfront, the house, to put it kindly, was cramped. It had two tiny bedrooms and a backyard barely big enough for a pair of swings. When the children had gotten older, Sean slept in the living room. Their one luxury, an indoor toilet, would have been unaffordable if Colonel Julius W. Adams hadn't successfully made Brooklyn a test case to improve sewage systems.

Jeffrey Handley had worked in the same butcher shop for twenty-five years. The owner appreciated Jeffrey and was as generous as he could be with him. That meant that Jeffrey brought home enough money to very modestly house, feed, and clothe his family, along with an occasional bonus of a nice piece of meat. Every unexpected bill was a major headache, but Jeffrey felt blessed. After all, he had done well enough for his family to avoid "Young Dublin," a section of Brooklyn where poor Irish immigrants lived in makeshift shanties. This positive attitude carried over to his family. He was supportive of both his children. Jeffrey found a light touch got better results when Elizabeth was being overly critical. In an imperfect world filled with imperfect relationships, Jeffrey and Elizabeth counterbalanced each other nicely and were, oddly, a good match.

Mary knew if her mother got wind of her being fired before Mary told her, she'd be harder on her. So before dinner, she informed Elizabeth and got the response she had expected: a look of disappointment. One fact remained resolute. No matter how well or poorly Mary felt about herself, her mother invariably made her feel worse.

The dining room was strangely quiet except for the sound of the ladle as Elizabeth doled out the stew she had made. Mary braced herself, knowing her mother was bound to start in on her. As the stew was passed out, Mary looked at her bowl and found it sparse.

"Could I please have more potatoes, Mother?"

"Mary dear, maybe you should be easin' up on the potatoes."

Elizabeth was obsessed with appearances. A woman needed to be slender and a man needed to stand up straight

in order to make the proper impressions. Since they were young, she had hammered into her children that they were lacking in these areas, even if they weren't. These subjects had become sore points with both children, but they also were Elizabeth's answer to all problems. In Mary's case, "slender" meant attractive enough to get a good husband. As absurd as it might have seemed that anyone could think Mary overweight, Elizabeth reasoned that she was not married because men found her physically lacking. It was a deep-seated belief to which Elizabeth clung as a way of explaining what she couldn't fathom: a daughter who aspired to the incomprehensible.

Jeffrey immediately jumped in, assuming his role as peacekeeper.

"The girl's skin and bones, Elizabeth."

"It's wise to err on the side of caution," she responded.

"A few more potatoes might be wise for all of us." He nodded to Elizabeth, meaning her. "I hear they take the edge off."

Mary and Sean looked at each other, amused, but a sharp look from Elizabeth put an abrupt end to their enjoyment. Jeffrey did accomplish his goal though. Elizabeth ladled out more potatoes to Mary. He winked at Mary, and she smiled.

"Sean, how's work, dear?" Elizabeth asked.

"I prevented a stabbing today in front of Chief Campbell. He was impressed."

Perturbed that he had conveniently left out her role in what had happened, Mary glared at Sean. A positive mention might have helped her get off the chopping block. But Sean ignored her.

"Excellent, son. I'm proud of you," exclaimed Elizabeth,

then tilted her head toward Mary. "At least one of my children is tryin' to make a future for himself."

"I don't have a lot of options," Mary chimed in. "You're well aware of that."

"Options, is it? Sarah McNish married a professional man. She has two children and one on the way. Have you no interest in betterin' yourself?"

"Not as someone's possession. I'll advance on my own terms."

"As an unemployed sweatshop worker? Time to start re-negotiatin' those terms." Elizabeth was the one person who had no problem trading barbs with Mary. Mary rose.

"Your mother's just upset," Jeffrey interjected. "Sit down, finish your dinner."

"Sorry, Father," Mary said, then faced Elizabeth, echoing her words. "But I've been taught it's wise to err on the side of caution."

She then left. Jeffrey knew he couldn't stop her. Disappointed, he turned toward Elizabeth, who shrugged as if she'd had nothing to do with it.

Enjoying this interplay, Sean chuckled. Both parents immediately stared daggers at him. His smile instantly disappeared as he buried himself in his stew.

It had been ten hours since the meeting at Pearl Street Station with Morgan and the encounter with Tesla, but Edison paid little attention to time. He had actually been up thirty-six hours straight. This was nothing unusual. He was a driven man who lamented that there were only twenty-four

hours in a day. As he and Batchelor examined a blueprint on the desk in his office, he sipped Vin Mariani. Vin Mariani was the most popular wine in the United States, due mostly to an important ingredient: cocaine. Cocaine was considered a wonder drug, hailed by such luminaries as Queen Victoria, Pope Leo XIII, Robert Louis Stevenson . . . and Thomas Edison.

Edison wholeheartedly endorsed the drug, proclaiming it helped him endure long nights of work, clearing the cobwebs when his mind was fuzzy. He was often quoted as saying, "Genius is one percent inspiration and ninety-nine percent perspiration." It might be said that a significant percentage of that perspiration was aided by cocaine.

"You look dreadful, Tom," Batchelor commented. "When did you last sleep?"

"Sleep? I can't shut my mind down," Edison replied, referring to the multiple projects they had going at all times. "We're climbing mountains, Batch, mountains."

As Edison poured himself some more wine, there was a knock at the door. They both turned as Goodrich tentatively entered.

"Sorry to bother you, but it's seven o'clock, sir . . . my last day."

"Oh, right, right." Edison had been so wrapped up in his work he had genuinely forgotten. Although Goodrich had been with him for years, he was a mere bookkeeper and could easily be replaced.

"I've enjoyed working with you," Goodrich said as he stepped forward to shake their hands. Edison and Batchelor obliged. It couldn't be over soon enough for them.

"Take care of those warehouses, Goodrich," Edison said.

"They're boardinghouses, sir."

"Yes, well, good luck."

Both men thought they were done, but on his way out, Goodrich paused.

"Sir, earlier, with Mr. Tesla—"

"Yes, awful business. Sorry about that."

"Like Mr. Tesla said, I was there. You did promise him the money."

He had their attention now. Edison stared at Goodrich, sizing him up.

"Hmm, looks like you took our little chat about taking a stand quite seriously."

"I always take you seriously, sir, and I know you'll do the proper thing." Goodrich smiled and took his leave. Edison stared after him.

Batchelor could read his thoughts. "It's Goodrich, Tom. He has no backbone."

"But apparently he's acquired a conscience. Make sure it doesn't become troublesome."

Though Edison and Batchelor were close, Edison was Batchelor's boss and he did whatever Edison said, no matter how distasteful it might be to him.

∽

Mary had been walking for some time. She was so mad she hadn't paid attention to where she was going. Her mother was the only person who could trigger that behavior, and she did it well. She looked around and noticed she was probably a mile or two from her parents' house, somewhere near the

docks in a run-down area occupied by mostly abandoned, dilapidated buildings. The streets were empty and ominous looking.

The one open establishment was a bar with a tilted sign that read MCGINTY'S TAVERN. Bright lights and loud voices wafted out into the night air as a piano blasted a lively tune. Respectable women didn't populate places like McGinty's, but Mary didn't care. She was angry, her feet hurt, and she wanted a drink.

McGinty's Tavern was a tough waterfront hangout that reeked of cigar smoke and booze. The men were mostly rough-and-tumble types who worked with their hands or not at all. The few women there were prostitutes trying to earn their evening's pay. Mary entered and marched up to the bartender.

"An ale, please," she announced too loudly, her desire to make clear her right to be there getting the better of her. It didn't matter. A woman like Mary entering an establishment like McGinty's was a rare enough event that most had already taken notice.

An exception to the crowd was a man halfway down the bar. He was a charming thirty-four-year-old Southerner, nursing his bourbon, who appeared to be a cross between a gentleman farmer and a riverboat gambler. He was neither. Charles Pemberton was his name, and he had a lost air about him. In better, more confident times, his smile was contagious. Catching Mary's eye, Charles summoned his most positive look, lifted his glass to her, and nodded. Mary frowned, then took a gulp of her ale. She turned and found herself facing a powerful-looking man who towered over her.

"Well, aren't you a pretty one, girlie. You can call me Burt."

"Though I'm sure I'll be utterly smitten by your charm and pithy repartee, Burt," Mary replied, "I'm just here for a drink."

She started to go around him, but the man's massive frame blocked her. Burt clearly thought that any woman in McGinty's was fair game. He had just happened to pick the one who was not, and he was too drunk to notice it.

"You won't sleep tonight, knowin' you got me riled up and then deserted me."

"Not when I know tight undergarments or a stiff breeze can perform the same task," Mary retorted, thinking it would dispatch him. It was a miscalculation.

Burt's disposition was much more fragile than his body. As Mary walked away, he raised his hand to smack her down, only to find it being grabbed by Charles.

"Didn't your mother teach you never to hit girls?" Charles asked.

His plan to be the hero then took a drastic turn for the worse. Burt came across his body with his other fist and landed a crushing blow to his chin, which propelled Charles into one customer, then another, and finally to the floor. Burt turned back to Mary, but Charles was determined. Still groggy, he stumbled to his feet, grabbed a stool, and smashed it over Burt's head. Burt dropped to the floor with a loud thud.

"Are you all right?" Mary said as she approached Charles.

"I've been hit harder," Charles said, feeling his chin, still somewhat dazed. "I think."

"Pity it was unnecessary. I'm well versed in several arts

of self-defense, including jujitsu, and thus more than capable of defending myself."

"Then I'm more than honored to make your acquaintance. Charles Pemberton." He nodded, introducing himself.

"Poor boy. Nowadays it seems like every Tom, Dick, and Harry is called Charles."

"My cousins are Tom, Dick, and Harry, so I'm afraid my parents had no choice."

Mary laughed. She found Charles handsome, bright, witty, but also suddenly in danger. She hastily shoved him aside. Fortuitously, the speed of her kick to a charging Burt's crotch landed at the point where the combination of the two forces was the most devastating. Burt froze, stunned at his pain, then crumpled to his knees. Mary clasped her hands and whacked him in the face, sending Burt down and out. The bar erupted in raucous cheers. To celebrate, Mary downed her ale in one gulp.

"I must take up jujitsu," Charles said, impressed by Mary's achievement.

"That's not jujitsu. That's good ol'-fashioned Brooklyn street fighting. The name's Mary Handley. Welcome to Brooklyn, Charles."

They shook hands. There couldn't have been a more perfect exit, so Mary left. He watched her go, thinking she was much more than the one-night stand he had envisioned.

In a much quieter tavern in another part of Brooklyn, Charles Goodrich entered, anxiously looking around. Goodrich soon spotted whom he was searching for and hurried

toward a secluded booth where Nikola Tesla was patiently sitting by himself.

"I hope you had no trouble finding this place, Mr. Tesla," Goodrich said. "Sorry you had to come to Brooklyn, but it's best to be discreet."

"No problem at all," said Tesla. "Please sit." And Goodrich joined him.

Outside the tavern, spying on them through the window, was a large and powerful man by the name of Samuel. Samuel had orders to follow Goodrich to make sure he did nothing untoward. His employer had given him the discretion to act if need be, and this meeting seemed odd to him. He would wait. He might need to take action.

In a cheap boardinghouse room with two small beds and a rickety desk, John Pemberton was seated, judiciously poring over some papers, when Charles Pemberton entered. A bearded man in his fifties, Pemberton rose to greet his son.

"Ah, the prodigal son back from a night of carousing." He noticed the bruise on Charles's face. "What's this?"

"A mark of gallantry. I interceded on behalf of a damsel in distress."

"A damsel who didn't succumb to your charms, or you wouldn't be home."

"Please try not to refer to this . . . room as home."

"It's a necessary sacrifice. The longer we can stay here, the better chance we have."

"You still honestly believe people will invest large sums in a fountain drink?"

"I feel it with every fiber of my being," said Pemberton. His conviction was so strong it bordered on being maniacal.

"I assume that's a yes?"

Pemberton laughed, and Charles joined in. It was good they could still amuse each other. Pemberton had his last dime riding on this venture. Pemberton's laugh soon turned into a cough. It was no ordinary cough. Charles went to him, concerned.

"Are you all right, Father?"

As Pemberton caught his breath, he nodded, then changed the subject. "I wangled us invitations for the governor's Salute to Thomas Edison," he said, his eyes lighting up. "Edison's an inventor. He'll understand what I've done. I know it."

"I hope so. I really do." Yawning, Charles stretched out on one of the beds.

"I've been fooling with the new name. It should look good on signs."

Pemberton tossed a sheet of paper to Charles. On it, there was a bright red background and across it in big, white letters were written the words COCA-COLA.

"Not bad," Charles said. "Not bad at all."

Goodrich walked down the row of brownstones on Degraw Street to the one in which he lived. He'd had too much to drink and was humming his favorite song, "Over the Waves." It had been an eventful day. Not only had he finally quit working for Edison, he had purged himself of the guilt that had been nagging at his soul, and to top it off, he was

in love. As he carefully mounted the stairs and entered his brownstone, Goodrich could say that he was finally happy.

A moment after he went inside, a gunshot flash crackled through one of the windows as its sound pierced the silent night. Charles Goodrich was dead.

7

It was a few days before spring, and the remnants of the blizzard were still quite evident. However, the sun was shining, and the temperature had edged up to fifty degrees, feeling twenty degrees warmer—the kind of deception the mind plays on the body after suffering through miserable weather. Spring was definitely in the air, and it reeked of hope for new beginnings. As Mary and Kate exited their tenement and strolled along Elizabeth Street, Kate's body surged with country exuberance.

"I'm so happy for you, Mary! Isn't it wonderful to be in love?"

"Please, I just met this man last night, I don't know if I'll ever see him again."

"You will," the ever-positive Kate said. "I have a second sense about these things. The two of you will fall hopelessly in love. I just know it."

Kate's prediction only made Mary regret her decision to leave the night before. True, it had been a perfect exit, but maybe she should have stayed and tried to get to know him

better. Charles Pemberton intrigued her. She sensed he was different, unconventional, and therefore the type of man with whom she could envision herself.

"Who knows?" Mary smiled. "You just may be right."

"Of course I am. You listen to this Haddonfield girl, Mary Handley. Brooklyn has nothing on me when it comes to intuition."

The two of them were laughing, enjoying each other's company and the day as they passed a newsstand. Mary was still laughing when she noticed Kate had stopped. Her brow crinkled as if processing information, then her face suddenly turned ashen.

"What's the matter?"

Unable to speak, Kate slowly raised her arm and pointed toward the newsstand.

Confused, Mary turned. At first, a steady stream of customers blocked her view. Finally, the newsstand was empty, and she realized Kate was pointing to the headline of the *Brooklyn Daily Eagle.* Big bold letters covered the front page—CHARLES GOODRICH MURDERED! GRISLY KILLING ON DEGRAW STREET!

Kate barely managed to say, "They . . . killed him . . . my Charlie." Then she collapsed.

∾

Nothing attracts people like a good murder, and with the added spice of celebrity, the Charles Goodrich case had the makings of a sensational one. After all, Goodrich was the brother of Brooklyn alderman W. W. Goodrich and an

employee of Thomas Edison. One of New York's luminaries could have been involved, and no one wanted to miss that.

Not long after the murder had been reported in the newspapers, curiosity seekers had rushed to Goodrich's brownstone on Degraw Street and spilled out into the street, covering half the block. Pushcart peddlers were out in force, selling their wares. One man's cart was full of pistols. He was proclaiming that if Charles Goodrich had owned a pistol he'd still be alive.

Mary shook her head. She already knew about the public's fascination with the macabre. She had once seen dozens gather around a fruit peddler's horse. Its leg had broken, and it was lying on the cobblestones, writhing in pain. They watched eagerly as the distraught owner put the poor animal out of its misery . . . and then, in an instant, they were gone. She was the only one who had stayed to console the man, who had lost his best friend and business partner of the past twenty-two years.

Mary had just left Kate in her room on Elizabeth Street after a doctor had seen her. He had prescribed nothing but rest. Mary knew that would be impossible until Kate found out what happened to her fiancé. As she worked her way through the throngs of people, many were reluctant to cede their hard-earned positions to a newcomer. Mary suffered several elbows, some pushes, and countless angry stares until she finally made it to the front. In this "prime" position, she was surrounded mostly by newspaper reporters as she faced Charles Goodrich's brownstone and three policemen on crowd control.

The excitement of being at a crime scene surged through

her. It was nothing like the morbid curiosity that most in the crowd were feeling. Hers was akin to that of an aspiring actor in the audience of a play, desperately yearning to be a part of it. For now though, she had to put these feelings aside.

Mary didn't know the three policemen in front of her. As she was trying to devise a plan of attack, another policeman came out of the brownstone, and for the first time she could see the man standing guard in the hallway.

"Billy!" she screamed, lurching forward, "Billy!"

The three policemen swiftly moved to contain her. Just as the crowd was beginning to enjoy the first real action they had seen, it ended as fast as it began.

"Unhand the girl, fellas," Billy's voice boomed, "and let her through."

Mary wasted no time in ridding herself of the policemen. Then, straightening her dress, she ascended the stairs in as ladylike a manner as possible, a vindicated woman.

Rumors tore through the crowd. "She's a Goodrich. No, she works for Edison," etc. Newspaper reporters peppered the three policemen with questions about Mary, but they had no idea who she was.

"Mary, darlin', what in God's name are you doin' here?" Billy whispered.

"Mr. Goodrich was my friend's fiancé, and she's absolutely devastated, Billy."

"Her fiancé, huh?" Billy shook his head. "The poor girl."

"When she got word of it, she passed out," Mary said, emphasizing the drama. "Please, Billy, I have to tell her something. She's very distraught, as you can imagine."

Billy took off his hat and wiped the sweat from his brow.

He stared at her for a moment, then announced loudly, so everyone could hear, "What's that, information about the murder? Why, go right in, Miss Handley."

Pleased, Mary smiled, continuing the charade. "Thank you, Sergeant," she said, trying to match his volume. "I certainly hope it will help." And she marched right in.

Charles Goodrich's brownstone was decorated very much in line with his personality. Every choice was safe, with little chance of offending anyone. The floors were pine and the furniture mahogany, all stained in a warm brown. Muted colors reigned, with only a hint of something brighter on an occasional throw pillow or in a painting. The most outrageous choice, and it was hardly that, was a large steamer trunk in his study next to his couch, as if it were a coffee table. The study was to the right of the entrance directly across from the living room, which was on the left. Chief Campbell was in the living room with W. W. Goodrich and Officer Russell. Older than Charles and very much his opposite, W. W. Goodrich was known for his stylish dress and for being outspoken. He was very upset. As a result, no one noticed Mary.

"My brother would never commit suicide," he protested, seeming more concerned with his family's name than his brother's death. "He's a Goodrich, for God's sake!"

So it wasn't murder. Evidently, the *Eagle* had rushed to press too quickly with a "hot" story. Mary saw Charles Goodrich's body lying in the study and couldn't resist going over to examine it. She had read many books on forensics and felt confident she could tell whether a man had committed suicide or not. There was a bullet hole through his temple, and he had a gun in his right hand.

"No reason to get excited, Alderman," Chief Campbell cautioned, his voice drifting over from the living room. "Nothing's official until the coroner examines him."

"He'll find the same, Chief," Officer Russell interjected. "Powder stains on his hand and black ones on his temple, showing he was shot at close range. It's a suicide."

Officer Russell sneered confidently, positive he had made a big impression on the chief. He had, but not in the way he had thought. Chief Campbell was trying to put out a fire, and one of his officers was pouring kerosene on it.

"It's not a suicide," Mary announced from the study, taking the three men by surprise. Almost in unison, they turned to see her rising from Goodrich's body. "You will probably find a second bullet in a wall or cushion where the killer fired the gun from Mr. Goodrich's hand after he was dead. Hence, the powder stains on his hand."

Officer Russell quickly responded. "I see we have a lady expert. How fortunate."

"They're teaching us to read now, too," Mary responded immediately. "It's highly experimental."

Chief Campbell walked toward the study, and the others followed. At the moment, he didn't care how Mary had gotten into a murder scene. He was hoping she might create a diversion for W. W. Goodrich until the coroner arrived. If that meant a sparring match of words between Officer Russell and Sean Handley's sister, so be it.

"Meet the woman who saved your life the other day, Russell. Mary Handley."

Mary held out her hand. Officer Russell didn't take it. "I see you make a habit of interfering."

Mary looked at her empty hand, then at him. "And they say chivalry is dying."

Officer Russell realized he was not going to win this war of words, so he just stood there, quietly steaming. But W. W. Goodrich didn't care that Mary was a woman. He just cared that someone was confirming a scenario that would avert a family scandal.

"How do you know this, young lady?" he asked.

"I have seen many gunshot victims, granted mostly in pictures or in drawings, and one thing is uniform. It's messy. As you can see on the floor, there are massive amounts of blood." She kneeled down next to Charles Goodrich's body. "Yet there is no blood at all on his clothes. That's highly improbable, and his body is positioned like an actor in a bad melodrama." She sniffed Goodrich's shirt. "His clothes are fresh. It's reasonable to assume the killer changed them, possibly because he got blood in the wrong places when positioning the body to pass as a suicide."

"See, it's not a suicide!" W. W. Goodrich shouted joyously. "I knew it wasn't!"

Just then the coroner entered with his assistant. It had been a busy morning. This was his fourth case. "Where's the unfortunate Mr. Goodrich, Chief?"

Chief Campbell stepped aside, revealing the body, and the coroner went to work.

With the situation under control, Chief Campbell turned to Mary. "In my office at the station in one hour, young lady," he said sternly.

Mary's heart sank. Officer Russell, who had a sneer for every occasion, had one of pure joy.

8

Mary sat on the bench outside Chief Campbell's office. He was already forty-five minutes late and each passing minute gave her more time to obsess over what she had done. She had always been bold about her knowledge, but this time she had gone too far. Her actions could reflect poorly on Billy and possibly Sean, too. Sean was trying hard to make a career for himself, and the last thing Mary wanted to be was a stumbling block.

When Chief Campbell finally arrived, he entered his office without even looking at Mary. After thirty seconds, he emerged.

"Well, Miss Handley, are you coming in or not?"

Chief Campbell had developed a technique for dealing with people during his twenty-two years on the police force. He found that if he was able to keep them off balance, he usually got an honest reaction. Unnerved, Mary entered his office.

"Do have a seat, Miss Handley," he said. "We have some

important matters to discuss, not the least of which is your unusual behavior on Degraw Street."

As Mary sat, Chief Campbell walked around his desk to his chair.

"I am sorry if my impetuous actions offended you in any way, Chief Campbell," Mary blurted out, then continued at breakneck speed about Kate being Goodrich's fiancée and how her brazen behavior was only intended to help her grieving friend.

Chief Campbell sat back in his chair, unconsciously scratching his neck just under his chin. After many versions of "I'm sorry," Mary concluded with, "You have my solemn promise I will never interfere ever again."

Chief Campbell stared at her briefly, then said, "That's reassuring, yet also unfortunate." Mary was confused. "I had hoped, Miss Handley, you would help us find Charles Goodrich's murderer."

Chief Campbell's technique worked. Mary was beyond off balance. She was absolutely stunned . . . and totally delighted.

~

Chief Campbell was late for his meeting with Mary because he had been forced to take a detour that would change everything. He had been summoned to police headquarters by his bosses, Police Commissioners James Jourdan and Daniel Briggs.

Jourdan sat behind his large desk. A natty dresser in his fifties, he was tall and thin with a thick crop of brown

hair. He smelled of too much cologne and sported the mustache of a dandy. Jourdan was hardly that; it was more wishful thinking on his part than anything else. Briggs was in his late forties and Jourdan's polar opposite. He was average height, balding, and heavyset with a pronounced double chin. Though he wore an expensive suit, there was always something amiss: a stain on his tie, a cigar burn, etc. Briggs was forever puffing on a cigar and would bark his displeasure if the minutest detail didn't go his way.

Briggs stood behind Jourdan, occasionally glancing out the window at the female protesters in front of their building. He grunted his disapproval of their chants, their signs, and their mere presence. Being more political, Jourdan kept his views to himself. However, he had been under pressure from both above and below him and thought this latest directive from the very top might get everyone off his back.

"We would like you to hire a woman to spearhead the Goodrich murder investigation," Jourdan said, clasping his hands on his desk. "As soon as possible."

"A woman?" Chief Campbell said, as if making sure he had heard Jourdan correctly.

"As a separate private investigator, of course," Jourdan hastily added, "not as part of the force. We definitely don't want to set that precedent."

"Absolutely not," Briggs chimed in.

"Did Goodrich's brother make this request?" Chief Campbell responded. "We already had to halt everything at the murder scene until he arrived. I realize he's—"

"Alderman Goodrich had absolutely nothing to do with it," Jourdan assured him. "This comes straight from

Chapin." He was referring to the mayor of Brooklyn, Alfred C. Chapin. Jourdan then nodded ever so slightly toward the window behind him. "The women's groups have been stirring up trouble. Apparently, some of them have friends in high places, and the mayor feels we need to placate them."

"They belong in the kitchen and the bedroom and no place else, damn it!" said the ever-combustible Briggs, capping it off by spitting out a piece of his cigar.

"I can't put an inexperienced female on a murder case. She's bound to falter."

Briggs put his two hands on Jourdan's desk and leaned forward. "That would be awful, a real crying shame."

"Naturally, you will give us progress reports on her activities, and we'll be conducting our own investigation while the press follows her," Jourdan continued, any attempt at subtlety already foregone by Briggs.

After pausing to consider his alternatives and finding none, Chief Campbell said, "I understand, gentlemen. I'll find someone."

Further discussion would be useless. Chief Campbell knew an order when he heard one. He stood, they all shook hands, and he left.

Briggs could no longer contain himself. "I hope this works. Any day I expect to see Campbell's goddamn name on my door."

His fear wasn't misplaced. Chief Campbell's reputation as a very competent detective was growing every day.

"Not after this," Jourdan calmly replied. "Trust me. Chapin has done us a favor." He smiled mischievously. "Definitely not after this."

~

It didn't take much thought for Chief Campbell to realize the commissioners were using Mayor Chapin's request to set him up. Subtlety was definitely not their strong suit. What they didn't know was that Chief Campbell had no desire to have either of their jobs. He liked being out in the field and didn't want to be trapped behind a desk. But he doubted they would believe him even if he told them so. They wouldn't be able to fathom not wanting a promotion.

Chief Campbell had to obey orders, and he'd been pondering how he could do so in the least damaging way. Mary Handley appeared to be bright and observant, and had apparently studied criminology. The coroner had confirmed her assessment of the crime and even found three books in the garbage with a bullet hole through two of them and a bullet in the third. That exhibited a reasonable level of competence, certainly more than had been displayed by that fool Russell. He was annoyed that she had hustled her way into the crime scene and had planned to reprimand her accordingly, but that kind of resourcefulness could also be a plus. The way he reasoned, in the short time he had, he could do worse.

"In addition to the fifteen-hundred-dollar reward the department is offering for catching the culprit, how does seven dollars a week sound?" he asked Mary, part of him hoping she'd walk out the door.

"To an unemployed sweatshop worker?"

Chief Campbell found himself liking Mary. He admired her spirit, her sense of humor, and unlike some men, he admired women with brains. His wife was always a step ahead

of him, and that suited him just fine. He couldn't tell her that her job was to be a dupe, but he could at least stress certain dangers that would be involved.

"I wouldn't take this lightly, Mary."

"Chief, one thing I've always been able to count on is my mind. When I'm put on an even playing field, I can compete with anyone."

"There will be nothing even here. You will be a woman in a sea of men working on a high-profile murder case. As far as I can recall, it's never been done before in Brooklyn, New York City, or any place in these United States. The press will be relentless, and your life will be fraught with danger. You'll have enemies everywhere, within the department, too, all the way to the top."

That was as far as he could go without revealing the commissioners' plan. But none of it mattered to Mary. This was her opportunity to fulfill her dream. All that was going through her mind was the saying she had seen on Wei Chung's charm years before.

Ji qing ru yi, she thought. *May your happiness be according to your wishes.* Holding her head up, Mary looked Chief Campbell directly in the eye and smiled.

"I'm used to adversity, Chief. I'm a woman."

He had done his part in trying to dissuade her and had failed. Chief Campbell hoped this experience wouldn't destroy her, but more important, he hoped it wouldn't kill her.

9

It was late morning when the Bowler Hat arrived at the Zuckerman farm after camping out the previous night. He had spent hours the day before searching Pithole and the surrounding area for his horse and buggy. As he plodded along, chastising himself for not preventing the gunfire that spooked his horse, he was reminded of an incident that had occurred during his boyhood in the Cuyahoga Valley of Ohio. His parents had a farm. While his father was plowing the field one day, a rattlesnake spooked his horses and they took off, trampling and killing the family dog, a collie. The Bowler Hat's parents and five siblings were distraught, and he thought the crying and wailing would never stop. The Bowler Hat was ten, and it was the first time he had realized he was different. He felt nothing, nothing except an overwhelming sense that his family was weak and that he was strong. His mother noticed, and she gave him a good whipping, calling him "an unfeeling godless child." He never broke; he never cried. That's when he realized he had a special skill.

He pulled his horse and buggy up to the farmhouse and stopped as Albert Zuckerman came out to see what he wanted. When the Bowler Hat first laid eyes on him, he found it hard to believe Zuckerman was Jewish. Six feet tall, muscular, with blond hair and blue eyes, he was Romanian with an accent to match.

He could easily pass for one of us, the Bowler Hat thought.

Any doubts he had were erased when, after having convinced Zuckerman he had a friendly business proposition, they entered his farmhouse. On the doorway was one of those Jewish decorations. Zuckerman saw the Bowler Hat stare at it.

"It's a mezuzah," he explained as he kissed his hand, then touched it. "It ensures that God will watch over our home no matter where we are."

The Bowler Hat smiled. Zuckerman would soon discover that God was nowhere to be found. Hell had come to pay him a visit.

An hour later, Zuckerman was tied to a chair. He had a broken cheekbone, a smashed nose, and two cracked ribs, but he still refused to sign over his land.

"Take our offer. You're going to, eventually," the Bowler Hat reasoned. "You might as well do it while you still have some semblance of a face left."

"Go to hell!" screamed Zuckerman as he spit blood in the Bowler Hat's face.

The Bowler Hat reacted swiftly with a fist to Zuckerman's cracked ribs. Zuckerman cried out in pain, but he wasn't budging. He looked up defiantly.

With each blow, the Bowler Hat's admiration for

Zuckerman grew. He was becoming weary from hitting him, and the place in his arm where he had been shot was starting to throb. Yet the Jew was still full of fight. At this pace, he might kill him before he signed over his land. That would be messy, and the Oil Trust didn't like messy.

There was a chance of a surprise with every job; some were unfortunate, some fortuitous. What happened next he could only describe as serendipitous.

A horse and wagon could be heard approaching. Seemingly out of the blue, Zuckerman got anxious. It was the first time he showed any concern at all.

"Firn avek!" he shouted in Yiddish. *"Firn avek!"*

The Bowler Hat was fluent in many languages. Yiddish was not one of them, but he didn't need a linguist to realize it was a warning. He stuffed his handkerchief in Zuckerman's mouth and forced it closed with his hands so he wouldn't make a sound.

Amelia Zuckerman was an exotic-looking beauty with a lithe, supple body. She was returning from a trip to Titusville, where she had bought food and supplies for the next few weeks. She was excited that the dress she had ordered from Philadelphia had arrived. She and Albert liked to dress for dinner once a week. It was their way of keeping some semblance of civilization in a place where there was none.

"Albert, come help me unload the—" Amelia stopped after entering and seeing her husband. "Albert!" she screamed in shock.

The Bowler Hat had never seen such a beautiful Jewess. At that moment, he knew exactly what to do. He punched Zuckerman in the face as hard as he could. Zuckerman's

last conscious moment was filled with his wife's horrified scream.

Later, Zuckerman awoke to cold water being splashed in his face. It was a jolt, but it meant he was alive. He soon realized he was still tied to the chair and had been moved to his bedroom. Zuckerman turned his head, then froze, petrified by what he saw. Amelia was totally nude, her hands and feet tied to the four corners of their bed. The Bowler Hat stood next to the bed wearing only his undershorts.

"Welcome back," the Bowler Hat said, grinning tauntingly.

"Amelia!"

"Amelia. So that's her name. Thank you for the introduction. It will make what we're about to do more personal." He pulled down his undershorts.

"Albert!" Amelia screamed, her anguish tearing at her husband.

"Leave her alone! Leave her alone, goddamn you, or . . ."

"Or you'll what?"

The Bowler Hat climbed on top of Amelia as Zuckerman struggled to get loose.

"You bastard!" Zuckerman yelled at the top of his lungs, but his anger soon turned to desperation. "Please, leave her alone," he pleaded. "I'll sign whatever you want. Just leave her alone." Then Zuckerman started crying. Not just crying, sobbing.

The Bowler Hat smiled. His job was done. He just needed to get the bill of sale signed, then leave. He was a businessman, and this was all about business.

As he started to get up, the Bowler Hat caught a glimpse

of Amelia. She looked at Zuckerman with such sympathy, such compassion, such love, that he was overcome with a desire to teach her a lesson. It was almost involuntary when he entered her. Zuckerman's sobbing and Amelia's struggling only excited him more. In no time, he was finished.

Riding away in his horse and buggy, the signed bill of sale in his breast pocket, the Bowler Hat reflected on what had just transpired. He had left the Zuckermans huddled on the floor together, both crying uncontrollably. It disgusted him. The Jew was tough; he'd give him that. But in the end he broke. Most men did. It was just a matter of finding their weak spot. The Bowler Hat was confident he didn't have one, though he was a little concerned about his transgression. Discipline was a way of life for him. Work demanded he be in total control. In this instance, he hadn't been. Again, he questioned himself. Was he slipping? Again, he immediately dismissed the thought as ridiculous and categorized what happened as no more than a perk of the job.

As he spotted Titusville in the distance, his mind wandered on to other matters, and he headed into town, hoping his train would be on time.

10

This was a big day for W. W. Goodrich, and he was determined to look his best. In the morning he went to his favorite barbershop for a shave and a coif. The barber there always did a superb job, especially when advised about the importance of the occasion, and on this day what he had achieved bordered on magnificent. When it came to dress, little thought was necessary. He would wear his favorite suit, the one he'd had specially tailored on Savile Row in London. His derby hat perfectly complemented it, as did his custom-made cane with the solid-gold handle.

His brother's funeral had taken place the day before. It was a large affair with an impressive turnout. Of course, most of the attendees had come to pay tribute to him, including political friends and foes and even the mayor. To be fair, there had also been a smattering of Charlie's acquaintances, but no matter. That was his brother's moment, and today was his. As he stood on the steps of Second Street Station, everything was going as planned. His proclamation at the funeral that he would have an announcement the next

day had attracted much attention. It was everything W. W. Goodrich had hoped it would be. There were about eighty or ninety people crowding the sidewalk and spilling onto the street. It wasn't the voluminous crowd that had appeared at his brother's brownstone when word of his murder had spread, but it was a good size. Of greater significance, there were reporters representing all the local newspapers and a reasonable number from Manhattan, too. The others, mere citizens and even the ubiquitous women protesters, also seemed anxious to hear what he had to say.

W. W. Goodrich had started formulating his speech shortly after he learned of Charlie's murder. It had to possess the perfect combination of determination, controlled outrage, and grief. The result was magical. He had the crowd in the palm of his hand. W. W. Goodrich had always known he had this ability, an ability that would take his political career far beyond Brooklyn. But opportunity was the key. He had to admit Charlie deserved credit for giving him that, but he knew it required a special man to take advantage of it, and it was more than evident how special he was.

He was beyond the halfway point of his speech. He had reached a crescendo and was heading toward his fleeting moment of grief, the one that would show his vulnerability yet also assert his manhood. He had rehearsed it over and over and was sure it would net him great results.

". . . And so I, Alderman Goodrich, am offering a reward of thirty-five hundred dollars to anyone who provides information leading to the capture and conviction of my brother's killer. This is not done out of disrespect to the Brooklyn Police Department. They are fine men who risk their lives for us every day. It is rather done in the belief that one man

can still make a difference and also, to be perfectly honest, so that my family . . ."

At that moment, the unthinkable happened. A murmur started to rumble through the crowd. At first, he thought it was merely people reacting to his generous offer. But soon he realized that, beyond all reason, he was losing them! He quickly searched his mind. What event in Brooklyn could possibly trump his?

"There's Mary Handley!" shouted Amanda Everhart, the leader of the protesters.

"She's right!" screamed one of the reporters, and everyone rushed toward Mary. In no time, W. W. Goodrich stood alone on the steps, delivering his speech to himself.

"One man can still make a difference," he repeated as loudly as he could in an attempt to recapture his audience, but he was drowned out by the women protesters.

"Who's the one? Mary's the one! Who's the one? Mary's the one!"

Mary hadn't expected this kind of reception. Chief Campbell had warned her of the notoriety that accompanied the job when he had hired her, but in truth, she hadn't given it much thought. She was consumed with the joy of having gotten her dream job, and with her concern for Kate. She had checked in on Kate the night before and had told her about the job and how she was going to catch Charlie's killer. Kate was in no mood to talk. It was understandable. The wound was still very fresh.

Mary had made an effort to dress well that day, not for her public but rather to make a good impression at her new job. Her choices, though, were very limited. She called what she was wearing "the best of the worst." It was a pale blue

dress, a hand-me-down from her mother that she had personally altered. The color matched her eyes, and it contrasted nicely with her blond hair and fair complexion. Underneath it was a corset, a bustle, and a host of undergarments that made movement difficult.

"Designers of women's clothes are either sadists or, at the very least, jealous husbands," she often ranted about her pet peeve. "They've made it abundantly clear that our comfort is irrelevant and that we're not expected to stray far from home."

As Mary saw the crowd approaching and braced for the onslaught, she made a vow to stand strong. She wasn't going to foster any stereotypes by acting meek.

The reporters immediately started tossing out questions. "As a woman, how do you expect to catch the Goodrich murderer?"

"Why, with both hands, of course," Mary calmly replied as she kept walking toward the police station. Laughter rippled through the crowd. They sensed a newspaper darling, and a barrage of questions followed.

"What's your hairdo called? Who made your dress? What brand of perfume are you wearing?" Close to the police station, Mary stopped.

"Please, this is a murder investigation."

"Our readers want the female angle," a reporter shot back.

Mary considered his point, then replied, "Tell them I prefer Paris chic but, like them, can't afford it."

Once again there was laughter. Mary paused and looked around. She realized she was good at this. All she had to do was be herself, and they seemed to love it.

"Now, if you'll all excuse me, I don't want to be late for my first day of work." She gently pushed by several in the crowd who were blocking her access to the stairs and started to make her ascent, reporters still shouting questions as she did.

W. W. Goodrich made one last, desperate effort to regain their attention. "I'm donating thirty-five hundred dollars," he shouted, repeating his offer, "thirty-five hundred from my own personal funds to anyone, anyone at all who provides information that . . ."

But he had become invisible. After Mary entered the police station, the crowd was still buzzing about her as they wandered down the steps.

Led by Amanda Everhart, the women protesters resumed their chanting.

"Who's the one? Mary's the one!"

Always the politician, W. W. Goodrich gritted his teeth and did his best to paste a smile on his face. He arched his back, forcing himself to stand up straight, as he jauntily made his way down the steps, then up the block, all the while haunted by the chanting. Only the occasional clanging of his cane revealed how furious he really was.

Mary was glad to be inside the police station. Dealing with the reporters was fun, but she was anxious to get to work. The evidence room was in the basement, and as she made her way to the stairs, no one stopped to say hello or to acknowledge her with a nod. She liked that everyone was busy. She wanted to do her work without interruption.

The basement consisted of a very long hallway off of which were numerous rooms on each side. The hallway was damp and very dark, the only light being flickers seeping out from under the closed doors of the rooms in use. A strong musty odor permeated the air, and though not seen, water could be heard slowly dripping from the ceiling. It was cool in the basement, and the hard stone walls made it chillier.

Mary stepped off the stairs into virtual darkness, barely able to see a few feet in front of her. A drop of water landed on her nose.

Nice greeting, she thought as she wiped it away.

She was slowly venturing forward when a figure materialized out of nowhere, startling her. She was relieved to see it was Billy.

"Oh, Billy, you gave me a fright. I'm looking for the evidence room . . ."

But Billy continued on and up the stairs, ignoring her. As she was rationalizing his behavior, another policeman emerged from the darkness and slammed her against the wall as he passed her.

"Excuse me," he said as he headed for the stairs. But there wasn't the slightest hint of apology in his voice. This was no accident, and Mary was realizing that Billy's slight probably wasn't either when she was grabbed from behind, a man's arm tightly around her throat. It was Officer Russell.

"Sorry," he said. "I thought you were an intruder."

He squeezed a little tighter, then he, too, shoved her against the wall and took off. Mary had had enough. She was about to go after Officer Russell when a door opened across from her, pouring light into the hallway. She instantly

turned and assumed her jujitsu stance, ready to take on all comers. It was Sean.

"A bit tense on our first day, sis?" he said, holding up his hands to show he meant no harm. "You need to calm down."

"Not until I know why I'm being bullied," she demanded, standing her ground.

Sean turned serious. "So it's started. You know I can't protect you, Mary."

"Protect me from what? Tell me. What kind of dilberry is this?"

"Dilberry, is it?" he said, his emotion rising. "We've worked like dogs, hoping one day to finally be promoted, and you get the big case just because you're a woman."

"So that's why," she replied, unable to resist a dose of sarcasm. "You boys are feeling neglected and passed over. Experiencing life from the other side, are you?" Mary leaned in toward him. "Better be careful, Sean. You may grow breasts."

She marched off into the darkness. It was another perfect exit, but as she'd learned back at McGinty's Tavern when she left Charles, perfect exits didn't always produce perfect results. She turned and headed back toward Sean.

"By the way, where exactly is the evidence room?"

11

Officer Hayworth cursed his fate. He had coveted the position in the evidence room for five years. While active on the streets, he had been seriously wounded twice, and he definitely didn't want to tempt fate a third time. When Officer Gleason retired, he lobbied hard for the job and had been thrilled to get it. At this point in his career, he'd rather file murder weapons than face them, and he looked forward to whiling away the rest of his working days in a tranquil place with plenty of time to read and take an occasional nap. Fate was not through fooling with him though, forcing him to face a new enemy—the plumbing. It rebelled, turning his personal utopia into a dripping hell. He was forever trying to keep the evidence dry and mopping the floor. If he had wanted to do custodial work, he would've followed in his father's footsteps. His father was always miserable, and now he was, too.

Officer Hayworth handed Mary Handley a large envelope wrapped in a towel. Mary looked at it askance, and he decided to make a preemptive move.

"It's as dry as it's gonna be. The pipes have been broken for over a month now, and my complaints fall on deaf ears. 'Budget cuts,' they say. 'Budget cuts' is all I hear."

He looked right at Mary, daring her to say something, and then returned to mopping the floors, periodically muttering complaints.

Mary spied a small table and chair nearby that were dry enough. She wiped some surface moisture off the chair with the towel, then emptied the contents of the envelope onto the table. They were all personal items: a wallet, a key chain, some change, and a date book. The gun was missing, but she was sure it was safely in the coroner's hands, so when he dug the bullets out of Charles Goodrich he could match the size, caliber, and markings to it. The science of making a match like that was not exact, but Mary was sure it didn't matter. It was simple. The gun placed in Charles Goodrich's hand was the murder weapon, or the murderer wouldn't have placed it there.

The wallet was empty, so Mary needed to concentrate on what was missing. Although there was no money, she immediately dismissed robbery as a motive. W. W. Goodrich had told Chief Campbell that, as far as he knew, no valuables had been taken from Goodrich's brownstone. If someone broke into your house, Mary reasoned, they would take more than what was in your wallet. She would check the brownstone herself later, but robbery seemed unlikely. Also, most men kept important papers in their wallets. Charles Goodrich could have been killed for something he was carrying, but it was more likely that he had everything important filed away. He was a bookkeeper, and a bent for organization usually went hand-in-hand with that profession.

Mary then opened the date book and noticed something odd.

"Pardon me, Officer Hayworth," she said, trying to be as polite as possible, "but none of the pages before the day of the murder are here. Did I overlook something?"

"Whatever you see is how it came in," he said defensively. "I don't alter evidence, I don't lose it. I file it, I protect it, and I mop." And he returned to mopping, muttering a little louder than before.

Mary rapidly thumbed through the date book. Besides a few water stains, most of it was extremely neat and orderly. Beyond the day of the murder, nothing seemed to be of any significance. There was a doctor's appointment and several dates when rent was due on the properties he owned. On the day of the murder, there were three entries:

8 A.M. to 7 P. M.—Last day of work at Edison Electric.
9 P.M.—Meet Tesla at Tavern by the Park.
10 P.M.—Meet Roscoe at his place.

Mary studied these entries for a while and then closed the book. It occurred to her that she knew someone who might be able to shed some light on what she'd just read.

～

Mary arrived at her tenement on Elizabeth Street late afternoon. She had been delayed at the police station by Chief Campbell, who had asked her to sit for newspaper interviews and pose for photographers with him and several local politicians. It was not his idea but rather a directive from

Commissioners Jourdan and Briggs, who were conveniently absent.

Kate was not in her room. She normally would not have been home at this time, but Mary assumed that, after what Kate had been through, she would have stayed home from work. Mary immediately headed to the Lowry Hat Factory and got there just after the shifts had changed. She could see Kate up the street at the corner.

"Kate," she called. "Kate." But Kate didn't respond and she started to cross the street. Mary had to catch up with her, and hurrying in women's fashions was no easy task. She lifted her skirt to give her some freedom of movement, and taking short steps, she felt very much like a mouse as she scurried across the street.

"Kate!" she cried out. This time Kate immediately turned toward her.

"What, Mary, what do you want?" She reacted impatiently, as if she'd known Mary was there all along.

Mary didn't take offense. Her friend was in pain.

"Why didn't you stay home from work? You need time to grieve, Kate. I'm sure even the Widow Lowry would understand."

"But would our landlord understand when the rent is due or the grocer when I go to buy food?"

Mary shrugged. "You could always share burnt French toast with me."

Mary's comment seemed to cut the tension, giving Kate a slight smile. "What's the matter? Don't you think I've suffered enough?"

Mary also smiled. She put her arm in Kate's, and they started walking.

"The truth is," Kate said, "I couldn't bear staring at the four walls in my room knowing that was where I was going to be for the rest of my life."

"That's not true, Kate . . ."

"I've done some soul searching, Mary. It's time for me to face reality. Charlie and I were not everything I made us out to be, but I'll never get any closer to love."

It upset Mary to see Kate in such a deep state of melancholy.

"Kate, what happened was absolutely dreadful and impossible to comprehend. But you're still young and pretty. In time—"

"It's late," Kate said as she broke from Mary and quickened her pace. "I need to get my mail from Haddonfield, since it seems they're the only family I'm ever going to have."

Mary saw that Kate was in no mood to be soothed. She needed to embrace her sadness before she could let it go. But Mary also had a job to do. Once again, she lifted her skirt and scurried to keep up with Kate. She was slightly winded when she spoke.

"On the day Charlie died, he met with Nikola Tesla and a man named Roscoe."

Kate stared ahead of her as she walked. When she spoke, her words were controlled and lacking in emotion. Mary knew she was trying her best not to fall apart.

"I met Roscoe. Dark-haired, a Spaniard. Charlie did some business with him."

"Roscoe may have been the last person to see him alive."

"Roscoe?" Kate responded, a far-off look on her face.

"Yes, Roscoe," Mary said emphatically, trying to get Kate to focus. "Do you know where I can find him?"

"I don't even know his last name," Kate replied, shrugging helplessly.

Mary knew the next question could be upsetting, but she had to ask it.

"Kate, where were you that night?"

Kate stopped short and recoiled. "You think I killed my Charlie?" With that one question, Kate went from hurt to betrayal to outrage.

"I'm sorry," Mary said, jumping in quickly. "It's my job. I have to ask."

"You want to know?!" Kate said, her pain and anger weighing on every word. "I was at home, all by myself, like a fool, planning our wedding!"

Fighting back tears, Kate picked up her pace again. Mary started to follow, then stopped. She had gotten most of the information she needed, and Kate was in no state to give out any more. She would speak with her another time. Mary had read about Nikola Tesla and his recent splash in the scientific world as a brilliant young mind. She would arrange a meeting with him. But Roscoe intrigued her more. She didn't know how or why, but her instinct told her that he was the key to Charles Goodrich's murder.

12

Mary quietly watched as the line of carriages leading to J. P. Morgan's mansion kept growing. The passengers, mostly from the upper strata of New York society, were amazingly tranquil. The endless complaints and egotistical fits that usually accompanied such a delay were virtually absent. No one, not even these people, wanted to risk creating a scene at a J. P. Morgan/Thomas Edison event. As carriages emptied, the men strutted out dressed in top hats and tails and the women in the latest fashions. Flash powder from newspaper cameras exploded with such regularity the scene rivaled Fourth of July fireworks.

Chief Campbell's carriage repeatedly stopped and started on the cobblestone street. Inside, Mary paused to take in what was happening. Everything was going so fast. Last week she had been an unemployed sweatshop worker with no prospects. Now she was on her way to an event hosted by Governor Hill and J. P. Morgan in honor of Thomas Edison. She normally had little regard for events of this nature, viewing them as mere excuses for affluent

people to parade around like peacocks, the women sporting whatever jewelry would garner the most attention and the men boasting about their latest business triumphs. But Mary believed this one might have more substance. Thomas Edison deserved the recognition; he had immeasurably enhanced people's lives. Unfortunately, that also made it difficult to get an appointment with him.

"I've ventured to West Orange every day for almost a full week," Mary had told Chief Campbell earlier that day as he was looking through some papers on his desk.

"I've only read about it. What's it like?" said Chief Campbell, cutting her off.

"It's massive, really, spread out over many acres. There's a three-story main building with laboratories, studios, and offices, not to mention four other structures containing more laboratories. He must have countless employees, and right next door he's just broken ground on a huge manufacturing complex."

"I heard it was impressive," said Chief Campbell. "All those busy bees slaving away to accomplish one common goal: making Thomas Edison absurdly rich." He looked up at her, a trace of a glint in his eye.

"I would be more impressed if I had been able to secure an interview with Mr. Edison. I've spent six full days dealing with delays. I realize he is an important man, but this is a murder investigation. He must have some obligation to cooperate."

"They do have a talent for making you feel like a nuisance. I'll attest to that."

"I searched Charles Goodrich's brownstone and found nothing of consequence. I had hoped to also search his

office, but Mr. Edison's secretary, a Mrs. Embry, has blocked my every move. She has made it abundantly clear that only Mr. Edison can grant that permission, and only after meeting the person asking for it."

"And since you haven't been able to see him . . ."

"Exactly," Mary said with a resigned shrug.

"I've met Mrs. Embry. Stalwart woman. She'd make an excellent prison guard."

Mary smiled her agreement.

Lost in thought, Chief Campbell scratched under his chin. "Would you accompany me to a formal gathering this evening at J. P. Morgan's house?"

Mary was stumped for an answer. Chief Campbell was married and older and . . .

"I'm not trying to court you, Miss Handley."

"No, certainly not, I—"

"My wife and I have been invited to Governor Hill's Salute to Thomas Edison. If you take her place, I might be able to arrange an introduction."

"That would be wonderful, Chief, but I don't want to deprive your wife—"

"Deprive?" Chief Campbell interrupted her. "You'd be doing her an enormous favor. At these things, she inevitably finds herself with a group of women who go on and on about the difficulty of running a household with multiple servants. She's afraid one day she may lose control and speak her mind."

Mary didn't have to meet Mrs. Campbell to know she'd like her. Yet, as cynical as Mary was about the merits of those in the upper crust, she was wide-eyed as she stared out of Chief Campbell's carriage at the parade before her.

"They still put both feet on the ground when they walk," Chief Campbell told her.

"I would have thought they'd have someone do the walking for them." Mary glanced back at Chief Campbell. "It's a larger gathering than I had anticipated. I borrowed this gown from my friend Sarah. I hope nothing happens to it."

"It's perfectly safe, Mary. No ruffians here, only pompous blowhards."

"I can see why you attend these affairs. You seem to love them so."

"I have no illusions about my status. At the moment, I'm one of a few who help fill their Admiration for Public Servants quota. When someone supplants me, I will be persona non grata at these events."

The carriage lurched forward again, then stopped. They had reached the entrance. Mary thanked the driver, who opened the door and held her hand to guide her down. She was wearing an evening dress that fastened in the back and had a low yet respectable neckline, most of which was covered by a garnet, diamond, and pearl necklace that she had also borrowed from Sarah. The dress was pale pink in color and flowed graciously from top to bottom, as form-fitting as good taste would allow. Long, formal white gloves rose almost to her elbows. Mary's hair was pulled loosely up and put into a chignon held by one of Sarah's jeweled combs. Short and curly bangs adorned her forehead. Sarah had told Mary how lovely she looked. It was an understatement.

Mary noticed that most of the reporters and photographers outside the entrance were gathered around a theatrical-looking man in his fifties. She instantly recognized

him as Edwin Booth, who, despite having the star-crossed disadvantage of being John Wilkes Booth's older brother, had persevered to become the premiere actor in America.

"I am presently converting my home in Gramercy Park into the Players Club," Booth announced with a theatrical flair. Like many actors, when in public he was always on-stage. "It will hopefully be a place where artists from all walks of life can interact with businessmen from all walks of life, so they can see that we are not all heathens."

The crowd laughed as a reporter tossed out a question. "Mr. Booth, when will you next do *Hamlet*?" It was a natural question. Booth's Hamlet was considered the greatest of the nineteenth century.

"Not until the fall," Booth responded. "However, I am currently at the Brooklyn Academy of Music rehearsing *An Enemy of the People,* a new play by that brilliant Norwegian playwright Henrik Ibsen."

More flash powder exploded. By now Chief Campbell had gotten down from the carriage and joined Mary. He whispered, "Let's get inside before they notice."

"Notice what?"

"You, of course."

He ushered her toward the entrance, positioning himself on Mary's right, trying to block her from the reporters. Mary had been at Edison's complex in West Orange, New Jersey, for the past few days and hadn't fully experienced the fervor her newspaper interviews and photographs had caused. On her way to and from West Orange, she had noticed looks of recognition. There was one woman who had approached her, asking if she was "that lady detective, Mary

Handley." Still, it was hard for Mary to fathom that she could attract as much attention as Edwin Booth!

Before she knew it, she was inside J. P. Morgan's mansion and dancing a waltz with Chief Campbell. Chief Campbell had not yet told her exactly how he planned to approach Edison, because he felt that amateurs often obsess and nerves cause mistakes. He obviously didn't know Mary very well.

As they danced, Mary looked around. It was a spacious room with a domed ceiling and a gigantic crystal chandelier. There was fine art everywhere. Along one wall was a huge marble fireplace. The wall facing the street had tall, over-sized windows framed by drapes, imported from the Orient, that were tied back with sashes. The orchestra was at the far end of the room, and the dance floor in the middle. It was surrounded by people chatting in groups, as waiters served drinks and hors d'oeuvres on trays. Most of them had already separated according to gender.

"What do you think of Mr. Morgan's house?" Chief Campbell asked.

"My parents live in a house," Mary replied. "This is a castle, and a rather large one at that."

"And J. P. Morgan is the king." Chief Campbell instructed her on the dynamics of the room. "Notice how they've gathered," he said, then indicated each group he identified with a tilt of the head. "There's Jay Gould's group, Andrew Carnegie's, Rockefeller, Westinghouse, and finally, J. P. Morgan with Mr. Edison."

"They have their own little fiefdoms."

He nodded. "New York society. They run in packs like rats. Those weasel-like fellows floating from group to group

currying favor are the Tammany Hall politicians who run New York government."

"And I thought Tammany was for the common man," Mary said with a touch of sarcasm.

"The only reason their former leader, Boss Tweed, got caught for swindling was that he temporarily ignored his obligation to these people."

"Shame on him," Mary replied, tongue still in cheek. "Thanks for the lay of the land, Chief. Hopefully, we'll be able to secure a meeting with Mr. Edison."

"It's akin to getting an audience with the Pope, but it's not impossible."

They danced by J. P. Morgan, Thomas Edison, and Charles Batchelor, who were conversing over cocktails, greeting the occasional intruder who came to pay homage.

"I realize purple signifies power and nobility," Mary whispered, "but dare I say J. P. Morgan's nose pushes the proverbial envelope?"

"It's a rare skin disease."

"I certainly hope so."

"Mary, if you are to get anything out of these men, they expect a certain behavior from women. You need to be pretty but harmless. A touch of savvy and they'll shut you out faster than they would a vagabond."

Mary was disappointed. "I've dreamed of meeting Thomas Edison since I was a little girl, and you want me to play the fool?"

"Are you aware of Machiavelli and his treatise *The Prince*?"

"The ends justify the means, and my means is to deny

my intellect." She sighed. "Don't mind me. You know what's best, Chief. I'll do as you say."

A man tapped Chief Campbell on the shoulder. When Chief Campbell turned, Mary was surprised to see Charles Pemberton, dressed in formal tails, looking even more handsome than he had at McGinty's Tavern.

"May I cut in, sir?" Charles asked, trying to squeeze as much Southern charm and tradition out of those few words as he possibly could. His request was followed by a silent pause until it dawned upon Mary that Chief Campbell was waiting for her reaction.

"I know this gentleman. It's perfectly fine . . . that is, if you don't mind, Chief."

"Go right ahead. I have some arrangements to make," he said, emphasizing this with a knowing nod. "And my wife is a great admirer of Edwin Booth. If I don't obtain his autograph, I might as well not go home." With that, Chief Campbell left the dance floor.

Charles took Mary in his arms, and as they began dancing, he spoke his first words to her since that night at McGinty's.

"You're a long way from Brooklyn, Mary."

"So are you. How are Tom, Dick, and Harry?" Mary was trying to rekindle their rapport. If it was a fluke or the result of drink, she wanted to know right away.

"Green with envy," he responded.

"And why is that?"

"Because I'm dancing with the most beautiful woman in New York City."

"Pardon me if I don't swoon," she said. "In the Irish parts of Brooklyn, we call that blarney."

"Really? In Atlanta, we call it a hefty load of bull."

His response would have sent most women running. Mary, however, was delighted, and her spontaneous laugh signaled her approval. This man definitely had potential.

Absorbed in each other, they danced past George Westinghouse, a fleshy man about forty years old with a large bushy mustache that stretched out to meet his longer, bushier sideburns. He was approaching Morgan and Edison's clique with Nikola Tesla at his side. A prolific inventor, Westinghouse had made a good deal of his fortune when he revolutionized the railroad system by inventing the air brake at the age of twenty-two. To put it mildly, he and Edison were rivals.

"Congratulations, Thomas," Westinghouse boomed out, trying to cover the fact that being there brought him no joy. He offered his hand to Edison. "It's a splendid tribute."

As Edison shook Westinghouse's hand, he, too, remained cordial. "Thank you, George. Glad you could make it." He wasn't glad, but gladness was required of him.

"Wouldn't miss it for the world," Westinghouse replied, continuing their mutual-admiration façade. "You truly deserve it."

Tesla, who had little patience for social games, cleared his throat. Westinghouse switched to the purpose of their visit: making Edison squirm.

"I believe you know Mr. Tesla," Westinghouse said, indicating his companion. "I've just pledged Westinghouse funds to back his AC system, give you and J. P. a run for the money in the electrical market."

This was the first Edison had heard of the alliance, but he'd be damned if he'd give them the satisfaction of showing

any concern. He smiled and shrugged. Morgan's reaction was different. This was his home, his domain, and any attempt at encroachment was immediately challenged.

"I always welcome competitors, George." Morgan's voice couldn't have been calmer. "It makes success that much sweeter."

The dance music stopped, and the orchestra played a brief and loud musical fanfare. The conductor had an announcement to make.

"Ladies and gentlemen, I have the distinct pleasure of presenting to you the Honorable David B. Hill, governor of the great state of New York." Then he signaled with his baton and the orchestra played "Hail to the Chief" as Governor Hill, a thin, balding man with a thick mustache, walked out and waved to an applauding crowd. He held his hand up for everyone to quiet.

"I'd like to thank the orchestra for the job promotion," he said as he turned to them. "I'm not president, gentlemen . . . not yet, that is."

The crowd responded with laughter and applause.

"But we are not here to talk about me tonight. Though our guest of honor's research facilities are in a neighboring state"—Governor Hill stared in mock disapproval, generating many laughs, none heartier than the one emanating from Edison—"we're forever indebted to him for his dedication, his generosity, and his genius. Tom."

Governor Hill gestured for Edison to join him, and thunderous applause followed. Edison motioned with his hands, implying that all the praise was too much, which it wasn't. It was a large part of what drove him.

Determined to ruin Edison's evening, Tesla moved

closer to him. "You know our system is superior," he whispered. "Admit it, Thomas. You're nervous."

"Poor boy, you still don't know how this works," Edison said under his smile as he waved to his admirers. "That's my name the governor just called, Nikola, not yours."

It was hard to say what frustrated Tesla more: Edison's seemingly cavalier attitude about the importance of scientific work or Tesla's fear that Edison was right and that his reputation would always trump Tesla's, regardless of their products' quality. Tesla announced he had urgent business and then stomped off, adding extra satisfaction to Edison's evening.

The party resumed. Charles and Mary were now standing by the marble fireplace.

"I've been reading in the newspapers about your meteoric rise since we met," Charles said. "Congratulations, Mary."

"Thank you, but I don't believe in congratulations until a person actually accomplishes something."

"Oh, my. Burdened with that requirement, many of the revered reputations in this room would vanish." Charles took two glasses of champagne from a waiter's tray. "Let's drink to your future accomplishments," he said as he offered a glass to Mary. "Only the best champagne for you."

Mary took the glass. "That's awfully generous, especially since it's free."

"If I had my way, we'd bathe in it." Then Charles very gently took her hand and kissed it. When their eyes met, Mary felt a tingly excitement shoot through her.

They were soon interrupted by the arrival of Chief Campbell.

"Ah, Mary, I need to wrest you back from this charming fellow," he declared, his look telling her it was time to get back to work. Mary and Charles made plans to meet for dinner at a later date, and as Charles watched them walk off, John Pemberton arrived, flushed with excitement over gaining an appointment with Edison. He noticed his son's attention was elsewhere.

"Another damsel in distress?" Pemberton inquired.

"*The* damsel, Father, *the* damsel." Charles raised his glass in a toast to Mary, then drank. Not used to seeing his son so intrigued by a woman, Pemberton was amused.

As Mary and Chief Campbell headed toward Edison, he reminded her of the role she needed to play. It was not necessary. Mary was fully aware she was to act demure and uninformed in front of a man she greatly admired.

Batchelor spotted Mary and Chief Campbell and immediately whispered in Edison's ear, filling him in on the situation.

Chief Campbell spoke first. "Mr. Edison, may I present to you—"

"No need for an introduction, Chief Campbell," Edison interrupted. "Everyone in New York knows who Mary Handley is." He extended his hand to shake Mary's, then continued in a tone that could only be described as condescending. "The first woman to conduct a murder investigation. Congratulations, Miss Handley."

Normally, when people addressed Mary in that tone, a quick witticism would soon dispel their erroneous notion of her. This was different.

"It's an honor to meet you, Mr. Edison. I don't know

how you men of science do what you do. You're very much like magicians. That's what you are."

"I often think we are, too, Miss Handley. I must confess that some of my inventions at times felt as farfetched as pulling a rabbit out of a hat."

They all laughed, then Mary interjected. "To be so accomplished and yet so modest; I am truly in awe."

"Thank you," responded Edison. "And how is the investigation going?"

Mary emitted her best exasperated sigh. "To be honest, I wish I could pull a rabbit out of my hat. The task before me seems quite daunting. The crime of murder is very complicated. Why one human being would actually want to obliterate another is troubling enough and, frankly, beyond me."

"I'm sure you'll eventually catch on," Edison said, casting a glance at Batchelor that indicated the opposite.

Mary knew it was time to strike. Trying to look as helpless as possible, she stared into Edison's eyes. "It would be so, so helpful if I could see Mr. Goodrich's office."

"Consider it done," he decreed.

"And I do have a few teeny questions for you. Would it be at all—?"

"Be delighted to. Arrange a time with Batch." Edison gestured toward Batchelor, eager to move on to more fruitful conversations. He would painfully submit to her simplistic questions at another time. Doing otherwise could invite bad press, and he was acutely aware of how important his image was to himself and to his business.

While Batchelor handed Mary his card, she glanced at Chief Campbell with admiration. His advice about handling these men was spot-on.

Governor Hill joined their group with a request. "Excuse me, but I need to borrow the guest of honor for a few minutes."

Edison welcomed the interruption. The two of them retreated, and soon Chief Campbell and Mary found themselves heading for the exit, their mission accomplished.

"Teeny?" Chief Campbell asked, giving Mary a look.

"Please, Chief, I already despise myself enough."

And that's when Mary saw it. Chief Campbell actually laughed.

Alone in J. P. Morgan's study with Edison, Governor Hill closed the door. "I'm under siege, Tom. I need to find a more humane method of execution."

"What, murderers are too good for hanging?"

"It's a new age. Bleeding hearts rule."

"Then inject the bastards with poison."

"I wish it were that simple. The hypodermic needle is far too new. We don't want to hold back medical science by making the public afraid of it."

Governor Hill waited as Edison pondered the conundrum. He wanted to help. It was always convenient to have a high-ranking politician in one's debt, though if necessity was indeed the mother of invention, Edison's interest hadn't reached that level. His mind wandered to his deeper concern: Westinghouse and Tesla. Then it suddenly all came together.

"I may have a solution to your problem," Edison announced.

Another idiom was rumbling through his brain—"kill two birds with one stone." One bird was doing a favor for Governor Hill. Two was destroying the competition for good. And the stone? Well, it was just an idea, but it had to be deadly.

13

No sooner had the Bowler Hat returned from Pithole than he was sent out on another assignment in Rock Springs, Wyoming. Even though he traveled in first class, it was a miserable six-day trip, because to him, any day he did not perform his duties was a complete waste.

As the Bowler Hat stepped off the train in Rock Springs, it was hard for him to imagine that this little pile of dust they called a town had such a violent history. But it did. During the Rock Springs Massacre, white coal miners, incensed at the huge influx of cheap Chinese labor, had rioted and burned down a section called Chinatown. When the smoke cleared, twenty-eight Chinese were dead, and the governor of Wyoming had brought in the army to restore peace. Now it was three years later, and the army was still there with no end to their occupation in sight.

The Bowler Hat had explicit instructions from the company. Everything had to be extremely low-profile. He was specifically told this could not be another Pithole.

Zuckerman had complained to the authorities in Titus-

ville. The Bowler Hat wasn't surprised. A man had to do something when his wife was violated, or he could never be a man again. As it turned out, the inconvenience it caused was minimal. Small-town sheriffs and judges were easily handled. Still, the Bowler Hat got paid a large fee to make his work undetectable. The slightest reflection upon his employers meant that he had failed. They were businessmen who used words like "convince" and "persuade." Violence was conveniently absent from their vocabulary, so they could deny any responsibility for it, not only to the public but to themselves.

The Bowler Hat didn't believe in excuses, and neither did his employers. He assured everyone that Pithole was an anomaly. He was sorely aware that this was his sole chance at redemption. He wouldn't get another.

In any case, his job seemed easy enough. A Chinaman was trying to forge a peace between the white workers and the Chinese. He needed to convince him to do otherwise. The Chinese were cheap nonunion labor. If they formed an alliance with the white workers, strengthening the labor union, they could force the company to pay them a decent wage. The company liked things the way they were.

The Bowler Hat was hungry. He would find the best tavern in town, have a big steak, then go about finding the man everyone in Rock Springs called Wei Chung.

Years earlier, when Wei Chung; his wife, Xin; and his daughter, Tina, left Brooklyn for San Francisco, it had been an especially difficult parting for Tina and her friend Mary.

Wei was sure that Tina would feel better when she made
new friends in San Francisco, and he was right. Tina blossomed, both socially and academically. She and Mary wrote
religiously to one another for a year or so, then the letters
gradually trailed off until they stopped completely. It wasn't
that they cared less about one another, but rather that their
lives continued separately.

The laundry Wei and his brother, Huan, started in San
Francisco had been doing well and slowly building business
year after year. Then tragedy struck. Huan Chung was delivering laundry to their biggest client, a large hotel. Huan
ran for the elevator but only had one foot inside when it
took off. There were no safety devices, and elevators flowed
freely up and down even if a gate or door was open. In a matter of seconds, Huan was dead. He had been flipped upside
down and had smashed his head against the hard hotel floor
before tumbling down the elevator shaft.

Huan's widow, Lien, filed a lawsuit against the hotel.
Wei knew it was a hopeless cause. They were Chinese, and
the hotel owners were white. She not only lost the lawsuit,
but the Chungs were also labeled as "difficult" and word
spread not to do business with them. Wei's efforts to save
the laundry failed. He reverted to handyman work, and Xin
went back to performing cleaning services.

Around the time Tina got married and was employed as
a teacher, the army was assuring the safety of Chinese workers in Rock Springs. The work was dangerous, but the pay
was well beyond what Wei and Xin currently made. So they
moved to Rock Springs, where Wei was hired as a miner and
Xin got a job as a maid for one of the mine officials. Wei figured if the two of them lived cheaply for several years, they

could save enough money to return to San Francisco. His dream was to open a store where hardworking Chinese like himself could buy expensive items like washing machines by paying out the cost in small monthly installments.

Wei and Xin paid the company absurdly high rent for a one-room wooden shack with an old stove that was part of a long row of shacks among many such rows in Chinatown. The slightest rainfall turned the streets into mud, and the cold winter air easily permeated the cracks of the shoddy construction. The communal outhouses were supposed to be cleaned regularly by the company, but it was done too infrequently. As a result, a foul odor often pervaded the air, especially on hot summer days.

The Chungs shared their shack with four other Chinese miners who worked the night shift. With only one room for all of them, the fact that Wei and Xin worked a day shift (if one could call twelve-hour days a day shift) gave them the luxury of some privacy.

Dusk was fading into darkness, and Wei was cutting vegetables for dinner. He heard a knock at his door, put down his knife, wiped his hands, and went to answer it.

"Ah, glad to see you're home," the Bowler Hat said, greeting Wei with a smile.

"I'm always home at this time," Wei responded. He could tell this man wanted something. White men did not stroll into Chinatown without a purpose. Wei noticed his family necklace with the ancient charm was dangling from his neck, and he quickly tucked it inside his shirt.

The Bowler Hat saw Wei Chung's wariness and that it wasn't just about the necklace. Although he did wonder why anyone would possess something of value while living

in such dire poverty. But that was not why he was here. He focused on the Chinaman. He was observant and cautious. Idle chatter was useless.

"Can we talk inside, Mr. Chung?"

Wei stared at this man who somehow knew his name and reasoned that if there were complications, it would be better for him in Chinatown than in company territory. Wei stepped aside and let the Bowler Hat enter.

When on a job, it had become second nature for the Bowler Hat to familiarize himself with his surroundings. Once he had found himself counting exits and possible weapons while at a gathering in the Rockefeller mansion. There wasn't much to consider here: the front door and two windows, one on each side wall. Six flimsy cots were lined up against one wall, and an old stove was in the far corner with a table and four makeshift chairs in another corner. A deck of Chinese playing cards was on the table. He knew the Chinese liked to gamble, but he couldn't imagine what these people possibly had to gamble with.

"We're inside," stated Wei, signaling the Bowler Hat to speak.

The Bowler Hat obliged. "There are certain parties who would prefer you be elsewhere, and they have asked me to assist them."

The warning signals that had been going off since Wei first saw this man now put him on full alert. The Bowler Hat tried to defuse the situation.

"No need to be alarmed. This is just meant to be a discussion."

"Then say what you have to say," Wei responded as he stood up straight, an accomplishment in itself since he was

working a portion of the mine that had four-foot ceilings. Still, his discipline, jujitsu, had kept him in shape, and he was fearless.

"These parties are very generous men. I am prepared to offer you five hundred dollars to go wherever you please." The Bowler Hat was authorized to offer Wei more, but having seen the squalor in which he was willing to live, he decided to lower the amount. He had found that saving people money, no matter how rich they were (and his employers were beyond rich), was an excellent way of ingratiating yourself. Considering recent events, ingratiating would be a wise move.

Five hundred dollars was a lot of money. It would take Wei and Xin many months of hard labor and deprivation to save up that much. However, Wei's desire to accept the money was countered by something he valued much more: his honor.

"Thank you for your offer, but I respectfully decline."

The Bowler Hat assessed the situation. He had found that all men have a number. Maybe he'd mistakenly assumed this Chinaman could be bought at fire-sale prices.

"One thousand dollars and two train tickets back to San Francisco," the Bowler Hat blurted out. He had found that when money was involved, the element of surprise often triggered an instinctive positive response. Judging from this Chinaman's circumstances, it could possibly spark a heart attack . . . and that would be fine, too. Either way, his job would be done.

The Bowler Hat wasn't very far off. Wei's heart was pounding strongly. Add one thousand dollars to what they had already saved, and he and Xin could go back to San

Francisco, be with their daughter, and start his dream. But Wei had made promises. He had been the driving force in negotiating a deal between the Chinese and white workers. Many of them were depending on him to improve their lives, and in his absence, he knew the deal would fall apart. If San Francisco represented Wei's heart's desire, Rock Springs represented his soul, and he couldn't live with betraying his soul.

"Tell your employers that I am humbled by their offer," Wei answered very thoughtfully. "Though it is indeed very tempting, I cannot accept it."

"That's my limit. I can't offer you more."

"It wouldn't matter if you could."

The Bowler Hat definitely did not want another physical altercation. He needed a peaceful, uneventful "Yes," and he had one last card to play.

"I doubt whether your daughter would agree with you," he said. "Tina, isn't it?"

Wei Chung was a peaceful man, but when he heard this man threaten his daughter, it touched a nerve in his core that ripped through his body like a hot coal. He was ready to hurt the man and hurt him badly. Then Wei's cooler, philosophical brain took over. He would not allow this man to provoke him. Even jujitsu, a discipline of which he was a master, had been taken up purely for reasons of self-defense.

The Bowler Hat spoke as he stepped toward Wei. "I didn't want this to happen. You forced this on your—"

Before he could finish his sentence, he was on the floor looking up at the ceiling. The Bowler Hat was familiar with many forms of self-defense. As his body crashed to the floor, he knew the Chinaman was using jujitsu and that he was

good at it, possibly an expert. He appreciated the irony. *Just when I actually want boring and uneventful,* he thought, *I get the surprise and challenge I always crave.*

"I have no desire to hurt you," Wei said. "Please leave."

But that was not going to happen. The fight had just begun. The Bowler Hat was an expert boxer who, as a younger man, had honed his skills in bare-knuckle contests throughout the nation. He had also studied savate, the French art of kickboxing, and had become quite proficient at it. However, Wei Chung had not just studied jujitsu. It was a way of life to him, part of a larger Neo-Confucian philosophy that required moral and ethical behavior. It didn't matter what forms of combat the Bowler Hat had mastered. It didn't matter that the Bowler Hat was larger and stronger than Wei. This wouldn't go well for him.

The Bowler Hat wasn't used to losing. Every move he made was countered by a faster and more efficient one by Wei. He was being bounced around the shack like a soccer ball, sometimes careening off walls and other times just being slammed to the floor. After a while, the Bowler Hat found it increasingly hard to recover from the thumping he was taking. He needed an edge. He pulled out a knife he kept hidden in his boot, but Wei immediately disarmed him. He went for the gun inside his coat and found himself flying through the air before he could get to the holster. He landed on the table, shattering it to pieces. When he looked up, he saw Wei with the gun, emptying the bullets and scattering them onto the floor. He then tossed the gun into the corner.

"You've had enough," Wei said. "It's time to leave."

Wei's generosity repulsed the Bowler Hat. It filled him with hatred, which he welcomed like an old friend. He

worked on it, nurtured it, allowed it to fill his soul and give him strength to continue. But what could he do? He had to stall.

"You're right," he uttered in a breathy voice, lying in a pile of wood and scattered playing cards. "I know when I've met a better man."

While propping himself up from the floor, the Bowler Hat's hand slid on one of the Chinese playing cards. It was highly unlikely, but it was all he had. He picked up a playing card. It was firm, more substantial than the American kind. That was good.

Trying to catch his enemy off guard, the Bowler Hat slowly rose. Then he put every ounce of energy into his arm and wrist as he flung the card toward the Chinaman. The Bowler Hat watched as it cut through the air, spinning rapidly, slicing its way toward the Chinaman's neck. He was amazed. Was it possible this could actually work?

Wei wasn't fooled by the man's weary manner. He knew opponents often played possum. What did puzzle him was what the man thought he could accomplish by throwing a playing card at him. This delayed his reaction, but just as the playing card neared his neck, he raised his left arm to deflect it.

The last-second move by Wei made the Bowler Hat's heart sink. He was done. All that was left was to wait for the Chinaman to finish him. But Wei didn't move toward him at all. He just stood there, completely bewildered as he looked down at his left arm. It was only then the Bowler Hat noticed the playing card was embedded deeply in the Chinaman's wrist. Blood was gushing out, more than even he had seen in a while.

Wei frantically searched for something to stop the bleeding. He quickly pulled out the card, removed his shirt, then wrapped it around his wrist. It had no effect. In seconds, the shirt was filled with blood. Wei knew he needed a doctor, but there were none in Chinatown. He'd never make it to the white part of Rock Springs in time.

The Bowler Hat was now in charge, and his swagger returned. Wei stumbled toward the door, trying to make it out of the shack, but the Bowler Hat threw him to the floor, where he stayed, crunched in a corner, too weak to move, a look of complete disbelief on his face.

"Before you slip into the next world, I suppose I should tell you why," the Bowler Hat boasted. "I once saw a man cut through a tree branch with an ordinary playing card. I thought it was a parlor trick, then I practiced it and discovered it wasn't. I never tried it on a human before. That's my next step, now that I know it works on chinks."

Wei was thankful he could no longer hear. He didn't want his last thoughts filled with the words of a beast. His mind wandered to Xin and Tina, how much he loved them, how he would not be able to fulfill his dream and thus make their lives easier. His heart filled with sadness. He would never meet his grandchildren, never see them grow up. He would never see any of his family again. Well, maybe in the next life. Maybe . . .

Wei Chung was dead. All the Bowler Hat had to do was straighten up the shack so there was no trace of a fight, and it would look like this Chinaman had committed suicide. Clean, no complications. The company would be happy. He removed the shirt that the Chinaman had wrapped around his wrist, and took the knife from the counter where Wei

Chung had been cutting vegetables and put it in the China-man's right hand. The appearance of a suicide was now complete, and as he was gathering his knife, his gun, and the bullets, he heard someone at the door.

Xin Chung always got off work one hour after Wei. The second she entered, she sensed something was wrong. Then she saw Wei hunched up in the corner, blood everywhere. Before she could scream, the Bowler Hat had grabbed her. He snapped her neck, breaking it, and having joined her husband in death, she fell to the floor.

Suicide would no longer be an option. The Bowler Hat had to stage something that would make sense. He remem-bered the Chinaman's necklace and realized a robbery was his only option. He ripped the necklace off Wei's dead body and stuffed it in his pocket. He searched the shack but found no other valuables. He hastily tossed the cots to make it look like a frantic search (which it was), and he was done. It would have to do.

The Bowler Hat quietly disappeared under the cloak of night, leaving Wei and Xin Chung on opposite sides of the shack, their dead eyes staring at each other.

14

Four days after the Edison tribute, Mary arrived at his West Orange complex to, once again, be informed of a last-minute cancellation of their meeting. This time, though, her reception was somewhat different. Edison had given the officious Mrs. Embry permission for Mary to inspect Charles Goodrich's office. A touch matronly, Mrs. Embry was in her mid-fifties and a widow. Mr. Embry, her childhood sweetheart, had been killed in the last throes of the Civil War, and she'd never remarried. She had been Edison's secretary for fourteen years, and she possessed all the qualities he needed: she was competent, efficient, and most of all, extremely protective of her boss. Mary remembered having joked with Chief Campbell about her and was sorry she had. Mrs. Embry was one of those people whose work had become her family, and she was just trying to do a very difficult job as well as she could. Everyone wanted to see Thomas Edison, and it was up to her to keep them in check.

Mrs. Embry ushered Mary down a long hallway at the

end of the second floor in the main building to Charles Goodrich's office.

"Help yourself," she said while letting her in. "I'll return later."

Goodrich's office was small and utilitarian. There was
a desk, a chair, a tall wooden filing cabinet, and a lamp. He
had some antiques scattered around, including a few vases
and a music box. Most of them were from the East.

Mary started going through everything. The files took
the longest. From what she could glean, there was nothing
unusual. He seemed like a typical bookkeeper: organized,
routine oriented, most probably a quiet, innocuous man. It
was the same conclusion she had drawn when she searched
his brownstone. A couple of hours had gone by, and Mary
was just about finished, albeit somewhat frustrated at not
finding anything, when Mrs. Embry appeared in the doorway. Somehow she instinctively knew how long it would
take Mary to complete her business. It was one of the many
mysterious powers that really good secretaries possessed.

"It's terrible what happened to Mr. Goodrich," Mrs.
Embry said, showing genuine sympathy. "No one is safe
anymore."

"Yes, terrible," Mary replied as she opened the music
box. It played a light and airy baroque-style tune, but there
was nothing inside pertinent to her case.

"I'm very fond of music boxes," said Mrs. Embry, then
she hummed along.

"It's a musical snuffbox," Mary responded. "It appears
to be very old and, judging from the music, probably of
French origin."

"Mr. Goodrich adored his antiques, especially those from the Orient."

"Really, where did he get them?" Mary was just making conversation. Her mind was elsewhere as she looked around the room again.

"I haven't the slightest idea," said Mrs. Embry. "Every so often a handsome Spaniard would appear with yet another one he had purchased."

Now Mrs. Embry had Mary's full attention. "Was his name Roscoe?" Mary asked. "The Spaniard," she said, eagerly awaiting an answer.

Mrs. Embry didn't know. Mary started examining the antiques in the room. On the bottom of one of the vases that looked Japanese in origin, she saw a company name, "Eastside Imports, New York." She felt a surge of excitement. It was her first real lead.

Lucette Myers was at police headquarters on a fishing expedition. She insisted she had information so vital she refused to impart it to a lowly police officer, but her real purpose was to hook a man, any man, who could rescue her from her meager existence. She didn't often get to fish in these waters, and she had made sure to emphasize her most enticing attributes. Her extra-tight corset trimmed her waist perfectly and allowed her ample breasts to stand out. She wore a bustle, and she celebrated it. Along with her bosom, it represented one of the two areas that most stirred men's fantasies. She had spent hours making sure her bright red hair was curled perfectly in front. Her makeup was overdone,

but she was still unattached in her thirties. That fact had to be hidden by whatever means.

Commissioner Jourdan's secretary, a Miss Whitehead, approached Lucette but stopped about ten feet from her, as if getting close would taint her. "The commissioner will see you now, Miss Myers."

It was painfully noticeable to Lucette that this drab and uninspired-looking woman felt threatened by her mere presence. She hoped Miss Whitehead would escort her to the commissioner and introduce them. She felt the contrast between them would benefit her greatly and set the meeting off on the right foot.

Jourdan was going over reports. He felt the only activity that could surpass it in boredom was to speak with a lady who insisted she had vital information. Such information was never vital, and he normally relegated these people to an underling. But Lucette Myers had been so persistent, so unrelenting in her pursuit of him, that he finally agreed. After all, he was a servant of the people, and no matter how distasteful it might be, once in a while he had to actually deal with one of them.

When Miss Whitehead opened his door, he was almost struck speechless. The lady standing next to her embodied everything he desired in a woman. His eyes devoured her. Lucette wanted to write Miss Whitehead a thank-you note for her assistance.

"Commissioner Jourdan, this is Lucette Myers," Miss Whitehead announced, barely concealing her disdain.

Jourdan immediately rose. Adrenaline shot through his body. His mouth opened but no words emerged. Miss White-head left, shaking her head.

Jourdan finally managed to blurt out, "How do you do, Miss Myers?"

A feeling of self-satisfaction filled Lucette. The fish was on the hook. All she had to do was to keep stroking his ego as she slowly reeled him in.

"Whoever thought a man in such a powerful position could also be so handsome?" Lucette said, adding a coquettish smile.

Jourdan beamed, then he smiled, then beamed some more. That was about all he could manage until he resorted to his annoying habit of nervously twirling his mustache.

"Please sit down, Miss Myers," he offered politely.

"Only if you call me Lucette," she replied.

She made sure their eyes connected for a moment. He wanted to take her in his arms, but he knew a proper lady like Lucette would take umbrage at that.

"So, Lucette, I'm told you have some information on the Goodrich murder."

"Indeed," she said. "I know who killed the poor man."

This was shocking news, but not shocking enough to stop Commissioner Jourdan from picturing Lucette naked.

∽

The name "Roscoe" kept appearing. Mary hoped she would find him at Eastside Imports, which was on the West Side. *Such are the vagaries of business names,* she thought. *Maybe it was once on the east side and moved, or maybe its name reflects that it specializes in antiques from the East.* The name also gave the impression that it was a large business, but

it turned out to be a small antique shop amid similar small shops and bars on lower Broadway.

As Mary entered Eastside Imports, a bell attached to the door announced her arrival. Space was limited. Antiques were strategically placed to show them off, but one couldn't avoid a sense of clutter. They ranged greatly, from sculptures to vases to opium pipe bowls and everything in between.

It didn't take long for Mary to realize she was the only "customer" in the store. There was a blond-haired, mousy-looking little man with glasses who was studiously dusting antiques in a section of the shop and would occasionally sneak quick, nervous glances at her. As Mary perused the inventory, she slowly inched closer to him.

"Lovely shop you have here. A lot of beautiful pieces, mostly from the Orient, aren't they?" Trying to avoid her, he kept dusting. She spoke louder and more pointedly. "Aren't they?"

He could ignore her no longer. His eyes on his dusting, he hastily mumbled, "Yes, the Orient, mostly."

She was now close to the man. She knew he was hiding something, and he wasn't good at it. She waited, watching the tension mounting in him.

"How often do you get shipments in?"

"Why, are you a collector, Miss Handley?" The second he uttered her name he looked stricken, as if he wanted to take those words back.

Mary faced him straight on. "I'm at a disadvantage. Have we met?"

"No, no," he said, avoiding her stare, then somewhat

frantically making his way behind the main counter by the cash register. "But everyone in New York knows you, Miss Handley. Everyone." Bending down, he disappeared behind the counter briefly. Mary readied herself. He could reappear with anything, including a weapon. But when he straightened, he was holding a newspaper in his hand. He pointed to the headline: LADY SEEKS GOODRICH KILLER. Underneath it, there was a photograph of Mary.

"Hmm." Mary nodded. "Makes discretion difficult."

With a cheery "Quite so, quite so, indeed," he returned the newspaper to its place, relieved that he had deflected her suspicion. But Mary was persistent.

"In that case, are you Roscoe?" She knew he wasn't. This man didn't come close to fitting any of the descriptions she had heard. She just wanted to see what the mention of the name would do to him. And it did plenty. A simple no would have sufficed, but he nervously began chattering on.

"Me? Do I look like a Roscoe? Clarence, maybe, possibly a Gerard, but no Roscoe, never . . . My name is Mortimer."

"But you do know Roscoe, don't you?"

"Roscoe, hmm, Roscoe," Mortimer babbled on, feigning to search his mind. "I know a Richard, a Roger, a Randall . . . Rodrigo. But no, no Roscoe."

"Think harder." Mary leaned on the counter, trying to rattle him even more. "Somewhere amidst all those acquaintances, there must be a Roscoe."

"I have a facility with names, Miss Handley. I'm certain I don't know a Roscoe."

"Speaking of names, Mortimer, do you know what *I* know for certain? It's what they call a person who hinders the police in a murder investigation—an accomplice." For

effect, she stared at him in silence for a moment. Then Mary opened the door, the bell rang, and she was gone.

Had Mortimer been a flower, he would have wilted.

~

Commissioner Briggs sat back in his desk chair, puffing on his cigar. Moments earlier, Jourdan had rushed into his office with some redheaded tart claiming it was urgent. Jourdan had made a habit of involving him in his pathetic attempts at romantic liaisons. Still, Jourdan was his colleague, so Briggs summoned as pleasant an expression as he could stomach and tried to be cordial.

"What does this lovely lady have to say that could possibly be so urgent?"

Lucette blurted out her answer. "A man named Roscoe killed Mr. Goodrich."

"What?!" Briggs exclaimed as he sat up in a flash. "Roscoe! You saw it?"

"Oh no, thank God. If I had, I'd have been too traumatized to speak." Lucette looked over at Jourdan, assuring him that she was but a helpless female.

She explained that she lived on Degraw Street, across from Mr. Goodrich. A few days before his murder, she had witnessed a heated row between him and a man she knew only as Roscoe. She didn't know exactly why they were fighting, but it was shortly after she had seen him flirting with Mr. Goodrich's fiancée right in front of Mr. Goodrich, visibly upsetting him.

"Roscoe is a swarthy Latin, the kind who compromises innocent young women," Lucette explained. "With these

men, there's always a wealthy father, husband, or fiancé involved from whom he extorts a tidy sum to disappear."

Jourdan decided it was time to reassure Lucette that he himself was a complete gentleman. He pounded on the desk, expressing his outrage.

"The scoundrel!" he shouted.

Lucette knew the game much better than he did and took it one step further.

"He tried his charms on me, but I prefer refined, educated gentlemen." Her eyes landed on Jourdan, who lost all powers of speech and twirled his mustache again.

Briggs was annoyed. This was important business, and Jourdan was behaving like a dog in heat. It was enough. They could make puppies later.

"Where can we find this Roscoe?" Briggs interrupted with a sense of urgency.

Lucette turned toward him. The blank look on her face told him she didn't know.

"Think," he pressed her. "It's very important."

After a moment, her face brightened. "It might take some time, but I'm certain I can furnish you with his whereabouts."

"Excellent," he said, commending her. "But for now, let's keep this between us."

Now part of the same conspiracy, they all smiled. Underneath his smile, Briggs was hoping Lucette and Jourdan's relationship would last long enough for her to lead them to Roscoe. If not, he was sure this trollop would blab everything she knew all over Brooklyn.

∼

Mary didn't stray far from Eastside Imports. She had no doubt Mortimer was hiding something. He most probably knew Roscoe, maybe also knew where he was and might even be involved himself. She had frightened him, and she hoped it was enough to send him running to Roscoe. Hiding in a storefront doorway across the street, waiting to see if her strategy worked, she didn't have to wait long.

About fifteen minutes after she had left him, Mortimer exited the shop, put up the CLOSED sign, and locked the door. He looked around uneasily and then headed up the street.

Mary smiled. Mortimer couldn't have behaved more suspiciously. He was actually rather comical. She followed him from across the street at a distance. He stopped periodically and looked around, obviously trying to see if he was being followed. Mary would duck into a doorway or behind a carriage, and he detected nothing. Then a trolley passed him, and he started to run for it. Mary quickened her pace, too.

Waiting in an alley, watching the cat-and-mouse game, was Samuel. It wasn't easy for a man his size to be invisible, but he'd had practice. Just like he had been given orders earlier to follow Goodrich, he had been instructed to keep an eye on this situation. As always, he was given the freedom to act if necessary. It was time.

Samuel emerged from the alley and collided with Mary.

"Excuse me, madam," he apologized in his thick German accent.

Mary needed to catch up with Mortimer and couldn't stop for pleasantries. As she hurried her way around him, Samuel extended his massive arms and grabbed her. She struggled to get free but to no avail. With one hand over her

mouth, he dragged her into the alley while whispering an edict in her ear.

"The Goodrich case is over for you. Now!"

With that Samuel squeezed her, cutting off her air supply until she lost consciousness. When he let go, Mary's limp body fell to the ground like a rag doll.

15

Waking after being unconscious can be an excruciating experience. It was decidedly better than the alternative, but Mary hardly had that thought in mind. A throbbing, sharp pain shot through her head, feeling like an arrow dividing her brain, and a debilitating nausea made it hard for her to focus. Slowly, other senses started to return. The morning light pierced her eyes, and she slowly opened them to find herself staring at a decaying ceiling with chipped paint. It took a while for her to process that she was indoors. Then the cold registered. It came from the hard surface beneath her. She slid her hands across it. It was cement. Groggy, Mary sat up. A cockroach ran across her leg, but that did little to rouse her. She casually swatted it away. It was the sight of the iron bars that shocked her into full consciousness.

Mary was in a jail cell. How she had gotten there, what she had done to get there, was a mystery. She had a hazy memory of being extremely giddy mixed with bouts of fear, yet her recollection was very dreamlike and certainly vague. Mary's senses came alive, and she noticed there was an

awful stench. She sniffed around and discovered it was her! To say she smelled like a bar minimized it. It was more like a bar floor the morning after a busy night.

She heard giggling and turned to see two women sitting against the back wall. Judging from their dress, she concluded they were prostitutes. Their lack of cleanliness led her to believe they weren't getting much for their services, but that didn't stop them from having a grand old time kissing and fondling one another.

"Care to join us, sweetie?" one of them asked Mary, and they both laughed, showing their rotted teeth. It wasn't a genuine invitation, but they reveled in the shock value it might have with this very establishment-looking young lady. It was hard to shock Mary, but that was soon to happen. She heard a tapping on the bars and turned. It was Chief Campbell.

"A rather auspicious beginning, eh, Mary?"

He was there to get her out, but her embarrassment at facing him almost made staying in jail with her two new friends a viable alternative. Almost.

Chief Campbell and Mary left in his carriage. They sat on opposite sides as far apart as possible, due in part to her shame but more to her strong odor. The chief told Mary what had happened. An officer had discovered her stumbling out of an alley, reeking of wine.

"You were screaming that snakes were attacking you, and then you passed out. A sad example to set for the Brooklyn Police Department," he said.

Mary couldn't explain her behavior, but she vehemently denied any drinking and told Chief Campbell of her encounter with the large German. He listened, nodding his head

periodically, occasionally asking a question for clarification but not indicating whether he believed her or not. After she was done, he picked up an empty bottle that was next to him on the seat.

"This was in the alley near where you were found." Then he sniffed the opening, crinkling his face in distaste. "If one were to judge by aroma alone, it's a match."

When he handed her the bottle, she simply stared at it, somewhat dumbfounded. Then she noticed the label. Suddenly, she became animated as she pointed to it.

"This proves I was set up, Chief," she practically shouted. "This is Vin Mariani. It's a coca wine, and cocaine's supposed to energize you, not rob you of consciousness."

The chief considered what she said, then nodded. "That's a valid point, Mary."

Mary breathed a sigh of relief, but her relief was short-lived.

"So," he continued, "either the wonder drug is no wonder or you were overmatched and ill suited to perform your duties. Which would you like me to believe?"

He was right. She had been careless and let the excitement of the chase distract her. Mary wouldn't let that happen again. But she knew better than to make that promise. She would have to show him with her deeds.

They rode the rest of the way in silence. When the carriage arrived at Second Street Station, Chief Campbell alighted, closed the door, and then turned to Mary.

"My carriage will take you home."

As Mary thanked him, her gaze soon wandered to the police station steps. A dummy wearing a thin black dress and a police hat was lying on them. An empty wine bottle

was attached to it, as was a note written in large letters that read, PARIS CHIC BROOKLYN COP. Mary winced.

"The men despise me enough as it is."

Chief Campbell picked up the dummy and turned to her.

"You can seek redemption next Wednesday night at Clancy's Bar, our monthly morale booster." Chief Campbell saw her dubious look and continued. "It's mandatory for all my 'boys,' Mary. Maybe you can give them pointers on hoisting a few."

He climbed the steps with the dummy. Mary sat back, but there would be no respite. Amanda Everhart had been waiting for Mary's return and rushed up to the carriage. She knew how demoralizing an event like the one Mary had experienced could be and wanted to encourage her to be tenacious.

"We know they're trying to discredit you, sister, but take heart—" That's as far as she got. The odor emanating from the carriage overwhelmed and repulsed her. "For God's sake, woman, if you have no respect for yourself, at least show some for your gender," she chastised Mary. "No matter how depraved your inclinations, you have a responsibility not to drag us into the sewer. The future of women in this city depends on you." After a stern look, Amanda Everhart marched off.

Mary had no desire to be the image of the Brooklyn Police Department or to be the torchbearer for femininity. She simply wanted to be a detective, but no variation of "simple" applied to her situation. She would have to learn to manage it better. She sagged in her seat, weighed down by the responsibilities thrust upon her, then took a deep breath and

signaled the driver to move on. She was going home to take a bath.

Bathing was not a simple ritual. Mary was fortunate her small tenement apartment had a sink with running cold water and a toilet in the hall. Many didn't. Waiting on line to use the toilet was much better than braving an outhouse on a cold winter's night. Bathtubs, though, were a luxury out of her reach. A bathtub attached to indoor plumbing was limited mostly to the very wealthy and to luxury hotels. Most people bathed infrequently, sometimes very infrequently. Rumors spread that regular bathing made a person more susceptible to disease. The scare of cholera and typhoid epidemics gave credence to those rumors, but the truth was that bathing was difficult and time-consuming. And odor wasn't an issue. People were used to it. Some would try to cover up with perfumes, but most, even elite ladies and gentlemen, would just stink.

Mary was an exception. She enjoyed bathing—not the lengthy, arduous process but the feeling she had at the end of being clean. It was as if she had washed the dirt of an imperfect world off of her. She had a large tin tub that, when not in use, she leaned against the wall under the only window in her apartment, not far from the sink. It was light, manageable, and just big enough to sit in. She'd fill it partway with cold water from the sink. Then she'd heat up pots of water on the stove and keep heating and pouring until the temperature was bearable. After the bath, she'd drag the tub to the window and use a pot to ladle the used water out into the back alley. Once the tub was light enough to lift, she would pour the rest out.

When Mary got undressed, she spotted a mark on her right arm and soon realized it was the result of a hypodermic needle injection. It enabled her to finally deduce what had happened. She had read in one of her scientific journals that the nausea and headache she had experienced along with her bizarre behavior, hazy memory, and extreme fatigue were consistent with the effects of a morphine overdose. The large German must have injected her after he had knocked her out. However, the answers to who he was and why he wanted her off the Goodrich case still eluded her.

In spite of what had transpired, Mary's bath proved to be invigorating. After it, she was ready to charge forward with the investigation no matter what obstacles were put in her way and in spite of the obligations that were placed upon her. But good feelings can be fleeting.

She returned to Eastside Imports and found it vacant except for a couple of items and empty crates left from a hasty move. She then checked moving companies. None of them had been hired. Mortimer, possibly Roscoe, and whoever might be helping them, must have moved their inventory by themselves during the twenty-four hours or so Mary had been incapacitated. Mary's one lead had gone cold.

16

Senator Conkling had finally died, succumbing to the ill-
ness he contracted after venturing out during the Great
White Hurricane. The former New York senator was a
popular figure, and normally his passing would have been
headline news, but not that day. What pushed it aside were
the dubious adventures of a young female detective. CASE
OVERWHELMS HANDLEY was the headline of the *Brooklyn Daily
Eagle,* among similar headlines in other papers. It was written in big block letters that consumed half of the front page.
Underneath was a photograph of Mary passed out in a police officer's arms as he carried her into the police station.
Reproducing photographs in newspapers was in its infancy.
It was more expensive than the artists' drawings normally
used, and yet whenever Mary was involved, the newspapers
decided the expense was worthwhile. And it was. The evening edition of the *Eagle* sold out in record time.

Mary sat with the *Eagle* at a booth in Longdon's, a modest restaurant in Brooklyn where people of lesser means
could dine reasonably. She held the newspaper high to avoid

being ogled. It was to no avail. She could feel stares penetrating through the newspaper. It gave her a modicum of relief that three men at a nearby table were drunk and rowdy,
thereby deflecting some attention. She also took some solace
in knowing it was Friday, and she was missing the ritual
dinner at her parents' house. She cringed imagining what
kind of hell her mother would have put her through.

The last thirty-six hours had been eventful in her young
career as a detective, mostly in a negative sense. After failing to find Mortimer, she had tried to see Nikola Tesla, the
other name in Goodrich's date book for that fateful day,
but Tesla couldn't meet with her until Monday. She then
proceeded to J. P. Morgan's mansion, hoping to ask him a
few questions. Morgan's butler informed her that Morgan
was having cocktails and would contact her when he was
available. He shut the door in her face without giving her a
chance to respond. The next day she was due to take yet another trip to West Orange to meet with Edison, though she
had no faith he would keep the appointment. She wondered
if she was being taken lightly because she was a woman or
if the wealthy and influential always got such preferential
treatment. She doubted a poor, uneducated person would be
able to avoid interrogation. She made a mental note to ask
Chief Campbell at the proper time, when he wasn't disappointed in her.

Mary had no intention of putting the newspaper down.
In order to thwart the curiosity seekers, she was determined to read it from beginning to end and then again. In
the middle of the first section, around page ten, there was a
tiny article in the lower right corner with a small headline
that read, CHINESE LABOR LEADER SLAIN. She casually glanced

at it, and that's when the name Wei Chung jumped out at her. This couldn't be her Wei Chung. The Chungs she knew lived in San Francisco. She frantically scanned the article, hoping it was merely a bizarre coincidence. When she read that Xin was also killed and that they had a daughter, Tina, who was a teacher in San Francisco, there was no escaping it. Mary's heart filled with sadness and despair. What kind of animal would kill such wonderful people? Her thoughts went to Tina. She couldn't fathom the enormity of what she was feeling. It made her own troubles seem minuscule. She put the newspaper down. Let the gawkers have their day. Three innocent people had been murdered: Goodrich, Wei, and Xin. That's what mattered. Nothing else.

After a few minutes, Charles entered. She was glad to see him.

"Sorry, delayed at the office," he said as he slid into the booth next to her.

"You don't have a job."

"I would've been delayed if I did. I'm a hard worker."

"And what exactly do you want to do?"

"I'm wavering between becoming a rag man and president of the United States. But since I have no discernible talents, I'm leaning toward the latter."

Mary shook her head and smiled. Charles was charming and entertaining, but he seemed determined to avoid any discussion relating to his personal ambitions. She saw the pain in his eyes flash ever so briefly before he resumed his evasive tactics.

"Hopefully, my hidden talents will surface as yours have." He pointed to the headline on the *Brooklyn Daily Eagle*.

"A minor bump in the road," she said. "I'm fully recovered." And Mary started to relate her experience. When she got to the point where Samuel grabbed her, Charles interrupted. He looked directly into her eyes. On this topic, he was completely earnest.

"Mary, you're bold, you're beautiful, and you're brash, all qualities that make you extremely attractive. They also make you an easy target. Please be careful."

Moved by his concern, Mary gently touched his hand. They spent dinner immersed in conversation. Charles was sympathetic and supportive as Mary told him about her heartache over the Chungs and her frustrations with her job. Eventually, she got to a problem she thought she'd never solve: her mother.

"Sometimes I wish I was the person she wants me to be," Mary confessed, "so that she would accept me, and I could be happy. I'm afraid I'm going to have that feeling the rest of my life, the feeling of falling short."

"Mary, you're living your dream now," Charles responded. "If you concentrate on the naysayers, you might miss precious moments of it." He gave his father as an example. "He's still longing for the type of opportunity you already have."

Mary was grateful for his words. She listened as he talked about his father's obsessive belief in Coca-Cola. Charles thought his chances for success were minute, but he desperately wanted it to happen for him.

A couple of hours later, when Mary and Charles left Longdon's, the three drunken men who had been sitting near them in the restaurant were down the block in the middle of a scuffle. Two of the men were restraining the

third, but Mary and Charles paid little attention to them. They were engrossed in each other.

"You'll never pry Coca-Cola's secret ingredient from my lips," Charles declared, purposely being overdramatic. "I'll go to my grave before I ever reveal that it's cocaine." He faked a shocked gasp. "Well, now you know."

"Yes, I do, and I will guard your secret with my life," said Mary, playing along. "But somehow I think the name betrays its secret."

"Nonsense. How could you ever get 'cocaine' from . . . ? My God, you're right!"

They both laughed, and their eyes met. Charles was leaning in for their first kiss when, out of the blue, a gunshot rang out and a bullet shattered the window next to Mary's head. She whirled around to see who it was.

"Mary, get down!" Charles shouted. "Get down!"

Another shot was fired. Charles threw her to the pavement, then jumped on top of her to shield her, and as he did, two more shots hit the building above them.

Mary looked up. By then the three drunks had run off. She saw a man across the street putting his pistol away before ducking into a nearby livery stable. It was Samuel.

"It's the same ape who attacked me!" she exclaimed, promptly rolling out from under Charles and springing to her feet. Holding her dress up to make moving easier, she charged across the street.

"Don't be insane, Mary. He has a pistol!"

But Mary paid no attention. She was already fearlessly heading for the stable in pursuit of Samuel. Charles mumbled something about her stubbornness, then followed her.

Just as they were arriving at the stable, the doors flung

open, and a horse and buggy galloped out, Samuel at the reins.

"There he is!" Mary screamed, then frantically looked around, trying to decide on her next move. A trolley had just come to a halt across the street, and Mary ran to it.

"Mary, what are—" But Charles stopped. He had already learned not to question.

The trolley was a horse-drawn omnibus, one of the older ones where the driver sat on a perch on top and he could freely guide it through the streets without the assistance of tracks. It had seats for sixteen passengers around its perimeter with poles in the center for those who stood. Mary climbed up next to the driver, a crotchety, heavyset forty-year-old man.

"Follow that buggy!" she commanded, pointing ahead at Samuel.

The surly trolley driver had never taken orders from his wife, his mother-in-law, or his ugly sister. He certainly wasn't going to take orders from this young woman.

"Says who?" he defiantly replied.

Mary had no time to discuss the matter, especially with someone of his limited understanding. She shoved him off the trolley. As the driver yelled and cursed from the street, Charles caught up with her and alerted the passengers.

"This is an emergency! Everyone out!" No one moved, so he decided to provide the incentive they lacked. "Those who are fascinated by dynamite and enjoy a good explosion are welcome to stay." At that, they all ran past him, making a mad dash for the exit.

Samuel had put enough distance between himself and his pursuers at the stable. There was no longer any need to

press his horse as hard as he had. He was a good, loyal animal who heeded him, certainly much better than any human ever had. Just as he was easing him into a trot, he heard a loud, thundering noise behind him and turned to look.

It was Mary, whip in one hand, reins in the other, standing at the helm of the trolley as it swayed from side to side, guiding the horses pulling it. With the full moon glowing behind her, its light bouncing off the cobblestones, the image she projected rivaled that of Washington Irving's Headless Horseman.

There would be no rest for Samuel's horse. He laid his whip into the animal's hide, urging him to go faster.

Clinging to a pole, Charles felt useless in the empty carriage, and he thought he could be of some help to Mary. The omnibus had paneless windows. He went to the one nearest to the driver and started climbing his way out and up to join Mary on the perch. He was slowly and carefully making progress when the trolley hit a huge hole. The jolt launched him into the air. Mary screamed when she saw him being ejected.

At the last second, he latched on to a small railing on the side of the perch with his left hand. He clung on for dear life, his body flailing about on the side of the trolley as Mary held out the whip.

"Grab it! Come on, grab it!" Mary urged him on.

Charles knew that even if Mary could pull him on board, she would need both hands to do it. That would involve her letting go of the reins, and then the unguided horses might do both of them in. He ignored her plea and carefully inched his fingers up on the railing until he had a firmer grip. Then, using that hand as a base, he threw the rest of his body

toward the perch, hoping to also grasp the railing with his right hand. For his efforts, his body slammed against the side of the trolley. The pain was instantaneous, and though his right hand had grabbed the rail, it slipped off.

"You've got to hold on!" Mary screamed.

Her advice riled him. Did she really believe he'd let go on purpose? Ignoring the pain, he lunged for the rail with his right hand again. This time he was able to hang on!

With both hands firmly on the rail, he climbed his way onto the perch. There he sat, emotionally and physically drained, clinging to the rail and muttering to himself.

"If you're praying," Mary said, "put in a word for me."

"I'm closer with the opposition," replied Charles, pointing downward.

The buggy made a last-minute sharp turn down a narrow street. Following it in the huge trolley would be incredibly dangerous, possibly suicidal.

Charles looked at Mary. "No, Mary, you're not going to—"

But there was never a doubt in her mind. She went for it, pulling hard on the reins. The horses obeyed, barely making the turn, but the trolley didn't. It slammed against a building and almost tipped over, then slowly righted itself.

"We made it! Maybe there is a God!" was Charles's jubilant cry. Then he saw Samuel turn down an even narrower street. "And he's a sadistic shit!"

This time proved too much for the trolley, and it all happened in a matter of seconds. The trolley slammed so violently against a stone building that the loud cracking sound it made was too ominous to ignore. The horses' hitch broke and they galloped off, leaving Mary and Charles still aboard

the trolley, which, still moving forward, was unsteady from the crash and teetering dangerously from side to side. Finally, the trolley completely flipped over, the top smacking into a building before it toppled onto the ground and splintered into pieces.

Charles had been thrown free from the trolley when it tipped over and lay dazed, sprawled out on a pile of garbage that had broken his fall. He soon realized that Mary wasn't next to him. He jumped to his feet and saw her on the sidewalk, unconscious. Panicked, he quickly ran to her and cradled her limp body in his arms.

"Mary. Can you hear me? Mary!" There was no response. Charles held her closer as he tried to figure out where the nearest doctor or hospital was. Then he felt her begin to move.

"Charles?" Mary said as if she were asking but really knew. Then she snapped back to her old self, exclaiming, "That bastard tried to kill me!"

Thrilled and relieved, Charles hugged her, and they held each other tightly.

17

Oddly, Mary woke up feeling well rested, as if nothing of significance had happened the night before. There were no ill effects of being shot at, destroying a trolley, and being knocked unconscious. However, Mary did smell a familiar scent. She smiled, put on her robe, and went to Charles, who was standing over the Franklin stove cooking, his shirt hanging out over his pants.

"I hope you like French toast," he said as he scooped his creation onto plates and put it on the table.

"It had better not be burned. That's my specialty."

"Really, French toast?"

"No, burning it." Mary smiled and Charles looked at her, thinking what a magnificent woman she was. He leaned over and kissed her. She welcomed it. A first kiss is very important. It can either live up to expectations or put a damper on the relationship. Charles's kiss exceeded what Mary had hoped it would be, and she let it linger. When they broke apart, Mary gently patted his cheek.

"Thank you for last night. Your gallantry was far beyond the pale."

And he had been gallant. Insisting she was perfectly fine, Mary had refused to go to the hospital, so Charles had taken her home. He had spent the night on two chairs, his feet propped up on one, making sure she was indeed fine. And now he had cooked her breakfast. This was a man she didn't want to let go.

They were about to sit down to breakfast when there was a knock at her door. Mary froze. Seconds later, there was another knock.

"Aren't you going to—?" Charles started to say.

"Shhh, male visitors aren't allowed," Mary whispered.

"Mary . . . Mary, I know you're in there," called a familiar voice. It was Kate.

Relieved, Mary opened the door, pulled Kate inside, and shut it in a hurry. Before Mary could say a word, Kate unloaded.

"I behaved awfully toward you, Mary. Can you ever forgive me?"

"Forgive you?" Mary replied, incredulous. "I never should have asked you those questions at that time. I was being ridiculously insensitive."

They had just hugged, their spat resolved, when Kate spied Charles over Mary's shoulder.

"This must be your Charles. My Charlie and I never got this far. He was consumed with being a gentleman." Kate somehow managed to be both happy and sad at the same time.

"Luckily, that problem has eluded me," responded Charles.

"But even I was not cad enough to take advantage of Mary in her state." And they told Kate what happened.

Kate reacted with shock. "My father always said a lady should know how to protect herself. You need a weapon, Mary."

"Maybe in Haddonfield," Mary responded, trying to make light of her friend's concern, "where you might encounter a bear on Main Street, but . . ."

"Actually, Mary," Charles chimed in, "that's an excellent suggestion."

Mary was a perfectionist. Unless she felt proficient in an area, she avoided it. And "proficient" to Mary was tantamount to being an expert. She had studied all aspects of detective work for most of her life. She had practiced jujitsu for even longer, but pistols, knives, and all other weaponry were not part of her repertoire.

"Weapons can be used against you," she offered as an excuse. "But I'll have the killer in my sights soon enough."

It was false bravado. Mary was concerned, and Charles knew it.

～

John Pemberton was placing a crumpled piece of paper under the leg of a club chair to stop it from wobbling when Charles entered their boardinghouse room.

"Good morning, son," Pemberton greeted him as he straightened himself. Charles was noticeably on edge, and Pemberton, forever the optimist, thought he could divert his attention and possibly cheer him. "You must be feeling pretty chipper."

Charles responded with a quizzical look.

"Your young damsel finally succumbed to your charms," Pemberton explained.

"Not yet. Fact is, she's quite marvelous." His words not only expressed his great admiration for Mary but also betrayed his own sense of unworthiness.

Charles took a case off the desk and opened it. Inside were hypodermic needles and a vial of liquid. He held up the vial for inspection.

"You've been hitting the morphine rather heavily, Father," he uttered matter-of-factly. "I guess we have to dismiss your theory about cocaine curing the habit."

Put on the defensive, Pemberton replied accordingly. "I was wounded in the war, dear son. What's your excuse?"

Charles filled his needle. "I have no ambition, no confidence, and no shame. I, Father, am the perfect addict."

He sat down on his bed, injected himself, then leaned back, relieved to know that he'd soon be lost in his escape.

Mary was right. Once again, Edison had canceled at the last minute with no regard for her time. Mrs. Embry tried to mitigate the damage her boss had wrought.

"Mr. Edison had an emergency meeting. I assure you, Miss Handley, it was totally unavoidable."

"I need to see him as soon as possible." No matter how strongly Mary uttered those words, she knew it would make no difference. She was powerless in this situation.

"I'll squeeze you in at the earliest possible spot. I guarantee it." They both knew her guarantee was of little value.

Before they could say their good-byes, a man burst through the door. Mary recognized him as Eadweard Muybridge, an odd name and an even odder man. She had seen him on a previous visit being forcibly removed by guards. An Englishman in his late fifties with a long gray beard, Muybridge seemed as off-balance now as he had then.

"Where is he?!" he shouted.

The ever-composed Mrs. Embry replied, "Mr. Edison isn't here, Mr. Muybridge."

The two guards who had disposed of him before and were now in pursuit rushed in. Muybridge immediately raised his hand to stop them.

"No need for mindless thuggery. I'm leaving." He turned once more to Mrs. Embry. "Tell that bloody thieving bastard I'll be back!"

His head held high, trying to salvage whatever dignity he thought he had, Muybridge strutted out with the guards close behind him.

"I'm sorry you had to witness that, Miss Handley. Geniuses like Mr. Edison seem to attract an equal share of the brilliant and the deluded."

"You're being kind, Mrs. Embry. 'Crackpot' seems more appropriate."

Mrs. Embry smiled, tacitly agreeing but knowing full well that verbally acknowledging her accord would give voice to an opinion, something a person of her position was not supposed to have.

As Mary left the complex, she wondered where she fell on Mrs. Embry's scale. She was a woman attempting to do a man's job in a man's world. The "deluded" category seemed

likely. Mary spotted Muybridge out of the corner of her eye sitting on the curb, his back propped up against a lamppost. By keeping her eyes ahead of her and quickening her pace, she hoped to avoid contact. But crackpots pay little attention to others' intentions.

"Be smart," Muybridge called out to Mary. "Leave now while you still have all your fingers and toes."

Mary walked faster, trying harder to ignore him, but he would have none of it. He jumped to his feet and jogged over to her, staying by her side.

"Ask yourself," he shouted, wanting the world to hear. "What kind of fellow steals another man's life? He requests a joint venture, then poof! My zoopraxiscope becomes his kinetoscope. No regrets, not so much as—"

"Sorry, but I need to go," she blurted out curtly, trying to discourage any further conversation.

"What you need," Muybridge declared, matching her step for step, "is to heed my words. Don't think being a woman will protect you. A scoundrel is a scoundrel."

"I have nothing that Mr. Edison could possibly want." She hastened her gait, but he also hastened his.

"Ah, famous last words of the swindled."

Mary finally stopped and faced him. "Look, I'm just here about Charles Goodrich. Now please let me be."

Muybridge strangely transformed before her. His demeanor completely calmed. His voice was genuine and devoid of rant. He actually seemed normal.

"You're the woman working on Charlie's murder?" he eagerly asked. It was the familiarity and warmth with which he referred to Goodrich that got her attention.

"You knew Mr. Goodrich?" she said. Charles Goodrich was a levelheaded man, not the type who befriended crackpots like Muybridge.

"Charlie had the proof I need. Without it, my accusations are just words."

"Proof?"

"Charlie was a stickler for detail. He recorded all of Edison's transactions."

"You mean a journal exists?" Mary was being drawn in deeper with each word. As Lewis Carroll's Alice would say, things were getting "curiouser and curiouser."

Muybridge nodded. "A journal that can expose Thomas Edison for the fraud that he is."

And curiouser.

had only felt it once before, when he was twelve. He had infuriated his mother, a regular occurrence, and she had cornered him at an abandoned well. She grabbed for him, he stepped aside, and she fell into the well. A month later when she had passed away, after having caught typhoid from the contaminated water in the well, the Bowler Hat went into their barn and there, amid the farm animals, he bawled like a little baby. He despised himself for being so weak, and he swore that it would never happen again. Yet, here it was.

He forced the sadness deep down inside of him, willing it to never come back. Feelings led to mistakes. He had already made too many of those, and he had to deal with his present situation.

Purportedly, his employers had arranged a temporary job for him, so he could earn a living while he was "mending." But what did it take to make promises? His knowledge of his employers' activities made him too great a risk to just be cast aside. He knew of others who had been deemed no longer useful and were eliminated. One was removed by his wife while making love, another by an usher at the opera, in the middle of *Don Giovanni,* for God's sake. Anything was possible.

The Bowler Hat looked around the park. There were couples walking arm in arm, people riding bicycles and high-wheel tricycles, and others seemingly just enjoying the beautiful spring weather. Everything looked innocent enough, but he knew better. It was at times like these, when the subject felt comfortable, that a really good assassin struck. And they would have to send their best to eliminate him.

The Bowler Hat rose. Any number of men could come at him, and he had to be ready. As he walked, he sensed

18

The Bowler Hat sat quietly on a bench in Central Park. He had just been put on indefinite suspension because he had "failed to handle matters in everyone's best interests."

He had raped a woman and killed a Chinese labor leader and his wife, but those words would never be spoken. It was business and would be handled with business vernacular. Besides, "publicity" was the dirty word, not "violence." Several Chinese workers had reported seeing a white man who fit the Bowler Hat's description by the Chungs' cabin at the time of the murders. That wasn't the concern. The word of a few Chinamen would never convict a white man. But should that information get in the hands of a crusading newspaperman, the "wheels of justice" might be forced into motion no matter how well they had been paid to remain still.

The Bowler Hat didn't take suspension lightly. He viewed it as tantamount to a death sentence. He loved his work and didn't know what he would do without it.

While he was thinking these thoughts, a strange sensation surged through him. He recognized it as sadness. He

danger all around him. There was a man sitting on a bench with a picnic basket, a basket that could easily contain weapons. Another man was pushing a baby carriage. It was suspicious. Only women did that. Then he saw a portion of a black derby hat through a large bush. Why was it not moving? Was the man lining him up in his sights? The Bowler Hat felt trapped. He suddenly started running, not just running but sprinting.

When he was safely outside the park and had stopped to catch his breath, the Bowler Hat began to realize that maybe his employers were right. Maybe he did need time to mend.

19

Mary's first stop after her encounter with Muybridge
was Charles Goodrich's brownstone. She had previously
searched it and so had the Brooklyn police. No one had
found anything they deemed relevant. She didn't remember
coming across a journal, though if someone had, it might
have easily been passed over. Charles Goodrich was a bookkeeper. It was only natural he would have logged numbers
and transactions. Muybridge seemed earnest enough, but
Mary gave little credence to his claim that those figures
would besmirch the pristine reputation of Thomas Edison.
Muybridge had an air of desperation about him, of a man
grasping at straws. Taking him at his word would be a giant
leap of faith. It would also make Edison a suspect, and the
whole notion of Thomas Edison's being a murderer was not
only absurd but anathema to her.

Mary did realize there could be many other reasons why
such a journal would be in demand. Even if the journal didn't
exist, the rumor that it did was a dangerous one. A man of
Edison's phenomenal success was bound to have business

rivals out to ruin him, and if he didn't, a good old-fashioned blackmailer would view the journal as a money machine. It didn't matter if Charles Goodrich had such information or not. Any refusal to cooperate could have been considered hostile, and it could have easily hastened his demise.

So far, searching the Goodrich brownstone a second time had turned up nothing new. Mary was in his office, rummaging around in his desk drawers, when the steamer trunk in front of the couch caught her eye. An image of it from her last visit drew her to the trunk. She lifted the lid. It was empty—as it had been before. This time she noticed something odd, though, and she chastised herself for not having detected it before. Searching the steamer, feeling around with her hands, Mary eventually found a small lever camouflaged by a luggage strap. When she turned it, the bottom popped up. Mary removed it, revealing a new bottom containing a lone book pressed against the right side of the trunk wall. She snatched it up and eagerly started leafing through it.

"Good work, Miss Handley. I never would have suspected the steamer trunk." Mary looked up. The voice belonged to a bony man of medium height. He was smiling, and she immediately pegged it as false bravado. He wasn't comfortable being there, and his clothes suggested that if he was a criminal, he wasn't very successful at it. She didn't think he would provide much trouble, but there was one complication. He was pointing a pistol at her.

"It makes perfect sense," she coolly and calmly explained. "A man of Mr. Goodrich's impeccable taste would never have a steamer trunk in his study, unless he had something of value hidden there." Her eyes fell on an ashtray

situated on the end of the desk. She slowly made her way toward it and closer to the bony man.

"Hand over the journal. And leave the ashtray where it is," he said with a cocky smirk. "That old trick won't work on me."

"Really? How about this one?"

Mary tossed the book at the bony man, and he hastily closed his arms to catch it. The pistol was now pointing away from her. She lunged for him, grabbed his hand, and twisted it, causing him to drop the pistol. She then elbowed him in the face. The bony man was both stunned and scared. A woman had tricked and overpowered him. It was too much. Clutching the book, he ran out. Mary didn't hesitate. She lit out after him.

Out on the street, Mary found herself severely hampered by her clothes. Unencumbered, pant-aided men had a distinct advantage over women in any footrace. The bony man was using that to his full advantage as he put more distance between them with each stride. Mary was frustrated. A lady walking her dog was shocked to see Mary stop, kick off her shoes, and shimmy her petticoat off. The lady protectively picked up her dog, as if Mary's insanity might be contagious. Feeling freer, Mary scooped up her things and took off again in her stocking feet, able to run much faster and more easily.

Still ahead by a large margin, the bony man slowed as he turned the corner. He knew there was no way she could catch him. It was rather comical the way she had feebly run after him. He smiled, then chuckled and broke into a full-throated laugh. He didn't notice Samuel until the huge man's powerful fist landed on his chin, instantly knocking him out.

Samuel despised incompetence. He shook his head at the pathetic thief, then grabbed the book and disappeared.

When Mary rounded the corner, shoes and petticoat in tow, she was tugging at her corset, trying to get some relief as she gasped for air. She saw the bony man on the sidewalk, the book nowhere in sight. As he started to gain consciousness, she leaned over him.

"Who are you?" she demanded, but he was in another world, thinking his grandmother was yelling at him. "I said, who are you?!"

"William Leeds," he replied before slowly realizing Grandma had been dead for a decade.

"Yes, yes, and?" Mary wasn't being specific, but Leeds knew what she wanted. He had practice being caught, and he had already capitulated.

"Nikola Tesla hired me to get the journal."

"I owe you a debt, Mr. Leeds, for allowing me to utter words I've wanted to say all my life—you're under arrest."

Bringing in her first arrest didn't earn Mary the respect she needed at Second Street Station. After all, William Leeds was no John Wilkes Booth or even a savvy bunco artist like Hungry Joe Lewis. True, a few eyebrows were raised, but Chief Campbell hardly paused on his way out as Mary entered with Leeds. He did break his stride though. That was something—for him. What Mary had that nobody else knew of was better than her first arrest. She had a new lead.

Her meeting with Nikola Tesla had been set for Monday. It was now Saturday, but it couldn't wait. She found Tesla

at a warehouse on the lower west side of Manhattan, not far from the water. Except for his reputation as a young, eccentric genius, she knew little about him.

She hadn't met Tesla at Governor Hill's Salute to Thomas Edison, but she had recognized him from the scientific journals she regularly read. He stood in the middle of the large, almost empty warehouse barking orders at men who were carrying in large crates. He was trying to be patient, but he had the tone of a man who was sure that at any moment some nitwit was going to ruin his day.

"In the corner"—he motioned to one of the men carrying a crate—"and be careful."

Mary took note of Tesla's combustible nature and approached him carefully.

"Nikola Tesla?" she asked tentatively.

Tesla was about to respond when a loud crash was heard in the far part of the warehouse. He froze for a moment, as if realizing the expected ineptitude of others had finally struck.

"I said careful!" he shouted as he abruptly spun around in the direction of the crash. He then turned back to Mary. "All I want is for the equipment not to be broken. Is that too much to ask?"

Mary ignored his question. "I'm Mary Handley. I'm working on the Goodrich murder. We were supposed to meet on Monday, but something—"

"That's right," he cut her off. "You're the woman they hired." He paused briefly, then shook his head. "Catching the killer must be a low priority."

Trying not to take the bait, Mary showed no reaction.

"You might be interested in whom I did catch—a Mr. William Leeds."

This stopped Tesla, but another crash soon stole his attention. He turned.

"What in God's name is your problem?!" When he turned back, he saw Mary patiently waiting for his response. He sighed. "What did Leeds do?"

"For starters, breaking and entering and armed robbery."

Tesla shook his head. "That's what happens when you have limited funds. You're forced to hire imbeciles."

"So you admit hiring him?" Mary was surprised.

"Yes, but not to steal. Just to locate, only locate . . . something."

"Charles Goodrich's journal?"

Tesla looked startled. "You know about it?"

"Your plan failed. The book Mr. Leeds stole was taken from him."

"Damn it! That means they have it!" As if punctuating his explosion, another loud crash was heard at the other end of the warehouse. In a flash, he was heading for it, motioning for Mary to come with him.

"I'm demonstrating my AC system tomorrow," he explained, then stared daggers at the men carrying his crates. "That is, if everything's still in one piece!" He turned back to Mary. "I'm sure Thomas Edison and J. P. Morgan are not thrilled about the competition. Billions are at stake. Those two would throw their mothers on the fire for much less, and Charlie was a mere bookkeeper."

They arrived at the crate that had been dropped. Tesla

opened and inspected it as the man who had carried it looked on and Mary responded, her words full of disbelief.

"You're not suggesting Thomas Edison—"

"I know," Tesla interrupted. "Not our all-American boy, the brilliant inventor of the lightbulb." He nodded to the man that the contents were all right, and the man carted it off.

"In spite of your sarcasm, it's the truth," she said pointedly.

Tesla laughed. "It's all a gigantic ruse. Thomas has a unique arrangement. His scientists do the inventing, and he gets the credit."

"So the journal would soil his image and propel you into the electricity game?"

"All I want is a fair chance to compete. Charlie knew that. He wanted to help me. 'Correct all the wrongs,' he said. But none of this matters now. They have the journal, and I'm going to jail."

Tesla held out his hands for Mary to cuff them. Mary paused as she studied him. He was a strange man, possessing an odd combination of attributes. Emotional and bombastic, he could fit the bill for a murderer without stretching logic. Yet he seemed honest almost to a fault and thoroughly incapable of deception. She couldn't help being charmed by the little boy in him who didn't understand the world and railed at its inequities. Still, none of it mattered. Arresting Nikola Tesla at this point was not an option.

"Mr. Leeds admitted stealing the journal was solely his idea," she said.

"An honest thief," he replied, surprised that fate was

giving him a break. "My God, he's a bigger imbecile than I thought."

"The book that was taken was a Bible—an old one, valuable, but not the journal."

Tesla finally realized she had been toying with him to extract information. Instead of being angry, he applauded.

"Bravo, Miss Handley. The money. Follow it, and you'll find Charlie's killer."

Mary considered Tesla's words as she left the warehouse. Her list of suspects was expanding instead of narrowing. There was Roscoe, and no matter what her instincts were, the facts showed that Tesla had to be added, along with his business partner George Westinghouse. Also, in spite of her feelings, she now had to include Edison. He had been mentioned twice. And if Edison was a possibility, so was his partner J. P. Morgan. The way things were going, her list would soon include President Grover Cleveland. Actually, some of these men were more powerful than the president. That should have made Mary very cautious, but she was mostly concerned with justice being served. Her concern rang of idealism, and idealists make excellent victims.

20

He was a very important man. No one with this kind of wealth was unimportant. He hadn't told her his name. He looked familiar, but she couldn't place him and he was hardly forthright. Some men enjoyed projecting an air of mystery. It was fine with her. She liked games. What she didn't like was that he was distracted. A problem was weighing on his mind. With a man of his stature, it could be various concerns. They weren't hers though.

Sighing, she looked out the window. Westchester County was an eerie place. Dark, not a flicker of light, and the quiet—she hated the quiet. So this was the country everyone raved about. They could have it. She loved the city with its constant sound of human voices. Laughing, crying, screaming—it was life. She missed the trolleys and carriages rolling by, the chanting of pushcart peddlers, the music emanating from the tavern below her apartment. The only sign of life outside here was the chirping of crickets. It was a grating noise that made her skin crawl.

Trying to encourage him, she flipped back her hair with

one hand and stretched out on the bed. One breast discreetly fell out of her negligee. It was no accident.

On the telephone in mid-conversation, he noticed her new position. Being the sort of man he was, he didn't change his expression. But she knew men, and she knew his interest was definitely piqued.

"You shouldn't have called me here about the Handley woman." He spoke in clipped tones, visibly perturbed. "Her stopping by again is irrelevant. She's of no import. None, do you hear me?" He returned the telephone to its cradle, then stepped toward her, sucking in his stomach and pushing out his chest.

Men were men. No matter how much he paid her, he wanted this woman to desire him. It was her job to convince him that she did. She had once wanted to become an actress, and it had often crossed her mind that she had become one. Slowly and sensuously, she slithered to the side of the bed where he was standing.

"You're an amazing man," she cooed, her voice dripping with false desire. She put her hand on his thigh and gently caressed it. "Brilliant, successful, handsome."

She worked her hand way up and . . . nothing. Limp.

This was the first time he had noticed her strong perfume, and it repulsed him. He looked forward to these Sunday-night trysts in his Westchester pied-à-terre, but this one was not going well. He made a mental note to fire the new man he had hired to handle delicate matters like these. True, he desired common, lusted after common, but this woman didn't have the touch. It was unfortunate, because he needed a diversion now. He was worrying about business, and that was not like him. He despised worriers.

She saw that she was losing him and thus her big pay-day. She had to think fast.

"I'm sorry. I do go on sometimes when I'm nervous. You see, I'm not often in the presence of such a prominent man, a man who is always in command."

"Really." He scoffed and stepped away from her.

"You don't feel it, do you?"

"Feel what?" He was ready to call it a night.

"Your power. Ordinary people like me can. We feed off it." His look told her she had his interest again. *So that's what he likes,* she thought. *He's one of those.* She needed to be humble, fawning, and reverent. She could do that, and do it well. "We try to stay close, hoping some way, somehow, it'll rub off on us."

"And how will that happen, pray tell?" Bemused, he stepped back toward her.

"Please don't laugh. It's all some of us have." Once again he was close to her, and she wrapped her hand around his thigh. Her voice got breathier and began to build in intensity. "Countless numbers depend on you. Their lives hang on your every word. People listen. Heed. Fear. And where does that leave us? In awe; in awe of your amazing, forceful, unyielding dominance."

She felt him, and this time he was ready. Not just ready, eager. In no time he was on top of her, spurred on by her moans of ecstasy. They weren't real, but they were convincing. Now he wanted her. He craved her. And she knew.

"Give me all your power," she demanded breathlessly between moans. "I want it all!"

He was also breathless, but it was real. "Call me by my name," he ordered her. "Call me J. P."

So that's who he was. She thought he looked familiar. The great J. P. Morgan. She would have laughed if she didn't have a job to do.

"Give it to me, J. P.," she screamed. "Give it all to me!"

~

Delmonico's had been a fixture on Beaver Street at the southern tip of Manhattan for fifty-one years. It provided fine dining and an extensive wine cellar surrounded by a décor of luxurious wood, elegant chandeliers, and tasteful artwork. Successful men who worked nearby were its main clientele, and besides always being a place for a good steak, it was rumored that more business deals were made at Delmonico's tables than up on Wall Street. So it was no surprise that J. P. Morgan chose Delmonico's for a lunch with Thomas Edison.

Morgan's tryst in Westchester the night before had reinvigorated him and given him a new perspective on his dilemma. He was the man with the power. He needed to put the problem on someone else's shoulders and let them worry about pleasing him. Morgan was in a good mood. Soon he would get to unload his burden and toy with Edison, two activities he enjoyed immensely.

Edison sipped a glass of Vin Mariani as Morgan tore into his steak. He was less than thrilled at the lunch invitation. Besides always feeling uncomfortable around Morgan, he knew being summoned by him meant that he wanted something, and Edison couldn't refuse. As expected, Morgan had secluded them in a private booth with the curtain drawn, making Edison a captive audience.

"Consuming a steak makes me feel utterly primal," declared Morgan, chewing vigorously, "as if I killed the beast myself."

"It comes from a cow, J. P. They're raised for slaughter."

"Please allow me my delusions, Tom. Are you sure you don't want to eat?"

"The wine will suffice." The cocaine content of the wine dulled his hunger, and Edison also wanted to get to the point and leave. "I assume this isn't a social lunch."

Morgan didn't break stride as he stuffed more steak into his mouth and chewed through his words. "I have a concern about my investment."

The expenses had been sizable. Morgan was a moneyman, and Edison had already prepared an answer. "I thought the costs might cause some—"

"Costs? Tom, we have a product that's opium to the masses. Once they taste it, they're not able to live without it."

"Sit on our golden throne," Edison agreed, "and charge outrageous fees without a whimper of protest."

"Outrageous is the precise fee I had in mind."

They laughed. Morgan patted his face with his napkin, and Edison took another sip of wine. Though Edison had joined in the frivolity, he was dismayed that, once again, he was unable to read Morgan. Fortunately, that was outweighed by the fact that Morgan was seemingly fine with the flow of money he had been pumping into their project.

"What's the problem then?" Edison asked. "Is it Westinghouse?"

"I can handle George. It's this Tesla fellow. Is his AD system—"

"AC, J. P.," Edison cut in. "It's called an AC system."

"Yes, yes." Morgan dismissed the correction. "Is it really less expensive and more powerful than ours, as he claims?"

It rankled Edison that Morgan knew so little about science, cared even less about it, and yet was going to make millions because of Edison's work. The answer to Morgan's question was a resounding yes, but Edison's ego wouldn't allow him to admit it out loud, and especially not to Morgan.

"It's irrelevant," Edison answered. Surely Morgan knew this. "Once the market is ours, they'll have to meet our terms."

"We're not there yet, and it would be a shame to allow someone in so late in the game. Competition lowers fees, and I'm rather fond of outrageous."

"And you shall have it, J. P. Trust me," Edison said. He boldly raised his glass and toasted Morgan, who, now mollified, dug back into his steak with renewed fervor.

So this is what was bothering J. P. Morgan, Edison thought, then he stretched and relaxed. He had begun planning Tesla's destruction right after his conversation with Governor Hill, starting with the demonstration he had planned for the next day. It was an added bonus that by doing so he also was a rare step ahead of Morgan. Edison smiled broadly, opened the curtain of their booth, sat back, and looked around the room. He decided he liked Delmonico's. He liked it very much.

21

Mary had read about Edison's upcoming demonstration in the newspaper and that it would take place on the day of her next appointment with him. He was going to unveil a new invention that was described as revolutionary, though it was not specified what the invention was or what it would revolutionize. It was obvious that Edison had an element of P. T. Barnum in him and no doubt wanted to ensure a maximum turnout. Mary could already envision the sympathetic look on Mrs. Embry's face as she broke the news that they would have to reschedule. She decided to go to the demonstration and somehow make sure Edison didn't dodge her afterward. At least that was her goal.

The demonstration was to be held on the vast property adjacent to Edison's West Orange laboratory, where he had already broken ground to build factories that would produce his products. When Mary arrived, the crowds had already begun to form, and she found a position somewhere in the middle. There were reporters from every newspaper in

the New York area, along with some who had traveled longer distances. They weren't alone. Spectators from all walks of life had flocked there to see what new miracle Thomas Edison would unfold before them. P. T. Barnum would have been proud. It was indeed a carnival-like atmosphere, the chatter and excitement similar to that of people standing in line to see the Bearded Lady, the Sword Swallower, or the Eighth Wonder of the World. Mary knew that scientists needed to do more than just innovate. Selling financed research. But she couldn't help feeling there was something cheap about the proceedings, more fit for a charlatan than a brilliant inventor.

The crowd stood in front of a raised platform that was blanketed with a large asbestos cover. In the rear, there were two generators, one substantially larger than the other. The larger one was on the left and the smaller on the right. In the center was an object covered with a silk sheet, draped very much like a sculpture before an unveiling.

A man was stationed at each generator, and Batchelor was there to supervise them. Finally, when it was twenty minutes past the scheduled time, when the antsy crowd had worked up enough fervor, Edison arrived in a Marcus car, one of the first passenger vehicles powered by an internal combustion engine. He hopped out of the car and stepped onto the platform, waving to everyone, exhibiting the mark of a true showman. His appearance was met with applause and random shouts of approval. After a short time, he held up his hand, and they eventually quieted.

"I heard there was a rumor about a new invention. Is that why all of you are here?" he asked, his tongue firmly planted in his cheek.

The crowd responded with an overwhelming roar of "Yes!"

"You know what they say about rumors? You should ignore them."

The crowd booed good-naturedly, shouting their protestations.

Edison paused as the reaction built to the desired frenzy, then continued. "But this time you would be wrong to do that." As he walked over to the center object covered with a silk sheet, he said, "For today, you will witness something that is at once revolutionary, utilitarian, and terrifying."

As he removed the sheet, he announced with great flair, "Ladies and gentlemen, I give you the electric chair."

The chair was made of wood with straps for both arms, both legs, and the body. It sat on a metal plate with wires protruding from it. The austere, scary-looking contraption elicited the requisite "oooh"s and "aaah"s from the crowd. Edison picked up a metal headband, also with wires attached to it. He held it above the chair where a person's head might be if that person was sitting in the chair. Gasps were heard from the crowd.

"I wouldn't try placing this chair at your dining room table," he joked, and nervous laughter erupted. Then Edison became very serious. "Our most heinous criminals will meet their ends here. Good riddance, I say."

Loud murmurs of agreement echoed his sentiment. Mary marveled at Edison's manipulation of the crowd. It impressed and disgusted her at the same time.

Edison patted the chair. "No need to fear this one yet. It is merely a model built by Tom Brown under my auspices and will be fueled by AC current."

A hand shot up from a reporter upfront. He didn't wait to be acknowledged.

"Mr. Edison, isn't AC current Mr. Westinghouse's brand?"

"Ah, the *New York Times,* always very astute and often lacking in manners." After a round of laughter, including the reporter's own chuckle, Edison continued. "Yes, AC is my competitor's brand. But Thomas Edison always provides the very best product, and AC has clear advantages here."

He motioned to Batchelor, who in turn signaled behind the platform. One by one, two men entered from a plank on the rear side, each escorting a calf on a rope. Edison went to the larger generator and was handed a rod attached to a wire by the man who was standing there. He held it up.

"This rod is attached to my DC generator."

In an unexpected move, Edison touched one of the calves with the rod. A shocked hush ran through the crowd as the calf's knees buckled. Then it whimpered, shook, and finally pissed. Mary was disturbed by Edison's willingness to harm an animal for the purpose of a press demonstration, but he wasn't finished.

Without hesitation, he took a rod from the man next to the smaller generator.

"This rod," he announced as he lifted the rod above the second calf, "is attached to the Westinghouse AC generator."

The crowd was transfixed as Edison placed the rod against the second calf. The calf emitted a deathly cry. In a matter of seconds it caught on fire. This was much worse. Screams emanated from the crowd as they watched the calf burn alive. Then, in complete agony, it fell to the ground and died. People were more than shocked. They were horrified.

Some were wobbly, on the verge of fainting. The total silence that had engulfed West Orange was shortly broken by sounds of vomiting.

Mary was sickened. Surely a man of science could have found a way to display his work without employing such abject cruelty. But Edison was seemingly unfazed.

"It's extremely clear which current is better suited for the electric chair," he said with a modicum of deference to the recently departed calf. "However, we need to ask which calf represents the current we want in our homes. This one"—he pointed to the first calf; it was still woozy but very much alive—"or the one that was Westinghoused?"

Smiling, Edison pointed to the second calf's charred remains.

As Mary entered Edison's outer office area, she was reassessing her estimation of him. His feet of clay had become evident, but the leap to murder was still a giant one. She couldn't draw that conclusion from the facts she had, though she no longer rejected the possibility. There was still much information to be gathered, and speaking with him had become a must.

When Mrs. Embry began to assume her apologetic pose, Mary paid absolutely no attention to her and headed straight for Edison's office.

"Miss Handley, you can't . . . !" exclaimed the shocked Mrs. Embry.

Mary was already at Edison's door. She opened it and charged in as Mrs. Embry scrambled after her.

Upon entering, Mary saw Edison hunched over a rectangular boxlike object about four feet high that was made out of wood. He seemed to be peering into some sort of viewer. "Mr. Edison," she began, prompting him to straighten and turn toward her. But Mrs. Embry had entered directly after Mary.

"She just burst right in, Mr. Edison," the dumbfounded Mrs. Embry apologized, speaking with the fear of an employee who was about to be chastised.

Mary didn't want that to happen. "Mrs. Embry did her best to stop me, but I had no choice. I have a job to do, Mr. Edison, and it requires your participation."

"Oh yes . . . Miss Handley," Edison said, apparently so wrapped up in his work that he had forgotten about the appointment and possibly, for a moment, who Mary was. "It's all right, Mrs. Embry."

He nodded to her, and she left. Mary had decided to continue following the chief's advice. She would try to put Edison at ease by beginning their conversation with something nonthreatening. It wasn't difficult, because no matter what Edison might have done, she was still very interested in his work.

"May I ask what that is?" Mary said, indicating the rectangular object.

Edison beckoned to her. "Come, take a look, Miss Handley."

Mary walked over and peered into the viewer. What she saw was a small black-and-white image of a man eating ice cream . . . and the picture moved! The man was chewing, smiling, and turning his head from side to side. He looked very lifelike.

"My Lord, what is this?" Mary was genuinely impressed.

"Simply a man eating ice cream," Edison replied.

Mary stood up, and her look told him she really wanted to know.

He smiled and patted the machine. "It's in the early stages of development. I intend to add my sound technology to it, but I call it the Edison Kinetoscope."

Mary immediately recognized the name from her conversation with Muybridge.

"Why, it's amazing, truly amazing," she said, and it was, so it took very little acting for her to say the words.

"What it is," Edison explained, "is a better and cheaper way for people to spend their leisure time. Helping others is my true reward." He conjured up the proper pious yet modest expression. However, considering what she'd just witnessed at his demonstration and what she had heard about him, Mary found it less than credible.

"You are a great humanitarian, Mr. Edison," she declared. "I mean, who cares if Eadweard Muybridge claims he invented this device before you did."

Edison paused, then smiled, trying to act amused. "He does, does he?"

"Yes. Calls it the zoopraxiscope. Sounds downright animalistic if you ask me."

Mary laughed, and Edison joined in as he took a bottle of wine and two glasses from a nearby cabinet, stalling for time to assess whether this woman was crafty or just plain dumb.

"You'll find, Miss Handley, that inventors are insanely territorial. If a mere thought crosses their minds, they claim that thought as an invention that is theirs in perpetuity."

Mary noticed the label on the bottle and couldn't help wondering if there was a connection with her attack in the alley and the bottle with the same label that was left to defame her. "I see you're a devotee of Vin Mariani."

"Yes. I was hoping you'd join me."

"I've had more than my fill, thank you," she said pointedly.

"Impossible," he exclaimed. "Cocaine's utterly medicinal. It clears cobwebs after being up all night."

"Your long hours are legendary."

"There's no substitute for hard work," he mused before uttering the statement that had become identified with him. "Creativity is one percent inspiration and ninety-nine percent perspiration."

"That doesn't leave much room for acquisition, does it, Mr. Edison?" Mary had finally dropped any pretense. She stared directly at him.

"Is this more of Mr. Muybridge's rubbish?" Edison asked, still trying to assess where this conversation was going.

"Confirmed by Nikola Tesla."

Now he knew. This woman was the enemy. Well, if she wanted to spar, she had picked the wrong partner. He poured himself some wine.

"You're not what I expected, you know," he said.

"First impressions can be misleading."

"Or used to mislead. Tread softly, Mary. You're playing with the big boys now."

"Oh, I see we're on a first-name basis . . . Tommy."

"Rather prickly, eh? It's a shame Chief Campbell hasn't

taught you to mind your words. You see, even I am subject to harmful rumors."

"So roasting calves in order to discredit a competitor is done in self-defense?"

In that instant, quicker than a flash, Edison exploded.

"You impudent little shit!"

He flung the wine bottle against the wall, shattering it, the wine splashing everywhere. His anger seemed out of character and was very scary. Shocked, Mary backed away, but Edison wasn't letting up.

"I'm not some lowly guttersnipe at McGinty's Tavern you can beat at will!" He paused, then nodded smugly. "Yes, I know more about you than your own mother does."

Confused and frightened, Mary stared at him for a moment, taking it all in, until they were interrupted by Mrs. Embry, who came in the room, looking worried.

"What happened, Mr. Edison?"

"An accident, no need to bother," he said, trying to hasten her exit. But the efficient Mrs. Embry headed straight for the mess in order to clean up.

"I said don't bother!" he snapped impatiently. Mrs. Embry was wisely out the door in no time.

Edison finally seemed to realize he had lost control. He sat down on the edge of his desk and rubbed his temples.

"I assure you, Miss Handley"—he spoke now in a modulated voice—"there are easier ways to turn a profit."

Mary was eager to encourage Edison's effort to regain his composure. "Many are envious of your success."

It seemed to work. Edison sounded more disappointed than angry when he said, "Nikola Tesla is an ingrate. I brought him over from Europe to work with some of the

greatest scientific minds in the world, and this is how he repays me."

Hoping Edison's guard was down, Mary jumped right to her case. "And what about Charles Goodrich, is there anyone he might have angered?"

"Goodrich?" Edison shook his head, dismissing him. "I don't like speaking ill of the dead, but the man had no gumption. He was a jellyfish."

"Even jellyfish can sting," she reminded him. "Did you know he kept a journal?" She paused to watch Edison's reaction and saw a glimmer of interest. "In which he recorded everything during his thirteen years working for you—every transaction, every deal."

"First time I heard of it," Edison said, shrugging.

"Well, thank you for your time, sir."

There was nothing more she could do for now. She shook his hand and turned toward the door. He didn't let her get far.

"That journal probably contains important business records," he said a little too casually. "Edison Electric will gladly pay a reward for its recovery."

Mary beamed inwardly. Edison's interest in the journal confirmed its value, whether the journal was real or not.

"No need for a reward. If I find it, I'll return it"—she strategically paused—"after our investigation, of course."

"Of course," he said, his smile forced.

She waved a friendly good-bye and was off.

Edison waited a moment after Mary left, then went back to his cabinet, took out another bottle of Vin Mariani, and poured himself a refill.

What a silly, brash young girl, he thought. Yet the news

she had brought him was troubling. He and Batch would discuss it, and they'd come up with a solution, one that he hoped wouldn't be too radical. He was always under a lot of scrutiny, but with this Tesla and Westinghouse thing, it was more intense than usual. Still, if it called for radical action, so be it.

22

"Thomas Edison! Are you insane?" Charles blurted out.

"Charles." Mary quickly signaled him to lower his voice. They had met for breakfast that Wednesday at a crowded coffeehouse, and she certainly didn't want anyone else to hear what they were discussing.

"Think about what you're saying," he whispered. "You can't go around telling people that Thomas Edison is unstable."

"I'm not telling people. I'm telling you," she said, also speaking in a low voice. "And you weren't there. It was eerie. The man's not right."

"What if he isn't? That doesn't make him a murderer."

"I said he was a suspect, just a suspect. Besides, he would never pull the trigger. People like him never do. They hire someone . . . someone like Roscoe."

"Mary, you know you can't go public with this."

"I know that. I would never consider it without having absolute proof."

"Absolute proof or not," he whispered intensely, alarmed

that she was not aware of the possible consequences, "these are very powerful men. They can destroy you."

"What can they do that hasn't already been done? The articles in the newspapers have ruined my reputation. If I don't do my job properly, I'll certainly return to being an unemployed sweatshop worker. What else—"

"Mary, people have disappeared for a lot less."

Mary looked straight into his eyes. "So you do agree that Thomas Edison could be a murderer?"

Charles sighed, frustrated by her stubbornness. There was nothing he could say or do to deter her.

That morning Commissioners Jourdan and Briggs had climbed four floors of the five-floor walk-up in which Lucette Myers lived. Naturally, she lived on the fifth floor. They were both out of shape and winded, but they kept in mind their promised reward: Roscoe. As part of his promise to give them progress reports, Chief Campbell had already informed them that Mary was looking for Roscoe. If she found him before they did, their whole plan would implode.

"This better be good," Briggs said as he sucked in more air. "Your little trollop has taken her sweet time arranging this rendezvous."

"I warn you, Briggs," responded Jourdan. "I won't tolerate such slander. Lucette is a remarkable woman of unassailable moral fiber."

It was true, in part. Jourdan and Lucette had not progressed to anything that could be labeled improper. Lucette had made sure they hadn't. She had been down that path

many times before and had intimate knowledge of how rudely a woman's generosity was treated. They had dinner one night, dinner and the ballet another. There was one innocent kiss good night, but that was it. She was determined it would stay that way until they said their vows before a minister.

Briggs looked at his love-struck colleague and decided not to pursue it any further. They climbed the remaining stairs, and Jourdan knocked on Lucette's door.

"Ah, gentlemen, please come in," Lucette said, playing the gracious hostess. In the far corner, a woman about forty years old, her black hair pulled back into a bun and wearing a conservative navy blue dress, sat erect and quiet in a wingback chair.

Lucette's apartment was only one room, and the furniture was cheap. She tried to camouflage that reality by placing colorful, lacy things everywhere. That meant frilly curtains patterned with large daisies, a lace-edged tablecloth adorned with pictures of fruit, and doilies of all sizes generously distributed, often strategically covering worn fabric or chips in wood.

"Welcome to my humble abode," said Lucette.

"It's magnificent, Lucette," cooed Jourdan. "You have a decorator's eye."

Impatient, Briggs got right to the point. "Where's Roscoe?"

"Of course, that *is* why you're here," replied Lucette. "Business is business." She and Jourdan exchanged a flirtatious glance as she led them to the woman in the wingback chair and gestured grandly.

"Gentlemen, meet Doctress Anna Parkes."

The woman solemnly rose. The title of "doctress" was given both to women who were gifted in medicine and to the few female medical doctors who existed. It was also given to women who practiced black magic.

"Doctress Parkes has graciously consented to help us locate Roscoe," Lucette informed them, and then added with great excitement, "We're going to have a séance!"

Jourdan shared her excitement. "What a brilliant idea!"

Briggs didn't say a word. He didn't have to. He merely shot Jourdan a look that said it all.

∼

After breakfast with Charles, Mary had hoped to catch W. W. Goodrich at his office but just missed him. She was told that he had left for a council meeting, and so she entered Brooklyn's city hall, hoping she'd find him before it started. Luck was on her side. She spotted W. W. Goodrich squashing a cigarette with his foot before heading toward the assembly room. She hurried along as she called to him, but he seemed not to hear.

"Councilman Goodrich," she called out once more.

He stiffened. "Ah, Miss Handley," he said with his back still to her, betraying that he knew who had been calling to him. He then turned around. "How unfortunate. You came at the wrong time. No reporters, no limelight to grab."

It took Mary a moment to process his jibe. "If you're referring to my arrival at the police station the other day, that certainly wasn't my intention."

"And what is your intention, Miss Handley . . . to ride the crest of my brother's murder for personal gain?"

"No. I leave that kind of opportunism to politicians, Councilman."

W. W. Goodrich wasn't insulted. He wasn't outraged. He was impressed. "Touché," he said admiringly.

He gestured toward the door of the assembly and opened it for the two of them to enter. Once inside, Mary eagerly looked around. Government and its workings were another area to which she had never been exposed except in books. What she saw, though, was only a large, empty auditorium. As she was getting a sense of the place, W. W. Goodrich casually sat down.

"We convene in five minutes. Knowing my political brethren, that gives us twenty to chat."

Mary got right to the point. "Did you by any chance find a journal in your brother's effects?"

"Don't tell me Charlie wrote a journal?" He chuckled at the prospect.

Mary knew his type only too well: a person born into privilege who thought himself exceedingly droll and clever. She needed to keep him on track and not allow him to wander.

"It was a diary of his time with Edison," she informed him.

"Knowing his bent for minutiae, it must be a foolproof cure for insomnia."

"It contained very sensitive information."

W. W. Goodrich decided it was time to educate this temporary hire on how a Goodrich behaves. "My brother was two things, Miss Handley: fiercely loyal and very private. Both would preclude him from exposing anything untoward that went on at Edison."

"And what would you say if I told you that your brother

was indeed about to divulge such information to several interested parties?"

W. W. Goodrich stiffened. "I'd say hogwash—pure, unadulterated hogwash."

Mary decided to drop it. He would never entertain a notion that might in some way betray the Goodrich image, or at least what he perceived the Goodrich image to be.

"Nevertheless, he owned boardinghouses, and I'd like to search them."

W. W. Goodrich paused for a moment to consider her request. Whatever damage such a search might uncover could not be worse than the publicity if he failed to cooperate with the police regarding his brother's murder. So W. W. Goodrich acquiesced, telling her he'd inform his secretary and she could pick up the keys at his office sometime after lunch. Mary thanked him and sat down facing him.

"From your positioning, I assume we're not through."

"Not yet." Mary smiled. "Your brother knew a man named Roscoe."

"Roscoe," he said as if searching his brain for any recollection of that name. "Never heard of him."

"Really? His fiancée said they had business dealings."

There was no mistaking it. This time the glib W. W. Goodrich showed a genuine reaction. "Charlie had a fiancée?" he said.

"Kate Stoddard. You didn't know?"

W. W. Goodrich explained that he and his brother had had a falling-out and hadn't spoken in four months. Mary wanted to know the cause of their disagreement.

"He told me he was quitting Edison to manage boarding-

houses," he explained. "Imagine, giving up working with Thomas Edison and . . . Well, you know the kind who lives in those places."

"Yes, my kind," she replied.

W. W. Goodrich realized he had firmly placed his foot in it this time. An awkward moment passed that he tried to fill by lighting a cigarette.

"And associating with your kind," Mary continued, "probably got him killed."

Furniture was moved in Lucette's apartment to clear a space. The séance had begun and she, Jourdan, Briggs, and Doctress Parkes were sitting on the floor in a circle, holding hands. Doctress Parkes's skills had been honed on the carnival circuit, then somewhat refined after a wealthy believer financed her move to New York. Still, her expressions and vocal intonations would be considered overdone by any theatrical critic of the day, and histrionics on the stage were entirely acceptable to most of them. She hemmed, hawed, hummed, and swooned, swinging her head back and forth as she called out, "It's Roscoe we seek, Spirit of the Night."

Briggs grunted. He had begrudgingly stayed to support his infatuated partner and to see that Lucette didn't make even more of a fool out of him. Chief Campbell's undoing would only come about with a joint effort, so he had to keep Jourdan from going off track.

"Wait," cautioned Doctress Parkes in a loud voice. "I'm getting an image." She froze as if it was being transmitted

into her brain at that very moment. "Three hamlets," she continued. "Yes! Three hamlets in one!"

"Must be Edwin Booth," muttered Briggs. But Jourdan gave Briggs a reproachful look for his attempt at humor.

"Have you seen his Hamlet?" said Briggs in mock defense of his comment.

Jourdan shushed him as Doctress Parkes deciphered her message from the beyond.

"It is far from here, in another state," she proclaimed. "No, New York. But not New York City. Miles away." She turned her head swiftly to the left and held up her hand to the left ear. "I hear a bell, a big loud one. I see some kind of seal, official. And men, very important men."

"Sounds like Albany," said Jourdan. It didn't matter whether he really believed this act or if he was blinded by his lust for Lucette. It was probably a little of both. His reaction, though, was enough to convince Doctress Parkes that he was a believer.

"Albany? I'll ask." But Doctress Parkes had already decided the show was over. It was better to leave them wanting more than thinking they'd had enough. "Oh no, she's fading," she lamented, appearing devastated as she prepared for the finale. "Don't go. Stay, Great Spirit! Stay!" She prolonged the "ay" in "stay" until it became a long whining plea. At the same time, she extended her arms, reaching out to the spirit, but alas, her reaction told all that it was not to be. Doctress Parkes hung her head in disappointment, her performance complete.

Jourdan jumped to his feet. "Official seal, important men—it has to be our state capital!"

"Or Queen Victoria's bed," Briggs sarcastically added.

Jourdan paid no attention to him. This was his chance to be supportive, brilliant, and, most important, to impress the hell out of Lucette.

"Three hamlets in one—Albany, Schenectady, and Troy," he declared, naming the area in New York State known as the Tri-cities. "Roscoe's in Albany!"

Lucette stood up and gave Jourdan what he wanted—a big, wet kiss. And Briggs also got what he wanted: permission to leave.

It was possible Charles Goodrich had hidden his journal in one of his boardinghouses—unlikely but possible—and Mary had to check out every possibility. That was why, after getting the keys from W. W. Goodrich's secretary, she was down in the dark and dusty basement of his boardinghouse in the Cobble Hill section of Brooklyn. It was a nice neighborhood, and Charles Goodrich had bought the building in observance of the well-accepted real estate belief that buying the least expensive property in an expensive area was a solid investment. The area wasn't exactly expensive, but the other properties would sell for more than what he'd paid for his. Goodrich had planned to gradually fix it up, to raise the rents, and to eventually sell it for a tidy profit . . . had he lived to see his plan through.

The kerosene lamp Mary was holding illuminated the room, revealing that Goodrich hadn't begun the "fix it up" stage of his plan. There was a pile of old wooden boards

full of rusty nails on one side, with another pile of broken-down furniture directly across from it. She also saw what appeared to be fresh mice pellets. And if fresh pellets were present, close by there were bound to be . . . Well, she had a job to do and really didn't want to think about that now. She was adhering to the idiom of "Leave no stone unturned." But having studied Charles Goodrich's lifestyle and habits, she had concluded the only thing he would put there was a cleaning crew.

Mary was winding up her search when she was literally blindsided, whacked on the back with what felt like a club. She fell to the ground, and sprawled out there, numb from the blow, she had the presence of mind to count her two saving graces: the kerosene lamp was still whole, and she hadn't fallen on the mice pellets.

"State your business or lose your head," boomed a loud female voice with a cockney accent.

"I'm Mary Handley," Mary answered, a little groggy from what had just transpired but not seriously hurt. "I'm investigating the murder of Charles Goodrich."

"No doubt, and I'm the Prince of Wales," the woman loudly proclaimed.

Mary got to her feet, picked up her kerosene lamp, and held it out to see her attacker. She was a large, wide woman who was wearing an apron. She was also wielding a cricket bat and was moving toward Mary for another strike.

Mary held the kerosene lamp up to her face. "I *am* Mary Handley. See?"

The woman stopped, stared at Mary, and in an instant, her demeanor changed.

"Well, I'll be. Cynthia Frump." She grabbed Mary's

hand and pumped it. "I used to help the late Mr. Goodrich look after this place. Chief cook and bottle washer, I am."

"It's a pleasure to meet you, Miss Frump," Mary said as the thought crossed her mind that she had finally discovered one advantage to her notoriety.

"Please excuse the nasty greetin'. Ya can't be too careful nowadays, right?" Cynthia Frump patted her cricket bat then laughed. It was a full, hearty laugh and contagious. Mary couldn't help joining in.

"Say," continued Cynthia Frump, "how come you're down here in the muck and not up in his flat?"

"Mr. Goodrich had a room here?"

"Mr. Goodrich ran a tight ship, he did. A real taskmaster, God bless his soul. He'd pop in from time to time. Made sure everything was on the up-'n'-up." She noticed Mary glancing at the monumental mess that surrounded them. "The poor man hadn't made it down here yet. It was on his list though."

She showed Mary to Charles Goodrich's room and was telling her which key on the ring of keys Mary had gotten from W. W. Goodrich would open the door when she noticed the door had been jimmied.

"My Lord, we've had a break-in. I better notify the police," exclaimed Cynthia Frump, then it occurred to her. "What am I sayin'? The police are already here."

Mary knew that meant her. "Not exactly, but I'll take care of it."

Cynthia Frump seemed satisfied, and she returned to her duties in the kitchen, but not before getting Mary's autograph for her scrapbook.

Mary entered Goodrich's room to discover it had been

completely ransacked. All the cabinets and drawers were opened and their contents spilled onto the floor. Chairs were turned over, the sofa cushions tossed.

If the journal had been there, it no longer was. Yet it was important that she search the place. Something might have been left behind. And no sooner had that thought crossed her mind than Mary spied a small chain protruding from under the couch. When she picked it up, it was attached to a pocket watch. On the back of the watch was an inscription that read, FOR MY DARLING NIKOLA . . . KATHERINE.

So Nikola Tesla had hired a criminal to find the journal, proclaiming it was just to locate it. Yet, the watch indicated that Tesla himself broke into this room to search for it. He hadn't mentioned that. If W. W. Goodrich was correct in his assertion that it was "hogwash" for anyone to think his brother would betray Edison, what would a desperate Tesla do if Charles Goodrich had agreed to cooperate, then changed his mind? Up until recently she had thought Edison was a calm, logical man of science, and she had been proven wrong. It was possible that Tesla, too, was capable of more than she thought.

23

It was early evening by the time Mary arrived at Tesla's warehouse. She didn't know if he'd still be there, but it was worth a try. The warehouse was markedly different from Mary's last visit, when there was a flurry of activity. Dark and very quiet, it seemed virtually deserted, and she now saw it for what it was: a vast, hollow building with tall stone pillars and a massive cement floor.

"Mr. Tesla?" Mary called out, her voice echoing off the walls. "Hello, Mr. Tesla?"

There was no response. She stepped further into the darkness, feeling like an intruder. She had the distinct impression that something intensely private was going on. It was just a feeling. Call it intuition, but her speculation was brought to an abrupt halt.

A gunshot rang out, its flash piercing the blackness. Mary instantly dropped to the ground, her body hugging its hard, cold surface. She watched carefully as the bullet ricocheted off the cement floor and stone pillars, flashing again with each hit and making a pinging sound as it bounced her

way. At the last minute, she rolled over to avoid it, the bullet
striking dangerously close to her before moving on. Another
shot was fired, causing more pings and flashes. Mary again
trained her eye on the zigzag path of the bullet and moved
just in time to elude it. A third bullet eventually ripped the
lower part of her dress, but she herself was unharmed. Mary
had to get out of there, and just as she was devising an escape plan, a shadowy figure staggered out of the darkness. It
was Tesla. He had a pistol in one hand and a bottle of vodka
in the other. And he was drunk, very drunk.

"I just prove scientifically by trial and error," he said,
slurring his words, his accent thicker than usual, "when
bullet hits cement, it bounces. Good thing no error, huh?"

Mary rose warily and dusted herself off, all the time
keeping her eyes on Tesla and his pistol. "Yes, very good
thing, Mr. Tesla."

"Please, Nikola. And I'll call you . . ."

He paused, searching for her name, victim no doubt of
an alcohol-induced memory lapse.

"Mary," she calmly reminded him. She wasn't feeling
calm at all, but she didn't want to reveal that to him.

"Mary, how could I forget? My mother's name."

"Really?"

"No."

He erupted in laughter, stumbled a few steps, and
tripped. Mary caught him, saving him from falling.

"I made joke," Tesla proclaimed. "People say I'm too serious. Ridiculous." He waved his pistol hand, dismissing his
detractors, and took a big swig of vodka.

"Yes, ridiculous. Now, may I have that?" In his state,

Mary figured that simply asking for the pistol could get the job done. It was worth a try anyway.

"Ah," Tesla said, chastising himself. "Where are my manners?" He held out the bottle, offering her a drink. "Vodka. Can't get it in United States. Had it sent specially from my homeland."

"Actually, I meant your pistol."

Tesla staggered backward as if absorbing a punch.

"No, never pistol." He petulantly waved it in the air. "Everybody cowboy in America. Nikola wants to be cowboy, too!"

He began shooting again, randomly pointing the pistol at the ground, then in the air, paying no attention to where he was aiming or to the possible consequences. One shot after another wildly ricocheted around the warehouse. Mary carefully followed the pings and flashes, dodging the bullets when necessary. When she spotted one bouncing back at Tesla, she dove and knocked him out of the way just in time. They both wound up on the floor. Tesla found this all terribly amusing.

"Whoops," he chirped out in a high voice, then broke into a hearty belly laugh.

Mary once again rose and dusted herself off. Dodging bullets was wearing thin. She had to get Tesla's pistol out of his hand.

"Mr. Tesla, I have a proposition for you. I propose we trade."

"What could you possibly have that I would want? Can you give me Thomas Edison's integrity? Oh no, you can't. He has none."

Tesla also found this incredibly funny. Ignoring him, Mary opened her pocketbook, slowly took out the watch she had found at the boardinghouse, and dangled it in front of him. Tesla's mood changed instantly. He silently stumbled toward her and gladly relinquished the pistol for the watch.

"I thought I'd lost it forever!" he said, cradling it as if it were a precious jewel.

Relieved, Mary put the pistol in her pocketbook, then resumed business.

"Who's Katherine?"

"She's a no-no. But she's also an oh-oh." Judging from his inflection and facial expression, he was most decidedly smitten.

"I found it in one of Mr. Goodrich's boardinghouses," Mary informed him.

"Yes, I was searching for the journal. No luck."

"Mr. Tesla . . ."

"Charlie promised it to me. A promise is a promise. It doesn't die 'cause he did." Before Mary could respond, he continued, "Come, I show you something."

He guided Mary to a workbench and turned on a light, illuminating a cylindrical object with wires leading to it and with what looked like a metal tower on top. Above the tower were two metal rods about three feet apart that were pointing at each other.

"This is work in progress, but it will change world!" He was extremely animated and filled with excitement as he pointed to it and announced, "The Tesla coil!"

He proudly flicked a switch, sending electricity to the rod, and within seconds, lightning bolts were jumping across open space between the two metal rods.

"See how energy jumps from one side to other, no wires guiding it, just air?" he explained.

Mary was truly mesmerized. "That's amazing. How do you do that?"

Tesla shrugged matter-of-factly. "I'm brilliant. That's how." Then his enthusiasm returned. "This energy transport will revolutionize communication! Talk in New York, be heard in Boston. Without wires, none!"

Then suddenly his excitement dissipated, and he became morose.

"Charlie told me Thomas and J. P. Morgan were going to steal my coil technology and finance someone else to develop it."

"There are laws to protect you. You could—"

"Laws!" an incredulous Tesla blurted out. "You think laws apply to people like Thomas and Morgan?" He stepped away from her, trying unsuccessfully to gain control of his emotions. "After Thomas's trick with his calves, everyone backed out of my demonstration."

"I am so sorry." Mary meant it. She was beginning to feel his pain.

"It's not true, you know. My current is safer than his." Then he turned to her, unable to mask the pain he was experiencing. "Why can't it be about work? Not who wins, but who produces best product!"

Mary looked at his innocent expression. It was that of a child who had just discovered the world was not fair. She couldn't help feeling sympathy.

"What happened between you two, Nikola?" she asked gently.

"Thomas promised me fifty thousand dollars if I could

improve efficiency of his DC generator by twenty-five percent. I improved it by fifty percent."

"I assume he welshed on the deal."

"He laughed. Said I didn't understand his American
sense of humor."

Suddenly, Mary felt a strong kinship with this man who
simply wanted to be judged on the merits of his work. "On
second thought, I could use a drink."

She grabbed the bottle from Tesla, took a big swig, and
then handed it back to him. They both sat down on the floor,
their backs propped up against a pillar while lightning bolts
from Tesla's coil flew back and forth above them. A few
drinks later, he divulged that the Katherine on his watch
was the wife of his best friend, and though he desperately
loved her, his sense of honor forbade him from taking any
action. As they continued to share the bottle and their personal frustrations, Mary decided this was not the type of
man who committed murder. He was more likely to be a
victim.

24

The monthly Wednesday morale booster, as Chief Campbell had put it, consisted of off-duty policemen from Second Street Station gathering for drinks. Clancy's Bar was mostly a policemen's hangout anyway, so it didn't take much effort to organize the gathering. The bar was always three deep, but the Second Street officers were in the back, where there were several tables and room to roam from group to group.

Chief Campbell was holding court in the center, surrounded by a handful of policemen, Sean among them. It looked as if he was spewing nuggets of wisdom to his flock, but he was just being congenial as men moved in and out to get in a word with him. Some of them tried to use these meetings as a chance to impress the chief, some to get to know him better, and others used them as a bulletproof excuse for going home to their wives completely smashed. Chief Campbell knew all his men: the ambitious ones, the loyal, the deserving, and the malcontents. He wasn't swayed by their behavior on Wednesdays.

"I'm feeling the effects of this good brew," he announced,

holding up his beer mug. "Excuse me, gentlemen." Chief Campbell headed for the bathroom, nodding along the way to his men, including Billy, who was standing next to Officer Russell and another policeman. Officer Russell had already imbibed far beyond his share. He nudged Billy.

"Look who's here. Our lady savior."

Mary had just entered Clancy's. She had already shared a good part of a vodka bottle with Tesla and was well on her way to being soused. But after the bad press she had received regarding the incident in the alley, she didn't want to appear the least bit tipsy, so she had splashed some cold water on her face. It did little to help, but what the water didn't do was aided considerably by the juvenile behavior of the policemen as she walked into their lions' den.

Boys will be boys, and when they make pacts, they're especially emboldened if they are all together and drink is involved. Mary got a good taste of this behavior at Clancy's that night. As she made her way to the rear, men stepped in front of her, blocking her way. It was annoying, but it made her determined and helped her focus, erasing some of the effects of the vodka. Trying her best to appear unaffected, she went around each and every one of them. In the back room, she got more of the same. She joined a group of three police officers, who quickly dispersed, leaving her alone. She scanned the crowd, and eventually she and Sean locked eyes. It was easy to read his mind. He had told her he couldn't help her, and he couldn't. Frustrated, he shook his head and walked away from her over to the bar.

Officer Russell turned to Billy and the others with them.

"Time to send our lady detective crying into the night."

"Leave her be," Billy said. "She'll be gone soon enough." Like the others, Billy was upset at Mary's appointment, feeling it was a slight to all the men at Second Street Station. But it wasn't personal to him. Mary was just a symbol, a symbol whom he happened to like. He wished her no harm and certainly no cruelty.

Officer Russell had different priorities, and getting revenge on the bitch who'd made him look bad in front of the chief was number one. "Am I the only one whose testicles are still intact?"

After his rallying cry, he gulped down the last of his drink, hoping someone would meet his challenge and join him. No one did, but his boast had made retreat impossible. He straightened up and swaggered out toward Mary. The swagger soon became more of a stagger, but he made it to her. He stood there for a brief moment, staring, grinning from ear to ear. He thought he was being intimidating, but he just looked dazed and stupid. Finally, he mumbled out some words.

"Detective, you know what a johnson is?"

"Sorry?" Mary couldn't make out what he had said. No one could.

Overcompensating, Officer Russell spoke much louder and slower, carefully enunciating each word. Now everyone in the bar could hear him, including Chief Campbell, who had just returned from his journey to the bathroom.

"Johnson. Do you know what it is?"

"No, pray tell, what?" Mary answered, humoring him.

The bar was suddenly silent. They all knew this routine. But would Officer Russell actually go through with it? They

soon got their answer. With drunken bravado, he dropped his pants. He was totally nude from the waist down. To emphasize his point, Officer Russell, who would never be accused of subtlety, did a pelvic thrust so that his penis flapped in the air.

"That's a johnson!" he proudly boasted.

All eyes were on Mary. She calmly looked down at his crotch.

"Oh, I see. Like a prick but infinitely smaller."

For a split second there was complete silence, and then they all burst out laughing. A horde of officers rushed by Officer Russell toward Mary. Billy was first.

"Ah, Mary, how can I stay mad at ya?" And he hugged her.

While the other officers gathered around Mary, Sean made his way through the sea of people at the bar to Officer Russell who had just pulled up his pants. Sean shoved him.

"That's my sister, you bastard!"

"Ah, piss off, Handley." Officer Russell shoved him back.

In no time fists were flying. Sean caught him with a roundhouse right that sent him stumbling back several feet. To his credit, Officer Russell was a scrapper. He came right back at Sean. It wasn't long before the other police officers descended upon the two men and pulled them apart. Within moments, Chief Campbell had gotten between them. Blood trickled down from Sean's mouth, but he was still struggling to get free from the officers restraining him and that didn't stop him from goading Officer Russell.

"Not so easy when you're fightin' a man!" he shouted.

Chief Campbell had had enough. "Shut up, Handley! Go clean yourself!"

Chief Campbell's word was law. The men holding Sean

let him go. They knew he wouldn't dare disobey the chief right in front of him.

Mary was all at once surprised and pleased at what had just transpired. She and Sean had had a contentious relationship their whole lives, and yet here he was defending her honor while risking a reprimand at work and maybe his job. Was it possible that, in spite of all their differences, deep down, he really loved his little sister? This thought made her extremely happy. She took out her handkerchief and tried to wipe the blood away from Sean's mouth, but he shrugged her off, stared daggers at Officer Russell, and then headed to the bathroom. It was typical Sean. Mary couldn't help smiling.

Chief Campbell put his arm around Officer Russell and took him aside as the rest of the gathering regained some semblance of normalcy. Chief Campbell was not one to mince words.

"You're fired, Russell," he said.

"What! You can't fire me for that!"

"I'm not. You see, you have the distinction of not only being an ass but also a lousy cop."

Even Officer Russell knew there was no changing Chief Campbell's mind. Frustrated, he stormed out of Clancy's, pushing aside anyone in his way.

Chief Campbell turned toward his men. He saw Mary in the middle of them chatting with the others, at last a real part of the group. He caught her eye. She was happy. So was he. He just hoped they'd both feel that way when all of this was over.

∼

Mary was not three sheets to the wind but she had surpassed two. Between the vodka she had drunk earlier and the beers she had with the men at Clancy's, she had consumed enough alcohol that later, at home, her mind kept wandering from the medical journals she had put aside to read. Edison's behavior fascinated her, and she wanted to learn more about the wonder drug cocaine, but not this night. She stared blankly at the stack of journals on the table in her apartment, looking for an excuse to procrastinate. It came in the form of a loud knock on her door, followed by a louder male voice with a heavy Brooklyn accent.

"Open up. It's Sal Dominick of the Brooklyn Trolley Car Company."

"What do you want?"

"What do ya think, lady? You turned our car into kindling wood, and I got two horses with a case of diarrhea that won't quit."

Mary had discussed the trolley incident with Chief Campbell, and he had said he would take care of it. Either he hadn't yet or nobody had told this Sal Dominick, who apparently possessed the gentility of a Brahma bull. How dare he bang on a person's door at a time when working people were getting ready for bed! Mary rose.

"Chief Campbell has probably already spoken to—" She opened the door and was stunned. "Charles!"

The ruse over, he exclaimed, "Thank God you're home!" He rushed by her and inside.

"Sal Dominick?" she asked as she closed the door.

"You can't have male visitors, but who would object to Sal Dominick?"

Mary laughed, but in spite of his playacting, Charles was

on edge. He paced, something clearly bothering him, as he absentmindedly reached into his coat pocket.

"Oh, here."

He took out a pistol and offered it to her. It was a Colt 1860 army revolver.

"What's this?"

"I believe it's a pistol, unless Cadbury's invented a new style of chocolate bar." Before Mary could protest, he charged ahead. "Father took it from a Union officer during the war. All it does is stir up bad memories. In your possession, at least I know it will be doing some good."

"What good?"

"Easing my conscience, for one. There are powerful people who would like to see you disappear. I, quite selfishly, would like you to remain visible and intact. Now, this is loaded, which means it can shoot six times. Have you ever used one?"

Mary recognized the pistol. Sean had practiced with one when he was preparing to join the police force. She had tried it out a few times but was by no means proficient.

"Yes, but—"

"Okay. Now where do you want me to put it?" Charles was not to going accept "no" for an answer, and Mary knew it. She got out a large roasting pan from a kitchen cabinet and lifted the lid.

"My mother gave this to me, also in spite of my protests. I doubt I'll ever be cooking a roast this huge in this little apartment—even if I knew how."

Charles placed the gun in the pan. "Hopefully you'll never need to use it. Done."

Mary was touched by his concern. She didn't want to

spoil his gesture, and she managed to utter a very sincere, "Thank you, Charles."

"I'm glad that's over." He went back to pacing. "My stomach's doing flips, and my mind's useless."

"It must be love," she quipped as she put the pan back in the cabinet.

"Certainly"—he smiled then—"but not this." He clutched his stomach.

"How could I forget? You're meeting with Edison tomorrow."

With so many things on his plate, Charles was easily distracted. He stopped and stared at the table. "Medical journals?"

"It's part of the job." She took a journal out of the stack and handed it to Charles. "In fact, I just read a study on cocaine in here. It says it causes loss of sleep, deadens the appetite, and can result in violent mood swings. And it is also highly addictive . . . Our Mr. Edison may have a serious problem."

But Charles's mind was on other things. Seeming to ignore Mary's findings, he put the medical journal down, then mused aloud, "I always wanted to marry a lady doctor."

"Not a lady detective?"

"The lady detective was going to be my sexy mistress."

It was the right reply; Mary's pleased reaction told him so. But Charles couldn't escape what was troubling him.

"I'm concerned about Father. He's not well, you know. He hasn't long to live."

"How awful! I am so sorry to hear that." She knew it sounded trite, but she took solace in the fact her words were heartfelt.

"He's convinced Coca-Cola is the legacy that will validate his existence on earth when he's gone."

"That's absurd. It's just a fountain drink. What about his family? He has you—"

Consumed with his emotion, Charles interrupted. "Me? I've failed to provide him with much joy."

"Don't, Charles. Don't do that."

"It's true. I can't point to anything I've accomplished on my own."

"Some people take longer to find the mountain they want to climb. That's not—"

"I never spent much time with Father growing up." Charles continued, "When I was little he was away at the war, and then he was always in the pharmacy fooling with his concoctions." He turned, facing Mary. "If I can ease his mind by helping him see that his creation will live on, then I've done something. Something significant, don't you think, Mary?" He looked into Mary's eyes, his expression very much like a little boy's.

"Of course. And you'll do it. I know you will."

She hated seeing him like this. Charles had so much to offer but so little confidence. He needed to find his calling and realize his worth. She was sure that in time she could help him do that. Mary's motherly instinct surfaced. She cradled his face in her hands and brought him to her, soothing him with kisses on his forehead, on his cheeks, trying to caress away the hurt. Eventually their lips met. It was like an explosion. A passion erupted inside of her, a passion she had never felt before. Mary knew it was too soon for them, even by her unconventional standards. Maybe the drink had

lowered her resistance, or maybe she just wanted to, but as their clothes started to come off, she welcomed it.

It was Mary's first time. She was confident, at times cocky, in many areas, but lovemaking was not one of them. The mystery of what it was like, if it would please her, if she would please him, were questions still to be answered.

Charles was a patient and gentle lover who saw how anxious she was and did everything he could to make her feel at ease. Unlike many men, he truly cared about her enjoyment and not just his. However, when he entered her, the amount of pain she experienced was greater than she had expected, and her instinctive grunt told him so. He stopped. She was actually relieved that he had, but she felt insecure and lied, telling him that everything was fine.

Not too much longer a wave of pleasure washed over the pain. It didn't erase it, but the word "stop" didn't occur to her again.

25

The next morning Mary and Charles made love again. This time she felt less pain and more pleasure. *I guess this love-making does have some merit,* she thought as she smiled at him, signaling her satisfaction.

The fact that a woman like Mary could care about him, possibly even love him, lifted Charles's spirits. When he left that morning, he had a sense of well-being he hadn't experienced in a long time. It was fortunate, because his father would need his support. He had proclaimed this day to be his finest hour, the day when he would present his invention to the "greatest inventor of all time." What John Pemberton didn't realize was that he was also selling to arguably the best salesman of all time.

"Coca-Cola contains cocaine, but not a drop of alcohol," he explained to Edison and Batchelor in Edison's office. "A temperance movement is sweeping our nation. We're primed to usurp the business of the coca wines, and millions will be ours."

Pemberton smiled at Charles, who was sitting next to

him with a pitcher of Coca-Cola in his lap. Pemberton knew he was doing a great job. There was much more to explain, but he paused for questions. He had no intention of monopolizing his conversation with Edison. That would be arrogant on his part.

"Sorry, Pemberton, not interested," was Edison's curt retort.

Pemberton blanched. Surely Edison had misunderstood something. He rose. "Please, Mr. Edison, wait. I . . . You see, I, too, consider myself a scientist. Not like you, there is only one you, but . . ."

Pemberton gestured to Charles to hand him the pitcher of Coca-Cola. Charles shook his head ever so slightly, urging his father not to proceed. He had studied Edison throughout his father's presentation, and he could see that Edison didn't have the slightest interest. But his father would never consider surrendering so easily. He had fought in the Civil War and still believed the South could win the battle when Sherman was burning Atlanta. He took the pitcher from Charles, then picked up an empty glass that was sitting near Edison's bottle of Vin Mariani. His hands shook as he poured a glass of Coca-Cola.

"I worked hours on end, day in and out, searching for the right formula. I had the cocaine, the cola, but I needed the taste. Then, miraculously—by accident mind you—I spilled carbonated water into the mix. The result? Well, you'll see."

Sweat was pouring down Pemberton's brow as he offered the glass of Coca-Cola to Edison. Edison stared indifferently, first at the glass, then at Pemberton, who helplessly stood there, not knowing what to do. The awkwardness increased

as the seconds ticked away. Charles rose, gently took the glass from his father, put it on the desk, and then relieved him of the pitcher.

"Thank you for your time, gentlemen," he said, then guided his father out the door, any sense of well-being Charles had felt earlier dashed along with his father's dream.

"That could've been had for pennies," Batchelor exclaimed after they had left.

"People expect me to change the world, not serve them fountain drinks," Edison said as he turned to examine some papers on his desk.

"Speaking of which," said Batchelor, already on to other business. He knew not to fight Edison once his mind was made up. "Our men have finished examining Tesla's coil technology."

Edison eagerly looked up. This was a subject in which he had great interest.

"As you thought, extraordinary. The possibilities are endless."

"Too bad Nikola's not a team player."

"Should I get the men to work on it?"

Edison shook his head. "Too risky with what's going on. Try Europe. I'm sure some young scientist will jump at the chance of working with Thomas Edison."

Their business completed, Batchelor left, and Edison returned to his papers. He spotted the glass of Coca-Cola on his desk and decided to take a sip. He nodded his head; it had a pleasing taste. He shrugged and returned to his work.

∾

The Bowler Hat was at work. It wasn't his usual work. There were men of means who needed a man they could trust to carry out certain delicate errands, and his employers had secured him a job with one of those men. The errands weren't difficult, but they needed to be accomplished discreetly by a reliable man. He thought the work was beneath him, but it still buoyed him considerably. It meant his employers did value him and want him to mend. That knowledge alone made him eager to go back out in the field, but he knew he would have to prove himself first.

As he entered the bookstore and looked around, he saw a preponderance of women. Women read more than men, and he wondered why. He decided it was a way for them to live out their fantasies while men like him lived them out in everyday life. The Bowler Hat approached a woman who was perusing the shelves.

"Hello, I work for Mr. J. P. Morgan. Mr. Morgan is ready to see you now."

Without turning, the woman responded, "And what happens if I'm not ready?" After all, J. P. Morgan had avoided meeting with her for quite a while now. Then she saw the face of the stern, humorless man before her. "Yet it appears I am."

And so Mary Handley left with him.

26

J. P. Morgan's carriage was larger than Mary's apartment; at least that's how it seemed. As carriages went, it fit comfortably into the classification of "gigantic and absurdly ornate." Mary looked around, marveling at the indulgences of the rich. "The pleasures of plenty," she remarked, indicating the carriage. "A most enticing narcotic. I can see it becoming quite addictive."

The Bowler Hat didn't respond. He had a job to do, and he had no delusions about its importance. He was essentially a delivery boy at the beck and call of J. P. Morgan. True, a well-paid delivery boy, and one who commanded respect, but no more than that. Delivery boys didn't overstep their bounds and engage in idle chatter. Nothing good could come from that.

Mary scrutinized him as he sat opposite her. Out of place in this environment, he appeared more military-stern than butler- or footman-dour. An air of danger surrounded him.

"How did you know where to find me?" she asked.

"Like I said, I work for Mr. J. P. Morgan." And he stopped there.

If he has verbal skills, he's loath to use them, Mary thought. She was curious to know who he was, his background, and the details of his life. She didn't deem the information essential, merely a mental exercise similar to her curiosity over Senator Conkling's ill-fated stroll during the Great White Hurricane. This man did look very familiar though.

"I can't help feeling we've met before, Mr. . . . ."

"We haven't," he responded, not willing to fill in her blank and give her a name.

"Is it possible I saw your picture in the newspaper?"

"You didn't."

Mary decided to drop the matter. *People with an air of mystery about them usually attract more attention than they deserve,* she thought, and turned to look out the window.

J. P. Morgan was intently watching a wrestling match. The matches were scheduled regularly at the New York Athletic Club to entertain its elite membership. Morgan enjoyed attending. He understood there was more to it than muscle. Strategy was key. Yet in wrestling, as in life, there was no substitute for brute strength.

Right now, strategy was winning. A smaller wrestler had the upper hand on a man who was much larger. The ring was brightly lit, and the surrounding stands where the spectators sat were in shadows.

George Westinghouse wasn't surprised to find Morgan

there. He had planned on it. Trading jibes with J. P. was one of his favorite pastimes. What good was all this money if you couldn't have a little fun? He sat down next to Morgan, who, though aware of his presence, didn't acknowledge it.

"Rumor is, we're in for an upset, J. P.," Westinghouse began, referring to the wrestling match. Morgan's answer was a mere shrug. Westinghouse had planned to wait awhile before bringing up business, but he lacked the patience. So, as the match on the floor continued, the one in the stands began with Westinghouse initiating the first volley.

"Quite a show Tom put on the other day."

"Yes," replied Morgan. "Set you back a bit, I trust."

"No need to fret. I have the superior technology, and whether it's one year or ten, you'll eventually come to me."

"Married to that firebrand Tesla for a decade. A hefty price to pay."

"I doubt he'll be around for the long haul. His passion to see his creations implemented is also his weakness."

The manager of the club appeared out of the shadows and whispered in Morgan's ear, delivering the news of his guest's arrival. Morgan nodded, and the manager left. Westinghouse sensed Morgan's imminent departure and delivered his coup de grâce.

"Of course, a turn of events could change our fortunes more rapidly. Rumors abound of improprieties and even murder."

As Morgan rose to go, the larger wrestler lifted the smaller one in the air, threw him to the ground, and pinned him. Morgan calmly pointed to the wrestlers.

"So much for rumors. Good day, George." And he left

with the satisfaction that he once again had gotten the better of Westinghouse.

~

Mary and the Bowler Hat sat silently in the study of the
New York Athletic Club, surrounded by leather furniture,
wooden tables, and walls covered with floor-to-ceiling book-
cases. Their relationship continued to lack any sign of
conviviality, and the quiet had begun to make Mary uncomfortable, a rare condition for her. The Bowler Hat showed
no signs of unease. In fact, he showed no signs of any feeling
at all.

Upon first meeting J. P. Morgan, people usually behaved
in three distinct ways; there were those who fawned, those
who cringed with fear, and those who combined the two. Yet
relief was what Mary conveyed when he let himself in. She
shot up from her seat, approached him, and shook his hand.

"Ah, Mr. Morgan."

"Miss Handley, glad you could make it."

His job done, the Bowler Hat headed for the door, his
only communication a slight glance at Morgan to see if anything more was required of him. It wasn't, and he left. Mary
couldn't resist commenting.

"Chatty fellow."

"Yes, sometimes it's impossible to get him to shut up."

Mary laughed, and Morgan gestured for her to sit. Not
wanting to make her feel too at home, he had pointed to a
straight-backed chair. She sat.

"I thought women were not welcome in here."

"An advantage of my position. People like to please me."

Morgan was in his club, on his terms, and was dealing with a woman. He had every reason to feel in total control. That's why, when he opened a humidor that was resting on a nearby table, he felt comfortable ceding personal courtesies.

"You mind?" he asked.

The shake of Mary's head indicated she didn't. In the unlikely event that she had minded, Morgan would have smoked anyway. He took out a cigar and lit up.

"I know you're a busy man, so I'll get to the point. Do you have any idea why someone would murder Charles Goodrich?"

As Morgan sat in a cushy club chair facing her, he rattled off possibilities. "Jealousy, greed, profit. Aren't those the usual motives for murder?"

"I was hoping you'd be more specific."

"Let's not play games, Miss Handley." He flicked cigar ash into an ashtray. "I'm fully aware Mr. Goodrich left a journal behind."

Having been summoned now made sense to her. Morgan wasn't granting her an interview. It was he who needed information.

"News travels fast from West Orange."

"Another advantage of my position. People tell me things."

"Could it be you're also concerned with the journal's contents?"

"Incentives other than self-preservation do exist."

"Like what?"

"Leverage."

He reached for a decanter filled with brandy on the table next to him. When Mary declined a drink, he poured himself one. Morgan held up his cigar and brandy glass.

"Brandy and a good cigar. I don't know who first thought of the combination. A true inspiration." He took a sip and breathed out a long, satisfied "Ahh." Morgan had deliberately digressed from their conversation. He wanted her to know that he was in charge and that he would only give her information when he decided it was time, and then only if he wanted to.

"I need Tom for his creativity," he said. "Yet I despise need. Need is weakness."

Mary was now certain of the purpose of this meeting. "With the journal, you can pull his strings and make him dance like a puppet."

"I see you're quick on the uptake."

"Greed is not hard to decipher."

Morgan wasn't fazed in the least. He stood, took another sip of his brandy and a big puff on his cigar, and then stretched out both his arms, gesturing expansively.

"With that in mind, Miss Handley, this is your lucky day. 'I am such stuff as dreams are made on.'"

"'We,'" Mary corrected him. "Your quote from Shakespeare, it's 'we are such stuff,' not 'I am.'"

"Well, Shakespeare didn't know me." Morgan paused for emphasis. "You may want to be the first policewoman. I can arrange that. It appears you're an avid reader. You may want to open a bookstore. Consider it done. Choose your fondest desire—"

Mary interrupted him in the middle of his oratory. "I don't have the journal, Mr. Morgan."

He didn't hesitate in the least. "You are pursuing it. It's an odds game, and I prefer them stacked in my favor."

Mary quietly studied Morgan, a man blessed with all the excesses of life, and was overcome with sadness. She rose quietly.

"You're one of the most powerful men in the world. You have money for a hundred lifetimes. When will you have enough?"

"Oh Lord, you're one of those."

"I'm afraid I am."

As far as Mary was concerned, there was nothing more to be said. If Morgan possessed information concerning Charles Goodrich, he didn't care to divulge it. She started to leave, but Morgan had no intention of yielding control. He was the one who had called this meeting, and he would be the one to end it.

"It's rather easy to take the moral high ground when you've accomplished nothing."

Mary stopped and listened as he steamrolled ahead.

"Men like Jay Gould, Andy Carnegie, John Rockefeller, and me transformed this country from being a cow's teat sucked on by Europe to being an industrial power. It took guts, it took fortitude, and it involved unspeakable risks. We damn well deserve whatever we can grab."

Mary viewed Morgan's diatribe as a rationalization for his abuse of power, and she had no intention of letting him get away with it. Her response took on a mocking tone. "Thank you for the lesson in ethics, sir."

Morgan winced. Ethics be damned. Everyone was out for himself. How could this child not have realized it by now? Besides, when J. P. Morgan benefited, so did every-one else.

"When our success trickles down, do you honestly think people will care how much we profited?"

"You imply it will rain gold, yet we know that at best it'll be a mild drizzle of pennies."

"How could you possibly know?" he harrumphed.

"Because that's all you could bear to let slip through your fingers."

If she hadn't insulted Morgan earlier, she was sure she had now and thought it would be prudent to leave posthaste.

"You haven't responded to my proposition."

"The problem is, I don't know if I'd get what I asked for."

"Nonsense. You'd be my partner."

"So is Thomas Edison."

And with that, she left the room, ending their meeting. Mary had refused Morgan's offer and had bested him. The rest of the day would not be pleasant for him or for anyone who came across his path.

27

The next morning Mary and Charles had just woken up, and she was lying on her bed after he had gone to the sink for a glass of water. He had come over the night before after the disastrous meeting he and his father had had with Edison. She had surprised him by being optimistic, assuring Charles they'd find a better deal somewhere else.

"And I thought we'd wallow in our mutual cynicism."

"I'm afraid your excessive negativity has made me see the folly of my ways."

"I don't deserve you, Mary."

"It's by plan. I always court beneath me."

Mary had enjoyed their lovemaking even more that night. She was beginning to relax, and there were times she was more the aggressor. That night though, Mary had felt a strong caring and vulnerability from Charles that was authentic and especially endearing. She was now certain their relationship had limitless possibilities.

"Come back to bed, Charles," she beckoned him.

"In a minute."

"That seems like such a long time," she said with a sigh.

Basking in her happiness, Mary didn't notice the change in Charles. He purposely stood with his back to her. He was sweating and shaking and desperately trying to control it. Withdrawal had started, and this wasn't his first experience with it. He gulped down the water and refilled his glass.

Mary got out of bed and headed for him. She was in a playful mood. "So, are you contemplating cooking another surprise for me?"

Charles was barely hanging on. Her proximity rattled him. The glass slipped out of his hand and crashed to the floor, shattering broken glass everywhere. She noticed the condition he was in for the first time.

"Charles!"

"I'm fine, just an upset stomach." Making a last-ditch effort to cover the state he was in, he tried to brush by her. She put out her hands to stop him and touched his shirt.

"Your shirt's soaking wet."

"I have to go. See how Father's doing."

As he hurriedly grabbed his coat, the image of Senator Conkling on his deathbed flashed through Mary's mind. She blocked the door. Charles knew he was at a breaking point and summoned his last ounce of self-control.

"Mary, please get out of my way."

"You're obviously sick, and you're not going to do your father any good by turning it into pneumonia."

His patience vanished. "Goddamn it! Get the hell out of my way!"

His outburst surprised, confused, and frightened her. She backed away. The adrenaline rushed through Charles's body.

"That's in one of your journals under violent mood swings. Not from cocaine. Morphine. We ran out yesterday."

Mary was speechless. She hadn't had the least suspicion. He laughed. It was a bitter one.

"Your new optimism blinds you," he said, then opened the door to go.

"Let me help, Charles. There are cures—"

"Damn it, Mary, I'm no good! Stay away! Stay far away or I'll bring you down, too!"

He bolted out the door. She had started to go after him when she realized she was still in her nightgown and rushed back to throw on some clothes.

Distraught and disheveled, Mary charged out of her tenement building. She looked up and down the block. Charles was nowhere in sight. As she was about to choose a direction in the hope that Charles had chosen the same, she heard a male voice.

"Are you that lady detective?"

The last thing Mary wanted to deal with now was her dubious popularity, or worse, a fan. She turned to quickly dismiss him. He was a wiry man in his thirties, wearing a white apron and large rubber boots. She didn't get a chance to speak.

"Barney Wallenski. I worked for Charles Goodrich. Thought you might be interested in a book he gave me."

Mary sat next to Wallenski on the trolley. They were on their way to the Fulton Fish Market, where Wallenski worked.

"I was a part-time fix-it man at his buildings," he explained. "Added to what I bring in at the fish market."

"And he just gave you the journal?" Mary was understandably incredulous.

"Paid me, for safekeeping. Said it was a family heirloom." Wallenski rose. "This is our stop." He headed toward the exit, and Mary followed.

"But he had a brother."

"Guess he trusted I'd never sneak a peek."

"And why is that?"

"I can't read." And he hopped off the train.

It made sense. Charles Goodrich couldn't trust his brother to protect the journal. W. W. Goodrich was too conscious of the family image. Why not leave it with someone who had no idea what it was? It was actually rather clever.

The Fulton Fish Market was in lower Manhattan next to the East River and close to the Brooklyn Bridge. The bridge was only five years old, and people were still marveling at the engineering genius that went into designing it and mourning the lives lost during its construction. The Fulton Fish Market had been around since 1822, and the routine was the same every day. From very early in the morning, the market was abuzz with activity. Fishermen unloaded their wares, fishmongers prepared and hawked them, and buyers ranging from restaurants to institutions to housewives flocked there to get their daily supply of fresh fish. There was no mistaking what business they were in. If you were sensitive to a fishy smell, you would be wise to stay several blocks away.

As Mary and Wallenski walked through, he waved to other fishmongers who were dressed just like him.

"See Sal for swordfish, José for shrimp." He banged a counter and proudly shouted, "The best fish in the world

is right here." Several fishmongers nearby bellowed their agreement.

Mary followed him to the back, where they entered a gutting room. The room wasn't large, about ten feet by twelve. On one wall there was a large tin tub with a pipe protruding from it into the floor. Buckets of various sizes, cutting instruments, and newspaper rested on a large table nearby. Wallenski made a hat out of newspaper and put it on as he explained the lay of the land.

"We gut the large ones here—your tuna, swordfish—and the blood drains through this pipe to the sewer." He indicated the buckets. "The guts get dumped here . . ."

"I appreciate the education, I really do. Can I please have the journal now?"

Mary was impatient but also trying to be polite. She could get her fish education at a later date.

Wallenski took a second to process her words. "I understand. Time for business."

With surprising swiftness, he grabbed a cleaver off the table and hurled it at Mary. She was startled but ducked just in time. The cleaver deeply embedded itself in the wooden door where her head had just been. Disappointed at his near miss, he picked a knife off the table and went for her. Mary had regained her composure and was ready for him. She studied Wallenski, measuring his moves. He jabbed at her twice, and she jumped back. The third time he lunged. Mary snagged his knife arm and flipped him over, sending him crashing into the wall and then to the floor. He was stunned but soon shook it off, rose, and charged at her again, meeting with the same result. Wallenski was confused.

"I see you're not familiar with the ancient art of jujitsu,"

Mary commented. "It's all about leverage, a specialty of your boss J. P. Morgan. Or is it Thomas Edison?"

Wallenski wasn't relinquishing any information. He responded by jumping to his feet and scooping another knife off the table. With a knife in each hand, he moved methodically toward her, slapping the two blades together, making a clicking sound.

"Slice and dice, slice and dice," he repeated with maniacal glee.

Not sure what to do, Mary grabbed two empty buckets, the larger one in her right hand. As they sparred, she fended off jabs with her buckets. She was becoming adept at it and was gaining confidence when Wallenski slipped through her defenses and cut her right forearm. She glanced at it and saw the blood streaming down. Wallenski became emboldened and closed in, sensing the kill.

"Slice and dice, slice and dice."

Mary kept desperately defending herself, lifting the left bucket, then the right; the right, then the left. Soon Wallenski was going only to her right. It was the smart move. He knew the wound would eventually take its toll, and Mary would be unable to hold the bucket up much longer. When her arm eventually lowered enough to make her vulnerable, he was ready. But so was Mary. She knew what he was doing and had exaggerated her weakened state. She purposely lowered her arm before she had to, knowing that he'd come in for the kill. When he did, she stunned him with her speed as she deftly deflected his knife and whacked him in the head with the bucket in her left hand. She hit him with such force that the bucket cracked open, and he tumbled, senseless, into the tin tub.

After a huge sigh of relief, Mary attended to her wound. She ripped off a piece of her dress and wrapped it around her forearm. She smiled, thinking of her habit of always lugging her pocketbook wherever she went. Sean had joked about it often and so had others. Even that morning when she was in a frantic rush to catch up with Charles, she had taken it with her. "Always carry a pocketbook," her mother had often told her. "You never know when it will come in handy." This time it was especially true, because in it, there were handcuffs.

Mary dragged a mortified Wallenski, handcuffed behind his back, into Second Street Station. Their reception reflected her change in status among the men. Some cheered. Others applauded. In response, Chief Campbell emerged from his office.

"Who's this sorry creature?" he asked.

"No one of import, Chief." After two policemen carted Wallenski away, Mary approached Chief Campbell, lowering her voice. "If he was hired by who I think he was, he won't be here long."

He spotted her wound. "You better have someone tend to your arm."

Chief Campbell went with her to the hospital to have her arm stitched and bandaged. On the way, she related her meetings with Morgan and Edison and also relayed her suspicions.

"This has gone much further than I ever imagined," he said. "I can't in good conscience allow you to continue."

"You have to let me, Chief. This job is my one chance."
She immediately regretted those words, knowing they
wouldn't persuade him. They wouldn't have persuaded her.

"So far, everything I've said can be attributed to the
ranting of an inexperienced woman. Once I have some concrete proof, then by all means, take over." She didn't want to
ever face that prospect, but one dilemma at a time. Sounding rational and devoid of any emotion that could be classi-
fied as "female behavior" was more important now.

Chief Campbell considered Mary's words. They made
sense. He also knew two attempts had been made on her
life, possibly three if one counted the escapade in the alley.
The question he asked himself was, if Mary were a man,
would he allow her to continue? Then he realized that question had no relevance. He would have never put an inexperienced man on this case. He actually had no power at all in
this matter. If he took Mary off the case, Briggs and Jourdan
would remove him from supervising her and reinstate her.
They wouldn't be satisfied until the case resulted in Mary's
utter failure or her death, and he was sure it didn't make a
difference to them which one it was.

"All right, Mary, you get your wish on one condition. I
want daily reports from you. If and when I decide you need
assistance, you will accept it gladly, or you're gone."

"That's perfectly fine with me, Chief. And in the spirit
of our new agreement, I would like to avail myself of your
assistance now. I need to borrow your carriage."

28

Refreshed and feeling chipper, Barney Wallenski nearly skipped out of Second Street Station and into the hired carriage that was waiting for him. He had been arrested twice before and had never experienced such a quick release or such royal treatment. He was moving up in the world. Work for powerful people, and you get powerful perks. As his carriage took off down the street, he was considering splurging on a steak dinner that night. Before that, he would stop by his ex-wife's apartment to flaunt his success. He was very much looking forward to the rest of his day.

Waiting down the block in Chief Campbell's carriage, Mary watched Wallenski drive off and signaled the driver to follow him. She had cautioned him not to get too close. She didn't want Wallenski to spot her. She was sure he would eventually meet up with his employer, and whether that person was an emissary from Edison or Morgan or someone else, she wanted to be there when he did.

Wallenski made two stops, one to buy cigarettes and another to purchase cologne. He liked finishing off a good

dinner with a smoke. He thought he might ask the woman who lived down the hall to join him. He sensed that after a fine dinner she might be the right kind of grateful.

Mary was becoming concerned. She had hoped he had a meeting planned, but there seemed to be no urgency to his actions. As Wallenski meandered, Mary's mind wandered to Charles and the bizarre twist their relationship had taken. How could she have been so blind to his condition? She would find Charles, and she was convinced that if she was patient, he would eventually let her help him. And patience would also net results with Wallenski. It had better. She didn't have any other choice.

The Bowler Hat was back in the game. It was earlier than even he had hoped, and though he had been specifically told it was only for one assignment and not to expect more so soon, it still felt good, a pleasant diversion from his current duties. Besides, words meant nothing. If he performed well and others took notice, it could lead to another assignment. He was to perform this service for a trusted ally of one of his regular employers. *One at a time,* he thought. Nothing was permanent in this business.

He had been informed the reason for this quick change of heart was that their most trusted men were presently on assignment. He took no offense at it. He was confident he would soon show them his value and return to the ranks of the most trusted.

As the Bowler Hat mopped the sweat that was beginning to stream down his brow, he grunted. He had always

detested those who sweat. It showed frailty and a pathetic lack of character. Yet here he was, sweating.

~

Wallenski made a third stop. Mary was beginning to think her theory about him was flawed. He didn't seem to be in a hurry to go anywhere. This time, though, when he got out of his carriage, it moved on without him, and he entered a building. Mary's driver had parked on an adjacent street before she directed him to take Wallenski's spot after he had gone inside. She glanced at the building he had entered and instantly slapped her leg in frustration. She couldn't follow him inside. She couldn't follow any man inside. It was the Russian baths!

Wallenski got a couple of towels and a key to a locker from the burly Russian attendant. He whistled as he entered the locker room and got undressed. Wallenski once again thought about the woman down the hall and his ex-wife, and he had an inspiration. What would it cost to get both of them in bed with him? He snickered, knowing how impossible that would be to arrange; even if he could, he'd probably die in the crossfire. But the woman down the hall was a definite possibility. He could tell she fancied him. He looked in the mirror and brushed his hair back. He was in no hurry. He was early.

~

So was the Bowler Hat. It had become a habit when he was on a job. He liked to get there first, peruse the lay of the

land, and prepare for all possibilities. Performing this ritual marked the territory as his own, much like a dog claimed home ground. It made him feel more in charge when the actual assignation occurred. The goal was to always get the edge, and the Bowler Hat was good at doing this, very good. The subject wasn't, and from what he had been told, he wasn't very good at anything. The man had been given orders to discourage someone who presented a problem. He had taken it upon himself to handle it by elimination, and he had failed to do so. That made his employer vulnerable.

The Bowler Hat fully understood the situation. The decision to eliminate wasn't the problem. That was always an option. No one would have been upset if it had been executed cleanly and couldn't be traced. But this man was unmistakably a bungler.

When he had heard the details of his assignment, the Bowler Hat was able to ascertain the identity of the ally who had engaged him. He was a very powerful man, and in his dealings with him, the Bowler Hat had found him to be a perfectionist. So he was surprised that he had been so careless in his choice of hire. Still, the man had every right to be upset that his hire couldn't even handle a woman.

As he started to sweat more profusely, the Bowler Hat wrapped another towel around himself as he waited patiently in the steam bath for Barney Wallenski.

∽

Mary had the driver move their carriage further up the block. When Wallenski exited, she didn't want him to see her there waiting for him. She was able to keep an eye on

the entrance from where she was. She alighted from the carriage to fully inspect the surroundings. In order to make sure she had everything covered, she walked to the corner and peered down the other side of the block. Alarmed, she immediately took off, running as fast as she could toward the entrance of the Russian baths. The meeting she had anticipated was taking place, and catching them together was essential to her plan. She hoped she wasn't already late, for what she had seen on the side street parked halfway up the block was J. P. Morgan's ornate carriage.

Whistling and naked except for a towel around his waist, Wallenski entered the steam bath to see the Bowler Hat all alone, covered with towels.

"Good of you to rent out the place for our meeting," he said, referring to the empty steam bath, as he stepped forward to greet the Bowler Hat.

"I value my privacy."

The Bowler Hat removed a towel, revealing that underneath he was fully dressed. In the same motion and with lightning-like velocity, he drove a dagger into Wallenski's throat. Wallenski never had a chance. As he gurgled and blood poured from his neck, it took him a second to realize what had happened. He grabbed at the Bowler Hat, got his hands as far as his neck, but it was too late. All of the energy seeped out of his body, and he sank to the floor, dead.

The Bowler Hat shed the rest of his towels. *Now, that's a clean elimination,* he thought, as if teaching the dead man a lesson.

He felt for the Chinaman's necklace and stuffed it under his shirt. Wallenski had almost broken it when he grabbed for him. The Bowler Hat had grown fond of the necklace, and he had recently found someone to translate the saying on the charm. *"Ji qing ru yi"* meant "May your happiness be according to your wishes." He felt that was especially meaningful to the way he led his life. He bent down and used a towel to wipe the blood off his dagger. Then he left as he had entered—through the back door.

At about this time, Mary had swung the door to the entrance open and was rushing inside. She was immediately stopped by the burly Russian attendant who was sitting with his feet on the counter. He pointed to a sign that read, MEN ONLY.

"Get out," he said.

Mary immediately broke into a thick Irish brogue. "Thought you'd wanna know. A couple of laddies are whizzin' on your front steps."

Her act worked to perfection. He jumped to his feet and stormed out.

"Careful," she called after him. "There's a mighty stiff wind blowin'."

Sure he was gone, she hurried inside to search for Wallenski. When she entered the steam bath, she found him, all alone, lying in a pool of blood. It was an ugly death, vastly unlike the neat, picture-perfect positioning of Charles Goodrich's nattily dressed body on the floor of his study. She was horrified, but there was nothing she could do for Wallenski now. Quickly gathering herself, she bolted out the door.

Once outside, Mary charged past the chief's carriage

and ran up the side street where she had seen J. P. Morgan's carriage. It was gone. The alley was empty.

Out of breath, frustrated by the terrible turns her case and her life were taking, haunted by the horrifying image of Wallenski's dead body, she dropped to her knees. There, in that deserted alley, Mary's emotions got the best of her. Her body revolted, and she started retching.

29

After Mary had reported Wallenski's murder and the coroner had arrived, Chief Campbell was kind enough to let her use his carriage to go home. Mary decided to take a bath, hoping to wash off the dirt of that day's events. It didn't work, not that she really thought it would. The pleasure of bathing was no match for the ugliness of the world. As she dried her hair with a towel, she spotted a large jagged piece of Charles's glass that she had somehow missed in her cleanup. She picked it up, carefully wrapped it in the same washrag she had used when she had burned her hand on the frying pan, and put it in her pocketbook. Charles was broken, too. She was going to keep that piece of glass until she found him and made sure he was whole again.

A while later, Mary stood in the ground-floor hallway of the boardinghouse where Charles and his father had been staying. She had no idea which room was theirs, so she knocked on the landlady's door. She was extremely pleasant until Mary mentioned the Pembertons.

"Those parasites? They snuck out before dawn, shorting me two weeks' rent!"

And she slammed the door in Mary's face.

Nothing was going right. Charles had disappeared, and her case had evaporated. Adding to her woes, it was Friday night, and she was due at her parents' house for dinner. She could have invented an excuse and missed it, but she decided not to. It was hard to explain, but she didn't want to be alone that night. The company might have been hostile, but at least it was familiar.

~

The aroma of a roast cooking engulfed Mary as she entered her parents' kitchen. Certain odors can set a mood. This one seeped into her blood, quieted her nerves, and blanketed her with an overall feeling of warmth and safety. It was a sensation Mary more than welcomed. Her mother stood in front of the stove, pouring the roast's own juices over it with a ladle as it sat in a pan on top. Mary inhaled deeply, sniffing the air.

"Smells delicious," she said.

Elizabeth turned. "Ah, Mary, you're here." She smiled hello, put the roast back in the oven, and went to kiss her. That's when she noticed Mary's bandage. It was also when Mary began to realize her wonderful sensation might be something she had invented, a façade created by a distant memory.

"My Lord, girl, what happened?" Elizabeth exclaimed.

"I'd rather not say."

"You might as well. I'm gonna find out sooner or later."

Mary knew she would, and she resented it. She was tired of worrying about her mother's opinions, always having to cushion her words so she wouldn't explode. She decided to tell her and not spare any gory details.

"A hired killer stabbed me while he was trying to gut me like a fish." Mary stared at her mother, daring her to respond.

Elizabeth didn't. Instead, she swiveled back toward the counter and began slicing an onion. Mary was well acquainted with all of her mother's techniques, and this one signaled her complete disapproval. It meant she would soon be berated. Elizabeth didn't disappoint.

"Why can't you be normal like other girls?" It was spoken quietly and controlled, as if it were a simple, harmless question.

"Do define 'normal,' Mother. I seem to—"

Elizabeth slammed down her knife with a thud, cutting Mary off. "People are laughin' at you!"

"Oh? And how do you respond, when they laugh? By defending your Mary?"

"There's nothin' to defend. You're an embarrassment, girl!"

Mary blanched. Her mother's words did more damage than Wallenski's knife had done.

"Predictable, so predictable." The emotion was building in her. It may have started with the events of the day, but it was multiplied by years of being told how odd and disappointing she was. She was tired and no longer had the strength to hold it in.

"Just once, Mother, just once, I'd like to hear, 'I'm with you, Mary girl, all the way.' That'd be nice. No, it'd be fuckin' great!"

Mary had purposely cursed, knowing it would increase her mother's upset. It had its desired effect. Elizabeth's mouth fell open, her hands flew to her chest, and she held her breath as if her lungs had ceased to function. Mary stormed out the door into the backyard.

She was about to collapse into tears when she spotted her friend Sarah sitting on the back porch. It wasn't that long ago that she had borrowed Sarah's dress, but her stomach appeared to have pushed out further since then, and Sarah looked very close to popping. The sight of her good friend was therapeutic. Mary rushed over to Sarah and hugged her.

"Sarah, it's so good to see you!"

"And there's so much more of me to see," Sarah joked as they separated and she stroked her protruding belly.

"You already have a boy and a girl. What do you want this time?"

"What I want," Sarah responded, "is for Walter to leave me alone. Every time he looks at me I get pregnant."

Mary knew Sarah was kidding. "Oh, Sarah, I'm so happy for you." Mary hugged her again but this time held her tight. She would never be a gusher; this was as close as she would ever come. When Mary let go, she continued, "This is a wonderful surprise."

"A surprise meant to inspire," Sarah said meaningfully.

Elizabeth's beliefs were no secret. Sarah was well aware the dinner invitation she had received had a purpose.

"Did you hear?"

Sarah nodded. "Reminded me of old times."

Sarah's presence calmed Mary. It made her less angry and more philosophical. She stepped off the porch and headed for the swings with Sarah by her side.

"The more things change, the more they stay the same," Mary recited reflectively.

"I wonder who makes up sayings like that." Sarah wasn't asking for a response, but she got one.

"Alphonse Karr," Mary stated, and Sarah looked at her, puzzled. "The quote. He's a French novelist."

Sarah smiled. "You would know that."

Each of them sat on a swing.

"Your life's turned out well, Sarah. I'm glad."

"I've made do with what I have." Mary looked at her askance, and Sarah quickly added, "Don't misunderstand. I love Walter and the children. I also recognized early on I wasn't marked for something special."

"Oh, come on . . ."

"But every time I read the newspaper, my buttons burst with pride. 'That's my friend Mary,' I say. 'She'll catch that killer, know why? She's the best-est chess player ever.'"

Mary laughed, and Sarah joined her.

"Sean still thinks I used to cheat."

"Naturally," said Sarah. "How else could a silly little girl outsmart a big, strong boy?"

They laughed some more, then Mary quieted. Sarah noticed. She could feel her friend's pain.

"Sometimes I wonder about the choices I've made," Mary mused. "Maybe I want too much, push too hard . . ."

"Don't do that, Mary."

"What?"

"Doubt yourself. You're brilliant and beautiful and special, and you should've been told that all your life."

Sarah's words couldn't have been more heartfelt or timely. And they were words Mary had longed to hear.

"Oh, Sarah," was all she could get out before tears started streaming down her cheeks. The hurt poured from the deepest part of her. It came from years of rejection and self-doubt inflicted by those who were supposed to protect her and a world that didn't understand her. Sarah wanted to erase Mary's anguish and was frustrated that she couldn't. Pretty soon she was crying, too. Eventually, Sarah took two handkerchiefs out of her pocketbook and handed one to Mary.

"Lord, I can't do anything right," Sarah wailed. "This is supposed to be a pep talk, and here we are bawling like two fools."

They wiped their tears and started reminiscing. New times, old times, it didn't make a difference. They wound up talking, laughing, and crying far into the night.

$\sim$

Briggs was working late. He had spent a good part of the last two hours trying to draft a reply letter to Mayor Chapin. His Honor wanted to know why there was no movement in the Goodrich case. Briggs was subtly attempting to blame Chief Campbell and Mary, but subtlety was not his forte. Hence, his wastepaper basket was filled with crumpled sheets of failed drafts when Jourdan burst in with a smug look on his face.

"That obnoxious grin is giving me the bends. Why are you still here?"

"I am here to save your rear." Full of himself, Jourdan delivered his statement with a flourish. He took a telegram out of his jacket pocket and waved it in front of Briggs.

"What's that," cracked Briggs, "an invitation to another séance?"

"Albany wired me back. They have in custody a Roscoe Rodriguez." He put the telegram in front of Briggs as he went on. "Arrested for counterfeiting, but—and take close notice of what follows the *but*—it was after he failed to elicit a five-thousand-dollar bribe from a man to stay away from the man's wife. Sounds very much like the type of swindle Lucette described to us."

Briggs was reading the telegram. "And he had just arrived from New York."

"Well?" Jourdan repeatedly tapped his foot. "I'm waiting for an apology."

Briggs didn't let that bother him. He also didn't point out that the séance and Roscoe's being in Albany could easily be coincidences. The possibility of not having to write that letter to Mayor Chapin was too appealing.

"We better dispatch two men to Albany to pick him up."

"Already done," replied Jourdan, pleased to be a step ahead of Briggs. "And we should send Handley out of town, to Philadelphia or someplace. Campbell's already told us she's searching for Roscoe. Tell her he's been spotted there."

"Good idea. That woman's a press magnet."

"And when we deliver the Goodrich killer, we want them all to ourselves."

They smiled like foxes in a henhouse with chicken feathers all over their faces.

30

In a way, Mary welcomed the trip to Philadelphia. A pleasant train ride and a change of environment could clear her head of all the recent trying events in her life and allow her to refocus on the Goodrich case. She had no illusions about the outcome of the trip. Purportedly, the commissioners had sent notice to Boston, Philadelphia, and other neighboring cities to be on the lookout for Roscoe, and Philadelphia had responded. However, the clues she had been given about Roscoe's whereabouts—more specifically sightings of the man—were too vague. No names were given, just places where he had supposedly "been seen." On that memorable night she spent drinking with Tesla, he had criticized Edison's scientific methods as "going straw by straw to find a needle in a haystack when ninety percent of that labor could be erased with simple theory and calculation." With the information provided to her, she would have to go straw by straw, and it was unlikely the needle would still be there, if it had ever been at all. When she had questioned Chief Campbell about the feasibility of such a trip, he'd skirted the issue.

"It came from upstairs. The department is built on orders, and we must all take them. We can only hope there is a greater plan."

That was all Chief Campbell could say. The fact was, he didn't know what Briggs and Jourdan had brewing, but he figured they had to be pretty sure of themselves if they were willing to spend department money on a trip to Philadelphia. Maybe they were planning to blame it on him when the trip proved to be a fiasco. One truth was sacrosanct: his and Mary's heads were on the chopping block, and he had to be on constant alert for the ax. It could come from any direction. Hopefully, they'd have enough time to duck.

Without unpacking, Mary dropped her bags at the William Penn Hotel, a place with modest accommodations but centrally located on Market Street. She hadn't chosen the hotel—the police department had—but she didn't care. Almost anything was nicer than her tenement. The search would be a long one, and she was eager to get started. Mary decided to go down the list of leads she had been given, taking them one at a time, straw by straw.

Her first stop was at the Philadelphia Baseball Grounds. Supposedly, Roscoe had been spotted there. She didn't have the luxury of the name of the spotter, just that an employee at the ballpark had seen him. Baseball was growing and becoming very popular, and so on game day, the Phillies had a lot of employees to handle the crowd, which often totaled ten thousand or more. There was also a reasonable amount of turnover, so whoever might have seen Roscoe the week before might no longer be working there. To somewhat prepare herself, Mary had had Kate describe Roscoe to an artist who sketched a rendering of him, but she knew finding him

on this type of search was highly unlikely. Still, Mary methodically went from employee to employee and received the answers she expected—a shake of the head or an emphatic no. One of the vendors thought he had seen Roscoe, then realized he was thinking of a baseball player, Charles Roscoe Barnes, and he didn't play baseball anymore and didn't look like the sketch. That was the way Mary's day was going.

After the baseball grounds, she proceeded to the Episcopal Church of St. Thomas, where a black woman pointed out the folly of her mission.

"You're looking for a white man? You see anyone white around here?"

The woman gestured toward the parishioners, who were all filing out of services and all black. Mary was just doing her job, no matter how ridiculous it made her feel.

It didn't help that the woman added, "They got you good. Like my kids. They love sending others on wild goose chases."

By now, Mary was certain the woman was right. She thanked her for her time and moved on. She spent the rest of the day and into the night chasing down phony leads at the U.S. Mint, up and down Market Street, and Benjamin Franklin's grave. When she got back to the hotel, she was so tired she lay down on the bed and fell asleep with her clothes on.

The next morning she woke up, somewhat refreshed, and went out again, expecting more of the same. Her expectations were met. At noon, she was at Independence Hall after suffering a morning of nos and a multitude of looks doubting her sanity. As always, the hall was crowded with patriotic tourists and history buffs who had flocked to the birthplace of the Declaration of Independence and

the Constitution before ambling across the street to see the Liberty Bell.

She was interviewing an eighteen-year-old security guard who was trying to impress her. There were eighteen-year-olds who were men, and there were those who were boys. This one was unquestionably a boy, a boy who had fantasies about pretty older women in their twenties.

"Never saw Roscoe," he said. "I'd remember. I have a keen eye for detail."

"No doubt. I could tell straightaway that you're a master observer."

He mistook Mary's sardonic response for flirting.

"Come back later. I'll provide you with a personal tour, and then we can have dinner. I've been told that I'm a wonderful cook."

"Really? What a delightful invitation." Mary's words dripped with sarcasm, but his adolescent exuberance interpreted it as encouragement.

"I have the whole house to myself. My parents are out of town in Haddonfield."

His comment almost demanded a wink, but even he stopped short of that. Mary had been preparing to let him down gently and wander on to conduct more pointless conversations when his remark stopped her.

"Did you say Haddonfield?"

"Yes, Haddonfield, across the river in New Jersey. They'll be there all week."

Mary immediately turned and started heading for the exit. The boy became anxious. He could see that he was losing the woman he'd never really had.

"Where are you going?"

"Haddonfield. I've had my fill of goose."

The boy looked confused. "Goose? I was thinking of hamburger steaks."

～

For over a year Mary had listened to Kate's stories about Haddonfield. As she traveled across the river on the ferry and took a buggy into town, Mary's mind was on her. From everything Kate had told her about her family, Mary felt she knew her parents, and they had to be worried. She wanted to assure them that though Kate had been through a traumatic experience, she had withstood it and was doing well. Besides, she needed a respite from this pointless Philadelphia sojourn, and if she could accomplish something positive and good, it would at least give some meaning to this wild goose chase of hers.

As Mary passed quaint vacation cottages, small farms, and quiet roads, she couldn't help smiling. Kate had painted a vivid picture of her small-town life where everyone was on a first-name basis and they all knew each other's business. For a multitude of reasons, people often exaggerate descriptions of their background. As far as Mary could see, Kate hadn't. It all appeared to be just as she had described it.

The town of Haddonfield was all of two blocks long and consisted of a bank, a post office, a print shop, a pharmacy, and a general store. The bank and post office took up the first block and the others the second. Mary had always lived in a big city. Though Haddonfield looked charming, she sympathized with Kate's desire to escape it. The lack of stimulation had to have been maddening.

The Haddonfield General Store was between the print shop and the pharmacy. It was a little larger than Mary had imagined, but she reasoned that it made sense. A general store had to stock a wide variety of products. When she got out of the buggy, the driver informed her that when she was ready to return to the ferry, she could find him at the pharmacy having an ice-cream soda. Mary nodded and went inside.

The store was a study in precision and tidiness. All the clothes were neatly folded and the cans evenly stacked. Products in boxes were lined up one behind another, and absolutely nothing was out of place. Evidently, an inordinate amount of care went into maintaining this store, and it was easy to conclude that Kate's parents took great pride in their business. As Mary browsed, trying to imagine Kate in the center of it, a slightly pudgy middle-aged woman approached her. Her pleasant smile was infinitely more inviting and sincere than that of any Brooklyn shopkeeper.

"Hello. Can I help you?"

"I was just admiring your store."

"We take great pride in it. Been in my husband's family for forty years now."

Mary studied the woman's face. This was Kate's mother, and she could see a resemblance.

"You must be Mrs. Stoddard."

"No, can't say I am. The name's King."

"King?" Mary wanted to make sure she heard her correctly.

"Been so for the twenty-seven years Isaac and I have been married."

"I'm sorry. I thought the Stoddards owned this store."

"Stoddards, huh? Never heard of 'em, and we're the only general store in Haddonfield."

Mary couldn't understand how she could have gotten her facts so confused. She slowly turned to leave and spotted a photograph. It was a framed photo portrait of the King family hanging on the wall behind the cash register. Besides the parents, there were two girls, one about nineteen, the other sixteen, and the latter was clearly Kate. Mary went to it and stared for a moment to make sure.

"Charming photograph, huh?" commented Mrs. King.

"Yes, lovely."

"Those are my girls, Franny and Lizzie."

"They're beautiful," said Mary, encouraging her to continue.

"Franny, my eldest, lives in Philadelphia now. Married to a very prominent lawyer." She was bragging, but within the limits of a proud parent. Mary liked that. She knew she'd never catch her mother boasting about her. What was more important, though, was that Mrs. King seemed to be in a talkative mood. Mary had questions.

"You must be very proud."

"Yeah, that Franny is something. Pregnant with her first child."

"Oh, wonderful. Congratulations."

Mrs. King smiled her thanks. Mary tried to be as nonchalant as possible as she asked, "And what about Lizzie?"

Mrs. King shook her head. "It's funny how one child goes one way and the other, well, nothin' ever goes right."

"Lizzie was trouble?"

"It happened sudden-like. One minute she was perfect,

the apple of her daddy's eye, the next . . ." Mrs. King stopped. "But you don't wanna hear . . ."

"No, no, go ahead, please."

"When Lizzie was seventeen, we sent her to Taunton to straighten her out."

"Did boarding school help?"

"Boarding school?" Mrs. King squinted at Mary. "Honey, Taunton's a lunatic asylum. Lizzie shot a boy, wounded him really bad, 'cause he broke their date to the school dance."

Mary was floored. She was having trouble absorbing this information. "Because he broke their date?" she repeated, trying to make sure she had heard correctly.

Mrs. King nodded solemnly. Whirling, Mary turned to digest Mrs. King's words. Everything suddenly took on a new perspective. It was as if she had entered a surrealistic world where formerly benign things were jumping out at her. For the first time she noticed that a large section of the store was devoted to hunting equipment and firearms. There were many varieties of rifles, including long-range ones that were American-made but also ones of German, French, and English origin. The pistols were displayed in order of size, from the double- and single-action revolvers down to palm pistols like the derringer. There were also bowie knives, hunting knives, brass knuckles, some by themselves and some incorporated into knife-and-gun combinations. If it could kill, this store had it. Statements Kate had made kept flashing through Mary's mind. "My father always said a lady should know how to protect herself," "Charlie and I were not everything I made us out to be," and "They think I'm crazy." The last one kept repeating and repeating in her brain.

Mary was finding it hard to breathe. Mrs. King noticed.

"Are you all right, honey?"

Mary was quick to cover. "Nothing, just a dizzy spell. Happens all the time. So, whatever happened to Lizzie?"

"God knows. She escaped from Taunton three years ago. Sure hope she's found peace."

Mary had been wishing for a magic answer that would absolve Kate, but all the magic had been sucked out of the air and she was left with only logic. It was very possible, more than possible, that Charles Goodrich had called off their engagement and that Kate had killed him. Mary chastised herself for her stupidity. Kate was the fiancée. She should always have been a viable suspect, but Mary had completely overlooked the possibility. What was it about her that made her completely miss gaping flaws in the people she liked? First there was Charles and now Kate.

She tried to maintain an appearance of normalcy while in the store, but once she had said good-bye to Mrs. King and had gone outside, she let go, stumbling a few steps toward a pole and clinging to it. Out of breath, the fresh country air did nothing for her. She forced herself to think, to put a plan together. When she got back to Philadelphia, she would send Chief Campbell a telegram telling him to detain Kate for questioning.

Mary planned to spend her train ride back to Manhattan trying to figure out how her friend might not be the killer. Having not yet found that rationale, she slowly made her way to the pharmacy to collect her driver, praying to God she'd get to Kate before she could hurt anyone else.

31

Jourdan and Briggs stood on the train platform of track nine in Grand Central Depot. The noon train from Albany had just arrived, and as the passengers streamed by, they anxiously peered through the crowd for their man. It didn't take long.

A handsome Spaniard in his late twenties was being escorted in handcuffs toward them by two police officers. Roscoe Rodriguez was back in New York. Jourdan slapped his companion on the shoulder, and Briggs smirked. The Goodrich killer was theirs, and so would be all the glory that went with him.

"We'll take him from here, boys," said Jourdan.

Jourdan and Briggs relieved the officers of Rodriguez and escorted him up the platform toward the main terminal by themselves. They wanted to shout for joy, but instead they put on their most official faces as they led him through the doors.

A throng of reporters mobbed them as they entered the main lobby area. Briggs and Jourdan acted surprised at the

presence of the press, even though they were the ones who had leaked the arrival of Rodriguez. Relishing the moment, they stood tall and preened as flash powder exploded from cameras. The reporters kept firing questions at them until Jourdan raised his right hand to quiet them. He and Briggs had rehearsed this moment and had flipped a coin to see who would go first.

"Hold on, gentlemen, please," said Jourdan. He paused for effect. He wanted to make sure everyone could hear him. If he had spoken any louder, he would have been heard on Lexington Avenue. "This poor excuse for a human being is Roscoe Rodriguez, the man responsible for the murder of Charles Goodrich."

"I never killed anybody," Roscoe Rodriguez shouted, protesting his innocence.

"You'll have a fair trial, sir," Jourdan responded calmly, "before you're hanged."

Briggs chimed in, "Or make history . . . by being the first to be fried in the electric chair."

There were some laughs mixed with chatter as more flash powder popped.

"Commissioner Jourdan and I spearheaded the investigation," Briggs continued as he returned to their planned speech, "and we are thrilled to finally get this vermin off the streets. Now, if you'll excuse us, boys, we have a job to do."

As they made their way through the crowd with Roscoe Rodriguez, they were barraged with questions. Briggs glanced at Jourdan. Everything was working perfectly.

On track four, Chief Campbell waited for a different train. He had gotten Mary's telegram and immediately dispatched officers to the Lowry Hat Factory and to Kate and Mary's tenement building. Lizzie King, a.k.a. Kate Stoddard, had vanished. Chief Campbell found it perplexing, but he wasn't aware of how fearful Kate was of getting caught. She was constantly on alert and had taken to carrying an umbrella with her, rain or shine. On her way home, Kate had spotted an officer inside the door of her tenement building. She shielded her face with the umbrella, kept on walking, and never returned.

Mary stepped off the Philadelphia train and was surprised to see Chief Campbell.

"Chief, you didn't have to meet me."

"I know." He took her arm and carefully guided her toward an exit that was in the opposite direction of the main lobby, where Briggs and Jourdan were performing their dog-and-pony show. He cautioned her not to speak, and it wasn't until they were out on the streets of Manhattan that he informed her of Kate's disappearance. It was the last piece of damning evidence. Mary was sure her friend was guilty.

"How could Kate have found out?"

"Forget about her for now," said Chief Campbell. He couldn't think of any good way to phrase it, so he just let it out. "I've been ordered to fire you."

Mary came to an abrupt halt. The last few days had been full of shocking surprises. She wondered when they were going to end.

"Commissioners Jourdan and Briggs believe they already have their man," he explained. "So your job is done."

"But we both know—"

"It doesn't matter what we know."

Mary saw her one chance at achieving her dream ending in utter failure. She couldn't let that happen.

"Give me an opportunity to bring her in. I can do it. I know I can. Please."

Chief Campbell hated the position the commissioners had put him in. He didn't resent authority. What he resented was that any authority had been given to those two idiots. He had grown to like Mary. She was smart and had good instincts. She deserved a break. And she was probably right about Kate Stoddard's being the one they were after.

"We never talked. You never saw me. And don't dare show up until you have her."

Incredibly grateful, Mary went to hug him. "Thanks, Chief! If you weren't married . . ."

"What?"

Her hands still in the air, she froze and lowered them. Not a good idea. Chief Campbell was not the hugging type.

"You . . . wouldn't be married. That's all."

Mary waved a self-conscious good-bye, then disappeared around the corner. Chief Campbell watched her as he wondered how long he would be able to keep Briggs and Jourdan at bay with the flimsy excuse that Mary had gotten lost in Philadelphia.

Jourdan and Briggs couldn't have been more pleased with their performance for the press at Grand Central Depot. All that was left were a few minor details, and Jourdan was

excited that Lucette was at the police station to see the conclusion of the case. He was sure she'd be impressed. They hadn't progressed beyond spooning, and he hoped she would finally succumb to his unbridled passion.

Lucette slipped her arm through his as she, Jourdan, and Briggs walked through the halls of the station to the interrogation area.

"I'm so proud of you, Jordy!" she squealed.

"Not here, Lucy," Jourdan whispered as he disengaged his arm. "This is business." Briggs snorted. In his opinion, Jourdan had thrown out any sense of decorum the second he took up with Lucette.

They reached the door to the interrogation room and stopped to savor the moment, Lucette quivering with anticipation. Briggs opened the door, and they went inside.

Still handcuffed, Rodriguez sat at a table with the two officers who had escorted him off the train. Lucette looked impatiently around the room.

"Okay," she said. "I'm ready. Where's Roscoe?"

Jourdan realized Lucette might be somewhat jittery. He patiently waited until he caught her eye, then pointed to Rodriguez. "Right there," he stated with a comforting smile.

"That's not Roscoe."

Jourdan got closer to Rodriguez and pointed again. "Sure it is. He's our Roscoe!"

"Well, he may be your Roscoe, but that certainly isn't the Roscoe I know."

Briggs had been watching this exchange with as much patience as he could muster. He was a time bomb, and the clock had ticked to zero.

"I knew we were being hornswoggled!"

Jourdan's head was swimming. "Wait a minute. There has to be an explanation!"

"An explanation," Briggs responded, pretending to consider his suggestion. "Ah, yes, of course. Here's one." He looked Jourdan directly in the eye. "Her tits are blocking your vision!"

Jourdan lunged for Briggs, knocking the cigar out of his mouth. Briggs retaliated with a knee to his groin. Lucette screamed. Jourdan had just socked Briggs in the abdomen when the two officers got between them to break it up.

During the scuffle, Roscoe Rodriguez was laughing hysterically.

32

Mary had spent two and a half days camped out at the Twelfth Street Post Office. She got there an hour before it opened and stayed until an hour after closing. Her reasoning was based on the premise that old habits die hard. Kate had consistently received her mail there since Mary had first met her, and if she was still in the city, chances were that wouldn't have changed.

On the third day at lunchtime, for those who had jobs that allowed for such a luxury, people poured in and out of the post office. Mary leaned on a lamppost, trying to appear casual but watching carefully for any sign of Kate.

A policeman rode up on a horse and stopped in front of her, blocking her view. She moved to the front of the horse, so she could still have a decent line of sight to the post office.

"Madam," the policeman declared, "you've been loitering here for days, and the storekeepers are nervous."

"Nervous?" Mary replied, keeping her eye on the post office. "Why in the world would . . ." And then she understood

his implication. "I'm no whore, sir. I defy anyone to say I left with a man."

"Madam, no one accused you of being good at it."

This was a delicate situation. She was lucky that the officer didn't recognize her, because she was supposed to be off the case and working incognito. Yet she couldn't divulge who she was in order to get rid of him for the same reason. She was pondering this problem when she spotted Kate across the street. She had just rounded the corner and was on her way to pick up her mail. Mary abruptly scooted to her right and hid behind the horse's rear. The policeman took exception.

"What in the world do you think you're—?"

"I'm leaving, Officer. Good day."

Having seen Kate enter the post office, Mary scurried across the street to position herself for when she left. The policeman watched her walk the length of the opposite block, then turn the corner. Satisfied that his job was done, he rode on.

Kate came out ten minutes later stuffing the last of the letters into her handbag. She didn't realize that some were actually sticking out as she headed to the corner from which she had come. Mary had counted on her returning in that direction, and to avoid detection, she was behind the opposite corner, checking periodically for Kate. She followed, keeping a safe distance behind, and watched Kate turn down a side street.

Mary turned down the same side street, but there was no Kate. She had disappeared. Looking from side to side, Mary ran along the rows of brownstones that covered each

side of the street. Still no Kate. It didn't make sense. It was possible Kate had an apartment in one of the brownstones, but this was a higher-rent district and Mary doubted she could afford one here.

Walking back up the block, Mary was more meticulous in her search and was rewarded when she spied an envelope on the sidewalk next to stairs that led down to the basement of a brownstone. It was addressed to Kate. Instead of walking down into the unknown, Mary climbed a few steps up toward the entrance and peered over the banister. Kate was there, hiding at the side of the bottom staircase, crouching and waiting.

"Hello, Kate," she called out.

Startled, Kate's head jerked up in the direction of her voice as Mary continued.

"I always loved games. Hide-and-seek was one of my favorites."

"If you had grown up in Haddonfield," Kate said as she stood, gathering herself, "you'd know not to hide behind the hind legs of a horse. Most times you'll get kicked."

Kate pulled out a pistol and pointed it at Mary. She motioned with it.

"Please join me."

Mary had no choice but to comply. At this point, she was convinced that Kate was good with weapons. Her voice had also taken on a strange detachment, which meant, Mary concluded, that Kate might be capable of anything.

"All of Brooklyn's looking for you, Kate," Mary said as she took her time descending the stairs toward the basement.

She was almost at the bottom when Kate pulled the

trigger. The bullet hit Mary in her right shoulder, the impact knocking her to the ground.

"I can't allow you to arrest me, Mary," Kate said, sounding genuinely apologetic. "Please don't be upset. It's not serious, I promise."

It certainly felt serious, but Mary knew she had to ignore the pain as much as she could. Keeping the conversation going became her priority, or one of two things was going to happen: Kate would either leave or kill her.

"Like the boy you shot in high school?"

"Oh, you know about that. You wouldn't have liked him, Mary. He was vulgar, nothing like your Charles."

"Was your Charlie vulgar?"

For the first time, Kate showed some real emotion. Remembering Charles Goodrich stirred up unpleasant feelings of anger, rejection, and resentment.

"He had it in his date book. 'Eight a.m. to seven p.m.—work. Eight thirty p.m.—Pick up clothes at Lin's Laundry. Nine p.m.—Break up with Kate.'" She turned to Mary, full of hurt and rage. "I came after laundry, Mary. Laundry!"

Now Mary knew who had torn the pages out of the date book. More important though, they had stopped talking, and that wasn't good, especially considering how angry Kate was.

"I don't know if it'll make you feel any better," Mary said, wracking her brain for topics to keep Kate engaged. "But I just discovered my Charles is a morphine addict."

"Well, what do you know," mused Kate. "Men are scum. You and I are too good for them, Mary."

"I couldn't agree with you more."

Mary was trying to figure out how she was going to get

to her feet and knock the pistol out of Kate's hand. She tested her shoulder by trying to move. The pain was too great, and she groaned. Luckily, Kate was lost somewhere in the recesses of her mind, traveling on a road meant only for the pathologically insane.

"I showed Charlie what true love is. I spent all night holding him, cleaning him, changing his clothes. My Charlie was going to look perfect. When I left, he was more handsome than when he was alive."

In spite of all that had transpired between them, Mary felt pity for her.

"Kate, let me get you help."

But Kate would have none of it. "I've been to Taunton. I'm not going back!" she vehemently declared, and started up the stairs to the street. Soon Kate's emotions did an about-face, and so did she. She returned and bent over Mary.

"I'm really going to miss you, Mary," she said sweetly. "Please don't make me kill you."

Then, in a flash, she disappeared onto the street above. Mary struggled to get to her feet. She knew she had to somehow overcome the pain. She thought of all that had taken place since she took the case—the giant German who attacked her twice, Edison, Morgan, Wallenski, the Chungs, Charles, and now Kate. She became angry, very angry. It soon turned to outrage, and it was more than enough to propel Mary to the railing, where she grabbed on to it with her left hand and lifted herself up. There was pain, but it didn't matter. She made her way up the stairs and stumbled onto the street.

Mary spotted Kate halfway down the block, and the folly

of chasing after her set in. In her state, it would be almost impossible to catch her, and if she did, what could she do? Frustrated, Mary anxiously looked around for an answer. She saw the policeman who had rousted her earlier coming down the block on his horse.

"Officer, officer!" she screamed. "That woman's the Goodrich killer!" And she pointed to Kate.

She was afraid he wouldn't believe her, but her being shot was evidence enough. The policeman broke into a gallop, heading toward Kate.

"Be careful," Mary called after him. "She has a pistol!"

The policeman pulled his pistol out of his holster and pointed it skyward as he was riding. Kate kept walking, minding her own business as if she hadn't the slightest idea what was going on.

The policeman closed in on her. "Halt, madam. Halt!"

With the cool alacrity of a trained killer, Kate turned, dropped to one knee, and shot the policeman. He fell like a duck in a shooting gallery, his horse galloping off down the street. Mary was shocked. She wanted to help him, but now was not the time. Pistol in hand, Kate was marching up the street toward Mary.

Mary scrambled for her life. She tried to run but soon discovered it was useless. Her wound slowed her down too much, and all the time Kate was gaining on her. She ducked down the stairs toward the basement of another brownstone and hid behind a wall where she couldn't be seen by anyone on the stairs. It was a desperate move. Mary didn't have a pistol or knife or anything to defend herself when Kate came down those stairs. And she was coming.

Then she remembered. Mary ripped open her pocket-book and took out the broken piece of glass she had wrapped in a washrag and had kept as a symbol of Charles. It needed to be a lot more useful than a symbol now. She re-wrapped the washrag to protect her skin before placing it in her left hand. The jagged edge exposed, Mary raised it high, poised to strike. She was breathing heavily, and she knew that would give her away. So, holding her breath, sweating, Mary stood there, opposite the basement, waiting to see if she was going to live.

At first sight of Kate, Mary lunged, slicing wildly at her, hoping that if she didn't hit her mark, she might scare her enough to have time to get the pistol out of her hand. How she was going to do that, she didn't know. But it didn't matter. Mary hit her mark. She cut a deep gash in Kate's right forearm, causing her to drop the pistol. Mary immediately kicked it away. Kate staggered back, her left hand covering the gash on her right arm, but that didn't stop the blood from oozing out. She was in a complete state of disbelief.

"But . . . you don't carry a weapon."

The adrenaline in Mary's body was working overtime. She had never felt such a surge of energy. She tossed the piece of glass aside.

"Something else you don't know about me. I'm a lefty, you crazy bitch!"

With everything she had, Mary drove her left fist into Kate's chin. Kate's head shot back, and the force of the blow propelled her against the wall, then down onto the cement. It would be a long while before she woke up.

~

The doctor patched up Mary's shoulder and put it in a sling. She was lucky. Kate's bullet hadn't broken any bones, and he assured her the healing process would be speedy. Kate had promised that the wound wasn't serious, and it wasn't. Unfortunately, the news wasn't as good for the policeman. He was going to live, but the recovery would take months and his career was over. Mary went to his hospital room and thanked him profusely, but she still felt awful. It had been his dream to be a policeman, and she knew only too well what it was like to have your dreams dashed.

Mary got a hero's welcome from the men at Second Street Station. They stood up and applauded when she entered. Sean even planted a kiss on her cheek in front of everyone.

"Good job, sis. I'm proud of you."

Mary searched his face to determine whether his display of affection was real or for show. It was real, and she was touched by it.

"Mary Handley," boomed Chief Campbell's voice as he came out of his office. "You were wounded in the line of duty and need to be home resting. Now go."

He waved his hand for her to leave, but Mary didn't budge. "I promise I'll go home, Chief. Right after I see Kate."

Chief Campbell turned to Sean. "My sympathies, Handley. Now I know why you were having so much trouble getting her to shoo when we first met. Your sister's incurably hardheaded."

"Yes, sir, Chief. Hardheaded and the smartest person I know."

It would be a while before Mary got used to Sean complimenting her.

It was a good walk to get to the cell where Kate was being held. Mary and Chief Campbell had to pass a row of offices before entering an anteroom to the holding cells. On the way, the two of them chatted about the crime, a normal occurrence after a big arrest. As they entered the anteroom and the guard took out his keys to unlock the iron-bar door leading to the cells, Chief Campbell scratched his head.

"He breaks it off with her, so she returns the next night and blows his brains out." It was hard for Chief Campbell to process. "I'm glad my courting days are over."

"Somehow I knew I'd find her at the post office," Mary said. "But I still don't completely understand it. If she wasn't writing her parents . . ."

"We looked through her letters. She was answering men's personal ads. Apparently, that's how she met Goodrich."

The guard had opened the door, and they entered. There were only four cells. Chief Campbell stopped at the fourth and pointed. "Well, here she is."

Mary froze. She had to see Kate, and yet she knew it was going to be difficult for her. She slowly edged closer. Kate was sitting on the cement floor, her back against the wall with her right arm bandaged. Without blinking, she stared ahead in what seemed like a complete state of stupor. Mary had read about this affliction in medical journals. Recently, doctors had given her condition the label of catatonia.

Chief Campbell pointed. "See that large locket around her neck?"

"Grandma Stoddard's," Mary said, remembering happier days. "That's where she was going to put the pictures of her and Charles Goodrich's grandchildren."

"Her plans changed. The inside is smeared with Goodrich's dried blood. She said it makes her feel closer to him."

The more Mary heard, the sadder she got. She couldn't help feeling that the part of Kate she had loved, the naïve country girl caught up in the big city, was real and was somehow being strangled by whatever disease it was that perverted minds like hers.

Mary got nearer to the bars. "Kate. Kate, it's me, Mary."

There was no response and no hope. They waited a little longer, then left.

When they were gone, Kate blinked. She thought she had heard something, a faint sound of a voice from long ago. There was no need to answer. That was another lifetime, when the world had waged war against her. Just the thought made her insecure. She desperately felt for her locket and found it. Its presence soothed her, and she slowly exhaled. It was silly to get upset. No one could take away what she had. Charlie was gone, but they would be together again someday. Their love was destined, and destiny could never be changed. She flipped open the locket, licked two fingers, then dipped them into the dry blood that lined its inside. She opened her mouth and eagerly pressed the two fingers to her tongue. Charlie was so thoughtful to leave her a part of him. This way they'd always have their moments together. Their passion would never die.

33

Just as you think the circus can't get any more exciting, in come the elephants. During the next couple of weeks, Mary's celebrity increased. One headline after another featured the miraculous woman who had done a man's job in capturing the Goodrich killer. Then, as happens, the news cycle changed. There was a series of murders in Manhattan, and everyone went off to cover them. The circus pulled up its tents and left. Mary dropped out of print.

It didn't bother her at all. It had been fun while it lasted. She had a wonderful evening with Sarah and her family. Chief Campbell invited her to his home for dinner, and she got to meet his wife. She was bright, observant, and really knew how to handle him: in short, she was everything Mary had imagined. Even Elizabeth congratulated Mary, though she soon backtracked, tempering her praise with suggestions on how Mary could use her celebrity to find a suitable husband. It became a full retreat when she concluded (out loud, of course) that most men would now be intimidated by

Mary, and that would lessen her chances of finding a mate. Alphonse Karr again: the more things change, the more they stay the same.

Being out of the spotlight gave Mary a chance to heal and think. Wondering about Charles was fruitless, so she concentrated on the case. There were still many things about it that bothered her. Who were these people who had tried to kill her? Kate couldn't afford to hire anyone. She had seen J. P. Morgan's carriage at the Russian baths and naturally assumed that in his determination to find Goodrich's journal, he had hired Wallenski and then had him removed. But that didn't explain the large German man who had attacked her before she knew there was a journal. And who was Roscoe? Was he just a business acquaintance or did he have some greater significance? The mere mention of his name had scared Mortimer, so there must have been something there. Questions like these plagued her. Merely solving the Goodrich murder was not enough. Being who she was, Mary would not rest until she had found answers.

During this period, she was able to come to one definite decision. She had had an acrimonious encounter with Edison. He had fallen from grace, her grace. She didn't approve of his business practices and his treatment of scientists, nor of her, but she possessed information that could help him. There was really no point in withholding it. She decided to rise above her feelings and extend an olive branch. She contacted Mrs. Embry and made an appointment.

As Mary waited in Edison's outer office, she couldn't help noticing her reception was quite different than it had been at any time before.

"Mr. Edison had a meeting with J. P. Morgan," said Mrs. Embry. "But he will return presently. He instructed me to request that you stay."

"I have no pressing engagement."

Just hearing J. P. Morgan's name was unsettling. It was frustrating to know she could do nothing about what he had done, but Mary was trying to put that behind her. She was no longer in a position to obtain Goodrich's journal, so the threat of another attack was minimal.

Mary glanced out of the window and saw J. P. Morgan's carriage pull up. Edison emerged, shortly followed by the Bowler Hat.

"Ah, here's Mr. Edison now with Mr. Morgan's man." Mary's tone betrayed her unease at what she was seeing.

Mrs. Embry corrected her. "I'm afraid you're mistaken. That man's a detective, a former Pinkerton, very thorough I understand, and quite discreet. Many people of means have used his services. So has Mr. Edison on numerous occasions."

Mary had assumed he was solely Morgan's employee, because that was the only capacity in which she had encountered him. She realized that was another oversight on her part. A good detective never assumes anything. She turned back to the window and saw that the Bowler Hat was all alone. He put on his hat, the black bowler, and adjusted it, tilting it slightly to the side. He casually looked around, turning full-on toward the window facing Mary, then got back in the carriage. She was overcome with a strong sense of familiarity. Her brain flashed on the image of the dead Frenchman she had seen hanging in the train when she was a little girl, but she didn't know why.

Edison entered in an unusually cheery mood. He pumped her hand.

"Good to see you, Miss Handley."

"Good to see you, too, sir."

Edison noticed that Mary seemed disconcerted.

"Don't just stand there. Come in."

He motioned to her, and she followed him into his office. Mary tried to regain her composure, but the image of the Frenchman kept haunting her. Edison grabbed a pen off his desk.

"Will five thousand be enough?" he asked.

"Five thousand?"

The images in Mary's brain were piling up. This time she saw the Bowler Hat exiting the Frenchman's compartment on the train.

"For the journal," Edison explained. "Mrs. Embry said . . . Are you all right, Miss Handley?"

Mary now understood the reason for her royal treatment. "I'm afraid there's a misunderstanding. I didn't bring the Goodrich journal. I don't have it, sir."

Edison's good humor instantly soured. Regardless, she had a mission to complete. She took a periodical out of her pocketbook and placed it on Edison's desk.

"What I brought is a medical journal, one with a revealing study on cocaine. I know we've had our differences, Mr. Edison, but—"

"You interrupted my day with this hogwash!"

Disgusted, he tossed the journal at her feet. Mary looked down at the journal and shook her head. She was only trying to help Edison. Surely he couldn't have known cocaine

was harmful, or he wouldn't have endorsed it. And most assuredly he wouldn't have been consuming it. But as these thoughts were rumbling around in her head, she was jolted by another memory. Her brain put her back on the train again. Outside of the Frenchman's compartment, the Bowler Hat turned toward her. She could see his face, and this time she recognized it. She cried out.

"It was you! You had him killed!"

"I did *what*? To whom? I say, Miss Handley, you really do seem ill."

"Louis Godard, a French inventor, murdered on a train bound for New York."

"Godard? Yes, twelve, thirteen years ago, but the poor man hung himself. Financial woes."

"Findings his wife strongly refuted. You see, he was about to patent a new invention that would provide untold riches, a device that played recorded sound, over a year before your phonograph."

Mary stared right at him. Instead of cracking, instead of denying, Edison laughed.

"My dear Miss Handley, I fear gossip from Eadweard Muybridge and Nikola Tesla has warped your pretty little brain."

His condescension was annoying, but Mary held the trump card.

"I was there. I saw your hired assassin, the man whom you were just with, leaving Mr. Godard's compartment with his invention in hand."

She studied Edison for a reaction. She couldn't read him. There was a reason he was Thomas Edison.

"What you think you might have seen as a child is irrelevant and most definitely a waste of my time."

"I was twelve, and I know what I saw."

"And a very mature twelve, too, no doubt," he said mockingly. "It appears you may have caught whatever awful disease plagues your friend Miss Stoddard. Before it consumes you, you should consult that fellow who's all the rage, Dr. Freud. He's making great progress in the area of female hysteria."

"Thank you for the suggestion. Maybe he can also explain why certain men crave glory, even if it's unearned."

"Miss Handley, you've had some modest success. Don't let it go to your head. Now, I don't personally care what you do, but if you make these unfounded and defamatory claims public, I guarantee you will become a laughingstock."

"Not if I locate Mr. Goodrich's journal. He was very thorough, I'm told. I'm sure there's a dated entry noting when Mr. Godard's device arrived, possibly along with a check made out to the man you hired."

"You truly are incorrigible. Good-bye, Miss Handley."

Edison hadn't so much as flinched. Mary picked up the medical journal. If he had been anyone else, she would have just left. But this was Thomas Edison, her hero, and she felt betrayed.

"You've achieved mythical status: a man who built an empire on pure intellect and foresight. How disappointing to find you're just a common thug, like your robber-baron cronies."

"I assure you, Miss Handley, there's nothing common about me."

"Incompetent then." Mary was flying without a net, based on a spur-of-the-moment hunch. "How else can one explain why you hired that nincompoop Wallenski to kill me?"

Mary got her flinch. Edison was momentarily silent. He knew only too well that hiring Wallenski was his mistake, and he hated making mistakes.

"You know, maybe I underestimated you. What's the saying? Oh, right," he said as he stared directly at her. "There's always next time."

She had squeezed out the truth, and it was sending shivers down her spine. Mary began to wish she had left earlier, much earlier, while still in a state of blissful ignorance.

Cutting up lettuce, tomatoes, and vegetables for a salad gave Mary time to analyze her situation. She only had herself to blame. Goading Edison into revealing himself was good detective work, but it did little for her. She couldn't arrest him, and it was a bad trade-off. When the case ended, she had felt free of threat. She no longer did.

Her terrified reaction to an unexpected knock at her door confirmed that. She immediately stopped cutting and listened, her heart pounding away. There was a second knock. Knife in hand, she slowly opened the kitchen cabinet and removed Charles's pistol from the roasting pan, then made her way to the door, grateful he had given it to her. She had even practiced with it a few times. Fully armed, she was ready.

"Who is it?"

"It's me, Mary. Charles."

"Charles! I've been looking everywhere for you!"

Thrilled, she threw the gun on her bed and opened the door. Charles looked at her, and his eyes wandered to the knife.

"Father warned me I might return a gelding."

Mary glanced at the knife, laughed, and then hastily put it with the salad fixings. Charles came in and closed the door. Mary had practiced what she might say if she ever saw him again, but now that he was here, she couldn't find the words. Neither could he, but he eventually managed to say, "I'm very proud of you, Mary."

"Charles, I've been so worried."

"I did it, Mary. The morphine's out of me."

"That's wonderful! I knew you could do it." Her impulse was to hug him, but their recent history made her tentative. She wound up fidgeting and feeling awkward.

"Father and I leave for Atlanta tomorrow."

Mary was confused. In her mind, one piece of news didn't follow the other.

"You're coming back, though? I mean, there's no reason why we can't—"

"I succeeded because I had to, but I don't know if I'll be able to keep it up."

Charles was being brutally honest about himself. Mary wanted to tell him how wonderful he was, how proud she was of what he had done. She wanted to list a litany of reasons why together they could conquer anything. But she knew it was no use. Only he could erase his self-doubt.

"You'll make it. I know you will."

"What, no sarcastic quip? I must confess, I'm not used

to this new, upbeat Mary. I guess accomplishment does that for a person."

"Charles, I . . ."

He had to stop her. He could feel his resistance weakening.

"I'm sorry if I caused you pain. You're truly magnificent, my darling."

He kissed her gently on the cheek. There was a finality to it she couldn't ignore.

"Surely we can at least correspond," she said tentatively. Letters weren't even close to what Mary had envisioned for their relationship, but it was the best she could do at this time. She tried to hide it, but her disappointment was palpable.

"I'd like that very much," Charles replied. "Yes, very much."

He paused for a moment, also trying to suppress the upset he was feeling. Covering his anguish with a smile, he took a card from his wallet and handed it to her. "Our address: pemberton pharmacy with two small p's. Father believes a lack of capital letters adds a smidgen of class."

"Charles . . ." Mary started to speak but could not continue. No words could fit what they were both feeling. Like a magnetic force, their bodies were drawn together, hugging one another tightly and clinging for what seemed like a long time. Neither had the willpower to let go, because they both knew that meant the end.

Finally, as if the same magnetic force that had drawn them together let them know it was time to part, they both let go. Charles and Mary stared at each other for a moment, sharing a sad but loving smile, and then he left. Mary took

several steps toward the door, determined to go after him, then stopped. Deep down, no matter how much it hurt, she had to let him find his own peace, or it wouldn't be his.

Mary turned back toward the kitchen and the salad she was preparing, briefly glancing at the card Charles had given her. Suddenly, her emotional state changed. She felt a flush of excitement, an excitement that had nothing to do with Charles. It involved Roscoe.

34

Mary had spent many a night bemoaning the fact that Charles Goodrich's final entry in his date book read only "Meet Roscoe at his place." It had always seemed too general for a man who was so exact. The lettering on John Pemberton's card changed her perspective. What if "his place" was the name of a restaurant or place of business rather than Roscoe's apartment? Mary did some research and soon discovered there was a tavern called "his place" down on the Bowery.

The Bowery was one of the most dangerous sections of New York. It bordered on an area called Five Points, which was infested with gangs and the bane of New York law enforcement. The Bowery had its own gang, the Bowery Boys, and the darkness, dirt, and noise brought on by the elevated subway, the Third Avenue El, made it a haven for criminals. As Mary trudged through the teeming streets, the sounds of poverty were all too familiar: a bloodied storekeeper screaming for police who never came, prostitutes calling to johns, a pushcart peddler chasing street urchins who regularly

pilfered from his cart, husbands and wives battling over the misery of their lives. Every so often, as an exclamation point, the Third Avenue train blanketed the area with its roaring, nerve-wracking clatter, shaking the ground below and any building nearby.

Mary wasn't scared. She knew how to handle herself in this environment. To her, the privileged world of Edison and Morgan was scarier. On the Bowery, you could spot your enemies, and the probability was that they'd come directly at you. The rich were more deceptive, being unwilling to dirty their own hands.

Mary entered his place and instantly realized it wasn't just a tavern. It was a full-fledged "resort." She had heard about resorts, meeting places for homosexuals, but she had never been to one, and his place was doing a booming business. Smoky, mobbed, and lively, the bar was packed with mostly men and some women, as were the tables. There was a dance floor on the far right next to a staircase, which led to a second floor that contained rooms for couples desiring more privacy. A man wearing full makeup and dressed in formal tails sat at the piano playing and singing "I'm Called Little Buttercup" from Gilbert and Sullivan's *H.M.S. Pinafore*. The waitresses were men dressed in drag who joked and flirted with the customers. There were two hostesses, also men in drag, one a redhead and the other a blonde. They noticed Mary.

"My God, as I live and breathe," the redhead exclaimed dramatically. "She looks just like that lady detective."

"If I had those cheekbones, I could look like Mary Handley, too," declared the blonde, sucking in his cheeks.

"In your dreams, dearie," the redhead replied, then

turned to instruct Mary. "Try more rouge and some wave in your hair."

"I'm looking for a man," Mary began to explain.

"Aren't we all?" the blonde interrupted, sighing.

"His name is Roscoe. Spanish, dark, handsome, late twenties."

"Oh, Señor Gorgeous," swooned the redhead, then pointed to the far left corner. "He's over there. But you're wasting your time. He's strictly for men only."

At that, both the redhead and the blonde ran off, hopping into the laps of two customers, laughing and flirting with them.

Mary walked the length of the floor and turned left at the bar. When she passed, a man at the bar stuck his neck out from the crowd and watched her go. It was Samuel. He had told his employer that Mary Handley would find his place. She was that good. Her presence there was important information, and he promptly left to report it.

Mary stopped before she got to the corner booth and set her eyes on Roscoe for the first time. By all reports, he was a handsome Spaniard. Mary would have added that he was also very masculine and sexy. If she had any doubts that this man was Roscoe, they were erased when she saw that sitting next to him was her old friend Mortimer.

"Roscoe?"

Roscoe rose and smiled charmingly. "Well, it's about time you found me," he said with a slight accent and a twinkle in his eye as he suavely took her hand and kissed it. He then nodded toward his companion. "I'm sure you remember Mortimer."

Mortimer waved and smiled meekly.

"Please join us," said Roscoe. "We have before us a recent invention by a bartender in San Francisco. It's called a martini, and it's quite scrumptious."

Mary joined them, and Roscoe ordered another pitcher of martinis for the table. They sat and drank and talked and drank some more. Mary had many questions, and Roscoe was not shy about giving answers.

"I couldn't come forward," Roscoe explained. "It would've been too easy to pin the murder on the homosexual, and then forget about it."

The fact that opposites often attract was a well-known phenomenon, but one would think Roscoe's open, debonair personality and Charles Goodrich's closed, reserved manner wouldn't have been remotely compatible. The reasons governing human attraction had been a puzzle since people had walked on this earth, and Mary wasn't going to solve it that evening. It was this factor though that tipped Mary's tone to the incredulous when she wanted to confirm what was now obvious.

"So you and Charles Goodrich were . . . ?"

"We were lovers. Why is it so hard for the world to understand? It's just love."

"We live in intolerant times," Mary said.

"Yet I suspect the intolerance will end for you before it will for me."

Mary raised her drink in a toast. "Here's hoping it ends for all of us, sooner rather than later."

They clinked glasses and drank. A good-looking man of about thirty came to the table and asked Roscoe to dance. Not in the mood for frivolity, he declined. Mortimer had no problem being second choice and left with the man. Mary

was trying to pace herself and was slowly sipping her second martini, which she found to be as delicious as described. By now, Roscoe had imbibed four that Mary had seen, yet the only effect she recognized was that he was much freer in expressing his emotions. His frustration and pain were very visible.

"Poor Charlie struggled so with who he was. That's the only reason he got involved with that Stoddard woman."

"He saw you the night he was killed, didn't he?"

"Charlie begged my forgiveness and asked if I still wanted him. Of course I said yes."

Trying to suppress his agony, Roscoe downed his drink and poured another one. Mary hated to keep probing into an issue that was clearly painful for him, but she couldn't stop. There was another piece to the puzzle, and she had to find out about it.

"Did Charlie ever mention a journal, one that contained sensitive information?"

Roscoe nodded. "He gave it to me that night to hold for him. He seemed quite concerned."

"I'm sure he was. He was about to expose Thomas Edison, opening a box of misdeeds that would make Pandora blush."

"Well then," he stated rather cavalierly, "we must finish what he started. Meet me tomorrow. The world will no doubt believe you before it will me."

He handed Mary his card. Her detective work over, she allowed herself to feel the tragedy of Charles Goodrich.

"Edison said he had no gumption," she told him. "Yet he was showing more guts than ten men."

Roscoe could stand no more and finished his drink. He

then delighted the man at the next table by asking him to dance. Before they left, Roscoe turned to Mary.

"Tomorrow," he said, and he was gone.

Mary was gathering herself to leave when she spotted someone at the bar. Samuel had returned, and he was trying to be inconspicuous. He was good at his job, but it was hard for a man his size to blend into the background. Mary grabbed a spoon off a table and stuck it in his back.

"You're feeling my derringer. It's small, but it can blow a hole clear through you."

As Mary guided Samuel to the exit, the piano player returned from his break. He dove right into "When I Was a Lad" from *H.M.S. Pinafore*. The redheaded and blond hostesses mimed the song and played with the customers while Mary pressed the spoon harder into Samuel's back, and they stepped out into the Bowery night.

Having managed to get Samuel outside, Mary hadn't figured out yet how she was going to get information from him before he realized she was threatening him with a spoon. Samuel started to fidget.

"Don't move," Mary warned him.

At that point, a man popped his head out of the window of a carriage that was parked in front. It was W. W. Goodrich.

"Can I give you a ride home, Miss Handley?" he said in a friendly manner, and then gestured toward Samuel. "Samuel won't hurt you. He works for me."

Taken aback, Mary slowly lowered the spoon. When Samuel turned and saw it, he smiled.

"Clever, very clever," he said, then climbed up onto the empty driver's perch.

This had been a night of surprises for Mary. Why not one

more? She shrugged, joined W. W. Goodrich in the carriage, and sat opposite him.

As the carriage traveled through the Bowery on the way to the Brooklyn Bridge, W. W. Goodrich put in place the last pieces of the puzzle. He explained that Samuel was a military assassin trained in Prussia. He could have easily harmed Mary, but that was never the plan. He had ordered Samuel to keep an eye on Roscoe. His brother's death was still fresh in his mind, and Roscoe was drinking heavily. In fact, Roscoe had been one of the three drunks outside of Longdon's restaurant when Samuel shot at her.

"When the poor drunken fellow decided to reveal himself, Samuel had to distract you. So you see, you were never in much danger at all . . . from Samuel, that is."

Mary listened to W. W. Goodrich's entire story. While his words enlightened her, they didn't offer her relief. Instead, she was overtaken by a strong sense of repulsion.

"You knew about this all along," she said.

"Charles told me four months ago of his . . . inclinations. I informed him there was no way I would allow him to stain the Goodrich name with a deviant lifestyle. After all, why should I have to give up my life because of him?"

"It works both ways, you know."

Either her comment went over his head, or he chose to ignore it and to continue.

"I suggested he immediately find a woman and marry her. I suppose I'll have to live with that for the rest of my life." And then W. W. Goodrich sighed, trying his best to approximate human emotion. He failed.

"Your remorse overwhelms me," Mary said drily.

W. W. Goodrich shrugged off his lack of theatrical talent

and got to his real purpose. He took a check out of his coat pocket. "Will this be enough to silence you?"

Just when Mary had thought her opinion of W. W. Goodrich couldn't get any lower, he managed to drop another notch.

"Your brother's private life is precisely that. I have no desire to reveal it."

"Scruples. What a pleasant surprise," he exclaimed as he stuffed the check back into his coat. He felt that he was on a lucky roll and took a wild guess. "You wouldn't by any chance also have his journal? It'll bring a tidy sum for both of us."

In addition to being despicable, his proposition was also an outright lie. Mary knew how ambitious W. W. Goodrich was, and Edison's sphere of influence was vast. "You mean you have no intention of using it as political collateral to advance your career?"

"Well, I suppose that is a possibility," he said, not at all fazed about being caught in a fabrication.

"I thought you were opposed to profiting from your brother's death."

"Only opposed to others profiting. It's perfectly all right if it's kept within the family."

They were in the middle of the Brooklyn Bridge, but she had reached her limit.

"The air has turned quite foul in here. Stop the coach. I'd rather walk."

If Mary couldn't provide W. W. Goodrich with his brother's journal, she could be of no further assistance to him. What she thought of him mattered not at all.

"If you wish," he said, and then banged the roof with his cane, signaling Samuel to stop.

As soon as Mary stepped onto the bridge, W. W. Goodrich's carriage took off. He didn't bother to look back. He stuck his cane out the window and waved it nonchalantly.

"*Au revoir,* Miss Handley." And he was gone.

Mary turned and looked back at Manhattan. It was a clear starry night, and the moon reflected off the water, highlighting the beauty of the island. It was hard to grasp that beneath the surface of that magnificence lay such greed, intolerance, and brutality. Mary vowed never to give in to it.

Straightening up, she started the long walk toward Brooklyn and home.

35

Mary met Roscoe the next day at his shop, formerly called Eastside Imports. It was now actually on the east side since their hasty move spurred by Roscoe's belief that, if found, he would be railroaded for murder. For the same reason, the name had been changed to Oriental Dreams. The visit was much different from her previous one. This time Mortimer was happy to see her, rather than scared, and Roscoe was there.

Roscoe was about to embark on a long buying trip to the Orient. It was necessary not only for business purposes but also for his emotional health. He needed to get away from the places that he and Charles Goodrich had frequented to clear his head. He was still a young man and needed to come at life from a different perspective. He hoped the trip would accomplish that.

"Do what you think is best in the name of Charlie. I don't know you very well, Mary. Call it instinct, but somehow I have faith in you."

And he handed her Charles Goodrich's journal. After all
Mary had gone through, it was as simple as that.

She left and spent the next twenty-four hours reading
and rereading it over and over again. It was everything she
had expected it to be and more. Dates and times of transactions and payments were on almost every page. Eadweard
Muybridge was not lying and neither was Tesla. There were
many more of whom Edison had taken advantage, beyond
the scope of anything Mary had imagined. And, in black and
white, there was an entry of the acquisition of a new invention the day after the Frenchman Godard was killed and a
check made out to "Cash" for "Detective Services." That
evidence was especially damning, but now she had to decide
what to do with it.

Commissioners Jourdan and Briggs had requested a
meeting with Mary that day. As the one who had hired and
supervised her, Chief Campbell was also going to be there.
She stopped at Second Street Station with ample time before the meeting at police headquarters and showed Chief
Campbell the journal. He expressed surprise that Mary was
still working on the case. Mary told him in no uncertain
terms that he needed to read it and read it now. Normally,
Chief Campbell would have thrown anyone who spoke to
him in that fashion out of his office, but he had learned
to respect Mary, so he obliged her.

Mary wandered around the station, saying hello to
Sean, Billy, and a few others. An hour later, Chief Campbell
emerged from his office, the journal tucked under his arm,
and he beckoned to her. She bade the others good-bye and
went inside with the chief. He closed the door and gestured
with the book.

"This is an amazing treatise," he said.

"It's not fiction, Chief."

"That's why it's so amazing and damaging and so incredibly disappointing."

"I had the same reaction. It's completely unforgivable."

"Completely. That's why you need to burn it."

Mary could not believe her ears. "But, Chief, this man has to pay for what he did."

"It will only bring you heartache and grief, and that's if you're lucky. You already know what else can happen."

Mary and Chief Campbell argued the point for a while, but they both had the same stubborn streak and neither one of them gave an inch. Mary was disappointed in Chief Campbell, who she had always believed was a protector of the weak and a purveyor of fairness. But as he explained to her, his reasoning was simple. He wanted Mary to live. Soon it was time to leave for the meeting with Jourdan and Briggs.

They didn't talk very much on the ride over to police headquarters. They weren't angry with each other. It was simply that the journal was too big a subject to avoid, so they decided not to speak at all. When they arrived at Jourdan's office, they were ushered right in, and Briggs joined them shortly afterward.

Jourdan and Briggs were overly solicitous and accommodating.

"You did such wonderful work in finding the Stoddard woman," said Jourdan.

"King," Briggs interrupted, correcting him. Confused, Jourdan looked at Briggs, and he explained further. "King was her name, not Stoddard."

"Yes," said Jourdan. "King, Stoddard, let's just call her the Goodrich killer. You nabbed her. Good job!"

"Yeah," Briggs muttered. No matter what the circumstances, complimenting Mary made him uneasy.

"Thank you, gentlemen," Mary replied. "I thoroughly enjoyed my work, and Chief Campbell's brilliant supervision was a great part of that."

"Really, Mary," said Chief Campbell, "it was all you."

"I mean it, Chief. I couldn't have done it without you."

By now, Jourdan and Briggs were wondering if they'd ever rid themselves of hearing Chief Campbell's praises being sung. They had to find a way to pluck this giant thorn out of their sides. But this meeting wasn't about him. Briggs cleared his throat, and Jourdan smiled through his distaste.

"We're well aware of Chief Campbell's significant attributes, but we're here to discuss you. It has been decided that we are going to hire a handful of matrons, and we want you to be the first."

"A matron? What does a matron's job entail?"

"As you may know, female crime is growing, and we're in need of women to search suspects, guard them, and tend to other female needs."

"You know," Briggs said, jumping in, "women things nobody wants a man to do."

Mary paused to fully take in their words before responding. "Please correct me if I misunderstood you. I solved Brooklyn's biggest murder case in the last couple of decades, maybe in its entire history, and you want me to be a nursemaid."

Chief Campbell had to suppress a laugh. Jourdan immediately started backpedaling.

"Well, I wouldn't exactly call it—"

"Absolutely not." Mary spared Jourdan his effort.

"Miss Handley, I really think you—"

"She doesn't want to do it," Briggs said pointedly to Jourdan, then turned to Mary. "It's okay. We understand." His delight in her refusal of their offer was evident, and he lit up a cigar as his exclamation point. "If there's nothing else . . . ," he said, puffing away on the cigar, indicating that the meeting was over.

Mary disappointed him. "As a matter of fact, there is." She took the Goodrich journal out of her pocketbook. "This is Charles Goodrich's journal. It contains evidence against Thomas Edison on an ethical and criminal level so profound that I dare only start at the top. That is why I've come to you."

"Yes, well, that was very wise of you," Jourdan said, doing a reasonable job of hiding his joy.

"Don't worry your pretty little head," said Briggs a little too eagerly. "Just leave the book here, and we'll take care of everything."

"I'm afraid I can't do that," responded Mary. "But what I will do is wait outside while you read it, then tell me what you plan to do. Is that all right?"

"Of course it is, Miss Handley," Jourdan said as he jumped up to escort Mary and Chief Campbell out the door. "Please have a seat, and we'll be right with you." Then he motioned to his secretary. "Miss Whitehead, please come in and bring your book."

As Miss Whitehead followed Jourdan inside, it occurred to Mary why they might need her, and when they were called

back in twenty minutes later, Mary whispered to Chief Campbell, "It appears the inmates are running the asylum, and I won't allow it."

"Be careful, Mary," he cautioned her.

They were barely seated in Jourdan's office when he started.

"We have a problem, Miss Handley," he said, and gestured toward the journal that was on his desk. "For all we know this book, or journal as you call it, is a work of fiction. Mr. Goodrich is not around to corroborate it."

"I'm sure you can verify the handwriting."

"Even so, the evidence is circumstantial at best. I'm sorry."

"How much of it did you read?"

"Enough to know that—"

"It doesn't matter. I'm sure you spent most of the time telephoning Thomas Edison. He has you in his pocket."

Chief Campbell was smiling inside. He was proud of his pupil. That exact thought had crossed his mind when Miss Whitehead was asked to bring her book with her.

Briggs stepped forward. "Watch your mouth, young lady!" he said, using his bullying tactics to back her down.

But bullying never worked on Mary. She went to collect the journal, and Jourdan pulled it back.

"We better keep it. It'll be safer here."

"Why does it need to be safe? You just told me it was worthless." Mary yanked Goodrich's journal from his hands. The commissioners' scheming had backfired on them, and she quickly left, before they could invent another reason to keep the journal.

Mary had reached the exit to police headquarters when she heard Chief Campbell calling to her. "Mary. Mary, where are you going?"

"To the newspapers," she said as she kept on walking. "Surely they'll be interested in what I have."

"You think Edison has no influence there?"

His words stopped her, and she turned to face him.

"He's too powerful," Chief Campbell said. "At least turn this into something positive. Secure enough to ensure your future and your family's. Please, Mary, make a deal with him."

Mary stood there, considering his plea.

"I can't, Chief. I wish I could. It may sound archaic, but I believe there's some justice left in this world." And with that, she pushed out onto the street.

All Chief Campbell could get out was, "Good luck." What he meant to say, what he would have said had he had time, was, "May God protect you. You're going to need it."

36

Chief Campbell was right. Every newspaper turned Mary down. The mayor refused to see her. Even George Westinghouse, Edison's competitor, didn't want any part in it. There seemed to be some bizarre code among these men that allowed them to trick, cheat, and sabotage each other, but tattling was somehow viewed as poor form. Mary considered Tesla, but, partially due to Edison, he already had a reputation as a crackpot, and no one would believe him. There was one option left. It wasn't a perfect one, but it would have to suffice.

It was dusk when Mary got home. She opened her apartment door to discover her place was a total mess. Her mattress was flipped, and her things had been tossed every which way. At the far end to the right of the window, cloaked in shadows, a man sat in a chair. The only thing she could definitively make out was the shape of the bowler hat he was wearing.

"So you were the little girl on the train," the Bowler Hat began.

"Get out of here."

He paid her no attention. Standing, he indicated her apartment. "And this is how your life turned out. It's really quite sad."

"I said get out!" Mary demanded.

He stepped toward her. She tried to flip him, but he was expecting it and avoided her grasp. After a quick kick to her stomach, she was the one who wound up crashing to the floor. Mary tried every move she had ever learned, but he had an answer for all of them. The Bowler Hat bounced her around the room. Books and pictures went flying. She crashed into a mirror, cracking it. He had been brushing up on his defense techniques, concentrating on jujitsu. Wei Chung had made him look foolish, and he was determined for that not to happen again. But it didn't matter. In this case, he was clearly the more skilled fighter.

Mary's energy was quickly fading, and the Bowler Hat was through toying with her. He punched her in the face. It was a crushing blow, and she went down hard.

"I heard about your jujitsu. I had hoped you'd be more competitive."

He kicked Mary, and she groaned. She had never felt this much pain.

"Give me the journal!" he commanded her.

"I don't have it."

The Bowler Hat landed another devastating kick. It didn't matter that she was a woman. He had a job to do. By now she was completely helpless. He grabbed Mary by her hair and dragged her to the cracked mirror. He pulled her head up, so Mary could see the reflection of her bruised and bloodied face.

"Look," he said, "a sweatshop girl going nowhere. You think anyone cares if you live or die?"

He pulled out the dagger he had used to kill Wallenski and put it to her neck.

"Last time. Give me the journal."

Mary was breathless, clinging to consciousness. She barely managed to say, "I don't have it. I gave it away, you baboon."

Through the years, the Bowler Hat had beaten information out of many people. He could easily tell a lie from the truth, and Mary sounded like she was telling the truth. He still needed verification.

"Who has it?"

"Your friend J. P. Morgan," Mary answered.

The Bowler Hat was frustrated. His job was to get the journal, and this woman was making it impossible. He had been fortunate enough to be trusted with yet another assignment to prove his worth. He couldn't fail, and Mary stood between him and success. He was ready to end this bitch's worthless life. Then he stopped and released her hair, letting her head bang to the floor. He needed to think this out thoroughly before acting. He had to decide if killing this woman was good business. He had been slipping lately, and he couldn't trust his instincts.

Before long, the Bowler Hat concluded that this killing would not be good business. Her death would not help him complete his mission and would only complicate matters. A dead former heroine creates much more attention than one who was simply beaten up. He would tell his employer who had the journal, and his employer could decide what the

next move would be. He sheathed his knife and started to clean up, looking for any clues of his presence that he might have left. The Bowler Hat was proud of himself for making this decision. It would serve him well.

Mary had suffered a terrible beating, but when the Bowler Hat had lifted her head up to the mirror, she hadn't seen her bruised face. She had seen only one thing: Wei Chung's necklace hanging down from his neck. It enraged her, it energized her, and it gave her purpose. While the Bowler Hat was covering his tracks, she quietly dragged herself to the kitchen cabinet. *The roasting pan,* she thought. She had to get to Charles's pistol. It was the only way.

The Bowler Hat was ready to leave when he heard a voice.

"You're the one who killed Wei Chung," stated Mary, coolly and calmly.

He turned to see her pointing a pistol at him. She had caught him off guard. Normally, he would have denied it immediately and started chatting as a distraction until he saw an opening to take her. But he knew he had waited too long.

Mary stared at the man before her. He had murdered the Chungs, the Frenchman, Wallenski, and countless more. He was not a man. He was a beast, a killing machine, and he had to be stopped.

The Bowler Hat could see the hate behind Mary's eyes, and he had no choice. He made his move. The first bullet that entered his body slowed him down. The second brought him to his knees, but he was still inching forward, reaching out for her. It was only then that he realized his slipping wasn't recent. It had started twelve years ago when he let

that little girl on the train live. The next three bullets propelled him backward, and he collapsed to the floor.

Mary stood over him. She'd had six bullets in her pistol, but it only took five to kill the Bowler Hat.

~

J. P. Morgan had requested yet another meeting with Thomas Edison. Edison was in the middle of many projects, and he was getting tired of dropping everything for Morgan. As his carriage stopped in front of Morgan's house, he made up his mind. He was going to put an end to these impromptu meetings. He would tell Morgan that if he wanted to see him, he could make an appointment like anyone else.

Morgan was seated at his desk when his butler escorted Edison in and left. Morgan smiled broadly, like Lewis Carroll's Cheshire Cat.

"Glad you could come, Tom," he said.

Edison sat, immediately knowing that he was in trouble. Before long, Edison found himself agreeing to cede control of Edison Electric to Morgan. He would stay on for as long as Morgan desired and then leave when Morgan no longer found him useful. He had become that dancing puppet and Morgan was holding all the strings.

As Edison left, Morgan happily drummed his fingers on the cause for Edison's immediate surrender. It was a book, a book that had eluded Edison and was known as the Goodrich journal.

~

Tina Chung was pregnant. That's why she was irritated when she was summoned to her principal's office during lunchtime. Tina was eating for two now, and she didn't want to miss a meal. It was hard enough continuing to work when she was in her ninth month, but Tina and her husband had their eyes on a house and they needed the income. She couldn't take a chance of being replaced because she took time off for her pregnancy.

The principal was not happy.

"I thought I made it perfectly clear, many times," he said, "that no one could receive personal mail here at the school."

"I'm well aware of that rule," said Tina, somewhat mystified. "I've never given this address to anyone."

"Then how did this happen?" The principal handed her a letter.

Tina looked at it. She had no idea where it came from. It had no return address, and the only writing on it was her name in care of the school. She opened the envelope, and there was no letter inside. But what it did contain was more than astonishing. It was a miracle. Her lips began to quiver, she lost all composure, and she burst into tears.

What Tina held in her hands was her father's necklace. Wei Chung had promised his daughter she could have it to pass down to her children. And now, somehow, from the grave, he had fulfilled that promise. Her family's legacy would continue.

Her sobbing increased.

The principal didn't know what to do. He offered her water. He asked if she wanted to lie down. He was afraid she was going to have the baby right there in his office.

Tina knew that was not going to happen. She knew from now on everything was going to be all right. And she was going to cry for a long while. They were tears of sadness and also tears of uncontrollable joy.

~

Mary slowly descended the steps of Second Street Station. It had been ten days since her encounter with the Bowler Hat, and she had finally been cleared of any wrongdoing. It was officially labeled "self-defense." Commissioners Jourdan and Briggs had ordered a full investigation, hoping to find some way to discredit her. Chief Campbell had followed their orders, had spent a reasonable amount of time investigating, and then had rendered a decision that he knew was correct from the beginning

It was a beautiful day, and Mary was in a mood for reflection. She decided to take a long walk around Brooklyn, the city in which she was born and raised. There was a movement afoot for it to become a part of New York City, but that hadn't happened yet, and right now it was still her Brooklyn.

She turned down Fifth Avenue, then east on Lincoln Place to where it all started, the brownstone in which Charles Goodrich had been murdered. It had been called Degraw Street, but the city council, in their infinite wisdom, decided that the infamy of the Goodrich case was too much and renamed the section east of Fifth. If the reasoning was to protect real estate values, they should have renamed all of Degraw. But political logic often escaped Mary. What made sense to her were actual facts. Charles

Goodrich was dead, Kate was locked up, and Mary was free of threats. Not all were happy occasions, but they were tangible.

Mary eventually found herself by the Sea Beach railroad line, and on a whim she took it to the end of Brooklyn, by the beach. She exited near the Sea Beach Palace Hotel, an expensive vacation destination that catered to the upper classes. Spotting an ice vendor, she bought a piece. The swelling on her face had almost completely subsided and the bruises were healing, but applying ice always made it feel better. The cool ocean breeze also helped. For the first time in a long while, Mary felt at peace with herself.

She heard a commotion by the hotel and turned. A group of women were in front protesting, demanding that women get the vote. As she drifted toward them, Mary remembered she had read in the newspaper that President Grover Cleveland was holding a fund-raiser at the hotel. Mary had done a lot of thinking about her beliefs, and this case had altered some of them. The "powers that be" were so strong and so corrupt that the common man and woman needed all the help they could get. She decided to put aside her petty notions of the women in the movement. It didn't matter that their privilege afforded them the luxury of protest. What mattered was numbers. That was all they had, and that was all the power brokers would understand.

Mary spotted Amanda Everhart among the protesters and approached her.

"Pass me a sign . . . sister," Mary said.

Amanda didn't say anything. She just handed Mary a sign and smiled. It was a welcoming smile with a touch of "It's about time."

Mary joined the other women. She faded into the crowd and pretty soon you couldn't tell one from the other. All that could be perceived, all that could be heard, and all that really mattered was their resounding chant.

"Women are better. Women are better."

EPILOGUE

A year after the Goodrich killer was caught, Mary Handley and Chief Campbell left the Brooklyn courthouse together, both happy the case was over. It wasn't the trial of Kate Stoddard or Lizzie King or whatever she was calling herself. She never had a trial. Under a new law, she had been sentenced to the State Lunatic Asylum at Auburn for the rest of her life. On this day, the particular case that had been tried was one that Mary had brought against the Brooklyn Police Department. They—meaning Jourdan and Briggs—had refused to pay her the fifteen-hundred-dollar bonus she was promised if she caught the Goodrich killer. W. W. Goodrich had weaseled out of paying the thirty-five-hundred-dollar reward he had pledged, using as a loophole the fact that he had stated the killer must be tried and convicted. He was technically right. Briggs and Jourdan weren't. They simply thought Mary would back down—another gross miscalculation on their part. She got her money.

Mary and Chief Campbell stood on the steps as they

watched two very sore losers leave the courthouse and hurry into their carriages.

"If they think they're upset now, this will seem like a picnic on Monday," said Chief Campbell. "That's when I start my job as superintendent of police."

"My Lord, Chief, that's fantastic! Congratulations!"

Mary had been concerned about Chief Campbell. Months before, Jourdan and Briggs had fired him, citing his incompetence in the Goodrich case. It was a lie, it was outrageous, but they were the commissioners and it stuck.

An entertaining thought crossed her mind. "Chief, that means you're their boss. You can . . ."

"Yes, I can," he said, and he didn't just smile. He grinned.

"I wish I could be there for that."

"Firing them will no doubt ease the pain of being confined to a desk. I'm contemplating hiring a photographer and memorializing the event for all eternity."

Mary and Chief Campbell laughed, enjoying their victories, then Mary got serious.

"Chief, I can't thank you enough for testifying on my behalf."

"You were only asking me to tell the truth," he said, and then reminded Mary of her lament the year before. "It seems there is some justice left in the world."

They shook hands and parted. They had formed a friendship that would last, whether they worked together or not.

On her way home Mary tried not to dwell on her disappointment that capturing the Goodrich killer hadn't resulted in her garnering any other cases. There were positives. Her notoriety had diminished, but there was enough to get her a job in a Brooklyn bookstore where customers

liked getting recommendations from the woman who had caught the Goodrich killer. It didn't pay much, but it was more than the Lowry Hat Factory and she enjoyed such amenities as occasional breaks and access to all that was new in the literary world. She had gotten used to the possibility that Goodrich was her first and last case and that settling for something less than detective work might not be that bad. She had recently started to plan how she could combine the fifteen-hundred-dollar reward money with hard work to accomplish her second choice in life: becoming a doctor. Mary never thought small.

She found two letters waiting for her at home. One of them was from Charles Pemberton, and she eagerly opened it. She hadn't heard from Charles in a while and was very curious how he was. The letter was long, rambling, and sometimes incoherent, but she was able to glean some information from it. John Pemberton had passed away, but not before selling Coca-Cola to a man named Asa Candler for a mere twenty-three hundred dollars. The family was experiencing serious financial difficulties, and though he didn't say so, it was clear to Mary that Charles's morphine habit had returned. He didn't even make an attempt at hiding his lack of lucidity. Mary wanted to write him back and print in big letters, "GET HELP!" But she'd just be stating the obvious, and it would do no good. Charles was right. It was best they had separated. It wasn't lost on Mary that her desire for an unconventional mate had resulted in unforeseen complications. Maybe she needed to reexamine that notion.

The second letter was from a woman in Chicago. Three weeks ago, during the worst rainstorm in Chicago history, her husband had gone for a stroll and never returned.

The police were treating her as a hysterical woman whose husband had just simply run out on her. She contended her husband would never do that, not because their marriage was so strong but rather because he would never leave their pet dog. He adored the despicable beast beyond any reason, and it was still living with her. If Mary could find a way to get to Chicago, she had a place for her to stay and could afford to pay her four dollars a week.

Mary put the letter down. She understood why the police hadn't responded to this woman. She sounded seriously off-kilter, just the type a husband might leave without a word. The offer was also a paltry one, and quite possibly not genuine. She could give up her bookstore job and travel all the way to Chicago for nothing. It was definitely not worth it. She had a new career plan, and she was going to follow it.

Mary was thirsty and decided to make herself some lemonade. She filled a glass with water, then took out a couple of lemons and sugar. As she squeezed the lemons into her glass, she admitted that she might be judging the Chicago woman too harshly. The fact that her husband would not leave his wife because he loved his dog seemed a little extreme, but then Mary knew of a man who had run into a burning house to save his cat. The cat was found outside, safe and sound, but the man had perished. It was unusual for the woman to express hatred of her pet. Pets were considered sacred by many, but so were children, and Mary had heard many parents, including her own mother, speak disparagingly about theirs.

Mary decided she would go down to the train station and find out the cost of a ticket to Chicago. Purely to gather information. How can a person make a decision without

having all the facts? Not that she would ever consider going. Well, at least it was highly unlikely. Though maybe, just maybe, if the ticket was cheap enough, and if the bookstore owner would give her a leave of absence . . . He might. He was a nice man and being involved in another case would raise her profile and help business. And if he did, it was just possible she would get the answer to a question that had been nagging at her for some time.

Why did men like this woman's husband and Senator Conkling take strolls in such inclement weather?

AUTHOR'S NOTE

Second Street Station is historical fiction and certainly should be read as part of that genre. However, it also contains many historical facts that are quite accurate. Though fictionalized, the murder case is based on a real one. Mary Handley, Kate Stoddard, Chief Detective Patrick Campbell, and Charles Goodrich were real people, as were many of the people involved in the case. Many of the events actually happened, some taken from newspaper articles of the day. Thomas Edison, Nikola Tesla, J. P. Morgan, and George Westinghouse are iconic figures in American history, and I have tried to reveal aspects of their characters that may not be commonly known. The problems encountered when first marketing Coca-Cola and the plights of the troubled John and Charles Pemberton are well documented. To give further examples, Vin Mariani was an extremely popular wine at that time, and Senator Conkling and Governor David B. Hill were actual politicos. Of course, there are other examples, but suffice it to say I have made a concerted effort

to weave my fictional tale with enough historical truth to make it as engaging and as authentic as possible.

It's interesting to note that the Edison/Tesla feud outlasted both their lifetimes. It prevented them from getting the Nobel Prize when they refused to share it with one another. Edison exited General Electric, the company he helped found, when they decided to switch to AC electricity. Of the two though, Edison certainly came out on top. He outmatched and outsmarted Tesla every step of the way. When he passed away in 1931, he was a very wealthy man and is still considered by many today as America's father of invention. Edison held 1,093 patents, though Tesla, were he alive, would be the first to point out that it's debatable how many of those inventions were really his work.

Tesla's experience was almost the polar opposite of Edison's. Unlike Edison, he made one bad business decision after another. He sold his interest in AC electricity to George Westinghouse in order to finance other projects and didn't profit when it became the standard. Though his Tesla coil made him the father of the wireless age, he was destitute when he died in a New York hotel room in 1943. Adding to his image as a "mad" scientist, he became attached to pigeons in his last years and was reputed to think he could converse with them. He had accused Edison of stealing his coil technology and giving it to Marconi to invent the radio. Months after his death, a court decided that Tesla's patents predated Marconi's, and he was posthumously declared the inventor of the radio. Though he wasn't around to gloat, Tesla had finally beaten Edison at something.

Lawrence H. Levy

ACKNOWLEDGMENTS

From day one, my agent Paul Fedorko was excited and passionate about my book. His notes were always positive, and I found his enthusiasm encouraging and invigorating. I'm sure it was key to getting it sold in a very short time.

I would also like to thank Lauren Friedman for introducing me to Paul.

Sammy Bina, who is Paul's assistant, read my manuscript and recommended it to him, as did Andrea Deignan. I'd like to commend them for their impeccable taste.

My editor, Meagan Stacey, is a very smart woman whose edits were extremely helpful. She has also been very patient and considerate in leading me through the process of getting my first novel published. I am fortunate to have her as my editorial champion.

Kim Silverton is Meagan's assistant, and she, too, has been incredibly helpful in shepherding me through this process.

My late and very talented friend Louis Turenne, whose mind trumped the Internet in knowledge, was a wonderful source of information, and I thank him for it.

I know I mentioned my daughter, Erin, in the dedication, but anyone who has read my book multiple times and still finds the strength to give great notes should be mentioned twice.

I'd also like to thank Jane Putch; Michael, Helen, and Adam Levy; Roz and Elliot Joseph; Charley and Nikki Garrett; Stan Finkelberg; Bob and Randy Myer; Tom Szollosi; Lois Feller; Ron Marks; and James Gleason. As the saying goes, "It takes a village," and these were just some of my many relatives, friends, and acquaintances who read my work, buoyed me with their genuinely positive responses, and made me believe my dream was possible.

A READER'S GUIDE FOR SECOND STREET STATION

1. Mary Handley seems to be very different from her nineteenth-century peers. What do you think sets her apart? What influences in her past shaped her personality and ambitions?

2. There are many historical characters in *Second Street Station* from J. P. Morgan to Nikola Tesla, Thomas Edison, and more. Which character did you enjoy reading about most and why? Did any historical character surprise you? How so?

3. Thomas Edison is made out to be a villain and is one of the prime suspects in the Goodrich murder case. Does this influence your opinion of this prominent historical figure?

4. What do you think of the author's description of late nineteenth-century Brooklyn? How does this differ from how Brooklyn is represented in modern pop culture?

5. *Second Street Station* is based on the true story of the first woman hired by the Brooklyn Police Department to sleuth a crime. How does the historical context influence your reading of the book?

6. If you were a woman in late nineteenth-century New York City, how would you see yourself fitting into society? Do you think you would search for similar opportunities that Mary did or do you think you might enjoy living within the cultural norm at the time? Do you find Mary to be an inspirational character?

7. Aside from Mary, who did you find to be the most relatable character and why?

8. Is Mary's strained relationship with her mother specific to the historical era or do you think you might see this type of mother-daughter strain in modern times?

9. Discuss Mary's relationship with Charles Pemberton. Do you think they made the right decision to part ways? Why or why not?

10. Do you think Chief Campbell was a positive mentor and influence in Mary's life? Do you think he had selfish motivations?

11. Throughout Mary's investigation, she finds herself in dangerous and compromising situations. Is there a point where you might have stopped for your own well-being before she did?

12. Were you surprised to learn the identity of the killer? If so, whom did you suspect?

13. Cocaine was considered the wonder drug back in the nineteenth century and such notables as Queen Victoria, the Pope, Thomas Edison, and Robert Louis Stevenson endorsed it. The most popular wine, Vin Mariani, contained it, as did Coca-Cola and other products. Do you think this endorsement was caused by a lack of scientific knowledge and government regulation, and, if so, how is it different today? Have our scientific advances and the FDA helped us prevent harmful drugs from being put into our food or have corporations just gotten smarter with their deceptions?

14. We never learn the Bowler Hat's name. How do you think this influenced your experience reading about him?

15. Are the Bowler Hat's crimes any less heinous because he is a hired hand and not the one orchestrating the crime?

16. The Bowler Hat performed his duties for ruthless business tycoons who were given the derogatory name of robber barons. Were you aware and do you believe that such practices took place just to grow a business and accumulate wealth? Who were the robber barons? Do you think such people exist today, and, if so, who do you think they are?

17. The author has spent a large part of his career writing for television. Did this book remind you of any TV shows or films you have seen?

18. There is a lot of discussion about dreams and meaning-ful goals in life. Mary has a dream of being a detective. John Pemberton has a dream of Coca-Cola becoming a viable and successful product. Nikola Tesla has a dream of becoming a successful inventor recognized for his in-novation and genius. How important do you think it is to have a dream? How much did not having one play a part in Charles Pemberton's problems? Are dreams good or bad? Can they destroy you?

BROOKLYN ON FIRE

began organizing the eastern half. Under Bridgeman's plan it was divided into three sectors—one for each corps of the BEF. Specifically, III Corps would hold the Dunkirk end, next to the French; I Corps would be in the middle; and II Corps would defend the eastern end, which stretched across the frontier into Belgium. Two major canals—one running from Bergues to Furnes, the other from Furnes to Nieuport—would be the main defense line. For the most part, the line lay five or six miles back from the coast, which would protect the beaches at least from small arms fire. To command this defense line, Adam had the services of Brigadier the Honorable E. F. Lawson, a competent artilleryman.

There was only one ingredient missing—soldiers. As of 8:00 a.m. on the 27th, when the Cassel meeting broke up, the British defense line existed only on paper. Lawson would have to man it with troops plucked from the horde tumbling into Dunkirk, taking pot luck from what turned up. Later he could replace these pick-up units, when the regular divisions holding open the corridor fell back on the coast; but for the moment improvisation was once again the order of the day.

For immediate help he depended largely on artillerymen who had destroyed their guns during the retreat and could now serve as infantry. Several units manned the line between Bergues and Furnes, bolstered by a party of nineteen Grenadier Guards, who had somehow been separated from their battalion. Farther east, the 12th Searchlight Battery dug in at Furnes, and a survey company of Royal Engineers moved into Nieuport.

While Lawson patched together his defense line, Colonel Bridgeman concentrated on getting the troops back to the coast. Basically his plan called for three main routes—III Corps would head for the beach at Malo-les-Bains, an eastern suburb of Dunkirk . . . I Corps for Bray-Dunes, six miles farther east . . . and II Corps for La Panne, four miles still farther east and across the Belgian frontier. All three towns were seaside resorts and provided an unlikely setting of bandstands, carousels, beach chairs, push-pedal cycles, and brightly painted cafés.

Of the three, La Panne was the logical place to establish headquarters. It was where the telephone cable linking Belgium and England entered the Channel, and this meant direct contact with Dover and London not available anywhere else. Adam set up shop in the *Mairie*, or town hall, and it was from here that Bridgeman did his best to direct the withdrawal.

Naturally his plans meant issuing orders, and this in turn meant paper, and this in turn raised a brand new problem: there was no paper. GHQ's entire supply had gone up in flames, as the BEF destroyed its stores and equipment to keep them from falling into enemy hands.

Major Arthur Dove, a staff officer under Bridgeman, finally managed to buy a pad of pink notepaper at a local stationery store. It was more suitable for *billets-doux*, but it was the only thing available. In payment Dove needed all his diplomacy to persuade Madame the proprietress to accept French instead of Belgian francs.

It's doubtful whether many of the addressees ever saw the Major's pink stationery. Dispatch riders did their best to deliver the orders, but communications were in a bigger shambles than ever. While the three corps did stick basically to their allotted sectors of the beachhead, many units remained unaware of any such arrangement, and thousands of stragglers went wherever whim—or an instinct for self-preservation—took them.

They swarmed into Dunkirk and onto the beaches—lost, confused, and all too often leaderless. In many of the service and rear area units the officers had simply vanished, leaving the men to shift for themselves. Some took shelter in cellars in the town, huddling together as the bombs crashed down. Others threw away their arms and aimlessly wandered about the beach. Others played games and swam. Others got drunk. Others prayed and sang hymns. Others settled in deserted cafés on the esplanade and sipped drinks, almost like tourists. One man, with studied indifference, stripped to his shorts and sunbathed among the rocks, reading a paperback.

And all the time the bombs rained down. The 2nd Anti-Aircraft Brigade was charged with protecting Dunkirk, and soon after arriving at La Panne, Colonel Bridgeman instructed the Brigade's liaison officer, Captain Sir Anthony Palmer, to keep his guns going to the last. Any spare gunners to join the infantry; any incapacitated men to go to the beach. Palmer relayed the order to Major-General Henry Martin, commanding all

Gort's antiaircraft, but somewhere along the line the meaning got twisted. Martin understood that all antiaircraft gunners were to go to the beach.

He never questioned the order, although it's hard to see why any force, as hard-pressed from the air as the BEF, would begin an evacuation by sending off its antiaircraft gunners. Instead, he merely reasoned that if the gunners were to leave, there would be no further use for their guns. Rather than have them fall into enemy hands, he ordered his heavy 3.7-inch pieces to be destroyed.

Sometime after midnight, May 27–28, Martin appeared at Adam's headquarters to report that the job was done. With rather a sense of achievement, one observer felt, he saluted smartly and announced, "All the antiaircraft guns have been spiked."

There was a long pause while a near-incredulous Adam absorbed this thunderbolt. Finally he looked up and merely said, "You . . . fool, go away."

So the bombing continued, now opposed only by some light Bofors guns, and by the troops' Brens and rifles. In exasperation some men even cut the fuses of grenades and hurled them into the air hoping to catch some low-flying plane. More were like Lance Corporal Fred Batson of the RASC, who crawled into a discarded Tate & Lyle sugar box. Its thin wooden sides offered no real protection, but somehow he felt safer.

Their big hope was the sea. The Royal Navy would come and get them. Gallipoli, Corunna, the Armada—for centuries, in a tight spot the British had always counted on their navy to save the day, and it had never disappointed them. But tonight, May 27, was different. . . .

Private W.B.A. Gaze, driver with an ordnance repair unit, looked out to sea from Malo-les-Bains and saw nothing. No ships at all, except a shattered French destroyer beached a few yards out, her bow practically severed from the rest of the hull.

After a bit, a single British destroyer hove into view . . . then three Thames barges, which moored 400 yards out . . . and finally fourteen drifters, each towing a couple of small boats. Not much for this mushrooming crowd on the beach.

The prospect was even worse to the east. At La Panne Captain J. L. Moulton, a Royal Marines officer attached to GHQ, went down to the beach to see what was going on. Three sloops lay offshore, but there were no small boats to ferry anybody out.

After quite a while a motor boat appeared, towing a whaler. As a Marine, Moulton knew something about boats and rushed to grab the gunwhale to keep the whaler from broaching to the surf. The skipper, sure that Moulton was trying to hijack the craft, fired a shot over his head.

Somehow Moulton convinced the man of his good intentions, but the incident underscored the ragged inadequacy of the whole rescue effort at this point. More ships were needed, and many more small boats.

Going to General Adam's headquarters, Moulton reported the shortage of vessels. Adam phoned London, hoping to stir some action at that end, and then approved a suggestion by Moulton that he go to Dover, armed with a map showing where the troops were concentrated, and speak directly with Admiral Ramsay.

Moulton now went back to the beach, got a lift to one of the sloops lying offshore, and had the skipper take him across the Channel. Perhaps he could explain the true dimensions of the job. Without enough ships, all the time so dearly bought in Flanders would be wasted.

5

"Plenty Troops, Few Boats"

In his office just off the Dynamo Room Admiral Ramsay listened politely as Captain Moulton described the desperate situation at Dunkirk, and the need for a greater naval effort if many men were to be saved. Moulton had the sinking feeling that he wasn't getting his point across ... that this was one of those cases where a mere Marine captain didn't carry much weight with a Vice-Admiral of the Royal Navy.

His mission accomplished, Moulton returned to France, reported back to General Adam's headquarters, and went to work on the beaches. Meanwhile, there were still few ships, but this wasn't because Ramsay failed to appreciate the need. Relying mainly on personnel vessels—ferries, pleasure steamers, and the like—he had hoped to dispatch two every three and a half hours, but the schedule soon broke down.

The first ship sent was *Mona's Isle*, an Isle of Man packet. She left Dover at 9:00 p.m., May 26, and after an uneventful passage tied up at Dunkirk's Gare Maritime around midnight. Packed with 1,420 troops, she began her return journey at sunrise on the 27th. Second Lieutenant D. C. Snowdon of the 1st/7th Queen's Royal Regiment lay in exhausted sleep below decks, when he was suddenly awakened by what sounded like someone hammering on the hull. This turned out to be German artillery firing on the vessel. Because of shoals and minefields, the shortest route between Dunkirk and Dover (called Route Z) ran close to the shore for some miles west of Dunkirk. Passing ships offered a perfect target.

Several shells crashed into *Mona's Isle*, miraculously without exploding. Then a hit aft blew away the rudder. Luckily, she was twin-screw, and managed to keep course by using her propellers. Gradually she drew out of range, and the troops settled down again. Lieutenant Snowdon went back to sleep below decks; others remained topside, soaking in the bright morning sun.

Then another rude awakening—this time by a sound like hail on the decks. Six Me 109's were machine-gunning the ship. All the way aft Petty Officer Leonard B. Kearley-Pope crouched alone at the stern gun, gamely firing back. Four bullets tore into his right arm, but he kept shooting, until the planes broke off. *Mona's Isle* finally limped into Dover around noon on the 27th with 23 killed and 60 wounded. Almost as bad from Ramsay's point of view, the 40-mile trip had taken eleven and a half hours instead of the usual three.

By this time other ships too were getting a taste of those German guns. Two small coasters, *Sequacity* and *Yewdale*, had started for Dunkirk about 4:00 a.m. on the 27th. As they approached the French coast, a shell crashed into *Sequacity*'s starboard side at the waterline, continued through the ship and out the port side. Another smashed into the engine room, knocking out the pumps. Then two more hits, and *Sequacity* began to sink. *Yewdale* picked up the crew, and with shells splashing around her, headed back for England.

By 10:00 a.m. four more ships had been forced to turn back. None got through, and Admiral Ramsay's schedule was in hopeless disarray. But he was a resourceful, resilient man; in the Dynamo Room the staff caught his spirit and set about revamping their plan.

Clearly Route Z could no longer be used, at least in daylight. There were two alternatives, neither very attractive. Route X, further to the northeast, would avoid the German batteries, but it was full of dangerous shoals and heavily mined. For the moment, at least, it too was out. Finally there was Route Y. It lay still further to the northeast, running almost as far as Ostend,

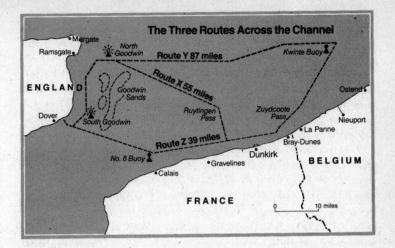

The Three Routes Across the Channel

Margate
Ramsgate
North Goodwin
Route Y 87 miles
Kwinte Buoy
ENGLAND
Goodwin Sands
Route X 55 miles
Ostend
Dover
South Goodwin
Ruytingen Pass
Zuydcoote Pass
Nieuport
La Panne
Bray-Dunes
Route Z 39 miles
No. 6 Buoy
Dunkirk
BELGIUM
Calais
Gravelines
FRANCE
0   10 miles

where it doubled back west toward England. It was easier to navigate, relatively free of mines, and safe from German guns; but it was much, much longer—87 miles, compared to 55 for Route X and 39 for Route Z.

This meant the cross-Channel trip would be twice as long as planned; or, put another way, it would take twice as many ships to keep Ramsay's schedule.

Still, it was the only hope, at least until Route X could be swept clear of mines. At 11:00 a.m. on the 27th the first convoy—two transports, two hospital ships, and two destroyers—left Dover and arrived off Dunkirk nearly six hours later.

The extra effort was largely wasted, for at the moment Dunkirk was taking such a pounding from the Luftwaffe that the port was practically paralyzed. The *Royal Daffodil* managed to pick up 900 men, but the rest of the convoy was warned to stay clear: too much danger of sinking and blocking the harbor. With that, the convoy turned and steamed back to Dover.

During the evening four more transports and two hospital ships arrived by Route Y. The transport *Canterbury* picked up 457 troops at the Gare Maritime, but then the Luftwaffe returned for a nighttime visit, and it again looked as though the harbor might be blocked.

As *Canterbury* pulled out, she received a signal from the shore to turn back any other vessels trying to enter. She relayed the message to several ships waiting outside, and they in turn relayed it to other ships. There was more than one inexperienced signalman at sea that night, and garbles were inevitable. By the time the warning was flashed by a passing ship to the skoot *Tilly*, coming over by Route Y, it said, "Dunkirk has fallen and is in enemy hands. Keep clear."

Tilly was one of six skoots that had sailed together from the Dover Downs that afternoon. Her skipper, Lieutenant-Commander W.R.T. Clemments, had no idea why he was going to Dunkirk. His only clue was a pile of 450 lifejackets that had been dumped aboard just before sailing—rather many for a crew of eleven. Now here was a ship telling him to turn back from a trip he didn't understand anyhow. After consulting with the nearest skoot, he put about and returned to Dover for further orders.

The other skoots hovered off Nieuport for a while. They too received signals from passing ships that Dunkirk had fallen. They too turned back. To cap off the day, two strings of lifeboats being towed over by a tug were run down and scattered.

This chain of mishaps and misunderstandings explained why the men waiting on the beaches saw so few ships on May 27. Only 7,669 men were evacuated that day, most of them "useless mouths" evacuated by ships sent from Dover before Dynamo officially began. At this rate it would take 40 days to lift the BEF.

As the bad news flowed in, Admiral Ramsay and his staff in the Dynamo Room struggled to get the show going again. Clearly more destroyers were needed—to escort the convoys, to fight off the Luftwaffe, to help lift the troops, to provide a protective screen for the longer Route Y. Ramsay fired off an urgent appeal to the Admiralty: take destroyers off other jobs; get them to Dunkirk. . . .

HMS *Jaguar* was on escort duty in the cold, foggy waters off Norway when orders came to return to England at once. . . . *Havant* was lying at Greenock, tucked among the green hills of western Scotland. . . . *Harvester* was a brand new destroyer training far to the south off the Dorset coast. One after another, all available destroyers were ordered to proceed to Dover "forthwith."

Saladin was a 1914 antique on escort duty off the Western Approaches when she got the word. The other escort vessels had similar orders, and all complied at once. The twelve to fourteen ships in the convoy were left to fend for themselves. These were dangerous waters, and Chief Signal Clerk J. W. Martin of the *Saladin* wondered what the commodore of the convoy thought as he watched his protection steam away.

On the destroyers few of the men knew what was up. On the *Saladin* Martin, who saw much of the message traffic, caught a reference to "Dynamo," but that told him nothing. He just knew it must be important if they were leaving a convoy in this part of the Atlantic.

Speculation increased as the destroyers reached Dover and were ordered to proceed immediately to "beaches east of Dunkirk." On the *Malcolm* the navigation officer, Lieutenant David Mellis, supposed they were going to bring off some army unit that had been cut off. With luck they should finish the job in a few hours. The *Anthony* passed a motor boat heading back to England with about twenty soldiers aboard. The officer of the watch shouted across the water, asking if there were many more to come. "Bloody thousands," somebody yelled back.

It was still dark when the *Jaguar* crept near the French coast in the early hours of May 28. As dawn broke, Stoker A. D. Saunders saw that the ship was edging toward a beautiful stretch of white sand, which appeared to have shrubs planted all over it. Then the shrubs began to move, forming lines pointed toward the sea, and Saunders realized they were men, thousands of soldiers waiting for help.

The whole stretch of beach from Dunkirk to La Panne shelved so gradually that the destroyers couldn't get closer than a mile, even at high tide. Since no small craft were yet on the scene, the destroyers had to use their own boats to pick up the men. The boat crews weren't used to this sort of work, the soldiers even less so.

Sometimes they piled into one side all at once, upsetting the craft. Other times too many crowded into a boat, grounding or swamping it. All too often they simply abandoned the boat once they reached the rescue ship. Motors were clogged with sand, propellers fouled by debris, oars lost. Operating off Malo-les-Bains in the early hours of May 28, *Sabre*'s three boats picked up only 100 men in two hours. At La Panne, *Malcolm*'s record was even worse—450 men in fifteen hours.

"Plenty troops, few boats," the destroyer *Wakeful* radioed Ramsay at 5:07 a.m. on the 28th, putting the problem as succinctly as possible. All through the day *Wakeful* and the other destroyers sent a stream of messages to Dover urging more small boats. The Dynamo Room in turn needled London.

The Small Vessels Pool was doing its best, but it took time to wade through the registration data sent in by owners. Then H. C. Riggs of the Ministry of Shipping thought of a short-cut. Why not go direct to the various boatyards along the Thames? With a war on, many of the owners had laid up their craft.

At Tough Brothers boatyard in Teddington the proprietor, Douglas Tough, got an early-morning phone call from Admiral Sir Lionel Preston himself. The evacuation was still secret, but Preston took Tough into his confidence, explaining the nature of the problem and the kind of boats needed.

The Admiral couldn't have come to a better man. The Tough family had been in business on the Thames for three generations. Douglas Tough had founded the present yard in 1922 and knew just about every boat on the river. He was willing to act for the Admiralty, commandeering any suitable craft.

The first fourteen were already in the yard. Supervised by Chief Foreman Harry Day, workmen swiftly off-loaded cushions and china, ripped out the peacetime fittings, put the engines in working order, filled the fuel tanks.

Tough himself went up and down the river, picking out additional boats that he thought could stand the wear and tear of the job ahead. Most owners were willing; some came along with their boats. A few objected, but he commandeered their vessels anyhow. Some never realized what was happening, until they later found their boats missing and reported the "theft" to the police.

Meanwhile volunteer crews were also being assembled at Tough's, mostly amateurs from organizations like the Little Ships Club or a wartime creation called the River Emergency Service. These gentleman sailors would get the boats down the river to Southend, where the Navy would presumably take over.

The Small Vessels Pool, of course, did not confine its efforts to Tough's. It tried practically every boatyard and yacht club from Cowes to Margate. Usually no explanation was given—just the distance the boats had to go. At William Osborne's yard in Littlehampton the cabin cruisers *Gwen Eagle* and *Bengeo* seemed to fill the bill; local hands were quickly rounded up by the harbor master, and off they went.

Often the Small Vessels Pool dealt directly with the owners in its files. Technically every vessel was chartered, but the paperwork was usually done long afterwards.

Despite a later legend of heroic sacrifice, some cases were difficult. Preston's assistant secretary Stanley Berry found himself dealing interminably with the executor of a deceased owner's estate, who wanted to know who was going to pay a charge of £3 for putting the boat in the water. But most were like the owner who asked whether he could retrieve some whisky left on board. When Berry replied it was too late for that, the man simply said he hoped the finder would have a good drink on him.

By now the Dynamo Room was reaching far beyond the Small Vessels Pool. The Nore Command of the Royal Navy, based at Chatham, scoured the Thames estuary for shallow-draft barges. The Port of London authorities stripped the lifeboats off the *Volendam*, *Durbar Castle*, and other ocean liners that happened to be in dock. The Royal National Lifeboat Institution sent everything it had along the east and south coasts.

The Army offered eight landing craft (called ALC's), but some way had to be found to bring them from Southampton. Jimmy Keith, the Ministry of Shipping liaison man in the Dynamo Room, phoned Basil Bellamy at the Sea Transport Division in London. For once, the solution was easy. Bellamy flipped through his cards and found that the cargo liner *Clan MacAlister*, already in Southampton, had exceptionally strong derrick posts. She began loading the ALC's on the morning of the 27th, and was on her way down the Solent by 6:30 p.m.

On board was a special party of 45 seamen and two reserve officers. They would man the ALC's. Like the crews for the skoots, they were drawn from the Chatham Naval Barracks. Sometimes a ship was lucky and drew an experienced crew. More often it was like the skoot *Patria*, which had a coxswain who couldn't steer and an engineer making his first acquaintance with marine diesels.

In the Dynamo Room, Admiral Ramsay's staff worked on.

There seemed a million things to do, and all had to be done at once: Clear Route X of mines. . . . Get more fighter cover from the RAF. . . . Find more Lewis guns. . . . Dispatch the antiaircraft cruiser *Calcutta* to the scene. . . . Repair damaged vessels. . . . Replace worn-out crews. . . . Send over water for the beleaguered troops. . . . Prepare for the wounded. . . . Get the latest weather forecast. . . . Line up some 125 maintenance craft to service the little ships now gathering at Sheerness. . . . Put some men to work making ladders—fast.

"Poor Morgan," Ramsay wrote Mag, describing the effect on his staff, "is terribly strained and badly needs a rest. 'Flags' looks like a ghost, and the Secretary has suddenly become old. All my staff are in fact completely worn out, yet I see no prospect of any let up. . . ."

For Ramsay himself there was one ray of light. Vice-Admiral Sir James Somerville had come down from London, volunteering to take over from time to time so that Ramsay could get a bit of rest. Somerville had an electric personality, and was worshiped by junior officers. He was not only a perfect stand-in but a good trouble-shooter as well. Shortly after his arrival on May 27 morale collapsed on the destroyer *Verity*. She had been badly shelled on a couple of trips across the Channel, her captain was seriously wounded, and the crew had reached the breaking point. One sailor even tried to commit suicide. When the acting skipper reported the situation to Dover Castle, Somerville went back with him and addressed the ship's company. Knowing that words can only accomplish so much, he also rested *Verity* overnight. Next morning she was back on the job.

To Somerville, to Ramsay—to the whole Dynamo Room contingent—the evacuation had become an obsession. So it seemed like a visit from another world when three high-ranking French naval officers turned up in Dover on the 27th to discuss, among other things, how to keep Dunkirk supplied.

From General Weygand on down, the French still regarded the port as a permanent foothold on the Continent. Admiral Darlan, the suave naval Chief of Staff, was no exception, and his deputy, Captain Paul Auphan, had the task of organizing a supply fleet for the beachhead. Auphan decided that trawlers and fishing smacks were the best bet, and his men fanned out over

Normandy and Brittany commandeering more than 200 vessels.

Meanwhile, disturbing news reached Darlan. A liaison officer attached to Gort's headquarters reported that the British were considering evacuation—with or without the French. It was decided to send Auphan to Dover, where he would be joined by Rear-Admiral Marcel Leclerc from Dunkirk and by Vice-Admiral Jean Odend'hal, head of the French Naval Mission in London. A firsthand assessment might clarify the situation.

Auphan and Odend'hal arrived first, and as they waited for Leclerc in the officers' mess, Odend'hal noticed a number of familiar British faces. They were strictly "desk types"—men he saw daily at the Admiralty—yet here they were in Dover wearing tin hats. Odend'hal asked what was up. "We're here for the evacuation," they replied.

The two visitors were astonished. This was the first word to reach the French Navy that the British were not merely "considering" evacuation—they were already pulling out. Leclerc now arrived, and all three went to see Ramsay. He brought them up to date on Dynamo. Auphan began rearranging the plans for his fleet of fishing smacks and trawlers. Instead of supplying the beachhead, they would now be used to evacuate French troops. The two navies would work together, but it was understood that each country would look primarily after its own.

Back in France next day, the 28th, Auphan rushed to French naval headquarters at Maintenon and broke the news to Darlan. The Admiral was so amazed he took the Captain to see General Weygand. He professed to be equally surprised, and Auphan found himself in the odd position of briefing the Supreme Allied Commander on what the British were doing.

It's hard to understand why they all were so astounded. On the afternoon of May 26 Churchill told Reynaud that the British planned to evacuate, urging the French Premier to issue "corresponding orders." At 5:00 a.m. on the 27th Eden radioed the British liaison at Weygand's headquarters, asking where the French wanted the evacuated troops to be landed when they returned to that part of France still held by the Allies. At 7:30 a.m. the same day the French and British commanders meeting at Cassel discussed the "lay-out of the beaches" at Dunkirk—they could only have been talking about the evacuation.

Informally, the French had been aware of Gort's thinking a good deal sooner. As early as May 23 a British liaison officer, Major O. A. Archdale, came unofficially to say good-bye to his opposite number, Major Joseph Fauvelle, at French First Army Group headquarters. Fauvelle gathered that evacuation was in the wind and told his boss, General Blanchard. He in turn sent Fauvelle to Paris to tell Weygand. The information was in the Supreme Commander's hands by 9:00 a.m., May 25.

And yet, surprise and confusion on the 28th, when Captain Auphan reported that the British had begun to evacuate. Perhaps the best explanation lies in the almost complete breakdown of French communications. The troops trapped in Flanders were no longer in touch with Weygand's headquarters, except by wireless via the French Navy, and their headquarters at Maintenon was 70 miles from Paris.

As a result, vital messages were delayed or missed altogether. The various commands operated in a vacuum; there was no agreement on policy or tactics even among themselves. Reynaud accepted evacuation. Weygand thought in terms of a big bridgehead including a recaptured Calais. Blanchard and Fagalde wrote off Calais, but still planned on a smaller bridgehead built around Dunkirk. General Prioux, commanding First Army, was bent on a gallant last stand down around Lille.

In contrast, the British were now united in one goal—evacuation. As Odend'hal noted, even senior staff officers from the Admiralty were manning small boats and working the beaches—often on the shortest notice.

One of these was Captain William G. Tennant, a lean, reserved navigation expert who normally was Chief Staff Officer to the First Sea Lord in London. He got his orders on May 26 at 6:00 p.m.; by 8:25 he was on the train heading for Dover. Tennant was to be Senior Naval Officer at Dunkirk, in charge of the shore end of the evacuation. As SNO he would supervise the distribution and loading of the rescue fleet. To back him up he had a naval shore party of eight officers and 160 men.

After a brief stopover at Chatham Naval Barracks, he arrived in Dover at 9:00 a.m. on the 27th. Meanwhile buses were coming from Chatham, bringing the men assigned to the shore party. Most still had no idea what was up. One rumor spread that

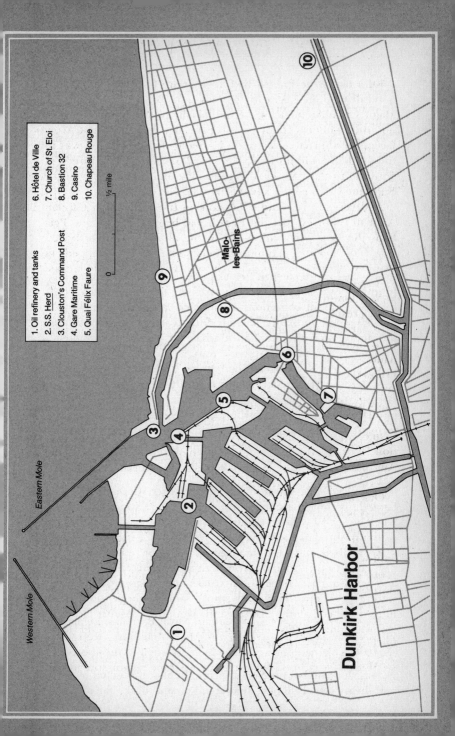

Dunkirk Harbor

Western Mole

Eastern Mole

Malo-les-Bains

1. Oil refinery and tanks
2. S.S. Herd
3. Clouston's Command Post
4. Gare Maritime
5. Quai Félix Faure
6. Hôtel de Ville
7. Church of St. Eloi
8. Bastion 32
9. Casino
10. Chapeau Rouge

0   ½ mile

they were going to man some six-inch guns on the Dover cliffs. Seaman Carl Fletcher was delighted at the prospect: he then would be stationed near home.

He soon learned better. On arrival at Dover the men were divided into parties of twenty, each commanded by one of Tennant's eight officers. Fletcher's group was under Commander Hector Richardson, who explained that they would shortly be going to Dunkirk. It was a bit "hot" there, he added, and they might like to fortify themselves at a pub across the way. To a man they complied, and Seaman Fletcher belted down an extra one for the trip over.

The destroyer *Wolfhound* would be taking them across, and shortly before departure her skipper, Lieutenant-Commander John McCoy, dropped by the wardroom to learn what his officers knew about conditions at Dunkirk. Sub-Lieutenant H. W. Stowell piped up that he had a friend on another destroyer who was there recently and had a whale of a time—champagne, dancing girls, a most hospitable port.

At 1:45 p.m. *Wolfhound* sailed, going by the long Route Y. At 2:45 the first Stukas struck, and it was hell the rest of the way. Miraculously, the ship dodged everything, and at 5:35 slipped into Dunkirk harbor. The whole coastline seemed ablaze, and a formation of 21 German planes rained bombs on the quay as *Wolfhound* tied up. Commander McCoy dryly asked Sub-Lieutenant Stowell where the champagne and dancing girls were.

The *Wolfhound* was too inviting a target. Captain Tennant landed his shore party and dispersed them as soon as possible. Then he set off with several of his officers for Bastion 32, where Admiral Abrial had allotted space to the local British command.

Normally it was a ten-minute walk, but not today. Tennant's party had to pick their way through streets littered with rubble and broken glass. Burned-out trucks and tangled trolley wires were everywhere. Black, oily smoke swirled about the men as they trudged along. Dead and wounded British soldiers sprawled among the debris; others, perfectly fit, prowled aimlessly about, or scrounged among the ruins.

It was well after 6:00 p.m. by the time they reached Bastion 32, which turned out to be a concrete bunker protected by earth and heavy steel doors. Inside, a damp, dark corridor led through a candle-lit operations room to the cubbyhole that was assigned to the British Naval Liaison Officer, Commander Harold Henderson.

Here Tennant met with Henderson, Brigadier R.H.R. Parminter from Gort's staff, and Colonel G.H.P. Whitfield, the Area Commandant. All three agreed that Dunkirk harbor couldn't be used for evacuation. The air attacks were too devastating. The beaches to the east were the only hope.

Tennant asked how long he would have for the job. The answer was not encouraging: "24 to 36 hours." After that, the Germans would probably be in Dunkirk. With this gloomy assessment, at 7:58 p.m. he sent his first signal to Dover as Senior Naval Officer:

> Please send every available craft East of Dunkirk immediately. Evacuation tomorrow night is problematical.

At 8:05 he sent another message, elaborating slightly:

> Port continually bombed all day and on fire. Embarkation possible only from beaches east of harbour. . . . Send all ships and passenger ships there. Am ordering *Wolfhound* to anchor there, load and sail.

In Dover, the Dynamo Room burst into action as the staff rushed to divert the rescue fleet from Dunkirk to the ten-mile stretch of sand east of the port. . . .

> 9:01, *Maid of Orleans* not to enter Dunkirk but anchor close inshore between Malo-les-Bains and Zuydcoote to embark troops from beach. . . .

> 9:27, *Grafton* and Polish destroyer *Blyskawicz* to close beach at LaPanne at 0100/28 and embark all possible British troops in own boats. This is our last chance of saving them. . . .

> 9:42, *Gallant* [plus five other destroyers and cruiser *Calcutta*] to close beach one to three miles east of Dunkirk with utmost despatch and embark all possi-

ble British troops. This is our last chance of saving them.

Within an hour the Dynamo Room managed to shift to the beaches all the vessels in service at the moment: a cruiser, 9 destroyers, 2 transports, 4 minesweepers, 4 skoots, and 17 drifters—37 ships altogether.

In Dunkirk, Captain Tennant's naval party went to work rounding up the scattered troops and sending them to the nearest beach at Malo-les-Bains. Here they were divided by Commander Richardson into packets of 30 to 50 men. In most cases the soldiers were pathetically eager to obey anybody who seemed to know what he was doing. "Thank God we've got a Navy," remarked one soldier to Seaman Fletcher.

Most of the troops were found crowded in the port's cellars, taking cover from the bombs. Second Lieutenant Arthur Rhodes managed to get his men into a basement liberally stocked with champagne and foie gras, which became their staple diet for some time. But this did not mean they were enjoying the good life. Some 60 men, two civilian women, and assorted stray dogs were packed in together. The atmosphere was heavy . . . made even heavier when one of the soldiers fed some foie gras to one of the dogs, and it promptly threw up.

Some of the men took to the champagne, and drunken shouts soon mingled with the crash of bombs and falling masonry that came from above. From time to time Rhodes ventured outside trying to find a better cellar, but they all were crowded and he finally gave up. Toward evening he heard a cry for "officers." Going up, he learned that the Royal Navy had arrived. He was to take his men to the beaches; ships would try to lift them that night.

Cellars couldn't hold all the men now pouring into Dunkirk. Some, looking desperately for cover, headed for the sturdy old French fortifications that lay between the harbor and the beaches east of town. Bastion 32 was here, with its small quota of British staff officers, but the French units holed up in the area were not inclined to admit any more visitors.

Terrified and leaderless, one group of British stragglers wasn't about to turn back. They had no officers, but they did have rifles. During the evening of the 27th they approached Bastion 32, brandishing their guns and demanding to be let in. Two Royal Navy officers came out unarmed and parlayed with them. It was still touch and go when one of Tennant's shore parties arrived. The sailors quickly restored order, and this particular crisis was over.

Seaman G. F. Nixon, attached to one of these naval parties, later recalled how quickly the troops responded to almost any show of firm authority. "It was amazing what a two-badge sailor with a fixed bayonet and a loud voice did to those lads."

Captain Tennant, making his first inspection of the beaches as SNO, personally addressed several jittery groups. He urged them to keep calm and stay under cover as much as possible. He assured them that plenty of ships were coming, and that they would all get safely back to England.

He was invariably successful, partly because the ordinary Tommy had such blind faith in the Royal Navy, but also because Tennant *looked* like an officer. Owing to the modern fashion of dressing all soldiers alike, the army officers didn't stand out even when present, but there was no doubt about Tennant. In his well-cut navy blues, with its brass buttons and four gold stripes, he had authority written all over him.

And in Tennant's case, there was an extra touch. During a snack at Bastion 32 his signal officer, Commander Michael Ellwood, cut the letters "S-N-O" from the silver foil of a cigarette pack, then glued them to the Captain's helmet with thick pea soup.

Unfortunately no amount of discipline could change the basic arithmetic of Dunkirk. Far too few men were being lifted from the beaches. Tennant estimated he could do the job five or six times faster if he could use the docks. Yet one glance at Dunkirk's blazing waterfront proved that was out of the question.

But he did notice a peculiar thing. Although the Luftwaffe was pounding the piers and quays, it completely ignored the two long breakwaters or moles that formed the entrance to Dunkirk's harbor. Like a pair of protective arms, these moles ran toward each other—one from the west and one from the east—with just enough room for a ship to pass in between. It was the eastern mole that attracted Tennant's special attention.

Made of concrete piling topped by a wooden walkway, it ran some 1,400 yards out to sea. If ships could be brought alongside, it would speed up the evacuation enormously.

The big drawback: the mole was never built to be used as a pier. Could it take the pounding it would get, as the swift tidal current—running as high as three knots—slammed ships against the flimsy wooden planking? There were posts here and there, but they were meant only for occasional harbor craft. Could large vessels tie up without yanking the posts loose? The walkway was just ten feet wide, barely room for four men walking abreast. Would this lead to impossible traffic jams?

All these difficulties were aggravated by a fifteen-foot tidal drop. Transferring the troops at low or high water was bound to be a tricky and dangerous business.

Still, it was the only hope. At 10:30 p.m. Tennant signaled *Wolfhound*, now handling communications offshore, to send a personnel ship to the mole "to embark 1,000 men." The assignment went to *Queen of the Channel*, formerly a crack steamer on the cross-Channel run. At the moment she was lifting troops from the beach at Malo-les-Bains, and like everyone else, her crew found it slow going. She quickly shifted to the mole and began loading up. She had no trouble, and the anxious naval party heaved a collective sigh of relief.

By 4:15 a.m. some 950 men crammed the *Queen*'s decks. Dawn was breaking, when a voice called out from the mole asking how many more she could take. "It's not a case of how many more," her skipper shouted back, "but whether we can get away with what we already have."

He was right. Less than halfway across the Channel a single German plane dropped a stick of bombs just astern of the *Queen*, breaking her back. Except for a few soldiers who jumped overboard, everyone behaved with amazing calm. Seaman George Bartlett even considered briefly whether he should go below for a new pair of shoes he had left in his locker. He wisely thought better of it, for the ship was now sinking fast. He and the rest stood quietly on the sloping decks, until a rescue ship, the *Dorrien Rose*, nudged alongside and transferred them all.

The *Queen of the Channel* was lost, but the day was saved. The mole worked! The timbers did not collapse; the tide did not interfere; the troops did not panic. There was plenty of room for a steady procession of ships. The story might be different once the Germans caught on, but clouds of smoke hung low over the harbor. Visibility was at a minimum.

"SNO requires all vessels alongside east pier," the destroyer *Wakeful* radioed Ramsay from Dunkirk at 4:36 a.m. on the 28th. Once again the staff in the Dynamo Room swung into action. They had spent the early part of the night diverting the rescue fleet from the harbor to the beaches; now they went to work shifting it back again. On the beach at Malo-les-Bains Commander Richardson got the word too and began sending the troops back to Dunkirk in batches of 500.

But even as the loading problem was being solved, a whole new crisis arose. Critical moments at Dunkirk had a way of alternating between the sea and the land, and this time, appropriately enough, the setting once again reverted to the battle-scarred fields of Flanders.

At 4 a.m.—just as the *Queen of the Channel* was proving that the mole would work—Leopold III, King of the Belgians, formally laid down his arms. The result left a twenty-mile gap in the eastern wall of the escape corridor. Unless it could be closed at once, the Germans would pour in, cut the French and British off from the sea, and put an abrupt end to the evacuation.

6

The Gap

General Gort heard the news by chance. Hoping to confer with General Blanchard about the evacuation, he had driven to Bastion 32 around 11 o'clock on the night of May 27. No sign of Blanchard, but General Koeltz from Weygand's headquarters was there, and casually asked whether Gort had heard that King Leopold was seeking an armistice.

Gort was amazed. He felt sure that the Belgians weren't capable of prolonged resistance, but he didn't expect them to crumble so soon. "I now found myself suddenly faced with an open gap of 20 miles between Ypres and the sea through which enemy armoured forces might reach the beaches."

General Weygand was even more astonished. He got the word during a conference at Vincennes, when somebody handed him a telegram from his liaison officer with the Belgians. "The news came like a thunderclap, as nothing had enabled me to foresee such a decision, no warning, not a hint of it."

Even Winston Churchill, who had his own special man, Admiral Sir Roger Keyes, at Leopold's headquarters, seems to have been caught off-guard. "Suddenly," the Prime Minister told a hushed House of Commons a few days later, "without prior consultation, with the least possible notice, without the advice

of his ministers, and upon his own personal act, he sent a pleni-
potentiary to the German command, surrendered his Army, and
exposed our whole flank and means of retreat."

The mystery is why they were so surprised. As early as May 25
Leopold had telegraphed King George VI that Belgian resistance was on the point of being crushed, "and so the assistance
which we can give to the Allies will come to an end if our Army
is surrounded." He added that he considered it his duty to remain with his people and not set up a government in exile.

On the 26th and 27th both Gort and the War Office received
from their Belgian liaison contacts seven separate messages
warning that the end was near, unless the British could counterattack—which was clearly impossible. In addition, Admiral
Keyes telephoned Churchill on the morning of May 27 that "he
did not think that the Belgian army's resistance could be main-
tained much longer." Keyes then wired Gort that Leopold

> fears a moment is rapidly approaching when he can
> no longer rely upon his troops to fight or be of any
> further use to the BEF. He wishes you to realize that
> he will be obliged to surrender before a debacle.

Leopold, on the other hand, had been told nothing about Allied
intentions. Although Gort felt that an active, fighting Belgian
Army was "essential for our extraction," its leaders were never
consulted, and not one ship was allocated for the use of Belgian
troops.

Finally, after a nudge from Eden, Churchill telegraphed Gort
on the morning of May 27, "It is now necessary to tell the Belgians. . . ." He then included a personal message for Admiral
Keyes, spelling out the approach to take with Leopold: "Impart
following to your friend. Presume he knows that British and
French are fighting their way to coast. . . ." Thus London explained away its failure to inform the King by simply "presum-
ing" that he already knew.

Churchill's message also urged Keyes to make sure that Leopold left the country and ended with a vague offer to include
Belgian troops whenever the BEF returned to France.

The message never reached Keyes, but it didn't matter. By

now Leopold had other ideas. Never an attractive personality—a haughty, aloof man who made his ministers stand in his presence—the King nevertheless had a strong sense of duty. On the mistaken assumption that he would continue to have influence under German occupation, he decided to surrender and remain with his people.

At 5:00 p.m. on the 27th a trusted staff officer, Major-General Derousseau, set out with a white flag for the German lines. Any hopes he had for favorable terms were quickly dashed. The Fuehrer insisted on unconditional surrender. Leopold agreed, and at 4:00 a.m. on May 28 Belgium formally laid down her arms.

Here and there a few fought on. After an exhausting day of retreat, Captain Georges Truffaut of the 16th Infantry Division was sleeping in the great hall of the chateau at Ruddervoorde when he woke up with a start at 4:30 a.m. The lights were on, and people were moving about. "The army has capitulated," somebody explained.

"What?"

"The liaison officer attached to Corps headquarters has just brought the order."

"Then I'm deserting." Truffaut, a member of Parliament and one of the young leaders of the Walloon Socialist Party, was no man for blind obedience to military orders.

He "borrowed" a staff car and was soon on his way to Dunkirk. Coming to a French outpost, he learned that staying in the war would be no easy matter. Enraged by the Belgian surrender, the officer in charge called him a traitor, a coward, and warned that the guard would start shooting if he came any closer.

Turned back, Truffaut now tried another road farther south . . . and ran head-on into a German column. Racing north again, he reached the sea at Coxyde. Here he cautiously approached a British officer and carefully explained he was no traitor. Could he enter the lines?

"I'm afraid it's impossible, sir. Sorry."

On to Nieuport, which he found full of Belgian soldiers, some as frustrated as himself. Here Truffaut and a few others appropriated a fishing smack lying in the fairway. They had trouble

with the engine, with the sail, and with a lone German ↓
that swooped down and buzzed them. It apparently decided
they weren't worth the ammunition, for it flew off and they safely reached the open sea.

It was now dark, and to attract attention they lit rags soaked
in petrol. There were plenty of ships, but no one wanted to stop
in these dangerous waters. Finally a British destroyer did pick
them up, and once again Truffant faced a hostile reception.

This time he managed to sell his case. In fact, the destroyer
was on its way to Dunkirk and could use these sturdy Belgians
with their boat. It had been a long, hard day, but Georges Truffant was at last back in the war.

There were not many like him. Private W.C.P. Nye of the 4th
Royal Sussex was on sentry duty at the Courtrai airfield when
he saw a mass of men coming down the road away from the
front. Hundreds of Belgian soldiers on bicycles swept by, shouting that the war was over. Tramping toward the coast from the
River Lys, the men of the 2nd North Staffordshire passed
swarms of disarmed Belgians standing by the roadside watching
the retreat. Some looked ashamed, but many shouted insults
and shook their fists at the weary Tommies. At Bulscamp a
plump gendarme appeared at British headquarters, announced
that Belgium had surrendered and he had been ordered to con-
fiscate all British weapons. There is no record of the language
used in reply.

All over the countryside white bedsheets blossomed from
windows and doorways. At Watou Lieutenant Ramsay of the
2nd Dorsets started to enter an empty house to get a bit of rest.
A woman who lived nearby rushed up crying, "*Non, non, non!*"

"*C'est la guerre,*" explained Ramsay, using the time-honored
expression that had served so well in two world wars to explain
any necessary inconvenience.

"*C'est la guerre, oui, mais pas pour nous!*" she retorted.

To most Belgians it was now indeed somebody else's war,
and they were relieved to be out of it. Many felt their country
had become just a doormat, to be stamped on by larger, stronger neighbors in an apparently endless struggle for power. "*Les
anglais, les allemands, toute la même chose,*" as one weary peasant
woman put it.

Technically, the Belgian surrender suddenly created a huge gap at the northeastern end of the Allied escape corridor. Actually, the gap had been steadily growing as Belgian resistance crumbled, and for the past 48 hours Lieutenant-General Brooke, the II Corps commander defending the line, had been juggling his forces, trying to fill it. He worked miracles, but on the afternoon of May 27 (just when Leopold was tossing in his hand) there were still no Allied troops between the British 50th Division near Ypres and some French on the coast at Nieuport—a gap of over twenty miles.

All Brooke had left was Major-General Montgomery's 3rd Division down by Roubaix near the bottom of the pocket. To do any good, it would have to pull out from its position near the right end of the line . . . move north for 25 miles across the rear of three other divisions . . . then slide back into place on the far left. The shift would be that most difficult of military maneuvers: a giant side-step by 13,000 men, made at night along back lanes and unfamiliar roads, often within 4,000 yards of the enemy. And it all had to be completed by daylight, when the moving column would make a prime target for the Luftwaffe.

Montgomery wasn't in the least fazed by the assignment. Although virtually unknown to the public, he was probably the most discussed division commander in the BEF. Cocky, conceited, abrasive, theatrical, he had few friends but many admirers in the army. Whatever they thought of him, all agreed that he was technically a superb soldier and a master at training and inspiring troops. All winter his men had practiced this sort of night march. They had drilled and drilled, until every detail was down pat, every contingency foreseen. Now "Monty" was sure he could pull it off.

Late afternoon, his machine gunners and armored cars went ahead as a light advance force. Then at last light the red-capped Military Police moved out to mark the way and keep the traffic properly spaced. Finally, after dark, the main body—2,000 vans, lorries, pick-ups, staff cars, and troop carriers. There were, of course, no regular lights. Every driver had to watch the rear axle of the vehicle in front of him. It was painted white, faintly illuminated by a small shielded lamp. Monty himself was riding in his regular Humber staff car, with his bodyguard Sergeant Elkin close by on his motorcycle. On their right the front, running parallel, was marked by the constant flicker of guns. On their left some British artillery kept up a lively fire from Mont Kemmel. Shells and tracers were passing overhead in both directions, forming a weird archway for the moving troops. Once a British battery, positioned by the roadside, let loose just as Monty was passing. It practically blew the Humber off the road, but the General didn't bat an eye.

By daylight on the 28th the 3rd Division was moving into position. Thanks to Montgomery's giant side-step, British troops now held the eastern wall of the escape corridor as far north as Noordschote. For the rest of the way to the sea—some thirteen miles—he counted on the remaining Belgians, for they were still in the war, as far as he knew. Then, shortly after 7:30 a.m., he learned for the first time of Leopold's capitulation.

"Here was a pretty pickle!" Montgomery later recalled in his memoirs. "Instead of having a Belgian Army on my left, I now had nothing. . . ." He quickly slapped together a scratch force of machine gunners plus some British and French armored cars. These fanned out and held the line until more substantial help could be mustered. It was often touch and go. Lieutenant Mann of the 12th Lancers barely managed to blow the bridge at Dixmude before Bock's advance entered the town.

Then, in the afternoon, more bad news. The Germans were at Nieuport, the eastern anchor of the perimeter. The Belgians were gone; Montgomery was stretched to the limit; there was no organized unit to defend the line from Wulpen to Nieuport and the sea.

Once more, improvisation. Brigadier A. J. Clifton happened to be available. Brooke packed him off to Wulpen to organize the defense. On arriving, he took over a scratch force of 200 artillerymen, bolstered from time to time by "unemployed" fitters, surveyors, transport drivers, and headquarters clerks. The unit never had a name; the officers came from five different regiments. Most of the men had never seen their officers before, and the officers had never worked with Clifton.

Somehow he welded them together and they marched off to the front in amazingly good spirits. Along the way, they met the disbanded Belgians trooping back. The Belgians were throwing away their weapons and shouting that the war was over. Taking advantage of the windfall, Clifton's men scooped up the discarded rifles and ammunition, and added them to their own meager arsenal. Positioned along the Furnes-Nieuport canal and the River Yser, they kept the enemy at bay for the next 30 hours. The hottest fighting swirled around the bridge at Nieuport. The Belgians had failed to blow it before the cease-fire, and the British sappers couldn't reach the demolition wires at the eastern end. Again and again the Germans tried to cross, but Clifton concentrated all his "heavy stuff" (four 18-pounders and some Bren guns) at this point and managed to fend them off. Once again the eastern wall held.

The west held too. At Wormhout, a strong-point twelve miles south of Dunkirk, the British 144th Brigade held off Guderian's troops all May 27 and most of the 28th. Every man was used. At the local chateau that served as Brigade headquarters, Private Lou Carrier found himself teaching some cooks and clerks how to prime a Mills bomb—even though he had never seen one before in his life.

Successfully completing this hazardous assignment, he was ordered to help man the chateau wall. As he made his way through the garden, he heard a terrible scream. Thinking some poor blighter had been hit, he spun around . . . and discovered that it came from a peacock perched in a tree.

"That is one bird who will frighten no one else," Carrier said to himself as he raised his rifle to bring it down. Before he could fire, a young lieutenant knocked the rifle aside, saying that he should know better. Didn't he realize it was unlucky to shoot peacocks? The officer added that Carrier would be courtmartialed if he disobeyed and shot the bird.

The next step was predictable. Carrier waited until the lieutenant moved out of sight, then took careful aim and fired. If shooting a peacock brought bad luck, he never noticed it.

But a large dose of bad luck did come to some men defending Wormhout who had probably never harmed a peacock in their lives. After a hard fight most of the 2nd Royal Warwicks were broken up and forced to surrender around 6:00 p.m. on the 28th. Prodded by their captors, the SS Leibstandarte Adolf Hitler Regiment, about 80 men and one officer were herded into a small open-ended barn just outside the village.

As they crowded in, the officer Captain J. F. Lynn-Allen protested that there wasn't enough room for the wounded. Speaking fluent English with a strong American accent, one of the SS guards snapped back, "Yellow Englishman, there will be plenty of room where you're all going to!"

With that, he hurled a stick grenade into the barn, and the carnage was on. For fifteen minutes the guards blasted away with grenades, rifles, tommy guns, and pistols. As an extra touch two batches of prisoners were brought outside and executed by an impromptu firing squad. Amazingly, some fifteen men somehow survived amid the jumble of bodies.

Eight miles farther south Cassel continued to hold. Perched on its hill, it had become—as Colonel Bridgeman foresaw—the "Gibraltar" of the western wall. For two days Kleist's tanks, artillery, and mortars battered the town ... waves of Stukas pounded it ... and still it stood. It was a minor miracle, for the principal defenders—the 5th Gloucesters—had little to fight with. Told to build a barricade, Lieutenant Fane could find only one farm wagon, one plough, a pony trap, and a water cart. When a tank broke into a nearby garden, he tried to stop it with a Boyes rifle—and watched his shots bounce off the armored plate.

The town was surrounded, yet on the evening of May 28 the Gloucesters' quartermaster Captain R.E.D. Brasington managed to get some rations through. The defenders settled down to an odd meal of bully beef washed down by vintage wine.

All the way south, at the bottom of the pocket, units of General Prioux's First Army still held Lille. In contrast to most of the French, they fought with passionate commitment, holding off six German divisions ... meaning six fewer divisions to harass the BEF farther up the corridor.

Most of the escaping troops were now well on their way. The time had come to abandon the strong-points farthest south, and pull the defending units back toward the coast as a sort of rear guard.

On the morning of the 28th Corporal Bob Hadnett, in charge of dispatch riders at 48th Division headquarters, was ordered to get a message to the troops holding Hazebrouck, one of these southern strong-points. The defenders were to disengage and make for Dunkirk that night. Hadnett had already lost two messengers on missions to Hazebrouck; so this time he decided to go himself.

The main roads were jammed with refugees and retiring troops, but he had been a motorcycle trials driver in peacetime and had no trouble riding cross-country. Bouncing over fields and along dirt lanes, he reached Hazebrouck and delivered his message at 143rd Brigade headquarters. After helping the staff work out an escape route north, he mounted his motorcycle and started back.

This time he ran smack into a German column that was just moving into the area. No way to turn, he decided to ride right through. Bending low over the handlebars, accelerator pressed to the floorboards, he shot forward. The startled Germans scattered, but began firing at him as he roared by.

He almost made it. Then suddenly everything went blank, and when he came to, he was lying in the grass with a shattered leg and hand. An enemy officer was standing over him, and a trooper was holding a bottle of brandy to his lips. "Tommy," the officer observed in English, "for you the war is over."

As the British troops streamed up the corridor toward the coast, General Gort's headquarters moved north too. On May 27 the Command Post shifted from Prémesques to Houtkerque, just inside the French border and only fourteen miles from the sea. For the first time since the campaign began, headquarters was not on the London-Brussels telephone cable. It made little difference: Gort wasn't there much anyhow.

He spent most of the 27th looking for General Blanchard, hoping to coordinate their joint withdrawal into the perimeter. He never did find him, and finally returned to Houtkerque weary and frustrated at dawn on the 28th. Then, around 11:00 a.m., Blanchard unexpectedly turned up on his own.

There was much to discuss, and Gort began by reading a telegram received from Anthony Eden the previous day. It confirmed the decision to evacuate: "Want to make it quite clear that sole task now is to evacuate to England maximum of your force possible."

Blanchard was horrified. To the amazement of Gort and Pownall, the French commander hadn't yet heard about the British decision to evacuate. He still understood that the strategy was to set up a beachhead based on Dunkirk which would give the Allies a permanent foothold on the Continent. Somehow Churchill's statement to Reynaud on May 26, Eden's message to the French high command on the 27th, the decisions reached at Cassel and Dover the same day, the information given Abrial and Weygand early on the 28th—all had passed him by. Once again, the explanation probably lay in the complete collapse of French communications.

Now that Blanchard knew, Gort did his best to bring him into line. He must, Gort argued, order Prioux's French First Army to head for Dunkirk too. Like the BEF, they must be rescued to come back and fight again another day. With the Belgians out of the war, there was no longer any possibility of hanging on. It was a case of evacuation or surrender.

Blanchard wavered briefly, but at the crucial moment a liaison officer arrived from Prioux, reporting that the First Army was too tired to move anywhere. That settled it. Blanchard decided to leave the army in the Lille area.

Gort grew more exasperated than ever. Prioux's troops, he exclaimed, couldn't be so tired they were unable to lift a finger to save themselves. Once again, evacuation was their only chance.

Blanchard remained adamant. It was all very well, he observed ruefully, for the British to talk evacuation. "No doubt the British Admiralty had arranged it for the BEF, but the French Marine would never be able to do it for French soldiers. It was, therefore, idle to try—the chance wasn't worth the effort involved."

There was no shaking him. He ended by asking whether the British would continue to pull back to Dunkirk, even though they knew that the French would not be coming along. Pownall exploded with an emphatic "*OUI!*"

Down at French First Army headquarters at Steenwerck a somewhat similar conversation took place that afternoon between General Prioux himself and Major-General E. A. Osborne, commanding the British 44th Division. Osborne was planning the 44th's withdrawal from the River Lys and came over to coordinate his movements with the French, who were on his immediate left. To his surprise, he learned that Prioux didn't plan to withdraw at all. Osborne tried every argument he knew—including the principle of Allied solidarity—but he too got nowhere.

Yet Prioux must have had second thoughts, for sometime later that afternoon he released General de la Laurencie's III Corps, telling them to make for the coast if they could. He himself decided to stay with the rest of his army and go down fighting.

The idea of a gallant last stand—saving the honor of the flag, if nothing else—seemed to captivate them all. "He could only tell us the story of the honor of the *drapeaux*," Pownall noted in his diary after hearing it from Blanchard one more time.

"I am counting on you to save everything that can be saved—and, above all, our honor!" Weygand telegraphed Abrial. "Blanchard's troops, if doomed, must disappear with honor," the General told Major Fauvelle. Weygand pictured an especially honorable role for the high command when the end finally came. Rather than retreat from Paris, the government should behave like the Senators of ancient Rome, who had awaited the barbarians sitting in their curule chairs.

This sort of talk, though possibly consoling at the top level, did not inspire the poilus in the field. They had had enough of antiquated guns, horse-drawn transport, wretched communications, inadequate armor, invisible air support, and fumbling leaders. Vast numbers of French soldiers were sitting around in ditches, resting and smoking, when the 58th Field Regiment, Royal Artillery, passed by on May 28. As one of them explained to a French-speaking Tommy, the enemy was everywhere and there was no hope of getting through; so they were just going to sit down and wait for the Boches to come.

Yet there were always exceptions. A French tank company, separated from its regiment, joined the 1st Royal Irish Fusiliers at Gorre and proved to be a magnificent addition. The crews bristled with discarded British, French, and German weapons and were literally festooned with clanking bottles of wine. They fought with tremendous *élan*, roaring with laughter and pausing to shake hands with one another after every good shot. When the Fusiliers were finally ordered to pull back, the tank company decided to stay and fight on. "*Bon chance!*" they called after the departing Fusiliers, and then went back to work.

General de la Laurencie was another exuberant Frenchman not about to fold his tent. Exasperated by the indecision and defeatism of his superiors, on two separate occasions he had already tried to get his III Corps transferred to Gort's command. Now, released by Prioux, he hurried toward Dunkirk with two divisions.

The first of the fighting contingents were already entering the perimeter. The 2nd Grenadier Guards moved into Furnes, still marching with parade-ground precision. The steady, measured tread of their boots echoed through the medieval market square. Here and there a uniform was torn, a cap missing, a bandage added; but there was no mistaking that erect stance, that clean-shaven, expressionless look so familiar to anyone who had ever watched the changing of the guard at Buckingham Palace.

Not far behind came the 1st/7th Middlesex. They were a Territorial unit far removed from the professionalism of the Guards, but raffishly engaging in their own way. They too had seen their share of rear-guard action. Now they continued through Furnes, finally halting at Oostduinkerke three miles to the east. Here they were a mile or so from Nieuport, the eastern anchor of the perimeter and the point most exposed by the Belgian surrender. Colonel Clifton's "odds and sods" were already in position, but spread very thin. The Middlesex battalion would beef up the line.

Spreading their camouflage nets and digging slit trenches, the new arrivals settled down in the dunes and scrub. As yet there was no sign of the enemy, and it was wonderful to flake out at last and sleep undisturbed. The war of movement had ended, and until the Regimental Sergeant-Major, "Big Ike" Colton, caught up with them and devised some new torment, it was a chance to soak up oceans of missed sleep. Private Francis Ralph Farley only hoped that "Big Ike" didn't find them too soon.

General Gort was also moving into the perimeter. At 6:00 p.m., May 28, GHQ opened up at La Panne, housed in a beachside villa at the western end of town. The place was well chosen. It had been the residence of King Albert during the dark days of the First War, and later served as a summer home for the old King during the twenties. As a result it had a large, reinforced cellar, ample wiring, and the London-Brussels telephone cable, which ran practically by the front door. Once again Gort was only a phone call away from Churchill, the War Office, and Ramsay at Dover.

The Corps commanders also moved into the perimeter on the 28th: III Corps at Dunkirk, II Corps at La Panne, and I Corps in between at Bray-Dunes. Lieutenant-General Michael Barker, commanding I Corps, was by now utterly exhausted. An elderly veteran of the Boer War, he was no man to cope with a *blitzkrieg*. Reaching corps headquarters at the western end of the beach promenade, he retired to the cellar. From here he constantly called up to his assistant quartermaster, Major Bob Ransome, to come and tell him what was going on.

Ransome found the scene on the beach appalling. A mob of officers and men from various service units milled around, firing haphazardly at German planes. Ransome tried to get the crowd into some sort of order but had no luck, even though he jammed his pistol into some very senior ribs. Finally he sent for Captain Tom Gimson, an assistant operations officer at III Corps headquarters. Gimson was an old Irish Guardsman, and his solution was to order the mob to fall in, as on parade. He then solemnly drilled them, running through all the usual commands. Surprisingly, the men complied, and order was soon restored. To Ransome the incident revealed not only what drill could accomplish but also the workings of that most austere of human mechanisms, a Guardsman's mind.

Reports of the confusion at Bray-Dunes soon reached Captain Tennant, busy organizing the embarkations at Dunkirk. So far he had no naval shore parties operating that far up the beach. But the eastern mole and Malo-les-Bains were now under control, and clearly Bray was the next problem to tackle. There were said to be 5,000 troops there, most without officers or any leadership.

Around 5:00 p.m. on the 28th Tennant met with Commander Hector Richardson and two of his other officers, Commanders Tom Kerr and Campbell Clouston. He explained that he wanted an officer to lead a party to Bray and embark the 5,000 men waiting there. At the moment all three commanders were available; so they decided to cut a deck of cards for the assignment—loser to get Bray-Dunes. Richardson lost, but said it was such a big job he really needed another officer to go with him. Kerr and Clouston then cut again. This time Kerr lost. Clouston, the "winner," took what all three considered the easiest assignment—pier master of the mole.

Richardson and Kerr then set off for Bray with fifteen men in a lorry. It was only seven miles, but the roads were so clogged with traffic and pitted with craters that it took an hour to get there. Arriving around 9:00 p.m., the party headed down to the beach to start organizing the embarkation.

It was dusk now, and in the fading light Seaman G. F. Nixon saw what he first thought were several breakwaters, extending from the sand out into the water. Then he realized that the "breakwaters" were actually columns of men, eight thick, leading from the shore right into the sea. The men in front were standing up to their waists, and even to their shoulders, in water.

Five thousand troops? It was more like 25,000. Richardson immediately signaled the situation to Dover and the Admiralty via a destroyer hovering offshore. Once again, an urgent appeal for small boats and motor launches.

Meanwhile they must "make do." Richardson set up headquarters in the back of the lorry. Some of his seamen began breaking up the troops into batches of 50; others rigged lifelines running down into the sea. The beach shelved so gradually that even small boats had a hard time getting in close.

"What a terrible night that was," Kerr wrote his wife a few days later, "for we had got hold of the odds and ends of an army, not the fighting soldiers. There weren't many officers, and those that were, were useless, but by speech and promise of safety and the sight of our naval uniforms we got order out of the rabble."

Those manning the boats were having an equally difficult time. The skoot *Hilda* had arrived early in the afternoon, and because of her shallow draft, her skipper Lieutenant A. Gray managed to nurse her within wading distance of the shore. Troops swarmed out, surrounding the boat completely, trying to scramble up ladders tossed over the bow. But the ladders weren't firmly secured; the men were exhausted; and the tide was rising. They began falling back into the sea. It took super-human efforts by the *Hilda*'s crew to haul them up and over the rail—a collection of inert, sopping bundles.

By 7:00 p.m. Gray had 500 men aboard—not many, considering that 25,000 were waiting—but all he could carry. These he ferried to a destroyer lying farther out, then returned for another load. The tide was now ebbing, and the *Hilda* soon sat on the sand in only two feet of water. Some 400 soldiers surged aboard, and he had another full load by the time the next tide refloated him around 1:30 a.m.

Not far away the skoot *Doggersbank* was doing similar work. Earlier her skipper Lieutenant Donald McBarnet had let go a kedge anchor, then ran himself aground. But he drew more than the *Hilda*, and he still lay in six feet of water—too deep for wading. He lowered his boat and a raft to ferry men out to the ship. On reaching shore, both were immediately mobbed and swamped. Bailed out, they went to work, and by 8:00 p.m. McBarnet had about 450 aboard. Enough. He then used the kedge to pull himself off the beach. Once afloat, he too carried his load to a destroyer farther out, then returned for more.

This became the pattern all along the beach—Bray, Malo-les-Bains, and La Panne as well. Dinghies, rowboats, and launches would load at water's edge and ferry the troops to small ships waiting offshore. These would then ferry the men to the growing fleet of destroyers, minesweepers, and packets lying still farther out. When filled, these would head for England—and one more bit of the army would be home.

It was a practical, workable scheme, but it was also very slow. Each skoot, for instance, averaged only 100 men an hour. No wonder nerves were frayed.

Most of the troops were not up front where they could see what was going on. They stood far back in line or waited in the dunes behind the beach. They couldn't imagine why it all took so long. In the blackness of the night they could see nothing, except the occasional silhouette of some boat caught in the glittering phosphorescence of the water. They could hear only the steady rhythm of the surf and every now and then the clank of oarlocks.

They were tired, cold, and hungry. May nights are chilly along the coast of Flanders, and the men longed for the greatcoats they had thrown away during the hot, dusty retreat. Regular rations had vanished, and it was no longer possible to live off the land. When Corporal R. Kay, a GHQ signalman, found a seven-pound tin of peas near the beach, it was a major discovery. He and a few lucky mates ate them with their fingers, like expensive chocolates.

At Malo-les-Bains Lieutenant-Colonel John D'Arcy was another who fretted over the seemingly endless delay. He had gathered his artillery regiment in a brickyard behind the dunes—splendid cover but no place to see what was going on. He finally ordered one of his officers, Lieutenant C. G. Payne, to take a signal lamp and "go down to the beach and call up the Navy."

Payne had no idea how to go about this, but he did find a signal manual with a section headed, "Call to an Unknown Ship." Pointing his lamp to sea, he carefully followed the instructions, little expecting any results. To his amazement, an answer came flashing out of the night. Instructed to bring the unit to the beach, he hurried back to the Colonel in triumph.

Around 1:30 a.m. on the 29th a stiff breeze sprang up, meaning much greater surf and even slower going. At Bray-Dunes Commander Richardson was making so little progress that he decided to suspend any further embarkations and began sending the troops back to Dunkirk. Maybe the mole would be faster.

Indeed so. Over 24 hours had now passed since Captain Tennant began using the eastern mole or breakwater of Dunkirk harbor as an improvised pier, and the gamble was paying off. A steady stream of destroyers, minesweepers, ferries, and other steamers eased alongside, loaded troops, then backed off and headed for England. The flow of men was regulated by Commander Clouston, who had won the "easy" assignment—pier master of the mole—when he, Richardson, and Kerr cut cards to decide who would be stuck with Bray-Dunes.

Clouston was a Canadian—big, tough, athletic, amusing. He was a fine ice hockey player, and when stationed at Portsmouth, typically he had organized the staff into a hockey team. He was a man bursting with energy, and in his new job he needed all of it.

Word of the mole had gotten around, and now thousands of

disorganized troops were flocking there, queuing up for a chance to embark. To Private Bill Warner, a headquarters clerk with the Royal Artillery, it was like the endless queue at the cinema when talkies first came in. To others it was more like London at rush hour or a rugby scrum. Planting himself at the foot of the mole, Clouston squarely faced the crowd. Megaphone in hand, he shouted instructions, matching the flow of men to the flow of ships.

At first they were mostly destroyers. During the morning of May 28 no fewer than eleven loaded up, and Commander Brian Dean of the destroyer *Sabre* showed how fast they could work. Earlier he had lifted 100 men off the beaches in two hours. His turn-around at Dover took only 58 minutes, and now he was back again, tying up at the mole at 11:00 a.m. This time he loaded 800 men, and headed back to Dover at 12:30 p.m.—a rate of 540 men an hour, compared to 50 men an hour at the beaches.

And he wasn't through yet. Reaching Dover at 6:20 p.m., he refueled and was on his way back to the mole at 10:30—his third trip of the day. This time he stayed only 35 minutes, picking up another 500 troops.

Dusk on the 28th, and the destroyers were joined by an assortment of other craft. The fleet minesweeper *Gossamer* arrived at 9:45 p.m., departed half an hour later with 420 aboard. The sweeper *Ross* loaded another 353 about the same time. The skoot *Tilly*, leading a procession of six small motor vessels, tied up at 11:15; they took on hundreds more. The paddle steamer *Medway Queen* arrived around midnight and picked up nearly 1,000. Her skipper Lieutenant A. T. Cook had warned Chief Cook Russell to expect "several hundred men who will no doubt feel somewhat peckish." The warning scarcely prepared Russell for the assault on his galley. These men weren't "peckish"—they were ravenous.

All through the night of May 28–29 the ships kept coming, while the men streamed out the long wooden walkway like an endless line of ants. For a while the ebb tide slowed the pace—it was hard for untrained soldiers to crawl down the makeshift ladders and gangplanks—but the flow never stopped. Tennant estimated that Clouston was getting men off at a rate of 2,000 an hour.

At 10:45 p.m. he sent Dover his first optimistic situation report:

> French general appreciation is that situation in port tomorrow will continue as for today. Provided aircraft fighters adequate, embarkation can proceed full speed. . . .

The Dynamo Room began to hope that more than a handful might be saved. The total evacuated on May 28 reached 17,804—more than twice the figure for the 27th. They would have to do far better than that, but at least they were moving in the right direction.

There was other good news too: the Admiralty had now released to Ramsay *all* destroyers in home waters. . . . Route X had at last been cleared of mines, cutting the passage to Dunkirk from 87 to 55 miles. . . . The beachhead was holding despite the Belgian surrender. . . . The surf was subsiding; a threatening storm veered away. . . . Smoke from the blazing oil refinery hid the port from the Luftwaffe. . . . Casualties were mercifully low.

Besides the *Queen of the Channel*, the only serious loss of the day was the little paddle steamer *Brighton Belle*. A charming antique looking like something out of a toy store, she was thrashing her way home with 800 men plucked from the sea at La Panne. Sapper Eric Reader huddled in the boiler room drying off, when the ship hit a submerged wreck with a frightful jolt. "Never touched us," an old cockney stoker called out cheerfully, but the sea gurgled in and the *Brighton Belle* began to sink. The troops tumbled on deck as the whistle tooted an SOS. Happily other ships were nearby and took everybody off—even the captain's dog.

If casualties could be kept at this level, there were valid grounds for the Dynamo Room's optimism. On the whole the evacuation was proceeding smoothly, and the greatest crisis of the day—the gap created by the Belgian surrender—had been successfully met. For the troops still pouring up the escape corridor, there was additional reason to hope. On either side of the raised roadways, the fields were beginning to fill with water.

The French were flooding the low-lying land south of the coast. Even German tanks would find the going difficult.

But already a new crisis had arisen, shifting the focus back from the land to the sea. It had been brewing for several days without anybody paying much attention. Now, in the early hours of May 29, it suddenly burst, posing a fresh challenge to Admiral Ramsay and his resourceful staff.

7

Torpedoes in the Night

What could the German Navy do to help prevent an evacuation? General Keitel asked Vice-Admiral Otto Schniewind, Chief of the Naval War Staff, in a phone conversation on May 26. Not much, Schniewind felt, and he formally spelled out the Navy's views in a letter to OKW on the 28th. Large ships were not suitable in the narrow, confining waters of the English Channel; the destroyers had been used up in Norway; U-boats were restricted by shallow water and the enemy's very effective antisubmarine measures.

There remained the *Schnellboot,* the small fast German motor torpedo boat. These "S-boats" were especially suited to narrow seas like the Channel, and new bases were now available in Holland, closer to the scene of action. The only problems were the possibility of bad weather and the short nights this time of year.

Overall, the prospects seemed so bright that SKL—the naval war command—had already shifted two flotillas, totaling nine boats, from the German island of Borkum to the Dutch port of Den Helder, 90 miles closer to Dunkirk. From here Captain-Lieutenant Birnbacher's 1st Flotilla and Captain-Lieutenant Peterson's 2nd Flotilla began operating along the coast.

They drew first blood on the night of May 22–23. The French

destroyer *Jaguar*, approaching Dunkirk, rashly radioed that she would be arriving at 12:20 a.m. German intelligence was listening in, and when *Jaguar* turned up on schedule, an unexpected reception committee was waiting. *S 21* and *S 23* sank her with a couple of well-placed torpedoes, then slipped away unseen.

On the Allied side nobody was sure what caused the loss. A submarine seemed most likely. The British were still unaware of the S-boats' nightly patrols as the destroyer *Wakeful* lay off the beach at Bray-Dunes, loading troops on the evening of May 28. Her skipper Commander Ralph Lindsay Fisher was chiefly worried about an air attack. This might require some violent maneuvering; he packed the troops as low in the ship as possible to get maximum stability. They crowded into the engine room, the boiler room, the store rooms, every inch of empty space.

At 11:00 p.m. *Wakeful* weighed anchor with 640 men aboard—all she could carry—and headed for Dover via the long Route Y. It was a black night, but the phosphorescence was brilliant. Under such conditions bombers often spotted ships by their wake; as Commander Fisher headed northeast on the first leg of his trip, he kept his speed down to twelve knots to reduce this danger.

Around 12:30 he spotted the winking light of Kwinte Whistle Buoy, where he would swing west for the final run to Dover. It was an important buoy; so important that it remained lit even in these dangerous times. It was also the most exposed point of the homeward journey—easy to reach for enemy planes, U-boats, or any other menace.

Fisher began to zigzag and increased his speed to twenty knots. You couldn't get by Kwinte too soon.

Not far away other vessels were also watching the winking light of Kwinte Whistle Buoy. The two German *Schnellboote* flotillas were now alternating their nightly patrols, and tonight was the turn of Captain-Lieutenant Heinz Birnbacher's 1st Flotilla. On *S 30* the skipper, Lieutenant Wilhelm Zimmermann, searched the night with his binoculars. There ought to be plenty of targets out by the buoy, but so far he saw nothing.

Then suddenly, about 12:40, he spotted a shadow even

darker than the night. "There, dead ahead!" He nudged the helmsman, standing right behind him. The shadows quickly took shape as a darkened ship rushing toward them. Zimmermann sized it up as a destroyer.

A few brief orders, and *S 30* turned toward the target, leading it slightly. On a *Schnellboot* the torpedo was aimed by aiming the boat itself. The gap quickly narrowed between the two vessels as the S-boat crew tingled with excitement. Would they get close enough before they were seen?

Another order from Zimmermann, and two torpedoes slapped into the sea. The crew began counting the seconds, waiting interminably. . . .

On the bridge of the *Wakeful*, Commander Fisher saw them coming—two parallel streaks, one slightly ahead of the other, racing toward his starboard side. They gleamed like silver ribbons in the phosphorescence. He ordered the helm hard-a-port, and as the ship began to swing, the first torpedo passed harmlessly across his bow.

The second hit. It exploded with a roar and a blinding flash in the forward boiler room, breaking *Wakeful* in half. She sank in fifteen seconds . . . the severed ends resting on the bottom, the bow and stern sticking out of the water in a grotesque V.

The troops far below never had a chance. Trapped by the slanting decks, engulfed by the sea, they were all lost—except one man who happened to be topside sneaking a cigarette.

A few hundred yards away Lieutenant Zimmermann watched with satisfaction as his torpedo finally hit. He had almost given up hope. He toyed with the idea of picking up survivors for questioning, then thought better of it. Occasional shadows and flashes of phosphorescence suggested that other ships were rushing to the scene—certainly alert and maybe even looking for him. Withdrawal seemed his best bet. The *S 30* eased off into the night and resumed its prowl.

Back at the wreck Commander Fisher floated clear of his ship, as did most of the gun crews. About 30 men ended up on the stern, some 60 feet out of the water. Fisher and the rest paddled about, hoping some friendly vessel would find them.

In half an hour they got their wish. Two small drifters, *Nautilus* and *Comfort*, appeared out of the night. Normally engaged in minesweeping, they were now part of Admiral Ramsay's rescue fleet, bound for La Panne via Route Y. As they approached Kwinte Buoy, crew members heard voices crying "Help!" and saw heads bobbing in the sea.

Nautilus managed to pick up six men, *Comfort* another sixteen, including Commander Fisher. Other rescue ships began to appear: the minesweeper *Gossamer*, packed with troops from the eastern mole . . . next the sweeper *Lydd*, also crowded . . . then the destroyer *Grafton*, with a full load from Bray-Dunes. All lowered their boats and stood by. Few yet knew what happened—only that a ship had sunk—and there were a number of flares and flashing signal lights.

Hidden by the night, a thousand yards away Lieutenant Michalowski, commanding the German submarine *U 62,* watched the confusion of lights with interest. Like the *Schnellboot*, he had been lying near Kwinte Buoy, waiting for some fat target to come along. These were indeed shallow waters for a U-boat—but not impossible. The *U 62* glided toward the lights.

Commander Fisher sensed the danger. Picked up by the *Comfort*, he had taken over from her regular skipper. Now he moved here and there warning the other ships. Hailing *Gossamer*, he shouted that he had been torpedoed and the enemy was probably still nearby. *Gossamer* got going so fast she left her skiff behind. *Comfort* picked up its crew, ordered *Nautilus* to get going too, then moved over to warn *Grafton* and *Lydd*. Easing alongside *Grafton*'s starboard quarter, Fisher once again called out his warning.

Too late. At that moment, 2:50 a.m., a torpedo crashed into *Grafton*'s wardroom, killing some 35 army officers picked up at Bray-Dunes. *Comfort*, lying alongside, was hurled into the air by the blast, then dropped back into the sea like a toy boat. Momentarily swamped, she bobbed back to the surface, but all the crew on deck were washed overboard, including Commander Fisher.

With no one at the helm, but her engines set at full speed, *Comfort* now moved into a wide circle that took her off into the night. Fisher grabbed a rope's end and hung on for a brief, wild ride. But she was going too fast, and there was no one to pull him aboard. He finally let go.

Just as well. *Comfort*, still in her circle, came back into view and was sighted by the nearby *Lydd*. Her skipper, Lieutenant-Commander Rodolph Haig, had been warned by a *Wakeful* survivor that an enemy torpedo boat, rather than submarine, was probably to blame. Now this seemed confirmed by what he saw in the dark: a small vessel dashing about at high speed.

Lydd opened up with her starboard guns, raking the stranger's wheelhouse and producing a satisfying cloud of sparks. The torpedoed *Grafton* joined in, and the stranger appeared disabled.

Swimming in the sea again, Commander Fisher realized that *Lydd* had mistaken *Comfort* for the enemy; but there was nothing he could do. On *Comfort* herself three survivors huddled below decks, equally helpless. Her engines had stopped now, probably knocked out by gunfire, and she wallowed clumsily in the Channel swell.

Suddenly something big loomed out of the night, racing toward her. It was *Lydd* again, coming to finish off the "enemy" by ramming. As her steel prow knifed into *Comfort*'s wooden side, two figures burst out of the hatch and leapt for *Lydd*'s bow.

"Repel boarders!" The ancient rallying cry rose above her decks as members of the crew grabbed rifles and pistols and blazed away. They fortunately missed the two survivors of *Comfort* who had climbed aboard, but a stray shot fatally wounded Able Seaman S. P. Sinclair, one of their own men. The mix-up was finally ironed out, and *Lydd* set course for home.

Meanwhile, confusion on the stricken *Grafton*. The torpedo hits (there was apparently a second) knocked out all her lights, and the 800 troops aboard blindly thrashed about. Among them was Captain Basil Bartlett of the Field Security Police, one of the last to board the ship at Bray-Dunes. There was no space left in the ward room, where the officers were assigned; he settled for a corner of the captain's cabin. Stunned by the explosion, he came to, groping for some way out. There seemed practically no chance of escape; still he was not overly worried. He remembered similar scenes in countless American war movies. "Gary Cooper always finds a way out," he consoled himself.

He finally stumbled onto the open deck, and found the night alive with gunfire. *Grafton* had joined *Lydd* in pounding the luckless *Comfort*, and probably other nearby ships were firing, too. Stray shots ripped into the *Grafton*'s bridge, killing the skipper, Commander Charles Robinson.

Gradually the firing died down, and a semblance of order returned. Word reached the sick bay to start sending the wounded up, and Private Sam Sugar, an RASC driver who had injured his hand, bolted for the ladder. He was stopped in his tracks by an orderly, who gave him a flashlight and told him to stay a bit. Someone was needed to hold the light while the orderly fixed a tourniquet on a sailor who had just lost both legs. Sugar had been on the verge of panic, but the sight of the orderly calmly going about his business at this desperate moment showed the power of example. He had to stay calm too; he just couldn't let this good man down.

By the time Sugar reached deck, the ferry *Malines* lay alongside taking off the troops. The *Grafton* was listing now, slowly sinking, but the men kept in ranks, patiently waiting for their turn to transfer. Captain Bartlett was one of the last to cross over. Gary Cooper had found a way out.

The destroyer *Ivanhoe* finished off *Grafton* with two well-placed shells, and at last there was time for postmortems. For Bartlett there was the lucky break of getting on board so late. Any earlier, and he would have died with the other officers in the ward room.

For Sergeant S. S. Hawes, 1st Division Petrol Company, there was a more ironical twist. He had briefly left his unit at Bray-Dunes to help a wounded comrade. Understandable, but orders were to stick together. By the time he got back, the others had put out in a launch, heading for a destroyer lying offshore. It was the *Wakeful*, and every man in the company was lost. For disobeying orders, Hawes was rewarded with his life.

The luckiest man of all was the indestructible Commander Fisher. Washed off *Wakeful*, he was one of the few picked up by *Comfort;* washed off *Comfort*, he was again picked up, this time by the Norwegian freighter *Hird*. A battered old steamer out of Oslo, *Hird* was engaged in the timber trade and was not even part of Admiral Ramsay's rescue fleet. She had made a routine stop at Dunkirk on May 13, and for the past two weeks had been taking her share of punishment as the Luftwaffe pounded the port. Now only one engine worked, and she could barely make six knots.

But these were desperate times. As the panzers approached, *Hird* was requisitioned by the French Navy to transfer some of the trapped poilus to Cherbourg, 180 miles to the southwest and presumably out of danger. They crowded aboard all through the evening of May 28, unofficially joined by some of the British soldiers pouring into Dunkirk. Sapper L. C. Lidster found the gangplank blocked by a queue of Frenchmen, so he grabbed a rope ladder hanging down. He and his mates scrambled aboard while the waiting poilus shouted in anger. In various ways other Tommies made it too—Private Sam Love of the 12th Field Ambulance . . . Corporal Alf Gill of the 44th Division . . . Staff Sergeant Reg Blackburn of the Military Police . . . maybe 1,000 men altogether.

The *Hird* finally crept out of the harbor about midnight, packed with 3,000 Allied troops and a handful of German prisoners. At six knots, her master Captain A. M. Frendjhem wasn't about to challenge the enemy batteries planted along the coast to the west, so he first steered east along Route Y. At Kwinte Whistle Buoy he would then swing west and make his run down the Channel, beyond the range of the German guns.

It was while rounding Kwinte that he picked up Commander Fisher and several other swimmers—all probably survivors of the *Wakeful*. Exhausted, Fisher slumped against the after cargo hatch among a crowd of French colonial troops. He saw no British soldiers, nor did it occur to him that any might be aboard.

Regaining his strength, he went to the bridge to urge that he be landed at Dover. Important charts might have floated clear when the *Wakeful* sank, and Admiral Ramsay must be warned. Captain Frendjhem replied that his orders were to go straight to Cherbourg. Fisher didn't persist: he knew that the *Hird* had to pass close to Dover breakwater anyhow; surely he could catch a ride into the harbor from some passing ship.

And so it proved. As the *Hird* approached the breakwater, Fisher hailed a passing naval trawler. It came alongside, and he jumped aboard.

Meanwhile on the *Hird*'s foredeck the British troops watched Dover draw near with mounting anticipation. It had been an exhausting trip—no food or water—made worse when one Tommy fell down an open hatch and lay groaning all night. Now at last life began perking up. The famous white cliffs never looked better.

Then to everyone's surprise the *Hird* turned out again and headed westward along the coast, past Folkestone . . . Eastbourne . . . Brighton. The men decided they must be going to Southampton and settled back to make the best of things. Sapper Lidster tried eating a tin of uncooked fish roe. It tasted awful, "but God! I was so hungry!"

Then another surprise. The *Hird* didn't go to Southampton after all. Instead, she veered off past the Isle of Wight and headed across the Channel toward France again. Howls of rage rose from the foredeck. Some men aimed rifles at the bridge, hoping to "persuade" Captain Frendjhem to change his mind. At the crucial moment an elderly British major named Hunt stood up in front of the Captain to protect him and try to calm the troops. He explained that the *Hird* was under French control, that the senior French officer aboard had ordered her to Cherbourg, that the poilus were desperately needed there, and finally that he personally would see that every British soldier got back to England. It was an inspiring performance, coming from an officer who was not a trained combat leader, but rather a mild father figure in the 508th Petrol Company of the supply troops.

The spell of mutiny was broken. The *Hird* continued on to Cherbourg, where the British troops each received two slices of dry bread and jam, then marched off to a transit camp outside of town. Here they settled down in tents, until Major Hunt—true to his word—got them all back to England.

Admiral Ramsay and the Dynamo Room staff were blissfully ignorant of the meandering *Hird*, but they were very much aware of the disastrous events off Kwinte Whistle Buoy. With characteristic energy they dived into the business of countermeasures.

At 8:06 a.m. on the 29th Ramsay radioed his entire armada: "Vessels carrying troops not to stop to pick up survivors from ships sunk but are to inform other near ships."

Next he took two minesweepers off troop-carrying duties and ordered them to search the area around Kwinte for any lurking torpedo boats. This was a drastic but realistic move. He needed every possible ship for lifting the BEF, but what good did it do, unless he could get them safely home?

There was still some suspicion that U-boats might be involved, so the Admiral also established an antisubmarine patrol in the waters west of Kwinte. In addition, antisubmarine trawlers patrolling off the Thames estuary were brought down to the critical area east of Margate and Ramsgate. A speedboat flotilla at Harwich was ordered to stand by as a striking force in case these various probes turned anything up.

Most important of all, the middle Route X was finally cleared of mines and opened to traffic. During the morning three destroyers tried it out, pronounced it safe from the German shore batteries both east and west of Dunkirk. At 4:06 p.m. Ramsay ordered all ships to start using the new route exclusively in daylight hours. This not only shortened the trip from 87 to 55 miles, but shifted the traffic 26 miles farther west of Kwinte Buoy—meaning 26 miles farther away from the S-boats' favorite hunting ground.

By midafternoon all possible countermeasures had been taken, and the Dynamo Room returned to what one staff officer called "its normal state of organized chaos." There were always fresh problems. New German batteries were shelling the mole from the southeast—could the RAF mount a quick strike? The Army's medical service had completely broken down on the beaches—could the Navy send over a team of good doctors? Refueling was becoming a major bottleneck. Peacetime Dover refueled commercial traffic at a leisurely pace of one ship at a time—how to cope with dozens of vessels, all clamoring for oil at once? The Admiralty reported twenty Thames barges, towed by five tugs, would be arriving at Ramsgate at 5:30 p.m.—could they be used on the beaches as an improvised pier?

Tennant was consulted about the barges, and he turned the idea down. The beach shelved so gradually that twenty barges weren't enough to make a decent pier. Better to use them for ferrying troops out to the destroyers and coastal steamers waiting offshore. He still didn't have the small boats he really needed for this work, but the barges were better than nothing.

Meanwhile the problems grew. Men were pouring onto the beach at a far faster rate than they could be lifted off. When Captain S. T. Moore led a mixed bag of 20 officers and 403 men into La Panne around 10:00 a.m. he hadn't the faintest idea what he was meant to do with them. Someone suggested he check II Corps headquarters; he left his charges in a hotel garden and trudged to the headquarters dugout about a mile up the beach.

Inside, it was another world—three lieutenant-colonels, about six staff assistants, a battery of telephones, and papers being shuffled back and forth. He was given a ticket, neatly filled out, authorizing him to embark 20 officers and 403 men from "Beach A." Presumably it was to be handed to some collector at some gate to some particular beach.

Then back to the beach the way it really was: no signposts, no ticket takers, just bewildered waiting. At La Panne, Bray-Dunes, and Malo-les-Bains, ever-growing lines of men curled over the sand and into the sea. The queues seemed almost stationary, and the troops whiled away the hours as best they could. The padre of the 85th Command Ammunition Depot moved among his flock, inviting them to join him in prayers and hymns. Some antiaircraft gunners at Bray-Dunes were calmly playing cards; they had run out of ammunition long ago. On the promenade east of the mole a group pedaled about on brightly-colored mini-bikes borrowed from some beachfront concession. Near Malo a soldier lay face down, clutching handfuls of sand and letting it run through his fingers, repeating over and over, "Please, God, have mercy . . ."

Some discovered a stiff drink could help. Corporal Ackrell of the 85th Command Ammunition Depot asked a comrade for a drink from his water bottle. He discovered, not entirely to his sorrow, that it was filled with rum. A few swigs, and he passed out. Others like Private Jack Toomey didn't trust the drinking water and had depended on wine and champagne for a fortnight. This morning some *vin blanc* finally caught up with him: "I was drunk as a lord."

As the queues inched into the water, panic sometimes took over. With so many thousands waiting, it was hard to remain calm when some skiff, holding perhaps ten people, finally came within reach. Working the beach at La Panne, Lieutenant Ian Cox of the destroyer *Malcolm* had to draw his revolver and threaten to shoot the next man who tried to rush the boats. Even so, one army officer went down on his knees, begging to be allowed off first. In another rush at La Panne a boat overturned, and seven men were drowned in four feet of water.

Wading out could be hell. Artillery Captain R. C. Austin felt his britches balloon out and fill with water till they were "heavy as masonry." His sodden jacket and water-logged boots seemed to nail him down.

The sea was up to his chin when a ship's lifeboat finally appeared, and Austin wondered how he could ever climb into it. He need not have worried. Strong arms reached out, grabbed him by the armpits and belt, and swung him over the gunwale. He heard someone in the boat shouting, "Come on, you bastards, wake up, blast you!"

Occasionally the more resourceful soldiers devised their own transportation. Separated from his artillery unit, Gunner F. Felstead discovered that none of the queues seemed to want stragglers, so he and six mates decided to go it alone. Walking along the beach, they found a canvas collapsible drifting offshore. It had only one oar, but using their rifles as paddles, the little group put to sea. They were ultimately picked up by a naval cutter and transferred to the paddle steamer *Royal Eagle*.

The minesweeper *Killarney* rescued three other adventurers about this time. Heading across the Channel, she encountered a raft made of a door and several wooden planks. Aboard were a French officer, two Belgian soldiers, and six demijohns of wine. All were safely transferred.

But it was Lieutenant E. L. Davies, skipper of the minesweeper *Oriole*, who had the most practical idea for breaking the bottleneck of the beaches this day. *Oriole* was an old River Clyde paddle steamer with a good, shallow draft. Taking advantage of this, Davies aimed her at the shore and drove her hard aground. For the rest of the day she served as a pier. The troops wading out scrambled aboard her bow and were picked up from her stern by a steady stream of boats from the larger vessels lying further out.

Even so, many of the soldiers stumbled and sank while trying to reach the *Oriole*. Sub-Lieutenant Rutherford Crosby, son of a Glasgow bookseller, dived overboard again and again, pulling them out. He got a rest when the tide went out, leaving the *Oriole* high and dry, but toward evening it flowed in again, ultimately refloating the ship. Her work done, she turned for Ramsgate with a final load of Tommies. Altogether on the 29th, some 2,500 men used her as a bridge to safety.

In Dunkirk Captain Tennant had his own solution to the problem of the beaches. The eastern mole was proving such a success, he asked that the whole evacuation be concentrated there. Admiral Ramsay turned him down. The BEF was now pouring into the perimeter in such numbers the Admiral felt that both the mole *and* the beaches were needed. Beyond that, he wanted to spread the risk. So far he had been lucky. Thanks to the smoke and a low cloud cover, the Luftwaffe had virtually ignored the mole. Ramsay wanted to keep it that way. A large concentration of shipping might draw unwelcome attention.

As it was, a steady stream of vessels pulled in and out all morning. The formula was working: a ship would come alongside . . . the pier master Commander Clouston would send out enough troops to fill it . . . the ship would load up and be off again—sometimes in less than half an hour. Working with Clouston was Brigadier Reggie Parminter, formerly of Gort's staff and now army embarkation officer. Totally imperturbable, he disdained a helmet and jauntily sported a monacle in his left eye.

All the time the queue of men waiting at the foot of the mole continued to grow. To keep it manageable, Parminter devised a "hat-check" system. The waiting men were divided into batches of 50; the leader of each batch was assigned a number; and when that number was called, it was time to go.

"Embarkation is being carried out normally now," Captain Tennant radioed Dover at 1:30 p.m. on the 29th. And everything was indeed "normal"—except for the number of ships alongside the mole. There were more than usual. On the harbor side the destroyers *Grenade* and *Jaguar*, the transport *Canterbury*, and a French destroyer were all loading troops. On the seaward side, the Channel packet *Fenella* was also loading.

Now at 1:30, just as Tennant was sending his message, six

more ships arrived. Lieutenant Robin Bill was leading in a flotilla of small trawlers. Normally engaged in minesweeping, today they were bringing some badly needed ladders for the mole. They too tied up on the harbor side, between the two British destroyers and the *Canterbury*.

Then a big paddle steamer, the *Crested Eagle*, also arrived, tying up on the seaward side, just astern of the *Fenella*. Altogether, there were now twelve ships clustered around the end of the mole.

At the same time the weather began to clear and the wind changed, sending the smoke inland instead of across the harbor. It was turning into a sparkling afternoon.

All these details were unknown in the Dynamo Room, but the message traffic was certainly reassuring. Every possible precaution had been taken against those torpedo attacks in the night. There had been no serious ship loss since early morning, when *Mona's Isle* had struck a mine. Fortunately, she was empty at the time. No fresh information was coming in from Dunkirk, but news from there was always late.

By the end of the afternoon spirits were soaring. At 6:22 p.m. Major-General H. C. Lloyd, doing liaison work with Ramsay, telegraphed the War Office in London:

> Naval shipping plan now approaching maximum efficiency. Subject to weather and reasonable immunity enemy action, expect lift about 16,000 Dunkirk, and 15,000 from beaches. . . .

But even as the General wired his optimism, awesome events were unfolding at Dunkirk . . . staggering the rescue fleet, turning the mole into a shambles, and throwing Admiral Ramsay's whole evacuation plan into wild disarray.

8

Assault from the Sky

To Captain Wolfgang Falck, these would always be "the golden days." As a *Gruppe* commander in Fighter Squadron 26, he flew an Me 110—a new two-engine fighter said to be even better than the fabled Me 109, but nobody really knew because there was so little opposition. So far the campaign had been a picnic: knocking down obsolete British Fairey Battle bombers ... shooting French planes as they sat in neat rows on the ground ... protecting the Stukas, the Heinkel 111's, the Dornier 17's from attacks that never came.

The only problem was keeping up with the panzers. As the army advanced, so did the squadron, and it required superb organization to keep fuel, spare parts, and maintenance flowing. Usually the ground personnel would move forward during the night, leaving a skeleton crew to service the planes before taking off on their morning missions. These skeleton crews would then move on too. When the squadron completed its mission, it would land at the new base, where everything would be set up and waiting.

Food and lodging were always the best. The squadron's administrative officer Major Fritz von Scheve was an old reservist who had a real nose for finding decent billets—and where a good wine cellar might be hidden. He usually selected some lo-cal chateau whose owner had fled, leaving everything behind. Falck forbade any looting—the place must be left as they found it—but there was no rule against enjoying life, and the pilots found themselves eating off Limoges china and sleeping in can-opied beds.

There was even time for nonsense. Near one captured airfield some member of the squadron found a number of French baby tanks, abandoned but full of petrol. Pilots tend to be good at tinkering, and they soon had the tanks manned and running. The men spent a glorious hour chasing and ramming one an-other—it was like a giant dodgem concession at some amuse-ment park.

May 27, and the German flyers got their first inkling that the golden days would not last forever. Now the target was Dunkirk itself, and as the Stukas and Heinkels went about their usual business, a new throaty roar filled the air. Modern British fight-ers—Hurricanes and Spitfires—came storming down upon them, breaking up the neat formations, sending occasional bombers spinning down out of control. These British squad-rons had been considered too valuable to base in France, but the fighting was in range of England now, and that was differ-ent. Taking off from a dozen Kentish fields, they poured across the Channel.

It's hard to say who was more surprised—the Tommies on the ground or the Germans in the air. The ordinary British sol-dier had almost given up hope of ever seeing the RAF again; then suddenly here it was, tearing into the enemy. For the Luftwaffe pilots, these new air battles were an educational expe-rience. Captain Falck soon discovered that the Me 110 was not better than the Me 109—in fact, it wasn't as good. On one mis-sion his plane was the only 110 of four to get back to base after tangling with the RAF. He landed, still quivering with fright, to find General Kesselring making an inspection. When they met again years later, the General still remembered Falck's shaky sa-lute.

Like many pilots, Falck was superstitious. On the side of his plane he had painted a large ladybug—the lucky symbol of his squadron in the Norwegian campaign. A big letter "G" also adorned the fuselage. G was the seventh letter of the alphabet and "7" was his lucky number. With the Spitfires around, he needed every talisman he could get.

Even the Me 109's had met their match. The Spitfires could make sharper turns, hold a dive longer, and come out of it faster. They also had a way of appearing without warning—once so suddenly that Captain Adolf Galland, a veteran 109 pilot flying wing on his skipper, lost his usual cool. Momentarily shaken, he made a false turn, leaving the skipper a wide-open target. In anguish, Galland managed to shoot one of the Spitfires down, then returned to his base fearing the worst. But the skipper, a veteran World War I pilot named Max Ibel, turned out to be an indestructible old bird. Run to earth by the Spits, he managed to crash-land and "walked home."

Happily for the Luftwaffe, there were never enough Spitfires and Hurricanes. The RAF's Fighter Command had to think ahead to the coming defense of Britain herself, and Air Chief Marshal Sir Hugh Dowding refused to allocate to Dunkirk more than sixteen squadrons at any one time. Even stretched thin, these planes could not provide full-time cover, and the Luftwaffe took full advantage of those moments when the beaches were without fighter protection. When the score for the 27th was finally added up, there were conflicting claims on British and German losses, but on one point there was complete agreement: the port of Dunkirk was wrecked.

May 28 promised to be an even more productive day for the Luftwaffe. The Belgian surrender, the crumbling French defenses, the capture of Calais—all released additional planes. But the weather turned sour; Fliegerkorps VIII, responsible for Dunkirk, remained on the ground. Its commanding officer General Major Wolfram von Richthofen (distant cousin of the famous Red Baron) had more than the weather to contend with. Hermann Göring was constantly on the phone. The General Field Marshal was now worried about his assurances to Hitler that the Luftwaffe could win the battle alone, and seemed to think that Richthofen could somehow chase away the clouds.

May 29 dawned even worse. A steady drizzle and ceiling only 300 feet. Fliegerkorps VIII steeled itself for another barrage of calls from Göring. But around noon it began to clear up. At 2:00 p.m. Richthofen gave the long-delayed orders to attack.

Gruppe leaders were summoned and briefed. The main point: by agreement with Army Group B only the beaches and shipping would be attacked. No targets inland. There was now too much danger of hitting friendly troops. At 2:45 the planes began taking off from various fields: Major Oskar Dinort's Stukas from Beaulieu . . . Major Werner Kreipe's Dornier 17's from Rocrai . . . Captain Adolf Galland's Me 109's from Saint Pol . . . and so on.

It was no ordinary raid. Fliegerkorps VIII had been specially reinforced: planes from four other *Fliegerkorps* . . . a wing of new Ju 88's from Holland . . . another all the way from Dusseldorf. Altogether some 400 aircraft headed for Dunkirk, led by 180 Stukas.

By 3:00 p.m. they were there. So far no sign of the RAF. Circling so as to come in from the sea, Corporal Hans Mahnert, a gunner-radio operator flying with Stuka Wing No. 3, looked down on a remarkable sight. Ships were crowded together everywhere. It reminded him, oddly enough, of an old print he had once seen of the English fleet gathered at Trafalgar.

Other more practiced eyes were also scanning the sea. They may have missed the eastern mole before, but not today. The smoke was blowing inland now, and there—directly below—was a sight no one could overlook. Clustered alongside the mole were a dozen ships. It was hard to imagine a better target. . . .

Lieutenant Robin Bill could easily see the bombs falling. They looked about the size of 15-inch shells as they tumbled out of the diving Stukas. No more time for comparisons: he threw himself face-down on the mole, as the world exploded around him.

One bomb landed squarely on the mole, twenty feet in front of him, hurling slabs of concrete into the air. A chunk sailed by his ears, killing a soldier further down the walkway. Shaken and covered with dust, Bill felt something oddly moist: it was a stray puppy licking his face.

He glanced to his left, where his six trawlers were moored. They were still all right. But this was just the start. The planes seemed to attack in twos and threes, dropping a couple of

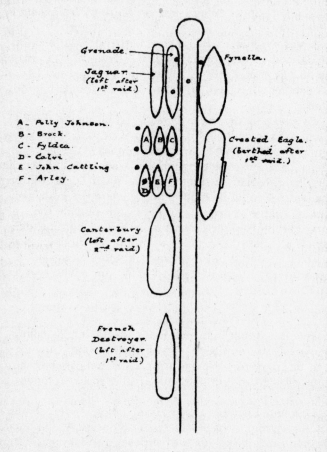

Position of ships berthed alongside
Dunkerque Pier.
~~1445~~ - 1815   29th May. 1940

Grenade.

Fynella.

Jaguar.
(left after
1st raid)

A - Polly Johnson.
B - Brock.
C - Fyldea.
D - Calvi.
E - John Cattling.
F - Arley.

A B C

Crested Eagle.
(berthed after
1st raid.)

D E F

Canterbury.
(left after
2nd raid)

French
Destroyer.
(left after
1st raid)

● = Position of bombs causing serious damage.

May 29, 2:45 p.m., the eastern mole (drawn at the time by Lieutenant Robin Bill) bombs every time. There were occasional lulls, but the attack never really stopped.

Lying at the very end of the mole, the destroyer *Jaguar* managed to cast off. Packed with troops, she headed for home as the Stukas dived on her again and again. They scored no direct hits, but several near misses did fearful damage. Shrapnel riddled her port side, slashing open fuel tanks and steam lines. *Jaguar* quickly lost headway and drifted toward the shore. Just in time the destroyer *Express* raced over, towed her clear, and took off the troops. Listing seventeen degrees, *Jaguar* ultimately crawled back to Dover empty—out of the evacuation for good.

At the mole it was the destroyer *Grenade*'s turn next. Standing by the forward capstan, Chief Stoker W. Brown watched a Stuka pass overhead, turn, and race in from the sea. It scored a near miss on the mole, spraying the *Grenade* with shrapnel. Brown fell wounded, and just as the ship's medical officer finished patching him up, along came another Stuka. This time the aim was perfect. One bomb landed aft, another on the bridge, exploding in an oil tank below. A great sheet of flame shot up through the deck as Brown managed to clamber onto the mole.

Seaman Bill Irwin was on the *Grenade* just by chance. One of his mates had been wounded on the mole, and Irwin brought him aboard, looking for medical attention. As they waited in a small compartment on the upper deck, a sudden blast threw them off their feet. Somebody's tin hat—turned literally red-hot—rolled crazily around on its rim as Irwin dodged out of the way.

He managed to get his friend back onto the mole, but had to leave behind a badly wounded petty officer lying in a bunk. Irwin promised to come back for him, but it was a promise he couldn't keep. Already Commander Clouston's men were loosening the ship's lines so that she wouldn't go down at her berth. Still blazing, *Grenade* drifted into the harbor channel. But if she sank here, it could be even worse. She might block the harbor completely. Finally one of Lieutenant Bill's trawlers towed her out of the way. *Grenade* burned on for several hours . . . then blew up, vanishing in a mushroom cloud of smoke.

Able Seaman P. Cavanagh managed to scramble from the burning *Grenade* onto the mole just before she cast off. Momentarily he was safe—but only momentarily. A German plane swooped down, machine-gunning the troops that crowded the walkway. A quick-thinking soldier pushed Cavanagh down, then lay on top of him. When the plane had gone, Cavanagh asked the soldier to get off his back, but there was no answer—he was dead. He had given his life to save a man he never even knew.

Cavanagh now went on board the *Fenella*, a large wooden steamer lying on the other side of the mole. "If this gets hit," someone observed, "it will go up like a box of matches." With that, a bomb landed alongside, splintering the ship's hull. Cavanagh hopped off, crossed the mole again, and decided to try one of Lieutenant Bill's trawlers. He picked the *Calvi*, but before he could climb aboard a bomb landed on her, too. She went down at her berth with stately dignity, resting on the bottom completely upright. Her funnel and masts remained above water, her battle ensign still flying from the foremast.

Cavanagh moved on to another of the trawlers—he never knew the name—and this time nobody dropped anything on him. Bombed out of three ships and machine-gunned once (all in 45 minutes), he sat down on the deck for a moment's rest. "Get off your arse and give us a hand," someone called, and he went wearily back to work.

On the *Fenella*, riddled by the near miss alongside the mole, Gunner Mowbray Chandler of the Royal Artillery sat below-decks sipping cocoa. He had been in Commander Clouston's queue since early morning; now that he was at last on board a ship, it was time to relax a little. Not even that near miss could interrupt his cocoa. Then someone looked out a porthole and noticed that the mole seemed to be rising. Since this was impossible, the ship must be settling. So it wasn't time to relax after all. Chandler and his mates hurried back to the mole, as *Fenella* sank at her berth.

Three ships gone—the mole strafed and damaged—it was all very unnerving. This long arm jutting out into the sea, once the goal of everyone, was no longer so popular. Some of the troops waiting at the seaward end wavered, then surged back toward the land. Commander Clouston was at the shore end talking to Lieutenant Bill, but his quick eye caught the movement. Taking Bill with him, he pulled his revolver and hurried out to meet the mob.

"We have come to take you back to the U.K.," he said quietly but firmly. "I have six shots here, and I'm not a bad shot. The Lieutenant behind me is an even better one. So that makes twelve of you." A pause, and then he raised his voice: *"Now get down into those bloody ships!"*

That ended the incident. The men turned back again, most of them boarding the steamer *Crested Eagle*, which lay just astern of the unlucky *Fenella*. A big wooden paddle-wheeler, the *Crested Eagle* was a familiar sight to many of the troops. In happier days she had taken them on excursions up and down the Thames. Going aboard her was almost like going home. By 6:oo p.m. her decks were packed with 6oo men, including a number of bedraggled survivors from the *Grenade* and *Fenella*.

Commander Clouston gave the signal to get going, and *Crested Eagle*'s big paddle wheels began churning the sea. Swinging clear of the mole, her skipper Lieutenant-Commander B. R. Booth headed east along the coast, planning to go home via Route Y.

It didn't take long for the Luftwaffe to find her. Standing by one of the paddle boxes, Chief Stoker Brown, safely off the *Grenade*, once again heard the familiar screech of a Stuka's bomb. It landed with a crash in the main saloon, sending tables, chairs, and bodies flying.

A deck below, Gunner Chandler, just off the *Fenella*, was watching the engines when the explosion came. It blew him along the deck until he hit the end bulkhead.

On the bridge Commander Booth noted that the paddles were still working, so he tried to hold his course. Maybe they could get out of this yet.

No such luck. The whole after end of the vessel was burning, and the engineer Lieutenant Jones came on the bridge to report that he couldn't keep the paddles going much longer. Booth decided to beach the ship, and turned toward shore opposite the big sanitarium at Zuydcoote, just short of Bray-Dunes. On the beach the troops momentarily forgot their own troubles as they watched this blazing torch of a boat drive hard aground.

"Get off, mate, while you can," a seaman advised Gunner Chandler as he stood uncertainly by the rail. Chandler decided it was good advice; he took off his shoes and jumped. There were other ships around, but none near, so he swam to the beach. It was easy; he had a life jacket and even managed to tow a nonswimmer along.

Once ashore he discovered for the first time how badly burned he was. In the excitement he hadn't noticed that the skin was hanging in shreds from both his hands. He was bundled into an ambulance and taken to the Casino at Malo-les-Bains, currently serving as a collection point for the wounded. It's hard to imagine a fuller day, yet he ended up only a few hundred yards from where he had started in the morning.

Except for the mole, the most inviting target this perilous afternoon was the 6,000-ton cargo liner *Clan MacAlister*. Loaded with eight assault landing craft and their crews, she had come over from Dover the previous night. Her skipper Captain R. W. Mackie felt that the prescribed route was unnecessarily dangerous, but when he complained to Captain Cassidie, in charge of the ALC's, Cassidie simply replied, "If you don't like to go, Captain, give me a course to steer, put the boats in the water, and I'll take them over myself." Mackie took this as a challenge to both his courage and his ability. On they went.

By 9:00 a.m. on the 29th they were lying off Dunkirk Roads discharging the boats. Two were damaged in lowering, but the other six were safely launched and soon hard at work. *Clan MacAlister* herself was told to wait around for further orders.

She was still waiting when the Luftwaffe struck. At 3:45 p.m. the Stukas scored three direct hits and set fire to No. 5 hold. Nearby the destroyer *Malcolm* dodged the same attack, and came alongside to help. Lieutenants Ian Cox and David Mellis leapt aboard the *Clan MacAlister* and began playing the *Malcolm's* fire hose down the blazing hold. Everyone ignored the fact that the hold was full of 4-inch ammunition. If it went off, it would be certain death for both officers—and probably both ships.

Luck was with the brave. The ammunition did not explode—but neither could Cox and Mellis put the fire out.

They finally returned to the *Malcolm*, and the destroyer cast off. With her went the *Clan MacAlister*'s wounded and a number of troops who had ferried out to the big steamer on the mistaken assumption that size meant safety. Captain Mackie stuck with his ship, still hoping somehow to get her home. But the Stukas kept attacking, knocked out her steering, and finally Mackie called for help.

The minesweeper *Pangbourne* eased alongside and asked if he wanted to "abandon ship." The sensitive Mackie refused to swallow that phrase. "Well, 'temporarily abandon,' " the *Pangbourne*'s captain tactfully suggested. That was all right, and Mackie crossed over.

There was no need to feel ashamed or embarrassed. The *Clan MacAlister* was just beginning to play her most useful role. She sank upright in the shallow water off the beach, and for the next several days the Luftwaffe would waste tons of bombs on her deserted hulk.

The *Clan MacAlister* was an especially tempting target, but no ship was safe this May 29th. As the minesweeper *Waverley* headed for home with 600 troops around 4:00 p.m., twelve Heinkels plastered her with bombs. For half an hour *Waverley* twisted and turned, dodging everything, but the Heinkels were insatiable. Finally a near miss tore off her rudder; then a direct hit blasted a six-foot hole in the bottom of the ship. The *Waverley* sank by the stern with a loss of over 300 men.

Now it was the *Gracie Fields*'s turn. Formerly a much-beloved Isle of Wight ferry, she left La Panne in the evening with some 750 troops. Forty minutes later a bomb exploded in her boiler room, sending up a huge cloud of steam that enveloped the ship. It was impossible to stop the engines, and with her helm jammed, she began circling at six knots. The skoots *Jutland* and *Twente* rushed over—one on each side—and for a while the three vessels waltzed around and around together, while the troops were transferred.

The minesweeper *Pangbourne*, already loaded with survivors from the *Crested Eagle* and riddled with holes herself, joined the rescue effort. She got a line on *Gracie Fields* and began towing her home. They never got there. With her crew safely removed, "Gracie" finally went down during the night.

The raid tapered off at dusk, and on the mole Commander Clouston surveyed a doleful scene. There was not a sound ship left. The *Fenella* and *Calvi* were sunk at their berths, and the rest of the vessels were gone—some to destruction, others to England with what troops they already had aboard. The bombing and the shelling were over, and the only sound was the barking of stray dogs. Abandoned by their fleeing owners, "half the canine population of France'' (as one man put it) had joined the BEF. Some were smuggled on the transports, but many had to be left behind and now forlornly prowled the waterfront—a continuing and melancholy phenomenon of the evacuation.

The mole itself was a sorry sight. Here and there it was pitted with holes and craters, not all of them made by bombs. At least two British ships rammed the walkway in their frantic maneuvers during the raid. Clouston went to work and soon had the gaps bridged with doors, hatch covers, and planking salvaged from the wrecked ships.

In the midst of these labors, the passenger steamer *King Orry* eased alongside. Her steering gear was gone and her hull badly holed by near misses. The last thing Clouston needed was another ship sunk at her berth; during the night her skipper took her out, hoping to beach her clear of the fairway.

He didn't get very far. Outside the harbor, but still in deep water, *King Orry* rolled over and sank. The naval yacht *Bystander* appeared and began picking up survivors. Manning the ship's dinghy, Able Seaman J. H. Elton dived into the sea to help the exhausted swimmers. He alone saved 25 men, and he was not done yet. He was the ship's cook, and once back on board the *Bystander*, he headed straight for his galley. Normally Elton had to feed a crew of seven, but tonight there were 97 aboard. Undaunted, he made meals for them all, then raided the ship's locker for dry clothes and blankets.

Often the evacuated troops were too exhausted to help themselves, but not always. Gunner W. Jennings of the Royal Artillery proved a tower of strength while transferring soldiers from the crippled *Gracie Fields* to the skoots alongside. Again and again he lifted men on his shoulders and carried them across, as if they were children.

When the escort vessel *Bideford* lost her stern off Bray-Dunes, Private George William Crowther, 6th Field Ambulance, gave up his chance to be rescued. He remained instead on the *Bideford*, helping the ship's surgeon. He worked for 48 hours, almost without a break, while the *Bideford* was slowly towed back to Dover.

All through the afternoon of May 29 the Dynamo Room remained blissfully ignorant of these staggering events. As far as the staff knew, the evacuation was proceeding smoothly—"approaching maximum efficiency," as liaison officer General Lloyd telegraphed the War Office at 6:22 p.m.

Three minutes later the roof fell in. The destroyer *Sabre* had been sent over with some portable wireless sets and reinforcements for the naval shore parties. Arriving at the height of the air attack, she wired Dover at 6:25:

> Continuous bombing for 1½ hours. One destroyer sinking, one transport with troops on board damaged. No damage to pier. Impossible at present to embark more troops.

Then, at 7:00 p.m. came a startling phone message. It was from Commander J. S. Dove, calling from La Panne on the direct line that linked Gort's headquarters with London and Dover. Dove had been helping out at Tennant's headquarters since the "lethal kite" fiasco, and was not part of the regular chain of command. He was calling on his own initiative, but it was not his status; it was what he said that seemed important. He reported that he had just come from Dunkirk, that the harbor was completely blocked, and that the whole evacuation must be carried out from the beaches.

Why Dove made this call remains unclear. He had apparently commandeered a car, driven it to La Panne, and talked the military into letting him use the phone—all on his own. He had been in Dunkirk since May 24, and had previously shown great coolness under fire. Perhaps, as Ramsay's Chief of Staff later speculated, he was simply shell-shocked after five extremely hard days.

In any event, the call caused a sensation in the Dynamo Room. Taken together with *Sabre*'s signal ("Impossible at present to embark more troops"), it seemed to indicate that the harbor was indeed blocked and only the beaches could be used.

First, Ramsay tried to make sure. At 8:57 he radioed Tennant, "Can you confirm harbor is blocked?" Tennant replied, "No," but the raid had left communications in a shambles, and the answer never got through. Not hearing from Tennant, he later tried the French commander, Admiral Abrial, but no answer there either.

At 9:28 Ramsay didn't dare wait any longer. He radioed the minesweeper *Hebe*, serving as a sort of command ship offshore:

> Intercept all personnel ships approaching Dunkirk and instruct them not to close harbor but to remain off Eastern beach to collect troops from ships.

Midnight, there was still no word from Dunkirk. Ramsay sent the destroyer *Vanquisher* to investigate. At 5:51 a.m. on the 30th she flashed the good news,

> "Entrance to Dunkirk harbor practicable. Obstructions exist towards outer side of eastern arm."

This welcome information was immediately relayed to the rescue fleet, but a whole night had gone by. Only four trawlers and a yacht used the mole during those priceless hours of darkness, despite calm seas and minimum enemy interference. "A great opportunity was missed," commented Captain Tennant a few days later. "Probably 15,000 troops could have been embarked had the ships been forthcoming."

But for Ramsay, the worst thing that happened on the evening of May 29 was not the false report from Dunkirk; it was a very real decision made in London. The day had seen heavy losses in shipping—particularly destroyers. The *Wakeful*, *Grafton*, and *Grenade* were gone; *Gallant*, *Greyhound*, *Intrepid*, *Jaguar*, *Montrose*, and *Saladin* damaged. The whole "G" class was now knocked out. To the Admiralty there was more than Dunkirk to think about: there were the convoys, the Mediterranean, the protection of Britain herself.

At 8:00 p.m. Admiral Pound reluctantly decided to withdraw the eight modern destroyers Ramsay had left, leaving him with only fifteen older vessels, which in a pinch could be considered expendable.

For Ramsay, it was a dreadful blow. The destroyers had come to be his most effective vessels. Withdrawing a third of them wrecked all his careful projections. Even if there were no further losses, he would now be able to maintain a flow of only one destroyer an hour to the coast—a pace that would lift only 17,000 troops every 24 hours.

The Admiralty's decision couldn't have come at a worse time. Every ship was desperately needed. The fighting divisions—the men who had defended the escape corridor—were now themselves moving into the perimeter. In the little Belgian village of Westvleteren, 3rd Division packed up for the last time. Headquarters was in a local abbey, and before pulling out, General Montgomery sought out the Abbot, Father M. Rafael Hoedt. Could the Father hide a few personal possessions for him? The answer was yes; so the General handed over a box of personal papers and a lunch basket he particularly favored. These were then bricked up in the abbey wall, as Monty drove off promising that the army would be back and he'd pick everything up later.

Only a general as cocky as Montgomery could make such a promise. Brigadier George William Sutton was more typical. He felt nothing but anguish and personal humiliation as he trudged toward Dunkirk, passing mile after mile of abandoned equipment. He was a career officer, and "if this was what it came to when the real thing came to a crisis, all the years of thought and time and trouble that we had given to learning and teaching soldiering had been wasted. I felt that I had been labouring under a delusion and that after all, this was not my trade."

Despite the disaster, some units never lost their snap and cohesion. The Queen's Own Worcestershire Yeomanry marched into the perimeter with the men singing and a mouth organ playing "Tipperary." But others, like the 44th Division, seemed to dissolve. Officers and men tramped along individually and in small parties. Private Oliver Barnard, a signalman with the 44th, had absolutely no idea where he was heading. Eventually Brigadier J. E. Utterson Kelso came swinging by. Barnard fell in behind him with the comforting thought, "He's a brigadier, he must know where he's going."

Parts of the French First Army north of Lille—finally released by General Prioux—were converging on Dunkirk, too. The plan was for the French to man the western end of the perimeter while the British manned the eastern end, but this caused all sorts of trouble where the poilus coming up the escape corridor had to cross over from east to west. It meant going at almost right angles to the generally north-south flow of the British.

There were some unpleasant collisions. As the Worcester-shire Yeomanry approached Bray-Dunes, they met the main body of the French 6oth Division moving west on a road parallel to the shore. Part of the Worcesters wriggled by, but the rest had to get down into a rugger scrum and smash their way through.

When a lorry fell into a crater, blocking the road north, Major David Warner of the Kent Yeomanry organized a working party to move it. French troops kept pushing the party aside, refusing to stop while the job was done. Finally, Warner drew his revolver and threatened to shoot the next man who didn't stop when ordered. The poilus paid no attention, until Warner actually did shoot one of them. Then they stopped, and the lorry was moved.

There were clashes even among the brass. General Brooke ordered the French 2nd Light Mechanized Division, operating under him, to cover his eastern flank as II Corps made its final withdrawal on the night of May 29–30. General Bougrain, the French division's commander, announced that he had other orders from General Blanchard, and that he was going to comply with them. Brooke repeated his previous instructions, adding that if the French General disobeyed, he'd be shot, if Brooke ever caught him. Bougrain paid no attention to this either, but Brooke never caught him.

All through this afternoon of tensions and traffic jams, the last of the fighting troops poured into the perimeter. Some went straight to the beaches, while others were assigned to the defenses, taking over from the cooks and clerks who had manned the line the past three days. As the 7th Guards Brigade moved into Furnes, cornerstone of the eastern end of the perimeter, the men spotted General Montgomery standing in the marketplace. In a rare lapse, the General had dropped his normally cocky stance and stood looking weary and forlorn. As the 7th swung by, they snapped to attention and gave Monty a splendid "eyes left." It was just the tonic he needed. He immediately straightened up and returned the honor with a magnificent salute.

Farther west, the 2nd Coldstream Guards were moving into

position along the Bergues-Furnes canal. Running parallel to the coast, about six miles inland, the canal was the main line of defense facing south. The Coldstream dug in along the north bank, making good use of several farm cottages that stood in their sector. The flat land across the canal should have offered an excellent field of fire, but the canal road on that side was littered with abandoned vehicles, and it was hard to see over them.

At the moment this made no difference. There was no sign of the enemy anywhere. The Coldstreamers whiled away the afternoon casting a highly critical eye on the troops still pouring into the perimeter. Only two platoons of Welsh Guards won their approval. These marched crisply across the canal bridge in perfect formation. The rest were a shuffling rabble.

The last of Lord Gort's strong-points were closing up shop. They had kept the corridor open; now it was time to come in themselves—if they could. At the little French village of Ledringhem, fifteen miles south of Dunkirk, the remnants of the 5th Gloucesters collected in an orchard shortly after midnight, May 29. The sails of a nearby windmill were burning brightly, and it seemed impossible that these exhausted men, surrounded for two days, could get away undetected. But the Germans were tired too, and there was no enemy reaction as Lieutenant-Colonel G.A.H. Buxton led the party north along a stream bed.

They not only slipped through the German lines; they captured three prisoners along the way. At 6:30 a.m. they finally stumbled into Bambecque, once more in friendly country. The adjutant of the 8th Worcesters saw them coming: "They were dirty and weary and haggard, but unbeaten.... I ran towards Colonel Buxton, who was staggering along, obviously wounded. He croaked a greeting, and I saw the lumps of sleep in his bloodshot eyes. Our Commanding Officer came running out and told the 5th Gloucesters' second-in-command to rest the troops a minute. I took Colonel Buxton indoors, gave him a tumbler of stale wine, and eased him gently to the floor on to a blanket, assuring him again and again that his men were all right. In a few seconds he was asleep."

The men holding the strong-point at Cassel, 19 miles south

of Dunkirk, were also trying to get back to the sea. For three days they had held up the German advance while thousands of Allied troops swarmed up the escape corridor. Now they finally had orders to pull back themselves, but it was too late. The enemy had gradually seeped around the hill where the town stood. By the morning of May 29 it was cut off.

Brigadier Somerset, commanding the garrison, decided to try anyhow. But not during the day. There were too many Germans. The only chance would be after dark. Orders went out to assemble at 9:30 p.m.

At first all went well. The troops quietly slipped out of town, down the hill, and headed northeast over the fields. Somerset felt there was less chance of detection if they traveled cross-country.

It really didn't matter. The Germans were everywhere. With Somerset in the lead, the 4th Oxfordshire and Buckinghamshire Light Infantry were overwhelmed near Watou; the East Riding Yeomanry were virtually wiped out in a minefield; the 2nd Gloucesters were trapped in a thick woods called the Bois Saint Acaire.

"*Kamerad! Kamerad!*" shouted the German troopers swarming around the woods, trying to flush out the Gloucesters. Crouching in the brush, the Tommies lay low. A pause, and then a voice speaking good English over a loudspeaker: "Come out! Come out! Hitler is winning the war, you are beaten. Come out, or we will shell you out. Lay down your arms and come out running."

Second Lieutenant Julian Fane of B Company wasn't about to buy that. He had heard of another British battalion that listened to such a broadcast, threw down its arms, and came out . . . only to be machine-gunned down. He told the men near him, and they decided to fight it out.

Since the Germans had them targeted, the first step was to find a new position. Fane led his men in a wild dash to another wood 100 yards away. It did no good. The enemy quickly spotted them, and they spent the rest of the day huddling under a hale of artillery and mortar fire.

Darkness at last, and the little group continued north. They moved in single file, keeping as silent as possible, making use of every bit of cover. But if they had any delusion that they were traveling unseen, it was dispelled when a red Very light suddenly soared into the night. Instantly machine guns, mortars, rifles, every kind of weapon opened up on them. They had been ambushed.

Tracers criss-crossed the sky; a nearby haystack burst into flames, illuminating the group perfectly. Men were falling on all sides, and Fane himself was hit in the right arm and shoulder. He finally reached a ditch, where he was relatively safe as long as he kept an 18-inch profile. He gradually collected about a dozen other survivors. Together they crept off into the darkness, managing somehow to work their way around the German flank. He didn't know it, but his little band was all that remained of the 2nd Gloucesters.

One British soldier outside the perimeter was still very much in the fight. Private Edgar G. A. Rabbets had been just another Tommy in the 5th Northamptonshires until the great retreat. Then a German thrust almost caught the battalion near Brussels. A fire-fight developed, and at one point Rabbets raised his rifle and took a potshot at an enemy soldier about 200 yards away. The man dropped in his tracks.

"Can you do that again?" asked the company commander. Rabbets obligingly picked off another German.

Then and there Ted Rabbets was designated a sniper, and henceforth he acted entirely on his own. He had no previous training for his new work, but did enjoy one unusual advantage: he had once known a poacher who taught him a few tricks. Now he could move so quietly he could "catch a rabbit by the ears," and he could make himself so small he could "hide behind a blade of grass."

As a sniper, Rabbets soon developed a few trade secrets of his own: never snipe from tree tops—too easy to get trapped. Keep away from farmhouse attics—too easy to be spotted. Best vantage point—some hiding place where there's room to move around, like a grove of trees.

Following these rules, Rabbets managed to survive alone most of the way across Belgium. He tried to keep in occasional touch with his battalion, but usually he was deep in German-held territory—once even behind their artillery. From time to time he matched wits with his German counterparts. One of them once fired at him from a hole in some rooftop, missed by six inches. Rabbets fired back and had the satisfaction of seeing the man plunge out of the hole. Another time, while prowling a village street late at night, Rabbets rounded a corner and literally ran into a German sniper. This time Ted fired first and didn't miss.

Rabbets ultimately reached the coast near Nieuport and slowly worked his way west, dipping into the German lines on an occasional foray. On May 31 he finally rejoined the BEF at La Panne—still operating alone and perhaps the last fighting man to enter the perimeter.

All the way south, five divisions of General Prioux's French First Army fought on at Lille. It was still early on the morning of May 29 when a French truck convoy, approaching the city from Armentières, met some armored vehicles moving onto the road. The poilus sent up a great cheer, thinking that at last some British tanks were coming to help them. Only when the strangers began confiscating their arms did the Frenchmen realize that they had run into the 7th Panzer Division.

Cut off from the north, General Prioux surrendered during the afternoon at his headquarters in Steenwerck. He had gotten his wish: to remain with the bulk of his army rather than try to escape. Most of his troops holed up in Lille, continuing to tie down six enemy divisons.

By now it didn't matter very much. With the escape corridor closed, Rundstedt's Army Group A and Bock's Army Group B at last joined forces, and the Germans had all the troops they needed for the final push on Dunkirk.

But this May 29 saw an important change in the composition of the German forces. Once again the tanks were gone—pulled out this time on the urging of the panzer generals themselves. Guderian summed up the reasons in a report he submitted on the evening of the 28th after a personal tour of the front: the armored divisions were down to 50% of strength . . . time was needed to prepare for new operations . . . the marshy terrain was unsuitable for tanks . . . the Belgian surrender had released plenty of infantry—far more effective troops for this kind of country.

Added to these very practical arguments was perhaps an intangible factor. Guderian and the other panzer commanders were simply not temperamentally suited to the static warfare that was developing. Theirs was a world of slashing thrusts, breakthroughs, long rolling advances. Once the battle had turned into a siege, they lost interest. By the evening of the 28th Guderian was already poring over his maps of the lower Seine.

In any event, OKH agreed. At 10:00 a.m. on May 29 General Gustav von Wietersheim's motorized infantry took over from Guderian, and later in the day General Reinhardt's tanks were also pulled out. But this didn't mean that the battered Allied troops were home free. On the contrary, ten German divisions—mostly tough, experienced infantry—now pressed against the 35-mile Dunkirk perimeter.

At the western end, the 37th Panzer Engineers hoisted a swastika flag over Fort Philippe around noon, and the port of Gravelines fell soon afterward. All the way east the 56th Division was marching on Furnes. About 3:30 p.m. Bicycle Squadron 25 reached the east gate of the old walled town. Here they ran into a French column trying to get into the perimeter. After a brief fire-fight, Captain Neugart of the 25th forced the Frenchmen to surrender.

Then along came two French tanks, so unsuspecting that their turrets were open. Corporal Gruenvogel of the bicyclists jumped on one of them, pointed his pistol down through the open turret, and ordered the crew to surrender. They complied . . . as did the crew of the second tank, even without such urging.

Captain Neugart now sent a captured French major along with two of his own men into Furnes to demand that the whole town surrender. But audacity has its limits, and this time he got only a scornful reply from the Allied troops now barricading the streets.

On the beaches no one knew how long the troops manning the perimeter could keep the Germans out. At Bray-Dunes Commander Thomas Kerr half-expected to see them burst onto the sands any minute. He and Commander Richardson continued loading the troops into boats; but they arranged for a boat

of their own to lie off Bray, ready to rescue the naval shore party, "just in case." This gave them some confidence, but talking
quietly together that night, they agreed they'd probably end up
in some German prison camp.

Dover and London knew even less. At one point on the 28th
the Admiralty actually told Tennant to report "every hour" the
number of people to be embarked—orders that could only have
come from someone who hadn't the remotest picture of the situation. Tennant patiently replied, "Am doing my best to keep
you informed, but shall be unable to report for hours."

But even at a distance one thing was clear: all too often the
ships weren't where they were needed the most. Sometimes
there were plenty of vessels at the mole, but no troops on hand.
Other times there were troops but no ships. The same was true
at the beaches. Someone was needed offshore to control the
flow of shipping, the same way Captain Tennant was directing
the flow of men between the mole and the beaches.

Rear-Admiral Frederic Wake-Walker got the nod. Fifty-two
years old, Wake-Walker was known as an exceptionally keen or-
ganizer, and a good seaman too. His last command had been
the battleship *Revenge*—a sure sign of talent, for the Royal Navy
gave the battleships to only its most promising officers. At the
moment, he held down a staff job at the Admiralty; he was
readily available for temporary assignment.

Returning to his office from lunch on Wednesday, May 29,
Wake-Walker learned that he was wanted by Rear-Admiral Sir
Tom Phillips, the Vice-Chief of Naval Staff. Phillips asked him if
he would like to go to Dunkirk and "try and get some organization into the embarkation there." Wake-Walker said that he'd
be "delighted," and the appointment was worked out. It was
important that he should not seem to be superseding Tennant.
The Captain would still be SNO on shore; Wake-Walker in
charge of everything afloat.

An hour later he was on his way by car to Dover. Arriving
about 6:00 p.m., he went directly to Ramsay's casemate for a
quick briefing. In the Dynamo Room he was shown a map, depicting the coast east of Dunkirk. The three beaches—Malo,
Bray, and La Panne—had been optimistically numbered, with
each beach in turn divided into three sections. The BEF would

be coming down to these particular beaches, while certain others west of Malo were reserved for the French.

This neat map, with its careful delineations, little prepared him for the chaos he found when he arrived off Bray on the destroyer *Esk* at 4:00 the following morning, May 30. Transferring to the minesweeper *Hebe*, Wake-Walker soon learned about the "real war" from Captain Eric Bush, who had been filling in until he got there. At dawn Wake-Walker could see for himself the dark masses of men on the beaches, the long lines that curled into the sea, the men standing waist-deep in the water . . . waiting and waiting.

"The crux of the matter was boats, boat crews, and towage," the Admiral later recalled. At 6:30 a.m. he radioed Dover that small boats were urgently needed, and at 7:30 he asked for more ships, and again stressed the need for small boats.

It was a familiar refrain, growing in volume these past few hours. At 12:10 a.m. Brigadier Oliver Leese of Gort's staff had telephoned the War Office, stressing that the perimeter could only be held for a limited time. Send as many boats as possible—quickly. At 4:00 the War Office called back with the welcome word that Admiral Ramsay was "going to get as much small craft as possible across as soon as he can."

But nothing came. At 4:15 the destroyer *Vanquisher*, lying off Malo, radioed, "More ships and boats urgently required off west beach." At 6:40 the destroyer *Vivacious* echoed the plea: "Essential to have more ships and boats."

By 12:45 p.m. Brigadier Leese was on the phone again, this time with General Dill, Chief of the Imperial General Staff. No ships yet, he complained. Off La Panne, Admiral Wake-Walker was getting desperate. He now sent Captain Bush back to Dover in the *Hebe*, to explain in person the vital necessity of sending out boats and crews.

By 3:00 p.m. Gort himself was trying. He first phoned Admiral Pound, then General Dill, pointing out that there were still no ships. Every hour counted, he stressed.

Headquarters could at least complain to somebody. The troops waiting on the beaches didn't even have that satisfaction. After a restless night curled up in the sand, Captain John Dodd of the Royal Artillery looked out to sea in the first light of dawn and saw—nothing. "No ships in sight," he noted in his diary. "Something must have gone wrong."

At Bray-Dunes Sapper Joe Coles felt "terrible disappoint-ment" and resigned himself to a day of troubled sleep in the Dunes. At Malo Chaplain Kenneth Meiklejohn couldn't under-stand it. There had been no air attacks, yet no one seemed to have embarked all night. A dreadful thought crossed his mind: "Has the Navy given us up?"

Plunging down from the sky, a German Stuka dive-bombs an Allied tank, as Hitler strikes west in May 1940. Together with the armored panzer division, the Stuka symbolized a new kind of lightning war—the *Blitzkrieg*—which the Allies were utterly unprepared to meet. German columns knifed through to the sea, trapping the British and French against the coast of Flanders. (Hergestellt im Bundesarchiv Bestand)

On the receiving end of the German onslaught were the Allied commanders, British General the Viscount Gort (left) and French General Maurice Gamelin. Within days Gamelin was fired and Gort was reeling back toward the French port of Dunkirk. Below, a file of British troops straggles into Dunkirk, hoping to escape by sea. (Top: Wide World Photos. Bottom: Hergestellt im Bundesarchiv Bestand)

Thousands of Allied soldiers soon crowded the beaches that stretched from Dunkirk to La Panne, a small Belgian resort ten miles to the east. Long lines of men curled out into the sea, patiently waiting to be picked up. (*Times*)

As the troops waited, German planes continued to pound them. For protection they dug foxholes in the dunes. Casualties were surprisingly light, since the sand tended to smother the exploding bombs. (Imperial War Museum)

Across the English Channel, a giant rescue operation was hastily organized under the command of Vice-Admiral Bertram H. Ramsay. Here Admiral Ramsay briefly relaxes on the balcony of his headquarters, carved out of the famous chalk cliffs of Dover. (Courtesy of Jane Evan-Thomas)

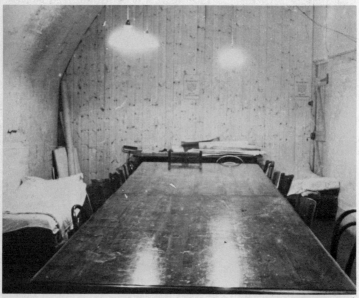

Command center for the evacuation was the austere "Dynamo Room," buried deep in the Dover cliffs. Here Ramsay's staff, using a battery of telephones, assembled and deployed a rescue fleet that ultimately totaled 861 ships. This photo is believed to be the only picture ever taken of the room. (Courtesy of W. J. Matthews)

Every kind of vessel was used for the evacuation, ranging from warships to small pleasure craft. Above, a "G" Class destroyer races toward Dunkirk "with a bone in her teeth." This entire class was eventually knocked out. Below, the yacht *Sundowner* was luckier. She rescued 135 men and escaped without a scratch. Her owner-skipper, Commander C. H. Lightoller, had performed earlier heroics as Second Officer on the *Titanic*. (Top: Imperial War Museum. Bottom: courtesy of Patrick Stenson and Sharon Rutman)

Dunkirk was easy to find. A huge pall of smoke from burning oil tanks hung over the shattered port. The smoke seemed to symbolize defeat and disaster, but had the happy side effect of concealing the harbor from German bombers. (Courtesy of W. J. Matthews)

In contrast, La Panne, at the eastern end of the evacuation area, looked deceptively tranquil. Rescue ships can be seen here, picking up troops near the shore. Gort's headquarters was in one of the detached houses on the far right. (Courtesy of J. L. Aldridge)

Picking up troops direct from the beach seemed to take forever—"loading ships by the spoonful" was the way one embarkation officer described it. Above, a trawler and a coaster take aboard men wading out from the shore. At right, British Tommies are up to their shoulders in water, approaching a rescue ship. (Top: Wide World Photos. Bottom: The Granger Collection)

Captain William G. Tennant (left) was finally appointed by Admiral Ramsay to take charge at Dunkirk and speed up the evacuation. As Senior Naval Officer (SNO), Tennant discovered that the eastern mole of Dunkirk harbor was ideal for loading ships. Here a destroyer could lift 600 men in 20 minutes, while it took 12 hours along the beaches. For most of the next week the mole was packed with an endless line of troops (below) trudging out to the waiting ships. (Top: ILN Pic Lib. Bottom: *Times*)

Ingenuity triumphed on the beaches too. Abandoned lorries were strung together, to form improvised piers leading out into the water. Here one of these "lorry jetties" is visible in the background. (Courtesy of D.C.H. Shields)

Soon an unbroken line of crowded ships could be seen carrying the men across the Channel to safety. (Culver Pictures)

The Luftwaffe did not leave the rescue fleet alone. These two pictures show how suddenly disaster could strike. In the top photo an Allied ship has just blown up, while two others lie nearby still untouched. In the bottom photo, taken an instant later (note that the configuration of smoke is still the same), the two nearby ships have now disappeared, obliterated by the rain of bombs. Troops on the beach are futilely firing their rifles at the planes. (Top: Imperial War Museum. Bottom: Fox Photos Ltd.)

The French destroyer *Bourrasque* joins the growing list of Allied casualties. Packed with troops, she struck a German mine and went down with a loss of 150 lives. (Imperial War Museum)

A fleet of French fishing trawlers was a late addition to Ramsay's armada. They concentrated on the inner harbor of Dunkirk, where hundreds of poilus swarmed aboard. (Wide World Photos)

Bombs and mines were not the only perils faced by the rescue fleet. The *Schnellboote*, fast German motor torpedo boats, prowled the seas at night, sinking and damaging Ramsay's ships. (Hergestellt im Bundesarchiv Bestand)

German artillery added to the toll. Nothing was safe—neither the ships, the harbor, the mole, nor the men on the beaches. "Greetings to Tommy" is the message painted on this shell. (Hergestellt im Bundesarchiv Bestand)

German troops finally broke into La Panne on June 1 and began moving down the beach toward Dunkirk itself. Below, the fall of Dunkirk, June 4. Weary but triumphant, German troops of the 18th Infantry Division stack their arms and rest. (Hergestellt im Bundesarchiv Bestand)

The quarry was gone. In nine desperate days Ramsay's fleet brought back more than 338,000 Allied troops. Typical was this batch, disembarking from the minesweeper *Sandown*. Naval officer in the lower-left foreground is Lieutenant Wallis, the ship's First Lieutenant. (Courtesy of J. D. Nunn)

Sometimes it seemed as if half the canine population of France had been evacuated too. Never was the Englishman's legendary fondness for dogs more ringingly affirmed. At least 170 dogs were landed in Dover alone. (Wide World Photos)

Disheveled but happy, the Tommies were sent by train to assembly areas all over Britain for rest and reorganization. At every station a relieved populace showered them with cigarettes, cakes, candy, and affection. (Wide World Photos)

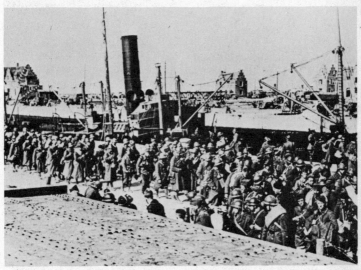

At Dunkirk, the captured French rear guard heard no cheers. They would soon be marching off to POW camp, most for the duration of the war. (Hergestellt im Bundesarchiv Bestand)

1940 DUNKERQUE LES ANGLAIS S'OPPOSENT A
L'EMBARQUEMENT DES DERNIERS FRANÇAIS
QUI VENAIENT DE PROTÉGER LEUR RETRAITE

In another two weeks France was knocked out of the war. The new pro-German Vichy government lost no time charging that the British had run out, leaving the French holding the bag at Dunkirk. Actually, Ramsay's rescue fleet saved over 123,000 French soldiers, 102,570 in British ships. Despite the statistics, French bitterness continues, even today. (Musée des Deux Guerres Mondiales—B.D.I.C., Universités de Paris)

9

The Little Ships

Lieutenant Ian Cox, First Lieutenant of the destroyer *Malcolm*, could hardly believe his eyes. There, coming over the horizon toward him, was a mass of dots that filled the sea. The *Malcolm* was bringing her third load of troops back to Dover. The dots were all heading the other way—toward Dunkirk. It was Thursday evening, the 30th of May.

As he watched, the dots materialized into vessels. Here and there were respectable steamers, like the Portsmouth–Isle of Wight car ferry, but mostly they were little ships of every conceivable type—fishing smacks . . . drifters . . . excursion boats . . . glittering white yachts . . . mud-spattered hoppers . . . open motor launches . . . tugs towing ship's lifeboats . . . Thames sailing barges with their distinctive brown sails . . . cabin cruisers, their bright work gleaming . . . dredges, trawlers, and rust-streaked scows . . . the Admiral Superintendent's barge from Portsmouth with its fancy tassels and rope-work.

Cox felt a sudden surge of pride. Being here was no longer just a duty; it was an honor and a privilege. Turning to a somewhat startled chief boatswain's mate standing beside him, he burst into the Saint Crispin's Day passage from Shakespeare's *Henry V*:

And Gentlemen in England, now abed
Shall think themselves accurs'd they were not here.

The efforts of the Small Vessels Pool and the Ministry of Shipping were at last paying off. The trickle of little ships that began in Tough's boatyard was turning into a deluge. There was still no public announcement of the evacuation, but England is a small place. In one way or another, the word reached those who were needed.

It was a midnight phone call from the Admiralty that alerted Basil A. Smith, a London accountant and owner of the 24-foot cabin cruiser *Constant Nymph*. Would Smith confirm that his boat was ready for sea and could sail on four hours' notice? Early next morning, May 27, the summons came: take her down to Sheerness at once.

Captain Lemon Webb was nursing the Ipswich spritsailing barge *Tollesbury* up the Thames on an ordinary cargo run. Then a motorboat eased alongside, and a naval officer ordered him to a nearby jetty. There a tug took her in tow, and *Tollesbury* was on her way to Sheerness, too.

The crew of the Margate lifeboat *Lord Southborough* were playing darts at their favorite pub when their turn came. A cryptic message said report to the boathouse at once. Within hours they were heading direct for Dunkirk—no stop at Sheerness for them. For Coxswain Edward D. Parker it was almost a family outing. His brother and nephew were in his crew; a son had already gone over with the Margate pilot boat; another son was one of Commander Clouston's men on the mole.

The cockle boat fleet of Leigh-on-Sea lay peacefully at anchor on May 30 when the call came for them. Bearing imposing names like *Defender*, *Endeavour*, *Resolute*, and *Renown*, they sounded like dreadnoughts; actually they were only 40 feet long with a 2½-foot draft. Normally they were engaged in the humblest of tasks—gathering in the cockle shellfish found in the mud flats of the Thames estuary. The crew were all civilians, but every man volunteered. Seventeen-year-old Ken Horner was considered too young and left behind, but he wasn't about to buy that. He ran home, got his mother's permission, and bicycled off in pursuit of the fleet. He caught up with his boat at Southend.

These vessels came with their crews, but that did not always happen. In the race against time, yachts were often commandeered before their owners could be located. Other weekend sailors just couldn't drop everything and sign up in the Navy for a month—the standard requirement. As the little ships converged on Sheerness and Ramsgate, the main staging points, Admiral Preston's Small Vessels Pool looked around for substitute crews.

Shipwright A. W. Elliott was working in Johnson & Jago's boatyard at Leigh-on-Sea when a bobby pedaled up on a bicycle. He announced that volunteers were needed to get "some chaps" off the French coast. Elliott needed no urging.

At Lowestoft on the east coast the Small Vessels Pool commandeered taxis to bring down a contingent of commercial fishermen. In London, Commander Garrett of the Pool spent three straight nights calling up various clubs . . . rounding up yachtsman members . . . packing them off in Admiralty cars to Sheerness and Ramsgate.

It was during these hectic days that Sub-Lieutenant Moran Caplat arrived in London for a few days' leave. An actor and yachtsman in peacetime, he was currently serving on a naval trawler in the North Sea, but the ship was being refitted, and for the moment he was free. He was aware that Dunkirk was coming to a boil, but felt it was no concern of his.

Going to the Royal Ocean Racing Club for breakfast, he was surprised to find nobody there. Even the steward was gone. He finally located the steward's wife, who explained that everyone had vanished after a call from the Admiralty a day or so ago. Mildly mystified, he settled down in a chair to relax alone.

The phone rang, and he answered. It was the Admiralty. A voice said they wanted "still more hands" and asked who he was. Caplat identified himself, and the voice said, "You're just what we need." He was then told to go to Sheerness immediately. Still baffled, he caught a train at Waterloo Station within an hour.

Five minutes' walk from the Royal Ocean Racing Club was the ship chandlers shop of Captain O. M. Watts on Albemarle Street. Downstairs the Captain cheerfully dispensed a hodgepodge of charts and nautical gear; upstairs he gave navigation lessons to young gentlemen who hoped for a commission in the

Royal Navy Volunteer Reserve. They were mostly professional men: solicitors, brokers, actors, bankers from the City, and such. Few knew much about the sea; some had never been out of sight of land.

John Fernald was a young American theatrical director attending the Captain's classes every Thursday evening. Usually the session was blackboard work, but not on Thursday, May 30. When he arrived with his friend David Homan, a scenery designer, Watts took them aside for a private chat. Quietly he explained there would be no regular class tonight; the Navy needed volunteers immediately for a "hazardous job."

Neither Fernald nor Homan liked the prospect of moving from navigational theory to practice so abruptly, but they couldn't see any graceful way out; so they volunteered. Captain Watts told them to grab what gear they could and report immediately to the Port of London Authority down by the Tower.

Fernald rushed back to his flat, picked up an old pea jacket, and hurried down to Tower Hill, as directed. Most of the others were already there. Some didn't even have time to change their clothes and were still wearing the cutaways and striped trousers of the City. Stockbroker Raphael de Sola, however, was resplendent in the jacket of the Royal London Yacht Club, blue trousers to match, a visored cap, and a greatcoat worthy of the First Sea Lord of the Admiralty.

Along with Captain Watts's scholars, there were a number of more obviously waterfront types: lightermen, dock workers, deckhands, barge men. High and low together, they milled around the lobby of the Port Authority building, still not knowing what they were to do.

Then a Royal Navy commander appeared and gave them a quick briefing. They were to man ship's lifeboats collected from vessels lying at the London docks. These would be towed down the river and across the Channel, where they would be used to help rescue the BEF.

A bus now took the group to Tilbury, where the lifeboats were waiting. The rule was four men to a boat; twelve boats to a tow. Fernald and Homan managed to stick together, and soon after midnight they were on their way. In the quiet of the night, broken only by the water rushing by and the throb of the tug up ahead, Fernald wondered at the incredible change in his life that had snatched him from a humdrum existence in London and put him in an open boat racing through the dark.

First stop was Sheerness. This bustling harbor on the Thames estuary had become the collecting point for all the little ships streaming down the river. Here they were sorted out and put into shape under the watchful eye of Commodore A. H. Taylor, a retired Rear-Admiral who could normally be found shuffling paper in the Economic Warfare Division of the Admiralty.

Engines were the big problem. Many of the boats had been laid up for the winter and were hard to get running again. Others had idiosyncrasies apparently known only to their absent owners. The Thames excursion steamers had boilers that couldn't use salt water. It was a miracle that Captain T. E. Docksey and his engineers managed to get more than 100 boats in good enough shape to cross the Channel.

Every ship also needed someone on board who could keep the engine running. By now there were plenty of weekend-sailor volunteers, but few of these bankers and shopkeepers really understood machinery. The Shipping Federation, an organization of operators, was asked to help and issued a call for volunteers. About 350 marine engineers responded.

From Sheerness most of the little ships moved on to Ramsgate. Here fuel tanks were topped off, provisions loaded, and convoys made up. Many of the craft had no compass, and some of the skippers had never been out of sight of land. Lieutenant-Commander Raymond Grundage, the Routing Officer, issued more than 1,000 charts, 600 with routes lined off for neophyte navigators.

Problems could be enormous—or exasperatingly minute. Robert Hilton, a physical education specialist, and Ted Shaw, a red-headed cinema manager, had teamed up to bring the motorboat *Ryegate II* down the river. They expected to pick up supplies at Ramsgate, but all they received were two cans of water. Otherwise the boat was bare—not even a tumbler for the water. The naval supply depot at Ramsgate seemed unable to cope; they finally went to a pub, had a drink, and pocketed the glasses.

Each little ship had its own tale of troubles, but at the start they all suffered from one common problem: none of them were armed. Lieutenant C. D. Richards carefully hoarded his stockpile of 105 Lewis machine guns, doling them out only to the tugs and escort vessels.

Later the crews would scavenge the beaches, gathering a plentiful supply of discarded Bren guns; and sometimes a BEF gunner might even attach himself to a vessel, but at first they were defenseless. It was enough to make a member of the crew feel a bit uneasy. "Even a record of the 1812 Overture would be better than nothing," observed one skipper.

It was 10:00 p.m., May 29, when the first convoy of little ships set out from Ramsgate on the long trip across the Channel. None of the eight launches in the group had any navigating instruments. Nevertheless, Lieutenant R. H. Irving, skipper of the escorting motorboat *Triton*, was confident. Unlike most, he knew these waters well. Waiting outside Ramsgate breakwater, he shouted to the other ships to close up and follow him. Three of the boats developed engine trouble and had to turn back, but the others stuck to *Triton* and arrived safely off La Panne at dawn.

At 1:00 a.m. on the 30th another convoy left Ramsgate—this time, nineteen launches led by the Belgian ferry *Yser*—and from then on the flow steadily increased. By late afternoon it was hard to tell where one convoy ended and the next began. All that night, and the 31st too, the little ships poured across the Channel.

Frequently they passed ships like the *Malcolm* heading back to England. Decks packed with troops, they were a sobering sight. For their part, the men on the returning vessels watched this armada of small craft with mounting excitement and pride. The very names seemed to say "England": *Swallow* . . . *Royal Thames* . . . *Moss Rose* . . . *Norwich Belle* . . . *Duchess of York* . . . *Blue Bird* . . . *Pride of Folkestone* . . . *Palmerston* . . . *Skylark* . . . *Nelson* . . . *Southend Britannia* . . . *Lady Haig* . . . *New Prince of Wales*.

Many of the names also had a personal quality, suggesting that this rescue effort was no mere naval operation; that it was really a family affair: *Grace Darling* . . . *Boy Bruce* . . . *Our Maggie* . . . *Our Lizzie* . . . *Girl Nancy* . . . *Handy Billie* . . . *Willie and Alice* . . . *Auntie Gus*.

Traveling in company, usually shepherded by an armed tug or skoot, the little ships moved across a smooth, gray carpet of sea. The English Channel has a reputation for nastiness, but it had behaved for four days now, and the calm continued on May 30. Best of all, there was a heavy mist, giving the Luftwaffe no chance to follow up the devastating raids of the 29th.

"Clouds so thick you can lean on them," noted a Luftwaffe war diarist, as the Stukas and Heinkels remained grounded. At Fliegerkorps VIII General Major von Richthofen couldn't believe it was that bad. At headquarters the sun was shining. He ordered Major Dinort, commanding the 2nd Stuka Squadron, to at least try an attack. Dinort took his planes up, but returned in ten minutes. Heavy fog over Dunkirk, he phoned headquarters. Exasperated, Richthofen countered that the day was certainly flyable where *he* was. If *Herr Generalmajor* didn't believe him, Dinort shot back, just call the weather service.

But cloudy weather didn't guarantee a safe passage for the little ships. Plenty of things could still go wrong. The Channel was full of nervous and inexperienced sailors.

"Periscope on the starboard bow," shouted the lookout of the 80-foot excursion steamer *New Prince of Wales*. It turned out to be the mast of a sunken ship, standing fifteen feet out of the water, complete with shrouds.

Next, *New Prince of Wales* was almost run down by a destroyer that mistook her for a German S-boat. The skipper, Sub-Lieutenant Peter Bennett, managed to flash a recognition signal just in time. A little later he ran alongside an anchored French cargo ship, hoping to get some directions. "*Où est l'armée britannique?*" he called. The reply was a revolver shot. These were dangerous days for strangers asking questions.

Uncorrected compasses were another source of trouble. It was easy to find the French coast, but the right spot was another matter. Sub-Lieutenant William Ronald Williams anchored his lighter a few hundred yards off an empty stretch of beach and had a boat row him ashore. Walking a quarter-mile inland in search of somebody in authority, he hailed a couple of soldiers he saw silhouetted against a distant blaze.

"*Lieber Gott!*" one of them cried, and they began shooting at him. Williams ducked behind a dune and shot back. Both Germans fell, but there were other voices now, and Williams raced back to the beach. In less than five minutes he had his lighter under weigh at her full six knots.

One way or another, most of the little ships eventually reached the right part of the coast and went to work. Essentially they were ferries, carrying or towing troops from the beaches to the larger vessels lying further out. Sometimes it was easy—just a matter of towing some rowboat or inflated raft; other times it was difficult and dangerous—especially when they had to pluck men directly from the sea.

"Well done, motorboat, wait for me," a voice hailed Lieutenant Irving, as he nursed *Triton* alongside a destroyer with one more load. An officer wearing a lambskin coat leapt aboard. It was Commodore Gilbert Owen Stephenson, a 62-year-old retired vice-admiral, who had been recruited for the crisis and put in charge of all offshore operations at La Panne. Hatless and wet through, he seemed oblivious to his own discomfort as he told Irving to carry on. He added that he might later have "one or two other jobs" for *Triton* to do.

Stephenson then threw himself into the rescue work too. Nothing was beneath him. He steered, passed lines, helped haul the exhausted troops aboard. Through it all he kept up a line of cheerful chatter. "Come on, the Army!" he would cry; or, to some half-drowned soldier, "Where have I seen you before? You're so good-looking I'm sure I know you."

Late in the afternoon Stephenson had *Triton* take him to a certain spot off the beach. Instructing Irving not to move, he explained he was going ashore to look for Lord Gort. If he brought back the General, Irving was to take him straight to England. With that, Stephenson plunged over the side and waded ashore through the surf, often up to his neck in water.

In an hour he was back, again wading through the surf, but there was no sign of Lord Gort. Stephenson offered no explanation, nor did Irving ask. They simply went back to their rescue work, the Commodore still hatless and soaked to the skin. Along with his words of cheer for the troops, he had plenty to say to Irving himself. Sometimes the lieutenant was a "good fellow"; other times, "a bloody fool." Irving didn't mind. He'd do anything for a senior officer like this.

Off Bray-Dunes to the west, the *Constant Nymph* was hard at work too. At first Basil Smith, her accountant-skipper, could find only French troops. These he ferried out to the skoot *Jutland*, which was serving as a "mother ship." Then a British army officer swam out to say there was a whole division of the BEF waiting a little farther west. Smith shifted his boat slightly and began picking them up.

It was never easy. On top of all the other problems, the Germans were now within artillery range, and began shelling the beach. East of La Panne an enemy observation balloon rode unmolested in the sky directing the fire. Smith was one of the few who didn't seem disturbed. As he later explained, he was deaf and had a lot to do.

Off Malo-les-Bains the *Ryegate II* was having less success. Coming over from Ramsgate, her engines broke down; then it turned out she drew too much water to get close to the beach; finally she fouled her propeller on some piece of wreckage. Disgusted, her skipper Sub-Lieutenant D. L. Satterfield tied up to the skoot *Horst* and assigned his crew to a couple of ship's boats.

Bob Hilton and Ted Shaw, the pair who had brought *Ryegate II* down the Thames, manned the *Horst*'s own lifeboat. As they pulled toward the shore, they could hear the skoot's radio blaring away. It was incongruously tuned into the BBC's "Children's Hour."

Coming through the surf, Hilton and Shaw were immediately mobbed and capsized. Gradually they learned the art of successful ferry-work. Basically, it consisted of getting close enough to pick up men, but not so close as to be swamped. For seventeen straight hours they rowed, side by side, carrying troops to the *Horst*.

Hour after hour the little ships worked the beaches, returning to Ramsgate only when they could find no more fuel, or when the crews were too tired to carry on. Then they discovered that the trip home could be perilous too. The motor launch *Silver Queen* had neither charts nor compass, but the crew felt they had a good idea where England was, and they headed that way.

Halfway over they found a soldier's compass, and this increased their confidence. Finally they sighted land, and then a friendly-looking harbor. Approaching the breakwater, they were greeted by a blast of gunfire. Hopelessly twisted around, they had stumbled into Calais by mistake.

Six batteries of German guns pounded away as *Silver Queen* frantically reversed course. One round crashed into her stern; another landed on the starboard bow. The Belgian launch *Yser*, traveling in company, was hit too. Someone on the *Yser* fired a Very pistol in a desperate call for help. Amazingly, a friendly destroyer did catch the signal, hurried over, and provided covering fire while the two strays crept out of range. Somehow *Silver Queen* limped back to Ramsgate, discharged a load of troops, and then quietly sank at her pier.

For most of the little ships, the time of greatest danger was not going over or coming back; it was at the beach itself. Even when the troops behaved perfectly, the boats were in constant danger of capsizing. The sea was still smooth, but the wind was veering to the east and the surf began rising. The loading went more slowly than ever.

At La Panne, Lieutenant Harold J. Dibbens of the Military Police had been puzzling over the loading problem ever since reaching the beach the previous afternoon. Unlike most of the BEF, Dibbens was thoroughly at home on the sea. He grew up on the Isle of Wight—always around boats—and even served a hitch in the Navy before settling into his career as a detective at Scotland Yard. When war came, his professional experience won him a direct commission in the Military Police, and until "the balloon went up" he spent most of his time fighting pilferage and chasing black marketeers. The great retreat ended all that, and now here he was, with the remnants of 102nd Provost Company, waiting on the beach like so many others.

Watching the confusion at the water's edge—some boats overturning, others drifting away untended—Dibbens decided that the biggest need at the moment was a pier or jetty stretching out to sea. Then the boats could come alongside and be loaded far more efficiently. But where to find the materials for such a jetty? His eye fell on the mass of abandoned trucks and lorries that littered the beach. Now all he needed was a little manpower.

"Want a sapper unit! Need a sapper unit!" Dibbens shouted, stalking through the dunes, where many of the troops were waiting. He was acting on his own initiative—had no authority at all—but it was a time when resourcefulness was what counted, and a colonel would listen to a corporal, if his idea was good enough.

Captain E. H. Sykes of the 250th Field Company, Royal Engineers, stepped forward. What was wanted? Dibbens couldn't order the Captain to do anything, but he suggested a deal: his own men would provide a supply of lorries, if Sykes's men would use them to build a jetty out into the sea. As a "sweetener" the sappers could be the first group to use the completed jetty.

Sykes agreed and detailed 2nd Lieutenant John S. W. Bennett's section to do the construction. These men threw themselves into the job with amazing enthusiasm, considering their mood until now. They had just completed a long march to the coast, and the last night had been hell. They had lost many of their officers somewhere in the dark, and most of the company just melted away. Normally 250 strong, they were down to 30 or 40 by the time they reached La Panne.

Lieutenant Bennett was one of the few officers who stuck with them all the way. He did his best, but in peacetime he was on the Faculty of Fine Art at Cambridge, and what they wanted right now was a professional soldier. There was a lot of grumbling, until in exasperation he finally told them, "If you want me to lead you, I'll lead you; if you want me to leave you, I'll leave you."

"Frankly, I don't give a damn what you do," someone called out from the ranks.

But the art professor was a better leader than they realized. The men were soon working flat-out. They lined up the lorries side by side, leading into the sea. They loaded them with sandbags and shot out the tires to keep them in place. They scavenged timber from a lumberyard for staging. They ripped decking from stranded ships for a plank walkway. They even added the touch of a rope railing.

When they began the tide was out, but now it came rolling in. Soon the men were up to their waists in the surf, lashing the lorries with cable. Sometimes they had to hold the jetty together by linking arms until a lashing could be made. Buffeted by the surf, they were soaked to the skin and covered with oil and grease.

The men of 102nd Provost Company had been good scavengers—sometimes too good. At one point an irate brigadier stormed up to Dibbens. Somebody had stolen four lorries he had earmarked for use as ambulances. Dibbens expressed appropriate dismay, said he couldn't imagine who could have done a thing like that, and quietly replaced the missing lorries with four others stolen from somebody else.

The "provost jetty," as it came to be called, was finished during the afternoon of May 30 and proved a huge success. All evening, and all the next day, a steady stream of men used it to board the growing fleet of small boats and launches engaged in ferry work. Ironically, Bennett's men were not among them. Corps headquarters decided that they had done such a splendid job, they now must maintain it. Down the drain went the promise that they would be the first "customers." Instead, they learned the hard way the old military maxim: never do a task too well, or you'll be stuck with it forever.

Later there would be considerable speculation over who first thought of the jetty. Besides Lieutenant Dibbens, credit has been given to Commodore Stephenson, Commander Richardson, and General Alexander, among others. Curiously, all these claims may be valid. It seems to have been one of those ideas "whose time had come," for examination of Luftwaffe photographs shows that no fewer than ten different lorry jetties were slapped together on May 30–31 between Malo-les-Bains and La Panne.

This in turn meant there were many builders besides the long-suffering 250th Field Company. One such unit was A Squadron of the 12th Lancers, who built a jetty about three miles west of La Panne. They were anything but experienced in this sort of work—they were an armored reconnaissance unit—but the perimeter was now fully manned, and all surplus fighting troops were being funneled to the beaches.

With the regulars moving in, there was a striking improvement in discipline. At Bray-Dunes Commanders Kerr and Richardson had their first easy night. As Kerr explained a little unkindly, they were at last dealing with "real officers."

The long shadow of tradition was now very much in evidence. When Colonel Lionel H. M. Westropp ordered the 8th King's Own Royal Regiment to head down the beach toward the mole, he first assembled his officers. He reminded them that they wore the badge of one of the oldest regiments of the line. "We therefore will represent the Regiment as we march down the beach this afternoon. We must not let it down, and we must set an example to the rabble on the beach."

The battalion set off in perfect step, arms swinging in unison, rifles correctly slung, officers and NCO's properly spaced. The "rabble on the beach" were suitably impressed.

Nineteen-year-old 2nd Lieutenant William Lawson of the Royal Artillery knew that appearances were important, but he felt he had a good excuse for looking a little scruffy. His artillery unit had been badly mauled on the Dyle, again at Arras, and had barely made it back to the perimeter—two rough weeks almost always on the run.

Now at last he was at La Panne, and it was the Navy's turn to worry. Wandering down the beach, he suddenly spied a familiar face. It was his own father, Brigadier the Honorable E. F. Lawson, temporarily serving on General Adam's staff. Young Lawson had no idea his father was even in northern France. He rushed up and saluted.

"What do you mean looking like that!" the old Brigadier thundered. "You're bringing dishonor to the family! Get a haircut and shave at once!"

The son pointed out that at the moment he couldn't possibly comply. Lawson brushed this aside, announcing that his own batman, a family servant in prewar days, would do the job. And so he did—a haircut and shave right on the sands of Dunkirk.

At the mole Commander Clouston had standards, too. Spotting one of the shore patrol with hair far longer than it could have grown in the last three or four days, he ordered the man to get it cut.

"All the barbers are shut, sir," came the unruffled reply. Clouston still insisted. Finally, the sailor drew his bayonet and hacked off a lock. "What do you want me to do with it now," he asked, "put it in a locket?"

Under the Commander's firm leadership, the mole continued

to operate all day, May 30. A steady stream of destroyers, mine-sweepers, Channel steamers, and trawlers pulled alongside, loaded up, and were off again. For one two-hour stretch, Clouston had the troops trotting out the walkway on the double. He embarked over 24,000 during the afternoon and evening.

Clouston's efforts got a big assist from a major policy reversal engineered in Dover. Early afternoon Admiral Ramsay phoned Admiral Pound in London, insisting that the modern destroyers be put back on the job. They were absolutely essential if he was to get everybody off in the time he had left. After a heated exchange, Pound finally relented. At 3:30 p.m. orders went out, sending the destroyers back to France.

German batteries were now firing on Dunkirk harbor from Gravelines, but the mole lay just out of range. German planes made occasional hit-and-run attacks on the shipping, but Kesselring's great fleets of bombers remained grounded. In sharp contrast to yesterday's fear and confusion, today the mood was cheerfully relaxed. While the *Malcolm* loaded some Cameron Highlanders, her navigator Lieutenant Mellis played his bag-pipes on the foc'sle. As one party of Royal Dragoon Guards moved along the walkway, a big Royal Marine stood ladling out hot stew. One Dragoon officer had no cup, but he did produce a long-stemmed cocktail glass picked up somewhere. The Marine filled it with gravy, solemnly inquiring, "Can I put a cherry in it, sir?"

But the greatest change was on the beaches. Discipline continued to improve; the columns of waiting men were quiet and orderly; the ever-growing stream of little ships methodically ferried the troops to the larger vessels lying offshore. As Captain Arthur Marshall's twelve-man internal security unit patiently waited their turn, a colonel bustled over. Apparently worried that the unit had nothing to do, he ordered the men to "tidy up the beach a bit."

At first Marshall felt the colonel must be joking; but no, he was dead serious. The smaller the mess they left, he explained, the less likely the Germans would think that the BEF had left precipitously. The result would decrease the enemy's feeling of triumph, thereby helping the war effort.

Finally convinced that the colonel meant what he said, Marshall's party glumly went to work—piling abandoned overcoats here, stowing empty crates there, neatly coiling stray lengths of rope. They kept at it as long as the colonel was in sight.

Overall, May 30 proved a very good day. Thanks to better discipline, the lorry jetties, and above all, the surge of little ships, the number of men lifted from the beaches rose from 13,752 on the 29th to 29,512 on the 30th. A total of 53,823 men were evacuated on this gray, misty day—much the highest daily figure so far.

Casualties were mercifully light. Thanks to the heavy overcast, the rescue fleet streamed across the Channel unchallenged by the Stukas and Heinkels. First loss of the day came when the French destroyer *Bourrasque*, bound for Dover, struck a floating mine. Nearby ships saved all but 150 of her troops.

Later, during the night of May 30–31, another French destroyer, *Siroco*, was torpedoed by S-boats lurking off Kwinte Buoy. For a while her skipper, Gui de Toulouse-Lautrec (cousin of the painter), thought he might save his ship, but she let off a huge cloud of steam which attracted the attention of a passing German patrol bomber. A bomb crashed down on the vessel's stern, igniting her ready ammunition. A column of flame shot 200 feet into the sky, and *Siroco* was gone.

But most of the ships reached England safely, landing their ragged passengers in Dover and other southeast coast ports. Herded toward waiting trains, their ordeal was mirrored in their faces—unshaven, hollow-eyed, oil-streaked, infinitely weary. Many had lost their equipment; but some clutched odd, new possessions picked up along the way. A pair of wooden sabots dangled from Private Fred Louch's gas mask . . . a French poilu carried a live goose . . . Bombardier Arthur May still had 6,000 of his 10,000 cigarettes . . . 2nd Lieutenant R. C. Taylor's batman had somehow rescued the Lieutenant's portable gramophone. Along with the men, the inevitable dogs trooped ashore—170 in Dover alone.

Everything about this motley crowd said "evacuation," but until now there had been a news blackout. With the men pouring home, this was no longer possible; so on the evening of the 30th London finally issued a communiqué announcing the withdrawal. It was, the *Times* sniffed, "what so many people in this country have seen with their own eyes."

Among the thousands of soldiers brought back, a select few

had been carefully hand-picked. Whatever else happened, Lord Gort hoped to get enough good men home to form the nucleus of a new army that might some day return and even the score. General Pownall, Gort's Chief of Staff, left on the evening of May 29th, as did the Commander-in-Chief's personal aide, Lord Munster. Now, on the 30th, it was General Brooke's turn. After a lunch of *petit poussin* and asparagus, miraculously conjured up by his aide, Captain Barney Charlesworth, he paid a final visit to his division commanders.

It was not easy. Brooke was known as a brilliant but rather cold man; this afternoon he was all emotion. Saying good-bye to General Montgomery, who would take over the Corps, he broke into tears. Monty patted him on the back, said all the right things. Finally they shook hands, and Brooke trudged slowly away.

One man absolutely determined not to leave was Lord Gort. The General's decision became known in London on the morning of May 30, when Lord Munster arrived from the beaches. Winston Churchill was taking a bath at the time, but he could do business anywhere, and he summoned Munster for a tub-side chat. It was in this unlikely setting that Munster described Gort's decision to stay to the end. He would never leave without specific orders.

Churchill was appalled at the thought. Why give Hitler the propaganda coup of capturing and displaying the British Commander-in-Chief? After discussing the matter with Eden, Dill, and Pownall, he wrote out in his own hand an order that left Gort no choice:

> If we can still communicate we shall send you an order to return to England with such officers as you may choose at the moment when we deem your command so reduced that it can be handed over to a corps commander. You should now nominate this commander. If communications are broken, you are to hand over and return as specified when your effective fighting force does not exceed the equivalent of three divisions. This is in accordance with correct military procedure, and no personal discretion is left you in the matter.

Whoever Gort appointed was to fight on, "but when in his judgment no further organised evacuation is possible and no further proportionate damage can be inflicted on the enemy, he is authorised in consultation with the senior French commander to capitulate formally to avoid useless slaughter."

These instructions reached Gort during the afternoon, and he read them aloud at a final GHQ conference that assembled in his beachfront villa at 6:00 p.m. Besides General Barker, commanding I Corps, and Monty, now in charge of II Corps, the meeting included Brooke, who had not yet pushed off. The final plans for the evacuation were discussed: I Corps would be the last to go, and its commander, Barker, would take over from Gort as directed by London.

As the meeting broke up, Montgomery lingered behind and asked to see Gort privately for a moment. Once they were alone, Monty unburdened himself. It would be a dreadful mistake, he said, to leave Barker in charge at the end. The man was no longer fit to command. The proper course was to send Barker home and appoint instead the 1st Division commander, Major-General Harold Alexander. He had just the calm, clear mind needed for this crisis. With luck, he might even get the rear guard back safely to England.

Gort listened but didn't commit himself.

Down on the beach General Brooke prepared to go. Usually a rather snappy dresser, he had discarded his new Huntsman breeches and Norwegian boots for a pair of old slacks and shoes. More practical, in case he had to go swimming. But he didn't have to swim at all. Instead he rode piggy-back out to a rowboat on the broad shoulders of the faithful Charlesworth. By 7:20 he was on his way to a waiting destroyer.

Around 8:00 a new visitor turned up at GHQ. Admiral Wake-Walker had come to see Lord Gort. With the small craft starting to pour in, he wanted to work out better coordination with the army. During the past few days, all too often the available ships weren't where the troops were, and vice versa.

Gort greeted him warmly. The Commander-in-Chief and his staff were about to have dinner; Wake-Walker must join them. They moved into a longish dining room with French windows opening on the sea. The conversation was mostly small talk, and as he sat there sharing the General's last bottle of champagne, Wake-Walker found it a remarkable experience. They were on the brink of the greatest military disaster in British history, yet here they sat, chatting idly and sipping champagne as though it were just another social evening at the seashore. Only one thing seemed out of the ordinary: his trousers were soaking wet from wading ashore.

Gort was charm itself, cheerful and unperturbed. He assured the Admiral that just by being here he would have a great stabilizing effect. Wake-Walker found it hard to believe that the mere presence of a desk-bound sailor like himself could prove so inspirational.

After a final dish of fruit salad, they got down to business. It soon became clear to Wake-Walker that Gort and his staff felt that their part of the job was done. They had gotten the BEF to the coast more or less intact; now it was up to the Royal Navy to get them home—and so far, the Navy hadn't tried very hard.

Wake-Walker said any lack of success was not through want of trying. He stressed the difficulty of lifting large numbers of men off the beaches and urged that more troops be shifted down to Dunkirk, where they could use the mole. Brigadier Leese remained unconvinced. The Army had marched enough. The ships should go where the men were. It should be perfectly possible to take men off the beaches . . . except for the "ineptitude of the Navy."

Wake-Walker bristled. He told Leese he had no business or justification to talk that way.

The discussion turned to getting the rear guard off. No matter how the others were evacuated, this was going to be a tight squeak. The Germans were pressing Nieuport and Furnes hard, and it didn't seem possible to hold the eastern end of the perimeter beyond the night of May 31–June 1. It was hoped to get everybody else off during the day, then quickly pull the rear guard back to the beaches at midnight. Ramsay had promised to make a supreme effort and was sending a whole new armada of small craft to lie off the coast. With luck they would be where needed, and the rear guard would swarm aboard before the enemy could interfere.

It was a very demanding timetable. Apart from the rear

guard, estimated at 5,000, there were tens of thousands of other troops to come off beforehand. Wake-Walker's heart sank at the prospect. The thought of that last-minute rush for the boats in the dark, with the enemy in hot pursuit, was not a pleasant picture.

By 10:00 p.m. they had talked themselves out. Wake-Walker headed back for the destroyer *Worcester*, which he was using at the moment as a flagship. Going down to the beach, he found a large inflated rubber boat, and recruited eight soldiers to paddle him out. As Tennant and Leese watched from the shore, they started off, but the boat was too crowded and began to swamp. They all jumped out and waded back to the beach for a new try with fewer paddlers. "Another example of naval ineptitude," Wake-Walker dryly told Leese.

Back at GHQ the staff prepared a situation report for the War Office, which went off at 11:20 p.m. It reported that the six remaining divisions in the beachhead were being thinned out tonight, and the eastern end of the perimeter should be completely clear some time tomorrow night, May 31–June 1. Evacuation of the rest of the BEF was proceeding satisfactorily. The report didn't say, but at the present pace, the lift should be complete by the end of June 1.

Thirty-nine minutes later, at 11:59, the Chief of the Imperial General Staff, General Dill, phoned from London. Gort assured him that the night was quiet . . . that all was going well on the beaches. Dill brushed this aside and got to the real purpose of his call. The Prime Minister wanted him to get off as many French as possible—not just a "fair" number, but an *equal* number. Winston Churchill himself came on the phone and confirmed the order.

It was an astonishing development. Instead of winding up the evacuation with a last-minute lift of a small rear guard on June 1, the whole French Army was now involved. Nobody—absolutely nobody—knew how many that meant, but it was clear that all the careful calculations and timetables worked out during the day were now meaningless.

10

"Bras-Dessus, Bras-Dessous!"

"Let's help the Froggies, too," Bob Hilton suggested to Ted Shaw as they began their seventeen-hour stint, rowing troops from the beach to the ships lying off Malo-les-Bains. Shaw agreed, and from then on, they never worried whether a soldier was French or English. Both were on the same side. It seemed simple enough.

Higher up, it wasn't that easy. When the evacuation began, the Admiralty simply assumed that British troops would be taken off in British ships, French troops in French ships. That was the way everything else had been done. Each of the Allies had conducted its own retreat to the coast, then manned its own part of the perimeter. In the same spirit the British had made their own decision to evacuate. Reynaud had been informed, and now it was up to the French to do the same.

As for the French, at this point they weren't even thinking evacuation. On May 19, the day Weygand took over, Admiral Darlan told Supreme Headquarters that such a step could lead only to "disaster." Darlan preferred to hold on to the beachhead, turn it into a continuing threat to the German flank. It was with this thought in mind that Captain Auphan began rounding up hundreds of French trawlers. They were to supply the beachhead, not evacuate it. In Dunkirk Admiral Abrial faith-fully reflected the same point of view.

The French finally faced reality on May 27, when Auphan, Admiral Leclerc, and Admiral Odend'hal met with Ramsay at Dover Castle. They had come to discuss supplying Dunkirk, only to discover that the British were already leaving. Now the French would have to catch up. Auphan's trawlers could be used, but they weren't remotely enough. Few French warships were available; most were stationed in the Mediterranean by ar-rangement with the Royal Navy.

An agreement was hastily hammered out between the French officers and Admiral Ramsay. Paragraph 5 declared that "all na-val means for evacuation shall be shared between Dover and Dunkerque." This was admittedly vague, but to the French it seemed to promise at least some access to British shipping.

They soon learned what "sharing" could mean. When Bel-gium surrendered on May 28, General Champon, head of the French mission to King Leopold, made his way to La Panne. With him came the mission staff, numbering 100 to 150 men. They were a hand-picked lot, and the Allied area commander General Georges ordered "immediate evacuation." Champon asked Lord Gort for space on some British ship.

Gort fired off a telegram to the War Office asking confirma-tion from Brigadier Swayne, British liaison officer at French Su-preme Headquarters. "Swayne should point out," Gort added helpfully, "every Frenchman embarked is a loss of one English-man." Why this argument would be persuasive at French head-quarters, Gort didn't say. But he did offer a final suggestion: "Why not send a French destroyer, using own boats?"

The next day—Wednesday, the 29th—found Champon and his staff still stranded at La Panne. General Georges again urged Gort to act, and Brigadier Swayne followed up with a telephone call to General Pownall, Gort's Chief of Staff. Pow-nall reported that orders had been issued covering Champon and "some of his officers," then asked rather pointedly if this mission was meant to have top priority, "thus displacing an equal number of British troops?"

No, said Swayne, he was certain that wasn't what Georges meant. The General just wanted to make sure that the Champon mission had equal status with the British.

The problem dragged on. Thirty-six more hours would pass before Champon finally got off at 8:00 p.m., May 30.

If it was that hard to make room for 100 hand-picked men, the prospects weren't bright for the thousands of ordinary poilus now pouring into the perimeter. From the south came remnants of the French First Army . . . from the east, the badly mauled 60th Division . . . from the west, the 68th Division retiring from Gravelines—all converging on the beaches at once. They were in for a long wait: on May 29 over 47,000 men were evacuated, but only 655 were French.

Winston Churchill understood both the arithmetic and the political ramifications. On the 29th he addressed a memo to Anthony Eden and to Generals Dill and Ismay:

> It is essential that the French should share in such evacuations from Dunkirk as may be possible. Nor must they be dependent only upon their own shipping resources. Arrangements must be concerted at once . . . so that no reproaches, or as few as possible, may arise.

Meanwhile General Georges appealed again to Lord Gort. This time his message concerned not just the Champon mission, but all the troops now gathering on the beaches. As relayed over the telephone by the accommodating Brigadier Swayne, Georges urged that the evacuation be carried out by the British and the French "with mutual co-operation and support."

"I am quite prepared to cooperate," Gort wired General Dill in London, "but support—by which is implied resources—is all on our side. Strongly urge that the French should take their full share in providing naval facilities."

This of course ignored the fact that the French had very little in the way of "naval facilities," with their fleet down in the Mediterranean. Pointing out that he had already evacuated "small parties of French," Gort once again reminded London: "Every Frenchman embarked is at the cost of one Englishman." His instructions said that the safety of the BEF came first. In light of that, he asked, what *was* the government's policy toward the French?

General Dill wrestled with this for some hours, finally wired Gort a little lamely that the safety of the BEF still came first, but he should try to evacuate "a proportion" of French troops.

In London that night, Churchill remained uneasy. Despite his directive, there was little evidence that the French were sharing in the evacuation. At 11:45 p.m. he shot off another telegram, this time for Reynaud, Weygand, and Georges:

> We wish French troops to share in evacuation to full-est possible extent, and Admiralty have been instruct-ed to aid French Marine as required. We do not know how many will be forced to capitulate, but we must share this loss together as best we can, and, above all, bear it without reproaches arising from inevitable confusion, stresses, and strains.

At this moment Admiral Wake-Walker, crossing the Channel to take charge offshore, had a very different view of Admiralty policy. Before leaving, he had been briefed by Admiral Pound, the First Sea Lord. Pound had told him that the French were not thought to be pulling their weight; he was to "refuse them embarkation, if British troops were ready to embark."

Next morning, May 30, Churchill summoned the three Service Ministers and the Chiefs of Staff to a meeting in the Admiralty War Room. An important guest was General Pownall, just back from La Panne. Once again the Prime Minister stressed the importance of getting off more French troops.

Pownall spoke up, defending the present figures. As usual, he trotted out the familiar argument: so long as the French did not produce ships of their own, "every Frenchman embarked meant one more Englishman lost."

Pownall felt that he had forced Churchill to face an "inconvenient truth," but the Prime Minister had been hearing this argument for two days now, and if he showed displeasure, it more likely stemmed from exasperation.

More phone talks with Gort followed during the day. At 4:20 p.m. General Dill confirmed that Gort's first consideration was the safety of the BEF, but he must also do his best to send off a "fair proportion" of the French. At 8:10 p.m. the War Office again notified Brigadier Swayne that French troops were to share in the evacuation "to fullest possible extent."

Then came Admiral Ramsay's figures for the total number rescued during the day: British 45,207; French 8,616.

Clearly phrases such as "fair share," "fullest possible extent," and "fair proportion" could mean what anybody wanted them to mean—thousands of troops, or just one soldier. If the French were really to share the British ships, the orders would have to be far more precise. It was almost midnight, May 30, when Churchill finally faced the matter squarely.

"British and French troops must now evacuate in approximately equal numbers," General Dill stressed in his telephone call to Gort, relaying the Prime Minister's new orders. Lest there be any misunderstanding, Dill repeated the instructions three different times in the conversation. When Churchill himself came on the wire, the Prime Minister emphasized that the whole future of the alliance was at stake.

He was right. Paris was full of rumors and recriminations these days, mostly to the effect that the British were running home, leaving the French holding the bag. Hoping to clear up any misunderstandings, Churchill flew to Paris the following morning, May 31, for a meeting of the Allied Supreme War Council. Accompanied by General Dill and a few top aides, he was met at the airport by his personal representative to Reynaud, Major-General Sir Edward Spears, who had been bearing the brunt of the French complaints these past few days.

At 2:00 p.m. the British and French leaders met at the Ministry of War on the rue Saint-Dominique. Joining the group for the first time was Marshal Pétain, an ancient gloomy figure in civilian clothes. General Weygand was there too, wearing a huge pair of riding boots that made him look, General Spears felt, like Puss in Boots. The French sat on one side of a large baize-covered table; the British on the other. Through the tall, open windows lay a garden basking in the sunshine. It was another of those glorious spring days—so many this year—that seemed to mock these grim statesmen and generals trying to ward off disaster.

Churchill opened the meeting on a cheerful note. The evacuation, he reported, was going far better than anyone had dared hope. As of noon this day, 165,000 men had been lifted off.

"But how many French?" Weygand asked sharply. The Prime Minister dodged a direct answer for the moment: "We are companions in misfortune. There is nothing to be gained from recrimination over our common miseries."

But the question wouldn't go away. After a brief survey of the Norwegian campaign, the discussion came back to Dunkirk, and it turned out that of the 165,000 evacuated, only 15,000 were French. Churchill did his best to explain this awkward disparity: many of the British were rear area troops already stationed near Dunkirk . . . the French had farther to come . . . if just the fighting divisions were counted, the disparity wasn't so bad.

Reynaud broke in. Whatever the reasons, the hard facts remained: of 220,000 British, 150,000 had been rescued: of 200,000 French, the number saved was only 15,000. He couldn't face public opinion at home with figures like these. Something had to be done to evacuate more French.

Churchill agreed and explained the new "equal numbers" directive. He also stressed that three British divisions still at Dunkirk would stand by the French until the evacuation was complete.

Darlan then drafted a telegram to Admiral Abrial in Bastion 32, describing the decisions taken by the Council. It mentioned that when the perimeter closed down, the British forces would embark first.

Churchill leapt to this feet. *"Non!"* he cried. *"Partage—bras-dessus, bras-dessous!"* His atrocious French accent was a legend, but this time there was no mistaking him. With dramatic gestures he vividly acted out an arm-in-arm departure.

Nor did he stop there. Emotionally carried away, he announced that the remaining British troops would form the rear guard. "So few French have got out so far," he declared, "I will not accept further sacrifices by the French."

This was a lot more than arm-in-arm, and to General Spears it was going too far. After more discussion, the final draft simply said that the British troops would act as rear guard "as long as possible." It also said that Abrial would be in overall command.

It was just as well that Lord Gort did not know of the Prime Minister's outburst. It was difficult enough to swallow the policy of "equal numbers." At least it wasn't retroactive. London agreed that the rule only applied *from now on*. Still, it could be costly. The War Office had instructed him to hang on longer, so that as many French as possible could be evacuated. But how long? This morning, May 31, everything pointed to a heavy German attack on Furnes. If he hung on too long just to save more Frenchmen, he might lose the whole Guard's Brigade.

He was still mulling over this problem when General Alexander—the calm, capable commander of the 1st Division—visited GHQ at 8:30 a.m. Gort glumly told him to thin out his division, since it looked as if he would have to surrender most of his men alongside the French. At least that was what the War Office's instructions seemed to mean.

At 9:00 a.m. Anthony Eden came on the phone with an interpretation of these orders that must have greatly eased Gort's mind. As Eden explained to Brigadier Leese:

> The instructions sent the previous night to hold on so as to enable the maximum number of Allied troops to be evacuated must be interpreted to mean that [Gort] should only do so as long as he was satisfied that he could continue to hold his position with the forces at his disposal, but he should not prejudice the safety of the remainder of his force by trying to hold his position beyond that time.

In other words, hanging on for the sake of evacuating an equal number of Frenchmen was desirable—as long as it was safe.

Enlightened, Gort now drove down to Dunkirk to meet with Admiral Abrial at 10:00 a.m. The Admiral was, as usual, in Bastion 32. Besides his staff of naval officers, he had with him General Fagalde, commander of the French military forces in the perimeter, and General de la Laurencie, who had just arrived with the only French troops to escape from the German trap at Lille.

Gort's sessions with Abrial were often strained. Tucked away in Bastion 32, the man never seemed to know what was going on. Today, all was cordial. Gort relayed the "equal numbers" policy, stated that he had already promised to evacuate 5,000 of de la Laurencie's men. Abrial said that Weygand preferred to use the space for some mechanized cavalry units, and de la Laurencie made no objection. Gort also offered the French equal access to the eastern mole. If it seemed a little odd for the British to be offering the French free use of a French facility in a French port, Abrial was tactful enough to keep silent.

Gort and Fagalde now exchanged full information on each other's positions along the perimeter—apparently the first time this had been done—and Gort announced that he had been ordered home. At this point General Blanchard turned up. Nominally the Army Group commander, these days he was virtually unemployed. Gort invited him and General de la Laurencie to accompany his own party to England. Both politely declined. As de la Laurencie put it: "My flag will remain planted on the Dunes, until the last of my men have embarked."

There were farewell toasts. Everyone promised to meet in France soon again.

Returning to La Panne, Gort summoned General Alexander to the seaside villa that served as GHQ. The Commander-in-Chief had reached a major decision: Alexander, not Barker, would take over after Gort's own departure for England. He never explained the switch. Perhaps he was impressed by Montgomery's fervent protest the previous evening, but the stolid Gort was not known to be easily influenced by the mercurial Monty.

In any case the orders were ready and waiting when Alexander arrived around 12:30 p.m. Technically, he would relieve Barker as Commanding Officer of I Corps, consisting of three rather depleted divisions. His orders were to "assist our French Allies in the defence of Dunkirk."

He would be serving under Abrial, as decided in Paris, but with an important escape clause added: "Should any order which he may issue to you be likely, in your opinion, to imperil the safety of your command, you should make an immediate appeal to His Majesty's Government."

That was all, as Gort originally dictated the orders to Colonel

Bridgeman, still acting as the General's Operations Officer. Yet there was an important omission. Gort had left out the War Office's instruction authorizing surrender "to avoid useless slaughter." Bridgeman felt it should be included, but didn't dare say so to his chief. Finally, he got a copy of London's original telegram, pointed to the passage in question, and asked whether he wanted it included, too. Gort said yes, and it was done. To the end they managed to avoid actually saying the dreaded word, "surrender."

Technically, Gort's orders would not take effect until 6:00 p.m., when GHQ was scheduled to close down. As a practical matter, they became operational almost right away. After a quick lunch, Alexander drove back to his headquarters and turned his division over to one of his brigadiers. Then he drove down to Dunkirk, accompanied by his Chief of Staff Colonel William Morgan and the ubiquitous Captain Tennant. At 2:00 p.m. they entered the candle-lit gloom of Bastion 32 for Alexander's first meeting with Admiral Abrial and General Fagalde.

It did not go well. Abrial planned to hold a reduced beachhead, running as far east as the Belgian border, with French troops on the right and a mixed French-British force under Alexander on the left. This force would act as a rear guard, holding the beachhead indefinitely while the rest of the Allied troops embarked. Then, presumably, the rear guard itself would scurry to safety at the last minute.

Alexander felt it would never work. Protracted resistance was impossible. The troops were in no condition to fight indefinitely. The proposed perimeter was too near the harbor and the beaches. Enemy artillery fire at short range would soon stop the evacuation completely. Instead, he proposed to wind up the evacuation as fast as possible, with the last troops pulling back to the beach the following night, June 1–2.

Abrial was unimpressed. If the British insisted on leaving anyhow, he added, "I am afraid the port will be closed."

Alexander decided it was time to invoke the escape clause in his orders. He announced that he would have to refer the matter to London. Then he drove back to La Panne, relieved to find that the telephone line was still open.

At 7:15 p.m. he managed to get through to Anthony Eden

and quickly explained the problem. An hour later Eden called
back with new and welcome instructions from the Cabinet:

> You should withdraw your force as rapidly as possible
> on a 50–50 basis with the French Army, aiming at
> completion by night of 1st/2nd June. You should in-
> form the French of this definite instruction.

The phrase "on a 50–50 basis with the French Army," Eden explained, did not require Alexander to make up for any past dis-
crepancies; it simply meant that equal numbers of French and
British troops must be withdrawn from now on. Supported by
the Cabinet, Alexander hurried back to Bastion 32.

Meanwhile, Abrial, too, had gone to his superiors. Wiring
Weygand, he protested that Alexander—who had been placed
under him—was refusing to follow instructions to fight on. Instead, the British commander planned to embark on the night
of June 1–2, whatever happened, "thus abandoning the defence
of Dunkirk."

Weygand could do little but buck the complaint to London.
At 9:00 p.m. he radioed Dill, Chief of the Imperial General
Staff, reminding him of the decisions reached by the Supreme
War Council that very afternoon. Paragraph 4 had specifically
put Abrial in charge.

The Admiral was still waiting for some word from Weygand,
when Alexander arrived back in Bastion 32 with the British
Cabinet's instructions. He announced that he would hold his
sector of the perimeter until 11:59 p.m., June 1—tomorrow
night—then would withdraw to the beaches under cover of
darkness. The French were welcome to come along and share
the British shipping, but whatever they did, he was pulling out.

Faced with no alternative, Abrial agreed.

It was now after 11:00 p.m. Alexander had shifted his headquarters to the outskirts of Dunkirk, but the roads were strange
and full of craters. It seemed safer to stay in Bastion 32 overnight, so he and Colonel Morgan curled up on the concrete
floor—as hard and as cold as relations were getting to be between the two great Allies.

Completely oblivious to all this high-level wrangling, an old soldier sat in his quarters at La Panne on the afternoon of May 31, snipping medal and campaign ribbons from a uniform blouse. General Gort was getting ready to go home. The evacuation was Alexander's headache now, and at the moment Gort's main concern was to see that no German soldier made a souvenir out of anything he had to leave behind.

He was to go at 6:00 p.m. Two separate plans had been made for his embarkation, and it was typical of these trying days that neither group of planners knew of the other's existence. Under one of these plans—developed by the Navy liaison at GHQ—four motor torpedo boats would dash over from Dover to pluck Gort and his staff off the beach. The orders were very vague. The commander of the little flotilla only knew that he was to pick up "a party." When he arrived, he checked with Admiral Wake-Walker, in charge offshore, for further directions.

Wake-Walker knew even less. No one had briefed him, and it never occurred to him that these motor torpedo boats had been sent to pick up the Commander-in-Chief. He thought that was *his* responsibility. He assigned the MTB's to courier chores and continued his own planning. Gort would leave his villa shortly after 6:00, going to a designated spot on the beach two miles west of La Panne. Here he and his staff would be met by a launch and taken out to the destroyer *Keith* lying offshore. The *Keith* would then run the party back to Dover. Commodore Stephenson would be in direct charge, with Wake-Walker himself supervising.

As planned, Gort's party left his villa at 6:00 p.m., but that was as far as they followed the script. For some reason the two staff cars carrying the group did not go to the designated rendezvous, but to a spot much closer to La Panne. This meant no small boats were waiting, and the departure from the beach became a very ragged affair. Ultimately Gort's staff wound up on the *Keith*, he himself on the minesweeper *Hebe*, and his batman, driver, and luggage all on the motor yacht *Thele*.

Safely aboard the *Hebe*, Gort went to the bridge to greet the skipper, Lieutenant-Commander J. S. Wemple. There was time for only the briefest exchange of niceties; then the sea, the sky, the ships all seemed to erupt with explosions. The weather had cleared, and the Luftwaffe was back—ten separate raids this evening. As the *Hebe*'s crew rushed to their gun stations, Gort learned how useless his role had at last become. He settled quietly in a corner of the bridge, raised his binoculars, and gazed absently around.

"Won't you go below and take cover, sir?" suggested Captain Eric Bush, one of Ramsay's coordinators working with Tennant and Wake-Walker.

"No, thank you, I'm quite happy where I am," the General replied politely. Finally the raid tapered off, and Gort—unruffled as ever—went below for a bite to eat.

The *Hebe* still did not head for England with her distinguished passenger. By now hundreds of ordinary soldiers were swarming aboard, delivered from the beaches by the ever-growing swarm of little ships. Wake-Walker decided to wait until she had a full load before sending her back.

Dover and London grew restless, then frantic. Seven hours had passed since the Admiralty had dispatched the four MTB's to pick up Gort, and still there was no sign of him. Those boats could do 40 knots; they should have been back long ago. Worse, the latest radio traffic indicated that the MTB's hadn't even been used to get the General. What had happened to him anyhow?

"Report immediately why MTB's sent for Commander-in-Chief were diverted to other duties," Admiral Phillips, the Vice-Chief of Naval Staff, radioed Wake-Walker at 11:36 p.m. "Take immediate action to embark Commander-in-Chief and report steps taken."

On the *Keith*, Wake-Walker sent one of the MTB's to the *Hebe* to get Gort, but he was no longer there. He had taken a launch, hoping to reach the *Keith*. A half-hour passed, and still no sign of the launch.

Now it was Wake-Walker's turn to agonize. The night was black; no lights showing. Had the launch missed the *Keith*? Was Gort out there somewhere drifting in the dark? Wake-Walker had visions of the disgrace that would be his if he botched this job and lost the Commander-in-Chief of the BEF.

It was after midnight, the opening minutes of June 1, when the launch finally loomed out of the dark. Gort climbed aboard the *Keith*, reunited at last with his staff.

But only briefly. He and Brigadier Leese quickly transferred to the speedboat *MA/SB 6* and headed for Dover. At 6:20 a.m. they landed at the Admiralty Pier, where Gort gulped a cup of tea and caught the next train to London.

Anthony Eden and members of the War Cabinet were on hand to greet him, but the little group passed almost unnoticed amid the crowds swirling around Victoria Station. By now bedraggled soldiers were tumbling off every train from the south coast into the waiting arms of friends and relatives. Gort seemed to be just one more of them. He was already a fading figure of the past.

Far more important than the escape of a discredited chieftain was the rescue on May 31 of 53,140 more men who could help form the nucleus of a new British Army.

Thousands of them used the lorry jetties that had been improvised at Bray-Dunes and La Panne. Despite the ingenuity of the builders, these were rickety affairs that heaved alarmingly in the surf and changing tides. Still, a steady stream of soldiers clambered out along the duck boards, dropping into the rowboats and launches that came alongside.

"Well, my lucky lad, can you row?" a sailor greeted Private Percy Yorke of the 145th Field Ambulance, as he tumbled into a boat. "No? Well, now's your time to bloody well learn." Yorke learned by doing, and managed to reach the excursion steamer *Princess Elizabeth*.

Major E. R. Nanney Wynn, 3rd Division Signals, reached the end of a jetty and peered down at a waiting motor whaler. Manning it, improbably, was a ship's steward immaculate in his short white jacket. It was almost like going Cunard.

Other troops made use of the growing mountain of debris that littered the beaches. Private C. N. Bennett of the 5th Northamptonshires came across a discarded army boat made of canvas. It was designed to carry six men across a river; now ten men jumped into it and headed across the sea. Using their rifles as paddles, they hoped to get to England. It was just as well that a motor launch soon spotted them and took them to the destroyer *Ivanhoe*.

Brigadier John G. Smyth, commanding the 127th Infantry Brigade, rallied nineteen men around a big ship's lifeboat stranded well up on the beach. A heavy, bulky thing, it required all their strength to shove it down to the water. Even then their troubles weren't over: it was a sixteen-oared boat, and not one of Smyth's recruits could row.

They shoved off anyhow, with Smyth at the tiller and the men at the oars. After a few strokes the "crew" began falling over backwards; the oars were tangled up; and the boat was turning in crazy circles. As he later recalled, "We must have looked like an intoxicated centipede."

There couldn't have been a worse time to give a lesson in basic rowing. The Luftwaffe chose this moment to stage one of its raids, and the Brigadier's instructions were punctuated by gunfire, exploding bombs, and geysers of water. The men tried again, this time with Smyth shouting out the stroke, "One-two, in-out!" The crew caught on, and the boat moved steadily toward a waiting destroyer. They even made a real race out of it, beating an overloaded motor launch carrying their division commander.

Farther along the beach, Private Bill Stratton of the RASC helped haul an abandoned lifeboat to the water's edge, then watched a stampede of men jump in and take it over. Determined not to let all his hard work go for nothing, Stratton made a flying leap and landed on top of the crowd. Predictably, the boat soon swamped. Stratton was a good swimmer, but his greatcoat dragged him down. He was about to go under when a navy launch appeared. Someone pulled him over the side and flung him down on the bottom, "like a fish."

Inevitably there were confrontations. Near Malo-les-Bains a column of wading men retrieved two small rowboats lying off-shore. Suddenly a voice called, "Halt, or I fire!" It was a Scots colonel heading up an adjoining column, and he clearly felt his men had first call on the boats. Finally, a compromise was worked out allowing both columns to use them.

Near La Panne, Yeoman Eric Goodbody set out in a whaler with eight naval signalmen from GHQ. As they shoved off, an officer on shore ordered him to bring back four soldiers who had also piled in. Goodbody refused—he was in charge of the whaler and everybody in her, he declared. The officer pulled a gun . . . Goodbody drew his . . . and for a moment the two stood face to face, aiming their pistols at each other. At this point the four soldiers quietly volunteered to go back, and another crisis was passed.

At Bray-Dunes Sapper Joe Coles was aroused by a friend who had found a large rowboat swamped and stranded on the beach. They bailed it out, then were hurled aside by a mob of soldiers piling in. About to swamp again, it was emptied by a Military Policeman at pistol point.

Order restored, Coles and his friend tried again. This time they shoved off safely and took a load of troops to a skoot, then headed back for another load. Dozens of men were swimming out to meet them, when they were hailed by an officer floating nearby on a raft. Brandishing his revolver, the officer ordered them to take him first. Coles felt the swimmers should have priority—the raft was in no trouble—but that pistol was very persuasive. The officer had his way.

One reason for frayed nerves was the state of the sea. For the first time since the evacuation began, the wind was blowing onshore, building up a nasty surf throughout the morning of May 31. The loading went more slowly than ever, and at Bray-Dunes Commander Richardson finally decided that nothing more could be done. He ordered the troops on the beach to head for Dunkirk: then he, Commander Kerr, and the naval shore party salvaged a stranded whaler, rounded up some oars, and began pulling for England.

They didn't realize how tired they were. Every stroke hurt. Soon they were barely moving, and they probably would have broached to and swamped; but the Margate lifeboat spotted them in time. It hurried over and picked them up.

At 10:35 a.m. Admiral Wake-Walker radioed the situation to Ramsay at Dover.

> Majority of pulling boats are broached to and have no crews: Conditions on beach very bad owing to freshening onshore wind. Only small numbers are being embarked even in daylight. Consider only hope of embarking any number is at Dunkirk. . . .

By "Dunkirk" he of course meant the eastern mole. For Tennant and his aides, the mole was more and more the answer to everything. They were constantly trying to concentrate the boat traffic in that direction. Ramsay knew its importance too, but he also guessed that there were still thousands to be evacuated, and everything had to be used—including the beaches, even though the going was slow.

At 11:05 a.m. Wake-Walker tried again. "Dunkirk our only real hope," he telegraphed Ramsay. "Can guns shelling pier from westward be bombed and silenced?"

This was a new problem. Until May 31, the German guns had been a nuisance, but that was all. Their aim was haphazard; the shells usually fell short. Now, batteries had been planted this side of Gravelines; and the result was soon apparent.

At 6:17 a.m. the minesweeper *Glen Gower* lay alongside the mole, ready to receive her first troops of the day. As the skipper Commander M.A.O. Biddneph waited on the bridge, he suddenly heard a whistling noise . . . then a bang, quickly followed by several more bangs. A mass of black fragments leapt up on the foredeck, just where the gunnery officer, Sub-Lieutenant Williams, was standing. At first Biddneph thought it must be a stick of bombs, but there wasn't a plane in the sky. Then he realized it was a salvo of shells, one of them piercing the deck exactly between Williams's feet. Miraculously, the gunnery officer wasn't touched, but twelve men were killed or wounded in the explosion below.

The mole itself continued to lead a charmed life. Since its discovery by the Luftwaffe on May 29 it had been bombed by Stukas, pounded by artillery, and battered by rescue ships coming alongside too heavily. Rammed by the minesweeper *King Orry*, the seaward tip was now cut off completely. Yet for most of its length, it remained usable. Here and there gaps appeared, but they were bridged with boards, doors, and ships' gangplanks. The loading went on.

Still, the dash to the waiting vessels was always unnerving. None felt it more than Private Alfred Baldwin of the Royal Artillery. He was carrying on his shoulders his friend Private Paddy Boydd, who had smashed a foot. Stumbling along the walkway, Baldwin came to a gaping hole, bridged by a single plank. Two sailors standing by said, "Take a run at it, mate," adding, "don't look down." Baldwin followed their advice, except that he did look down. Dark water swirled around the piles twenty feet below. Somehow he kept his balance, and another pair of sailors grabbed him at the far end, cheering him on: "Well done, keep going!"

He struggled on, panting and stumbling, until he ran into two more sailors, who helped him maneuver Boydd up the gangplank to a waiting ship. She turned out to be the Channel packet *Maid of Orleans*, the very same vessel that had brought him to France at the start of the war.

Baldwin made his dash when the tide was high. At low tide the mole could be even more trying. Corporal Reginald Lockerby reached the destroyer *Venomous*, only to find there was a fifteen-foot drop to the ship's deck. Several telegraph poles leaned against the side of the mole, and the troops were expected to slide down them to get aboard. Trouble was, neither ship nor poles had been made fast. Both were unpredictably swaying and heaving up and down. One slip meant falling into the sea and being crushed between boat and dock.

"I can't do it, Ern," Lockerby gasped to his friend Private Ernest Heming.

"Get down there, you silly sod, or I'll throw you down!" shouted Heming. "I'll hold the top of the pole for you."

Somehow Lockerby mustered the strength and courage. He slid down the pole, then held it from the bottom as Heming followed.

No French troops were yet using the mole, but starting May 31, the new policy of equal numbers was very much in evidence along the beaches. When the motor yacht *Marsayru* arrived from Sheerness about 4:00 p.m., her first assignment was to help lift a large number of French waiting at Malo-les-Bains. The yacht's civilian skipper G. D. Olivier sent in his whaler, but it was stormed by about 50 poilus, and immediately capsized. He edged farther east, "where the French troops appeared to be a little calmer," and tried again. This time no problem, and over the next 48 hours he lifted more than 400 French soldiers.

Nearby a small flotilla of Royal Navy minesweeping craft was doing its bit. The *Three Kings* picked up 200 Frenchmen . . . the *Jackeve*, 60 . . . the *Rig*, another 60. The same sort of thing was happening at Bray-Dunes and La Panne.

How many French troops remained to be evacuated under

this policy of equal numbers? Neither Paris nor Admiral Abrial in Bastion 32 seemed to have any idea. To the weary organizers of the rescue fleet in London and Dover, it didn't make much difference. They were already sending everything that could float. . . .

In all her working years the 78-foot *Massey Shaw* had never been to sea. She was a Thames fire boat—or "fire float," as Londoners preferred to say—and until now her longest voyage had been down the river to fight a blaze at Ridham. She had no compass, and her crew were professional firemen, not sailors.

But the *Massey Shaw* drew only 3.9 feet, and to the Admiralty this was irresistible. There was also a vague notion that she might come in handy fighting the fires sweeping Dunkirk harbor, an idea that conveys less about her effectiveness than it does about the innocence still prevailing in some quarters at the Admiralty.

A call for volunteers went out on the afternoon of May 30. Thirteen men were picked, with Sub-Officer A. J. May in charge, and in two hours the *Massey Shaw* was on her way. There had barely been time to buy a small marine compass. On the trip down the river, the crew busied themselves boarding up the cabin windows and dabbing gray paint on the various brass fittings and hose nozzles. The situation must be serious indeed: the *Massey Shaw*'s bright work had always been sacred.

At Ramsgate she picked up water and a young Royal Navy sub-lieutenant with a chart. Then across the Channel with the additional help of a pocket tide table that somebody found. Arriving off Bray-Dunes late in the afternoon of May 31, the crew studied the beach with fascination. At first glance it looked like any bank holiday weekend—swarms of people moving about or sitting in little knots on the sand. But there was one big difference: instead of the bright colors of summer, everybody was dressed in khaki. And what first appeared to be "breakwaters" running down into the surf turned out to be columns of men, also dressed in khaki.

The *Massey Shaw* sent in a rowboat toward one of the columns. It was promptly swamped and sunk by the troops piling in. Then a stranded RAF speedboat was salvaged in the hope it might be used, but 50 men crowded aboard, putting it out of action too. Toward 11:00 p.m. still another boat was found. A line was now strung between the *Massey Shaw* and the beach, and the new boat was pulled back and forth along this line, rather like a sea-going trolley car. The boat carried only six men at a time, but back and forth it went, ferrying load after load.

Finally the *Massey Shaw* could hold no more. There were now 30 men packed in the cabin, which had seemed crowded with six the night before. Dozens more sprawled on the deck; there didn't seem to be a square foot of empty space.

It was dark when the *Massey Shaw* finally weighed anchor and started back for Ramsgate. So far, she had led a charmed life. The Luftwaffe was constantly overhead, but not a plane had attacked. Now, as she got under weigh, her screws kicked up a phosphorescent wake that caught the attention of some sharp-eyed enemy pilot. He swooped down and dropped a single bomb. It was close, but a miss. The *Massey Shaw* continued safely on her way, bringing home another 65 men.

Like the *Massey Shaw*, the Tilbury Dredging Company's steam hopper dredge *Lady Southborough* had never been to sea. Plucked from rust-streaked obscurity in Portsmouth harbor, she checked in at Ramsgate, then set out for Dunkirk with three other Tilbury hoppers early on the morning of May 31. Arriving at 12:30 p.m., *Lady Southborough* anchored off Malo-les-Bains, lowered her port lifeboat with three hands, and began lifting troops off the beach.

As the *Lady Southborough* hovered several hundred yards offshore, a German plane dropped a stick of four bombs. No hits, but they lifted the ship's lifeboat clear out of the water and whacked it down again, springing every plank. Nobody was hurt, but the boat was finished. Seeing that it was ebb tide, skipper Anthony Poole now drove *Lady Southborough* head-first onto the beach, so that he could pick up the troops directly from the water. They swarmed out, and one Frenchman—who evidently had not heard of the new British policy of equal numbers—offered to pay acting Second Mate John Tarry to get aboard.

Nearby, another Tilbury hopper dredge, *Foremost 101*, lay at anchor. The usual signs of disorder were everywhere: boats swamped by the surf . . . others sinking under the weight of too many men . . . others drifting about without oars or oarsmen. Amid this chaos was a single note of serenity. A petty officer had found a small child's canoe in some boating pond ashore. Now he was ferrying soldiers one by one out to the waiting ships. As he threaded his way through the debris, none of the swimmers ever bothered him. By common consent he seemed to have a *laissez-passer* to work in peace, without interference.

Going home in the dark was the hardest part. As *Lady Southborough* groped uncertainly through the night, a destroyer loomed up, flashing a signal. None of the dredge's crew could read Morse; so there was no answer. The destroyer flashed again; still no answer. Finally one of the soldiers on board said he was a signalman: could he help? Some more flashes, and the soldier announced that the destroyer had now demanded their identity three times; if they didn't answer at once, she would blow them out of the water. Watching the signalman flash back the ship's name, Second Mate Tarry cursed the day she had been christened *Lady Southborough*. Those sixteen letters seemed to take forever. But at last the destroyer was satisfied, and *Lady Southborough* crawled on to Ramsgate.

Meanwhile the cascade of little ships continued in all its variety—the stylish yacht *Quicksilver*, which could make twenty knots . . . the cockle fleet from Leigh-on-Sea . . . the Chris Craft *Bonnie Heather*, with its polished mahogany hull . . . the Dutch eel boat *Johanna*, which came complete with three Dutch owners who couldn't speak a word of English . . . to name just a few. Countless other boats, which Admiral Ramsay called "free lances," were now heading out of south coast ports like Folkestone, Eastbourne, Newhaven, and Brighton. Most never bothered to check with Dover; no one would ever record their names.

The French and Belgian fishing vessels requisitioned by Captain Auphan were beginning to turn up too, adding an international flavor to the rescue effort. Names like *Pierre et Marie, Reine des Flots,* and *Ingénieur Cardin* joined *Handy Billie, Girl Nancy,* and at least nine *Skylarks*. The French mailboat *Côte d'Argent* began using the east mole like any British steamer.

Most of the French crews were from Brittany and as unfamiliar with these waters as the cockle boatmen from the Thames estuary, but there was the inevitable exception. Fernand

Schneider, assistant engineer on the minesweeping trawler *St. Cyr*, came from Dunkirk itself. Now he had the agony of watching his hometown crumble into ruins, but at the same time the comfort of visiting his own house from time to time.

Knowing the area, Schneider also knew where food was to be had, and the *St. Cyr*'s skipper occasionally sent him on foraging expeditions to bolster the trawler's meager rations. He was on one of these forays on May 28 when he decided to check his house on the rue de la Toute Verte. It was still standing, and better yet, his father Augustin Schneider was there. Augustin had come in from the family refuge in the country, also to see how the house was faring. They embraced with special fervor, for the occasion was more than a family reunion, more than a celebration that the house was intact—it was Fernand's 21st birthday.

The old man went down in the cellar and brought up a bottle of Vouvray. Then for an hour the two forgot about the war while they joyfully killed the bottle. Parting at last, father and son would not see each other again for five years.

Fernand Schneider was the only sailor at Dunkirk who celebrated his birthday at home, but the rescue fleet was full of improbable characters. Lieutenant Lodo van Hamel was a dashing Dutch naval officer, always conspicuous because he flew the only Dutch flag in the whole armada. Lieutenant-Colonel Robin Hutchens was an old Grenadier Guardsman, mired in a dull liaison job at the Admiralty. An experienced weekend sailor, he headed for Dover on his day off; now he was in charge of the War Department launch *Swallow*. Captain R. P. Pim normally presided over Winston Churchill's map room; today he wallowed across the Channel commanding a Dutch skoot. Samuel Palmer served on the Plymouth City Patrol, but he was an old navy "stripey," and that was good enough. In charge of the seven-ton *Naiad Errant*, a cranky motor yacht that was always breaking down, he split up the cabin door and told the soldiers on board to start paddling.

Robert Harling was a typographical designer, but as a student in Captain Watts's navigation class, he had volunteered with the rest. Now he found himself one of four men assigned to a ship's lifeboat stripped from some liner at Tilbury docks. His companions turned out to be an advertising executive, a garage proprietor, and a solicitor. They had practically nothing in common—yet everything, joined as they were in an open boat on this strange adventure.

The boat was one of twelve being towed across the Channel by the tug *Sun IV*, skippered at the moment by the managing director of the tugboat company. The afternoon was beautiful, and the war seemed very far away. For a long time there was little to do but shoot the breeze. As they neared the French coast, marked by the pillar of black smoke over Dunkirk, the conversation fell off, and the mood in Harling's boat became tense.

"There they are, the bastards!" someone suddenly called, pointing up at the sky. Harling looked, and soon made out more than 50 planes approaching with stately precision. They were perhaps 15,000 feet up, and at this distance everything seemed to happen in slow motion. Gradually the planes drew closer . . . then were directly overhead. Fascinated, he watched the bombs fall lazily toward the earth. Then suddenly they were rushing down at breakneck speed, crashing into the sea, just missing two nearby destroyers.

Soon some RAF fighters appeared, tearing into the German formation. Harling was mildly surprised that the Hurricanes and Spitfires really did rout the enemy—just as the communiqués said. But that wasn't the end of it. In a last gesture of defiance, one of the German fighters swooped down, strafing the *Sun IV* and her tow. Watching it come, Harling felt mesmerized—he couldn't even duck in time—then in a second it was over. The bullets ripped the empty sea; the plane zoomed up and out of sight. *Sun IV* and her charges steamed on untouched.

The sky was not the only source of danger. After a night of ferry work, the six cockle boats started back for Ramsgate at 3:00 a.m., June 1. Most had fared very well, but *Letitia* had now broken down and was being towed by the drifter *Ben and Lucy*. Then *Renown*'s engine went, and she latched onto *Letitia*. The three vessels limped along, with *Renown* yawing wide at the end of the tow.

It was about 3:30 when *Renown* brushed a German mine, freshly laid by some bomber or S-Boat. There was a blinding flash, and every trace of *Renown* and her crew of four vanished completely.

The methodical German shelling continued taking its toll

too—often with frightening suddenness. As the pleasure steamer *New Prince of Wales* lay off Bray-Dunes on the 31st, Sub-Lieutenant Bennett left the bridge to help start a balky engine. He
had just reached the deck when there was a shrieking, tearing
sound, coming at him straight from above. There was a shattering explosion . . . a momentary glimpse of gray streamers of
smoke laced with bits of shell . . . pain in his left foot, left thigh,
and the left side of his face . . . and he found himself lying on
deck. As he lost consciousness, he decided this must be the end.
He had seen enough war movies showing men dying with blood
running out of their mouths. That was the way they always
went, and that was what was happening to him.

He came to a few minutes later, happy to find he was still
alive. But two of his men were killed, and the *New Prince of Wales*
was a write-off. The motor boat *Triton* was nearby, and Lieutenant Irving eased her over to take off the survivors. By now Bennett was on his feet again and even feeling belligerent. His face
was a bloody mess, but his mind was clear, and he took over as
coxswain for Lieutenant Irving.

They weren't all heroes. Off Bray-Dunes one Dutch skoot lay
motionless for hours, doing little or nothing. The skipper was
tipsy, and the second in command seemed less than enthusias-
tic. Troops rowed out to her anyhow, and finally she was reasonably full. At this point Corporal Harold Meredith of the
RASC heard the skipper explain, "I'm supposed to take you out
to the destroyers, which are lying farther offshore, but I've had
a very rough day, and tonight I am Nelson. I've unfortunately
put my telescope to my blind eye, and I cannot see any destroyers; so I'm taking you all the way home."

One way or another, 68,014 Allied troops were evacuated this
May 31. As usual, the most dramatic incidents occurred off the
beaches, but the most effective work was again done on the east
mole. The destroyer *Malcolm* showed what one ship could do—
1,000 men lifted at 2:15 a.m. . . . another 1,000 at 2:30 p.m. . . .
still another 1,000 lifted in the early hours of June 1. Her efficiency made the job look easy, yet it was anything but that. War-
rant Engineer Arthur George Scoggins nursed his machinery in
a steam-filled engine room where the temperature hit 140° to
150°.

For the first time British ships were carrying a really respectable number of Frenchmen—10,842 were rescued this day. Not enough to satisfy Premier Reynaud, but it was a start. And the difficulties were more than the critics in Paris could ever realize. Usually the poilus wanted to bring all their equipment. Many refused to be separated from their units. They seemed unable to comprehend that if too many people got into a small boat at once, it might capsize or run aground. The British crews were inclined to think that the French were just naturally landlubbers, in contrast to "our island race." The evidence suggests that much of the trouble stemmed from the language barrier.

"*En avant mes héros! Courage mes enfants!*" Sub-Lieutenant A. Carew Hunt summoned up his limited store of French, trying to tempt some hesitant soldiers to wade out to his boat. Minutes later he was waving his revolver at them to stop the rush.

"*Débarquez!* You bloody fools, get out! Get out! *Nous sommes ensables!*" shouted one of Captain Watts's scholars as his boat grounded under the weight of too many Frenchmen. Nobody understood, and nobody moved. Finally a French NCO caught on, reworked the language, and the order was obeyed.

Sub-Lieutenant Michael Solomon, who knew French well, never had any trouble during a brief stint as interpreter for Commander Clouston on the eastern mole. English officers shouting "*Allez!*" got nowhere—that was insulting—but the right words, plus a little tact, could work wonders.

So the loading went on, and one more crisis was passed. The equal numbers rule did not upset Ramsay's timetable after all. Thanks to Clouston's organizing ability, far more men were evacuating from the mole than anyone had dared hope. The surge of little ships across the Channel helped too. By now there were enough boats for everyone—both French and British.

But already a new crisis was at hand. All day May 31, German shells had been falling on the beach and shipping at La Panne. Now, as dusk settled over the battered town, the bombardment grew worse than ever. It suggested that all was far from well along the eastern end of the perimeter. If it collapsed, Bock's seasoned troops could break into the beachhead and end the evacuation for good.

11

Holding the Perimeter

German shells screeched overhead as Captain P. J. Jeffries of the 6th Durham Light Infantry leaned over and plucked a small flower in the garden of the chateau at Moeres, a Belgian village toward the eastern end of the perimeter. Jeffries didn't know what this flower was—sort of a cross between an azalea and a rhododendron—but he vowed to find out and plant some in his own garden . . . if he ever got home again.

At the moment his chances didn't look too good. Jeffries was second in command of the 6th DLI, one of the units assigned to hold off the Germans while the rest of the BEF and the French escaped to England. For two days enemy pressure had been growing on the Durhams' section of the canal defense line, and now on the morning of May 31 German shells began landing uncomfortably close to battalion headquarters.

The first actual penetration came not at Moeres, but still farther east near Nieuport, the coastal town that served as the perimeter's eastern anchor. Here at 5:00 a.m. German infantry crossed the canal in rubber boats and stormed the brickworks held by the 1st/6th East Surreys. By noon they were in danger of being outflanked. Their "sister" battalion, the 1st East Surreys, rushed to the rescue just in time. Together they managed to stop the enemy, but it took every man. At one point the two battalion commanders manned a Bren gun together. One colonel fired the gun, while the other acted as "No. 2," feeding it with ammunition.

Next, an even closer squeak. While the Surreys were clinging to their brickyard, a new German attack hit the British 8th Brigade three miles to the west. At 12:20 p.m. a hysterical sapper stumbled into Furnes, the main town in the area, blurting that the front had been broken and the Germans were pouring across the canal unopposed.

No time to lose. Reinforcements from the crack 2nd Grenadier Guards were rushed to the scene under a quick-thinking 2nd lieutenant named Jones. He found two battalions of the brigade about to retire without orders. If this happened, a gaping hole would open up in the perimeter, allowing the Germans to pour in behind the defenders. The few remaining officers were trying to rally their men, but nobody would listen.

Jones took more drastic measures. He found it necessary to shoot some of the panic-stricken soldiers, and others were turned around at bayonet-point. He then reported back to headquarters that the brigade was once again stabilized but in desperate need of experienced officers and ammunition. Lieutenant J. Trotter of the 2nd Grenadier Guards was then sent to help him, along with 14,000 rounds of ammunition. By 3:00 p.m. the men were all back in position and morale was high—proving once again the importance of that elusive quality, leadership, in shaping the fortunes of war.

During the afternoon the Germans shifted their efforts to the area southwest of Furnes, but with no better results. They managed to storm across the canal at Bulscamp, but soon bogged down on the other side. Flooded terrain and a spirited defense blocked any further advance. In such a predicament the standard remedy was to soften resistance with artillery, and shells were soon raining on the Durham Light Infantry's chateau at Moeres. Toward evening the DLI abandoned the place with few regrets. This country was meant to be an epicure's delight, but for three days they had lived on a diet of tinned pilchards in tomato sauce.

Evening, and the target was Nieuport again. It's doubtful

whether the exhausted East Surreys could have stood up to any serious attack. Fortunately, just as the German columns massed, help came from an unexpected direction. Eighteen RAF bombers, supported by six planes from the Fleet Air Arm, swept in from the sea, smashing and scattering the enemy force. The British troops forgot their weariness; leapt and waved and shouted with excitement. Until now they thought that only the Germans could pull off this sort of stunt.

While the British brigades to the east desperately parried the German thrusts, the Allied troops to the west had a relatively quiet day. The line from Fort Mardyck to the ancient walled town of Bergues was a French responsibility; General Beaufrère's 68th Infantry Division lay waiting behind a patchwork of ditches. A mixed garrison of French and British held Bergues itself. Some long-range guns were shelling the place, but the medieval walls stood up to modern artillery amazingly well.

It was the Bergues-Furnes Canal Line to the east of town that seemed most exposed. While the flat fields were bound to reveal an advancing enemy, they also gave away the defenders. There was no cover, except for an occasional tree or farmhouse.

The 2nd Coldstream Guards eyed uneasily the 2,200 yards assigned to them. Lieutenant Jimmy Langley of No. 3 Company moved his platoon into a small brick cottage directly north of the canal. He was anything but a picture-book guardsman—he stood only five feet eight—but he was lively and immensely resourceful. He lost no time converting the cottage into a miniature Gibraltar.

From scores of trucks and lorries abandoned along the canal bank, Langley's men brought back a vast haul of booty. The weapons alone were impressive—12 Bren guns, 3 Lewis machine guns, 1 Boyes antitank rifle, 30,000 rounds of ammunition, and 22 hand grenades. Considering there were only 37 men left in the company, this was fire power indeed.

Nor was food neglected. Stacks of bully beef, canned vegetables, and tinned milk were piled in the kitchen. And since Langley was especially partial to marmalade and Wiltshire bacon, there was a liberal supply of these too. They might, he decided, be there a long time; so they should be prepared for the good life as well—he added two cases of wine and two crates of beer.

During the afternoon the company commander, Major Angus McCorquodale, dropped by and made his contribution too: a bottle of whiskey and two bottles of sherry. McCorquodale was one of those throwbacks to a glorious earlier age in British military history. Gleaming with polished brass and leather, he scorned the new battle dress. "I don't mind dying for my country," he declared, "but I'm not going to die dressed like a third-rate chauffeur."

He liked Langley's set-up so much he decided to make the cottage the Company's forward headquarters, and the two of them bedded down in a small back room for some rest. They were up before dawn, June 1, removing roof tiles and turning the attic into a machine-gun nest. Neither the roof nor the end walls were really strong enough, but it was too late to worry about that now. Langley settled down to wait for Jerry with a pair of binoculars and two buckets of cold water by his side. The buckets were for cooling the wine, or the beer, or the Bren-gun barrels—whichever seemed to need it most.

There was no night of quiet waiting at Furnes. Shells poured down on the old Flemish town, as they had all day. The 1st Grenadier Guards huddled under an avalanche of falling slate and masonry from the seventeenth-century buildings that ringed the marketplace. The churchyard of venerable Saint Walburge was so thick with shrapnel that walking on the grass was like tramping over a carpet of jagged glass.

In the roomy cellar that served as battalion headquarters, Signalman George W. Jones hunched over a portable radio listening to the BBC evening news. It was the first voice he had heard from the outside world in three weeks. It assured him that two-thirds of the troops trapped at Dunkirk were now evacuated and safely back in England.

Jones felt anything but assured. Here he was, stuck with the rear guard in a collapsing town miles from home, and now he heard that the best part of the army was safely back in England. It was a very lonely feeling.

Lance Sergeant John Bridges, also of the 1st Grenadier Guards, was sure they would never get away. He had originally joined the regiment as a drummer boy, hoping to see the world, play a little football, and ultimately become a writer. But now the dream was buried in the rubble of Furnes. His company commander, Major Dickie Herbert, showed him how to dig a round foxhole, so he could shoot in any direction. That could only mean they were about to be surrounded.

Then an unexpected reprieve. Toward evening Major Herbert returned from a brigade conference and immediately called a meeting of his own officers and NCO's. He lost no time getting to the point: his first words were, "We're going home." A map was produced, and a staff lieutenant lined off the route to the beaches. There were no histrionics, no exhortations. It was all so matter-of-fact that to Bridges it seemed rather like planning a family outing.

At 10:00 p.m. the battalion began "thinning out"—first the headquarters personnel, the signalers, the quartermaster units; then the infantry companies, one by one; and finally certain hand-picked parties from No. 2 and No. 4 Companies, especially skilled in rear-guard work. Everything went very smoothly. After all, they had been doing it since Brussels.

The premium was on silence. The enemy must not find out. The rear-guard parties wrapped sandbags around their boots to deaden the sound on the cobblestone streets. Still, there were heart-stopping moments as the columns, tramping single file, noisily scrambled over piles of rubble, bricks, broken glass, and tangled telephone wire. How could the Germans miss hearing them?

Yet there was no sound of unusual activity in the sections of town now occupied by the enemy. Only the steady pounding of shells that had gone on for two days. By 2:30 a.m., June 1, the last Grenadier had pulled out.

For Sergeant Bridges the march to La Panne was a three-mile nightmare. He especially hated mortar fire, and tonight every mortar in the German Army seemed concentrated on him. Most of the shells landed ahead of the column, which meant few casualties but gave the terrifying impression that the battalion was always marching straight into hell. At one point Bridges's rifle got caught in a tangle of telephone wire, and the more he tried to get it loose, the more he himself became enmeshed in the tangle. On the verge of panic, he was finally freed by his sergeant major, who also brought him to his senses with a good slap.

Adding to the confusion, hundreds of abandoned cattle, sheep, pigs, and chickens were loose and running among the stumbling men. They reminded Bridges of the stories he had heard about wild animals fleeing before a great forest fire.

All along the eastern end of the perimeter—the II Corps area—the battalions were thinning out and falling back on La Panne. As with the 1st Grenadier Guards, the process usually began about 10:00 p.m. and continued to around 2:30 a.m., when the last rear-guard parties retired. Probably the last unit of all to pull out was the carrier platoon of the 1st Coldstream, which hung around Furnes till 2:50 a.m., covering the withdrawal of the battalion's infantry.

As always, silence was the rule—which could fool a friend as well as foe. Private F. R. Farley was on sentry duty that night in a lonely copse east of Furnes. He knew his battalion, the 1st/7th Middlesex, would be withdrawing, and he was to be called in when the time came. Hours passed, and nothing happened. From time to time he heard faint sounds: a car starting, a muf-fled word of command. Then complete silence. He listened—a sentry did not leave his post lightly—then decided to slip back, and see what was happening.

Everyone had gone. The NCO had forgotten to call him in. Desperately he sprinted through the copse to the main road. He was just in time to leap onto the last truck of the last column of the battalion, as it started down the coastal road for La Panne.

The convoy stopped on the edge of town; the men piled out; and the trucks were disabled in the usual way—a bullet in the radiator, the engine left running until it seized. Moving into La Panne, Farley joined a flood of troops converging on the place from every direction. The whole eastern end of the perimeter was being abandoned; all had instructions to make for La Panne.

Beyond that, there seemed to be no orders. Some men slumped in doorways; others lay exhausted on the *pavé*; others wandered aimlessly about, as officers and NCO's called out unit numbers and rallying cries, trying to keep their men together.

The shelling had unaccountably stopped, and for the mo-ment all was relatively quiet. As the men waited to be told what to do, a thousand cigarettes glowed in the darkness.

Eventually there was a stirring, but instead of moving onto

the beach, the troops were ordered back a couple of streets. They were now further from the sea, but much better dispersed. It was just as well, for at this moment a spotter plane droned overhead, dropping flares that brilliantly lit up the whole scene. Then came the thump of distant guns, followed by the shriek of falling shells.

There was a shattering crash as the first salvo landed at the intersection near the beach. The hotels and shops in the area were mostly built in the "modern" style of the 30's, full of chrome and plate glass. Now the glass came cascading down, adding to the general din.

"Into the shops! Off the streets!" The cry went up, and the troops needed no further urging. Rifle butts went to work on the doors and windows remaining, and the men swarmed in, just as a second salvo was landing.

Farley and several others from the 1st/7th Middlesex broke into a large corner shop, and once inside were thankful to find stairs leading down to a basement. Here they crouched in comparative safety as the shelling swept methodically up and down the streets salvo after salvo, turning the town into a dust-choked ruin. Flames began to lick through upper windows as fires took hold.

It was important not to go entirely underground. There was always the danger of missing some important order. The men took turns keeping watch at the door—very unpleasant duty with the town collapsing around them. Farley found the knack was to leap back to the stairs whenever a salvo seemed likely to be close. He got very good at it.

After an hour and a half, Captain Johnson of Headquarters Company slipped in with the latest orders: listen for some whistle blasts as soon as there is a lull in the shelling . . . then clear out and run for the beach at the double . . . turn left at the bandstand and keep going for half a mile. That would be where the battalion would reassemble and embark.

No one was to stop for anything. Casualties to be left where they fell. The medical orderlies would take care of these. The essential thing was to clear the streets without delay at the first feasible moment.

Just before 2:45 a.m. Private Farley heard the whistle loud

and clear. His group raced up the cellar steps and out into the street. Other units were pouring out of other buildings, too. Jumbled together, they all surged toward the beachfront. The flames from the burning buildings lit their way; the crash of bursting shells spurred them on. The "lull," it turned out, meant only a shift in targets. But the most unforgettable sound—a din that drowned out even the gunfire—was the steady crunch of thousands of boots on millions of fragments of broken glass.

Soon they were by the bandstand . . . across the esplanade . . . onto the beach—and suddenly they were in a different world. Gone was the harsh, grating clatter; now there was only the squish of feet running on wet sand. The glare of the fire-lit streets gave way to the blackness of the dunes at night. The smoke and choking dust vanished, replaced by the clean, damp air of the seaside . . . the smell of salt and seaweed.

Then the shelling shifted again, aimed this time right at the beach where the men were running. Private Farley of the Middlesex saw a flash, felt the blast, but (oddly enough) heard no "bang" as a close one landed just ahead. He was untouched, but the four men running with him all went down. Three lay motionless on the sand; the fourth, propped up on one hand, pleaded, "Help me, help me."

Farley ran on. After all, those were the orders. But he knew in his heart that the real reason he didn't stop was self-preservation. The memory of that voice pleading for help would still haunt his conscience forty years later.

Half a mile down the beach was the point where the Middlesex had been ordered to reassemble for embarkation. Private Farley had imagined what it would be like. He pictured a well-organized area where senior NCO's would stand at the head of gangway ladders taking name, rank, and serial number as the troops filed aboard the waiting ships. Actually, there was no embarkation staff, no waiting ships, no organization whatsoever.

Nobody seemed to be in charge. The 2nd Royal Ulster Rifles had been told that reception camps would be waiting for them when they got to the beach, that a Division Control Staff would take over from there and guide them to the ships. They found no trace of either the camps or the Control Staff, and of course no sign of the ships.

The 1st Grenadier Guards reached the beach intact, but with no further orders, the battalion soon broke up. Some men headed for Dunkirk; others joined the columns hopefully waiting at the water's edge; Sergeant Bridges led a small group of six or eight into the dunes to wait for dawn. Maybe daylight would show them what to do.

But would they last that long? At one point Bridges heard an ominous rumble coming toward them. It sounded like the whole German Army, and he crouched in the sand, awaiting that final confrontation. It turned out to be only horses, abandoned by some French artillery unit, galloping aimlessly up and down the sand.

But the next big noise might always be the enemy, and still there was no sign of any ships. To Lieutenant-Commander J. N. McClelland, the senior naval officer remaining at La Panne, the situation was turning into a hideous exercise in arithmetic. It was now 1:00 a.m.; the British couldn't expect to hold La Panne beyond dawn at 4:00. Some 6,000 troops were pouring onto the beach; they had lifted off only 150 since nightfall. At this rate, nearly the whole force would be lost.

He conferred briefly with Major-General G. D. Johnson, the senior army officer on the beach at this point. Yes, McClelland assured the General, he had made a personal reconnaissance both above and below the position. No, there weren't any ships. Yes, they were meant to be there. No, he didn't think they would come now—something must have gone wrong. To McClelland the Royal Navy's absence was almost a matter of personal shame. He formally apologized to Johnson for the nonarrival of the boats.

They decided that the only course left was to march the bulk of the troops down the beach toward Dunkirk and try to embark from there. Or perhaps they would run across some ships at Bray-Dunes along the way.

A few men—mostly wounded and exhausted stragglers— were not fit to march. These would be left behind, and McClelland headed down to the lorry jetties to look after them, on the chance that some ships might still turn up.

More German guns were ranged on the beach now, and McClelland was twice knocked down by shell bursts. One smashed his signal lamp; the second wounded his left ankle. As often happens, it didn't hurt much at first—just a numb feeling—and he hobbled on down the beach.

At the embarkation point it was the same old story: no boats for over half an hour. McClelland now ordered the remaining troops to join the trek to Dunkirk. Even if they couldn't keep up with the main body, they must try. He himself rounded up all the stragglers he could find and sent them on their way. Then he limped off after the rest.

About two miles toward Bray-Dunes he suddenly saw what he had been searching for all night—ships! Three vessels lay at anchor not far from the shore. A small party of soldiers stood at the water's edge firing shots, trying to attract attention. There was no response from the ships. They just sat there, dark and silent.

McClelland looked farther down the beach. The night was filled with explosions, and in the flashes he could make out swarms of troops, but no trace of any other boat. These three anchored ships were the only chance. Somehow they must be told that the troops were moving steadily westward toward Dunkirk. Once these ships knew, they could alert the others, and the rescue fleet could finally assemble at the right place.

He plunged into the sea and began swimming. He was dead tired; his ankle began acting up; but he kept on. As he thrashed alongside the nearest ship, somebody threw him a line and he was hauled aboard. She turned out to be HMS *Gossamer*, one of Ramsay's hard-working minesweepers. Taken before the captain, Commander Richard Ross, McClelland managed to pant out his message: La Panne abandoned; all shipping should concentrate much farther west. Then he collapsed.

For Commander Ross, it was the first piece of solid intelligence to come his way since leaving Dover at 6:00 p.m. The *Gossamer* was one of the group of vessels earmarked for lifting the rear guard at the eastern end of the perimeter, amounting to some 4,000 men. The plan called for three big batches of ships' lifeboats to be towed by tugs across the Channel and stationed at three carefully designated points off La Panne. The rear guard would be instructed where to go, and at 1:30 a.m. the lifeboats would start ferrying the men to minesweepers waiting at each of the three points. Escorting destroyers would provide covering fire if the enemy tried to interfere. ("All tanks hostile," the orders reminded the destroyers.) The final directives were issued at 4:00 a.m., May 31, and the "special tows," as Ramsay called them, began leaving Ramsgate at 1:00 p.m.

Every possible contingency had been covered—except the fortunes of war. German pressure on the perimeter was too great. The covering position could no longer be held by the 4,000-man rear guard. Under heavy enemy shelling the troops were pulling back sooner than expected, and farther west than planned. The special tows must be alerted to go to a different place at a different time.

But Dover no longer had any direct communication with the special tows. Ramsay could only radio the accompanying minesweepers, hoping that the change in plans would be passed along to the tugs and their tows. He did this, but predictably his message never got through.

The armada chugged on to the originally designated spots, but now, of course, there was no one there. With no further directions, they groped along the coast, hoping somehow to make contact. *Gossamer* had, in fact, just stumbled on a sizable contingent when McClelland swam out, gasping his advice to look farther west.

The alert radio interception unit at General Georg von Kuechler's Eighteenth Army headquarters knew more than the BEF about the special tows and where they could be found. At 7:55 p.m. on the 31st, Captain Essmann of Headquarters phoned XXVI and IX Corps command posts, giving the latest information along with some instructions on what should be done.

Beginning at twilight, a heavy harassing fire was to be concentrated on the approach roads leading to the supposed embarkation points. . . . Armored reconnaissance patrols were to check whether the enemy had managed to evacuate. . . . If so, an immediate thrust was to be made to the coast.

Not exactly an inspiring blueprint for an army closing in for the kill. A lackadaisical mood, in fact, seemed to permeate most German military thinking these past two days. To Colonel Rolf Wuthmann, Operations Officer of General von Kluge's Fourth Army at the western end of the perimeter, it was a cause for alarm. "There is an impression here that nothing is happening today, that no one is any longer interested in Dunkirk," he complained to General von Kleist's Chief of Staff on May 30.

Quite true. All eyes were now on the south. "*Fall Rot*"—Operation "Red"—the great campaign designed to knock France out of the war, would jump off from the Somme in just six days. Its immense scope and dazzling possibilities easily diverted attention from Dunkirk. Guderian and the other panzer generals—once so exasperated by Hitler's halt order—now wanted only to pull out their tanks, rest their men, prepare for the great new adventure. Rundstedt, commanding Army Group A, had already shifted his entire attention to the Somme. On the 31st Bock, commanding Army Group B, received a fat bundle of papers from OKH regrouping his forces too. At OKH, General Halder, the Chief of Staff, spent most of the day far behind the lines, checking communications, the flow of supplies, the status of Army Group C—all for the great new offensive.

As for Dunkirk, it was hard to escape the feeling that it was really all over. Some ten German infantry divisions now pressed a few thousand disorganized Allied soldiers against the sea. Kluge's Chief of Staff Kurt Brennecke might scold, "We do not want to find these men, freshly equipped, in front of us again later," but no German command was more thoroughly preoccupied with the coming drive south than Brennecke's own Fourth Army. General Halder might complain, "Now we must stand by and watch countless thousands of the enemy get away to England right under our noses," but he didn't stand by and watch very much himself. He too was busy getting ready for the big new push.

It always seemed that one more try would finish up Dunkirk, but no one was quite in the position to do it. With the closing of the trap, there were too many overlapping commands and too little coordination. Finally, in an effort to centralize responsibility, General von Kuechler's Eighteenth Army was put in complete charge. On May 31, at 2:00 a.m., all the various divisions along the entire 35-mile length of the perimeter passed under his control.

It wasn't long before Kuechler was getting advice. The following evening General Mieth of OKH telephoned a few "personal suggestions" from the highest levels. General von Brauchitsch suggested the landing of troop units from the sea in the rear of the British forces . . . also, the withdrawal of German units from the Canal Line so as to open up opportunities for the Luftwaffe without endangering friendly troops. And finally, an idea from Adolf Hitler himself: Kuechler might consider the possibility of using antiaircraft shells with time fuses to compensate for the reduced effectiveness of ordinary artillery fire on the beaches, where the sand tended to smother the explosions. Like many shakers and movers of the earth, the Fuehrer occasionally liked to tinker.

For the moment, these intriguing ideas were put aside. Kuechler had already made his plan, and it called for nothing as offbeat as a landing behind the British forces, even if that were possible. Instead, he simply planned an attack by all his forces at once along the entire length of the perimeter on June 1.

First, his artillery would soften the enemy up with harassing fire, starting immediately and continuing the whole night. The attacking troops would jump off at 11:00 a.m., June 1, closely supported by General Alfred Keller's Fliegerkorps IV.

Everything was to be saved for the main blow. During the afternoon of the 31st, Eighteenth Army issued a special directive warning the troops not to engage in any unnecessary action that day. Rather, their time should be spent moving the artillery into position, gathering intelligence, conducting reconnaissance, and making other preparations for the "systematic attack" tomorrow.

All very sound, but this inflexibility also suggests why so little use was made of the radio intercept about Ramsay's special tows. It clearly indicated that the British were abandoning the eastern end of the perimeter this very night—leaving themselves wide open in the process—yet the German plans were frozen, and nothing was done.

If anybody at Eighteenth Army headquarters sensed a lost

opportunity on the evening of May 31, there's no evidence of it. Preparations went steadily ahead for the unified attack tomorrow. The artillery pumped out shells at a rate the British Tommies would never forget, and the Luftwaffe joined in the softening-up process.

Special emphasis had been placed on the Luftwaffe's role, and for the duration of the attack Eighteenth Army was virtually given control of its operations. General Kesselring's Air Fleet 2 was simply told to attack Dunkirk continuously until the Eighteenth told it to stop.

Making use of his authority, around noon on the 31st Kuechler requested special strikes every fifteen minutes on the dunes west of Nieuport, where the British artillery was giving his 256th Infantry Division a hard time. Kesselring promised to follow through, but later reported that ground fog was keeping some of the planes from taking off.

Bad weather was a familiar story. It had scrubbed almost all missions on the 30th, and curbed operations on the 31st. It was, then, good news indeed when June 1 turned out to be bright and clear.

12

"I Have Never Prayed So Hard Before"

As the growl of approaching planes grew louder, veteran Seaman Bill Barris carefully removed his false teeth and put them in his handkerchief pocket—always a sure sign to the men on the destroyer *Windsor* that hard fighting lay ahead. It was 5:30 a.m., June 1, and the early morning mist was already burning off, promising a hot sunny day.

In seconds the planes were in sight, Me 109's sweeping in low from the east. Gun muzzles twinkling, some strafed the eastern mole, where the *Windsor* lay loading; others hit the beaches . . . the rescue fleet . . . even individual soldiers wading and swimming out to the ships. Normally the German fighters did little strafing. Their orders were to remain "upstairs," flying cover for the Stukas and Heinkels. Today's tactics suggested something special.

Tucked away in the dunes west of La Panne, Sergeant John Bridges of the 1st Grenadier Guards safely weathered the storm. Around him clustered six to eight other Grenadier Guards, the little group he had formed when the battalion dissolved during the night. At that time nobody knew what to do, and it seemed best to wait till dawn.

Now it was getting light, and the choice was no easier. Joining the trek to Dunkirk looked too dangerous. Bridges could see nothing but gun flashes and towering smoke in that direction. On the other hand, joining one of the columns waiting on the beach below looked futile. There were so few boats and so many men. In the end, Bridges opted for the beach; perhaps the group could find some shorter queue where the wait would be reasonable.

A pistol shot ended that experiment. An officer accused the group of queue-jumping and fired a warning blast in the general direction of Bridges's feet. Undaunted, the Sergeant turned his mind to the possibility of getting off the beach without queueing up at all. Noticing an apparently empty lifeboat drifting about 100 yards off shore, he suggested they swim out and get it. Nobody could swim.

He decided to go and bring it back himself. Stripping off his clothes, he swam out to the boat, only to find it was not empty after all. Two bedraggled figures in khaki were already in it, trying to unlash the oars. They were glad to have Bridges join them, but not his friends. They weren't about to return to shore for anybody. Bridges hopped out and swam back to the beach.

But now the group had vanished, scattered by an air raid. Only Corporal Martin was left, faithfully guarding Bridges's gear. Looking to sea, they saw yet another lifeboat and decided to make for that. Martin, of course, couldn't swim, but Bridges—ever an optimist—felt that somehow he could push and pull the Corporal along.

It would have been easier if Bridges had been traveling light. But he was dressed again, carrying his pack and gas cape, and there was much on his mind besides Corporal Martin. While in Furnes, their unit had been stationed in a cellar under a jewelry and fur shop. There was much talk about not leaving anything for the Germans to loot, and first thing Bridges knew, he had turned looter himself. Now his pack and gas cape were filled with wristwatches, bracelets, and a twelve-pelt silver fox cape.

The two men waded into the sea, Bridges trying to help Martin and hang onto his riches at the same time. Somehow they reached the lifeboat, which turned out to be in the charge of a white-haired, fatherly-looking brigadier, still wearing all his ribbons and red trim. He was skillfully maneuvering the boat about, picking up strays here and there. Martin was hauled aboard, and Bridges prepared to follow.

"You'll have to drop your kit, Sergeant," the brigadier sang out. Every inch of space was needed for people. With a lack of hesitation that surprised even himself, Bridges let it all go—bracelets, watches, jewelry, furs, and perhaps most important, the load on his conscience.

Pulled aboard, he took an oar, and with the brigadier steering, they gradually approached a destroyer lying not far away. Planes began strafing, and the man rowing next to Bridges was hit. They crawled on, and were almost there when an officer on the ship called out to stay clear. She was stuck on a sandbar, running her screws full speed ahead to get free.

The brigadier tried, but whether it was tide, current, suction, or plain inexperience, they were relentlessly drawn to the side of the ship. A rising swell caught Bridges's oar against the hull, and through some play of physics he could never hope to understand, he was catapulted upward, clear out of the boat. He caught hold of a grid, which served as a ship's ladder, and willing hands hauled him on board.

Next instant the lifeboat plunged down again and was caught under the racing screws. The boat, the brigadier, Martin, and everyone else were chewed to bits. Bridges looked back in time to catch a brief, last glimpse of Martin's startled face as it disappeared beneath the sea.

He sank to the deck, leaning against the bulkhead. The destroyer turned out to be the *Ivanhoe*, and as Bridges began stripping off his wet clothes, a sailor brought him a blanket and a pack of cigarettes. He did not have much time to enjoy them. Once again the sound of aircraft engines warned of new danger from the skies.

The German bombers had arrived. Luckily, the *Ivanhoe* had at last wriggled free of the sandbar, and Commander P. H. Hadow was able to dodge the first attacks, delivered by level-bombing Heinkels. No such luck with the Stukas. At 7:41 a.m. two near misses bracketed the ship, and a third bomb crashed into the base of the forward funnel.

Down in the boiler room Private J. B. Claridge, who had been plucked from the sea at La Panne, was drying out his uniform when the ship gave a violent shudder, the lights went out, and a shower of burning embers fell about him. He was standing near a ladder to the deck, and he raced up through a cloud of swirling steam. He and another man were the only two to get out alive.

Sergeant Bridges watched from his resting place against the bulkhead. He was still stunned by his own ordeal, but he was alert enough to note that the *Ivanhoe*'s crew were beginning to take off their shoes. That could only mean they thought the ship was sinking.

He needed no better proof. Slipping off his blanket, he went over the side, naked except for his helmet, which he always managed to keep. He swam slowly away from the ship, using a sort of combination breast-and-side stroke that he especially favored. He could keep it up forever—or at least until some ship appeared that looked like a better bet than the *Ivanhoe*.

But the *Ivanhoe* was not finished. The fires were contained; the foremost magazine flooded; and the damaged boilers sealed off. Then the destroyer *Havant* and the minesweeper *Speedwell* eased alongside and removed most of the troops. As *Speedwell* pulled away, she picked up one more survivor swimming alone in the sea. It was Sergeant Bridges.

On the *Ivanhoe* the engineering officer Lieutenant Mahoney coaxed some steam out of his one remaining boiler, as the ship started back to England. Creeping along at seven knots, assisted by a tug, she made an ideal target and was twice attacked by the Heinkels. Each time, Commander Hadow waited until the first bombs fell, then lit smoke floats inside various hatches to simulate hits. The ruse worked: both times the planes flew off, apparently convinced that the destroyer was finished.

On the *Havant*, the troops transferred from the *Ivanhoe* barely had time to settle down before the Stukas pounced again. Two bombs wrecked the engine room, and a third landed just ahead of the ship, exploding as she passed over it.

The lights went out, and once again hundreds of soldiers thrashed about in the dark, trying to get topside. *Havant* took a heavy list, compounding the confusion. But once again help lay close at hand. The minesweeper *Saltash* came alongside, taking off some troops. Others transferred to a small pleasure steamer, the *Narcissa*, which used to make holiday cruises around Margate.

The crew of the *Havant* stayed on for a while, but for her there was no clever escape. The hull was ruptured, the engine room blown to bits. At 10:15 a.m. *Havant* vanished into the sea.

"A destroyer has blown up off Dunkirk," someone laconically observed on the bridge of the destroyer *Keith* lying off Bray-Dunes. Admiral Wake-Walker looked and saw a ship enveloped in smoke just off Dunkirk harbor, six miles to the west. At the time he didn't know it was the *Ivanhoe*—or that she would survive. He only knew that the German bombers were back on the job, and might be coming his way next. It would be hard to miss the concentration of ships working with the *Keith* off Bray: the destroyer *Basilisk*, minesweepers *Skipjack* and *Salamander*, tugs *St. Abbs* and *Vincia*, and the skoot *Hilda*.

Sure enough, a compact formation of 30 to 40 Stukas appeared from the southwest. Every gun in the fleet opened up, and a curtain of fire seemed to break up the formation. But not for long. Shortly before 8:00 a.m. three Stukas came hurtling down, right at the *Keith*.

The ship heeled wildly. In the wheelhouse everyone was crouching down, with the helmsman steering by the bottom spokes of the wheel. Teacups skidded across the deck. Then three loud explosions, the nearest just ten yards astern. It jammed the helm, and the *Keith* began steering in circles.

Captain Berthon switched to manual steering, and things were beginning to get back to normal, when three more planes dived. This time Wake-Walker saw the bombs released and watched them fall, right at the ship. It was an odd sensation waiting for the explosion and knowing that he could do nothing. Then the crash . . . the teeth-rattling jolt . . . a rush of smoke and steam boiling up somewhere aft.

Surprisingly, he could see no sign of damage. It turned out that one of the bombs had gone right down the second funnel, bursting in the No. 2 boiler room far below. Power gone, plates sprung, *Keith* listed sharply to port.

Not far away, Lieutenant Christopher Dreyer watched the hit from his motor torpedo boat *MTB 102*; he hurried over to help. Wake-Walker decided he was doing no good on the crippled

Keith, and quickly shifted to Dreyer's boat. It was the Admiral's eighth flagship in twenty-four hours.

On the *Keith*, now wallowing low in the water, Captain Berthon gave the order to abandon ship. Scores of men went over the side, including most of General Gort's staff. Colonel Bridgeman was sure of only one thing: he didn't want to swim back to La Panne. He splashed about, finally joined two sailors clinging to a piece of timber. Eventually they were picked up by the tug *Vincia* and taken to Ramsgate.

The Stukas were far from finished. About 8:20 they staged a third attack on the *Keith*, hitting her again in the engine room, and this time they saved something for the other ships nearby. The minesweeper *Salamander* escaped untouched, but her sistership *Skipjack* was a different story. The leader of the German flight scored two hits; then a second Stuka came roaring down. On the range-finder platform Leading Seaman Murdo MacLeod trained his Lewis gun on the plane and kept firing even after it released its bombs. The Stuka never came out of its dive, plunging straight into the sea.

But the damage was done—three more hits. *Skipjack* lurched heavily to port, and the order came to abandon ship. It was none too soon. In two more minutes *Skipjack* turned turtle, trapping most of the 250 to 300 troops aboard. She floated bottom-up for another twenty minutes, then finally sank.

The *Keith* lingered on, attended by a typically mixed assortment of small craft picking up survivors. After a fourth visit from the Stukas, the Admiralty tug *St. Abbs* came alongside around 8:40 and took off Captain Berthon and the last of the crew. Before leaving, Berthon signaled *Salamander* and *Basilisk* to sink the ship, lest she fall into enemy hands.

Both vessels replied that they were out of control and needed help themselves. Concentrating on his own ship, Berthon apparently didn't see the Stukas pounding the other two. *Basilisk* especially was in a bad way. A French trawler took her in tow, but she grounded on a sandbar and had to be abandoned around noon. The destroyer *Whitehall* picked up most of her crew, then finished her off with a couple of torpedoes.

Meanwhile the Stukas staged still another attack on the abandoned *Keith*—the fifth of the morning—and at 9:15 they finally sank her. The sea was now covered with fuel from sunken ships, and the surviving swimmers were a pathetic sight—coated black with oil, half-blind, choking and vomiting as they tried to stay afloat.

The tug *St. Abbs* poked about picking them up, twisting and turning, using every trick in the book to shake off the Stukas. Besides survivors from the sunken ships, she took aboard Major R.B.R. Colvin and a boatload of Grenadier Guards trying to row back to England. About 130 men jammed the tug's deck— some dreadfully wounded, others unhurt but sobbing with fright. An army doctor and chaplain passed among them, dispensing first aid and comfort. As the bombs continued to rain down, the padre told Major Colvin, "I have never prayed so hard before."

Eventually the Stukas moved off, and *St. Abbs* steamed briefly in peace. Then at 9:30 a single level-bomber passed overhead, dropping a stick of four delayed-action bombs right in the tug's path. They went off as she passed over them, tearing her bottom out.

Knocked down by the blast, Major Colvin tried to get up, but one leg was useless. Then the ship heeled over, and everything came crashing down. He felt he was falling into a bottomless pit, pushed along by rushing water, surrounded by falling coal. Next thing he knew, he was swimming in the sea some 50 yards from a lot of wreckage. *St. Abbs* was gone, sunk in just 30 seconds.

There were only a few survivors. Most had originally been on the *Keith* or *Skipjack*; this was their second sinking of the morning. This time they found themselves struggling against a strong tide that carried them along the coast, almost due east. They would soon be in German-held waters, but there seemed nothing they could do about it. Suddenly they saw a chance. A wrecked steamer lay directly in the way. The more agile swimmers managed to get over to her.

Passing under the stern, Major Colvin grabbed a gangway hanging in the water, and despite his bad leg, he pulled himself aboard. The wreck turned out to be the cargo liner *Clan MacAlister*, bombed and abandoned on May 29. She now lay partially sunk and hard aground about two miles off La Panne.

Some fifteen other survivors of *St. Abbs* also reached the hulk. Climbing aboard, they found themselves in a setting worthy of the legendary *Mary Celeste*. In the deserted deckhouse everything was still in place. Some sailors helped Major Colvin into a bunk, found him a couple of blankets and a set of dry clothes.

Midshipman H. B. Poustie of the *Keith* did even better. Covered with oil, he wandered into the captain's cabin and found the perfect uniform for an eighteen-year-old midshipman: the captain's dress blues, resplendent with four gold rings around the sleeves.

There was food too. Exploring the galley, someone came up with a light luncheon of canned pears and biscuits. To the tired and hungry survivors, it seemed like a feast.

The big question was: What next? Clearly they couldn't stay here much longer. It was ebb tide, and the *Clan MacAlister* now stood high out of the water on an even keel. From the air she looked undamaged, and the planes bombed her vigorously. Soon, the enemy artillery would be in La Panne, a stone's throw away.

One of the ship's boats still hung in the davits, and Captain Berthon—late of the *Keith* and senior officer present—ordered it loaded with provisions and lowered. With luck, they could row to England.

They were just about to start when a Thames lighter hove into view. She looked like a far better bet, and the castaways attracted her attention with yells and pistol shots. The lighter transferred them to a cement carrier so lowly she had no name—just Sheerness Yard Craft No. 63. She was, however, staunch enough to get them home.

On the beach west of La Panne, the 1st Suffolks had a grandstand view of the Stuka attack on the *Basilisk*. Still farther west, on a dune near Zuydcoote, the staff of the 3rd Grenadier Guards watched the *Keith*'s ordeal. All the way west, the sailors on the mole saw another swarm of Stukas sink the French destroyer *Foudroyant* in less than a minute. Captain Tennant himself watched the assault on the *Ivanhoe* and *Havant*.

There was something distant and unreal about it all—especially the battles in the sky that erupted from time to time. Any number of separate vignettes were frozen in the men's minds, like snapshots in an album: the thunderclap of a fighter and bomber colliding . . . a plane's wing fluttering to earth . . . the flash of flame as a Heinkel caught fire . . . the power dive of an Me 109, right into the sea . . . parachutes floating down . . . tracers ripping into the parachutes. It was hard to believe that all this was actually happening, and not just the familiar scenes from some old war film.

To Squadron Leader Brian Lane and the fighter pilots of No. 19 Squadron it was very real indeed. On June 1 their working day began at 3:15 a.m. at Hornchurch, a small field east of London. Still half-asleep, they gulped down tea and biscuits and hurried out onto the tarmac, where the Spitfires were already warming up. The roar of the engines rose and fell as the mechanics made final adjustments, and the exhaust flames still burned bright blue in the first light of the new day.

Lane climbed aboard his plane, checked his radio and oxygen, made sure that the others were ready, and waved his hand over his head—the signal to take off. Once airborne, he listened for the double thump that meant his wheels were up, and cast a practiced eye over the various dials and gauges that made up his instrument panel. It looked as though he had been doing this all his life; actually he had been a civilian making electric light bulbs until a short time before the war.

In fifteen minutes he was crossing the English coast, heading out over the North Sea. A glance at his mirror showed the other planes of the squadron, properly spaced behind him, and behind them were three more squadrons—48 Spitfires altogether—roaring eastward toward the sunrise and Dunkirk.

Ten more minutes, and they were over the beaches, bearing left toward Nieuport, the eastern limit of the patrol. It was 5:00 a.m. now, light enough to see the crowds waiting on the sand, the variety of vessels lying offshore. From 5,000 feet it looked like Blackpool on a bank holiday.

Suddenly the Spitfires no longer had the sky to themselves. Ahead and slightly to the right, flying toward Nieuport on a converging course, twelve twin-engine planes appeared. Lane flicked on his radio: "Twelve Me 110's straight ahead."

The Germans saw them coming. On both sides the neatly spaced formations vanished, replaced by the general melee that so reminded the men on the ground of something concocted by Hollywood. Lane got on the tail of a Messerschmitt, watched it drift into his sights, and pressed the firing button that controlled his eight machine guns. Eight streams of tracer homed in on the 110. Its port engine stopped. Then, as it turned to get away, he got in another burst, this time knocking out the starboard engine. He hung around long enough to watch it crash.

That job done, Lane searched for more targets, but could find nothing. His tanks only had enough petrol for 40 minutes over the beaches, and now he was getting low. Flying close to the water, he headed back across the Channel and home to Hornchurch. One by one the other members of the squadron came in too, until finally all were present and accounted for.

As they excitedly swapped experiences on the tarmac, the squadron intelligence officer toted up the score—7 Me 110's claimed; also 3 Me 109's, which had apparently turned up at some point during the free-for-all. Slowly the pilots drifted into the mess. It was hard to believe, but it was still only 7:00 a.m. and they hadn't even had breakfast yet.

It's worth noting that this aerial battle did not follow the standard script. Usually a very few British fighters took on a very great number of German planes, but this time the Spitfires actually outnumbered the Me 110's, four to one.

This was no coincidence. It was part of a tactical gamble. Originally Fighter Command had tried to provide continuous cover over the beaches, but the few planes available were spread so thin, the result was virtually no protection at all. On May 27, for instance, 22 patrols were flown, but the average strength was only eight planes. The Luftwaffe easily smothered this effort and devastated the port of Dunkirk.

After that disaster the RAF flew fewer patrols, but those flown were much stronger. There was also extra emphasis on the hours when the beachhead seemed most vulnerable—dawn and dusk. Hence the 48-plane patrol led by Brian Lane, and he in turn was followed by another patrol of similar strength.

But the total number of planes always remained the same— Air Marshal Dowding wouldn't give an inch on that, for he was already thinking ahead to the defense of Britain herself. As a result, there were inevitably certain periods when there was no protection at all, and on June 1 the first of these periods ran from 7:30 a.m. to 8:50 a.m.—that harrowing hour and twenty minutes when the *Keith* and her consorts were lost.

By 9:00 a new patrol was on the line, and the German attacks tapered off, but there were four more periods during the day when the RAF could provide no fighter cover, and the Luftwaffe cashed in on them all. Around 10:30 a.m. bombs crippled the big railway steamer *Prague* and turned the picturesque river gunboat *Mosquito* into a blazing wreck.

Then it was the Channel packet *Scotia*'s turn. As she slowly capsized, 2,000 French troops managed to climb the deck against the roll, ending up perched on her hull. The destroyer *Esk* plucked most of them to safety. No such luck with the French destroyer *Foudroyant*. Hit during another gap in fighter protection, she turned over and sank in seconds.

The carnage continued. During the afternoon a 500-pound bomb landed on the deck of the minesweeper *Brighton Queen*, killing some 300 French and Algerian troops—about half the number aboard. Later the destroyer *Worcester* and the mine-sweeper *Westward Ho* were badly damaged but managed to get home. *Westward Ho* had 900 French troops aboard, including a general and his staff. When she finally reached Margate, the general was so overjoyed, he decorated two members of the crew with the Croix de Guerre on the spot.

Seventeen ships sunk or knocked out of action. That was the Luftwaffe's score this June 1. All day the human residue—the hollow-eyed survivors, the pale wounded on stretchers, the ragged bundles that turned out to be bodies—were landed on the quays of Dover, Ramsgate, and other southeast coast towns. The effect was predictable on the men whose ships happened to be in port.

At Folkestone the crew of the railway steamer *Malines* were especially shaken by the ordeal of the *Prague*. The two vessels belonged to the same line, and there was a close association between the crews. Some of the *Malines*'s men were already survivors of a ship sunk at Rotterdam, and *Malines* herself had been heavily bombed there. After two hard trips to Dunkirk she was now at Folkestone waiting for coal, when nerves began to crack. The ship's doctor certified that three engineers, the wireless operator, the purser, a seaman, and several engine room hands were all unfit for duty.

Malines was ordered to Dunkirk again on the evening of June 1, but with the crew on the edge of revolt, her captain refused to go. He was supported by the masters of two other steamers also at Folkestone, the Isle of Man packets *Ben-My-Chree* and *Tynwald*. They too refused to go, and when the local naval commander sent a written inquiry asking whether *Ben-My-Chree* would sail, her skipper simply wrote back, "I beg to state that after our experience in Dunkirk yesterday, my answer is 'No.' "

Trouble had been brewing for some time, particularly among the larger packets and passenger steamers. They were still manned by their regular crews and managed by their peacetime operators. These men had no naval training whatsoever, nor much of that special *élan* that the weekend sailors and other volunteers brought to the job.

As early as May 28 the steamer *Canterbury* refused to sail. She had been there twice, and that was enough. The Dynamo Room finally put a naval party aboard to stiffen the crew. This worked, and a hurried call was made to Chatham Barracks for 220 seamen and stokers. They would form a pool of disciplined hands, ready for duty on any ship where the crew seemed to be wavering.

When the *St. Seiriol* refused to sail on the 29th, an officer, armed guard, and seven stokers went on board at 10:00 a.m., and the ship left at 11:00. On the packet *Ngaroma* the engineers were the problem. They were quickly replaced by two Royal Navy stokers, and an armed party of six hands was added for good measure. *Ngaroma* went back to work.

But these were individual cases. The dismaying thing about *Malines*, *Tynwald*, and *Ben-My-Chree* was that the three ships seemed to be acting in concert. A hurried call was sent to Dover for relief crews and armed guards, but it would be some hours before they arrived. All through the night of June 1–2 the three ships—each able to lift 1,000 to 2,000 men—lay idle.

Other men were losing heart too. When the tug *Contest* was commandeered at Ramsgate for a trip to Dunkirk, the crew deliberately ran her aground. Refloated, the engineer refused to put to sea, claiming his filters would be blocked by sand.

Off Bray-Dunes, Admiral Wake-Walker signaled another tug to help a stranded minesweeper. The skipper paid no attention, wanted only to get away. Wake-Walker finally had to train a gun on him and send a navy sub-lieutenant to take charge.

There was also trouble with the vessels of the Royal National Lifeboat Institution. The boat from Hythe flatly refused to go at all. The coxswain argued that he had been asked to run his boat onto the beach, and once aground he could never get off. He would not try at Dunkirk what he could not do at Hythe—apparently ignoring the fact that at Dunkirk the tide would do it for him.

He managed to talk the Walmer and Dungeness boats out of going too. In disgust the Navy then took over the whole RNLI fleet, except the Ramsgate and Margate craft. They had already sailed for Dunkirk with their own crews.

These lifeboat crews were no sniveling cowards. The coxswain of the Hythe boat had been risking his life in the service for 37 years, 20 of them in charge of the boat. He had won the Institution's silver medal for gallantry. Yet there was something different about Dunkirk—the continuing danger, the inability to control events, the reality of being under fire. Such factors could undermine the resolve of even the staunchest men.

Nor was the Royal Navy immune. There was a tendency to feel that "it can't happen here," that naval training and discipline somehow insulated a man from the fear and uncertainty that beset civilian hearts. Yet this was not necessarily so. Morale on the destroyer *Verity*, shaky since May 27, seemed to collapse after a trip to Dunkirk on the 30th. Twelve men broke out of the ship, with six still absent on the 31st. Those who returned simply explained they couldn't "stand it" any longer. *Verity* was ordered to remain in Dover harbor.

Acute fear could be like a disease—both physical and highly contagious. The minesweeper *Hebe* was hit perhaps worst of all. She had been a sort of command ship off Bray-Dunes; few of the crew slept for five days. On the evening of May 31 the ship's sub-lieutenant collapsed, going into fits and convulsions. Next day, 27 members of the crew came down the same way. Finally, as *Hebe* returned to Dover on the morning of June 1, the ship's surgeon collapsed too, mumbling that he could not face another trip to Dunkirk.

Rest was the answer, but rest was a luxury they couldn't have. After especially grueling trips the *Malcolm* and the *Windsor* did get a day off, but usually the ships just kept going. The main hope for relief came from the steady stream of new vessels and fresh hands that kept pouring in.

The Navy continued to comb its lists, searching for officers who could be borrowed from other duties. Commander Edward K. Le Mesurier was assigned to the aircraft carrier *Formidable*, building at Belfast. Important, but he could be spared for a week. He arrived at Ramsgate at noon, June 1, and by 5:30 he was on his way to Dunkirk. He found he had exchanged carrier duty for command of a tug, a launch, and five rowboats.

Sub-Lieutenant Michael Anthony Chodzko was a young reserve officer attending navigational school at Plymouth. Buried in his books, he didn't even know there was serious trouble until he was yanked out of class on May 31 and sent by train to Dover. Then, as the train ran along the chalk cliffs just before the station, he glanced out the car window and saw gunfire across the Channel. It was his first inkling of what lay ahead. Next morning, June 1, he was heading for Dunkirk with his first command—a small cabin cruiser called the *Aura*.

David Divine wasn't in the Navy at all. He was a free-lance writer and amateur sailor who naturally gravitated to Dover at the end of May, because that's where the big story was. Like the other journalists in town, he would stand in the grass that crowned the white cliffs and focus his binoculars on the incredible procession of vessels pouring across the Channel. But unlike the others, the sea ran in his blood, and the more he watched, the more he wanted to be part of this show.

It wasn't hard to join. Through his naval writing he had plenty of contacts at the Admiralty, and by May 31 he had the necessary papers that put him in the Navy for 30 days. He went to Ramsgate, looked over the mass of small craft now piling up in the harbor, and picked out for himself a small motor sailor called the *Little Ann*. With no formal assignment whatsoever, he jumped aboard and began getting her ready for sea. He was soon joined by a kindred soul—Divine never learned his name—and the two of them, with a couple of others, set out for Dunkirk early on June 1.

Charles Herbert Lightoller was another man who liked to do

things his own way. No stranger to danger, he had been Second Officer on the *Titanic*, where his coolness helped save countless lives that famous night. Now he was 66, retired from the sea, raising chickens in Hertfordshire, but he still had that combination of courage and good humor that served him so well in 1912.

And he still enjoyed life afloat. His 58-foot power cruiser *Sundowner* had been carefully designed to his exact specifications, and he liked nothing better than an occasional jaunt up and down the Thames with a party of friends. Once he even had 21 people aboard.

It was 5 p.m. on May 31 when Lightoller got a cryptic phone call from a friend at the Admiralty, requesting a meeting at 7:00 that evening. It turned out that the Navy needed *Sundowner* at once. Could he get her from the yacht basin at Chiswick down to Ramsgate, where a Navy crew would take over and sail her to Dunkirk?

Whoever had that idea, Lightoller bristled, had another guess coming. "If anybody is going to take her over, my eldest son and I will."

They set out from Ramsgate at 10 on the morning of the 1st. Besides Lightoller and his son Roger, they also had aboard an eighteen-year-old Sea Scout, taken along as a deck hand. Halfway across they encountered three German fighters, but the destroyer *Worcester* was near and drove them away. It was just as well, because *Sundowner* was completely unarmed, not even a tin hat aboard.

Midafternoon, they were off Dunkirk. It was ebb tide, and as he drew alongside the eastern mole, Lightoller realized that the drop was too great from the walkway to *Sundowner*'s deck. The troops would never be able to manage it. Instead, he berthed alongside a destroyer that was already loading, and his troops crossed over from her. He loaded *Sundowner* from the bottom up, with Roger in charge below decks.

No one ever tackled such an unglamorous assignment with more verve than Roger. To lower the center of gravity, he made the men lie down whenever possible. Then he filled every inch of space, even the bath and the "head."

"How are you getting on?" Lightoller called below, as the tally passed 50.

"Oh, plenty of room yet," Roger airily replied. At 75 he finally conceded he had enough.

Lightoller now shifted his efforts to the open deck. Again, the troops were told to lie down and stay down, to keep the ship more stable. Even so, by the time 50 more were aboard, Lightoller could feel *Sundowner* getting tender. He called it a day and started for home.

The entire Luftwaffe seemed to be waiting for him. Bombing and strafing, the enemy planes made pass after pass. Fortunately *Sundowner* could turn on a sixpence, and Lightoller had learned a few tricks from an expert. His youngest son, killed in the first days of the war, had been a bomber pilot and often talked about evasion tactics. The father now put his lost son's theories to work. The secret was to wait until the last instant, when the enemy plane was already committed, then hard rudder before the pilot could readjust. Squirming and dodging his way across the Channel, Lightoller managed to get *Sundowner* back to England without a scratch.

Gliding into Ramsgate at 10 that night, he tied up to a trawler lying next to the quay. The usual group of waterfront onlookers drifted over to watch. All assumed that the 50 men on deck would be *Sundowner*'s full load—an impressive achievement in itself. But troops continued to pour out of hatches and companionways until a grand total of 130 men were landed. Turning to Lightoller, an astonished bystander could only ask, "God's truth, mate! Where did you put them?"

So the evacuation went on. Despite bombs and frayed nerves, 64,429 men were returned this June 1. They ranged from the peppery General Montgomery to Private Bill Hersey, who also managed to embark his French bride, Augusta, now thinly disguised in British battle dress. The number lifted off the beaches fell as the troops pulled back from La Panne, but a record 47,081 were rescued from Dunkirk itself. The eastern mole continued to survive the battering it took from bombs, shells, and inept shiphandling.

At 3:40 p.m. the small minesweeper *Mare* edged toward the mole, hoping to pick up one more load of British soldiers waiting on the long wooden walkway. Nothing unusual about that, but then something happened that was completely unprecedented. The captain of a British destroyer lying nearby ordered

Mare to proceed instead to the western mole and embark French and Belgian troops. For the first time a British ship was specifically diverted from British to Allied personnel.

Mare crossed the harbor and found a Portsmouth steam hopper and drifter already working the western mole. Three more minesweepers joined in, and between them the six ships lifted 1,200 poilus in little more than an hour.

Such endeavors helped produce statistics that were far more significant than any single incident: on June 1 a total of 35,013 French were embarked, as against 29,416 British. At last Winston Churchill had some figures he could take to Paris without embarrassment. For the Royal Navy, *bras-dessus, bras-dessous* had become an accomplished fact.

All morning the top command at London, Dover, and Dunkirk watched the pounding of the rescue fleet with growing alarm. Around noon Admiral Drax of The Nore Command at Chatham called the Admiralty's attention to the mounting destroyer losses. The time had come, he suggested, to stop using them during daylight. Ramsay reluctantly agreed, and at 1:45 p.m. flashed the message, "All destroyers are to return to harbour forthwith."

The *Malcolm* was just starting out on one more trip across the Channel. No ship had better morale, but even Lieutenant Mellis's bagpipes were no longer enough to lift the men's spirits. The air was full of stories about sinking ships, and the general feeling was that *Malcolm* would get it next. Then, as she cleared the breakwater, Ramsay's message arrived, ordering her back. Mellis felt he now knew how a reprieved prisoner feels.

The *Worcester* was just entering Dunkirk harbor, and her skipper, Commander Allison, decided it didn't make sense to return without picking up one more load at the mole. Packed with troops, she finally pulled out at 5:00 p.m. and immediately came under attack. Wave after wave of Stukas dived on her— three or four squadrons of about nine each—dropping more than 100 bombs. They pressed their attacks home, too, diving as low as 200 to 300 feet. Miraculously, there were no direct hits, but near misses sent giant columns of water over the ship, and bomb splinters riddled her thin steel plates. By the time the attacks tapered off, 46 men lay dead, 180 wounded.

Watching *Worcester*'s ordeal from his command post at the foot of the mole, Captain Tennant decided this was enough. At 6:00 p.m. he radioed Ramsay:

> Things are getting very hot for ships; over 100 bombers on ships here since 0530, many casualties. Have directed that no ships sail during daylight. Evacuation by transports therefore ceases at 0300. . . . If perimeter holds, will complete evacuation tomorrow, Sunday night, including most French. . . .

But *could* the perimeter hold another day? London had its doubts. "Every effort must be made to complete the evacuation tonight," General Dill had wired Weygand at 2:10 p.m. At 4 o'clock Winston Churchill warned Reynaud by telephone that the evacuation might be stretched out a day longer, but "by waiting too long, we run the risk of losing everything." As late as 8:00 p.m. Ramsay sent a ringing appeal to his whole rescue fleet, calling for "one last effort."

At Dunkirk General Alexander originally felt the same way, but by now he wanted more time. He was determined to get the rest of the BEF home, yet on the morning of June 1 there were still 39,000 British troops in the perimeter, plus 100,000 French. Applying the equal numbers policy, that meant lifting at least 78,000 men in the next 24 hours—obviously impossible.

At 8:00 a.m. he dropped by Bastion 32 with a new withdrawal plan, extending the evacuation through the night of June 2–3. Admiral Abrial gladly went along: the French had always had greater confidence than the British in holding the perimeter. Toward evening Captain Tennant agreed too. There was no alternative once he made the decision to end daylight operations.

London still had its doubts, but in the end the chairborne warriors at the Admiralty and War Office had to face an unpleasant truth: they just didn't know enough to make the decision. At 6:41 General Dill wired Alexander:

> We do not order any fixed moment for evacuation. You are to hold on as long as possible in order that the maximum number of French and British may be

evacuated. Impossible from here to judge local situation. In close cooperation with Admiral Abrial you must act in this matter on your own judgment.

So Alexander now had a green light. The evacuation would continue through the night of June 2–3, as he and Captain Tennant proposed. But success still depended on Tennant's precondition: "*if* the perimeter holds." This was a very big "if" and the answer lay beyond the control of the leaders in London, Dover, or Dunkirk itself.

13

"BEF Evacuated"

On the 2nd Coldstream Guards' segment of the defense line along the Bergues-Furnes Canal, Lieutenant Jimmy Langley waited in the cottage he had so carefully fortified and stocked with provisions. He had no idea when the British planned to pull out—company officers weren't privy to such things—but his men were ready for a long siege. In the first light of the new day, June 1, Langley looked through the peephole he had made in the roof, but could see nothing. A thick mist hung over the canal and the flat meadows to the south.

Sunrise. The mist burned off, and there—600 yards away on the other side of the canal—stood a working party of German troops. There were perhaps 100 of them, armed only with spades, and what their assignment was, Langley never knew. A blaze of gunfire from the cottage mowed them down—the last "easy" Germans he would meet that day.

The firing steadily increased as the enemy troops joined in. At one point they wheeled up an antitank gun, and Langley watched with interest as they pointed it right at his cottage. A few seconds later an antitank shell came crashing through the roof, ricocheting wildly about the attic. The Coldstreamers tumbled down the stairs and out the front door as four more shells arrived. The enemy fire slackened off, and Langley's men reoccupied their fortress.

The big danger lay to the right. At 11:00 a.m. General von Kuechler launched his "systematic attack," and around noon the enemy stormed across the canal just east of Bergues. The 1st East Lancashires were forced back and might have been overrun completely but for the prodigious valor of a company commander, Captain Ervine-Andrews. Gathering a handful of volunteers, he climbed to the thatched roof of a barn and held off the Germans with a Bren gun.

Just to the left of the East Lancs were the 5th Borderers. Now across the canal in strength, the enemy smashed at them too. If they collapsed, the 2nd Coldstream, to their left, would be hit next. An officer from the Borderers hurried over to Major McCorquodale's command post to warn that his battalion was exhausted and about to withdraw.

"I order you to stay put and fight it out," the Major answered.

"You cannot do that. I have overriding orders from my colonel to withdraw when I think fit."

McCorquodale saw no point in arguing: "You see that big poplar tree on the road with the white milestone beside it? The moment you or any of your men go back beyond that tree, we will shoot you."

The officer again protested, but the Major had had enough. "Get back or I will shoot you now and send one of my officers to take command."

The Borderer officer went off, and McCorquodale turned to Langley, standing nearby: "Get a rifle. Sights at 250. You will shoot to kill the moment he passes that tree. Are you clear?"

McCorquodale picked up a rifle himself, and the two Coldstreamers sat waiting, guns trained on the tree. Soon the Borderer officer reappeared near the tree with two of his men. They paused, then the officer moved on past McCorquodale's deadline. Two rifles cracked at the same instant. The officer fell, and Langley never knew which one of them got him.

Such measures weren't enough. The 5th Borderers fell back, leaving the Coldstream's flank wide open. Jimmy Langley's fortified cottage soon came under fire. The afternoon turned into a jumble of disconnected incidents: knocking out a German gun with the much-despised Boyes antitank rifle . . . washing down a delicious chicken stew with white wine . . . using the Bren guns in the attic to set three German lorries on fire, blocking the canal road for precious minutes. At one point an old lady appeared from nowhere, begging for shelter. Langley told her to go to hell; then, overcome by remorse, he put her in a back room where he thought she might be safe.

Another time he went to the battalion command post to see how McCorquodale was getting along. The Major was lying beside his trench, apparently hit. "I am tired, so very tired," he told Langley. Then, "Get back to the cottage, and carry·on."

By now the Germans had occupied a house across the canal from Langley's place, and the firing grew more intense than ever. In the attic one of the Bren guns conked out, and Langley ordered the other downstairs. It would be more useful there, if the enemy tried to swim the canal and rush the cottage. Langley himself stayed in the attic, sniping with a rifle.

Suddenly a crash . . . a shower of tiles and beams . . . a blast of heat that bowled Langley over. In the choking dust he heard a small voice say, "I've been hit"—then realized that the voice was his own.

It didn't hurt yet, but his left arm was useless. A medical orderly appeared, slapped on a dressing, and began bandaging his head. So that had been hit too. He was gently carried down from the attic, put into a wheelbarrow, and trundled to the rear—one of the few Coldstreamers small enough to make an exit this way.

By now it was dark, and the battle tapered off. Firmly established across the canal, Kuechler's infantry settled down for the night. Resumption of the "systematic attack" could wait until morning. The British began quietly pulling back to the sea. It was all very precise: each battalion took along its Bren guns and Boyes antitank rifles. The 2nd Hampshires marched by their commander, closed up in three's, rifles at the slope. Most positions were abandoned by 10:00 p.m.

As the gunners of the 53rd Field Regiment marched cross-country toward Dunkirk, a sharp challenge broke the silence of the night, followed by a blaze of rifle fire. French troops, moving into defensive positions along the network of waterways that laced the area, had mistaken them for Germans.

No one was hit; the mix-up was soon straightened out; and the British gunners continued on their way, but with new respect for their ally. These Frenchmen were all business. Part of the 32nd Infantry Division, they had escaped with their corps commander, the feisty General de la Laurencie, from the German trap at Lille. Together with the local garrison troops of the *Secteur Fortifié des Flandres*, they were now taking over the center of the perimeter from the retiring BEF.

At the same time, the French 12th Division, which had also escaped from Lille, was moving into the old fortifications that lined the Belgian frontier. Dug in here, they would cover the eastern flank of the new shortened defense line. Since General Beaufrère's 68th Division had always defended the west flank, the entire perimeter was now manned by the French.

It was hard to believe that only yesterday, May 31, Winston Churchill had emotionally told the Allied Supreme War Council that the remaining British divisions would form the rear guard so that the French could escape. Since then there had been, bit by bit, a complete turn-around. Instead of the British acting as rear guard for the French, the French were now acting as rear guard for the British.

Later the French would charge that the switch was yet another trick by "perfidious Albion." Actually, the British weren't all that pleased by the arrangement. They had little faith left in their ally. As the 5th Green Howards pulled back through the French guarding the new defense line along the Belgian border, Lieutenant-Colonel W. E. Bush collected his company officers and paid a courtesy call on the local French commander. The real purpose was not to cement Allied unity, but to see whether the French were up to the job. They turned out to be first-rate troops under a first-rate officer.

These French had their first test on the afternoon of the 1st, as Kuechler's "systematic attack" cautiously approached from the east. General Janssen's 12th Division stopped the Germans cold.

All the way west it was the same story. The Germans had some armor here—the only tanks that hadn't gone south—but General Beaufrère's artillery, firing over open sights, managed to hold the line.

Covered by the French, the remaining British units converged on Dunkirk all through the night of June 1–2. As the 6th Durham Light Infantry trudged through the ruined suburb of Rosendaël, the steady crunch of the men's boots on broken glass reminded Captain John Austin of marching over hard ice crystals on a cold winter's day. It was a black, moonless night, but the way was lit by burning buildings and the flash of exploding shells. The German infantry might be taking the night off, but not their artillery. The DLI's hunched low, as against a storm, their steel helmets gleaming from the light of the flames.

Admiral Ramsay's ships were already waiting for them. Lifting operations were to run from 9:00 p.m. to 3:00 a.m. but when the first destroyer reached the mole, few of the troops had arrived from the perimeter. Those who came down from Bray-Dunes were mostly huddled in the houses and hotels along the beach promenade, seeking cover from the rain of shells.

Commander E. R. Condor couldn't see anybody at all when he brought the destroyer *Whitshed* alongside the mole soon after dark. Just smoke, flames, and a few dogs sniffing around. Spotting a bicycle lying on the walkway, Condor mounted it and pedaled toward shore looking for somebody to rescue. Eventually he found some poilus, and then some Tommies near the base of the mole. He sent them all out, along with a few other troops who now began to appear.

At 10:30 p.m. Major Allan Adair led out the 3rd Grenadier Guards, still carrying their Bren guns; they boarded the Channel steamer *Newhaven* . . . at 11:00 hundreds of French joined the crowd, and for a while the troops moved out four abreast—unconsciously symbolizing the troubled alliance . . . at 12:00 the gunners of the 99th Field Regiment marched out to the destroyer *Winchelsea*. Occasional shells prodded them along. "I've been hit," the man next to Sergeant E. C. Webb quietly remarked, dropping out of line.

"Hand out the wounded". . . "Lay out the dead". . . "Wounded to the front" . . . "Watch the hole." The sailors of the shore party kept up a running stream of orders and directions as they guided the troops along. An effort was made to keep a lane open for the stretcher bearers, but there was no time for the dead. They were simply pushed off the mole onto the pilings below.

It was after midnight when the 1st/6th East Surreys finally

reached the mole. There was a long queue now, and the wait stretched into hours. The mole itself was so packed that the line barely moved, and the East Surreys were still inching forward when word came at 2:00 a.m. that the last two ships of the night were alongside—a big paddle steamer, and just ahead of her a destroyer. It was almost 3:00 by the time the East Surreys reached the paddle steamer. Deciding there was no time to lose, the battalion commander Colonel Armstrong quickly divided his men in two, sent the first half up ahead to the destroyer, and ordered the rear-guard half to go aboard the steamer. A few East Surreys were still waiting to embark, when the cry went up, "No more!" Armstrong emphatically pushed the last men down the gangway, then slid down himself as the vessel cast off.

The 5th Green Howards were halfway down the mole at 3:00. They had spent most of the night coming down from Bray-Dunes. It was only six miles, but the sand, the darkness, their utter weariness all slowed them down, and they took nearly five hours to make the march. Now, mixed in with other British units and a great horde of French, they slowly moved along the walkway, with frequent stops that nobody could explain. It was during one of these halts when the word came down, "No more boats tonight. Clear the mole!"

Bitterly disappointed, the Green Howards turned back, only to run headlong into other troops who hadn't gotten the word yet. For a while there was much pushing and shoving, and all movement came to a standstill. At this point a salvo of German shells landed squarely on the base of the mole, mowing down scores of men.

If Commander Clouston had been on hand, things might have gone more smoothly, but he had returned to Dover for the night. He had served as pier master for five days and nights without a break—had sent off over 100,000 men—now he wanted to confer with Ramsay about the last, climactic stage of the evacuation, and perhaps get a good night's sleep.

While the destroyers and Channel steamers lifted troops off the mole, Ramsay's plan called for the minesweepers and smaller paddle-wheelers to work the beach just to the east, going as far as Malo-les-Bains. Thousands of British and French soldiers stood in three or four queues curling into the sea as far as a man could wade. Gunner F. Noon of the 53rd Field Regiment waited for two full hours, while the water crept over his ankles ... his knees ... his waist ... and up to his neck. Then, as the first trace of dawn streaked the eastern sky, somebody shouted, "No more! The ships will return tonight!"

The 2nd Coldstream Guards was another unit to reach the harbor late. After their long stand on the canal, the men were bone-tired, but they still had their Brens. As they moved down the paved promenade at Malo-les-Bains, they marched in perfect step, arms swinging. Most of the waiting troops watched in awe and admiration, but not all. "I'll bet that's the bloody Guards," called a caustic voice in the dark. "Try marching on tiptoes!"

One Coldstreamer who wasn't late was Lieutenant Jimmy Langley. Groggy from his wounds, he was vaguely aware of being trundled from the battlefield by wheelbarrow and loaded into an ambulance. The ride was one of those stop-and-go affairs that seem to take forever. He still felt no pain, but he was thirsty and dreadfully uncomfortable. Blood kept dripping onto his face from the man above him.

At last the ambulance stopped, and Langley's stretcher was lifted out. "This way," somebody said. "The beach is 200 yards ahead of you."

The stretcher party reached the water's edge. A ship's lifeboat lay waiting, rubbing gently against the sand. An officer in a naval greatcoat came over and asked Langley, "Can you get off your stretcher?"

"No, I don't think so."

"Well, I'm very sorry, we cannot take you. Your stretcher would occupy the places of four men. Orders are, only those who can stand or sit up."

Langley said nothing. It was hard to be turned back after coming so close, but he understood. The stretcher bearers picked him up and carried him, still silent, back to the ambulance.

About this time another Coldstreamer, Sergeant L.H.T. Court, joined one of the queues on the beach. Attached to 1st Guards Brigade HQ, he was carrying the brigade war diary, an imposing volume inscribed on a stack of Army Forms C 2118.

As he slowly moved forward into the sea, Court found his mind absorbed by three things: his bride of less than a year; his brother, just killed in Belgium; and the mountain of Forms C 2118 he was trying to save.

As the water reached his chest, he once again thought about his young wife. They had no children yet, and if he didn't return she'd have nothing to remember him by. This lugubrious thought was interrupted by his sudden discovery that some of the Forms C 2118 were floating away. A good headquarters man to the end, he put aside all else, and frantically splashed around retrieving his files.

Eventually Court neared the front of the queue, where a naval launch was ferrying men to a larger vessel further out. Then, at 3:00 a.m. a voice called out from the launch that this was the last trip, but added that there would be another boat later on. Court continued waiting, but no other boat ever came. Some of the men turned back toward the shore, but Court and a few others waded over to a grounded fishing smack lying nearby. He was hauled aboard, still clutching the brigade war diary.

The tide was coming in, and around 4:30 the boat began to move. By now some 90 to 100 men were aboard, most of them packed in the hold where the fish were normally put. A few knowledgeable hands hoisted the sails, and a course was set for England. But there was no wind, and nearly twelve hours later they were still only a mile and a half from Dunkirk. At this point a passing destroyer picked them up, including Court and the lovingly preserved papers.

There were others, too, who weren't inclined to wait eighteen hours for the Royal Navy to come back the following night. Thirty-six men of the 1st Duke of Wellington's Regiment took over a sailing barge appropriately called the *Iron Duke*. Colonel L. C. Griffith-Williams salvaged another stranded barge, loaded it with artillerymen, and set off for Britain. He knew nothing about navigation, but he found a child's atlas and a toy compass aboard. That would be enough. When a patrol boat later intercepted them, they were heading for Germany.

While the more adventuresome improvised ways to escape, most of the troops trudged back to the shore to wait out the eighteen hours. They passed the time in a variety of ways. It was now Sunday, June 2, and some men joined a chaplain celebrating Holy Communion on the beach at Malo-les-Bains. Ted Harvey, a fisherman stranded when his motor launch conked out, joined an impromptu soccer game. The 4th/7th Royal Dragoon Guards enjoyed motorcycle races in the sand and bet on which waterfront building would be hit by the next German shell.

But the most important game was to stay alive. Most of the waiting troops crowded into any place that seemed to offer the faintest hope of shelter. One group settled down in the shattered hulk of the French destroyer *l'Adroit*, lying just off Malo. Wrecked though she was, her twisted steel seemed to offer a measure of security. Others picked an old watchtower left over from Napoleon's time; its thick stone walls also seemed to promise safety.

Others packed the cellars of nearby buildings. The remnants of the 53rd Field Regiment chose the Café des Fleurs—flimsy, but it was right on the *plage*. Headquarters of the 5th Green Howards was established at 22 rue Gambetta, a comfortable house about a block from the beach. Here the battalion also adopted a stray poilu, who made right for the kitchen. True to the great tradition of his country, he soon produced a superb stew of beef and wine. Promptly christened "Alphonse," he was made an honorary member of the battalion and from now on sported a British tin hat.

The 5th Green Howards offered something very rare at Dunkirk: a sizable body of organized troops, complete with their own officers and accustomed to working together. Recalling the chaos at the mole when the loading stopped the previous dawn, the battalion commander Lieutenant-Colonel W. E. Bush decided the Green Howards had a useful role to play during the coming night, June 2–3. They would form a cordon to control the traffic and insure an orderly flow of men to the ships as they arrived. Four officers and 100 men should be enough to do the job. Those selected would, of course, be last off and might very well be left behind. The officers drew lots for the honor.

Plans for the evening were moving ahead at Dover too. Early in the morning Admiral Wake-Walker came over by MTB from Dunkirk. After a couple hours' rest, he attended a joint naval and military conference in the Dynamo Room. No one knew how many troops were left to be evacuated, but Wake-Walker gave an educated guess of 5,000 British and anywhere from 30,000 to 40,000 French.

Fortunately there were plenty of ships on hand. The suspension of daylight evacuation made it possible to collect virtually the whole fleet at Dover and the other southeast ports. Ramsay planned to use this vast concentration for what he called a "massed descent" on Dunkirk harbor. All troops to leave from Dunkirk itself; no more lifting from the beaches. Embarkation to start at 9:00 p.m. and continue until 3:00 a.m. Staggered sailings to insure a steady flow of ships. Three or four vessels to be alongside the mole continuously. Slow vessels to start first; fast ones later, to keep the flow even.

Captain Denny argued that the plan was too complicated—it would only result in confusion. It would be better simply to send everything over, and let the men on the spot work the details out. But most of the staff felt the scheme was worth trying.

As finally worked out, the plan provided for enough large ships to lift 37,000 men, plus whatever number might be picked up by the small craft that continued to ply across the Channel. In addition, the French would be using their own ships to lift troops from the beach just east of the mole, and from the west pier in the outer harbor. That should finish the job, and at 10:52 a.m., June 2, Ramsay signaled his whole command:

> The final evacuation is staged for tonight, and the Nation looks to the Navy to see this through. I want every ship to report as soon as possible whether she is fit and ready to meet the call which has been made on our courage and endurance.

"Ready and anxious to carry out your order" . . . "Fit and ready"—the replies were bravely Nelsonian. But beneath the surface, most of the rescuers felt like Sub-Lieutenant Rutherford Crosby on the paddle-sweeper *Oriole*. His heart sank when he heard they were going back again. He thought the evacuation was all over. Ramsay had said as much yesterday, when he called for "one last effort."

But, like Crosby, most of the others soon resigned themselves to facing another desperate night. "We were going," he later wrote, "and that was all there was to it."

Not everyone agreed. The three passenger steamers at Folkestone—*Ben-My-Chree*, *Malines*, and *Tynwald*—continued to give trouble. Most of the day they were kept anchored in the harbor, but at 6:50 p.m. *Ben-My-Chree* came alongside the jetty to be readied for the night's work. The crew lined the rails, demonstrating and shouting that they were going to leave the ship. When they tried to go ashore a couple of minutes later, they were turned back by an armed naval guard advancing up the gangplank with fixed bayonets. A relief crew quickly took over, and *Ben-My-Chree* finally sailed at 7:05. Only the chief officer, three gunners, and the wireless operator remained from the original crew.

Then it was *Tynwald*'s turn. Her crew didn't try to leave, but as she docked at 7:10 p.m., they hooted and shouted down at the naval sentries. At 7:30 she was still sitting at the pier.

Meanwhile, nobody had paid any attention to the *Malines*. At 4:30 p.m she quietly weighed anchor, and without any authorization whatsoever, stood off for Southampton. Her master later explained, "It seemed in the best interests of all concerned."

There was, in fact, good reason for the civilian crews on these Channel steamers to be afraid. They were virtually unarmed and presented the biggest targets at Dunkirk. If any further proof were needed, it was supplied by a series of incidents that began at 10:30 on the morning of June 2. At this time the Dynamo Room received an urgent message from Captain Tennant in Dunkirk:

> Wounded situation acute. Hospital ship should enter during the day. Geneva Convention will be honourably observed. It is felt that the enemy will refrain from attack.

The plight of the wounded had been growing steadily worse for several days, aggravated by the decision to lift only fit men in the regular transports. Now Tennant was trying to ease the situation with this special appeal for hospital ships. He had, of course, no way of knowing whether the enemy would respect the Red Cross, but he sent the message in clear, hoping that the Germans would intercept it and order the Luftwaffe to lay off.

The Dynamo Room swung into action right away, and at 1:30 p.m. the hospital ship *Worthing* started across the Channel. Gleaming white and with standard Red Cross markings, it was impossible to mistake her for a regular transport. But that didn't help her today. Two-thirds of the way across, *Worthing* was attacked by a dozen Ju 88's. No hits, but nine bombs fell close enough to damage the engine room and force her back to Dover.

At 5:00 p.m. the hospital ship *Paris* sailed. She got about as far as the *Worthing*, when three planes tore into her. Again no hits, but near misses started leaks and burst the pipes in the engine room. As *Paris* drifted out of control, Captain Biles swung out his boats and fired several distress rockets. These attracted fifteen more German planes.

The Dynamo Room sent tugs to the rescue and continued preparing for the coming night's "massed descent." With so many vessels involved, it was essential to have the best men possible controlling traffic and directing the flow of ships and men. Fortunately the best was once again available. Commander Clouston, fresh from a night's rest, would once more be pier master on the mole. To help him, Captain Denny assigned an augmented naval berthing party of 30 men. Sub-Lieutenant Michael Solomon, whose fluent French had been a godsend to Clouston since the 31st, would again serve as interpreter and liaison officer.

The Clouston party left Dover at 3:30 p.m. in two RAF crash boats: *No. 243*, with the Commander himself in charge, and *No. 270*, commanded by Sub-Lieutenant Roger Wake, an aggressive young Royal Navy regular. They were going well ahead of the other ships in order to get Dunkirk organized for the night's work.

It was a calm, lazy afternoon, and as the two boats droned across an empty Channel, the war seemed far away. Then suddenly Lieutenant Wake heard "a roar, a rattle, and a bang." Startled, he looked up in time to see a Stuka diving on Clouston's boat about 200 yards ahead. It dropped a bomb—missed—then opened up with its machine guns.

No time to see what happened next. Seven more Stukas were

plunging on the two motor boats, machine guns blazing. Wake ordered his helm hard to port, and for the next ten minutes played a desperate dodging game, as the Stukas took turns bombing and strafing him. In an open cockpit all the way aft, Lieutenant de Vasseau Roux, a French liaison officer, crouched behind the Lewis machine gun, hammering away at the German planes. He never budged an inch—not even when a bullet took the sight off his gun six inches from his nose. One of the Stukas fell, and the others finally broke off.

Now at last Wake had a moment to see how Clouston's boat had weathered the storm. Only the bow was visible, and the whole crew were in the water. Wake hurried over to pick up the survivors, but Clouston waved him off . . . told him to get on to Dunkirk, as ordered. Wake wanted at least to pick up Clouston as senior officer, but the Commander refused to leave his men. There was no choice; Wake turned again for Dunkirk.

Clouston and his men continued swimming, clustered around the shattered bow of their boat. A French liaison officer clinging to the wreck reported an empty lifeboat floating in the sea a mile or so away. Sub-Lieutenant Solomon asked permission to swim over and try to bring it back for the survivors. Clouston not only approved; he decided to come along. This was their best chance of rescue, and Solomon alone might not be enough.

Clouston was a splendid athlete, a good swimmer, and confident of his strength. Perhaps that was the trouble. He didn't realize how tired he was. After a short while, he was exhausted and had to swim back to the others clinging to the wreck. Hours passed, but Solomon never returned with the empty boat. As the men waited, they sang and discussed old times together, while Clouston tried to encourage them with white lies about the nearness of rescue. One by one they disappeared, victims of exposure, until finally Clouston too was gone, and only Aircraftsman Carmaham remained to be picked up alive by a passing destroyer.

Meanwhile Sub-Lieutenant Solomon had indeed reached the empty boat. He too was exhausted, but after a long struggle managed to climb aboard. He did his best to row back to the wreck, but there was only one oar. After an hour he gave up: the boat was too large, the distance too far; and it was already dark.

He drifted all night and was picked up just before dawn by the French fishing smack *Stella Maria*. Wined, rested, and wearing a dry French sailor's uniform, he was brought back to Dover and transferred to the French control ship *Savorgnan de Brazza*. His story sounded so far-fetched he was briefly held on suspicion of being a German spy. Nor did his fluent French help him any. *"Il prétend être anglais,"* the French commander observed, *"mais moi je crois qu'il est allemand parce qu'il parle français trop bien."* In short, he spoke French too well to be an Englishman.

An hour and a half after Clouston's advance party left Dover on the afternoon of June 2, Ramsay's evacuation fleet began its "massed descent" on Dunkirk. As planned, the slowest ships led the way, leaving at 5 p.m. They were mostly small fishing boats—like the Belgian trawler *Cor Jésu*, the French *Jeanne Antoine*, and the brightly painted little *Ciel de France*.

Next came six skoots ... then the whole array of coasters, tugs, yachts, cabin cruisers, excursion steamers, and ferries that by now were such a familiar sight streaming across the Channel ... then the big packets and mail steamers, the minesweepers and French torpedo boats ... and finally, kicking up great bow waves as they knifed through the sea, the last eleven British destroyers of a collection that originally totaled 40.

The Southern Railway's car ferry *Autocarrier* was a new addition. Lumbering along, she attracted a lot of attention, for in 1940 a car ferry was still a novelty in the cross-Channel service. The Isle of Man steamer *Tynwald* wasn't new, but in her own way she was conspicuous too. At Folkestone her crew had balked at making another trip. Now here she was, steaming along as though nothing had happened.

It hadn't been easy. Learning of the trouble, Ramsay sent over Commander William Bushell, one of his best troubleshooters. The Commander arrived to find *Tynwald* tied up at the quay, her crew in rebellion. Dover's instructions were a masterpiece of practical psychology: Bushell was on no account to consider himself in command of the ship, but was to make whatever changes were necessary to get her to Dunkirk. The chief officer relieved the master ... the second relieved the chief ... a new second was found ... other substitutes were rushed down from London by bus ... naval and military gun crews were added. At 9:15 p.m. *Tynwald* was on her way.

More than ever the ships were manned by a crazy hodge-podge of whoever was available. The crew of the War Department launch *Marlborough* consisted of four sub-lieutenants, four stokers, two RAF sergeants, and two solicitors from the Treasury who had come down on their day off. David Divine, the sea-going journalist, left the *Little Ann* stranded on a sand bar, hitched a ride home, shopped around Ramsgate for another boat, found a spot on the 30-foot motor launch *White Wing*.

"Where do you think you're going?" a very formal, professional-looking naval officer asked, as *White Wing* prepared to shove off.

"To Dunkirk," Divine replied.

"No you're not," said the officer, as Divine wondered whether he had broken some regulation. After all, he was new at this sort of thing. But the explanation had nothing to do with Divine. *White Wing*, of all unlikely vessels, had been selected as flagship for an admiral.

Rear-Admiral A. H. Taylor, the Maintenance Officer at Sheerness Dockyard, had now serviced, manned and dispatched over 100 small craft for "Dynamo." He was a retired officer holding down a good desk job in London; he had every reason to go back feeling he had done his bit—so he went to Ramsgate and wangled his way across the Channel.

There was a rumor that British troops were still at Malo-les-Bains, somewhat blocked off from the mole. Taylor quickly persuaded Ramsay that he should lead a separate group of skoots and slow motor boats over to Malo and get them. He picked *White Wing* for himself; so it was that almost by accident David Divine became an "instant flag lieutenant" for a genuine admiral.

At 9:30 p.m. Captain Tennant's chief assistant, Commander Guy Maund, positioned himself with a loudhailer at the seaward end of the eastern mole. As the ships began arriving, he became a sort of "traffic cop," ordering them here and there, wherever they were needed. Admiral Taylor's flotilla was directed to the beach at Malo, but there was nobody there. His ships then joined the general rescue effort centered on the mole. As Denny had predicted, it was impossible to draw up a detailed blueprint at Dover; Maund used his own judgment in guiding the flow of ships.

The mole itself got first call. As the destroyers and Channel steamers loomed out of the dusk, Maund gave them their berthing assignments. A strong tide was setting west, and the ships had an especially difficult time coming alongside. Admiral Wake-Walker, hovering nearby in the speedboat *MA/SB 10*, used her as a tug to nudge one of the destroyers against the pilings. At the base of the mole, Commander Renfrew Gotto and Brigadier Parminter, imperturbable as ever, regulated the flow of troops onto the walkway. The Green Howards, bayonets fixed, formed their cordon as planned, keeping the queues in order. There was plenty of light from the still-blazing city.

Shortly after 9:00 the last of the BEF started down the mole. Lieutenant-Colonel H. S. Thuillier, commanding the one remaining antiaircraft detachment, spiked his seven guns and guided his men aboard the destroyer *Shikari*. The 2nd Coldstream Guards filed onto the destroyer *Sabre*, still proudly carrying their Bren guns. With only a handful of men left, the Green Howards dissolved their cordon and joined the parade. The last unit to embark was probably the 1st King's Shropshire Light Infantry.

These last detachments ignored the order to leave behind their casualties. On the *Sabre* there were only fourteen stretcher cases, but over 50 wounded were carried aboard by their comrades. Commander Brian Dean, *Sabre*'s captain, never heard a complaint "and hardly ever a groan."

In the midst of the crowd streaming onto the mole walked two officers, carrying a suitcase between them. One was a staff officer, worn and rumpled like everyone else. The other looked fresh, immaculate in service dress. Calm as ever, General Alexander was leaving with the final remnants of his command. By prearrangement the *MA/SB 10* was waiting, and Admiral Wake-Walker welcomed the General aboard. They briefly checked the beaches to make sure all British units were off, then headed for the destroyer *Venomous*, still picking up troops at the mole.

Commander John McBeath of the *Venomous* was standing on his bridge when a voice from the dark hailed him, asking if he could handle "some senior officers and staffs." McBeath told them to come aboard, starboard side aft.

"We've got a couple of generals now—fellows called Alexander and Percival," Lieutenant Angus MacKenzie reported a few minutes later. He added that he had put them with a few aides in McBeath's cabin, "but I'm afraid one of the colonels has hopped into your bed with his spurs on."

Venomous pulled out about 10:00 p.m., packed with so many troops she almost rolled over. McBeath stopped, trimmed ship, then hurried on across the Channel. At 10:30 the destroyer *Winchelsea* began loading. As the troops swarmed aboard, Commander Maund noticed they were no longer British—just French. To Maund that meant the job was over, and he arranged with *Winchelsea*'s captain to take him along on the trip back to Dover.

Captain Tennant also felt the job was done. At 10:50 he loaded the last of his naval party onto the speedboat *MTB 102*; then he too jumped aboard and headed for England. Just before leaving, he radioed Ramsay a final signal: "Operation completed. Returning to Dover." Boiled down by some gifted paraphraser to just the words, "BEF evacuated," Tennant's message would subsequently be hailed as a masterpiece of dramatic succinctness.

Sub-Lieutenant Roger Wake was now the only British naval officer on the mole. With Tennant, Maund, and the other old hands gone—and with Clouston lost on the way over—Wake became pier master by inheritance, and it was not an enviable assignment. He was short-handed, and he was only a sub-lieutenant—not much rank to throw in a crisis.

At the moment it didn't make much difference. The mole was virtually empty. The British troops had left, and there were no French. "Plenty of ships, cannot get troops," Wake-Walker radioed Dover at 1:15 a.m. In two hours it would be daylight, June 3, and all loading would have to stop. Time was flying, but half a dozen vessels lay idle alongside the deserted walkway.

"Now, Sub, I want 700. Go and get them," Lieutenant E. L. Davies, captain of the paddle-sweeper *Oriole*, told Sub-Lieutenant Rutherford Crosby, as they stood together on the mole wondering where everybody was. Crosby headed toward shore, ducking and waiting from time to time, whenever a shell sounded close. At last, near the base of the mole, he came to a mass of poilus. There was no embarkation officer in sight; so he summoned up his schoolboy French. "*Venez ici, tout le monde!*" he called, gesturing them to follow him.

The way back led past another ship berthed at the mole, and her crew did their best to entice Crosby's group into their own vessel, like carnival barkers at a country fair. The rule was "first loaded, first away," and nobody wanted to hang around Dunkirk any longer than necessary. Crosby made sure none of his charges strayed—let the other crews find their own Frenchmen.

They were trying. Captain Nicholson, substitute skipper of the *Tynwald*, walked toward the shore, shouting that his ship could take thousands. The *Albury* too sent out ambassadors, hawking the advantages of the big minesweeper. She eventually rounded up about 200.

But other ships could find no one. The car ferry *Autocarrier* waited nearly an hour under heavy shelling . . . then was sent home, her cavernous interior still empty. It was the same with the destroyers *Express*, *Codrington*, and *Malcolm*. Wake-Walker kept them on hand as long as he dared; but as dawn approached, and still no French, they went back empty too.

Where were the French anyhow? To a limited extent it was the familiar story of the ships not being where the men were. As Walker made the rounds on *MA/SB 10*, he could see plenty of soldiers at the Quai Félix Faure and the other quays and piers to the west, but very few ships. He tried to direct a couple of big transports over there, but that was a strange corner of the harbor for Ramsay's fleet. When the steamer *Rouen* ran hard aground, the Admiral didn't dare risk any more.

There were still the little ships, and Wake-Walker deployed them to help. The trawler *Yorkshire Lass* penetrated deep into the inner harbor, as far as a vessel could go. Her skipper Sub-Lieutenant Chodzko had lost his ship the previous night, but that didn't make him any more cautious now. Smoke and flames were everywhere—buildings exploding, tracers streaking across the sky—as *Yorkshire Lass* ran alongside a pier crowded with Frenchmen. Chodzko called on the troops to come, and about 100 leapt aboard . . . then three Tommies, somehow left behind . . . then, as *Yorkshire Lass* threaded her way out again, a Royal Navy lieutenant-commander, apparently from one of the naval shore parties.

A little further out, Commander H. R. Troup nudged the War Department's fast motor boat *Haig* against another pier. Troup was one of Admiral Taylor's maintenance officers at Sheerness, but he too had wangled a ship for this big night. He picked up 40 poilus, ferried them to a transport waiting outside the harbor, then went back for another 39.

By now every kind of craft was slipping in and out, plucking troops from the various docks and quays. Collisions and near collisions were the normal thing. As *Haig* headed back out, a French tug rammed her. The hole was above the waterline; so Troup kept on. Two hundred yards, and *Haig* was rammed again by another tug. As Troup transferred his soldiers to the minesweeper *Westward Ho*, he was swamped when the minesweeper suddenly reversed engines to avoid still another collision. Troup now scrambled aboard *Westward Ho* himself, leaving *Haig* one more derelict in Dunkirk harbor.

Forty men here, 100 there, helped clear the piers, but most of the French weren't in Dunkirk at all. They were still on the perimeter, holding back General von Kuechler's "systematic attack." To the east the 12th Division fought all day to keep the Germans out of Bray-Dunes. Toward evening General Janssen was killed by a bomb, but his men fought on. Southeast, flooding held the enemy at Ghyvelde. In the center, Colonel Menon's 137th Infantry Regiment clung to Teteghem. Southwest at Spycker, two enterprising naval lieutenants commanded three 155 mm. guns, blocking the road for hours. All the way west, the 68th Division continued to hold General von Hubicki's panzers. A French observer in the church tower at Mardyck had an uncanny knack of catching the slightest German movement.

Corporal Hans Waitzbauer, radio operator of the 2nd Battery, 102nd Artillery Regiment, was exasperated. The battery had been promised Wiener schnitzel for lunch, but now here they were, pinned down by that sharp-eyed fellow in the church tower.

Waitzbauer, a good Viennese, wasn't about to give up his Wiener schnitzel that easily. With Lieutenant Gertung's permission, he darted back, leaping from ditch to ditch, to the company kitchen. Then, with his pot of veal in both hands, a bottle of red wine in his trouser pocket, and half a loaf of white bread in each of his jacket pockets, he scurried back again. Shells and machine-gun bullets nipped at his heels all the way, but he made it safely and distributed his treasures to the battery. Lieutenant Gertung's only comment was, "You were lucky."

With Kuechler's men pinned down in the east and west, the key to the advance was clearly Bergues, the old medieval town that anchored the center of the French line. If it could be taken, two good roads ran directly north to Dunkirk, just five miles to the north.

But how to take it? The town was circled by thick walls and a moat designed by the great military engineer Vauban. For a defense conceived in the seventeenth century, it was amazingly effective in the 20th. A garrison of 1,000 troops was well dug in, and they were supported by strong artillery plus naval guns at Dunkirk. The RAF Bomber Command gave help from the air.

Kuechler had been trying to take the place for two days, and it was still a stand-off. On the afternoon of June 2 it was decided to try a coordinated attack using Stukas and specially trained shock troops drawn from the 18th Regiment of Engineers.

At 3:00 p.m. the Stukas attacked, concentrating on a section of the wall that seemed weaker than the rest. Nearby the engineers crouched with flame-throwers and assault ladders. At 3:15 the bombers let up, and the men stormed the wall, led by their commander Lieutenant Voigt. Dazed by the Stukas, the garrison surrendered almost immediately.

Bergues taken, the Germans pressed on north toward Dunkirk, capturing Fort Vallières at dusk. They were now only three miles from the port, but at this point French General Fagalde scraped together every available man for a counterattack. It was a costly effort, but he managed to stop the German advance. Toward midnight the weary poilus began disengaging and working their way to the harbor, where they hoped the rescue fleet was still waiting.

Kuechler did not press them. In keeping with his orders for the "systematic attack," he took no unnecessary risks, and the Germans did not usually fight at night anyhow. Besides, there was a feeling in the air that the campaign was really over. Outside captured Bergues, one unit of the 18th Division sat in the garden of a cottage "singing old folk-songs, soldier-songs, songs of love and home." General Halder spent a good part of the day distributing Iron Crosses to deserving staff officers.

More than ever, all eyes were on the south. To the Luftwaffe, Dunkirk was now a finished story; it would be staging its first big raid on Paris tomorrow, June 3. Flying Officer B. J. Wicks, a Hurricane pilot shot down and working his way to the coast disguised as a Belgian peasant, noticed long columns of German troops—all heading south toward the Somme.

It was about 2:30 a.m. on the 3rd when the first of the French defenders, relieved from the counterattack, began filing onto the mole. Most of the ships had now gone back to Dover, but a few were still there. Sub-Lieutenant Wake struggled to keep order. He might lack rank, but he did have an unusual piece of equipment— a hunting horn.

It didn't do much good. The French seemed to know a thousand ways to slow down the embarkation. They tried to bring all their gear, their personal possessions, even their dogs. Many of them had inner tubes around their necks—improvised life preservers—and this bulky addition slowed them down even more. They invariably tried to crowd aboard the first boat they came to, rather than space themselves out over the full length of the mole. They insisted on keeping their units intact, never seemed to realize that they could be sorted out later in England. Right now the important thing was to get going before daylight.

Wake and his handful of seamen did their best, but his schoolboy French never rose to the occasion. What he really needed was someone like Clouston's assistant Michael Solomon, who was fluent in the language and could deal with the French officers. Lacking that, neither shouts of *"Allez vite"* nor blasts on the hunting horn could help. It was almost symbolic when some "damned Frenchman" (Wake's words) finally stepped on the horn and put it out of commission for good.

As it grew light, Admiral Wake-Walker—still patrolling in *MA/SB 10*—ordered all remaining ships to leave. The minesweeper *Speedwell* cast off; in an hour alongside the mole she had taken aboard only 300 French soldiers. Sub-Lieutenant Wake caught a small French fishing smack, and transferred to a large Channel steamer outside the harbor. The skoot *Hilda* lingered long enough for a final check of the beach at Malo— nobody there.

At 3:10, as the last ships pulled out, three new vessels slipped in. These were block ships, to be sunk at the harbor entrance under the direction of Captain E. Dangerfield. The hope was, of course, to deny the Germans future use of the port. But nothing seemed to go right this frustrating night. When the block ships were scuttled, the current caught one of them and turned it parallel to the Channel, leaving plenty of room to enter and leave.

"A most disheartening night," noted Admiral Wake-Walker on his return to Dover in the morning. He had hoped to lift over 37,000 men, actually got off only 24,000. At least 25,000 French—some said 40,000—were left behind. Wake-Walker tended to blame the French themselves for not providing their own berthing parties, but the British were the people used to running the mole. On May 31 Captain Tennant had, at Admiral Abrial's request, taken charge of both the British and French embarkation. It was asking a lot now to expect the French to take over on the spur of the moment.

To General Weygand sitting in Paris, it was a familiar story. Once again "perfidious Albion" was walking out, leaving the French to shift for themselves. Even before the night's misadventures, he fired off a telegram to the French military attaché in London, urging that the evacuation continue another night to embark the 25,000 French troops who were holding off the Germans. "Emphasize that the solidarity of the two armies demands that the French rearguard be not sacrificed."

Winston Churchill needed little convincing. He wired Weygand and Reynaud:

> We are coming back for your men tonight. Please ensure that all facilities are used promptly. For three hours last night many ships waited idly at great risk and danger.

In Dover at 10:09 on the morning of June 3, Admiral Ramsay signaled his command that their work was not over after all:

> I hoped and believed that last night would see us through, but the French who were covering the retirement of the British rearguard had to repel a strong German attack and so were unable to send their troops to the pier in time to be embarked. We

cannot leave our Allies in the lurch, and I call on all
officers and men detailed for further evacuation tonight to let the world see that we never let down our
Ally. . . .

On the destroyer *Malcolm* the morning had begun on a high
note. She was just back from her seventh trip to Dunkirk, and
was still in one piece. The last of the BEF had been evacuated,
and everyone assumed that the operation was over. Breakfast in
the ward room was a merry affair.

Lieutenant Mellis fell on his bunk hoping to catch up on his
sleep. He was so tired he didn't even take his clothes off. Several hours later he was awakened by the sound of men's feet on
the deck overhead. He learned that the crew was assembling for
an important announcement by Captain Halsey, who had just
returned from Ramsay's headquarters. Halsey came quickly to
the point: "The last of the BEF was able to come off because
the French took over the perimeter last night. Now the French
have asked us to take them off. We can't do anything else, can
we?"

No. But it was still a shock. For Mellis, it was the worst moment of the whole show. To enjoy that delicious feeling of relief
and relaxation—and then to have it all snatched away—was almost more than he could stand. The ward room had planned a
festive mess that evening, and decided to dress festively anyhow. When the *Malcolm* sailed on her eighth trip to Dunkirk at
9:08 p.m., June 3, her officers were wearing their bow ties and
monkey jackets.

14

The Last Night

"If you've never seen any Germans, here they are." The announcement sounded strangely calm and detached to Edmond Perron, a minor Dunkirk official who had fled the blazing city with his family. The Perrons had found shelter on the farm of M. Wasel at Cappelle-la-Grande, a couple of miles to the south. As the fighting surged toward them, the Wasels and their guests retired to the stable for added protection. Now it was 3:00 p.m., June 3, and M. Wasel was peeking through the stable door and issuing bulletins on what he saw.

M. Perron peered out, too. Men in green uniforms covered the plain to the south—running . . . lying down . . . getting up . . . crouching . . . always advancing. But they did not come to the Wasel farm. Reaching its edge, they veered to the left to get around a water-filled ditch, then continued north toward Dunkirk.

General Lieutenant Christian Hansen's X Corps was closing in from the south. By 3:30 the 61st Division had passed the Wasel farm and occupied Cappelle itself. By evening the 18th Division, advancing from the southeast, had Fort Louis, an ancient landmark about a mile south of the port. Stukas helped reduce another little fort two miles to the east.

The French were also crumbling farther east. Colonel Men-on's 37th Infantry were finally overwhelmed at Teteghem. By this time his 1st Battalion was down to 50 men. One machine gunner was working two guns, feeding them with scraps of ammunition picked up on the ground. Held up the better part of two days, the battered victors joined the other German units now converging on the port.

General Fagalde threw in everything he had left: the last of the 32nd Division . . . the coastal defense troops of the *Secteur Fortifié des Flandres* . . . the remains of the 21st Division Training Centre . . . his own *Gardes Mobiles*. Somehow he stopped them, although machine-gun bullets were now clipping the trees of suburban Rosendaël.

The end seemed very near to Sergeant Bill Knight of the Royal Engineers, who had somehow missed getting away with the last of the BEF. Now he was holed up in a cellar in Rosendaël with four other men from his unit. They had a truck, arms, plenty of food, but the German firing was so heavy that Knight felt they could never get to the harbor, even assuming the evacuation was still on.

The little party was pretty much resigned to surrender when two Belgian civilians, who had also taken cover in the cellar, began talking about slipping through the lines to their farms near the village of Spycker. Listening to them, an idea suddenly occurred to Knight: they might be cut off from the harbor, but why not go the other way? Why not slip through the encircling German Army and rejoin the Allies on the Somme?

A deal was quickly struck. Knight would give the Belgians transportation, if they would show him the little lanes and cow paths that might get them through the enemy lines unnoticed. Knight felt sure that the Germans were sticking to the main roads, and once through the cordon, it wouldn't be too hard to reach the Somme.

They set off at dusk, June 3, bouncing along the back streets that led southwest out of town. All night they continued driving, guided by the Belgians and by a road map picked up at a garage they passed.

Dawn on the 4th found them near Spycker. Here they dropped the two Belgians, and after a few final instructions continued heading southwest. They still used back roads, and when even these seemed dangerous, they lay low for a while in a field. Toward evening they had a lucky break. A German convoy appeared along the road, made up entirely of captured vehicles. They fell in behind, becoming the tail end of the convoy.

They made 20 to 25 miles this way, with only one narrow escape. A German motorcycle was escorting the convoy, and at one point it dropped back to make sure that none of the trucks were missing. Feeling that it would be just as jarring to find one truck too many, Knight slowed down, dropping far enough behind the convoy to appear to be no part of it. When the motorcycle returned to its regular position up front, Knight closed up again.

Wednesday, June 5, and the truck at last reached the Somme at Ailly. Here the British party had another break: a bridge still stood intact. It was not a highway bridge—just a cattle crossing—but it would do. Knight barreled across it into Allied lines.

No one else at Dunkirk was that enterprising. One and all believed that June 3 would be the last night, and at Bastion 32 the mood was heavy with gloom. There was no more fresh water; the medics had run out of bandages; communications were failing. "Enemy is reaching the outskirts," ran Abrial's last message, sent at 3:25 p.m. "I am having the codes burned, except for the M Code."

At 4:00 p.m. Admiral Ramsay's rescue fleet started out again. As before, the plan called for the big ships—the destroyers, the Channel steamers, the largest paddlers—to concentrate on the eastern mole. But this time the naval berthing party would be greatly strengthened. Commander Herbert James Buchanan would be in charge; four officers, fifty seamen, and several signalmen would be on hand. Four French officers were added to provide better communication. With luck, Ramsay hoped that 14,000 troops would be lifted off the mole between 10:30 p.m. and 2:30 a.m.

The minesweepers, skoots, and smaller paddle steamers would concentrate on the west pier, a shorter jetty just across from the mole, where crowds of French soldiers had waited in vain the previous night. This smaller flotilla should be able to take off another 5,000 men. The little ships—there were still scores of launches, motorboats, and small craft about—would again probe deep into the harbor where the larger vessels couldn't go. They would ferry the troops they found to the gunboat *Locust*, waiting just outside the port.

The ever-growing fleet of French trawlers and fishing smacks would take care of the Quai Félix Faure, cover the outer mole all the way west, and make a final check of Malo beach. These French boats were late arrivals, but now seemed to be everywhere.

All understood that this really would be the last night, and Ramsay tried to make sure of it with a strongly worded telegram to the Admiralty:

> After nine days of operations of a nature unprecedented in naval warfare, which followed on two weeks of intense strain, commanding officers, officers, and ships' companies are at the end of their tether. . . . If, therefore, evacuation has to be continued after tonight, I would emphasize in the strongest possible manner that fresh forces should be used for these operations, and any consequent delay in their execution should be accepted.

It was true, but hard to tell from the jaunty procession of vessels that once again streamed across the Channel. The destroyer *Whitshed* pulled out, her harmonica band playing on the foredeck. The cabin cruiser *Mermaiden* was manned by a sublieutenant, a stoker, an RAF gunner on leave, and a white-haired old gentleman who normally helped take care of Horatio Nelson's flagship *Victory* in Portsmouth. The motor launch *Marlborough* had lost her two solicitors—they only had the weekend off—but she boasted two equally dapper replacements: a retired colonel and an invalided army officer, said to be a crack shot with a Lewis gun.

The destroyer *Malcolm* looked especially dashing, with her officers dressed in their monkey jackets for the festive evening that never came off. The tug *Sun IV*, towing fourteen launches, was still skippered by Mr. Alexander, president of the tugboat company. The *MTB 102*, again carrying Admiral Wake-Walker, now sported a real admiral's flag—made from a red-striped dish cloth.

Wake-Walker arrived off the eastern mole at 10:00 p.m. and was relieved to find that tonight plenty of French troops were waiting. But once again the wind and the tide were against him, and he couldn't get alongside. When the *Whitshed* appeared at 10:20 with Commander Buchanan's berthing party, she had no better luck. The other ships too were unable to land, and a huge traffic jam built up at the entrance to the harbor.

Nearly an hour passed before Wake-Walker managed to get some lines ashore, and the berthing party was able to move into action. By 11:30 loading operations were under way, but a whole hour had been lost. What had been planned for four hours would have to be done in three.

Fortunately the Luftwaffe had turned its attention to Paris, and there was little shelling tonight. Many of the guns too had gone south, and Kuechler's advance was so close that his artillery were leery of hitting their own infantry. On the mole the British berthing party could hear machine-gun fire in the town itself. "*Vite, vite,*" a sailor shouted as the poilus tumbled aboard the *Malcolm*, "*Vite*, God damn it, *VITE!*"

Admiral Taylor's flotilla of small craft headed deeper into the harbor, to the Quai Félix Faure. The Admiral himself had gone ahead in the War Department's fast boat *Marlborough* to organize the loading. He understood there would be thousands of French waiting, but when he arrived, he found the quay deserted. Finally 300 to 400 French marines turned up and announced there was nobody else.

But they were enough, considering the size of Taylor's little ships. Most held fewer than 40 at a time. The *Mermaiden* was so crowded the helmsman couldn't see to steer. Directions had to be shouted over a babble of French voices.

As Taylor loaded the last of the marines, a German machine gun began chattering less than half a mile away. No more time to lose. Packing a final load into the *Marlborough*, he shoved off around 2:00 a.m. on the 4th. Dodging one of the many small craft darting about the harbor, *Marlborough* scraped over some fallen masonry and lost both her propellers and rudder. She was finally towed home by the large yacht *Gulzar*, piloted by a Dominican monk.

Mishaps multiplied. Nobody really knew the port, and the only light was from the flames consuming the waterfront. The Portsmouth Admiral's barge ran into a pile of rubble and was abandoned. . . .The trawler *Kingfisher* was rammed by a French fishing boat. . . .The minesweeper *Kellet* ran aground against the western breakwater. A tug towed her off, but she was too badly damaged to be of further use. Wake-Walker sent her home empty—one of only two ships not used this last hectic night.

The Admiral himself nipped about the harbor in *MTB 102*, busily juggling his fleet. The Quai Félix Faure was cleared . . . the eastern mole was under control . . . but the short jetty just west of the mole was a problem. The whole French 32nd Infantry Division seemed to be converging on it. At 1:45 a.m. Wake-Walker guided over a large transport, then the packet *Royal Sovereign* to help lift the crowd.

On the jetty, Commander Troup landed from the War Department's boat *Swallow*, took one look at the confusion, and appointed himself pier master. His chief problem was the usual one: the French troops refused to be separated from their units. Enlisting the help of a French staff officer, Captain le Comte de Chartier de Sadomy, Troup urged the poilus to forget their organization. In two hours they would all meet again in England. Take any boat. They seemed to understand: the big *Tynwald* came alongside, loaded 4,000 men in half an hour.

2:00 a.m., June 4, two small French torpedo boats, *VTB 25* and *VTB 26*, rumbled out of the harbor. Admiral Abrial and General Fagalde were leaving with their staffs. Behind them the massive steel doors of Bastion 32 now lay open and unguarded. Inside there was only a clutter of smashed coding machines and burnt-out candles.

2:25, gunboat *Locust,* stationed off the harbor mouth, received her last load of troops from Admiral Taylor's little ships. Her skipper, Lieutenant-Commander Costobadie, had done his duty, and it must have been a temptation to run for Dover. But he still had room; so he went instead to the eastern mole and topped off with another 100 men. Finally satisfied that *Locust* could hold no more, he headed for home.

2:30, the last French ships, a convoy of trawlers commanded by Ensign Bottex, emerged from the innermost part of the harbor. Packed with troops fresh from the fighting, he too turned toward Dover.

2:40, "heartened by bagpipes playing us out," the destroyer *Malcolm* slipped her lines at the eastern mole. Twenty minutes later the last destroyer of all, *Express*, left with a full load, including Commander Buchanan's berthing party.

3:00, French troops still crowded the short jetty just west of the mole. Commander Troup had been loading transports all night, but the jetty continued to fill up with new arrivals. Now the last big transport had gone, and Troup was waiting for a motorboat assigned to pick up himself, General Lucas of the French 32nd Division, and the general's staff at 3:00. The minutes ticked by, but no sign of the boat—not surprising on a night like this when a thousand things could go wrong.

Troup was beginning to worry, when at 3:05 the War Department's boat *Pigeon* happened by. She was miraculously empty, making a final swing through the harbor. Troup hailed her, and Sub-Lieutenant C. A. Gabbett-Mullhallen brought his craft alongside.

A thousand French soldiers stood at attention four deep, as General Lucas prepared to leave. Clearly they would be left behind—no longer a chance of escape—yet not a man broke ranks. They remained motionless, the light from the flames playing off their steel helmets.

Lucas and his staff walked to the edge of the pier, turned, clicked their heels, and gave the men a final salute. Then the officers turned again and made the long climb down the ladder to the waiting boat. Troup followed, and at 3:20 Sub-Lieutenant Gabbett-Mullhallen gunned his engines, quickly moving out of the harbor.

As these last ships left Dunkirk, they met a strange procession creeping in. Destroyer *Shikari* was in the lead. Following her were three ancient freighters, and flanking them were two speedboats, *MTB 107* and *MA/SB 10*. Captain Dangerfield was once again trying to bottle up the harbor by sinking block ships across the entrance. As the little flotilla moved into position, they were buffeted by the bow waves of the last ships racing out. Lieutenant John Cameron, skipper of the *MTB 107*, pondered the trick of fate that had brought him, "a settled barrister of 40," to be an actor in this awesome drama.

Suddenly an explosion. Enemy planes had apparently mined the channel—a parting present from the Luftwaffe. The first did no damage, but a second exploded under the leading block ship *Gourko*, sinking her almost instantly. As the two speedboats fished the survivors out of the water, the remaining block ships steamed on. But now there were only two of them, and the job would be that much harder.

While the block ships edged deeper into the harbor, *Shikari* paid a final visit to the eastern mole. It had been nearly empty when *Express* left, but now it was beginning to fill up again. Some 400 French troops tumbled aboard, including General Barthélémy, commanding the Dunkirk garrison. At 3:20 *Shikari* finally cast off—the last British warship to leave Dunkirk.

But not the last British vessel. Occasional motorboats were still slipping out, as Captain Dangerfield's two block ships reached the designated spot. With helms hard over, they attempted to line up at right angles to the Channel, but once again the tide and current were too strong. As on the previous night, the attempt was largely a failure. Hovering nearby, *MA/SB 10* picked up the crews.

Dawn was now breaking, and Lieutenant Cameron decided to take *MTB 107* in for one last look at the harbor. For nine days the port had been a bedlam of exploding bombs and shells, the thunder of artillery, the hammering of antiaircraft guns, the crash of falling masonry; now suddenly it was a grave-yard—the wrecks of sunken ships . . . abandoned guns . . . empty ruins . . . silent masses of French troops waiting hopelessly on the pierheads and the eastern mole. There was nothing a single, small motorboat could do; sadly, Cameron turned for home. "The whole scene," he later recalled, "was filled with a sense of finality and death; the curtain was ringing down on a great tragedy."

But there were still Englishmen in Dunkirk, some of them very much alive. Lieutenant Jimmy Langley, left behind because the wounded took up too much room in the boats, now lay on a stretcher at the 12th Casualty Clearing Station near the outskirts of town. The station—really a field hospital—occupied a huge Victorian house in the suburb of Rosendaël. Capped by an odd-looking cupola with a pointed red roof, the place was appropriately called the Chapeau Rouge.

The wounded had long ago filled up all the rooms in the house, then overflowed into the halls and even the grand staircase. Now they were being put into tents in the surrounding gardens. A French field hospital also lay on the grounds, adding to the crowd of casualties. The total number varied from day to day, but on June 3 there were about 265 British wounded at Chapeau Rouge.

Tending them were a number of medical officers and orderlies. They were there as the result of a curious but most fateful lottery. Even before the decision to leave behind the wounded, it had been clear that some would not be able to go. They were simply too badly hurt to be moved. To take care of them, orders had come down that one medical officer and 10 orderlies must be left behind for every 100 casualties. Since there were 200 to 300 wounded, this meant 3 officers and 30 orderlies would have to stay.

How to choose? Colonel Pank, the Station's commanding officer, decided that the fairest course was to draw lots, and at 2:00 p.m. on June 1 the staff gathered for what was bound to be a very tense occasion. Two separate lotteries were held—one among the 17 medical officers, the other among the 120 orderlies.

In each case all the names were put in a hat, and appropriately enough an English bowler was found in the cellar and used for this purpose. The rule was "first out, first to go"; the last names drawn would be those left behind. The Church of England chaplain drew for the enlisted men; the Catholic padre, Father Cockie O'Shea, drew for the officers.

Major Philip Newman, Chief of Surgery, listened to the drawing in agonized silence as the names were read out. Ten . . . twelve . . . thirteen, and still his name remained in the hat. As it turned out, he had good reason to fear: he was number seventeen of seventeen.

Later that afternoon a farewell service was held in the cupola. At the end Father O'Shea took Newman by the hand and gave him his crucifix. "This will see you home," the padre said.

One of those who stayed took no part at all in the lottery. Private W.B.A. Gaze was strictly a volunteer. An auctioneer and appraiser in peacetime, Gaze had been a machine gunner with a motor maintenance unit until the great retreat. Separated from his outfit, he had taken over an ambulance abandoned by its regular driver and was now a fixture at 12th CCS. The other men might know more about medicine, but he had skills of his own that came in handy at a time like this. He was a born scrounger, could fix anything, and had even located a new well, when Chapeau Rouge was running out of water. Major Newman regarded him as an "honorary member" of the unit, and Gaze reciprocated—of course he wasn't going to leave.

Most of the staff pulled out on the night of June 1. The 2nd was largely spent making futile trips to and from the docks, as false reports circulated that a hospital ship had arrived. That night a dispatch rider roared up with the news that walking wounded could be evacuated, if brought to the eastern mole. This last chance of escape was seized by many men who, under any normal definition, were stretcher cases. They rose from their cots and limped, hobbled, even crawled to the waiting trucks. One man used a pair of crutches made from a coal hammer and a garden rake.

June 3 was a day of waiting. The French troops were falling back, and Newman's main job was to keep them from occupying the house and using it for a last stand. A large red cross, made from strips of cloth, had been laid out on the lawn; the Luftwaffe had so far respected it; and Newman wanted to keep things that way. The French commandant seemed to understand. He didn't occupy the house, but he did continue digging on the grounds. Occasional shells began falling on the garden.

At dusk the French began pulling out, retiring still further into Dunkirk, and it was clear to everyone at Chapeau Rouge that the next visitors would be German. When, was anybody's guess, but the white German "victory rockets" were getting close.

While the wounded lay quietly on their cots and stretchers, the staff gathered in the basement of the house for a last dinner. They ate the best food they could find, topped off by some excellent red wine from the Chapeau Rouge cellar. Someone produced a concertina, but no one had the heart to sing.

Upstairs, Major Newman sought out a wounded German pilot named Helmut, who had been shot down and brought in several days earlier. It was clear to both that the roles of captor and captive were about to be reversed, but neither made much of it. What Newman did want was a crash course in German, to be used when the enemy arrived. Patiently Helmut taught him phrases like *Rotes Kreuz* and *Nichts Schiessen*—"Red Cross" . . . "Don't shoot."

By midnight, June 3–4, the last French defenders had retired toward the docks, and there was nothing to do but keep waiting. As a sort of reception committee, Newman posted two enlisted men by the gate. An officer was stationed on the porch outside the front door. They had orders to call him as soon as the first Germans appeared. Then he laid out a clean uniform for the surrender and curled up on the stone floor of the kitchen for a few hours' sleep.

On the front steps Jimmy Langley lay on a stretcher just outside the front door. It was so hot and sticky—and the flies were so bad—he had asked to be moved into the open. He too was waiting, and even as he waited, he began thinking about what might happen next. He was a Coldstream Guards officer, and in the last war, the Coldstream were not known for taking prisoners. Had that reputation carried over? If so, there seemed a good chance that the Germans would pay him back in kind. He finally had a couple of orderlies carry his stretcher to a spot near the gate and set it down there. If he was going to be killed, he might as well get it over with.

15

Deliverance

"The Germans are here!" a voice was shouting, as an unknown hand shook Major Newman awake at 6 o'clock on the morning of June 4. Dead tired, Newman had been deeply asleep, even though lying on the stone floor of the kitchen at Chapeau Rouge. He gradually pulled himself together and began putting on the clean uniform he had laid out for the surrender.

Down near the gate Jimmy Langley lay on his stretcher watching a small party of German infantrymen enter the grounds. They might be about to kill him, but they looked as tired as the British. As they walked up the drive toward him, Langley decided his best chance lay in playing to the hilt the role of "wounded prisoner." Pointing to the Red Cross flag on the cupola, he gasped a request for water and a cigarette. The leader of the squad gave him both. Then Langley asked, a little tentatively, what would they like from him.

"*Marmelade,*" was the reply. For the first time Langley felt there was hope. No one about to kill him would be thinking primarily of marmalade.

Troops were pouring into the grounds now—some dirty and unkempt, but most freshly washed and cleanly shaven, the way Supermen should look. They fanned out over the yard, check-

ing the tents and stretchers to make sure no armed Allied soldiers were still lurking about. "For you the war is over," a
trooper curtly told Guardsman Arthur Knowles, lying wounded
on his stretcher.

Satisfied that Chapeau Rouge met the standards of Geneva,
the Germans relaxed and were soon mixing with their captives,
swapping rations and sharing family pictures. Major Newman
stood on the porch watching the scene, resplendent in his clean
uniform but with no officer to take his surrender.

In two hours these Germans pushed on, replaced by administrative personnel who were far less friendly. The curious bond
that sometimes exists between enemies at the front is rarely felt
in the rear.

"*Wo ist das Meer*?" a departing infantryman asked Jimmy Langley, still lying on his stretcher. Langley had no idea where the
sea was, but pointed confidently where he thought it might be.
This couldn't be "helping the enemy"—they'd find it anyhow.

The French guns were completely silent now. As the Germans moved into town, white flags began sprouting everywhere. Sensing no opposition, Major Chrobek of the 18th
Infantry Division piled his men into trucks and lurched through
the debris-filled streets right to the waterfront. "Then our
hearts leapt," exulted the division's normally staid Daily Intelligence Summary: "Here was the sea—the sea!"

At 8:00 a.m. a detachment of German marines took over Bastion 32. There was, of course, nobody there except a handful of
headquarters clerks left behind by the departing generals and
admirals.

Twenty minutes later a German colonel rolled up to Dunkirk's red brick *Hôtel de Ville* in the center of town. Here he was
met by General Beaufrère, commanding the 68th Infantry and
senior French officer left in the city. Beaufrère had taken off his
steel helmet and now sported a gold-leaf kepi for the surrender
ceremony. Sometime between 9:00 and 10:00 a.m. he met with
General Lieutenant Friedrich-Carl Cranz, commanding the
18th Division, and formally handed over the city.

By 9:30 German units reached the foot of the eastern mole,
but here they faced a problem. French troops were packed so
tightly on the mole, it was impossible to round them up quickly.

As late as 10:00 o'clock, a French medical officer, Lieutenant Docteur Le Doze, escaped from the seaward end of the mole with 30 men in a ship's lifeboat.

It's hard to say exactly when Dunkirk officially fell. The Army Group B war diary put the time at 9:00 a.m. . . . X Corps said 9:40 . . . the 18th Army, 10:15. Perhaps the most appropriate time, symbolically anyhow, was the moment the swastika was hoisted on the eastern mole—10:20 a.m.

Now it was a case of mopping up. While Beaufrère dickered with Cranz, small parties of his 68th Division tried to escape to the west, but they were soon run down and captured. General Alaurent led a group from the 32nd Division in an attempt to break out via Gravelines, but they were rounded up at Le Clipon, just outside Dunkirk.

By 10:30 the last shots had been fired and the city was at peace. At Chapeau Rouge Major Newman could hear a golden oriole singing from the top of the oak tree close to the mansion. "This was his day."

A handful of dazed civilians began emerging from the city's cellars. Staring at the blackened walls and piles of rubble, a gendarme—covered with ribbons from the First World War—cried like a child. On the rue Clemenceau a small fox terrier sat guarding the body of a French soldier. Somewhere in the ruins a portable radio, miraculously intact, was playing "The Merry Widow Waltz."

Father Henri Lecointe, assistant curate of Saint Martin's parish, picked his way through the rubble to his church. The door was blown in, the windows gone, but it still stood. Entering, he was surprised to hear the organ playing a Bach chorale. Two German soldiers were trying it out—one at the console, the other in the loft, pumping the bellows.

Foreign correspondents—never far behind when the Wehrmacht was victorious—poked among the ruins, interviewing survivors. The Assistant Chief of Police, André Noël, remarked that he was an Alsatian from Metz and had served in the German Army during the First War.

"Now you can go back to your old regiment," dryly observed a lieutenant-colonel standing by.

As Georg Schmidt, one of Joseph Goebbels's propaganda men,

photographed the scene, his section chief drove up and reminded him that Goebbels expected pictures of British POW's—did
Schmidt have any?

Schmidt replied that the British were all gone.

"Well," said his chief, "you're an official photographer. If
you don't get any pictures of British POW's, then you *were* an
official photographer!"

Schmidt needed no further encouragement. He hurried over
to the POW compound, where he found 30,000 to 40,000
French, but still no British. He looked harder and was finally rewarded. Scattered here and there were two or three dozen
Tommies. Schmidt put them up front and began taking his pictures. The day was saved.

Most of the British were indeed gone, but they took an aston-
ishingly large number of French troops with them. Over 26,000
jammed the decks of the last ships to leave Dunkirk. As the *Medway Queen* groped through an early-morning fog toward Dover,
an officer strummed a mandolin on the after deck, trying to
cheer up the already homesick poilus. On the destroyer *Sabre*
Commander Brian Dean drew cheers by addressing his passengers in French. There was much banter comparing the accommodations on the crowded *Sabre* with those on the luxury liner
Normandie.

Generally speaking, the passage back was uneventful—but
not always. As the Belgian trawler *Maréchal Foch* neared the
English coast, the minesweeper *Leda* loomed out of the fog and
rammed her. The *"Foch"* sank instantly, pitching 300 soldiers
into the water.

The French motorboat *VTB 25*, carrying Admiral Abrial and
other high-ranking officers, heard cries and rushed to the scene.
But the fog knew no favorites: *VTB 25* ran into a piece of wreckage and lost her propeller. Now she wallowed helplessly in the
sea.

Eventually the destroyer *Malcolm* came up. Captain Halsey's
smooth-working crew picked up 150 survivors and threw a
line to *VTB 25*. Somewhat ignominiously, Admiral Abrial was finally towed into Dover around 6:00 a.m.

About this time the fog lifted, but that didn't help a young
French ensign named Tellier, commanding the auxiliary dredge

Emile Deschamps. He was thoroughly lost, and when he asked directions from a passing ship, he couldn't understand the answer. He tried to follow the crowd, and was just off Margate when the *Emile Deschamps* struck a magnetic mine and blew up. She sank in less than half a minute with most of the 500 men aboard.

Lieutenant Hervé Cras managed to swim clear of the wreck. He was getting accustomed to this sort of thing, having also gone down on the destroyer *Jaguar* the previous week. Now, as he tread water gasping for breath, he was hailed by a shipmate, Lieutenant Jacquelin de la Porte de Vaux: "Hello, Hello! Let's sing."

With that, de la Port de Vaux burst into *"Le Chant du Départ"*—"The Song of Departure"—a well-known French march. Cras was in no mood to join in, and gradually drifted away. Later, after both men were rescued, de la Porte de Vaux chided him for not singing in the water, "as all sailors with their hearts in the right place must do in such circumstances."

Perhaps he was right. Certainly the men who manned the evacuation fleet needed every conceivable device to keep up their spirits. The *Emile Deschamps* was the 243rd vessel lost, and many of the crews had now reached the breaking point. During the morning of the 4th, Admiral Abrial met with Ramsay in Dover Castle, and they agreed that the time had come to end "Dynamo." Abrial observed that the Germans were closing in; the French had now used up all their ammunition; and the 30,000 to 40,000 men left behind weren't combat units. He was wrong only on the last point: the troops standing forlornly on the pierheads of Dunkirk included some of France's best.

Paris gave its formal approval at 11:00, and at 2:23 p.m. the British Admiralty officially announced the end of Operation Dynamo. Released at last from the strain and tension, Ramsay drove up to Sandwich and celebrated with a round of golf. He shot a 78—by far the best score in his life.

The past several days had been so all-consuming that he never had time even to write "darling Mag," but she had kept the asparagus and gingerbread coming, and now on June 5 he once again took up his pen: "The relief is stupendous, and the results beyond belief." He tried to describe what had been achieved, but it sounded awkward and full of self-praise. He was really a man of action, not a man of letters. He quickly wrapped his effort up: "Tons of love, darling Mag, you are such a comfort to me."

Along with relief went a deep feeling of vindication. Ramsay had never gotten over his years in eclipse; his break with Admiral Backhouse hurt too deeply. Now Dunkirk made up for everything, and the grateful letters that poured in seemed doubly sweet.

He cherished them all, including one from his barber. But the most touching was a letter signed simply "Mrs. S. Woodcock," a British soldier's mother he had never met:

> As a reader of the Daily Express and after reading in today's paper of your wonderful feat re Dunkirk, I feel I must send you a personal message to thank you. My son was one of the lucky ones to escape from there. I have not seen him, but he is somewhere in England, and that's good enough. My youngest boy John Woodcock died of wounds received in Norway on April 26; so you can guess how thankful I feel and grateful to you. . . .

It was a nation already overflowing with gratitude and relief when Winston Churchill went to the House of Commons on the evening of June 4 to report on the evacuation. The benches were filled; the Public Gallery, the Peers Gallery, and the Distinguished Strangers Gallery all packed. The crowd welcomed him with a rousing cheer, then sat enthralled by that rarity—a speech devoted mainly to bad news but which, nevertheless, inspires men with hope and courage.

He thrilled the House with his ringing peroration—"We shall fight on the beaches, we shall fight on the landing grounds, we shall fight in the fields and in the streets"—but what impressed astute observers the most was his frankness in facing unpleasant facts. The *News Chronicle* praised the speech for its "uncompromising candour." Edward R. Murrow called it "a report remarkable for its honesty, inspiration, and gravity."

This was as Churchill wanted it. The rescue of the Army must not lull the nation into a paralyzing euphoria. "We must be very careful," he warned, "not to assign to this deliverance the attributes of a victory. Wars are not won by evacuations."

For the moment his warnings did little good. The returning troops were greeted—often to their own amazement—like conquering heroes. Captain John Dodd of the 58th Field Regiment, Royal Artillery, had expected sullen and angry faces, possibly hostile crowds, and a stigma that would stick for all time. Instead, he found nothing but joy and thankfulness, as if the BEF had been the victors, not the vanquished.

When the troops tumbled ashore at Ramsgate, the women of the town swamped them with cups of cocoa, buried them in sandwiches. The manager of the Pavilion Theatre gave away all his cigarettes and chocolate. A director of the Olympia Ballroom bought up all the socks and underwear in town, and handed them out as needed. A grocery store at Broadstairs gave away its entire stock of tea, soup, biscuits, butter, and margarine. A wealthy Scotsman at St. Augustines bought every blanket in town, sending them all to Ramsgate and Margate.

As fast as possible the returning troops were loaded into special trains and taken to assembly points scattered over England and Wales. Here the various units would be rested and reorganized. As the trains moved through the countryside, crowds gathered at the station platforms along the way, showering them with still more cigarettes and chocolate. Bedsheet banners hung from the windows of London's suburbs with messages like "HARD LUCK, BOYS" and "WELL DONE, BEF." Children stood at road crossings waving Union Jacks.

Lady Ismay, wife of Churchill's military adviser, was changing trains at Oxford when one of these "Dunkirk Specials" pulled in. The people on the platform, until now bored and apathetic, saw the weary faces, the bandages, the torn uniforms, and suddenly realized who these new arrivals were. In a body the crowd rushed the station refreshment stand and showered the exhausted soldiers with food and drink. That night when General Ismay told her how well the evacuation was going, she replied, "Yes, I have seen the miracle with my own eyes."

"Miracle"—that was the word. There seemed no other way to describe such an unexpected, inexplicable change in fortune. In his address to Parliament Winston Churchill called it a "miracle of deliverance." Writing a naval colleague, Admiral Sir William James of Portsmouth could only "thank God for that miracle at Dunkirk." Gort's Chief of Staff, General Pownall, noted in his diary, "The evacuation from Dunkirk was surely a miracle."

Actually, there were several miracles. First, the weather. The English Channel is usually rough, rarely behaves for very long. Yet a calm sea was essential to the evacuation, and during the nine days of Dunkirk the Channel was a millpond. Old-timers still say they have never seen it so smooth.

At one point a storm seemed to be heading for the coast, but veered up the Irish Channel. Northerly winds would have kicked up a disastrous surf, but the breeze was first from the southwest, later shifting to the east. On only one morning, May 31, did an on-shore breeze cause serious trouble. On June 5— the day after the evacuation was over—the wind moved to the north, and great breakers came rolling onto the empty beaches.

Overhead, clouds, mist, and rain always seemed to come at the right moment. The Luftwaffe mounted three all-out assaults on Dunkirk—May 27, 29, and June 1. Each time the following day saw low ceilings that prevented any effective follow-up. It took the Germans three days to discover the part played by the eastern mole, mainly because the southwesterly breezes screened it with smoke.

Another miracle was Adolf Hitler's order of May 24, halting his tanks just as they were closing in for the kill. That day Guderian's panzers had reached Bourbourg, only ten miles southwest of Dunkirk. Nothing stood between them and the port. The bulk of the BEF still lay near Lille, 43 miles to the south. By the time the tanks began rolling again in the predawn hours of May 27, the escape corridor had been established, the BEF was pouring into Dunkirk and Ramsay's rescue fleet was hard at work.

Hitler's "halt order" seems so mysterious that it has even been suggested that he was deliberately trying to let the BEF escape. With her army still intact, the theory runs, Britain might feel she could more honorably sit down at the peace table.

Anyone who was at Dunkirk will have a hard time believing that. If Hitler was secretly trying to let the British go home, he was slicing it awfully thin. He almost failed and caught them all.

Nor did he confide this secret to the Luftwaffe, the artillery, or the S-Boats. All were doing their best to disrupt the evacuation; none were told to go easy. Finally, there were the ideas tossed off by Hitler himself, suggesting better ways to raise havoc on the beaches.

The most convincing evidence indicates that Hitler was indeed trying to block the evacuation, but wasn't willing to risk his armor to do it. The British looked finished anyhow; Flanders was poor tank country; his lines were already stretched thin; the brief counterattack at Arras disturbed him; 50% of his tanks were said to be out of action; he needed that armor for the next phase of the campaign, the drive across the Somme and into the heart of France.

It was understandable, especially for any German who had been through the First War. France was crucial, and Paris was the key. It had eluded them then; there must be no mistake this time. Far better to risk a miracle at Dunkirk than risk a second "Miracle of the Marne."

The decision was all the easier when Hermann Göring announced that his Luftwaffe could handle Dunkirk alone. Hitler didn't buy this for very long—he lifted the "halt order" several days before it became clear that Göring couldn't deliver—but the General Field Marshal's boast certainly played a part.

By May 27, when the tanks got going again, the great German drive had lost its momentum, and the panzer generals themselves were thinking of the south. Guderian, once an impassioned advocate for using his armor at Dunkirk, now only had eyes for the Somme.

Still another miracle was provided by the Luftwaffe itself. Perhaps Göring could never have stopped the evacuation, but he could have caused far more mischief. The German planes rarely strafed the crowded beaches; they never used fragmentation bombs; they never attacked tempting targets like Dover or Ramsgate. None of this was through lack of desire; it was through lack of doctrine. The Stuka pilots had been trained for ground support, not for interdiction. The fighters were expected to stay upstairs, covering the bombers, not to come down and mix it up. Whatever the reasons, these lapses allowed additional thousands of men to come home.

"Had the BEF not returned to this country," General Brooke

later wrote, "it is hard to see how the Army could have recovered from the blow." That was the practical significance of Dunkirk. Britain could replace the 2,472 lost guns, the 63,879 abandoned vehicles; but the 224,686 rescued troops were irreplaceable. In the summer of 1940 they were the only trained troops Britain had left. Later, they would be the nucleus of the great Allied armies that won back the Continent. The leaders—Brooke, Alexander, and Montgomery, to name only three—all cut their teeth at Dunkirk.

But the significance of Dunkirk went far beyond such practical considerations. The rescue electrified the people of Britain, welded them together, gave them a sense of purpose that the war had previously lacked. Treaty obligations are all very well, but they don't inspire men to great deeds. "Home" does, and this is what Britain was fighting for now.

The very sense of being alone was exhilarating. The story was told of the foreigner who asked whether his English friend was discouraged by the successive collapse of Poland, Denmark, Norway, the Lowlands, and now France. "Of course not," came the stout-hearted reply. "We're in the finals and we're playing at home."

Some would later say that it was all clever propaganda that cranked up the country to this emotional peak. But it happened too quickly—too spontaneously—for that. This was a case where the people actually led the propagandists. The government's fears were the opposite—that Dunkirk might lead to overconfidence. It was Winston Churchill himself who stressed that the campaign had been "a colossal military disaster," and who warned that "wars are not won by evacuations."

Ironically, Churchill was a prime mover in creating the very mood he sought to dispel. His eloquence, his defiance, his fighting stance were almost bewitching in their appeal. Like Abraham Lincoln in the American Civil War, he was perfectly cast.

Another ingredient was the sense of national participation that Dunkirk aroused. Modern war is so impersonal, it's a rare moment when the ordinary citizen feels that he's making a direct contribution. At Dunkirk ordinary Englishmen really did go over in little boats and rescue soldiers. Ordinary housewives really did succor the exhausted troops reeling back. History is

full of occasions when armies have rushed to the aid of an embattled people; here was a case where the people rushed to the
aid of an embattled army.

Above all, they pulled it off. When the evacuation began,
Churchill thought 30,000 might be saved; Ramsay guessed
45,000. In the end, over 338,000 were landed in England, with
another 4,000 lifted to Cherbourg and other French ports still
in Allied hands. "Wars are not won by evacuations," but, for
the first time, at least Adolf Hitler didn't have everything his
own way. That in itself was cause for celebration.

Curiously, the Germans felt like celebrating too. Years later,
they would see it differently. Many would even regard Dunkirk
as the turning point of the whole war: If the BEF had been captured, Britain would have been defeated. . . . If that had happened, Germany could have concentrated all her strength on
Russia. . . . If that had happened, there would have been no Sta-
lingrad. . . . and so on. But on June 4, 1940, none of these "ifs"
were evident. Except, perhaps, for a few disgruntled tank commanders, the victory seemed complete. As the magazine *Der Adler* put it:

> For us Germans the word "Dunkirchen" will stand
> for all time for victory in the greatest battle of annihi-
> lation in history. But for the British and French who
> were there, it will remind them for the rest of their
> lives of a defeat that was heavier than any army had
> ever suffered before.

As for the escape of "a few men" back to England, *Der Adler* reassured its readers that this was no cause for alarm: "Every
single one of these completely demoralized soldiers is a bacillus
of disintegration. . . ." The *Völkischer Beobachter* told how wom-
en and children burst into hysterical tears as the battered troops
staggered home.

And they would never be back. Landing craft, "mulberries,"
fighter-bombers, sophisticated radar, the whole paraphernalia
of the 1944 counterstroke hadn't even been invented. Viewed
with 1940 eyes, it wasn't all that important to annihilate the
BEF. It had been thrown into the sea, and that was enough.

Only the French were bitter. Whether it was Weygand sniping at General Spears in Paris or the lowliest poilu giving up on the eastern mole, the overwhelming majority felt abandoned by the British. It did no good to point out that 123,095 French *were* rescued by Ramsay's fleet, 102,570 in British ships.

Goebbels joyfully fanned the flames. The crudest propaganda poured out of Berlin. In a little book called *Blende auf-Tiefangriff*, correspondent Hans Henkel told how the fleeing British in one rowboat forced several Frenchmen at pistol-point to jump into the sea. The survivors now stood before Henkel, cursing the "*sales anglais.*"

> Then I asked, "But why do you have an alliance with these '*sales anglais*,' these dirty Englishmen?"
>
> "But we didn't do this! It was done by our wretched government, which then had the nerve to save them!"
>
> "You didn't have to keep that government!"
>
> "What could we do? We weren't asked at all." And one added, "It's the Jews who are to blame."
>
> "Well, fellows, what if we now fought the English together?"
>
> They laughed and said with great enthusiasm, "Yes, we'd join up immediately."

In London the French naval attaché Admiral Odend'hal did his best to put the matter in perspective. He was a good Frenchman, but at the same time tried to give Paris the British point of view. For his pains, Admiral Darlan wrote back asking whether Odend'hal had "gone into the British camp."

"I have not gone into the British camp," Odend'hal replied, "and I would be distressed if you believed it." To prove his loyalty he then reeled off some of his own run-ins with the British, adding:

> But it is not with the English but with the Boches that we are at war. Whatever may have been the British faults, the events of Dunkirk must not leave us with bitterness. . . .

His advice was ignored.

———

Such matters of state made little difference to the men of the BEF these early days of June. They only knew that they were home, and even that was hard to believe. As the train carrying Captain John Dodd of the Royal Artillery steamed slowly through the Kentish countryside, he looked out the window at the passing woods and orchards. "Good gun position . . . good hideout for vehicles . . . good billets in that farm," he thought—then suddenly realized he was at last free from such worries.

Signalman Percy Charles, wounded at Cassel, boarded a hospital train for Northfield. It traveled all night and at 7:00 the following morning Charles was awakened by brilliant greenish lights streaming through the window. He glanced around and noticed that the other men in the compartment were crying. Then he looked out the window, and the sight he saw was "what the poets have been writing about for so many centuries." It was the green English countryside. After the dirt, the blackened rubble, the charred ruins of northern France, the impact of all this fresh greenness was too much. The men simply broke down.

General Brooke, too, felt the contrast. After landing at Dover, he checked in with Ramsay, then drove up to London in a staff car. It was a lovely sunny morning, and he thought of the horror he had just left: burning towns, dead cows, broken trees, the hammer of guns and bombs. "To have moved straight from that inferno into such a paradise within the spell of a few anguished hours made the contrast all the more wonderful."

In London he conferred briefly with General Dill, then caught the train to Hartley Wintney and home. He was overwhelmingly sleepy now, and walked up and down the compartment in a desperate effort to stay awake. If he so much as closed his eyes, he was afraid he'd fall asleep and miss the station.

His wife and children were waiting on the platform. They whisked him home for a nursery tea, and then to bed at last. He slept for 36 hours.

How tired they all were. Major Richardson of the 4th Division staff had managed only sixteen hours of sleep in two weeks. During one stretch of the retreat he went for 62 hours straight without even a nap. Finally reaching the Division assembly point at Aldershot, he threw himself on a bed and slept for 30 hours. Captain Tufton Beamish, whose 9th Royal Northumberland Fusiliers saved the day at Steenbecque, topped them all with 39 hours.

The rescuers were just as weary. Lieutenant Robin Bill, whose minesweepers were in constant demand, had five nights in bed in two weeks. Lieutenant Greville Worthington, in charge of unloading at Dover, stumbled groggily into the mess one morning. When bacon and eggs were put before him, he fell asleep with his beard in the plate. Commander Pelly, skipper of the destroyer *Windsor*, discovered that his only chance for a rest was during turn-around time at Dover. Even then he never took a nap, fearing that he wouldn't have a clear head when he woke up. Instead, he simply sat on the bridge, nursing a whisky and soda. It must have worked, for he never went to sleep for ten days.

No one was more tired than civilian volunteer Bob Hilton. He and his partner, cinema manager Ted Shaw, had spent seventeen hours straight rowing troops out to the skoots and small paddlers from the beach near the mole. Not even Hilton's training as a physical education instructor prepared him for a test like that, but somehow he managed it. Now the job was done, and they were back at Ramsgate.

They could have used some rest, but they were ordered to help take the little ships back up the Thames to London. To make matters worse, they were assigned the *Ryegate II*, the balky motor yacht they had sailed to Dunkirk and abandoned when her screws fouled. Wearily they set off, around the North Foreland . . . into the Thames estuary . . . and on up the river itself.

The cheering really began after Blackfriars Bridge. Docklands and the City had been too busy to watch the passing of this grimy, oil-stained fleet. But as *Ryegate II* passed the training ship *Discovery*, moored alongside the Embankment, her Sea Scouts set up a mighty cheer. It grew ever louder as the yacht continued upstream. Chelsea . . . Hammersmith . . . Twickenham . . . every bridge was lined with shouting people.

Hilton and Shaw ultimately delivered *Ryegate II* to her boatyard and walked to the tube, where they parted company. After rowing together, side by side, for seventeen hours, it would be reasonable to suppose they remained lifelong friends. As a matter of fact, they never met again.

Hilton took the tube home. As he entered the train, any idea he may have had that he would be greeted as a hero quickly vanished. He had a three-day growth of beard; his clothes were covered with oil; he reeked to high heaven. His fellow passengers quickly moved to the far end of the car.

He reached the front door and discovered he had forgotten his keys. He rang the bell, the door opened, and his wife Pamela was standing there. She took one look at "this tramp" and threw her arms around him. He was a hero to someone, after all.

Written Source Materials

"I am sorry I am unable to get the details and events to dates," writes Sapper Joe Coles of the 223rd Field Park Company, Royal Engineers. "That was an impossibility even a few days after Dunkirk. This I can only put down to continual fatigue and the atmosphere of continual emergency, 24 hours a day."

He isn't the only one with this problem. The days had a way of merging into one another for most of the participants, and the passage of more than 40 years doesn't make memories any sharper. Personal recollections are indispensable in recapturing the atmosphere and preserving many of the incidents that occurred, but overreliance on human memory can be dangerous too. For that reason, I spent even more time examining the written source materials on Dunkirk than in interviewing and corresponding with those who were there.

The Public Record Office in London was the starting point. The basic Admiralty files dealing with the evacuation are ADM 199/786-796. These have been well mined, but fascinating nuggets still await the diligent digger. For instance, ADM 199/792 contains not only Admiral Wake-Walker's familiar 15-page account, but an earlier, far more detailed 41-page account that has lain practically untouched through the years—apparently because it is so faint and hard to read. A powerful magnifying glass pays handsome dividends.

ADM 199/788-B and ADM 199/796-B, dealing with ships reluctant to sail, are still "off-limits" to researchers, but it is possible to work around this restriction and piece together the story from other documents.

Additional Dunkirk material pops up elsewhere in the Admiralty files. ADM 199/360 contains day-by-day information on the weather. ADM 199/2205-2206 includes much of the radio traffic between Dover and Dunkirk, and between ships and the shore. ADM 116/4504 has the story of the bizarre "lethal kite barrage."

The RAF role at Dunkirk can be traced through the Operational Record Books at the PRO, but most of these are too detailed for all but the most exacting scholars. AIR 20/523 does include a useful overview of the Fighter Command's contribution. The War Office records tend to mire the reader in the campaign, although occasionally some documents bear specifically on the evacuation. WO 197/119 has an excellent account of Brigadier Clifton's improvised defense at Nieuport; also a report by Colonel G.H.P. Whitfield, area commandant, depicting the chaos in Dunkirk itself until Captain Tennant arrived.

In some ways the most valuable materials at the PRO are the War Cabinet Historical Section series, CAB 44/60-61 and CAB 44/67-69, not released until 1977. The telephone played an enormous role in the decisions involving Dunkirk, and these CAB files contain detailed accounts of many of the calls, along with the texts of pertinent letters and telegrams.

The PRO is not the answer to everything. Probably the most useful single source of information on the evacuation is the three-volume annotated index of participating ships at the Ministry of Defense's Naval Historical Branch. Labeled "Alphabetical List of Vessels Taking Part, with Their Services," these volumes are occasionally updated as new information trickles in. They include valuable data on the French ships contributed by the French naval historian Hervé Cras.

Another extremely useful source is an account of RAF operations prepared by historian Denis Richards for the Air Historical Branch. Entitled *RAF Narrative: The Campaign in France and the Low Countries, September 1939–June 1940*, this volume gives day-by-day coverage of the evacuation.

Then there are the records so lovingly kept by most of the famous British regiments. These usually include battalion war diaries and often individual accounts. I paid most rewarding visits to the regimental headquarters of the Coldstream Guards, the Grenadier Guards, the Queen Victoria's Rifles, the Gloucestershires, and the Durham Light Infantry.

The formal dispatches of Lord Gort and of Admiral Ramsay complete the official side of the Dunkirk story. Gort's dispatch appeared as a Supplement to the *London Gazette*, October 17, 1941; Ramsay's account as a Supplement to the *Gazette* of July 17, 1947. They are helpful in fixing dates and places, but neither could be called a distinguished piece of battle literature.

There's no end to the unofficial material on Dunkirk. The Imperial War Museum is a cornucopia of unpublished diaries, journals, letters, memoirs, and tapes. I found the following especially valuable: Corporal P. G. Ackrell's account of early turmoil on the Dunkirk waterfront; W.B.A. Gaze's recollections of the 12th Casualty Clearing Station; Commander Thomas Kerr's letters to his wife on conditions at Malo and Bray-Dunes; Admiral Sir L. V. Morgan's reflections as Ramsay's Chief of Staff; Chaplain R. T. Newcomb's impressions as a padre caught up in the great retreat; Signalman L. W. Wright's manuscript, "Personal Experience in the Defence of Calais."

Few of the shipping companies that provided vessels have saved their records (many were destroyed in the blitz), but the Tilbury Contracting Group has preserved accounts by three of its skippers. Tough's Boatyard has a useful file of papers and clippings describing its contribution.

Numerous unpublished accounts have been made available to me by participants and their families. These include no fewer than fourteen diaries. Contemporary letters have been another important source, especially an almost-running commentary from Admiral Ramsay to his wife.

The voluminous published material on Dunkirk began to appear even before the evacuation was over. The *Times* and the other London papers are curiously bland, but not so the local press of the south and southeast coast. Their accounts make fresh, vivid reading even today. The cream of the crop: *The Evening Argus* (Brighton), June 5; *Bournemouth Times and Directory*, June 14; *The East Kent Times* (Ramsgate), June 5; *The Kentish Gazette and Canterbury Press*, June 8; *Folkestone, Hythe and District Herald*, June 8; *Isle of Thanet Gazette* (Margate), June 7; *Sheerness Times and Guardian*, June 7. The Dover *Express* is, of course, a "must" for the whole period.

A number of eyewitness accounts also appeared in various periodicals at the time. Some good examples: *The Architectural Association Journal*, September-November, 1940, "And So—We Went to Dunkirk" (Anonymous); *Blackwood's*, August 1940, "Prelude to Dunkirk" by Ian Scott, and in November 1940, "Small Change from Dunkirk" by M.C.A. Henniker; *Fortnightly Review*, July 1940, "Dunkirk" by E. H. Phillips; *King's Royal Rifle Corps Chronicle*, 1940, an important letter by Sub-Lieutenant Roger Wake, RN, who served as acting pier master on the eastern mole, night of June 2-3.

The magazine *Belgium*—published in London during the war and frankly Allied propaganda—occasionally carried articles on Belgian participants at Dunkirk. Georges Truffant's piece in the issue of July 31, 1941, deserves special mention.

Through the years newspapers have often marked the anniversary of Dunkirk with fresh material. The Scarborough *Evening News*, for instance, commemorated the tenth anniversary with a splendid series by "A Green Howard," appearing April 24, 26, and May 1, 1950. Just about every paper in England must have marked the 40th anniversary. Especially striking was the series in the Manchester *Evening News*, March 10, 11, 12, 13, 14, 1980.

Magazines and service journals are another continuing source of information. Hitler's role is analyzed in the *Army Quarterly*, January 1955, "The Dunkirk Halt Order—a Further Reassessment" by Captain B. H. Liddell Hart; and again in the *Quarterly*, April 1958, "Hitler and Dunkirk" by Captain Robert B. Asprey. The Belgian surrender is examined in *History Today*, February 1980, "The Tragedy of Leopold III" by James Marshall-Cornwall. Alexander's takeover and the last days are recalled in the *Army Quarterly*, April 1972, "With Alexander to Dunkirk" by General Sir William Morgan. But beware of General Morgan's contention that Admiral Abrial still didn't plan to evacuate as late as May 31. Alexander himself refutes this in his report.

Particular ships get their due in a host of articles through the years: *Malcolm,* in "Mostly from the Bridge" by Captain David B. N. Mellis, *Naval Review,* October 1976; *Harvester,* in "Dunkirk: The Baptism of a Destroyer" by Hugh Hodgkinson, *Blackwood's,* June 1980; *Massey Shaw,* in "New Bid to Save London Fireboat," *Lloyd's Log,* October 1981; the sprit-sailing barges, in "The Little Ships of Ipswich" by J. O. Whitmore, *East Anglian Magazine,* July 1950. The medical effects of continuing fear and exhaustion are intelligently discussed by James Dow in *Journal of the Royal Naval Medical Service,* Spring 1978.

No discussion of periodicals would be complete without some mention of the *Dunkirk Veterans Association Journal.* This little quarterly not only keeps the DVA members in touch, but serves as a clearinghouse for all sorts of questions and answers concerning the evacuation. It was through its columns, for instance, that the indefatigable Sam Love tracked down the story of the *Hird,* the ship that returned to France before unloading at Dover.

The books on Dunkirk could fill a warehouse. At least fifteen different titles are devoted entirely to the evacuation or the events leading up to it. From John Masefield's *Nine Days Wonder,* 1941, to Nicholas Harman's *Dunkirk: The Necessary Myth,* 1980, I have learned from them all. Two stand out especially: A. D. Divine's *Dunkirk,* 1944, and Gregory Blaxland's *Destination Dunkirk,* 1973. Mr. Divine was there himself with the little ships, while Mr. Blaxland has written the very model of a campaign history—clear, candid, and complete.

Not limited to Dunkirk, but covering the campaign in detail, are two official histories: Captain S. W. Roskill, *The Navy at War, 1939–45,* 1960; and Major L. F. Ellis, *The War in France and Flanders, 1939–1940,* 1953. Ellis's maps should be the envy of every military historian.

Published memoirs and diaries abound, written by both the known and the unknown. The leaders include: Clement R. Attlee, *As It Happened,* 1954; Duff Cooper, *Old Men Forget,* 1953; Hugh Dalton, *The Fateful Years,* 1957; Anthony Eden, *The Reckoning,* 1965; General Lord Ismay, *Memoirs,* 1960; R. MacLeod, (ed.), *The Ironside Diaries*, 1962; Field-Marshal the Viscount Montgomery, *Memoirs*, 1958; Lieutenant-General Sir Henry Pownall, *Diaries*, 1972; Major-General Sir Edward Spears, *Assignment to Catastrophe*, 1954; Sir Arthur Bryant, *The Turn of the Tide*, 1957, based on the diaries of Field Marshal Lord Alanbrooke. In a class by himself: Winston S. Churchill, *Their Finest Hour*, 1949.

Others are less famous but sometimes more revealing: Sir Basil Bartlett, *My First War*, 1940; Eric Bush, *Bless Our Ship*, 1958; Sir H. E. Franklyn, *The Story of One Green Howard in the Dunkirk Campaign*, 1966; Gun Buster (pseud.), *Return via Dunkirk*, 1940; Sir Leslie Hollis, *One Marine's Tale*, 1956; J. M. Langley, *Fight Another Day*, 1974; A.R.E. Rhodes, *Sword of Bone*, 1942; General Sir John G. Smyth, *Before the Dawn*, 1957; Colonel L.H.M. Westropp, *Memoirs*, 1970.

Useful biographies cover some of the leading figures. For Admiral Ramsay, see David Woodward, *Ramsay at War*, 1957; and W. S. Chalmers, *Full Cycle*, 1958. Lord Gort is gently handled by Sir John Colville in *Man of Valour*, 1972. Lord Alanbrooke is examined by General Sir David Fraser in *Alanbrooke*, 1982. Field Marshal Montgomery gets full-dress treatment from Nigel Hamilton in *Monty: The Making of a General*, 1981. *John Rutherford Crosby* by George Blake, 1946, is a touching, privately published tribute to a young, little-known sub-lieutenant (later a casualty) that somehow captures the glow of Dunkirk better than many more ambitious books.

Then there are the unit and regimental histories. I have made use of 54 of these volumes, and have come to appreciate the loving care with which all have been prepared. I have relied especially on D. S. Daniell, *Cap of Honour* (Gloucestershire Regiment), 1951; Patrick Forbes and Nigel Nicolson, *The Grenadier Guards in the War of 1939–1945*, 1949; Jeremy L. Taylor, *Record of a Reconnaissance Regiment,* section headed "The Fifth Glosters," by Anothony Scott, 1950. David Quilter, *No Dishonourable Name* (2nd Coldstream Guards), 1947; David Russik, *The DLI at War,* 1952; W. Whyte, *Roll of the Drum* (King's Royal Rifle Corps), 1941; and Robin McNish, *Iron Division: The History of the 3rd Division,* 1978.

Other books are important for specific aspects of the story.

The defense of Calais: Airey Neave, *The Flames of Calais*, 1972. The role of the railways: Norman Crump, *By Rail to Victory*, 1947, and B. Darwin, *War on the Line*, 1946. Reaction along the southeast coast: Reginald Foster, *Dover Front*, 1941. The air battles: Douglas Bader, *Fight for the Sky*, 1973, Larry Forrester, *Fly for Your Life*, 1956; B. J. Ellan (pseud.), *Spitfire!* 1942, and Denis Richards, *The Royal Air Force, 1939–1945*, 1953.

Many of these titles concern the rescue fleet. The little ships: Nicholas Drew (pseud.), *The Amateur Sailor*, 1946; and A. A. Hoehling, *Epics of the Sea*, 1977. Role of the Royal National Lifeboat Institution: Charles Vince, *Storm on the Waters*, 1946. The MTB's and MA/SB's: Peter Scott, *The Battle of the Narrow Seas*, 1945. The *Massey Shaw*: H. S. Ingham, *Fire and Water*, 1942. The *Medway Queen*: The Paddle Steamer Preservation Society, *The Story of the Medway Queen*, 1975. The *Clan MacAlister*: G. Holman, *In Danger's Hour*, 1948.

For the French side of Dunkirk I found especially useful the official French Navy study, *Les Forces Maritime du Nord, 1939–1940*, prepared by Dr. Hervé Cras. It is not generally available to the public, but I was given access to a set, and also to several important letters written by Admiral J. Odend'hal, head of the French Naval Mission in London, to his superiors in Paris.

Published memoirs of the French leaders are not very satisfactory. Premier Reynaud's *In the Thick of the Fight*, 1955, is heavy and self-serving. (He even calls it his "Testimony.") General Weygand's *Recalled to Service*, 1952, comes from an obviously bitter man. Jacques Mordal's *Dunkerque*, 1968, tries to combine a memoir with straight history. "Jacques Mordal," incidentally, is a pseudonym used by the historian Hervé Cras. Edmond Perron's *Journal d'un Dunkerquois*, 1977, depicts what it was like to be an ordinary citizen of Dunkirk trapped in the battle.

Good general histories include Rear-Admiral Paul Auphan (with Jacques Mordal), *The French Navy in World War II*, 1957; General André Beaufre, *1940: The Fall of France*, 1967; Guy Chapman, *Why France Collapsed*, 1968; and William L. Shirer, *The Collapse of the Third Republic*, 1969.

The German archival sources are amazingly complete. It's

difficult to understand how, in the final *Götterdämmerung* of the Third Reich, so much could have survived, but the very swiftness of the collapse enabled the Allied armies to seize vast quantities of records intact, to be examined and later returned to the owners.

It's all now in the lovely city of Freiburg, meticulously filed in the Bundesarchiv/Militärarchiv, and the Dunkirk material can be easily located. I found most useful the war diaries and situation reports of Army Groups A and B; the Sixth and Eighteenth Armies; IX, X, XIV, and XIX Corps; 18th Infantry Division; 1st, 2nd, and 10th Panzer Divisions; Luftwaffe Air Fleet 2; Fliegerkorps VIII; First Naval War Command; the motor torpedo boat *S 30*; and the submarine *U 62*.

The Bundesarchiv also contains a number of unpublished firsthand accounts covering the Dunkirk campaign. File Z A₃/50 includes recollections of Field-Marshal Kesselring and Luftwaffe Generals Hans Seidemann and Josef Schmidt. File RH37/6335 contains a vivid account by an unidentified soldier in XIX Corps, covering the whole period from the dash to the sea on May 20 to the fall of Bergues, June 2. File Z 305 is the published diary of Hans Waitzbauer, an observant young radio operator serving in the 102nd Artillery Regiment.

The most important diary of all was that kept by General Franz Halder, Chief of the Army General Staff at the time of Dunkirk. It provides not only an hour-by-hour record of events but candid comments on the various personalities at OKH and OKW. The copy I used is an English translation on file at the Bibliothek für Zeitgeschichte in Stuttgart.

The contemporary published material faithfully follows the Nazi line, but the press does convey the feeling of euphoria that swept Germany that intoxicating May and June of 1940. Three good examples: *Der Adler*, June 11 and 25; *Die Wehrmacht*, June 19; and *Völkischer Beobachter*, almost any day.

The German books of the period are just as slanted, but occasionally something useful turns up. Fritz Otto Busch, *Unsere Schnellboote im Kanal* (no date) gives a good picture of S Boat operations. Herbert W. Borchert, *Panzerkampf im Westen* (1940) has interesting anecdotes on the thrust of the panzers. Heinz Guderian, *Mit den Panzern in Ost und West* (1942) is really a compilation of eyewitness stories brought out under Guderian's name, but it does include a good piece on Calais by a Colonel Fischer, who was there. Hans Henkel, *Blende auf-Tiefangriff* (1941) has a chapter on Dunkirk that gives a vivid picture of the utter desolation that greeted the entering German troops.

The years since the war have seen an enormous output of German articles and books touching on Dunkirk. The propaganda is gone, often replaced by wishful thinking, second-guessing, and buck-passing. Some of these sources have English translations: Guenther Blumentritt, *Von Runstedt: The Soldier and the Man*, 1952; Adolf Galland, *The First and the Last*, 1954; Heinz Guderian, *Panzer Leader*, 1952; Hans-Adolf Jacobsen, *Decisive Battles of World War II*, 1965; Albert Kesselring, *Memoirs*, 1953; Werner Kreipe, *The Fatal Decisions*, 1956; Walter Warlimont, *Inside Hitler's Headquarters*, 1964. Pertinent interviews can be found in B. H. Liddell Hart, *The German Generals Talk*, 1948.

Hitler's "halt order" is picked apart by all these authorities, as it is by other, less familiar writers who have not yet been translated into English: Wolf von Aaken, *Inferno im Westen*, 1964; Peter Bor, *Gespräche mit Halder*, 1950; Gert Buchheit, *Hitler der Feldherr; die Zerstörung einst Legende*, 1958; Gerhard Engel, *Heeres-Adjutant bei Hitler, 1938–1943*, 1974; Ulrich Liss, *Westfront 1939–1940*, 1959.

For general background I often turned to Len Deighton's *Blitzkrieg: From the Rise of Hitler to the Fall of Dunkirk*, 1980; William L. Shirer's classic *The Rise and Fall of the Third Reich*; Telford Taylor's *The March of Conquest*, 1958; and John Toland's immensely readable *Adolf Hitler*, 1978. All helped fill me in, and Taylor's appendices proved indispensable.

Acknowledgments

"My own feelings are rather of disgust," writes a member of the 67th Field Regiment, Royal Artillery. "I saw officers throw their revolvers away ... I saw soldiers shooting cowards as they fought to be first in a boat."

"Their courage made our job easy," recalls a signalman with the Naval Shore Party, describing the same men on the same beaches, "and I was proud to have known them and to have been born of their generation."

To a clerk in 11th Brigade Headquarters, the evacuation was "absolute chaos." To a man in III Corps Headquarters, it was a "debacle" ... a "disgrace." But to a dispatch rider with the 4th Division, it was thrilling evidence "that the British were an invincible people."

Could they all be talking about the same battle? As I pieced the story together, sometimes it seemed that the only thing the men of Dunkirk agreed upon was their desire to be helpful. Over 500 answered my "call to arms," and there seemed no limit to the time and trouble they were willing to take.

Lieutenant-Colonel James M. Langley spent three days showing me around the perimeter, with special attention to the segment of the line held by the 2nd Coldstream Guards. Harold

Robinson, Hon. General Secretary of the Dunkirk Veterans Association, arranged for me to join the DVA's annual pilgrimage in 1978. It was a splendid opportunity to get to know some of these men personally, listen to their recollections, and feel the ties that bind them together. I'm especially grateful for the time given me by the Reverend Leslie Aitken, Fred Batson, and Arthur Elkin.

The DVA Headquarters in Leeds generously put me in touch with the organization's branches all over the world, and as a result I've received valuable assistance from such varied places as Cyprus, Zimbabwe, Malta, Libya, Italy, Canada, Australia, and New Zealand. The London Branch was particularly helpful, which calls for an extra word of thanks to Stan Allen, Ted Rabbets, and Bob Stephens. For making my cause so widely known, I'm indebted to Captain L. A. Jackson ("Jacko"), editor of the DVA's lively *Journal*.

Everyone was helpful, but as the work progressed, I found myself leaning more and more on certain individuals, whom I came to regard as "my" experts in certain areas. These included the Viscount Bridgeman on events at GHQ; Captain Eric Bush on the Royal Navy; Air Vice-Marshal Michael Lyne on the RAF; Captain Stephen Roskill on the Dynamo Room; John Bridges on the Grenadier Guards; Sam Love on the *Hird*; W. Stanley Berry on the Small Vessels Pool; and Basil Bellamy on the Ministry of Shipping. General Sir Peter Hunt gave me a crash course on British Regiments, and it's a lucky American indeed whose tutor on such an intricate matter is a former Chief of the Imperial General Staff.

The participants not only poured out their recollections; they cheerfully rummaged through trunks and attics for long-forgotten papers that might throw further light on their experiences. Old diaries were dusted off by A. Baldwin, J. S. Dodd, F. R. Farley, A. R. Jabez-Smith, W. P. Knight, J. M. Langley, R. W. Lee, I.F.R. Ramsay, and N. Watkin. Others sent in detailed accounts originally written when memories were green— for instance, G. W. Jones, E. C. Webb, and R. M. Zakovitch. Fred Walter contributed a remarkable 31-page handwritten account of Calais, which gave a better picture of that controversial episode than anything else I've seen.

Families gallantly pitched in where the participants themselves had passed on. Mrs. E. Barker sent in the diary of her father, Major J. W. Gibson; Roy L. Fletcher contributed a fascinating account by his father, Seaman C. L. Fletcher. Mrs. D. Forward extracted an interesting letter from her brother Syd Metcalf. Helpful widows included Mrs. Nancy Cotton and Mrs. C. Smales.

Two cases deserve special mention. First, David F. Ramsay made available some personal correspondence of his distinguished father, Admiral Sir Bertram Ramsay, including a file of letters to Mrs. Ramsay that vividly depicts the blend of desperation and determination that permeated the Dynamo Room. Second, through the good offices of my friend Sharon Rutman, Mrs. Sylvia Sue Steell contributed a letter from her gallant uncle, Commander Charles Herbert Lightoller. It mirrors the spirit of the men who sailed the little ships, and shows that Commander Lightoller had lost none of the zeal that served him so well as Second Officer on the *Titanic*.

Other firsthand accounts were collected and forwarded to me by various branches of the DVA, and for this good work I'm particularly grateful to E. C. Webb of the Glasgow Branch and A. Hordell of the Stoke-on-Trent Branch. A special word of thanks, too, for my friend Edward de Groot, who called my attention to Lieutenant Lodo van Hamel, the only skipper in Admiral Ramsay's rescue fleet to fly the Dutch flag. Further details on van Hamel's service were generously provided by Commander F. C. van Oosten, Royal Dutch Navy, Ret., Director of Naval History.

In France I was lucky to have the all-out assistance of Hervé Cras, Assistant Director of the Musée de la Marine, who survived the destroyer *Jaguar* and the minesweeper *Emile Deschamps*, both lost at Dunkirk. Besides being a participant, Dr. Cras lent me important French records and arranged for two key interviews: one with Rear-Admiral Paul Auphan, who explained the thinking at Darlan's headquarters; and the other with Vice-Admiral Gui de Toulouse-Lautrec, who described the loss of his destroyer, *Siroco*. I only wish Hervé Cras were still alive to read these words of heartfelt gratitude.

At a different level F. Summers (then Fernand Schneider)

provided a fascinating glimpse of life on a French minesweeping trawler. Mr. Summers came from Dunkirk, and he enjoyed the unusual distinction of starting the war in the French Navy and ending it in the Royal Navy—all in all, a unique point of view.

In Germany I concentrated on old aviators, since so much of Dunkirk revolved around the successes and failures of the Luftwaffe. I felt my questions were answered with candor, and I'm deeply grateful to Wolfgang Falck, Adolf Galland, and Hans Mahnert. Colonel Rudi Erlemann was only a small boy in 1940, but by the time I cornered him he was Air Attaché at the German Embassy in Washington, and full of insight on the Luftwaffe's performance.

For other glimpses of the German side, I'm indebted to Willy Felgner, a signalman with the 56th Infantry Division; Vice-Admiral Friedrich Ruge, a wise old sailor full of thoughtful comment on the German Navy's performance; Georg Smidt Scheeder, photographer with Goebbels's propaganda company; and Albert Speer, who had at least one conversation with Hitler touching on Dunkirk. Speer felt, incidentally, that anyone who believed that Hitler wanted to "let the English escape" didn't understand the Fuehrer very well.

The written material on Dunkirk is voluminous; fortunately an army of dedicated archivists and librarians stands ready to aid the probing scholar. At the Imperial War Museum in London, Dr. Noble Frankland's helpful staff made me feel like one of the family. Rose Coombs, Keeper of Special Collections, is a heroine to countless American researchers, and I'm no exception.

David Brown, head of the Naval Historical Branch, gave me a warm welcome, and his assistant, Miss M. Thirkettle, made available her encyclopedic knowledge of what ships were and what were not at Dunkirk. Andrew Naylor, Librarian of the Royal United Services Institute, and Richard Brech of the Royal Air Force Museum both had many useful suggestions.

The Secretaries of the various Regimental Headquarters scattered throughout Britain were invariably helpful. I'm especially grateful to Lieutenant-Colonel F.A.D. Betts of the Coldstream Guards; Major Oliver Lindsay of the Grenadier Guards;

Lieutenant-Colonel R. E. Humphreys of the Durham Light Infantry; Lieutenant-Colonel H.L.T. Radice of the Gloucestershire Regiment; and Lieutenant-Colonel W.R.H. Charley of the Royal Irish Rangers. Miss E. M. Keen of the Queen Victoria's Rifles Association not only produced records but organized a session where I could meet and talk with several of the veterans of Calais.

On the nautical side, the Association of Dunkirk Little Ships was always helpful in identifying various vessels. This organization must be the most unusual yacht club in the world: the boat, rather than the owner, is elected to membership. Through the Association's efforts, 126 of the Dunkirk little ships have now been carefully preserved. The group's Archivist, John Knight, knows them all and generously shares his knowledge. A special word of thanks to Harry Moss, owner of *Braymar*, who hosted me at the 1978 Fitting-Out Dinner.

A visit to Tough's Boatyard paid great dividends in learning how these little ships were collected and manned. Mr. Robert O. Tough, present head of the family enterprise, took time off from a busy day to dig out the yard's files on the evacuation. I was unable to get to Tilbury, but that didn't deter Mr. C. E. Sedgwick, Group Secretary of the Tilbury Contracting Group. He generously struck off for me photocopies of the actual reports submitted by the masters of three of the company's dredges at Dunkirk.

The German archivists matched their British counterparts in patience and helpfulness. Nothing seemed too much trouble, as they tirelessly pulled books and records for my perusal. Heartfelt thanks to the splendid staffs at the Bundesarchiv/Militärarchiv in Freiburg, at the Bibliothek für Zeitgeschichte in Stuttgart, and at the Institut für Zeitgeschichte in Munich. The Bundesarchiv in Koblenz is a treasure house of photographs, and I appreciate the effort here, too, in providing everything I needed.

A writer can always use helpful leads, and fortunately there were any number of knowledgeable people on both sides of the Atlantic willing to point me in the right direction. In England this loyal band included Leo Cooper, David Curling, David Divine, Dick Hough, Peter Kemp, Ronald Lewin, Roger Machell,

Martin Middlebrook, Denis Richards, Stephen Roskill, and Dan Solon. In America there were Dolph Hoehling, Tom Mahoney, Sam Meek, Drew Middleton, Roger Pineau, Ed Schaefer, Jack Seabrook, Bill Stump, and John Toland. Some, like Ronald Lewin and John Toland, took time out from their own books to help me—a sacrifice that perhaps only another writer can truly appreciate.

One bit of unusual generosity deserves separate mention. In 1970 the late Robert Carse wrote *Dunkirk—1940*, an interesting book that made use of many firsthand accounts. Ten years later—to my grateful surprise—Mr. Carse's daughter Jean Mitchell and a family friend, Vice-Admiral Gordon McLintock, USN (Ret.), turned over to me Mr. Carse's notes and correspondence with various Dunkirk participants. Although in the end I did not include any of this material in my book, it served as valuable background and a useful cross-check on my own sources. I deeply appreciate the thoughtfulness of both Mrs. Mitchell and Admiral McLintock.

There remain those who worked directly on the project over the long haul. Marielle Hoffman performed all sorts of heroics as my interpreter/translator in France. Karola Gillich did the same in Germany. I'm also indebted to my friend Roland Hauser, who scanned for me the German press coverage of Dunkirk in 1940 and took on several special research assignments.

In England Caroline Larken excelled in lining up interviews, checking various points, and helping me screen the press. Alexander Peters did useful reconnaissance at the PRO. Susan Chadwick efficiently handled the traffic at Penguin as the accounts poured in. My editor there, Eleo Gordon, constantly performed services above and beyond the call of duty.

In New York Scott Supplee came to town intending to write short-story fiction—and stayed to become the city's greatest authority on British regimental histories. Preston Brooks, whose father did research for me in 1960, carried on the family tradition. His fluent knowledge of French also came in handy at a critical time. Patricia Heestand not only carried out her share of research, but did yeoman work in compiling the List of Contributors and the Index. Colin Dawkins lent his shrewd eye to the selection and arrangement of illustrations. At Viking my editor, Alan Williams, was as patient and perceptive as ever.

Finally, there are those who lived with the book on an almost daily basis. Dorothy Hefferline handled the voluminous correspondence and helped out on all sorts of dire emergencies. The long-suffering Florence Gallagher deserves a medal for completing her 34th year of deciphering my foolscap.

But all these people—helpful as they were—would not have been enough without the cooperation of the participants listed on the following pages. They get no blame for my mistakes, but a full share of the credit for whatever new light is thrown on the events that unfolded at Dunkirk in the memorable spring of 1940.

List of Contributors

The miracle of Dunkirk was largely the achievement of British soldiers, sailors, fliers, and civilians—all working together—so it is fitting that the same combination has made possible this book. All contributors are listed alphabetically, regardless of rank or title. Where supplied, retired rank and honors are indicated.

Each name is followed by the participant's unit or service, to give some idea of vantage point; where appropriate, ship names are also included. In a few cases the participant is no longer living, and his account has been made available by some member of the family. These names are marked by an asterisk.

Lt.-Col. G. S. Abbott, TD, JP—BEF, Royal Artillery, 57th Anti-Tank Regiment
Douglas Ackerley—BEF, The King's Own Scottish Borderers
E. Acklam—BEF, Royal Artillery, 63rd Medium Regiment
L. J. Affleck—BEF, 2nd Division, Signals
Lt.-Cdr. J. L. Aldridge, MBE—HMS *Express*
Andrew Alexander—BEF, GHQ Signals; HMS *Calcutta*
P. D. Allan—BEF, Royal Artillery; HMS *Vimy*

George Allen—BEF
Stanley V. Allen—RN, HMS *Windsor*
H. G. Amphlett—BEF, 14th City of London Royal Fusiliers
Michael Anthony—RNVR, *Aura, Yorkshire Lass*
G. W. Arnold—BEF, Royal Engineers, 573rd Field Squadron
E. W. Arthur—RN, HMS *Calcutta*
Jean Gardiner Ashenhurst—nurse, Royal Victoria Hospital, Folkestone
C. J. Atkinson—RN, HMS *Basilisk*
Thomas Atkinson—BEF, RASC, 159th Welsh Field Ambulance
Mrs. M. Austin—Red Cross nurse, southern England

William H. Bacchus—BEF, RAMC, 13th Field Ambulance
Lt.-Col. L.J.W. Bailey—BEF, Royal Artillery, 1st Heavy Anti-Aircraft Regiment
Alfred Baldwin—BEF, Royal Artillery; *Maid of Orleans*
Brigadier D. W. Bannister—BEF, Royal Artillery, 56th Medium Regiment
R. H. Barlow—BEF, RAOC, 11th Infantry Brigade; HMS *Sandown*
Oliver D. Barnard—BEF, 131st Brigade, Signals; *Dorrien Rose*
A. F. Barnes, MSM—BEF
Douglas Barnes—BEF, Royal Artillery, 1st Heavy Anti-Aircraft Regiment; HMS *Javelin*
S. Barnes—RN, HMS *Widgeon*
A. F. Barnett—BEF
R. Bartlett—personnel ships, detached duty from Royal Artillery, 64th Regiment, *Queen of the Channel*
D. F. Batson—BEF, RASC
R. Batten—BEF, 48th Division, Royal Engineers
F. A. Baxter—BEF, RAOC, No. 2 Ordnance Field Park; *Bullfinch*
H. J. Baxter, BEM—RN, HMS *Sandhurst*
Ernest E. Bayley—BEF, 3rd Division, Signals; HMS *Mosquito*
J. Bayliff—BEF, 2nd Division, RASC; HMS *Mosquito*
C. E. Beard—BEF, RASC; *Bullfinch*
J. Beardsley—BEF, Royal Engineers
L. C. Beech—BEF, 3rd Division, Signals
Basil E. Bellamy, CB—civilian, Ministry of Shipping
R. Bellamy—BEF, Middlesex Regiment

C. N. Bennett—BEF, 5th Northamptonshire Regiment; HMS *Ivanhoe*

Lt.-Col. John S. W. Bennett— BEF, Royal Engineers, 250th Field Company

Lt.-Cdr. the Rev. Peter H. E. Bennett—RN, *New Prince of Wales, Triton*, HMS *Mosquito*

Myrette Bennington—WRNS, Naval HQ, Dover

W. S. Berry—civilian, Admiralty, Small Vessels Pool

Herbert V. Betts—Constable, Police War Reserve, Ramsgate

Cdr. Robert Bill, DSO, FRICS, FRGS—RN, Naval HQ, Dover; HMS *Fyldea*

Tom Billson—BEF, RASC; *Royal Daffodil*

R. H. Blackburn—BEF, CMP; *Hird*

L. Blackman—BEF, Royal Artillery, 1st Light Anti-Aircraft Battery

Robert Blamire—BEF, Infantry

R. J. Blencowe—BEF, Royal Artillery

G. Bollington—BEF, RASC, 3rd Division

Capt. L.A.A. Border—BEF, RASC, 44th Division; *Prudential*

George Boston—BEF, 143rd Infantry Brigade

Frank H. Bound—BEF, 2nd Cameronians

D. Bourne—BEF, RASC; HMS *Beatrice*

Eric Bowman—BEF, 7th Green Howards

Cdr. V.A.L. Bradyll-Johnson—RN, Eastern Arm, Dover breakwater

E. P. Brett—BEF, Signals; HMS *Calcutta*

Maj. Anthony V. N. Bridge—BEF, 2nd Dorset Regiment

Viscount Robert Clive Bridgeman, KBE, CB, DSO, MD, JP— BEF, GHQ, acting Operations Officer; HMS *Keith, Vivian*

John Bridges—BEF, 1st Grenadier Guards; HMS *Ivanhoe*, HMS *Speedwell*

Maj.-Gen. P.H.W. Brind—BEF, 2nd Dorset Regiment; HMS *Javelin*

W. Brown—RN, HMS *Grenade, Fenella*, HMS *Crested Eagle*

D. A. Buckland—BEF, Royal Artillery, 54th Light Anti-Aircraft Regiment

K. S. Burford—BEF, 1/7th Middlesex Regiment

Frederick J. Burgin—BEF, Royal Engineers

Lord Burnham, JP, DL—BEF, 2nd Division, Royal Artillery; HMS *Worcester*

G. H. Burt—BEF, 2nd Dorset Regiment

Capt. Eric Bush—RN, Adm. Ramsay's staff, Dunkirk beaches; HMS *Hebe*

Charles K. Bushe, SJAB—BEF, Royal Artillery, 52nd Field Regiment

R. G. Butcher—BEF, 1st Division

George H. Butler—BEF, Royal Artillery, 2nd Field Regiment; HMS *Worcester*

Olive M. Butler—civilian, Basingstoke, return of troops

Charles V. Butt—BEF, RASC

Capt. J.S.S. Buxey—BEF, Royal Artillery, 139th Field Regiment; *Lady of Mann*

Maj. Donald F. Callander, MC—BEF, 1st Queen's Own Cameron Highlanders

Lord Cameron, Kt, DSC, LLD, FRSE, HRSA, FRSGS, DI—RNVR, *MTB 107*

Lt.-Col. T.S.A. Campbell—BEF, 3rd Division, Signals

Moran Caplat—RNVR, *Freshwater*

David H. Caple—BEF, RASC, 3rd Division, 23rd Ammunition Company

Maj. B. G. Carew Hunt, MBE, TD—BEF, 1/5th Queen's Royal Regiment

D. C. Carter—BEF, 2nd Division, 208th Field Company; *Fisher Boy*

Robert Carter—BEF, 48th Division, Signals

P. Cavanagh—RN, HMS *Grenade*

P. C. Chambers—BEF, Royal Engineers

Mowbray Chandler—BEF, Royal Artillery, 57th Field Regiment; *Fenella*, HMS *Crested Eagle*

R. Chapman—BEF

Percy H. Charles—BEF, 44th Division, Signals; *Canterbury*

J. Cheek—BEF, RASC, 44th Division; HMS *Sabre*

Lord Chelwood, MC, DL—BEF, 9th Royal Northumberland Fusiliers; HMS *Malcolm*

Col. J.M.T.F. Churchill, DSO, MC—BEF, 2nd Manchester Regiment; HMS *Leda*

J. B. Claridge—BEF, 4th Division, 12th Field Ambulance; HMS *Ivanhoe*

Charles Clark—BEF, 4th Royal Sussex Regiment

E. Clements—RN, HMS *Gossamer*

D. J. Coles—BEF, Royal Engineers, 223rd Field Park Company

Col. J. J. Collins, MC, TD—BEF, GHQ Signals

Sir John Colville, CB, CVO—Assistant Private Secretary to Winston Churchill

A. Cordery—BEF, RASC; HMS *Icarus*

W. F. Cordrey—BEF, 2nd Royal Warwick Regiment

Henry J. Cornwell—BEF, Royal Engineers, 250th Field Company

*Walter Eric Cotton—BEF, Signals

L.H.T. Court—BEF, 2nd Coldstream Guards

David F. Cowie—BEF, 1st Fife and Forfar Yeomanry

Lt.-Cdr. I.N.D. Cox, DSC—RN, HMS *Malcolm*

F. J. Crampton, RSM—BEF, II Corps, Signals, attached to 51st Heavy Regiment, RA

George Crane—BEF, 12th Royal Lancers

Joyce Crawford-Stuart—VAD Guildford, Surrey

Maj. H. M. Croome—BEF, 5th Division, Field Security

Thomas Henry Cullen—BEF, RAOC, 19th HQ Field Workshops, attached to 1st Division

Frank Curry—BEF, 1st East Lancashire Regiment

R. G. Cutting—BEF, 44th Division, Signals

Maj. F. H. Danielli—BEF, RASC, 3rd GHQ Company

George David Davies—RNR, *Jacinta*, *Thetis*

F. Davis—BEF, Royal Artillery, 4th Heavy Anti-Aircraft

John Dawes—RN, Naval Shore Party; HMS *Wolfhound*

H. Delve—BEF, RASC, II Corps; *Westwood*

Raphael de Sola—civilian, ship's lifeboat

Charles James Dewey—BEF, 4th Royal Sussex Regiment

C.C.H. Diaper—RN, HMS *Sandown*

Harold J. Dibbens—BEF, I Corps, 102nd Provost Company; HMS *Windsor*

Robert Francis Dickman—BEF, 4th Division, Signals; *Ben-My-Chree*

G. W. Dimond—BEF, Royal Artillery, Brigade Anti-Tank Company

A. D. Divine—civilian, *Little Ann*, *White Wing*

K. Dobson—Infantry, Suffolk coast defense

John S. Dodd, TD—BEF, Royal Artillery, 58th Field Regiment; HMS *Sabre*

A. H. Dodge—BEF, Royal Artillery, 13th Anti-Tank Regiment

Harry Donohoe—BEF, 1st Division, Signals

Maj.-Gen. Arthur J. H. Dove—GHQ; HMS *Wolfhound*

James Dow—Royal Naval Medical Service; HMS *Gossamer*, HMS *Mosquito*

James F. Duffy—BEF, Royal Artillery, 52nd Heavy Regiment

F. G. Dukes—BEF, Signals, Division HQ; HMS *Shikari*

Reginald E. Dunstan—BEF, RAMC, 186th Field Ambulance

Col. L. C. East, DSO, OBE—BEF, 1/5th Queen's Royal Regiment

R. G. Eastwell—BEF, 5th Northamptonshire Regiment; HMS *Niger*

G. Edkins—civilian, Surrey, return of troops

R. Edwards—BEF, RASC, ambulance driver

R. Eggerton—BEF; HMS *Esk*

A. L. Eldridge, RMPA, RMH—BEF, 3rd Grenadier Guards

Arthur Elkin, MM—BEF, 3rd Division, Military Police, General Montgomery's bodyguard

A. W. Elliott—civilian, *Warrior*

C. W. Elmer—BEF, 2nd Coldstream Guards

Charles J. Emblin—RN, HMS *Basilisk*

Lt.-Col. H. M. Ervine-Andrews, VC—BEF, 1st East Lancashire Regiment

Alwyne Evans—BEF, 5th Gloucestershire Regiment; hospital carrier *Paris*

Col. H. V. Ewbank—BEF, 50th Division, Signals; HMS *Sutton*

Cdr. R. G. Eyre.—RN *MA/SB 10*

Julian Fane—BEF, 2nd Gloucestershire Regiment

F. R. Farley—BEF, RAOC, 1/7th Middlesex Regiment; HMS *Halcyon*

F. A. Faulkner—BEF, 1st Division, Signals

H. W. Fawkes—BEF, RAOC, electrician

Rosemary Keyes Fellowes—WRNS, Naval HQ, Dover

F. Felstead—BEF, Signals; HMS *Royal Eagle*

John Fernald—civilian, ship's lifeboat

Col. John H. Fielden—BEF, 5th Lancashire Fusiliers

Maj. Geoffrey H. Fisher—BEF, RASC

Rear-Adm. R. L. Fisher, CB, DSO, OBE, DSC—HMS *Wakeful, Comfort, Hird*

*Carl Leonard Fletcher, DSM—RN, HMS *Wolfhound*, HMS *Crested Eagle, Fenella*, HMS *Whitehall*

B.G.W. Flight—BEF, RASC, No. 1 Troop Carrying Company

E. H. Foard, MM—BEF, Royal Engineers, No. 2 Bridge Company, RASC

Capt. R. D. Franks, CBE, DSO, DSC—RN, HMS *Scimitar*

K. G. Fraser—Merchant Navy, *Northern Prince*, London docks

Brig. A. F. Freeman, MC—BEF, Signals, HQ II Corps

W. C. Frost—BEF, RAMC, 1th Casualty Clearing Station

Mrs. D. M. Fugeman—civilian, Wales, return of troops

Ronald Wilfred Furneaux—BEF, 1/5th Queen's Royal Regiment

H. E. Gentry—BEF, Royal Artillery, 32nd Field Regiment; HMS *Malcolm*

Lottie Germain—refugee; *Sutton*

*Maj. J. W. Gibson, MBE—BEF, 2nd East Yorkshire Regiment; HMS *Lord Howe*

Alfred P. Gill—BEF, RASC, 44th Division, 132nd Field Ambulance; *Hird*

Air Marshal Sir Victor Goddard, KCB, CBE, MA—RAF, Air Adviser to Lord Gort

Eric V. Goodbody—RN, Yeoman of Signals, GHQ; HMS *Westward Ho*

Mark Goodfellow—BEF, RASC, 55th West Lancashire Division

Thomas A. Gore Browne—BEF, 1st Grenadier Guards

Bessie Gornall—civilian, London, return of troops

S. E. Gouge—BEF, RASC; HMS *Intrepid*

William Douglas Gough—BEF, Royal Artillery, 1st Medium Regiment

Captain J. R. Gower, DSC—RN, HMS *Albury*

Air Vice-Marshal S. B. Grant, CB, DFC—RAF, 65 Squadron, Hornchurch

Col. J.S.S. Gratton, OBE, DL—BEF, 2nd Hampshire Regiment

D.K.G. Gray—BEF, RAMC, 12th Casualty Clearing Station
A. H. Greenfield—BEF, Royal Artillery, Anti-Tank Regiment
G. A. Griffin—BEF, RASC, driver
E. N. Grimmer—BEF, Royal Engineers, 216th Field Company;
   HMS *Malcolm*

Bob Hadnett, MM—BEF, 48th Division, Signals, Dispatch Rider
E. A. Haines—BEF, 1st Grenadier Guards; HMS *Speedwell*
David Halton—BEF, 1st Division, Signals
V. Hambly—civilian, Ashford, Kent, return of troops
M. M. Hammond—BEF, RAMC, 1st Field Ambulance
Lt.-Col. C. L. Hanbury, MBE, TD, DL—BEF, Royal Artillery,
   99th Field Regiment
E. S. Hannant—BEF, Infantry, Machine-Gunner
W. Harbord—BEF, RASC
George Hare—BEF, I Corps, 102nd Provost Company; HMS
   Windsor
S. Harland—BEF, 2nd Welsh Guards
R. A. Harper—BEF, RAF, Lysander spotter plane, attached to
   56th Highland Medium Artillery; HMS *Grafton*
K.E.C. Harrington—BEF, 48th Division, RAMC, 143rd Field
   Ambulance
E. Harris—BEF, Royal Engineers, 135th Excavator Company;
   HMS *Calcutta*
F. H. Harris—BEF, 4/7th Royal Dragoons
Leslie F. Harris—BEF, RAMC, 7th Field Ambulance
Tom Harris—BEF, Royal Engineers, I Corps, 13th Field Survey
   Company; hospital carrier *Paris*
Thomas Collingwood Harris—BEF, RAOC, No. 1 Recovery
   Section
Ted Harvey—civilian, *Moss Rose*, Cockle Boats, *Letitia*
Jeffrey Haward, MM—BEF, 3rd Division, Machine Gun Battal-
   ion
Maj. S. S. Hawes—BEF, RASC, 1st Division; HMS *Grafton*, HMS
   Wakeful
E. A. Hearl—BEF, RAMC, 132nd Field Ambulance
Ernest A. Heming—BEF, RAOC, Field Rank Unit
Oliver Henry—BEF, Infantry, Machine Gun Battalion
Col. J. Henton Wright, OBE, TD, DL—BEF, Royal Artillery,
   60th Field Regiment; *Royal Sovereign*

Sam H. Henwood—BEF, 3rd Division, Signals; HMS *Sandown*

Maj. John Heron, MC, TD—BEF, 2nd Dorset Regiment

Thomas Hewson—BEF, RAOC, attached to Field Artillery Unit

Col. Peter R. Hill, OBE, TD—BEF, RAOC, II Corps, 2nd Ordnance Field Park

C.F.R. Hilton, DSC—civilian, *Ryegate II*

Michael Joseph Hodgkinson—BEF, RAOC, 14th Army Field Workshop

William Holden—BEF, 3rd Division, Signals; HMS *Sandown*

Robert Walker Holding—BEF, Royal Sussex Regiment; HMS *Codrington*

F. Hollis—BEF, 7th Green Howards

Brig. A. Eric Holt—BEF, 2nd Manchester Regiment

C. G. Hook—BEF, RASC; *Tynwald*

Alan Hope—BEF, Royal Artillery, 58th Field Regiment

R. Hope—BEF, 2nd Manchester Regiment

Ronald Jeffrey Hopper—BEF, RASC, 50th Division

Richard Hoskins—BEF, RASC, driver

Brig. D.J.B. Houchin, DSO, MC—BEF, 5th Division

H. Howard—BEF, RASC, 4th Division

Jeffrey Howard, MM—BEF, 1/7th Middlesex Regiment

Dennis S. Hudson—RN, signalman, HMS *Scimitar*

Mrs. Pat Hunt—civilian, Portland and Weymouth, return of troops

Gen. Sir Peter Hunt, GCB, DSO, OBE—BEF, 1st Cameron Highlanders

Major Frank V. Hurrell—BEF, RASC

Freddie Hutch—RAF, 4th Army Cooperation Squadron; *Maid of Orleans*

L. S. Hutchinson—BEF, Royal Artillery, Medium Regiment

W. J. Ingham—BEF, Field Security Police; HMS *Sabre*

A. R. Isitt—BEF, 2nd Coldstream Guards; HMS *Vimy*

Byron E. J. Iveson-Watt—BEF, Royal Artillery, 1st Anti-Aircraft Regiment; HMS *Worcester*

A. R. Jabez-Smith—BEF, 1st Queen Victoria's Rifles

Albert John Jackson—Army sergeant attached to HMS *Golden Eagle*

Evelyn Jakes—civilian, return of troops

Maj. H. N. Jarvis, TD—BEF, Royal Artillery, 53rd Medium Regiment

Alec Jay—BEF, 1st Queen Victoria's Rifles

E. Johnson—BEF, Royal Artillery

Walton Ronald William Johnson—RN, HMS *Scimitar*

Gen. Sir Charles Jones, GCB, CBE, MC—BEF, 42nd Division, 127th Brigade

George W. Jones—BEF, 1st Grenadier Guards

Dr. Adrian Kanaar—BEF, RAMC, Field Ambulance; HMS *Calcutta*

R. Kay—BEF, GHQ, Signals

Maj. E. E. Kennington—BEF, Royal Engineers, 203rd Field Park Company; HMS *Wolsey*

Professor W. E. Kershaw, CMG, VRD, MD, DSC-RNVR, HMS *Harvester*

A. P. Kerstin—BEF, RASC, 1st Division

A. King—BEF, III Corps HQ; HMS *Impulsive*

Major H. P. King-Fretts—BEF, 2nd Dorsetshire Regiment

John F. Kingshott—BEF, RAOC, First A.A. Brigade Workshop

F. W. Kitchener—BEF, Royal Artillery

Jack Kitchener—BEF, RASC; *Isle of Gurnsey*

William P. Knight—BEF, Royal Engineers, No. 1 General Base Depot

Arthur Knowles—BEF, 2nd Grenadier Guards, 12th Casualty Clearing Station

George A. Kyle—BEF, 1st Fife and Forfar Yeomanry; *Killarney*

A. E. Lambert—BEF, Royal Artillery, 5th Heavy Regiment

Col. C. R. Lane—BEF, 3rd Division, Signals

Lt.-Col. J. M. Langley—BEF, 2nd Coldstream Guards, 12th Casualty Clearing Station

A. Lavis—BEF, Royal Artillery, Anti-Tank Regiment

George Lawrence—BEF, Middlesex Regiment

John Lawrence—BEF, 42nd Division, 126th Brigade

W. G. Lawrence—BEF, Royal Artillery; HMS *Vivacious*

W. Lawson—RNVR, HMS *Codrington*, LDG Signalman

A. E. Lear—BEF, 2nd North Staffordshire Regiment; HMS *Codrington*

David Learmouth—BEF, RASC, Ammunition Company

Robert Lee—BEF, Royal Artillery, 57th Field Regiment; HMS *Worcester*

Robert W. Lee—BEF, RASC, 44th Division; *Mersey Queen*

T. J. Lee—BEF, 3rd Division, Royal Artillery, 7th Field Regiment; *Isle of Thanet*

Ron Lenthal—civilian, Tough's Boatyard, Teddington

A. E. Lewin—BEF, 2nd Middlesex Regiment

W. C. Lewington—BEF, RASC, 2nd Corps

Cyril Lewis—BEF, Royal Artillery, 139th Anti-Tank Brigade, attached to Northamptonshire Regiment

G. E. Lille—RAF, 264th Fighter Squadron

Thomas H. Lilley—BEF, Royal Engineers, 242nd Field Company

Lt.-Col. S. J. Linden-Kelly, DSO—BEF, 2nd Lancashire Fusiliers; HMS *Shikari*

Maj. A. E. Lindley, RCT—BEF, 11th Infantry Brigade; *Pangbourne*

Margaret Loat—civilian, Warrington, Lancashire, return of troops

Reginald Lockerby, TD, Dip. MA, Inst. M—BEF, RAOC, 2nd Ordnance Field Park; HMS *Venomous*

Frederick Louch—BEF, RAMC, 13th Ambulance Train

S. V. Love—BEF, RAMC, 12th Field Ambulance; *Hird*

R. J. Lovejoy—BEF, RASC, 2nd Buffs

G. E. Lucas—BEF, Royal Artillery, 2nd Anti-Aircraft Battery

D. L. Lumley—BEF, 2nd Northamptonshire Regiment; Motor Torpedo Boat

Air Vice-Marshal Michael D. Lyne, CB, AFC, MBIM, DL—RAF, 19th Fighter Squadron

George M. McClorry, MM—RNR, Whale Island

Ivan McGowan—BEF, 57th Medium Regiment, Royal Artillery; HMS *Express*

Capt. B.D.O. MacIntyre, DSC—RN, HMS *Excellent*

Capt. A. M. McKillop, DSC—RN, Block Ships, *Westcove*

W. McLean—BEF, 1st Queen's Own Cameron Highlanders; *St. Andrew*

A. A. McNair—BEF, Royal Artillery, 5th Division

H. P. Mack—RN, HMS *Gossamer, Comfort*

Brig. P.E.S. Mansergh, OBE—BEF, 3rd Division, Signals

A.N.T. Marjoram—RAF, 220th Bomber Squadron

Frederick William Marlow—BEF, 44th Division, Signals; *Royal Daffodil*

Douglas J. W. Marr—BEF; HMS *Venomous*

R. W. Marsh—BEF, Royal Engineers, 698th General Construction Company

Arthur Marshall—BEF, 2nd Corps, Internal Security Unit

J. W. Martin—RN, HMS *Saladin*

A. J. Maskell—BEF, The Buffs

R. T. Mason—BEF, Signals, attached to 2nd Medium Regiment, Royal Artillery

Lt.-Cdr. W. J. Matthews—RN, Secretary to Commander of Minesweepers, Dover

Arthur May—BEF, Royal Artillery, 3rd Medium Regiment

H. T. May—BEF, 1st Oxfordshire and Buckinghamshire Light Infantry

Pip Megrath—civilian, village near Guildford, return of troops

Kenneth W. Meiklejohn—BEF, Royal Artillery, 58th Field Regiment, and 65th Field Regiment, Chaplain; *Isle of Man*

Capt. D.B.N. Mellis, DSC—RN, HMS *Malcolm*

Harold Meredith—BEF, RASC, with Royal Engineers at Maginot Line

*Syd Metcalfe—BEF, Signals

N. F. Minter—BEF, RAMC, 4th Division, 12th Field Ambulance

Wilfrid L. Miron—BEF, 9th Sherwood Foresters

E. Montague—civilian, return of troops

Philip Moore—BEF, RASC, 50th Division, 11th Troop Carrying Company

Maj. S. T. Moore, TD—BEF, RASC, attached to 32nd Field Regiment; HMS *Oriole*, HMS *Lord Collingwood*

R. W. Morford—Merchant Navy, captain of *Hythe*

T. J. Morgan—civilian, *Gallions Reach*

Maj.-Gen. James L. Moulton, CB, DSO, OBE—Royal Marines, Staff officer, GHQ

W. Murphy—civilian, Dover, return of troops

R. A. Murray Scott, MD—BEF, RAMC, 1st Field Ambulance, 1st Guards Brigade

Arthur Myers—BEF, RASC, Mobile Workshop
F. Myers—BEF, Royal Artillery, attached to 2nd Grenadier Guards

Lt.-Col. E. R. Nanney Wynn—BEF, 3rd Division, Signals; HMS *Sandown*
John W. Neeves—RN, HMS *Calcutta*
Eddie Newbould—BEF, 1st King's Own Scottish Borderers
Philip Newman, MD—BEF, RAMC, 12th Casualty Clearing Station
R. Nicholson—BEF, GDSM Company Runner
G. F. Nixon—RN, naval shore party; *Lord Southborough*
F. Noon—BEF, Royal Artillery, 53rd Field Regiment, 126th Brigade; HMS *Whitshed*
W.C.P. Nye—BEF, 4th Royal Sussex Regiment

W. Oakes—BEF, 7th Cheshire Regiment
W. H. Osborne, C.Eng., FRI, NA—civilian, William Osborne Ltd., boatyard, Littlehampton

George Paddon—BEF, 2nd Dorset Regiment; HMS *Anthony*
Leslie R. Page—BEF, RAOC, 44th Division
T. Page—BEF, RASC, II Corps
Mary Palmer—civilian, Ramsgate, return of troops
James V. Parker—RN, 2nd Chatham Naval Barracks, beaches; HMS *Grenade*
Maj. C. G. Payne—BEF, Royal Artillery, 69th Medium Regiment; *Tynwald*
Thomas F. Payne—BEF, 4th Royal Sussex Regiment; HMS *Medway Queen*
Grace Pearson—civilian, GPO, Bournemouth, return of troops
L. A. Pell—BEF, Royal Engineers
Rear-Adm. Pelly, CB, DSO—RN, HMS *Windsor*
N. J. Pemberton—BEF, 2nd Middlesex Regiment
Brig. G.W.H. Peters—BEF, 2nd Bedfordshire and Hertfordshire Regiment
Pamela Phillimore—WRNS, naval headquarters, Dover
Lt.-Col. John W. Place—BEF, 2nd North Staffordshire Regiment

H. Playford—civilian, Naval Store House of H. M. Dockyard, Sheerness

T. J. Port—RN, HMS *Anthony*

F. J. Potticary—BEF, 1st/5th Queen's Royal Regiment; *Royal Daffodil*

J. W. Poulton—BEF, Royal Artillery, 65th Heavy Anti-Aircraft Regiment

Lt.-Cdr. H. B. Poustie, DSC—RN, HMS *Keith*, *St. Abbs*

Stan Priest—BEF, RAMC, III Corps; *Mona's Isle*

Kathleen M. Prince—civilian, Bournemouth, return of troops

David W. Pugh, DSO, MD, FRCP—RNVR, HMS *Whitshed*, HMS *Hebe*

M. F. Purdy—civilian, London, return of troops

Edgar G. A. Rabbets—BEF, 5th Northamptonshire Regiment

Mrs. R. L. Raft—civilian, Ramsgate, return of troops

Maj. I.F.R. Ramsay—BEF, 2nd Dorset Regiment

R.R.C. Rankin—BEF, GHQ Signals

Maj.-Gen. R. St. G. T. Ransome, CB, CBE, MC—BEF, I Corps HQ

Col. M. A. Rea, OBE, MB—BEF, RAMC, Embarkation Medical Officer

Eric Reader—BEF, Royal Engineers, 293rd Field Park Company, III Corps; HMS *Brighton Belle*, HMS *Gracie Fields*

Edith A. Reed—ATS, BEF, GHQ 2nd Echelon, Margate

James Reeves—BEF, 2nd Essex Regiment

A. G. Rennie—BEF, Royal Artillery, 140th Army Field Regiment; *Côte d'Argent*

Walter G. Richards—BEF, RASC, No. 2 L of C Railhead Company, based at Albert (Somme)

Gen. Sir Charles Richardson, GCB, CBE, DSO—BEF, 4th Division, Deputy Assistant Quartermaster General

D. G. Riddall—BEF, Royal Artillery, Heavy Anti-Aircraft Regiment

C. A. Riley—BEF, Royal Engineers; HMS *Codrington*

H. J. Risbridger—BEF, RASC; HMS *Icarus*

George A. Robb—RN, *Isle of Thanet*

Kenneth Roberts—BEF, RAMC, 141st Field Ambulance; HMS *Worcester*

W. Roberts, MM—BEF, 1st East Lancashire Regiment

Maj. R. C. Robinson—BEF, Royal Artillery, 85th Heavy Anti-Aircraft Regiment

H. Rogers—BEF, Royal Artillery, Signals

Alfred Rose—BEF, Royal Artillery, 63rd Medium Regiment

Capt. Stephen Roskill—RN, Dynamo Room, Dover

Tom Roslyn—BEF

P. H. Rowley—BEF, 4th Division, Signals

R. L. Rylands—BEF, HQ, 12th Infantry Brigade

F. C. Sage—BEF, RASC, I Corps, Petrol Company

E. A. Salisbury—BEF, 4th Division, Signals

Dr. Ian Samuel, OBE—BEF, RAMC, 6th Field Ambulance

A. D. Saunders, BEM—RN, HMS *Jaguar*

Frank Saville—BEF, 2nd Cameronians

Maj. Ronald G. H. Savory—RASC, Ramsgate, Dunkirk beaches; *Foremost 101*

W.J.U. Sayers—BEF, Royal Sussex Regiment; HMS *Wolsey*

E.A.G. Scott—BEF, Royal Engineers

Guy Scoular, OBE, MBChB, DPH—BEF, RAMC, 2nd North Staffordshire Regiment; HMS *Codrington*

Maj. M.C.P. Scratchley—BEF, RAOC, 3rd Army Field Workshop

Lt.-Col. W. H. Scriven—BEF, RAMC; HMS *Shikari*

Robert Seviour—BEF, 2nd Dorset Regiment

Herbert G. Sexon—BEF, RAOC, 1st East Surrey Regiment

R. Shattock—BEF, Royal Artillery, 32nd Field Regiment

Reginald B. Short—BEF, Royal Artillery, 57th Field Regiment

Leslie R. Sidwell—civilian, Cotswolds, return of troops

A. E. Sleight—BEF, Royal Artillery, 60th Army Field Regiment; HMS *Salamander*

Maj. A. D. Slyfield, MSM—BEF, Royal Artillery, 20th Anti-Tank Regiment; *Hythe*

*B. Smales—BEF, headquarters clerk, Signals

Douglas H. Smith—BEF, 5th Northamptomshire Regiment

Evan T. Smith—BEF, RASC; HMS *Jaguar*

Leslie M. Smith—BEF, Royal Artillery, 58th Field Regiment; *Beagle*

Capt. George G. H. Snelgar—BEF, RASC, motor transport company

Col. D. C. Snowdon, TD—BEF, 1st Queen's Royal Regiment; *Mona's Isle*

Mrs. Gwen Sorrill—Red Cross nurse, Birmingham, return of troops

Christopher D. South—BEF, Hopkinson British Military Mission, Belgium; HMS *Worcester*

E. J. Spinks—BEF, Royal Artillery, gunner

H. Spinks—BEF, 1st King's Own Scottish Borderers

James Spirritt—BEF, RASC, 4th Division; HMS *Abel Tasman*

Kenneth Spraggs—BEF, Royal Artillery, 92nd Field Regiment

Raie Springate—civilian, Ramsgate; *Fervant*

J. S. Stacey—RNR, HMS *Brighton Belle*

John W. Stacey—BEF, Signals, No. 1 HQ Signals; HMS *Javelin*

A. Staines—RN, HMS *Hebe*

Wing Commander Robert Stanford-Tuck, DSO, DFC—RAF, 92nd Fighter Squadron

Jeanne Michez Stanley—French civilian married to BEF S/Sgt. Gordon Stanley

R. J. Stephens—BEF, Royal Artillery, 2nd Searchlight Regiment

Charles Stewart—BEF, Royal Engineers, 209th Field Company

Rowland Stimpson—civilian, Burgess Hill, return of troops

G. S. Stone—RAF, Lysander spotter plane

W. Stone—BEF, 5th Royal Sussex Regiment

H. W. Stowell, DSC, VRD—RNVR, HMS *Wolfhound*

William Stratton—BEF, RASC, troop carrier; HMS *Harvester*

Samuel Sugar—BEF, RASC, 50th Division; HMS *Grafton*

F. Summers—French Navy, *St. Cyr*; Dunkirk itself

Mrs. E. J. Sumner—civilian, Kent, return of troops

S. Sumner—BEF, Royal Fusiliers

Lt.-Col. G. S. Sutcliff, OBE, TD—BEF, 46th Division, 139th Brigade; HMS *Windsor*

John Tandy—BEF, 1st Grenadier Guards

John Tarry—Merchant Navy, *Lady Southborough*

Lt.-Cdr. Arthur C. Taylor, MM, Chevalier de l'Or—RNR, Calais

Billy Taylor—BEF, Royal Artillery, Heavy Anti-Aircraft

Gordon A. Taylor—BEF, RASC, 1st Division

L. Taylor—civilian, Local Defence Volunteer Force, Isle of Sheppey

Maj. R. C. Taylor—BEF, 1st East Surrey Regiment, Signals; *St. Andrew*

James E. Taziker—BEF, Royal Artillery, 42nd Division

Col. N.B.C. Teacher, MC—BEF, Royal Artillery, 5th Regiment Royal Horse Artillery

A. H. Tebby—BEF, 1st King's Shropshire Light Infantry

Dora Thorn—civilian, Margate, return of troops

J. P. Theobald—BEF, Royal Artillery, 58th Medium Regiment

Syd Thomas—BEF, I Corp, 102nd Provost Company

S. V. Holmes Thompson—BEF, Royal Artillery, 3rd Searchlight Regiment; *Queen of the Channel*

D. Thorogood—BEF, 2nd Coldstream Guards

W. H. Thorpe—RNR, HMS *Calvi*

H. S. Thuillier, DSO—BEF, Royal Artillery, 1st Anti-Aircraft Regiment; HMS *Shikari*

F. Tidey—BEF, 2nd Royal Norfolk Regiment

S. V. Titchener—BEF, RASC

Col. Robert P. Tong—BEF, Staff officer, GHQ

C. W. Trowbridge—BEF, Royal Artillery, 1st Medium Regiment

Joseph Tyldesley—BEF, RASC, attached to No. 2 Artillery Company GHQ

Derek Guy Vardy—BEF, Royal Artillery; HMS *Dundalk*

W. R. Voysey—BEF, 3rd Division, Signals

Maj.-Gen. D.A.L. Wade—BEF, GHQ Signals

C. Wagstaff—BEF, Royal Artillery, searchlight detachment

Dr. David M. Walker—BEF, RAMC, 102nd Casualty Clearing Station; *Prague*

George Walker—RN, HMS *Havant*

William S. Walker—BEF, Royal Artillery, 5th Medium Regiment

Fred E. Walter—BEF, 1st Queen Victoria's Rifles

Rupert Warburton—BEF, 48th Division, Provost Company

Alwyn Ward—BEF, RAOC, 9th Army Field Workshop

W. J. Warner—BEF, Royal Artillery, 60th Heavy Anti-Aircraft Regiment

Noel Watkin—BEF, Royal Artillery, 67th Field Regiment; *Prague*

J. T. Watson—BEF, RAMC, General Hospital No. 6

Maj. Alan G. Watts—BEF, 2nd Dorset Regiment

Capt. O. M. Watts—civilian, London, recruiting for Little Ships

E. C. Webb—BEF, Royal Artillery, 99th Field Regiment; HMS *Vrede*, HMS *Winchelsea*

S. G. Webb—BEF, Royal Artillery, 52nd Anti-Tank Regiment

Frank S. Westley—BEF, Signals

F.G.A. Weston—BEF, RASC; *Maid of Orleans*

George White—BEF, 7th Green Howards

Sir Meredith Whittaker—BEF, 5th Green Howards

H. Whitton—BEF, 4th Division, Signals

Miss G. E. Williams—nursing sister, hospital ship *St. David*

Maj. G. L. Williams—BEF, 3rd Division, 8th Field Ambulance

S/Sgt. W. G. Williams—BEF, RASC, 44th Division

Maj. Gordon D. Wilmot—BEF, 2nd Royal Scottish Fusiliers

George T. Wilson—BEF, King's Own Royal Regiment

S. J. Wilson—BEF, Royal Engineers

Brigadier R. C. Windsor Clive—BEF, 2nd Coldstream Guards

C. E. Wingfield—BEF, 3rd Division, Royal Engineers

Mrs. F.A.M. Wood—Public Health Nurse, Bournemouth, return of troops

C. Woodford—BEF, Infantry, The Buffs; HMS *Whitehall*

G. N. Woodhams, TD—BEF, Royal Artillery, Anti-Aircraft

N. D. Woolland—BEF, Royal Engineers

Frank Woolliscroft—BEF, RASC, 42nd Division

E. S. Wright, MM—BEF, 42nd W/T Section, Signals

Percy H. Yorke—BEF, RAMC, 149th Field Ambulance; HMS *Princess Elizabeth*

Robert M. Zakovitch—BEF, French interpreter, attached to 4th Brigade

Index

Aa Canal, 27, 29, 30, 36, 69. *See also* "Canal Line"

Abbeville, 6, 16, 26

Abrial, Admiral Jean, 76, 78, 94, 110, 143, 179–83, 229–30, 252, 256, 259, 268, 269

Ackrell, Corporal P. G., 55, 128

Adam, Lieutenant-General Sir Ronald, 37, 76, 78, 81

Admiralty: "Dynamo" implemented, 37, 41, 46, 58; French, relations with, 91, 109; destroyers, use of, 86, 144–45, 168, 228; Wake-Walker sent, 152; daylight operations ended: 229–30; "Dynamo," ends, 259. *See also* Little Ships; Small Vessels Pool

Ailly, 256

Alaurent, General, 267, 274

Albert, 3, 21

ALC (Army Landing Craft), 89, 140. *See also* Little Ships

Alexander, Major-General Harold: 166, 171, 180–83, 229–30, 246–47

Allan, Gunner P. D., 76

Allison, Commander, 228

Amiens, 6, 16, 18, 21

Anthony, 87

Antiaircraft guns, 80–81

Antitank guns, 3, 13, 21

Archdale, Major O. A., 92

Armentières, 35, 54, 150

Arras, 1, 13, 14, 15, 16, 21, 29, 30, 51, 167; counterattack at, 18–19, 27, 273

Atrocities, by SS units, 74, 106–7

Audresselles, 69

Auphan, Captain Paul, 90, 92, 174, 175, 193

Aura, 225

Austin, Captain John, 76, 235

Austin, Captain R. C., 129

Autocarrier, 244, 248

Bacchus, Private Bill, 52

Backhouse, Admiral Sir Roger, 42, 270

Baker, Sergeant Jack, 70

Baldwin, Private Alfred, 189

Barker, Lieutenant-General Michael, 112, 171, 181

Barnard, Private Oliver, 145

Barris, Seaman Bill, 212

Barthélémy, General, 261

Bartlett, Captain Basil, 123–24

Bartlett, Seaman George, 98

Basilisk, 216–17, 219

Bassett, Colonel Sam, 48

Bastion 32 (French Headquarters, Dunkirk), 36, 76, 94, 100, 179–83, 229, 256, 259, 266

Batson, Lance Corporal Fred, 81

Beamish, Captain Tufton, 13, 278

Beaufrère, General, 200, 234, 266, 267

Beckwith-Smith, Brigadier, M. B., 34

Belgium: Allied advance into, 8, 12; Allied withdrawal from, 2, 6, 8–12; participation in fighting, 19, 21, 22, 23, 24, 33, 36, 78; surrender of, 100–104, 134, 150, 175

Bellamy, Basil, 45, 89

Ben-My-Chree, 223, 241

Bennett, Private C. N., 186

Bennett, 2nd Lieutenant John S. W., 165

Bennett, Sub-Lieutenant Peter, 161, 196
Bergues, 36, 76, 78, 79, 200, 232, 250
Bergues-Furnes Canal, 147, 200, 231–33
Berry, W. Stanley, 40, 41, 46, 89
Berthon, Captain, 216–17, 219
Biddneph, Commander M. A. O., 189
Bideford, 142
Bill, Lieutenant Robin, 131, 135, 138–39, 278
Billotte, General Gaston, 16, 18, 20, 21
Birnbacher, Captain-Lieutenant Heinz, 119, 120
Blackburn, Staff Sergeant Reg, 125
Blanchard, General J. G. M., 18, 21, 22, 23, 24, 76, 78, 92, 100, 108, 110, 146, 181
Block ships, 251–52, 260–61
Blumentritt, Colonel Guenther, 64
Bock, General Colonel Fedor von, 3, 21, 22, 25, 32, 33, 105, 150, 197
Bonnie Heather, 193
Booth, Lieutenant-Commander B. R., 139
Border Regiment, 5th Battalion, 232
Bougrain, General, 146
Boulogne, 16, 17, 18, 21, 26, 33, 41–43, 48, 61, 62, 69
Bourbourg, 25, 27, 272
Bourrasque, 169
Boydd, Private Paddy, 189
Boyes Anti-Tank Rifles, 13, 107, 200, 233
Brammall, Lieutenant C. V., 68
Brauchitsch, General Colonel Walther von, 30, 31, 210
Bray-Dunes, 79, 112–15, 120, 122, 123, 124, 128, 139, 146, 151, 152, 153, 162, 186, 188, 190, 196, 207–8, 216, 224, 235, 249
Brennecke, General Major Kurt, 209
Bridgeman, Lieutenant-Colonel the Viscount, 15, 20, 22, 36, 37, 78, 79, 80, 107, 182, 217
Bridges, Lance Sergeant John, 201–2, 206, 212–15
Brighton Belle, 117
Brighton Queen, 222
British Expeditionary Force (BEF), 3, 6, 24. General Headquarters (GHQ): Arras, 1, 2, 7, 15, 16, 51; Boulogne, 19, 61; Hazebrouck, 16; La Panne, 80, 81, 111, 171, 180–82, 184; Dunkirk, 19, 183. Corps: I, 22, 79, 112, 171, 181; II, 10, 79, 104, 112, 128, 146, 171, 203; III, 10, 49, 79, 112. Divisions: 1st, 171, 180; 2nd, 33, 34, 74; 3rd, 15, 104–5, 145, 186; 4th, 22, 36, 49, 278; 23rd, 13; 44th, 34, 49, 50, 109, 125, 145; 48th, 34, 35, 107; 50th, 49, 54, 104. Brigades: 7th Guards, 146, 180; 8th, 199; 30th, 61, 62; 127th, 186; 143rd, 108; 144th, 106. Corps of Military Police, 11, 104, 125, 188; 102nd Provost Company, 164–66. Royal Army Medical Corps (RAMC), Field Ambulance: 6th, 142; 12th, 125; 13th, 52; 145th, 186; RAMC, Casualty Clearing Station: 12th, 261–66. Royal Army Ordnance Corps, 55; 2nd Ordnance Field Park, 35, 49, 50,

52. Royal Army Service Corps (RASC), 49, 52, 81: 1st Division Petrol Company, 124; 508th Petrol Company, 126; 85th Command Ammunition Depot, 128; No. 1 Troop Carrying Company, 49. Royal Artillery, 6: Anti-Aircraft, 2nd Brigade, 80; Field Regiments: 32nd, 8–10; 53rd, 233, 237, 239; 58th, 76, 110, 271; 99th, 235; 229th Field Battery, 70; 60th Heavy Anti-Aircraft Regiment, 35; Medium Regiments: 3rd, 54; 5th, 50; Searchlight Regiments: 2nd Battalion, 35; 12th Battery, 79. Royal Corps of Signals (Signals), 10. Royal Engineers, Corps of, 53, 79, 106: 216th Field Company, 1; 250th Field Company, 76, 165–66; 573rd Field Squadron, 49. *See also* individual regiments
Brooke, Lieutenant-General A. F., 22, 23, 25, 104, 146, 170–71, 273–74, 277
Brown, Chief Stoker W., 137, 139
Brownrigg, Lieutenant-General Sir Douglas, 19, 61, 62
Buchanan, Commander Herbert James, 256, 258, 260
Bush, Captain Eric, 153, 185
Bush, Lieutenant-Colonel W. E., 234, 239
Bushell, Commander William, 244
Buxton, Lieutenant-Colonel G. A. H., 147
Bystander, 142

Calais, 17, 21, 26, 33, 41–43, 48, 57, 60–70, 92, 134
Calcutta, 90, 95
Calvi, 138, 141
Cameron, Lieutenant John, 260
Cameron Highlanders, Queen's Own, 168; 1st Battalion, 34, 72
"Canal Line," 27, 31, 33, 69, 72. *See also* Aa Canal; La Bassée Canal
Canterbury, 85, 130, 131, 223
Caplat, Sub-Lieutenant Moran, 157
Carew Hunt, Sub-Lieutenant A., 197
Carmaham, Aircraftsman, 243
Carrier, Private Lou, 106
Carvin, 35
Cassel, 34, 36, 76, 91, 107, 109, 147, 277
Cassidie, Captain, 140
Cavanagh, Able Seaman P., 137
Chamberlain, Neville, 18, 41
Champon, General, 175
Chandler, Gunner Mowbray, 138–40
Chapeau Rouge, 261–66, 267
Charles, Signalman Percy, 277
Chartier de Sadomy, Captain le Comte de, 259
Chatham Naval Depot, 44, 47, 89, 92, 223
Cherbourg, 125–26
Chodzko, Sub-Lieutenant Michael Anthony, 225, 248
Churchill, Captain Jack, 70–72
Churchill, Winston: support of Weygand Plan, 18, 21–23, 28; decision to evacuate Dunkirk, 33, 37, 41, 109, 112; defense of

Calais, 60–63, 68; meetings with Reynaud, 2, 20, 24, 58, 178–79; Belgian surrender, 100–101; policy on evacuating French, 91, 173, 177–79, 228, 234, 252; reports on evacuation, 170, 229, 270–72, 274

Clan MacAlister, 89, 140, 141, 218

Claridge, Private J. B., 214

Clemments, Lieutenant-Commander, W. R. T., 86

Clifton, Brigadier, A. J., 105

Clouston, Commander J. Campbell: at Dunkirk, 112–13; pier master at eastern mole, 113, 115, 116, 130, 137–39, 141, 142, 167–68, 197, 236; loss of, 242–43

Cockle boats, 156, 195

Coldstream Guards, 12, 264; 1st Battalion, 11, 203; 2nd Battalion, 7, 12, 146–47, 200–201, 231–33, 237–38, 246

Coles, Sapper D. J., 13–14, 154, 188

Collard, Group Captain R. C. M., 1

Colton, Sergeant-Major "Big Ike," 111

Colvin, Major R. B. R., 218

Comfort, 122–24

Command Post, shifts of, 15–18, 20, 21, 23, 36, 108

Communications breakdown, 14–16, 65, 80, 92, 101, 109, 256

Condor, Commander E. R., 235

Constant Nymph, 156, 162

Contest, 223

Cook, Lieutenant A. T., 116

Corap, General André-Georges, 1, 3, 6

Costobadie, Lieutenant-Commander, 259

Court, Sergeant L. H. T., 237–38

Courtrai, 22, 103

Cox, Lieutenant Ian, 129, 140, 155

Cranz, General Lieutenant Friedrich-Carl, 266, 267

Cras, Lieutenant Hervé, 269

Crested Eagle, 131, 139, 141

Crick, Lieutenant T. S., 44

Crosby, Sub-Lieutenant John Rutherford, 130, 240, 247

Crowther, Private George William, 142

Dangerfield, Captain E., 252, 260

Darlan, Admiral François, 90, 91, 174, 179, 276

Davies, Lieutenant E. L., 129, 247

Day, Chief Foreman Harry, 88

Deal, 57, 58

Dean, Commander Brian, 116, 268

Demolitions, 53–55, 66, 106

Dendre, River, 10

Denny, Captain Michael, 43, 240, 242, 245

Destroyers: collecting and organizing, 38, 86; losses, 135–44; modern, withdrawn, 144–45, 228; returned, 168. *See also* ships' names

Dewing, Major-General R. H., 17

Dibbens, Lieutenant Harold J., 164–66

Dickens, Sub-Lieutenant Peter, 47

Dill, Lieutenant-General Sir John, 22, 24, 37, 38, 153, 170, 173, 176–78, 183, 229, 277

Dinort, Major Oskar, 135, 161

Discipline problems, 55, 96–97, 112–13, 128–29, 138–39, 147, 166–69, 187–88, 199, 213, 232–34, 236–37

Dive bombing, 8–10, 34–35, 65, 94, 107, 135–40, 214–17, 219, 228, 242. *See also* Stuka

Divine, David, 225, 245

Docksey, Captain T. E., 159

Dodd, Captain John S., 70, 153, 271, 277

Doggersbank, 114

Dornier 17 (German plane), 55, 132, 135. *See also* Luftwaffe

Dorrien Rose, 98

Dorsetshire Regiment, 2nd Battalion, 33, 72–73, 103

Dove, Major Arthur, 80

Dove, Commander J. S., 56, 143

Dover, 48, 58

Dover Castle, 43–44

Dow, Surgeon-Lieutenant James, 47

Dowding, Air Chief Marshal Sir Hugh, 134, 221

Dreyer, Lieutenant Christopher, 216

Duke of Wellington's Regiment, 1st Battalion, 238

Dunkirk, 17, 20, 24–26; decision to evacuate from, 95; destruction of port, 55, 251–52; last night, 244–49, 251–64; capture of, 266–67

Durham Light Infantry, 6th Battalion, 76, 198, 199, 235

Dyle, River, 6–8, 167

"Dynamo," Operation: activating, 44, 58; collecting and manning ships, 44–46, 87, 223; equiping and provisioning ships, 47–49; communications, 142–44, 152; morale, 90, 117, 186–87, 222–25, 228, 241, 253; numbers lifted, xi, 116–17, 125, 168–69, 176, 178, 179, 197, 228, 252, 268, 274–76; decision to end, 239–40, 269. *See also* Admiralty; Chatham Naval Depot; Destroyers; Little Ships; Small Vessels Pool

Dynamo Room, 43–44, 47, 48, 58, 83, 84, 89–90, 95–96, 99, 152, 239, 242

East Lancashire Regiment, 1st Battalion, 232

East Riding Yeomanry, 148

East Surrey Regiment: 1st Battalion, 12, 51, 76, 198–200; 1st/6th Battalion, 198–200, 235–36

Eastern mole, 97–99, 112, 115–16, 130–31, 135–38, 142, 181, 188–90, 212, 227, 235–36, 251, 266–67, 272

Eden, Anthony, 17, 22, 24, 25, 60–63, 91, 101, 108, 109, 170, 176, 180, 182–83, 186

Elkin, Sergeant Arthur, 15, 104

Elliott, A. W., 157

Ellison-McCartney, Lieutenant-Colonel L. A., 66

Elton, Seaman J. H., 142

Emile Deschamps, 269

Epinette, 70–72

Ervine-Andrews, Captain H. M., 232
Escaut, River, 7, 11, 12
Esk, 153, 222
Essex Regiment, 2nd Battalion, 7
Estaires, 73, 74
Express, 137, 248, 260, 261

Fagalde, General Marie B. A., 36, 62, 63, 76, 78, 92, 180–82, 250, 255, 256
Falck, Captain Wolfgang, 132–34
"Fall Rot," Operation, 209–11
Fane, 2nd Lieutenant Julian, 107, 148
Farley, Private Francis Ralph, 111, 203–5
Fauvelle, Major Joseph, 92, 110
Felstead, Gunner F., 129
Fenella, 130, 131, 138, 139, 141
Fernald, John 158, 159
Festubert, 33, 72, 73, 74
Field Security Police, 54, 123
Fieseler Storch (German observation plane), 9
Fife and Forfar Yeomanry, 1st Battalion, 49
Fifth Columnists, 10–11
Fisher, Captain John, 44, 45
Fisher, Commander Ralph Lindsay, 120–25
Fletcher, Seaman Carl, 94, 96
Flooding, 20, 118, 199, 249
Folkestone, 126, 193, 222, 244
Foremost 101, 192
Fort Mardyck, 200
Fort Philippe, 151
Foudroyant, 219, 222
Franklyn, Major-General H. E., 19
French Army: Somme line, 19, 23, 24, 255–56; defense of Calais, 62–65; withdrawal to Dunkirk, 24, 109–11; holding the perimeter, 109–11, 145–46; reluctance to evacuate, 24, 76, 90–92, 109–10; discipline of, 197; rearguard, 182–83, 229–30, 234, 249–50, 255; evacuation of, 173–83, 190–91, 197, 228, 247–48, 251, 258–60; surrender of, 266–67. Armies: First, 15, 16, 18, 21, 24, 34, 92, 107–11, 145, 150, 176; Second, 3; Seventh, 21; Ninth, 1, 3. Corps: III, 110–11. Infantry Divisions: 12th, 234, 249; 21st, 255; 32nd, 234, 255, 259, 260, 267; 60th, 34, 146, 176; 68th, 69, 78, 176, 200, 234, 249, 266, 267; 71st, 3; 137th, 255. 2nd Light Mechanized Division, 146. *See also* Weygand Plan
French Navy: participation in evacuation, 90–92, 109, 125–26, 175, 176, 193, 244, 257, 259–60; casualties, 169, 222, 269
Furnes, 78, 79, 111, 146, 151, 172, 180, 199, 201, 203, 213
Furnes-Nieuport Canal, 106

Gabbett-Mullhallen, Sub-Lieutenant C. A., 260
Galland, Captain Adolf, 134, 135
Gallant, 95, 144
Gamelin, General Maurice, 3, 16, 18

Garrett, Paymaster Lieutenant-Commander Harry, 41, 46, 156
Gaze, Private W. B. A., 81, 262–63
Gentry, Lance Bombardier H. E., 9–10
George VI, King, 101
Georges, General Alphonse-Joseph, 7, 15, 16, 175, 176, 177
German Army. Army Groups: A, 3, 21, 22, 25, 26, 28, 30, 31, 32, 33, 64, 150, 209; B, 3, 21, 22, 25, 29, 30, 31, 32, 135, 150, 197, 209, 267; C, 209. Armies: Fourth, 27, 28, 30, 31, 32, 33, 209; Eighteenth, 208–10. Corps: IX, 208; X, 254, 267; XIX, 3, 26, 31, 33; XXVI, 208. Infantry Divisions: 18th, 210, 250, 254, 266, 267; 56th, 151; 61st, 254; 256th, 211. Panzer Divisions: 1st, 6, 26, 27, 28, 64, 69; 2nd, 6, 26; 6th, 13, 69; 7th, 150; 10th, 26, 63, 64, 69. SS Totenkopf Division, 74. Regiments: 102nd Artillery Regiment, 249; 18th Regiment of Engineers, 250; 37th Panzer Engineers, 151; SS Leibstandarte Adolf Hitler, 106. Bicycle Squadron 25, 151
German Navy, 119
Gill, Corporal Alf, 125
Gimson, Captain Tom, 112
Glen Gower, 189
Gloucestershire Regiment: 2nd Battalion, 11, 34, 148; 5th Battalion, 107, 147–48
Goddard, Group Captain Victor, 37–39
Goebbels, Joseph, 267–68, 276
Goodbody, Yeoman Eric, 187–88
Göring, Hermann, 28–33, 55, 134, 273
Gort, General the Viscount: early career, 7, 15; advance into Belgium, 2–3, 6–8; withdrawal toward coast, 7, 17, 37–39, 69, 70, 72, 78, 81, 153; Weygand Plan, 18–24; decision to evacuate, 16, 20, 22–24, 41, 76, 91, 92, 108; Belgian surrender, 100–6; policy on evacuating French, 91, 173–82; evacuated, 162, 170–73, 183–86
Gossamer, 47, 116, 122, 207
Gotto, Commander Renfrew, 246
Gracie Fields, 141, 142
Grafton, 95, 122–24, 144
Grand Quartier Général, 20
Gravelines, 30, 33, 69, 78, 151, 168, 176, 189, 267
Gray, Lieutenant A., 113, 114
Green Howards: 5th Battalion, 234, 236, 239, 246; 6th Battalion, 33
Gregson-Ellis, Colonel Philip, 36
Grenade, 130, 137, 139, 144
Grenadier Guards, 12, 79, 218; 1st Battalion, 201–3, 206, 212; 2nd Battalion, 111, 199; 3rd Battalion, 219, 235
Greyhound, 144
Griffith-Williams, Colonel L. C., 238
Grimmer, Sapper E. M., 1
Guderian, General Heinz, 3, 6, 26, 28–33, 64, 69, 106, 150–51, 209, 272, 273
Gulzar, 68, 258

Hadnett, Corporal Bob, 35, 107, 108
Hadow, Commander P. H., 214–15
Haig, 249
Haig, Lieutenant-Commander Rodolph, 123
Halder, General Franz, 30, 31, 32, 209, 250
Halsey, Captain T. E., 253, 268
"Halt Order," 29–33, 69, 209, 272–73
Hamel, Lieutenant Lodo van, 194
Hampshire Regiment, 2nd Battalion, 233
Hansen, General Lieutenant Christian, 254
Harling, Robert, 194–95
Harvester, 86
Harvey, Ted, 239
Harwich, 45, 127
Havant, 86, 215–16, 219
Hawes, Sergeant S. S., 124
Hazebrouck, 16, 49, 70, 74, 107, 108
Hebe, 144, 153, 184–85, 224
Heinkel 111 (German plane), 55, 132, 133, 141, 161, 169, 212, 214, 215. *See also* Luftwaffe
Heming, Private Ernest, 190
Henkel, Hans, 276
Herbert, Major Dickie, 202
Hersey, Augusta, 51, 227
Hersey, Private Bill, 51, 227
Hilda, 113, 114, 216, 251
Hill, Major Peter, 50
Hilton, Robert, 159, 163, 174, 278–79
Hird, 124–26
Hitler, Adolf, 2, 28; and Belgian surrender, 102; "Halt Order," 29–33, 272–73; his suggestion for preventing evacuation, 210
Hoedt, Father M. Rafael, 145
Homan, David, 158
Hondschoote, 54
Hornchurch, 57, 220
Horner, Ken, 156
Horst, 163
Hospital Ships, 241–42
Houtkerque, 108
Hubicki, General Major A. R. von, 249
Hunt, Major (RASC), 126
Hunt, Major Peter, 72
Huntziger, General Charles, 3
Hurricane (British plane), 57, 133, 134, 195, 251. *See also* RAF
Hutchens, Lieutenant-Colonel Robin, 194
Hythe, 224

Ibel, Max, 134
Ingham, Lance Corporal W. J., 54
Interservice Topographical Department, 48
Iron Duke, 238
Ironside, General Sir Edmund, 17, 18, 19, 21, 23, 25, 37, 38
Irving, Lieutenant R. H., 160, 162, 196
Irwin, Seaman Bill, 137
Ismay, Major-General Sir Hastings, 20, 21, 176, 271
Ismay, Lady, 271
Ivanhoe, 124, 186, 214, 219

Jaguar (British), 86, 87, 130, 137, 144
Jaguar (French), 120, 269
James, Admiral Sir William, 272
Janssen, General, 234, 249
Jeffries, Captain P. J., 198
Jennings, Gunner W., 142
Jeschonnek, General Major Hans, 32
Jodl, General Major Alfred, 29, 32
Johnson, Major-General G. D., 206
Johnson & Jago's Boatyard, 157
Jones, 2nd Lieutenant, 199
Jones, Signalman George W., 201
Jonkerick, Mlle., 52
Ju 87 (German plane). *See* Stuka
Ju 88 (German plane), 135, 242. *See also* Luftwaffe

Kay, Corporal R., 115
Kearley-Pope, Petty Officer Leonard B., 84
Keitel, General Colonel Wilhelm, 29, 32, 119
Keith, 184–85, 216–19, 222
Keith, Jimmy, 89
Keller, General Alfred, 210
Kerr, Commander Tom, 112, 113, 115, 151, 166, 188
Kesselring, General Albert, 32, 133, 211
Keyes, Admiral Sir Roger, 100–101
King Orry, 142, 189
King's Own Royal Regiment, 8th Battalion, 167
King's Royal Rifle Corps, 2nd Battalion, 60, 61, 63, 65
King's Shropshire Light Infantry, 1st Battalion, 246
Kirchner, General Lieutenant Friedrich, 27
Kitchener, Corporal Jack, 52
Kleist, General Ewald von, 27, 32, 107
Kluge, General Colonel Guenther Hans von, 27, 28, 32, 33, 209
Knight, Sergeant Bill, 255–56
Knowles, Guardsman Arthur, 266
Koeltz, General Louis M., 78, 100
Kuechler, General Georg von, 208–11, 232–34, 249–50, 258
Kwinte Whistle Buoy, 120–25, 169

La Bassée Canal, 7, 33, 72, 74
Lady Southborough, 45, 46, 192–93
Lane, Squadron Leader Brian, 220
Langley, Lieutenant James M., 12, 200–201, 232, 237, 261, 264, 265
La Panne: evacuation operations: 79, 81, 87, 88, 95, 112, 114, 117, 122, 128, 129, 141, 143, 150, 152, 153, 162–67, 175, 177, 186, 187, 190, 202–8, 212, 214, 217, 219; Gort establishes headquarters, 79–80, 111–12; withdrawal from, 207, 227
Laurencie, General Fourmel de la, 110, 111, 180, 181, 234
Lawson, Brigadier the Honorable, E. F., 79, 167
Lawson, 2nd Lieutenant William, 167

Leclerc, Rear-Admiral Marcel, 91, 175
Lecointe, Father Henri, 267
Le Doze, Lieutenant Docteur, 267
Ledringhem, 147
Lee, Gunner Robert, 76
Leese, Brigadier Sir Oliver, 16, 153, 172–73, 180, 186
Leigh-on-Sea, 156, 157, 193
Le Mesurier, Commander Edward K., 225
Leopold III, 19, 99, 100–102, 175
Le Paradis, 74
"Lethal Kite Barrage," 56, 143
Letitia, 195
Lidster, Sapper L. C., 125–26
Lightoller, Commander Charles Herbert, 225–27
Lille, 10, 12, 16, 25, 34, 50, 51, 107–11, 145, 150, 180, 234, 272. *See also* French Army: First
Lindsell, Lieutenant-General W. G., 78
Little Ann, 225–27, 245
Littlehampton, 89
Little Ships: collecting, equiping, and manning of, 44–49, 88–89, 157; operations of, 155–64, 191–95. *See also* Ministry of Shipping; Small Vessels Pool; Tough Brothers Boatyard
Little Ships Club, 88
Lockerby, Lance Corporal Reginald, 35, 49, 56, 190
Locust, 257, 259
Long Price, Captain, 7
Looting, 34, 55, 134, 213–14, 263
Lord Southborough, 156
Lorry jetties, 164–66, 169, 186
Lossberg, Colonel Lieutenant Bernard von, 32
Louch, Private Fred, 169
Love, Private Sam, 126
Lucas, General, 260
Luftwaffe: early superiority of, 28, 31, 32, 50, 55, 56, 74, 132–33; mission to prevent evacuation, 104, 192, 204, 212–22, 228, 242, 273; raids on Calais, 64–66; raids on Dunkirk, 85, 97, 117, 125, 130, 133–42, 187, 221–22; RAF opposition to, 134–42, 195, 219–22; weather as a factor, 131, 134, 161, 168, 169, 184, 211, 272; shifts south, 251, 258; tactics, 135, 189, 195, 210–12, 273; 2nd Air Fleet (Luftflotte), 32, 55, 211; Fliegerkorps IV, 210; Fliegerkorps VIII, 32, 134, 135, 161; Fighter Squadron 26, 132; 2nd Stuka Squadron, 161. *See also* Göring; Stuka; and other German entries
Lydd, 122–24
Lyne, Flying Officer Michael D., 57–58
Lynn-Allen, Captain J. F., 107
Lys, River, 22, 24, 103, 109

McBarnet, Lieutenant Donald, 114
McBeath, Commander John, 246
McClelland, Lieutenant-Commander J. N., 206–7

McCorquodale, Major Angus, 12, 201, 232–33
McCoy, Lieutenant-Commander John, 94
MACFORCE, 7, 13
MacKenzie, Lieutenant Angus, 247
Mackie, Captain R. W., 140–41
MacLeod, Leading Seaman Murdo, 217
Mahnert, Corporal Hans, 135
Maid of Orleans, 95, 190
Maintenon (French Naval Headquarters), 91, 92
Malcolm, 87, 88, 129, 140, 155, 160, 168, 196, 224, 228, 248, 253, 257, 258, 260, 268
Malines, 124, 222–23, 241
Malo-les-Bains, 79, 81, 87, 95–99, 112–15, 128, 140, 152, 153, 163, 166, 174, 187, 190, 192, 236–39, 245, 257
Manchester Regiment, 2nd Battalion, 72
Mann, Lieutenant, 105
Mardyck, 78, 249
Mare, 227–28
Maréchal Foch, 268
Margate, 89, 156, 224, 269, 271
Marlborough, 245, 257, 258
Marsayru, 190
Marshall, Captain Arthur, 168
Martin, Major-General Henry, 80, 81
Martin, Chief Signal Clerk J. W., 87
MA/SB 6 (motor antisubmarine boat), 186
MA/SB 10, 246, 248, 251, 260–61
Mason-MacFarlane, Major-General Noel, 7
Massey Shaw, 191–92
Maund, Commander Guy, 245, 247
May, Sub-Officer A. J., 191
May, Bombardier Arthur, 11, 54, 169
Medway Queen, 48, 49, 116, 268
Meiklejohn, Chaplain Kenneth W., 154
Mellis, Lieutenant David, 87, 140, 168, 228, 253
Menon, Colonel, 249, 255
Meredith, Corporal Harold, 196
Mermaiden, 257, 258
Messerschmidt (German plane): Me 109, 57, 84, 132–35, 212, 220; Me 110, 132–35, 220, 221
Meuse, River, 1, 3
Michalowski, Lieutenant, 122
Middlesex Regiment, 1st/7th Battalion, 111, 203–5
Military Police. *See* British Expeditionary Force: Corps of Military Police
Ministry of Shipping, 41, 44, 45, 88, 89, 156
Moeres, 198
Mona's Isle, 83, 84, 131
Montgomery, Major-General Bernard, 15, 104–5, 145, 146, 170–71, 227, 274
Moore, Captain S. T., 128
Morale problems: Belgian, 102–3; British, 90, 105; French, 16. *See also* "Operation Dynamo": morale
Morgan, Lieutenant-Colonel William, 182, 183
Mosquito, 222

Motor Torpedo Boats, 184–85, 239; *MTB 102*, 216, 247, 257, 259; *MTB 107*, 260, 261
Moulton, Captain J. L., 81–83
Munster, Lord, 170
Münstereifel, 28

Naiad Errant, 194
Nanney Wynn, Major E. R., 186
Nautilus, 122
Naval shore parties, 92–94, 96–97
Navy, Army and Air Force Institute (NAAFI), 14, 54
Nelson, 46
Newcomb, Chaplain Reginald, 49, 54
Newhaven, 235
Newhaven, 193, 235
Newman, Major Philip, 262, 263, 265, 267
New Prince of Wales, 160, 161, 196
Ngaroma, 223
Nicholson, Brigadier Claude, 60–63
Nieuport, 78, 79, 86, 102, 104, 105, 106, 111, 150, 172, 198, 199, 211, 220
Nixon, Seaman G. F., 47, 97, 113
Noon, Gunner F., 237
Nore Command, 44, 85, 228
Northamptonshire Regiment, 5th Battalion, 149–50, 186
North Staffordshire Regiment, 2nd Battalion, 103
Nye, Private W. C. P., 103

O'Callaghan, Private Bill, 74
Odend'hal, Vice-Admiral Jean, 91, 92, 175, 276
OKH (Oberkommando der Heer), 30, 31, 150, 209, 210
OKW (Oberkommando der Wehrmacht), 26, 28, 32, 119
Orchies, 14
Oriole, 129–30, 240, 247
Osborne, Major-General E. A., 49, 109, 110
Osborne, William, 89
O'Shea, Father Cockie, 262–63
Ostend, 20, 84
Oxfordshire and Buckinghamshire Light Infantry, 4th Battalion, 148

Page, Private Leslie R., 50
Palmer, Captain Sir Anthony, 80
Palmer, Samuel, 194
Pangbourne, 140–41
Pank, Colonel, 262
Panzers, 3, 16, 25, 29, 30, 36, 41, 61, 70, 72, 125, 132. *See also* German Army; Tanks
Paris, 242
Parker, Coxswain Edward D., 156
Parminter, Brigadier R. H. R., 95, 130, 246
Payne, Lieutenant C. G., 115
Peirse, Sir Richard, 39
Pelly, Commander P. D. H. R., 278
Perimeter: planning, 37, 78–79; manning, 79, 99; defending, 104–11, 145–51, 153, 172–73, 181, 197–211, 229–39, 249–51

Péronne, 3, 21
Perron, Edmond, 254
Pétain, Marshal Henri, 58, 178
Peterson, Captain-Lieutenant, 119
Phillips, Rear-Admiral Sir Tom, 46, 152, 185
Pigeon, 260
Pim, Captain R. P., 194
POLFORCE, 13
Pooley, Private Bert, 74
Poperinge, 35, 54
Porte de Vaux, Lieutenant Jacquelin de la, 269
Portsmouth, 46, 155, 192, 257, 259, 272
Pound, Admiral of the Fleet Sir Dudley, 37–39, 144, 168, 177
Poustie, Midshipman H. B., 219
Pownall, Lieutenant-General H. R., 16–18, 20–21, 33, 36, 108, 110, 170, 175, 177, 272
Prémesques, 20, 21, 23, 36, 37, 108
Preston, Admiral Sir Lionel, 40, 46, 88, 89
Princess Elizabeth, 186
Prioux, General R. J. A., 92, 107–11, 150

Quai Félix Faure, 248, 257, 258, 259
Queen of the Channel, 98, 99, 117
Queen's Own Worcestershire Yeomanry, 145–46
Queen's Royal Regiment, 1st/7th Battalion, 83
Queen Victoria's Rifles, 1st Battalion, 61, 65–66

Rabbets, Private Edgar G. A., 149–50
Ramsay, Vice-Admiral Bertram, 41; early career, 42; letters to wife Mag, 47, 58, 90, 270; gathering ships, 44, 83, 86, 89; relations with the French, 91; dispatching ships, 99, 130, 143–44, 188–89, 236, 240, 252–53, 256; obtaining destroyers, 117, 168, 228–29; S-Boat threat, 126, 127; evacuating the French, 172–73, 178; "Special Tows", 207–8; decision to end Dynamo, 257, 269–70
Ramsay, 2nd Lieutenant I. F. R., 33, 73, 103
Ramsgate, 46, 48, 127, 157, 159, 160, 163, 164, 191–93, 217, 222–26, 245, 271, 273, 278
Ransome, Major Bob, 112
Reader, Sapper Eric, 117
Refugees, civilian, 8, 103, 254
Reinhardt, General Lieutenant Georg-Hans, 151
Renown, 156, 195
Resolute, 156
Return of troops, 169–70, 186, 227, 271, 277–78
Reynaud, Paul, 2, 20, 24, 58, 91, 92, 109, 174, 177–79, 197, 229, 252
Rhodes, 2nd Lieutenant Arthur, 96
Richards, Lieutenant C. D., 160
Richardson, Major Charles, 36, 277
Richardson, Commander Hector, 94, 96, 99, 112, 113, 115, 151, 166, 188

Richthofen, General Major Wolfram von, 32, 134, 161
Rifle Brigade, 1st Battalion, 61
Riggs, H. C., 45, 88
River Emergency Service, 88
Robinson, Commander Charles, 124
Rommel, General Major Erwin, 13
Rosendaël, 235, 255, 261
Ross, Commander Richard, 207
Roubaix, 104
Rouen, 248
Routes across the Channel, 84–86, 90, 94, 117, 120, 122, 125, 127, 139
Roux, Lieutenant de Vasseau, 243
Royal Air Force (RAF), 9, 17, 20, 24, 37, 38, 56–58, 90, 117, 127, 133–35, 200, 219–22, 250; 19th Fighter Squadron, 57, 220–21. *See also* Dowding, Air Chief Marshal Sir Hugh
Royal Daffodil, 85
Royal Dragoon Guards, 168; 4th/7th Battalion, 239
Royal Eagle, 129
Royal Irish Fusiliers, 1st Battalion, 110
Royal Kent Yeomanry, 146
Royal Lancers Regiment, 12th Battalion, 22, 105, 166
Royal Marines, 67, 81, 168
Royal National Lifeboat Institution, 89, 224
Royal Norfolk Regiment, 2nd Battalion, 74
Royal Northumberland Fusiliers Regiment, 9th Battalion, 13, 278
Royal Ocean Racing Club, 157
Royal Sovereign, 259
Royal Sussex Regiment: 4th Battalion, 103; 5th Battalion, 53, 76
Royal Tank Regiment, 3rd Battalion, 6
Royal Ulster Rifles, 2nd Battalion, 205–6
Royal Warwickshire Regiment, 2nd Battalion, 106
Rundstedt, General Colonel Gerd von, 3, 6, 15, 21, 22, 25, 26, 28, 29, 31, 32, 60, 150, 209
Russell, Chief Cook Thomas R., 48, 116
Ryder, Major, 74
Ryegate II, 159, 163, 278

Sabre, 87, 116, 143, 246, 268
St. Abbs, 216–19
Saint Eloi, Church of, 30
Saint-Omer, 13, 30, 61, 69
Saint Pierre-Brouck, 27
Saint Pol, 13, 135
St. Seiriol, 223
Saladin, 87, 144
Salamander, 216–17
Salisbury, Signalman E. A., 11
Sandford, Private T. W., 65
Saunders, Stoker A. D., 87
Savorgnan de Brazza, 244
Schaal, General Lieutenant Ferdinand, 64, 65
Scheve, Major Fritz von, 132
Schmidt, Georg, 267–68

Schmundt, Colonel, 32
Schneider, Augustin, 194
Schneider, Fernand, 194
Schnellboote (German speedboats), 119–21, 127, 169; S 21, 120; S 23, 120; S 30, 121
Schniewind, Vice-Admiral Otto, 119
Scotia, 222
Secteur Fortifié des Flandres, 234, 255
Sedan, 2, 3
Seine, River, 26, 150
Sequacity, 84
Servins, 51, 52
Shattock, Gunner R., 8
Shaw, Ted, 159, 163, 174, 278
Sheerness, 48, 90, 156, 157, 159, 190, 245
Shikari, 246, 260, 261
Shipping Federation, the, 159
Silver Queen, 163, 164
Siroco, 169
Skipjack, 216–18
SKL (German Naval War Command), 119
Skoots, 44–45, 86, 196
Skylark, 160, 193
Small Vessels Pool, 40–41, 46, 88–89, 156–57
Smith, Basil A., 156, 163
Smyth, Brigadier John G., 186–87
Snelgar, Sergeant George, 49
Snowden, Second Lieutenant D. C., 83, 84
Sola, Raphael de, 158
Solent, 89
Soloman, Sub-Lieutenant Michael, 197, 242–44, 251
Somali, 47
Somerset, Brigadier, 148
Somerville, Vice-Admiral Sir John, 90
Somme, River, 17, 18, 19, 23, 24, 209, 256, 273
Southampton, 44, 89, 126
Southend Britannia, 160
Spears, Major-General Sir Edward, 178, 179
"Special tows," 208, 210
Speedwell, 215, 251
Spitfire (British plane), 57, 133–34, 195, 220. *See also* RAF
Spycker, 78, 249, 255
Stanley, Staff Sergeant Gordon, 51, 52
Stanley, Jeanne Michez, 51, 52
Steenbecque, 13, 278
Steenwerck, 109
Stephens, Private Bob, 35
Stephenson, Lieutenant-Colonel E. L., 73
Stephenson, Commodore Gilbert Owen, 162, 166, 184
Stone, Private Bill, 53
Stopford, Lieutenant James, 43
Stowell, Sub-Lieutenant H. W., 94
Stratton, Private Bill, 13, 187
Stuka (German plane), 3, 8, 10, 29, 34, 35, 51, 52, 55, 57, 64–66, 94, 107, 132–40, 161, 169, 189, 212, 214–17, 219, 228, 242, 254, 273. *See also* Dive bombing; Luftwaffe
Suffolk Regiment, 1st Battalion, 219

Sugar, Private Sam, 124
Sun IV, 195, 257
Sundowner, 226–27
Sutton, Brigadier George William, 145
Swallow, 160, 194, 259
Swayne, Brigadier J. G., 175, 176, 178
Sykes, Captain E. H., 165

Tanks: British, 19, 21, 61; French, 3, 22, 34, 110; German, 2, 3, 13, 15, 20, 26, 34, 64, 66, 107, 118, 133, 150, 234. *See also* Panzers
Tarry, acting Second Mate John, 45, 192
Taylor, Commodore A. H., 159, 245, 249, 258, 259
Taylor, Driver Gordon A., 51
Taylor, 2nd Lieutenant R. C., 12, 169
Tennant, Captain William G.: sent to Dunkirk, 92–97; decision to use eastern mole, 97–99, 115; shore parties, 112, 130, 182, 188–89, 219, 241, 252; communications, 142, 152; stops daylight evacuation, 229–30; returns to England, 247
Teteghem, 249, 255
Thames estuary, 44, 89, 127, 156, 159, 193
Thames, River, 88, 156, 278
Thoma, Colonel Wilhelm Ritter von, 30
Thuiller, Lieutenant-Colonel H. S., 246
Tidey, Private Fred, 74
Tilbury, 158, 194
Tilbury Dredging Company, 45, 46, 192
Tilly, 85, 116
Titanic, 226
Tollesbury, 156
Toomey, Private Jack, 128
Tough Brothers Boatyard, 88, 156
Tough, Douglas, 88
Toulouse-Lautrec, Commander Gui de, 169
Tournai, 11, 35
Tresckow, Lieutenant-Colonel von, 32
Trippe, Corporal, 51
Triton, 160, 162, 196
Trotter, Lieutenant J., 199
Troup, Commander H. R., 249, 259
Truffaut, Captain Georges, 102–3
Twente, 141
Tynwald, 223, 241, 248, 259

"Useless Mouths," 19, 41, 55, 86
Utterson Kelso, Brigadier J. E., 145
U-Boats, 122, 127; *U 62*, 122

Vanquisher, 144, 153
Venomous, 190, 246–47
Verity, 90, 224
Vervins, 1
Vincennes, 20, 100
Vincia, 216–17
Vivacious, 153
VTB 25 (French torpedo boat), 259, 268
VTB 26, 259

Wahagnies, 16
Waitzbauer, Corporal Hans, 249
Wake, Sub-Lieutenant Roger, 242–43, 247, 251
Wakeful, 88, 99, 120–25, 144
Wake-Walker, Rear-Admiral Frederic, 152–53, 171–73, 177, 184–85, 188, 216, 224, 239–40, 245, 251–52, 257–59
Walker, Private W. S., 50
Walter, Colour Sergeant Fred, 65, 66
War Office, 16, 17, 24, 37, 41, 62, 101, 111, 143, 153, 176, 180
Warner, Private Bill, 35, 116
Warner, Major David, 146
Watkin, Lance Bombardier Noel, 6
Watou, 103, 148
Watts, Captain O. M., 157–58, 194, 197
Waverley, 141
Weather, 272
Webb, Sergeant E. C., 235
Webb, Captain Lemon, 156
Welsh Guards, 50, 147
Wemple, Lieutenant-Commander J. S., 184
Westropp, Colonel Lionel H. M., 167
Westward Ho, 222, 249
Weygand, General Maxime, 19, 21, 33, 62, 76, 78, 90–92, 100, 110, 174, 177–79, 181, 183, 229, 252, 275–76
"Weygand Plan," 19–23
Whitehall, 217
White Wing, 245
Whitfield, Colonel G. H. P., 95
Whitshed, 235, 257
Wietersheim, General Gustav von, 151
Williams, Sub-Lieutenant William Ronald, 161, 189
Wilson, Major, 7
Winchelsea, 235, 247
Windsor, 212, 224, 278
Wolfhound, 94, 98
Woodcock, Mrs. S., 270
Worcester, 173, 222, 226, 228–29
Worcestershire Regiment, 8th Battalion, 147
Wormhout, 106
Worthing, 242
Worthington, Lieutenant Greville, 278
Wounded, evacuation of, 237, 241–42, 246, 263
"Wrens" (Women's Royal Naval Service), 43
Wright, Lance Corporal E. S., 1–2
Wright, Signalman Leslie W., 66–68
Wuthmann, Colonel Rolf, 209

Yewdale, 84
Yorke, Private Percy, 186
Yorkshire Lass, 248
Ypres, 19, 20, 23, 100, 104
Yser, 160, 164

Zimmermann, Lieutenant Wilhelm, 120–21
Zuydcoote, 95, 139, 219